# BASTANTE

*a novel*

*by*

*s. jaen black*

To the tree
2998
I love you men

First Edition

Illumina Publishing
P.O. Box 2643, Friday Harbor, WA 98250
www.illuminapublishing.com
360.378.6047

Cover design and interior layout by Bruce Conway

Printed in the U.S.A. on recycled paper

ISBN: 978-0-9818092-0-5

Library of Congress Control Number: 2008929470

This book is dedicated to John Coffee...

# Acknowledgements

At the time that I signed up for typing class, I had no intent of becoming a secretary, which was the main reason girls were directed to tuck typing in their resume along with home economics for a well-rounded pre-wife education. Still, I learned this skill well, and I am thankful to you Miss Dora Helms, my high school typing teacher, for your thorough instruction.

Despite what emanates from my southern mouth, I do have great affection for the English language and the puzzle of grammar. Thank you Miss Cecelia Malone from Dothan High School in south Alabama who first gave me compliments on my writing.

Bless you my dear Aunt Maryella from Memphis who was one of the rare positive voices that always met my creativity with delight, appreciation, and encouragement. Thank you for your love and generosity at very critical times in my life.

I would like to thank the couple of dozen people who have read various issues of the six drafts of this novel I have written over the past fifteen years. They were thoughtful and daring friends who helped me continue to believe that all of these pages and thoughts really did add up to a book.

Then, there's the matter of the gazillion people I have been privileged to know and love as a result of walking through the doors of Coffee's Gym in Marietta, Georgia back in 1983. A hardcore iron gym is a holy place to people whose psyches rely on physical strength, and, like other holy places, you will find an array of personalities. But Coffee's Gym was like no other. I always said you could go around the world twice, or sit in the office of Coffee's Gym, where a truly world class education in humanity was there for those willing to take time to smell the Icy Hot.

From the ether, here's to you Angie Boatenreiter, one of the last great splitters and a true friend that always clapped and cheered for every word I ever wrote. I regret you are not in this physical plane to toast with me in celebration of this book. I will never forget you, dear Angie, and my tears of your departure surely colored the pages of this book although I understand that you had to go.

And, of course, there is you to thank, John Coffee, who gave me enlightenment by shoving untold number of weird books, articles, and comments into my consciousness. It is because of you showing me the works of so many renegade authors that gave me the thought that maybe I did have something to say. Thanks to a conversation we had about Tennesse Williams, the next

morning at five a.m., I started writing this book. I will be forever grateful for you taking me into the fold, for your very great generosity and love, for all the laughs we've had, and yea to our mantra there at Coffee's Gym, "Only the Strange Survive".

I always knew somehow, someday, this book would be published. So much time has passed since the first draft, I had, more than once, run the scenario of how, upon my death, my poor friends sifting through the rubble of my things… might come upon this manuscript, and publish it to pay the junkman to come haul all my stuff off. But, here we are, and I'm alive and well...

There was a spark that ignited me last August at the San Juan County Fair when I came upon Bruce Conway, of Ilumina Publishing. It was like he had the plan and enthusiasm I lacked, and the expertise in the subjects about publishing that I had not a clue.

Bruce, you have been a true spirit guide here, and patted me on the back just enough to keep me from spooking about it all. Thank you so much, my friend, for being a part of one of the most exciting periods of my life.

To my editor, Judith Carter, I appreciate your gentle hand with me. Thank you for your hard work and kindness.

# INTRODUCTION

I have had the great fortune to have my life collide with many unique individuals. For many years, I managed one of the most infamous iron gyms on the planet, Coffee's Gym out of Marietta, Georgia. Through the doors strolled many strength aficionados whose sole purpose in life was to be big, to win big.

We had athletes from many disciplines use our gym as their temple to work their magic. I hung with the Olympic lifters. Our sole purpose in life was to have the strength and the courage to heave barbells over our heads.

As a child of the sixties, the drug culture has always been a part of the landscape of my life. However, through my adventures in physical culture, the rituals I have witnessed with steroids and the like made any acid trip pale in comparison to the surreal lives of those seeking bodybuilding trophies. The rigors of competitive bodybuilders amazed me with their grand pathological pursuits. Yet, I honor the dedication of anyone who fosters a dream and can commiserate with the goal to win. I don't stand in judgement of decisions to go that route, and been grateful, and completely fascinated to be privy to these observations.

Along that sixties theme, I survived the realization and subsequent joyful embrace of my life as a homosexual. Despite the opportunities credit cards and the medical community provide these days, I never considered changing my sex, but like bodybuilding, my intrigue with the premise of transsexuality inspired me to present this subject here, as well as the backstage life of a drag queen who walks the walk 24/7.

Childhood sexual abuse changed not only my life but countless young souls. Some of us come back around to entertain intimacy in our lives, and some of us never do. All of us have to work to smooth out our psyches with a variety of tools. In this book, daily sedation of sorts assists the main character here enough—bastante to keep as happy of a life as a perpetual low grade heartache allows.

Overall, I view this novel as an exercise in observation of change—as Charles Darwin spoke, "It is not the strongest nor most intelligent animal who survives, but the ones most responsive to change."

# CHAPTER 1

She perched upon that stool with an attitude every bit as gigantic as her butt. That white woman, with a body carved out of pure Spam, sat there with mean eagle eyes glued to anyone that dared to pass through the door. The confines of the cash register cubicle were wired as hot as the front gate at Fort Knox. Munio found this familiar; he moved very carefully in these places, so as to not cause a sudden flex of the trigger that was always engaged just below the waterline of the counter top.

He could hear her breathing clear across the store. He could hear her fat lying on her lungs like a ton of bricks. She pushed a finger to cock her glasses a little higher, coughed, and hacked up a wad of mucous that she spit into the trashcan behind the counter. Munio made the rounds down every aisle.

"Whatcha looking for?" she questioned gruffly.

"Oh, ah, a few things, you know." Munio smiled and nodded.

"No, I don't know. Git what you came for and git on out, all right? Comprendo?"

Munio said nothing in reply as he settled for a couple of cans of beans for his dinner, two cans of Puss and Boots mackerel, and a six pack of Schlitz malt liquor. He plopped the items on the counter and made eye contact with the woman that you could almost hear. She reluctantly raised her right hand from below the counter to conduct the cash register business.

"Seven eighty-six," she said, as the drawer flew open with a ding.

Munio gave her a wadded up ten-dollar bill and enjoyed her struggle with it. Her uneasiness grew with her finger away from that gun for so long. He studied the little beads of sweat lined up on her upper lip just from the exertion of sitting on that stool. She plopped down his change, and with no bidding of good nights or be carefuls, he walked away.

He pointed the old white Ford truck towards the Louisiana line, cranked the window down halfway and breathed deeply the cool air. The dark emptiness of the interstate highway soothed like a warm bath. Stolen moments of peace occurred rarely, these first few days in the land of the free and the home of the brave. He looked over at the gray kitten who had surfaced from the mass of black plastic garbage bags, his luggage, on the floorboard. This little silver lining represented the only friendly face he had seen in days.

Ten miles down the road, he pulled off onto the shoulder of the highway. With can opener in hand, Munio proceeded to fix dinner. The kitten paced and mewed as the opener made its way around that can. With the last crank,

the truck became transformed into a fish factory. Munio cursed, coughed, and raced to roll the window down a few more turns.

"Jesus Christ, kitty, is that stuff really good? I guess you don't want any of my beans either, do you?"

He gave the kitten a pat as he raked half the can onto a paper plate. After he served himself a can of beans, they enjoyed a peaceful dinner in silence as the meteors of red tail-lights passed them and disappeared into the night. With the last scrape of the can, Munio felt satisfied and awake enough to continue. The kitten sat up straight, in a sophisticated fashion, and methodically licked his paws and cleaned his face. Munio smiled and chuckled as he cranked up the truck.

"Kitty, let's go to Georgia, OK? OK. We go to see my friend there, ok? He'll put us up for a while, maybe."

Through the night they drove, and when the sun was at high noon, they were fifty miles deep into Georgia. Several times Munio stopped to look at a map, but it might as well have been a blank piece of paper for all the sense it made to him. He could barely read English or Spanish. All the words and numbers gave him were vague hunches about his destination.

Fortunately, he intuitively possessed a keen sense of direction. The time he navigated boats all along the Caribbean enhanced this natural ability.

Illiteracy haunted Munio like a blind man on a bluff with a pervasive deep ache, a tense fear that his next step might be his last. He made it a point, as best he could, to have that fact remain his best-kept secret. It wasn't that he had not had opportunities to learn to read and write, but Munio, as a child, could not bear confinement in a classroom when he could be out in the world. Though Belize's literacy rate ranked high, Munio's mother, a native Mayan, believed organized book learning was unimportant compared to fishing and drug-running skills. She would say, "After all, Munio, you cannot eat books."

Still, the older he became the more often the issue of his illiteracy surfaced, and it rested in his heart as a shameful thing that he refused to directly acknowledge. Poor vision caused the problem, he claimed, and he stuck to the story.

A few staples of the written word he had down pat. One of those was cold, and another was beer. Munio kept his eye peeled for one of those signs, and at the next one, he pulled off the highway and headed for it like a sea weary sailor to a harbor.

"Little kitty, I'm going to have a couple of beers and find out which way it is to this town of my friend's. You go to sleep, OK?"

Perched on top of the black plastic bags, the little kitty did not protest. From experience, he knew Munio would eventually return to the truck.

ZZ Top and cigarette smoke filled the room. Munio choked and coughed a few times till his respiratory system got its footing. He took a seat on a stool at the bar as the bartender approached him.

"What'll it be, bud?"

"Yes, that will be fine, please."

"Huh?"

"I said that will be fine. Bud, you know?"

"Oh," he laughed, "oh, right."

The bartender, a chunky man of medium height with a long blonde ponytail, shook his head and chuckled as he stepped away to fetch the beer.

Munio sat with his back to the bar. His eyes scanned the darkened room and zeroed in on a brightly lit area where a dartboard was hung. The wall surrounding it had thousands of little stab wounds from bad misses. A daydream began to steal his consciousness.

*"You think you can just cheat in this way? Hey, where are you going? This game is not ended. You owe me my money!"* Munio spoke this to the backside of a man decked out in cowboy trappings.

*"Can't you just play fair as you should? You fucking rip-off cowboy! You're just a damn cheater, aren't you? Why won't you just talk to me? Hey, fuck you! Can you hear that, motherfucker? Maybe your big ass hat's just too big! Maybe that hat's pulled over your ears so you cannot hear, eh?"*

*The cowboy leaned on the bar, sipped from his frosted mug, rolled his eyes in mock fear for the entertainment of the bartender and others watching, and remained oblivious to Munio's requests for dialogue or money.*

*Munio threw an arm up in disgust as he turned away from the man and walked toward the dartboard to retrieve his darts. The bar was packed with drunken people on a Friday night in the south Texas town. Many of them snickered at Munio's verbal pursuit of the cowboy.*

*"Hey wetback, you ought to be glad he lowered himself just to play with you, you son of a bitch."*

*"Hell yeah, Jose. You better just shut the fuck up."*

*He made his way through the sea of voices; his body burned hot with anger and the pain of this humiliation. As his hand reached for a dart, a whizzing object flew past his ear, landed without a sound through the back of his hand, and pinned it to the dartboard. Munio held perfectly still and watched as blood trickled across the back of his hand and down his brown muscled arm. He felt it disappear over his shoulder, and off his back onto the sawdust covered floor.*

The bartender plopped the longneck on the counter and cleared his throat, but Munio sat pupils fixed and dilated, still entranced by the sight of his bleeding hand.

"Hey, man, wake up."

Munio snapped to and turned around on his stool. "Oh, sorry, how much?"

Munio noticed the bartender's muscularity. His thick-veined forearms stuck out of his short-sleeved shirt like the hind legs of a pit bull. The man's forehead hung over his eyes in Cro-Magnon fashion.

"You lift weights?" Munio asked, knowing the answer.

"Yeah, I lift a little," The bartender produced a toothy grin, eager for the attention.

"Is that right? What do you do, body build?"

"Uh huh, yeah, I've been in a few shows around, you know."

"Ever win one?"

"Well, I come in second at the Southeastern Cup a few months ago. It was a tough class. There was this big ol' boy from Atlanta showed up. He was awesome. If he hadn't been there, I'd've won for sure."

"Where do you train?"

"I train down at a place called Dixie Ironworks. It's hard-core. You know what I mean, man?"

"Yes, I know what you are saying."

"Hey, where's your accent from?"

"Belize."

"Belize, where the hell is that? I ain't never heard of it. Is that in Mexico?"

"Central America." Munio tipped the brown bottle high.

"Is that right? Well, I ain't ever met anybody from there. To tell you the truth, I ain't ever heard of the place, but I ain't what you would call a worldly individual."

Munio laughed and drained his beer dry. "Let me have another one please."

"Do y'all speak Belizian or what down there?"

"Spanish and English."

"Sure sounds like a Mexico accent." The bartender sat the new beer in front of Munio.

Munio picked up the bottle. "Well, I am not from Mexico, I assure you." He tipped the bubbling beer down his throat.

"It'd be ok if you was, man. I ain't prejudiced or nothin."

" What if I asked if you were from New York or commented that you have a New York accent. How would you feel?"

"I'd probably kick your teeth in. I don't want nobody thinking I'm from yankee land." The bartender grinned and nodded, " So, I reckon I got your point. Hey what's your name, man?"

"Munio." He offered his hand to the bartender.

"Munio, my name is Eddy." They grasped hands, and their eyes met, dark brown and light blue, in an intimate moment that hung in the air like a seventy- yard pass.

"You know, Munio, you got quite a grip yourself. You ever lift any weights?"

"Oh yes, I lifted weights probably before you were born. How old are you?"

"Twenty-five."

"Yes, see, I am fifty years old. I am old enough to be your father."

Eddy doubted the extent of this slight, though wiry, man's weightlifting experience. Besides, as a bartender, Eddy constantly heard exaggeration about physical prowess. They spoke of the longing, the regret about their bodies, their lives. In the darkness of their minds, all were almost champions, who would forever live and wonder in the lonely world of "what ifs".

"I did the overhead lifts." Munio slid a cigarette from the pack stuffed in his T-shirt pocket.

"The what?" Eddy asked.

"The overhead lifts. You mean you spend all that time in a gym, and you don't know what the overhead lifts are?"

Eddy chuckled nervously, glancing both ways. He would feel mighty embarrassed if somebody found out that he didn't know everything there was to know about the iron game. The many furrows on his massive forehead wrinkled like convolutions of a brain and twisted with inquisitiveness.

"So what you talking about, man?"

Munio let out a halfhearted snicker and said, "Does the sport of Olympic lifting, the snatch or the clean and jerk, ring a bell, brother?"

"Oh, yeah, uh huh, yeah, I know what you're talking about now. Yeah, I used to do power cleans in high school for football. You really do that shit, man?"

"For many years, I trained every day."

"Now, ain't that the thing you need them big rubber plates for?" Munio was pleased to be quizzed on this matter. A half smile formed upon his lips.

"In 1993, in these times, people use those plates, which are called bumper plates by the way, but when I began my lifting, I had no such equipment." Munio ground his cigarette butt into the ashtray.

"Oh, I didn't know they was so new and all. So what did you use, just iron plates?" Eddy dangled his legs from his seat atop a stack of beer cases.

"In competition, yes, I used them, but, at home, I learned on a weight set I made myself."

Eddy cackled and looked both ways once more to see if anybody else heard Munio's crock of shit. As far as conversations went, this was by far the most entertaining one he had had all day.

"What you talking about? Made your own weights? Shit, man."

"I did really, brother. Give to me another beer, please, and I will tell you how I accomplished this feat."

"Oh, you bet. I can't wait to hear this shit."

Eddy plopped a third beer down for Munio. Munio took a long swig, then lit up another cigarette.

Eddy sat, childlike, with his hands in his lap, riveted to this exotic man's every word.

"Much experimentation was necessary, but I finally figured it out." Mu-

nio continued with his mesmerizing voice, a Spanish/Jamaican clip. "By use of an old axle rod, lead collected from discarded batteries, and a cast iron cake pan, I molded the plates.

"We had a fire pit in the yard where we sometimes cooked food and burned all our garbage. Oh, I forgot that, first, I weighed out some lead in a box on the scales. I made several different weights, you see. For instance, like ten pound, twenty-five pound, you know?" Eddy nodded with his face cupped in his hands, and leaned on the bar. "I took the lead, put it in the cake pan, and then put it on the fire. I don't know if you have this information, but lead has a very quick melting point, you see." Eddy nodded. "So, on this fire, the lead melted, and I take it from the fire. I stick the axle rod in the center of the cake pan with no delay until it cools, which it does very quickly. After that, I dump the lead out of the cake pan, and I label the weight of the plate on one side with a screwdriver and hammer. You know, like, ah, like engraving or like chiseling. Then, I have a plate." He threw his hands out to the side in the "Voila!" fashion of a magician.

Eddy yawned, stood up straight, stretched and scratched, "Damn, man, that's some story, you got any pictures of that? I bet you couldn't drop that shit in the house, huh?" He laughed out loud.

"Oh no, I totally trained out of doors." Munio smiled at Eddy and drained his beer. "The one trouble with these weights was when I dropped them from overhead, they would bury in the dirt clear up to the bar, and I had to dig them out to do another lift."

"Well, how much weight did you ever lift with them?"

"One time I did a two hundred pound snatch."

"Shiiit! That's hell, man. I wish I'd seen that. Uh, what is a snatch again? I forgot."

"You young guys don't know nothing at all about weightlifting! You bodybuilders!" Munio waved in disgust at Eddy and smiled. "The snatch is done with a wide grip." He hopped off his barstool and maneuvered a shadow lift.

"Oh yeah, I remember. I seen that done before."

Munio pointed at Eddy and smiled. "I'm going to go out to my truck and bring something to show you. I'll be right back." He turned quickly towards the door.

Eddy piped up sharply, "Hey, wait a minute, Bud. You got to pay for your beers before I can let you go, now."

"Oh, I see, you can't trust a man for one second in this country, can you?"

"Hey, don't take it personal, man. I just got to keep up with this shit, you know."

Munio stopped, stared at him for a moment, started to go away on one of his daydreams, but resisted the rip tide of his mind. A faint smile crept across

his face, and he came back to earth.

"Yeah, I know man. It's cool. Here, how much?" Munio rifled through his jeans and extracted some bills.

"Six seventy-five."

"OK, I'll be right back." Munio slapped the money on the bar.

The air, a hot, thick, invisible fog, did not bother Munio, who relished the heat, that smothering feeling of jungle air. It was all he had ever known. Now, it helped center him and those beers. The little gray kitten, perched up on the garbage bags, greeted him when he opened the truck.

"Hey, kitty, kitty. What you doing, huh?"

The kitten watched Munio rustle paper and plastic behind the front seat. He withdrew two photographs, studied them, and a small smile came over his face.

"Well, little kitty, let's see what this dumb muscle head thinks of this, huh?" Munio slammed the truck door. The little kitten, frozen in his spot on top of the black plastic garbage bags, seemed unfazed by his comings or goings.

Munio strode purposefully across the parking lot and into the bar, where he flipped the photos Frisbee style in front of Eddy. Eddy picked one up in each hand and studied them for a moment.

"So what the hell is this, man? Was this some contest somewhere?"

Munio shook his head slowly and looked him in the eyes. He attempted to run his fingers through his incurably tangled black hair. "Contest? Yes, it was some contest, the fucking Olympic games! In the 1972 Olympic games in Munich, Germany, I was the first man to ever represent Belize as a weightlifter."

Eddy looked up like he had just seen God. "No shit, man? Is that what this is?"

"Yes, look." Munio pointed to himself in the lineup of lifters in the photograph.

Eddy continued to look at the picture. Although it had been twenty-one years, Munio did not look that different. "Damned if that ain't you."

Eddy looked Munio up and down and snorted, "I sure wouldn't have figured you for no weightlifter, man. Just goes to show you, you know."

"That is right!" Munio slapped the bar hard. "I'm just not a real big man, you know. Lifters come in all sizes. Of course you know this, eh?" Munio chugged the remainder of his beer. "Let me have another one of those beers, Eddy."

"Hey, you got it. Listen, I get off in a little while. What do you say we go over to my gym?"

"That would be good. We can do that."

Eddy plopped a new beer on the counter and moved down the bar to serve other customers. Munio lit a cigarette and turned on the stool so his

back was against the bar. He breathed deeply, and began to relax finally from the tension of the trip. He closed his eyes, and in an instant, a memory swept him far away from south Georgia.

Monkey River Town, a little village in southern Belize, did not express any desire to move into the twenty-first century. Munio had a desire though, and always gathered information about modern ways, especially pertaining to America. He liked the slick cultures he had experienced through his contacts with the drug dealing Columbians and Americans.

Six weeks ago he began the travels, which had landed him on this bar stool in Rosedale, Georgia. His mother, brother, and a few neighbors watched him load the black plastic garbage bags into the rusty Ford truck. A home-made but well-built wooden toolbox spanned the width of the bed of the truck where Munio stored a nice collection of tools.

Up the north coast of Belize, at the port town of Chetumal in the state of Quintana Roo, he crossed into Mexico. After a quick delivery here, he would earn enough money to finance his adventures for some time. He stopped at a pay telephone and dialed a number.

"Hello," a man said on the other end.

"Yes, my name is Munio. I am looking for Ramon."

"This is Ramon, Munio. How was your drive?"

"Good, thank you."

"Where exactly are you?"

"I, ah, am at the old cliff road on the beach at the first gasoline station as you come into town."

"Yes, I know where you are. You stay there, and I'll be there in a few minutes, ok?"

"Yes, ok. I'll be right here."

"Good."

Munio hung up the phone and lit a cigarette. By the time he had taken the last puff, a man on a red scooter came to an abrupt halt next to the phone booth. Munio and the man made knowing eye contact, and Munio retrieved a small box of Tampax from his truck. The man chuckled when he saw the container. As Munio handed him the box, the man slipped some rolled-up bills in Munio's hand. They nodded, smiled, and parted company. Munio slipped behind the wheel and counted his delivery fee. The sight of two thousand American dollars inspired Munio to let out a loud, melodic whoop as he started the truck.

"Hey, hey, man! What the hell's wrong with you?" Eddy was in Munio's face.

Munio jumped off the stool as he snapped back to reality and saw Eddy's bewildered and angry face. "What's the matter? What did I do?"

"You was hollerin' at the top of your lungs, that's what, man. You can't be doing that now. Freak me the fuck out. You got seizures or something?"

Munio laughed because the dramatic look on Eddy's face seemed comical. "I'm sorry, man, but I guess I was just daydreaming or something. I do that sometimes. I'm cool. I have no seizures or anything."

Eddy wiped the sweat off his face with a napkin. "Well, goddamn, I hope you don't ever have a damn seizure if this is what you do in a fucking daydream. Scared the shit out of me and everybody else. Damn. Hey, I'm about ready to get off. You still want to go over to the gym?"

"Yes, definitely." Munio smiled, secretly pleased that he had scared Eddy.

# CHAPTER 11

They drove a few blocks in Eddy's beat up sedan, and pulled into a gravel parking lot. A big barbell-shaped sign with "Dixie Ironworks" painted in the middle of it towered above the small cinder block building.

"What's the name of this gym?"

"Dixie Ironworks, see? See that sign?" Eddy pointed to the sign.

Munio looked and frowned. These words were not on his vocabulary list.

As the door opened, a deafening sound of heavy metal music escaped along with the clank of iron and the anguished cries of the people who hoisted it. Eddy waded through this small and crowded room with Munio in tow. He stopped at a long wall at the back of the gym. Inscribed in huge letters across the top of the wall were the words "Grow or Die."

"Hey, man, " Eddy said grinned proudly and pointed, "How 'bout that shit?"

Munio felt a streak of terror run through him, lest his secret be on the line here. Even though this overgrown redneck meant nothing to him, he would almost rather die than admit he could not completely read this phrase.

Munio squinted hard and glanced over to make sure Eddy saw him. "I left my glasses in my truck. I can't quite make it out, man. What does it say?"

"You can't fucking see that, man? You need to buy a goddamn German Shepherd, buddy. It says grow or die. Ain't that some shit? You really can't see that?"

Munio smiled and ignored the question, "That is a good motto, yes."

"I need to go change. You want to stay here and look around or what?"

"Yes, I'll be right here. You go."

Munio sat down on a bench, leaned back against the wall, and absorbed the ambience of the Dixie Ironworks. The grungy equipment with its scuffed paint and worn upholstery with caked-on dirt excited him. A sense of reckless abandon saturated the gym as he watched and listened to the people pouring their sweat and hearts out making love to the iron.

Munio chewed on a toothpick and offered subdued smiles as he made eye contact with one and then another. Many of those people did not smile back. Since Munio did not display a great deal of muscle hypertrophy, his presence would have to pan out over time to gain real acceptance. Munio took no offense, as he possessed a feeling of superiority that no one there could ever have imagined. Unlike any of the Arnold wannabes at the Dixie Ironworks, Munio's fifteen minutes of fame had gone down in history in Munich, Monkey River Town, and places in between. No matter what else would or would not happen in his life, it seemed to Munio that event would remain the most important.

Most of the crowd were men, anabolically inflated, distorted, and in heaven as they went about their business. As the drugs created an optical illusion that filled their bodies, their eyes burned hot with hope, the hope that they would loom large in the world and unforgettable.

Many of the women loaded up, too. The side effects varied. Some had gone to great lengths to disguise their consequences with huge silicone globes surgically mounted on their chests. Mime-thick makeup covered their faces to hide the abundance of skin eruptions and the five o'clock shadows that crept across their chins. In weak defense of their lost femininity, they wore an array of pastel shades of tights, with neat matching socks. Some wore halter-tops to brandish their exaggerated sculpted chests for all to review.

The members generally worked in pairs. They alternated roles; the partner not lifting played the role of master, lover, and conscience. In an attempt to motivate their partners, they dictated the same catch phrases over and over. Munio was familiar with this format and, in his half-drunk state of mind, became somewhat aroused as he eavesdropped on these intimate moments.

One young bulldog of a man, crew-cut, clean-shaven, and testosterone-nasty bloomed like an orchid in a hot house in this hard-core environment. His classic all-boy look, not pretty but not homely either, epitomized a face which decorated any military lineup in West Point, Moscow, or anywhere discipline reigned. He was powerful, two hundred thirty pounds at a moderate height of five foot seven, and one of the few men in the gym who had not shaved away his body hair. His clothes were old-style workout clothes, a white T-shirt and tight, short gray knit shorts that followed every contour of his body like wax.

The bulldog boy teamed up with, Simon, a cute-as-a-button blonde, with a sugary sweet face, lit by big blue eyes. Simon wore stylish workout clothes, striped Spandex shorts and a baggy muscle-T. With his body shaved sleek, he allowed not even one hair to interfere with a full view of his muscularity.

Munio caught them in the middle of a hot and heavy squat session. After several warm-up sets, they loaded the bar to four hundred and five pounds. It was Simon's turn to take to the rack. He sat on a bench and wrapped one knee and then the other with long, dingy knee wraps. With each successive turn

around his leg, he pulled the elastic cloth tighter. As part of his psyching up ritual, Simon took big breaths, exhaled fiercely, and muttered profanity. The bulldog boy's excitement grew. He paced back and forth and watched Simon wrap his knees.

"Come on now, Simon. Let's git after it now! Show me something, hoss! Come on now, got to grow, boy, got to grow!"

"Let's fucking do it!" Simon spat as he shot up off the bench and approached the squat rack like a boxer coming off a break. He placed his hands carefully on the bar, ducked under it, and rested it on the back of his shoulders. After a quiet moment of concentration, he stood with the weight with a loud grunt. He stepped back and adjusted his stance. His image was formidable, bearing that barbell with four forty-five pound plates on each end. After inhaling a huge breath, he squatted all the way down and up again. By the time he had reached five repetitions, he was shaky and his fair face burned beet red in the mirror that he faced.

"Come on Simon! Don't you quit!" The bulldog boy shouted, and Simon went down again. "Get up! Get up!" He shadowed Simon's every move, ready to spot him should his strength run out altogether.

Simon looked like a desperate man who might not live through this. Munio's heart pounded too as he watched from the sidelines.

Two more reps went by, and bulldog boy commanded in Simon's ear, "Don't you quit you mother fucker! A double, you can do a double! Come on, Simon!"

Simon let out bloodcurdling screams every time he struggled to stand, and every eye in the gym stared to see if he would make it through to ten reps. In slow motion, Simon eventually produced the tenth rep then hurried forward to rack the weight as if it were red hot. He turned to get assorted congratulatory rewards from the bulldog boy and others standing around, but collapsed in his tracks. He lay on the floor, gasping for breath, and winced from the pain of exhaustion. No one moved to help him because, at this gym, it was just another day in the squat rack. Simon sat up after a minute or so and unfastened the knee wraps that still choked the life out of his legs. When he finally stood up, the bulldog boy hugged him and said, "Hell of a set, man. Shit, I didn't think you was going to make that. Way to hang, way to hang, bro."

"You and me both. To tell you the truth, I don't know how I got those last five. I swear to God I was sucking wind." Simon dropped to the bench for further rest.

Munio, like a dark and beautiful cat, his lambent beauty in sharp contrast to the synthetic blue blaze fluorescent world of the gym, shook his head and grinned as he chewed on a toothpick. He walked over to Simon. "Hey, man, that was some good set. Very nice form. You hung in there really good."

"Thanks man, I 'preciate it." Simon shot him a beautiful full-toothed smile and looked over at the bulldog boy, who gave Munio the eagle eye.

"You new here, ain't you?" bulldog boy asked.

"Belize."

"Belwho?"

"Belize."

Bulldog boy checked around to see who was watching him, and then chuckled, "Hell, I thought a Belize was a fucking Chevrolet." A few halfhearted laughs went out around the area.

"It isn't. It is a country in Central America below Mexico." He had encountered this attitude all too often since the border crossing in Brownsville, Texas.

"Is that a fact, ah, Julio, or ah, I don't believe I caught your name there, bud." The bulldog boy moved slowly closer to Munio.

Eddy appeared just in time to hear the last line and answered the bulldog boy. "Who is he? Don't you know an Olympic athlete when you see one, boy? This here is Munio, ah, damn I forgot to ask you your last name." Eddy slapped him on the back affectionately.

"Morelos." Munio aimed a small thin-lipped smile toward Eddy.

"This man, Munio Morelos," Eddy stumbled over the words, "was in the motherfucking Olympics, man, as a weightlifter. How 'bout that shit?" Eddy continued to grin and pat Munio on the back.

Bulldog boy's obnoxious edge vanished, and he joined Eddy in the adoration of Munio. It was as if Munio was a friendly space ship that had descended in their lives.

"Really? Well, I'll be damned. Which one was you in?"

"It was in Munich in 1972, long before you were born, I expect."

The bulldog boy was giddy. "I'll be. You're right, though. I wasn't even here 'til, well, 1973."

Simon walked over to Munio, and stuck out his hand. "Pleased to meet ya, man. My name is Simon."

Munio smiled appreciatively and stuck out his hand.

"Hey, you going to do your set or what, man?" Simon asked the bulldog boy.

"Damn, I got so carried away. Yeah, let me wrap here."

Simon slipped on another forty-five and started his coaching sermon. It was he who now paced while the bulldog boy wrapped his knees tighter and tighter.

"All right now! This is it, Jerry! Show me what you got! Last set, best set!"

Jerry's knees were bound so tight his white thighs cast a bluish hue. He rose and snapped a small white ammonia cap in half. With each of several huge snorts, Jerry's fury intensified.

He let out a whoop and headed for the squat rack. His eyes filled with ferocious intent, his fair face stained a grotesque shade of red, as he walked

20

out with the weight.

"'At's it, Jer!" Simon shouted as the bulldog boy ascended from the first rep with a roar. After eight successful repetitions, the drama escalated.

Jerry paused and trembled. He had become a raging beast for this moment in time. He took a deep breath and descended once more. As he rose in slow motion, a vein exploded in his nose that sent a gush of blood down his face. The taste of blood intensified his efforts, along with the frenzied crowd who yelled more aggressively.

The bulldog boy stared in the mirror. Blood continued to stream down his nose onto his white T-shirt, and from it, he summoned the will to continue.

"One more, Jerry! Don't quit, dawg! You can make it! Just one, Jerry! A single! Come on now! Fight through it!" Simon and the others shouted.

Munio watched with reserved excitement as he still held a grudge against the bulldog boy for his earlier disrespect. He did not expect him to rise with the last one. Sure enough though, Jerry managed to stand, and after he traipsed through splatters of his own blood, he set the bar in the rack. Eddy and Munio turned away as the bulldog boy dropped to the floor, to retch and heave all over himself.

Eddy adjusted the pin for two hundred pounds, grabbed the long, chrome curved bar that hung from the overhead cable, and used his body weight to pull the bar down low enough so he could sit on the seat of the lat pull station. He took a good breath and forced the bar down to his chest for a ten-rep set. Afterwards, he stood and hung onto the bar until the weight hit the stack like the resounding clank of two hundred pound castanets. Eddy turned loose of the bar and chomped his mouthful of bubble gum. He winked at Munio as he blew a big bubble and popped it.

"Hey, you want to go, Munio?"

"OK, sure." Munio adjusted the pin in the machine for one hundred pounds and performed ten reps.

"It has been a while since I used one of these," Munio said, shaking his woolly head as the stack clanked again upon completion of his set.

"Hell, I wouldn't have thought they'd even have these things down in Belize," Eddy laughed as he set the pin on two hundred fifty and went about his second set.

"Oh well, there are a couple of resorts that have exercise equipment in Belize City. I worked in them at times, and at others in the Yucatan. It's not…" Munio stopped talking as he realized Eddy, engrossed in the exercise, was not listening. Eddy leaned way back with his body weight instead of his back muscles.

"Whoooeee. Feeling good, Munio! I'm getting a good pump today," he said exuberantly as he stood with the bar and let it clank.

"You know that you are not using your back muscles efficiently, Eddy."

"What the hell you talking about?" Eddy's face wrinkled up, and he put his hands on his hips.

"Watch this." Munio set the pin on one hundred twenty, pulled the bar down smoothly with his lats for a set of ten. "See? You can't be all herky jerky. You have to stay in one position. Use less weight, do better work."

Eddy grabbed at his crotch defensively and then scratched his head. "Yeah, I know what you're saying. You're right, too, man. See, I don't usually train with anybody, and so my form gets a little sloppy, I reckon."

Munio stood tall, wiped his nose, and took on his most arrogant posture. "Yeah, well, I reckon you better get it together. Make it worth your while. Proper technique is most important. Now, you try again."

"Don't let it go back so fast, resist it, work your negatives." He put his fist in the middle of Eddy's back so that he could not lean any further back than ten degrees past upright. "Stop right there. That's it. Slow it down. Pull with your lats. Squeeze your shoulders together. That's better."

Eddy let the bar go to its resting spot. "Yeah, OK, that was better. I felt the hell out of that. Thanks, man."

Eddy looked at the clock on the wall. He looked at Munio and said, "I tell you what. I don't give a rat's ass about nothing right now but gittin' this god-damn workout over with. I am hongry, boy, hongry. I'm gonna do three sets of seated rows over here, and we're gittin' the hell out of Dodge."

"What does that mean, Dodge ?"

"For crying out loud. It don't mean nothing. It means like fucking va-moose. Ain't that Spanish?"

Munio shook his head and smiled. "I need to smoke a cigarette. You do your rows, and I'll be outside."

Munio was glad to get outside. The sky was winding down from a full day of blistering the town of Rosedale. Munio fired off a match, inhaled deep-ly and sighed at the comforting aromas of tobacco and sulfur. He thought of Eddy and smiled at his amusement of him.

An image of Simon passed through his mind, which caused thoughts of his Uncle Armando to surface. Uncle Armando would have loved Simon's looks.

Munio was Armando's favorite nephew and spent much time with him. For his tenth birthday, his uncle gave him a guitar and taught him how to play it. A meticulous dresser, Uncle Armando always wore tight, custom-fit clothes and thin, carefully drawn lines of eyeliner above and below his eyes. Though one of Monkey River Town's most flamboyant citizens, he was a man of money, cash money, which earned him much respect.

He imparted to Munio many things, and one of them was sex. With that thought, Munio pulled deeply on the cigarette and brought his attention back to the stoop outside the Dixie Ironworks. He flicked his ashes and blew hard on the orange glowing stub of the cigarette, a brilliant tangerine that matched

the sky of this deep hot sunset.

*The screen door slammed, and the woman looked up quickly from the counter where she chopped onions.*

*"Armando!" She dropped her knife on the counter, wiped her hands on her apron, and shuffled over to a man dressed in a midnight blue tuxedo with a hot pink ruffled shirt. He stood silently, statue still, with his arms fully extended. When the woman reached him, his arms sprang to grip her tightly, and they laughed and danced in circles. "Armando, where have you been? We missed you for so long now. You were to come to dinner three weeks past, and you just don't show! You are so bad to me, Armando."*

*"I'm sorry, Angelic." With both hands, he stroked her face moving his head animatedly from side to side as he spoke. "You forgive me, no? I had business that could not be put aside. I have been in Guatemala for two weeks, in fact."*

*The woman returned to her onions. "Yes, I know, I know. You always got something going on, Armando. I never understand, but it's ok, it's ok."*

*"Where is my boy? Is he out playing somewhere?"*

*Armando peeked in the door of the next room and turned his head back and forth. His thinly plucked eyebrows arched high. He stepped back from the doorway and bumped right into a wild-haired boy who came up to his chest.*

*Armando shrieked, "Oh my God, boy, you scared me to death!*

*The boy laughed and jumped around. The man reached out to grab him, but the giggling boy leaped out of his way.*

*"Munio, you are such a bad boy. Angelica, this boy is so mean to me. He scared me so bad, I thought I would pee in my pants." Munio and Angelica looked at each other and laughed.*

*"Munio, I have planned a special trip for you if your mother will consent?" His voice trailed off in a high-pitched question. Armando leaned back on the counter and crossed his legs carefully after checking to make sure he would not encounter anything that might soil his spectacular outfit.*

*"Where to now, Armando?" Angelica asked as she dumped the chopped onions into a bowl.*

*"Well, we will go to Belize City for a few days, and then possibly to the Yucatan for a few more. At the most, we will be gone maybe ten days. So mama, could you live without this boy for that long, I wonder? This scary boy who terrifies me so." Armando grinned at Munio, and lunged at him. Munio giggled and moved to the other side of his mother to escape.*

*"What will you do for so long?"*

*Armando pulled out a nail file and fine-tuned his already immaculately manicured nails. His eyes never ventured from his hands as he spoke in an even yet severe tone. "Angelica, you know my business, I must keep it private, but you know Munio is always safe with me. Eh, Munio?"*

*"Yes, Uncle. I want to go, mother." Armando winked at Munio.*

*"Ok, ok, you go, you go." She stirred and stirred the bowl without looking*

up.

Armando motioned with his head. "Well, go, boy, go! Pack some things."

"How old are you now, Munio?" Armando asked as they drove along the beach road in the big black Chevrolet.

"Eleven, I'll be twelve next month. You going to get me a car like this for my birthday, Uncle?"

" I don't think so this birthday, Munio. You are too young to drive."

"Why? You don't have to have a driving license here, do you?"

"No, it is just not time, but this trip I will let you do some new grownup things."

"Like what kind of things?"

"Oh, you will see soon enough, but you will like it because I will show you how to make a whole bunch of money. You like money, eh, Munio?" Uncle Armando laughed and lit a cigarette.

The bright sunny day disappeared as they entered the darkened barroom. Munio's eyes took forever to adjust, and when they did, he felt uneasy in the foreign room. The smoke hovered like a cloud. Men sat at little tables with small lamps that hung down over each one. Other bars Munio attended with his uncle resonated with music and laughter. Here, the men whispered, and their mood, so somber.

He followed Uncle Armando to the bar.  His uncle and the bartender exchanged words so quietly that Munio could not hear what was said.

The bartender looked Munio in the eye and smiled. Munio smiled back and fidgeted with the pile of coasters on the bar.

"Munio, I want you to meet a friend of mine, ok?"

"Sure, Uncle. Why is it so dark in here?"

Armando gazed into the boy's innocent eyes. He put his hand under Munio's chin as he spoke. "Baby, these people are just having fun. It is so cool in here out of the sun, out of the light, don't you think? Anyway, we're going to meet a nice man in a minute. So be patient. Don't you always have fun with me?" Munio nodded.

"Armando, come on back! So glad you made the trip." A beaming man walked briskly to Armando and shook his hand.

The man seemed enormous to Munio. He was so broad he filled the doorway, and to clear it height-wise, he had to duck. "Who is this little man you have here?" he asked, and gave Munio a big, warm smile.

"Felipe, this is Munio, my nephew," Armando winked at Felipe and extended his arm to present Munio.

"Well, what a big boy you have here. So handsome. Munio, pleased to meet you, son. Welcome! Welcome!"

Munio smiled faintly and nodded to the big man.

"Munio, can't you say hello to this nice man, eh?"

Armando drew his thin eyebrows together in mock sternness.

24

"Hello, sir," Munio said shyly.

"Hello to you, Munio. Come, Armando, into my office. Let me get you two some drinks. You must be tired from the drive."

They walked down a short hall that frightened Munio because it was more dimly lit than the bar, but then Felipe opened a door into a room that nearly blinded him. Gigantic windows on one side offered a spectacular panorama of the city; beyond the buildings, the Caribbean Ocean glimmered like liquid emeralds. Mesmerized by the view, Munio raced to the windows and paid no attention to his uncle and Felipe who sat at a table talking amiably. After a few minutes, Felipe mixed some drinks. He brought one over to Munio.

"Here you go, my boy. You like guava nectar, don't you?"

"Yes, thank you," Munio said shyly.

"Nice boy you got here, Armando," Felipe lit a cigarette as he stood over Munio and studied him in a way that made him nervous. Felipe put his hand on Munio's head and stroked it softly. "Yes, Armando, a very nice boy, so polite and handsome. I like the curls." He pointed with his other hand to Munio's head as he turned to look at Armando and laugh. Armando tilted his head, took a sip of his drink, and winked at Felipe.

"Munio, do you like Felipe?"

Munio looked over at his uncle and not knowing what to say. "Yes, uncle, he's a nice man."

Armando and Felipe laughed.  Munio, confused, turned to the window once more and hoped the men would go back to their talk so he could daydream about the buildings, the people moving about them, and the green sea beyond.

"Munio, could you come over here to me, please?" Armando motioned for the boy to sit on his lap. "There now. You having a good time, my boy?" Munio nodded. "Good, good. Now, remember I was telling you I knew a way you could make a lot of money, Munio?" Again, Munio nodded. "Yes, yes, well." Armando's eyes looked up nervously to meet Felipe's. Felipe took a deep drag off his cigarette, listened, and watched Munio.  "Felipe here likes you a whole lot, and he would like to get to know you better.  He has said that if you spend some time with him, he will give you $100."

Munio's eyes grew large, and a big smile of disbelief came across his face. He laughed, "Why would he do that, Uncle? What must I do for this money?"

Uncle Armando chuckled and hugged Munio. "Munio, Felipe has more money than he knows what to do with. Right, Felipe?" Armando grinned at Felipe. "He is just a real friendly guy with too much money, ok?" Munio laughed. "So, I am going to go out for a little while, and Felipe is going to stay here with you and play. Then, when I return, maybe, we'll go down to the harbor, have lunch, and watch the big ships pass, ok?"

"Yes, that will be fun." Munio wiggled around on Armando's knee and clapped his hands enthusiastically.  "I want to do that, Uncle."

"Ok then, we will do just that." He eased Munio off his lap and straightened

*out several developing wrinkles on his tuxedo pants.*

*"Ok, Munio, you do what Felipe asks, and be a good boy, eh?" He patted Munio on the head and said emphatically to Felipe, "Go slow, Felipe, ok?"*

*"Yes, yes, don't worry, Armando. Go. I do this all the time."*

*Felipe opened the door for Armando.*

*"Hurry back, Uncle," Munio called after him.*

*Felipe closed the door and looked back at Munio with a big grin. "Now, young man, would you like another drink, or how about a cupcake? I have some right over here if you like."*

*"Yes, please, I would like that." Munio felt pretty comfortable with the man. He was used to meeting strangers. Belize, because of its lush terrain and stunning coast, attracted many tourists. Munio, as long as he could remember, made money from them. He would help moor their boats or run errands while they stayed aboard.*

*Felipe set a clear glass full of the light-green guava juice and a golden brown cupcake in front of the boy. "There now. You enjoy. My mother made the cupcakes just this morning."*

*"Thank you sir," Munio said politely as he bit into the cupcake. It filled his mouth with a sweet, soft vanilla taste.*

*Felipe took a seat in front of the big windows. The man watched Munio eat his snack, and then he motioned for Munio to come to him. Munio walked over, and Felipe picked the boy up and sat him on his knee. He wrapped his arms around Munio as Munio munched on the cupcake and stared out the window.*

*"This is quite a good view, eh, Munio?" Felipe smiled and patted Munio on the leg. "Have you ever been in any tall buildings like those?" Felipe pointed to the skyline.*

*Munio shook his head back and forth. "No, but I can climb real far up trees in my town. I climb so far I could see the next town. I can climb up the highest coconut tree, higher than anyone I know," Munio proudly announced.*

*"Oh, is that so? You are some big boy, aren't you? Strong too, I bet. Let me see you make a muscle."*

*Munio responded by flexing his bicep with all his might. Felipe put his large hand all the way around Munio's small arm. "Ooooeeee, you are some boy, I'm telling you. You are going to be a big strong man someday, aren't you Munio?" Munio nodded and smiled and chewed, swinging his bare legs back and forth as he sat on Felipe's knee.*

*Felipe's hand traveled from Munio's bicep to one of his legs. He squeezed the boy's calf and moved up to his thigh. "Can you make a muscle here?" He pointed to Munio's leg with his other hand. Munio straightened his leg and squeezed it hard, still steadily chewing bites of the cupcake. Felipe touched it and moved his hand quickly, as if it were hot, which got a laugh out of Munio. "Boy, you are some little man. Munio, tell me, what do you want to be when you grow up, eh?" Felipe began to rub both of the boy's legs slowly from his sock line up to the bot-*

*slipped the boy's little penis into his mouth. From here, Munio retreated into a place of unknowing--unsure if this strange act was harmful, despite the pleasurable sensation. He just sat and watched the top of Felipe's bald head bob up and down, until a powerful feeling gripped him as the flood of his first orgasm rolled down Felipe's throat.*

"Hey! Hey boy! Hey man! Munio, you crazy mother fucker! Look! You done burnt your hand! Hey, wake up man!"

Eddy attempted to rouse Munio by shaking him. When Munio opened his eyes, Eddy was six inches from his face and looked like a caricature in a fisheye lens. Munio jerked awake and assumed an air of nonchalance.

"Damn," Munio hacked a nervous laugh. "I must have been tired from driving. I, I just passed out for a minute."

"You sure as hell did. Does your hand hurt?"

Munio inspected his left hand. A brown cigarette butt was stuck between his index and second finger. The cigarette, now burned away, had seared dime-sized circles on both fingers. Munio's stomach turned as he pulled the cigarette butt from his burnt skin. It was hard for him to believe how badly such a small area could hurt. His fingers throbbed like a heart that pulsed at the end of his arm.

"Does it hurt?" Eddy repeated.

"Hurt? No, it's not bad. It's not so bad. It definitely won't be so bad as soon as I get a cold beer, eh? You ready to leave this..." he looked above him at the sign that hung above the gym, "this place. What you say the name is again?"

"Dixie Ironworks, man. Damn, you must wear some thick ass glasses. Shoueeee. Let's go."

# CHAPTER III

Eddy, hyped from his workout, babbled nonstop on the drive back to the bar, while Munio sat silently and nodded from time to time. He forced himself to smile and make eye contact with Eddy. Munio pretended to listen, but his thoughts were on his daydream. For a long while, memories about those times with his Uncle Armando and Felipe and the many others he "visited" for money had remained submerged.

In some ways, he felt lucky to have gone on excursions outside of Monkey River Town. Few children ever left, even when they became adults. He knew he had been privileged for the chance to see all the different kinds of ways people can live, and he enjoyed the attention most of the men gave to him as well, especially Uncle Armando.

"Hey, are you listening to me, man?"

"Yes, I'm sorry, Eddy. I have a lot on my mind just now. I was thinking

about my trip and everything."

"I tell you what. If you want to crash here tonight, it's no problem. You can stay at my place. Have a few drinks, smoke some shit. You smoke, don't you?"

To stay with Eddy for the night seemed like a good idea. Maybe he could work himself into a comfortable little situation for a few days. It would be nice to be off the road.

"Eddy, I like that idea. I'll take you up on that offer. This is an interesting place to me, this Rosedale. I am in no rush to go to my friend's in Atlanta."

"Cool then. We'll stop off here and get some beer and some chow, and we'll be set, buddy." Eddy pulled into the parking lot of a grocery store. "You like spaghetti, man?"

"It's ok."

"All right. Give me five bucks for beer, and I'll buy the food. How's that?" Munio nodded and pulled a five from his pocket. "You just wait here, and I'll be right back."

Munio lit a cigarette and exhaled a great cloud of smoke with a sigh. He was tired from the day, and he knew he looked it as he caught a glimpse of his weary face in the rear view mirror. However, the last golden waves of sunset cast a light on him that illuminated his beauty. His hair hung around his shoulders in thick, soft, black ringlets and in overgrown bangs across his face, too, so that his ebony eyes peeked out. He pushed his T-shirt sleeve up to the armpit and exposed his smooth brown skin and the taut muscles of his arm. A few minutes later Eddy lumbered out with his arms full of brown grocery bags.

It was a short drive to the bar where Munio's Ford truck was parked. The kitten surfaced from the black plastic garbage bags and greeted him with loud meows.

Munio cranked the truck and threw it in gear. "Hello, little kitty. I'm sorry I leave you for so long, but we are going to have a little dinner now. I'll bring you into Eddy's house so you can roam around, stretch your legs." Munio had trouble following Eddy, who drove rather fast and had no concept of turn signals. "This man is crazy. Why is he driving so fast?" The kitten responded with drawn-out, wide-mouthed meows all the way to Eddy's.

Eddy sped through a neighborhood of small rundown clapboard houses. The front yard at Eddy's house had, in years past, been groomed with great care. Beds of grand old rose bushes filled with large fragrant blooms graced the perimeter. Huge hydrangea bushes in each front corner of the yard burst with purple and blue blossoms. Gardenia bushes, loaded with withering white flowers, flanked the porch steps and emitted a delicious bouquet.

"Come on in, boy." Eddy motioned to Munio as he quickly jumped out of his car and slammed the door. "It ain't too fancy, but the rents' paid. Know what I mean, man?" Eddy laughed. He walked over to inspect Munio's truck.

"You got a bunch of shit in that truck, ain'tcha, boy? That's a good old truck though, ain't it?"

"Yes, it is everything I own in this world, really. Hey Eddy, do you mind if I bring my kitten in?"

Eddy scowled and big wrinkles formed on his massive forehead. "Cat? You got a fucking cat in that damn truck?" Eddy broke into a hysterical giggle and pointed to Munio's truck. "Naw, you ain't got no cat in there. Don't tell me you got a fucking cat in there, man. You are a crazy mother fucker, aren't you?"

Munio laughed along with Eddy and shrugged.

"Hey, where's that cat? I want to get a look at this cat you got." Eddy peeked in the passenger window. His voice went up an octave when he spoke. "Will you look at this? The man has got a cat he's travelin' with. Well, I'll be. I ain't ever known nobody to travel with a damn cat." Eddy laughed and clapped his hands one good pop.

"He ain't gonna piss all over hell now is he?" The furrows of concern returned to Eddy's forehead.

"No, no, he's a good kitty. I got a box and everything for him. He's cool, man, really. Don't worry." Munio opened the passenger door, and the kitten leapt into his arms and promptly climbed up his shirt to perch on his shoulder.

Eddy threw his hand up. "Hell, go ahead and bring the little bastard in, I reckon."

Munio reached up and patted the kitten. "You lucked out here, little kitty. Come on, I'll feed you now." Munio grabbed a couple of bags from the truck and followed Eddy into the house.

Munio was shocked to find it immaculate. The living room housed two couches, a couple of arm chairs, all covered in a thick, plastic material with drab brown-flowered pattern. All the furniture circled around a square wooden coffee table and looked like a display from a cheap furniture rental store. Over the windows hung matching curtains that were pulled open. The spotless kitchen featured frilly lace curtains as well as a needlepoint plaque that read "Thank God for Our Happy Home."

Eddy stood with his growth-hormone-induced big ears, his three-day-stubble on his pockmarked face, his inflated muscles, and that big goofy grin with his arms open. "What do you think, man? Ain't this nice?" He rotated in a half circle, arms extended, like a busty blonde displaying door number three on a game show.

Munio shook his head. "Ok, where's your grandmother? That's who fixed all this stuff up this way, right?"

"My mama brung me up right, boy. Well, she did rig it all up, but I keep it up good. Here, have a brewsky." Eddy snapped open a beer for Munio and himself.

30

"Thank you." Munio took a big drink and put his bags down on the table. "Eddy where can I put his bathroom box?" He pointed to the kitten who still roosted on Munio's shoulder.

Eddy screwed his mouth up and looked around. "Let's see. Now, you swear that cat is housebroke?"

"Yes, oh yes, no problem."

"All right, put it out here on this little back porch. I'll leave the door open for the little bastard."

Eddy put a big pot of water on to boil and began to chop onions and mushrooms. Munio sat down at the blue Formica table to observe. The kitten returned from his bathroom and rubbed figure eights around Munio's ankles.

"You want some dinner too, kitten? I guess so. Ok, I fix you dinner." Munio took a can of cat food from a bag, pulled back the pop-top, and set it over in the corner. The kitten attacked it voraciously.

"Where'd you get that damn cat, Munio?" Eddy asked as he chopped.

"In Mexico, at a little bar as I was making my way up here to the US."

"In a bar? What was it, a door prize?" Eddy laughed loudly at himself.

"You might say that. I won him in a dart game." Munio lit a cigarette. "Eddy, you got an ash tray?" Eddy picked a clean one out of the dish drainer.

"On my way here, I entered a cantina about one hundred miles south of the border, the US border. I ordered a beer and noticed these men, six of them, drunk as shit, playing darts. They started to argue about who was the best player, and one of these assholes said he knew of a perfect test to decide. So, he went running from the bar and returned with a kitten, my little kitty here. I could not believe it, but he took twine, you see, and tied it around every one of his paws, ok?" Eddy nodded. "Then, he got one of the other guys to help him, and with four darts, nailed this kitten, belly up, spread eagle to the dartboard."

"How could a couple of darts hold that cat down? You'd think him squirming and all."

"He was a baby, just a few weeks old, very weak, and his little white belly was just out there, man. I knew what was coming next, and boy, I just turned my back to them because I could not bear to watch, you know." Munio took a hard draw off his smoke. "But I couldn't stand by and let them do this, and I knew they could not be talked out of this stunt. So." Munio tapped his temple with an index finger. "I thought fast, Eddy, real fast. I happen to be an expert dart player, and I had this idea, ok? I go over to these fuckers and asked them if they would really like to see who was the champion." Munio snickered. "They stood up, staggered really, they were so drunk, and bowed up their chests like they were so bad, you know. The man who started all of it asked me who that might be? I, of course, said me. And then I say, I think the hardest part of that cat to hit would be his tail, no? They laughed and got excited about that idea.

So, I say, ok, if I can hit that cat's tail the cat is mine. They agreed, and then, I stepped up to the line with a dart. I was pretty loaded myself, and that cat's tail was wiggling like a worm. I was not sure at that point I could do it, but I threw the dart anyway. I missed. I took a second one and watched the tail for a pattern, and finally again I tossed. Boom! Right through that cat's tail, and boy, did he scream. I dashed up there, released him, and ran out of that place. Those guys were on the floor laughing, and that damn cat bit the shit out of me as I ran to the truck. So, that's the story. Here." Munio picked up the kitten, "you can still feel where the tail broke."

Eddy rubbed his hand along the tail and felt the noticeable lump halfway down the cat's tail.

"Damn, Munio," Eddy shook his head and put the kitten down on the floor, "that's a hell story. That's a good deed that ought to last you a while. What's that cat's name?"

"I just call him little kitty. I don't know."

"Hell, you ought to give him a name other than 'little fucking kitty'. Shit, that cat's lived through hell."

"Little kitty's good enough," Munio replied.

Eddy shrugged and tended the pots on the stove like a master magician. His bare back was exposed to Munio, and his lat muscles sat on his back like wings. A deep groove formed where his spine lay at the bottom of the canyon created by his dense spinal erectors. Numerous big, angry pus-filled pimples appeared on his shoulders and midback amidst a thick crop of blonde hair.

"Let's have a toast." Munio pulled out two beers from the twelve-pack and put the rest in the refrigerator.

"To Eddy, for his friendliness." They clinked cans and downed a big gulp. They laughed, and Eddy went on with the dinner preparation.

"Hey, Munio, you want to smoke one?"

"Let me turn you on. I'll be right back."

Munio pulled out rolling papers and cleaned a couple of buds. "This is some terrific reefer, Columbian."

"Hey, this is great. I bet that is some good shit. I ain't had nothing but home grown for a while. It's all right, but it ain't ass-kicking shit, you know?"

"Well, you sit back because I am going to kick your shit in just a minute, brother."

"Hey, let's go sit out on the porch, and let this cook for a while," Eddy suggested.

The wooden screen door banged softly behind them as Eddy, Munio, and the kitten sauntered onto the porch. Munio had never seen furniture like this before. The faded green metal glider delighted him with its smooth rocking. Eddy took a seat in a lawn chair made of evenly spaced strips of curved spring steel fastened to the frame. He sighed as he was enveloped by the lulling, bouncing effect the springy steel provided. The kitten padded silently

32

over the whole perimeter of the porch, which spanned the entire length of the house. With great confidence, as if it were his kingdom, he slipped halfway through the spindles of the railing, stood on the edge, and overlooked the yard, six feet below.

The men passed the joint back and forth without a word, absorbing the deep green of the southern summer evening as it yielded to the night. The scorching day left a residue of heat, but a light, sporadic breeze danced in the hot air. It was a breeze that could scarcely bend a flower, nor could it even be heard; yet it moved sensuously, lightly as the passionate intent of a lover's finger might trail down a chest.

Munio breathed with an ease he had not felt in a long while. The gardenia blooms at the corner of the house filled the air with a thick, sweet smell. As the golden pink light faded, lightning bugs started their night show. At first, out of the corner of his eye, Munio saw a flash appear here and there. By the time the full force of darkness arrived, Eddy's yard and beyond pulsed with the silent, yellow-green flashes. Munio melted in the glider's slow, rocking rhythm. Engaged in mock combat, the kitten batted at real and imagined objects until his energy expired, and he hopped up with Munio to sleep. Munio smiled and stroked his fur. All the elements of this fine night whispered a welcome, welcome to the South.

"That's some bad ass weed, dude." Eddy's voice broke the deep silence like a stone thrown in the middle of a glass-glazed lake.

Munio snickered. "Well, dude," he mocked, "I'm glad you approve it. It is a special batch. My grandmother grew it herself."

Eddy's jaw dropped. "You are shitting me. Your grandmama?"

"Oh yes, haven't you heard about the natives chewing on plants to, ah, keep up their energy, or you know, for religious purposes?"

"Well, I've heard of them chewing on coke leaves, but I ain't never heard of them chewing on pot leaves, for crying out loud." Eddy bounced restlessly in the spring steel chair and scratched his head. "Your grandmaw? How about that."

Munio exploded with laughter and pointed at Eddy. " You will believe anything, won't you?"

Eddy chuckled and shook his head in disgust. " I thought that was fucked up, man. I ain't never heard of nobody's grandmaw sucking on no pot leaves. Sheesh. Tell you what. You stay out here and tell some more lies to yore goddamn cat, and I'm going to get dinner on the table. Your grandmaw. Sheesh." Eddy got up and headed for the door.

Munio reviewed the day as he slowly rocked back and forth on the glider. He stretched and yawned. He could use a workout himself, or at least some kind of movement. The thought of dancing went through his head. From the time he was small, he had always danced. Uncle Armando taught him to dance. He thought about how it might not be bad to just hang around this

Rosedale for a few days.

"Munio! Chow's on, man," Eddy called from the screen door.

Eddy heaped his plate with spaghetti and garlic bread. Munio sat down slowly and looked around the room.

"What's the matter, man?"

"Oh, nothing, I'm just taking my time."

"Well, I ain't. I'm so hungry I could eat a fucking horse."

Munio smiled and began to fill his plate. The noodles were hard to capture, and Munio wondered why anybody would invent food that was so difficult to handle. Eddy watched intently as Munio sliced his food like a surgeon. With knife and fork, he cut the wad over and over again until he had a plateful of inch long pieces.

"You got it under control over there, bud?"

"Oh yes, now I do. I don't see how you eat this stuff any other way."

"Like this. Look here." Eddy had a huge mouthful that trailed down to his plate, and as soon as he had Munio's attention, he sucked and chewed until the wad disappeared between his powerful jaws. Munio shuddered at Eddy's demonstration.

"If I try to do that, I would choke to death. You ate more in that bite than I will in the whole meal." A huge belch made its way out of Eddy's throat.

"So, Eddy, do you have any plans to enter a competition for your body-building?"

"Yeah, I thought I might do the Mr. Dixie Contest. It's a national qualifier, you know. Hell, if everything goes right, I might turn pro in another year, year and a half."

"When is this Mr. Dixie?"

"Uh, let's see. It is the last Saturday in October. So that gives me," Eddy counted on his fingers in the air, "that gives me about twelve weeks."

"That's not much time. You think you'll be ready?"

"Oh yeah, man, I can be righteous. In twelve fucking weeks? Uh huh, yes indeedy. You don't think so?"

"No, no, if you say so, you're the man that must do the thing. I am sure you know what you are doing."

"Well, I know some things about what I'm doing. Hey, Munio, did you ever load up when you was lifting?"

"I never did. I had no access to that stuff in my country, but," Munio smiled, "I probably would have if I could have. Everybody else was loading."

Eddy scanned the room left and right as if he were afraid of being overheard. "I have got a fucking dream connection, Munio!" He slammed his fist down on the table, looked Munio right square in the and gnawed off a big piece of garlic bread.

"You ever heard of people using growth?"

"Growth?"

"Yeah, growth hormone. It's the shit that the pituitary gland, I believe, produces to make you grow, like from when you was a little kid."

Munio listened intently. His soft brown face and big dark eyes looked innocent for a man of fifty years.

"So, I got a connection to get the real stuff, not that artificial shit."

Munio wiped his mouth with a paper towel and set down his fork so he could better concentrate on this information. He took a big drink of his beer. "Artificial? How could that be made artificially?"

"I don't know, man, but they do it. The best stuff is taken from dead people's pituitary glands." Munio's eyebrows shot up, and his eyes opened wide. "Well," Eddy looked around again, left to right. "I got an unlimited connection that will sell it to me for two fifty a bottle. Unbelievable, unbelievable!"

"Two dollars and fifty cents?"

"No, you idiot, two hundred and fifty dollars, two hundred and fifty dollars! Usually-well, hell, there ain't no usual about it. You just can't buy that shit at any price these days, but I damn sho' can." Eddy beamed and took a big slug of his beer.

"Tell me about it then."

Eddy's face lit up like a Christmas tree. He sat on the edge of his chair, and his forehead wrinkled with sincerity. Munio suppressed his laughter at Eddy's enthusiastic disclosure.

"All right, I'll tell you, but you can't tell nobody. Not that you know anybody or anything, but just in case you do. You promise?" Munio nodded his promise. "Ok, so one day I was down at the mall, and this guy came towards me walking this little baby boy. When they got right up on me, I saw that it ain't really a little baby, because he just looked, you know, older in the face and all. I made eye contact with the daddy and realized that he's this guy I went to high school with. I ain't seen the mother in forever. He was a pretty good guy and all. We got drunk a few times, you know. So we sat down on a bench and started talking, and he introduced me to the kid, who turned out to be eight years old. I'm telling you though, this boy looked, size-wise, about two years old. Come to find out the little bastard's a dadgum midget or dwarf, I forget which. There is some official name for it that I can't pronounce. The point is he's a tiny motherfucker. Anyhow, the guy starts telling me how they are doing hormone treatments on him, and it's kicking in pretty good. Buddy, when he said that," Eddy slapped the table, "a damn light bulb went off in my head, big time." Eddy giggled a few seconds, remembering his excitement. "I asked him specifically what it was the kid took, and he said Myoply 2000. Well, I about shit! I thought it was outlawed a few years ago. Nobody at all, not even God can get the shit. Then, the guy starts talking about how expensive it has been and all. The dude can't make much. I mean he works in the mobile home factory. I let him ramble on for a little bit, and he told me how good I looked." Eddy laughed and bounced in his chair while he spoke. "I tell him

I'm bodybuilding and all. Then, I go in for the kill. I asked him if he would like to make a bunch of money, and naturally, he said yes. So I told him I'd pay him two hundred and fifty dollars for every bottle of that growth he could get his hands on. Boy, did his eyes light up. He looked down at that little sawed-off fucker and said, 'You done had a couple of doses this week.' So anyhow, I bought a bottle the next day. Can you believe that?"

Munio shook his head over and over. "No, I can't. That's the strangest story I ever in my life have heard."

"Let me tell you, I can hardly believe it myself. That little old fucker, poor little guy. Although they think by the time he reaches puberty, they'll have him up a foot or so."

"So how long has gone by since you first took this stuff?"

Eddy looked up at the ceiling and counted on his fingers. "Uh, I think I've had six shots in about the last two weeks. Yeah, that's right."

"How long will you stay on it?"

"Buddy, I'm gonna stay on it til my pecker hits me in the damn chin." He cracked up, leaned over, and punched Munio playfully on the shoulder, which caused Munio to giggle, too.

"That stuff makes that grow, too?" Munio's eyebrows hung in half moon arches.

"Hell yeah, it does. I swear it does. It makes everything grow, bud--your fingers, the size of your fingernails, your hair."

"Your hair? Hell, your hair's already growing. How you can tell your hair is growing different?"

"Well, Munio, all I know is two weeks ago I had a damn crew cut. Look here at this shit," He held his ponytail to the side, and gave Munio a serious look.

"No way, no way. Your hair didn't grow that much in two weeks." Munio sat there with his jaw dropped.

"Gotcha!" Eddy pointed his finger and laughed.

"Oh," Munio leaned back and groaned, "I knew you were lying. I knew that."

"I tell you what, and I ain't lying about this neither." Eddy pointed his index finger emphatically at Munio. " I've growed my damn wisdom teeth. I ain't cut them fuckers in all this time, but suddenly they have shot up like weeds." Eddy nodded at his own testimony and opened his mouth wide for Munio to inspect.

Munio frowned and squinted as he peered into his mouth. "Eddy, why do you want to do all this shit? Aren't you afraid it will mess you up?"

"I'll worry about that shit when I get old. Anyhow, I don't think it's all that bad for you. The media always exaggerates stuff, but I don't care whether they do or not. I like bodybuilding, you know, and I really think I can turn pro. Then I could get them big shots to buy my drugs instead of chasing down

fucking midget kids in fucking malls, man. I just feel so good the bigger I get. People look at me like when I'm out in public and stuff. I tell you what. People respect me more, I think."

Munio looked at his dinner plate, abandoned now to conversation, scratched his head, and pulled a cigarette out of his pocket. He took a couple of long drags before he spoke.

"Everybody got to do what they got to do. Nobody knows what it feels like to be you. So, you have to use your judgment. Muscles make a man feel powerful. Who does not want to feel powerful? You want to do drugs that make your pecker grow, why not? Show me a man that don't want his pecker to grow!" They both chuckled.

"Damn right. This is my ticket out of this podunk town, man. I mean, it's a good place to grow up and all. Everybody I know in the world lives right here, except you, but I want to go somewhere else. You know I ain't even ever been out of Georgia, except to Florida. I have been down there, but that's so close. Hell, it seemed like Georgia to me. I tell you what else. I ain't got a hell of a lot going for me in the way of potential cash flow. I got to face facts, Munio. One, I ain't smart, you know, like book learnin' smart." Eddy counted on his fingers. "Two, I ain't got rich folks that's gonna give me a bunch of money one day, and three, I don't like getting dirty all day. About the only damn thing I do got is muscles—well, really, genetics. I got me some bitchin' genetics, and I got me some drugs. With them drugs? Buddy, it's through them I get my diploma, startin' with the Mr. Dixie."

"Eddy, if you feel so strong in this way, you should do it. Some things you can do only when you are young, and this bodybuilding is one of those things. Before I went to the Olympics, people in my town said I was crazy to practice. They said I was crazy to make the weights and everything like that. People said I could never do it. They said I could never be good, never go to Olympics, but, " Munio pointed at an emphatic finger at Eddy, "they were wrong, Eddy. They were wrong. So you go for it. If that is what you want to do, you go ahead and go for it. What you say is true about your body. You got a good start if you just continue."

"Thanks, bud, I appreciate you saying that." Eddy's spoke softly as he locked eyes with Munio. He leaned back in his chair and balanced on its two back legs. "Hey, lets go back out on the porch and talk. You want to?" Munio nodded and stood. "I'm gonna roll us up another one. I'll be out in a minute. I'm gonna let you get a taste of some Georgia homegrown."

The intermittent glow of billions of lightning bugs danced, providing the main source of light outside. The tops of the trees were silhouetted against the backdrop of the navy blue sky, and above them, many white, twinkling stars shone. The wind blew in erratic gusts. Munio reclaimed his seat on the glider. The kitten lay on top of the wide porch railing and watched the night with that famous tail twitching in thought, cat thoughts of the secrets of the darkness,

or of fantasies dredged by ancient tiger genes. Periodically, he would hold his head high, and stretch his neck out after catching a whiff of some particularly interesting odor.

Munio suddenly noticed that his feet felt very tight inside his shoes. They had, after all, been cooped up for a day and a half. He untied the well-worn black canvas Converses and quickly removed them along with his socks. Munio rubbed his feet and moaned passionately.

The screen door slammed, and Eddy appeared and fired up the after-dinner joint. After a long toke, he passed the cigarette to Munio.

"Say, Munio, what are your plans, man? Where do you figure on heading and all?" Eddy scratched his crotch and his head, and reached to receive the joint.

"Oh, I suppose I will continue north to the house of my friend in Atlanta. Maybe he will be there, and maybe he won't. I don't know. I will have to wait and see. It's no big deal one-way or the other. I still just wanted to see what is here in this country, you know."

"Well, I was thinking, and I don't know if you're interested or not, but maybe you would like to stick around here for a while. If you wanted to help me train, you know, you could stay here for free. Maybe you could chip in for food and stuff. You got a little money stashed, don't you?" Eddy's wrinkled forehead and big blue eyes called to Munio.

Munio looked away, took a long drag off the joint, held it for what seemed to be forever to Eddy, and dramatically stoked the silence for at least another thirty seconds. All the while, Munio stared at the stars, with a saint-like expression upon his handsomely weathered brown face. The phone rang. Eddy got up to answer it and left Munio, who pretended to be locked deep in thought. Munio held his pose until Eddy was out of sight and then relaxed. There was no doubt what Munio's answer would be.

The longer Eddy took on the phone, the more impatient Munio became. He tapped his foot, bounced his legs, like a nervous player on game day, an actor on opening night.

Finally, Eddy reappeared on the porch and announced with no particular excitement, "That was Destiny."

Munio smiled confidently and thought somehow this news had to do with his entrance in Eddy's life. "I'm not surprised." Munio inspected his nails.

Eddy, puzzled by Munio's comment, said. "This girl, this friend of mine is coming over."

"Ok," Munio nodded his head.

"So, anyhow, what do you think about what I said?"

Munio turned his head sharply and made direct eye contact with Eddy. "Eddy, I think I would enjoy that very much. I appreciate your generous offer, and I accept." Munio spread his arms wide in Eddy's direction. "I will stay."

"Cool, dude. That's great. We'll have a good old time. I ain't lying." Eddy slapped Munio on the back so hard he almost flew off the glider.

"Damn, Eddy, what you are trying to do, kill me?" They both laughed, and Munio stood up. "You want another beer?" Eddy nodded.

Headlights turned into the driveway, and out jumped a woman who made her way toward the porch.

Eddy stood up and waved. "Hey, come on up here. I want you to meet somebody. Munio, I'd like you to meet Destiny. Destiny, this here is Munio."

Munio smiled, then laughed out loud as he realized he had mistakenly thought Eddy was being philosophical earlier. He rose from the glider and stuck out his hand to greet her.

Although the light was dim on the porch, it was plain to see Destiny was a very pretty woman with a trim and shapely body. Her long brown hair swayed around her in a free and easy manner and hung down to her breasts. Her teeth shone evenly in the night as she smiled a big wide easy grin.

"Munio?" Destiny looked over at Eddy for reassurance that she had pronounced it correctly, "Munio, Eddy tells me you're from way down south of the border." She smiled politely and nodded her head.

"Yes, that is correct. I am from Belize."

"Well, how about that? That is so neat. I don't get a chance to meet foreigners much." She smiled and chuckled a little. "You know, I took Spanish in high school. Eddy, did you?" Munio and Eddy returned to their seats while Destiny sat down in an old caned-back rocker that had been painted white.

"Nooooo, not me. I couldn't understand all that mumbo jumbo. Hell, I damn near didn't graduate high school on account of almost flunking English."

"Let's see, if can I remember any." Destiny laid a finger along side her nose and wrinkled her eyebrows and mouth for concentration. Her green eyes brightened up, and she jumped a little in her seat from the excitement of stirring her memory. "Let's see. Uh, me llamoes Destiny. Uh, hable espanol? Si, um poquito, and Puerto Viarta. That's it! That's my whole repertoire." She threw her hands up as if in surrender, looked at Eddy and Munio and laughed.

"That's not too bad." Munio was amused at her efforts.

"Seriously, Destiny, that was hell. I'm impressed. You're just a, a, damn smart babe, I reckon." Eddy slugged his beer.

"Hey, you want a beer?" Eddy asked her.

"You ever known me to not want a beer? Especially after all those brain cells I just fired up remembering that Spanish shit. I'm thirsty as hell." Eddy went in the house for the beer.

"Are you Eddy's girlfriend?" Munio pried because he wanted to know her availability status.

"Hell no! I ain't fucking that crazy pumped up wild man!" Destiny

laughed and so did Munio. "I used to be, but we're just friends now, good friends too. Ever now and then we get it on." She ran her fingers through her long hair.

The screen door slammed behind Eddy. He handed Destiny a can of beer. "Oh, ah, mucho gracious, senõr. Hey, I forgot about that one." She held her beer up to Munio and Eddy in a toast. "Cheers. Or maybe it's Cheerios." She giggled, but Munio didn't.

"I want to go down there to Mexico. My sister went. She brought me a bottle of that tequila with the worm in it, and some of them sandals that was made out of old tires. Can you believe that? We had the best time drinking that stuff. Got drunk, shewweee! Lord, we was wiped out, you know?" Destiny chattered relentlessly, and the sound of her voice lowered the quality of serenity that Eddy and Munio had shared before she arrived. "She ate some weird fish one night. What was that shit? Hell, I can't remember. As many of 'em as are in the US, I ain't ever met a Mexican like you face to face."

Munio's temper sparked. "Lady, I am not Mexican. I am from Belize. It is a different country."

"Oh, well, you look like a Mexican. It's all about the same down there, ain't it? Rice and beans? Y'all speak Spanish, don't you?"

"We don't speak the same as Mexicans. Don't refer to me as Mexican because I am not. Belize is a much more civilized place. We are quality like you. We speak English and so on."

"Are you saying y'all look down on the Mexicans?" Destiny was confused.

"Well, yes, in some ways. It is just that I consider myself closer to American in status than to Mexican."

Destiny looked over at Eddy for help, but Eddy just shrugged his shoulders and shook his head. "Y'all are getting too deep for me. I don't know what the hell y'all are even talking about."

"Well, whatever, I hope I didn't make you mad. I'm glad to meet ya anyhow."

"It's ok. It's ok. You don't know about us. It's ok." Munio wanted to change the subject because he knew he was on the verge of a nasty recoil in response to her innocent insult. The whole conversation reminded him of many Americans who sailed up to the docks in Monkey River Town. They would say similar things, call him Mexican, thinking he was the same. Munio felt more privileged because the English had established his country, even though they enslaved his ancestors to work the docks, tend their animals, and farm the plantations.

Eddy broke in. "Anyhow Destiny, Munio was in the Olympics as a weightlifter."

"Is that right? What sport? Oh hell, I heard you say that." Destiny put her index finger to her temple and pulled a mock trigger. "I can't remember shit

these days. When is what I meant to say." She laughed and got a snicker from Eddy and Munio.

"In 1972," Munio said quietly and smiled.

"How about that? I ain't ever met a bona fide Olympic athlete. How much did you lift? Did you win a medal?"

"No, no, I did not win a medal, but I was the first man to ever represent Belize in the Olympic competition as a weightlifter."

Destiny joked, "Lots of pencil necks down there, bud?" She looked first at Eddy, then at Munio, neither of whom did not shared the humor.

"As I was saying," Munio cleared his throat and continued. I pressed 225, snatched 250, and clean and jerked 300 pounds. That was at a body weight of 148."

"Wow weee, that's a lot. Can you do that much, Eddy?"

"I can't do none of them Olympic lifts at all. I ain't flexible enough. Besides, you need a lot of technique. I can press two and a quarter, but that's about it."

Destiny noticed the kitten who woke up. "Awww, who are you?" She reached down and scooped him onto her lap. "He's so cute. I didn't know you got a kitty, Eddy. When did you get him?"

" I didn't. He's Munio's."

"Really? I love cats. I've always had cats. I have three now. One's named Peachtree, then Libby, and, ah, Jed," she drawled.

"How would you like to have four?" Munio asked matter of factly.

"You looking to give him away?" Destiny looked down in her lap at the kitten who was now nearly asleep.

"Sure, why not?" Munio slugged his beer.

"Don't you want him? I mean, he's awful cute and all."

Eddy sat up in his chair, surprised at this dialogue.

"No, I don't have any use for him really. You can have him if you want him."

"Damn, Munio, I thought y'all was kind of bonded after that dramatic rescue story." Munio shrugged and looked away.

Destiny glanced at Eddy, unsure of what to do. Eddy shrugged and shook his head, confused at Munio's attitude.

"Well, I will take the little fellow if you ain't going to keep him." Destiny stroked the sleeping kitten.

"Take him. Take him. It's fine. That's good." Munio lit a cigarette.

"All right then, I will." Destiny shrugged over at Eddy.

The three talked for a while longer on the porch and watched the lightning bugs. Far away, heat lightning lit up the sky with orange and white puffs of light.

A fleeting whiff of rain wafted on the breeze, and grew until its balmy aroma overwhelmed all others. The buildup of the shower entertained them

from their grand viewing stand, safe and dry on the porch. Like popping corn, the drops started with a split-splat rhythm. Then, every two or three seconds another and another dropped until the sound of the steady, gentle rain on the steps, on the sidewalk, on the cars, on the porch's tin roof became the only sound in the world.

They sat in mesmerized silence, each of them relieved to have a focus other than themselves or the previous conversation. Their relaxation deepened, and they all nearly fell asleep. When the rain abruptly stopped half an hour later, the change in sound caused them to stir.

"Well y'all, I better get going . I got to get up early tomorrow. Munio, has this cat got himself a name?" Destiny yawned and rubbed her eyes.

"I call him little kitty, but I think you might change it if you wish."

"Whatever. I'll see about it." Destiny said, tired and cranky.

The three stood up, stretched, groaned, and headed into the house. The living room was dark, but a light on in the hall enabled them to make their way. In the kitchen, Munio and Destiny got their first good look at each other. Munio was surprised to see a terrific scar on Destiny's face. The scar blazed a trail through the left eyebrow, distinct as a power line right of way through an overgrown hillside. It clipped the outer edge of the left nostril, traveled right through her lips and dissected them into uneven halves. The trail stopped short of her chin. Most of the disfigurement was thin as a razor cut, but on the nostril and the upper lip, the scar tissue accumulated like congealed pink solder residue.

The sight stunned Munio and flooded his mind with frightening fantasies of what might have caused such a brutal injury.

"You want to know about this shit?" She pointed to her face. "See, they had to open up my face to give my oversized brain breathing room. I got a damn IQ of 500, you know, and I'll be dogged if it ain't been a tremendous help." She nodded her head sincerely and winked at Eddy on the sly.

Munio didn't quite know what to say, as he stumbled through a response. "Hmmm, how about that. I never heard of that. Do you go to college or anything?"

Destiny guffawed. "Yeah, right, you idgit. I was just joking."

Eddy laughed out loud now and enjoyed this moment with Destiny. Just below the surface, Munio's anger simmered. He did not like to be fooled, and since the last thing he needed was to screw up the home situation he had just created for himself, a few deep breaths helped stave off his impulse to lash out at her.

"Well, lady," Munio coughed out a weak laugh, "You seem plenty smart to me. Hell, I don't know all the medical procedures available this day."

"No, ok, what really happened is I, ah," Destiny again winked at Eddy. "I'm dyslexic, and I cut myself shaving. She held her hand up sideways and pretended to hold a razor..

42

Munio laughed out loud. "You did not do that, lady. I do not know what has happened for you to get that big ass scar, but this thing you say was not it."

"All right, all right, I was drunk as hell, and walked through a giant plate glass window in a Texaco station. That is the truth. I had to get a hundred and thirty stitches. I might get plastic surgery, but I ain't sure yet. They say it won't always look this bad."

""Wow, that must have been some great shock, eh?"

"'Eh' hell," she mocked Munio, accent too. "I liked to bled to damn death. It put a definite crimp in my party that fine day. I tell you what. Why don't you round up that cat if he's going with me."

Munio picked the kitten up off the glider and spoke softly, "Kitty, it's time for you go now. You are to go with the lady. She has got other cats you will like and play with." Munio patted him gently. He placed the kitten on Destiny's shoulder.

"I reckon I'm out of here, y'all. It's been real. It's been fun, but it ain't been real fun."

"Destiny, you take it easy, girl," Eddy said as he and Munio followed her to the door.

Munio stepped onto the porch and leaned against the wall with his hands in his pockets. He watched Destiny until the red tail-lights disappeared completely into the darkness.

"I'm going to bed, Munio. You ready?" Eddy called from the door.

Munio, leaning on the porch railing, turned to face him. "You go on." Munio waved him on.

"Ok, but let me show you to your room." Eddy talked as Munio followed him down the hall. "We got to get up early tomorrow to go train, all right?"

"Yes, ok, that is no problem. I always stay up late at night. I think better late at night."

"What the hell you got to think about tonight? I don't know about you, but I'm stoned as hell and half drunk. I can't very well think about shit when I'm like this."

"See, that is the difference between you and me, Eddy, my friend. I feel like my brain thoughts are enhanced when I am a little high."

"Enhanced?" Eddy mocked Munio, "Don't go intellectual on me, Munio."

Munio laughed and slapped Eddy on the back affectionately. Eddy walked into the room that was to be Munio's and turned on the light. Munio's head snapped back in shock.

The walls, papered in a deep pink satin material, presented a three-dimensional effect as he moved about the room. The furniture, fancy and Victorian in nature, the woodwork, the curtains, the carpet were bright white.

Dolls of all sizes were piled on top of the pink taffeta bedspread, all Cau-

casian, all dressed in pink. Literally, not one spot was available to even perch on the edge of the bed. The white shelving units along the walls burgeoned with more dolls, many of them identical. They sat silently, eyes fixed and dilated, with slight smiles upon their faces and hats upon their heads, in fine southern belle style. In the corner, a lone chair, white Victorian with a pink-covered seat, was full of dolls as well.

Munio blinked several times and shook his head.

Eddy sensed his shock. "I know. It's fucked up, ain't it? It was my mama's room. She was into dolls. She died a couple of years ago, but I just don't know what to do with all of 'em, you know? You're actually the first person to stay in here since she passed. Is this gonna be ok? I mean, we can shovel em off the bed and all."

"Sheesh. Eddy, no disrespect to your mother, but this is weird. How many dolls are in this room? There must be two, three hundred?"

"Uh, there's, uh, two hundred fifty-eight." Eddy bowed his head, seemingly embarrassed. "My mama knew. She wrote it down somewhere."

Munio smoothed over the awkwardness of the moment. "Well, girls," he addressed the dolls, "My name is Munio, and I'll be the man of your dreams tonight. Easy now, stay back everybody, one at a time please!" Munio joked.

"Well, you just make yourself comfortable, and pile the damn things over in that corner so you can get in the bed."

Munio chuckled, "Ok man, you go to bed. I'm a big boy. I can figure this out. I got to have another beer and maybe a joint also after this sight. Wow."

"Whatever, make yourself at home, and I'll see you in the morning." With that, Eddy disappeared.

Munio leaned on the door jamb and studied the panorama. Most of the dolls were brunettes, except for a few blondes, but they all shared the same glassy brown eyes, the same faint smiles, the same sheen bouncing off their high cheekbones. Munio laughed out loud again as he absorbed the view.

"Girls, I'm going to go out to the porch, get a little more liquored up, and I'll be back to show you a real good time." He flipped off the light switch.

Munio roosted on the metal, porch glider in the sweet and silent night. He drank and puffed in celebration of his new temporary home. He wondered what he would find in this Georgia town. What women or men would he woo? Whatever he would do, he knew he would not have to work for a while. On that thought, he smiled, raised his beer can, and silently toasted Eddy.

"Ok, I guess I am ready go sleep with some dolls, eh? I am the only man in the world that tonight can say his bed is full of dolls." Munio laughed as he stood and staggered.

Down the dark hall, he groped his way, reached in, and felt for the light switch. He peeked his head in and somehow hoped the dolls had gone away. As if not to startle them, he tiptoed into the room. There was the chance, he thought, they might all attack. The bright pink color on the walls made him

dizzy. He undressed and lay his clothes on the back of the chair. When he turned toward the bed, he stopped and put his hands across his chest with a self-consciousness spawned by dozens of glassy brown eyes. Suddenly he felt as if the dolls were all looking at him.

"Oh boy, this is harder than I thought." He sat down on the edge of the bed after raking an armful of dolls out of the way.

"Ok girls, we're getting down to it now. Who wants to go first?" He laughed and grabbed the crotch of his tight lavender jockey shorts. His body, superior for a man of his age, was smooth, brown, symmetrical and lean, every muscle's definition could be seen, even his abdominals.

"I hate to be rude, girls, but I prefer to sleep alone this evening." He stood by the bed and pointed his finger at the dolls. "OK, so you and you and you and you, and you, girl over there, all of you must leave right now, and don't make me call the policeman. All right, I'm going to have to get rough. I asked you nice, now." With that, he crawled onto the bed and began scooping armloads of the dolls, which he deposited in the one deserted corner of the busy room. Three more trips finally cleared the bed, and Munio pulled back the covers so he could crawl in. To his chagrin, the pattern on the sheets was covered in little dolls.

"Jesus fucking Christ! When will it end? I will probably shit a doll in the morning, for crying out loud." He muttered to himself in Spanish as he switched on a lamp next to the bed, and turned off the wall switch.

He breathed a deep sigh and realized he had an erection. While the dolls watched on in silence, he worked himself into a swift and breathless orgasm on this sweet, August Georgia night.

A scream--the next thing Munio heard was a loud scream, a war cry really. He jumped from the sheets and moved quickly and quietly down the hall toward the sound. At the edge of the door to the kitchen, he peeked his head around cautiously. There he met Eddy who wore nothing but a big, goofy grin and holding an empty syringe in his hand.

"Eddy, what in the world is the matter with you?"

"Ain't a goddamn thing wrong with me, bud. I feel like a million bucks." Again, he made a loud whoop, and blew on the syringe as if it were a smoking gun. "God o' mighty damn, if that ain't a rush, I don't know what is."

"What did you do?" Munio asked, letting the rest of his body slip around through the doorway.

"I just took a shot of growth, man."

"Growth hormone?"

"Yeah, you 'sposed to do it first thing in the morning. See, I keep it loaded in the freezer. You hit up right in the stomach, but I'm gonna tell you what though. It stings like a mother fucker, but after that goes away, you feel a hell of a rush."

Munio looked out the window, and saw that it was still dark. " What time

is it?" He rubbed his stomach gently and cringed inside at the thought of having a shot there.

"Six o'clock. I'm gonna go back to bed now for a couple of hours. Then I'll get up, eat breakfast, and go train. Hey, sorry I woke you up, man. I should have warned you, but when that shit hits you, you just gotta yell." Eddy laughed and slapped Munio on the back as he passed on the way back to his bedroom.

Enough light filtered in at six in the morning to silhouette the dolls on the shelves. Munio scanned them, sighed, muttered a few words in Spanish, and crawled back under the sheets.

He fell instantly into a deep sleep and began to dream. The dream took him out to a reef off the coast of Monkey River Town.

*The sun shone intermittently, hiding behind gigantic banks of white and gray clouds. With all its multishades, the water appeared like the coat of a green and blue calico cat. His bare skin felt warm, and the breeze was light. He paddled to a spot where he felt lucky, and threw out the heavy rock that served as an anchor. The splash splattered him. He tasted the salt water that dripped down his face to his lips.*

*He donned his mask and snorkel, and with spear gun in hand, he jumped from the canoe. The water felt warm, and the bubbles tickled him seductively. He looked around to get his bearings. His long black curls radiated out from his mask and waved like some strange sea plant. With a good breath sucked into his lungs, Munio swam down under the water a few feet. He held that position for a bit to see if he could spot a big fish. The sea was full, as always, with an abundance of life. The array of shapes and colors of the fish dazzled, a display of fireworks with fins. He returned to the surface for another breath and on the way back down, found himself suddenly face-to-face with an enormous red Oscar fish twice the size of his canoe. The sight so terrified Munio that he lost all his air when he gasped. He started to dash for the surface when the fish called to him.*

*"Hello, Munio. Don't be afraid. I'm here to speak to you," the fish said in Spanish.*

*Munio stopped his attempt to flee. With no effort, he began breathing right there underwater, just like the fish. His fear abated, and he studied the beauty of the fish.*

*It was so large that each of its scales was as big as a saucer, and sparkled like an opal. All the scales blended together gave off a scarlet color, and the fish had three thick, wavy, black stripes that ran the length of its body. The fins by its gills calmly vacillated back and forth like large transparent fans.*

*"What is it you seek this day, Munio Morelos?" The fish let out a big deep laugh and a flood of basketball-sized bubbles.*

*"Supper, I was fishing for my supper."*

*"Well, haven't you gotten lucky? I would represent many suppers, now wouldn't I?" Again, the fish roared with laughter and released a great amount*

*of bubbles.*

"Yes." Munio relaxed a bit more and chuckled at the fish, as well as this whole unbelievable scene. "You would be a good catch all right, except you are bigger than my boat. Not only that, my spear gun would feel like a pin prick to you."

"I am not here to feed your stomach, Munio. I am here to feed your soul. I am your guardian angel, so to speak. Don't be afraid to come close, examine me." The fish remained motionless like an idling dirigible.

Munio swam right up to the fish now, worked his way around it, and marveled at each detail.

He stared right into its eye, which was bigger than his own head and colored gold with a shiny black center. He ran his hands along the fish's side, feeling its smooth, slick surface.

"You are such a beautiful fish. I feel like a minnow next to you."

"That diminishes your sense of power, does it not? Do you miss that power, Munio?"

"Not at the moment, since I feel you not to be a great white shark or a raging barracuda. I am no longer afraid you will eat me."

The fish laughed a great laugh. "Don't be so foolish. The day is young. My appetite has not yet developed today. I might eat you, and then again, I might not. Tell me, do you think you would be tasty?"

"Ah, no, maybe not. I drink and smoke a great deal. I would probably be bitter." Munio broke a sweat on his brow behind his mask and longed for a cigarette.

"That is perfect. I very much like smoked meat, don't you?" The fish laughed a deep scary laugh.

"I guess you got a point, all right. I like smoked fish very much."

"Things aren't always as they seem, Munio. I want you to close your eyes because I have a surprise for you."

Munio closed his eyes and continued to tread water.

"All right, you may open them now."

Munio opened his eyes to find that the fish had turned into a gigantic cat, his ex little kitty. He growled ferociously, and had the same gold eyes as the fish, only they were filled with rage. His gray fur looked much longer wet, waving there in the blue-green water. Big streams of bubbles left his mouth and nose in a race for the surface. He tread water too as naturally as the fish. The cat reached out for Munio and quickly caught him. Munio struggled, but was unable to escape. The big kitty held Munio at arm's length and studied him carefully.

Finally, he spoke. "Ah, just what I've been wanting, a good Cuban cigar."

"But I'm not Cuban!" Munio screamed. His eyes were big as pies from fear and from the pressure of the big cat's paw that squeezed his waist and rib cage.

"Whatever, close enough. I'll make believe." The cat waved his other paw as he spoke.

*With that, the big cat raised Munio to his mouth, promptly bit off his head and spit it out. Minnows picked on it enthusiastically as it floated lazily to the bottom of the sea. Then the cat stuck the stub of Munio's neck into his mouth and held it there between his lips. Munio's body was stiff as a board. The cat reached out and struck a giant match on a piece of the reef. It sparkled an orange flame as the cat held it under Munio's bare feet. He sucked hard on Munio's neck until he drew smoke out. He took Munio out of his mouth and blew out the smoke.*

*"Ah, now that's a good smoke, old boy!" The cat let out a great big evil laugh and thumped Munio.*

Munio's heart beat wildly as he sat up in bed. He breathed deeply and exhaled as he reviewed the wild dream. He slowly raked his fingers through his thick hair.

He lay back quietly on the bed as tears ran down his cheeks. Motionless and expressionless, he stared at the ceiling as the stream flowed steadily from his eyes, down his face, and onto his ears before finally they dripped onto the pillow. After a few minutes, the tears soothed him into sleep.

Munio awoke to the smell of coffee and food cooking. He opened his eyes to see the multitude of dolls in the light of day. Many of them, he observed, were covered in dust, a condition that was not obvious to him last night.

"I see you don't look so good first thing in the morning either, eh?" Munio looked at his own face in the dressing table mirror. There were lines on his face and bags under his eyes. He picked at his hair to fluff out the flat spots, and then got dressed.

"Good morning to ya," Eddy said a little too cheerfully for Munio to appreciate.

"Morning." Munio walked to the back door to look out the window for a weather report.

"Want some pancakes and oatmeal? There's some coffee right over there on the counter, too."

Munio nodded, "That's what I need, coffee."

"You want cream or sugar?"

"Yes, both please." Munio filled a cup, and Eddy set the sugar bowl and a small container of milk by him on the counter. Eddy watched him pour a flood of milk into the cup and then proceed to dump spoon after spoon after spoonful of sugar into the cup.

"Damn, Munio, I'm getting sugar diabetes just fucking watching you do that shit. You need a sugar rush this morning special, or do you always do that?" Eddy's face crinkled up in a combination of disgust and concern as he stared at the cup of coffee.

Munio grinned when he looked at Eddy. "Yeah, right, my man here is concerned about a little sugar. The man who injects dead monkey glands into his stomach. That is pretty funny, you know, Eddy? Pretty funny." Munio took a big swig of the coffee.

48

Eddy's intensity melted into a giggle as he continued to stir and flip the food on the stove.

"Well, I guess you got a point there, buddy. Speaking of which, I got to get me some more of that stuff today. That growth is some weird shit. Look here what it's done to my fingers."

He held up his hands for Munio to see. Eddy's left index finger was abnormally large and long. The nail was huge, nearly twice the size of the one on the other hand. The ring finger of the right hand stuck out about an inch further than the left. Both thumbs looked unusually large as well.

"Wow, that's pretty strange."

"Yeah, and sometimes it gets ugly. Like, um, it can make your ears grow a bunch, or your cheekbones grow real weird. Most people get spaces between their front teeth. Hey, let's eat."

Munio's stomach was generally a little queasy in the morning, but all this graphic talk about deformities had him close to puking. When Eddy set a heaping, steaming platter of food in front of him, he had to leave the room.

Munio smoked and sipped coffee on the porch. He wore sunglasses in self-defense on this already blinding, white-hot cloudless day. At seven-thirty in the morning the temperature was close to eighty-five. The yard buzzed with activity. Bees harvested the bounty from various blooming flowers. Huge double-winged dragonflies hovered like small helicopters to investigate this and that. They amazed Munio, who had never seen a dragonfly.

Munio felt old this morning, tired, and worse still, lost. He questioned everything. Why had he come here? He took a big drag off his cigarette, exhaled, and shook his head slowly. Consumed with sadness and confusion, a part of him just wanted to walk out to that truck and leave without a word. These bouts of depression surfaced often, and he could acknowledge the feelings only for a fleeting moment until another part of him would call a halt to it. It was too painful to figure out so he snuffed out the thoughts as deftly as he put out his cigarette butt. A roach found in the ashtray lifted his spirits as its kind smoke filtered relief through his head.

A month flew by as Munio and Eddy established a routine that would persist until the Mr. Dixie contest. The days began and ended the same. Eddy's morning howl signaled the dawn, his workouts filled the days, and for Munio, beer and reefer on the porch alone finished the evenings.

# CHAPTER IV

The Dixie Ironworks was busy. Even at eight forty-five in the morning, the clientele ranted and raved at the weights to cooperate with their efforts. The stationary bikes and stepping machines were full of tortured sweating souls buying time from the devil.

Today presented a change in Eddy and Munio's routine. Eddy had made a date to train legs with an old friend.

"What time is this man to arrive?" Munio asked.

"Nine. I don't see him yet, but it's early."

"I think I will wait outside til he comes."

Eddy turned his attention to the finishing touches of his workout outfit. He tied a lime green bandanna pirate-style around the top of his head. His face was a bright reddish-brown color from tanning bed treatments. The pants he wore were a blinding orange Spandex that stopped at the knee. Despite the fact it was hot and steamy in the gym, Eddy wore a thick, traffic-yellow sweat shirt that included a furious image of a grizzly bear, with bold black lettering: "If you're going to be a bear, be a grizzly", and on the back, "Go heavy or go home." He had cut the neck out of it, creating a plunging neckline effect. This allowed a generous view of his neck, trapezius, upper chest, and one shoulder. Instead of boosting Eddy's manly image, the shirt created a perversely feminine look.

Suddenly, a cry rang out. "Ouuu Lawd, brother, I'm feeling good today!" A wild man had entered the gym, and even if he had not spoken a word, his presence was such that it was felt. Everyone's eyes were on the man, which is just exactly the way he wanted it.

"Hey, Jimmy Ray!" Eddy threw out his hand to the man, who promptly grabbed it and shook it with a vengeance.

"Are you ready for God to work a miracle in yore life this mornin'? Do you believe, brother Edward, in the power of Jesus? Well, do you now?" Jimmy Ray let out a big belly laugh.

"Fuck, Jimmy Ray, don't start with that shit today. Hell, I am always ready for God or any other damn body to work a miracle on leg day. I tell you what. More than anything, I beeeelieve in the power of knee wraps, brother." Eddy laughed.

Jimmy Ray was a great big man of God. He stood about six feet four, and believed God had made him to rise above most everybody else so he'd be closer to the home office of heaven. At just over three hundred fifty pounds, his imposing frame and aggressive charisma made it easy for him to attract attention. Above all, he was a handsome man, and he knew beauty to be a wonderful tool of coercion. His long dark brown hair, full beard and mustache, plus his overdeveloped physique, made him look like a loaded-up steroid Jesus. He did not pretend to be the actual son of God, but he did indeed fancy himself to be at least, perhaps, a distant stepson.

His clothes was equally as flashy and obscene as Eddy's. His color theme for the day was an electric blue, the hue of both his Spandex knee pants and his sawed-off sweatshirt, which displayed, in white ink, a scene of Jesus on the cross in great distress, and read "go heavy for Jesus because he went heavy for you."

50

"What we going to do, son?" Jimmy Ray spoke in his booming southern voice.

"Squats." Eddy counted on his fingers as he spoke. "Uh, hack squats, leg presses. That's about e-damn-nough, don't you reckon?"

"Yeah, I do, sure do. Let me stretch out here a minute. You stretched out?"

"Naw, I ain't either."

"Hey, did you see that weird yahoo out there on the stoop, long old curly hair. Man, looked like he just stepped out of the jungle. Ain't never seen nobody around here like that. Out there smoking a dadgum cigarette."

"I know who that is, man. He's all right. He's been helping me train. He's going to stay with me for a while. He's cool, man." Eddy said defensively.

"Whaaaaat? Help you train? Well, where in the world did you pick up this fellow? I thought he was some bum just hanging out. What you want to take up with him for?"

"He came in the bar a few weeks ago. We got to talking. Come to find out he used to be a weightlifter, Olympic weightlifter. He even went to the Olympics in 1972 in Germany."

"Olympic lifter, eh? Like good old Paul Anderson. Now there was a strong man of God. Strongest man in the world for years. Did I tell you I met him? Did you know that?" Jimmy Ray's smile had faded and was replaced with a furrowed brow and emphatic eye contact.

Eddy continued. "The man knows a lot about training. He came here from Belize, down below Mexico. He's just traveling around, so I think he's going to stay here until after my show."

"Oh, uh huh, I see." Jimmy Ray got a stern and suspicious look about his face. "Eddy, brother, I don't want to tell you how to run your business, but you don't hardly know this man well enough to let him in your house and all, do you?"

"Aw, he's all right. I like him. He ain't up to nothing."

"You don't know how them people down there work. They're lost and desperate, them people from Mexico, Central America. We've got some missionaries covering some of the territories, but not near enough. They ain't civilized like us. I ain't saying he's not basically a nice guy, but he don't know our ways, Eddy." He shook his head and pointed a finger, with his thick eyebrows furrowed.

Eddy laughed and said sarcastically, "Some damn good Samaritan you are, Jimmy Ray. Boy howdy, a friend to all." Eddy threw out his arms. "You know what? You don't know what you're talking about. Now, just shut up, and let's talk about them pencils you call legs."

"Pencils, my foot! The Lord's spotting me this morning, Edward! I can do no wrong! Let's go, brother!" he boomed, causing heads to turn.

With that, the men took to the squat rack. By the time they had added

four hundred and five pounds on the bar, the sets were getting serious. Munio returned from smoking and had his first formal introduction to Jimmy Ray.

"Munio, I want you to meet Reverend Jimmy Ray Jones, and Jimmy, this here is Munio Morelos, ex-Olympian weightlifter."

"How you doing there." Jimmy Ray was cool.

"Pleasure to meet you." Munio lied and smiled. Jimmy Ray had given Munio a hard cold stare as he walked arrogantly in the door.

"All right Jimmy Ray, it's all you. Let's get twenty big ones." Eddy coached him as the reverend wrapped his knees tightly around and around with the long white knee wraps. When he was finished, he stood and sounded off with a mighty roar.

"Lord, help me get twenty. Lord, bless my soul, won'tcha? Bless my spotter too! Sweet Jesus, I'm goin' in!" Jimmy Ray let out a whoop and attacked the squat rack, quickly stepping out with the weight on his back. His white face reddened more every second as he drew a great breath and began to squat. After he got ten reps, he was in big trouble. Munio knew there was no way he would get ten more. He smiled silently at the pain and anguish Jimmy Ray was in. Eddy virtually spooned with Jimmy Ray in order to spot him. His arms were around him, and he dug his thumbs into Jimmy Ray's chest when he hit sticking spots as he tried to stand with the weight.

On rep thirteen, Jimmy Ray seemed to lose his faith in the whole situation. He was afraid and tired, and didn't want to play anymore. After Eddy cranked him up with the fifteenth rep, Jimmy Ray hesitated.

"Come on, dog! Don't you quit on me, mother fucker! Get on down there, boy!" Eddy screamed, thus provoking Jimmy Ray to try one more against his better judgment. His legs could barely descend with the weight, much less stand back up. With every bit of strength he had, Eddy managed to pull Jimmy Ray to the surface once more, and Jimmy Ray immediately headed for the pins on the squat rack.

He was so anxious to be relieved of the load that he forgot to bring his hands in so that they wouldn't get pinched at the spot the bar came to rest in the squat rack. As he set the weight down, he realized what was about to happen, but did not have the strength to stop himself. The outside edge of his hands and both pinkie fingers lay trapped under four hundred and five pounds of weight.

Jimmy Ray screamed and fell to his knees, his arms outstretched and caught. Blood streamed down each sleeve of the electric blue sweatshirt as he knelt helplessly, looking a lot like the crucified Jesus.

"Munio, help me!" Eddy screamed as he raced to lift up one end of the bar. Munio was with him in a flash; as they lifted one end up swiftly, one arm fell limply to the floor. They ran to the other side, lifted it, and freed Jimmy Ray once and for all. Jimmy Ray had fainted in a big, electric blue heap. Eddy knelt down by him, slapped him in the face, and shook the big man as best as

he could, but Jimmy Ray didn't respond right away.

Munio picked up one of the man's hands to survey the damage. The pinkie was flat and mangled, and big gouges let blood escape through the meaty side edge of his hand. Eddy picked up the other hand only to see that damage was practically identical. By now, big Jimmy Ray began to stir.

"Hey. Man, you all right?" Eddy asked as Jimmy Ray's eyes fluttered open.

"What happened?" He asked weakly.

"You set the motherfucking bar down on your damn hands, boy!" Eddy laughed, feeling relieved that Jimmy Ray was moving.

"Good Lord in heaven, why in the world did I do that? I just wasn't worth a good God damn today, was I?"

"Hell no, you sure as shit wasn't. Now, I got to train legs by my damn self." Eddy kidded.

Jimmy Ray sat up slowly and brought his hands together in front of his face to see his stigmata.

"Well, that looks nasty as hell, don't it?" Jimmy Ray exchanged his red face for gray.

"Yeah, it does. You better go to the emergency room and get them to look at it, I reckon. Although I don't know what they can do for that shit. It's going to be sore, I can guarantee that, bud." Eddy shook his head. "Yuck."

"God damn that hurts," Jimmy Ray cursed and spit on the floor. The pain began to sink in.

Munio observed on the periphery of the scene. He personally felt great pleasure that this accident had befallen Jimmy Ray.

Jimmy Ray's head started to clear a little more, and Eddy sat loyally by him with his hand on his shoulder, patting him from time to time.

"You want me to take you over to the hospital or something?"

"No, I believe I'll call my mama. She'll carry me."

At that moment, Jimmy Ray looked up and caught sight of the ever so slight smile on Munio's face.

"What the hell you looking at, you fucking wild-haired jungle man? I'll get up from here and kick yore wetback ass if you don't get that smirk off your damn face! You hear me, boy?" he thundered.

Munio didn't twitch a muscle, but gave Jimmy Ray a good long piercing beam of direct eye contact before he spoke.

"You must have been sinning today, preacher man, for him," pointing upward, "to treat you so badly, eh? What is it, hmmm? Perhaps, you don't treat your fellow man with enough respect. That is what I think it is, personally. Also, you don't go deep enough in your squats. You use too much back. You're cheating, as well as wearing out your spotter."

"Damn Munio, the man just got hurt. Could you give him a break?" Eddy looked worried and caught in the middle.

Jimmy Ray spat. "You a lying sack of shit that don't know a squat from a hole in the ground. I take that back. You probably live in a hole in the ground when you ain't mooching off other people."

"And God bless you too, preacher man," Munio said and turned to go outside, working his way through the crowd that had gathered to look at Jimmy Ray

"Jimmy Ray, you are a real son of a bitch sometimes, you know that?" Why'd you talk to him that way? He ain't never did nothing to you. Hell, you just met the guy." Eddy looked away.

"I just don't like his kind, all right! I just don't trust these illegal aliens! Comin' up here, crowdin' up America. Bringin' all them diseases and shit. Anyhow, fuck him! I want my mama, damnit! Go call her, Eddy! I thought we was friends, and there you go taking up for that wetback like that! Jesus!"

"I'll go call her, but you know what he said was right. That thing about respecting people and all."

"Let me get something straight with you once and for all, Eddy Jackson. I ain't a preacher man to all people. I am the preacher man for the white folks that lives around here that I preach to! I don't preach to colored, no time, no how, never. My God is white! I am white, and each and every day, I thank almighty God for it!" He looked straight up as he spoke. "That, my friend, is as big as my world is! That's as big as I want it to be! My rainbow is white, snow white, washed in the lamb white! You got that?" He got so worked up a few tears rolled out of his angry blue eyes.

Eddy silently rose to call Jimmy Ray's mama. The crowd quietly broke up, exchanging looks as they snickered under their breath.

Eddy was back in just a couple of minutes. He had a small plastic bottle of soda pop for bodybuilders. It bore big bold letters that said "Pumped and Ready". He opened it and handed it to Jimmy Ray.

"I reckon this'll cure it, won't it," Jimmy Ray chuckled as he slugged the drink. Little streams of the orange liquid ran out of both sides of his mouth. "Ahhhh. That's damn good. Thank ya, buddy. Was she home?"

"Yeah, she'll be here in a minute."

"Hey, will you take these knee wraps off of me. I forgot I had 'em on. My dadgum legs is about to die. Look how blue my calves are."

"Good lord, Jimmy Ray, you gonna lose everything you got today if you don't watch it. This ain't your lucky day, is it, man?" Eddy joked as he quickly unwrapped his legs. The wraps left deep welts up and down his legs.

"Shooowwwee, if that don't feel better, Lawd Jesus, I'll eat your hat." Jimmy Ray laughed out loud for the first time since the accident.

Shortly, Jimmy Ray's mama burst through the door of the Dixie Ironworks. Her speed was impressive for a roly-poly woman twice as big around as she was tall. The hem of her dress flew in her wake, flip flops smacking against her heels.

"Where's my baby?" she hollered blindly into the room, looking back and forth. "Oh," she said as she saw her baby on the floor.

"Hey, mama," Jimmy Ray said.

"Lord, Jimmy Ray, what have you gone and did? I told you this dang liftin' weights is dangerous, ain't I?" She peeked over at Jimmy Ray's hands. "Ouuuuu, Lord! Oh, my God in heaven, you has broke both yore hands slap off, boy." With that, she started to cry. "My baby's prayin' hands has been broke off. Lord, why, why oh why?" She looked upward with the last question.

"Mama, I just think I broke my pinkies. I'll be all right. Settle down now. Eddy, help me get up so I can get out of here before my mama faints."

Eddy got behind Jimmy Ray, and on the count of three, lifted up on his armpits while Jimmy Ray engaged all the leg strength he had to rise. Jimmy Ray's hands were now so swollen they looked like exploded softballs. Eddy walked them out to Jimmy Ray's mama's car and waved at the trail of dust in the gravel parking lot as they drove away. When he turned around to go back inside, he saw Munio on the stoop. He sat down beside him.

"Well, that got the day off to a fun start, huh?" Eddy laughed and threw a pebble out into the parking lot.

"Yes, that was a real fun time, Eddy. I would love to get together with that man again real soon." Munio raised his eyebrows at Eddy.

"He's all right really. He's just an asshole Jesus freak that hates anybody that ain't white, that's all." Eddy laughed.

Munio looked over at him and laughed too. "Oh, is that all? Well, I'll see if I can get a whitewash so that Reverend Jimmy Ray will shine on me."

"Hell, he don't really like me much anymore because I ain't no Jesus freak. I hardly ever see him, actually. Now and then we get together and train legs, and that's about it. Speaking of which, I still got to train. You gonna help me or what?" Eddy winked and poked him.

"Sure, sure, I'm ready." He took one last toke off his cigarette and thumped it into the parking lot.

"Hey, you want to eat at the Waffle House for lunch?" Eddy asked.

"Do they serve beer there?"

"Naw, but why don't you just come over to the bar this afternoon, and I'll give you some free beers, ok?"

"Yes, that is the best offer I've had all day. I'll take it." he said with great enthusiasm.

Munio loved bars, the darkness, the neutral environment, and most of all, the drinks. Since his arrival in Rosedale, he had laid low, doing his drinking on Eddy's porch. This opportunity sounded like a good change of pace.

In the Waffle House, Eddy and Munio sat down. Eddy picked up a menu and scanned it, while Munio gazed out the window.

Eddy looked up at him. "Aren't you going to eat?"

"Sure, I'm going to eat."

"Why aren't you looking at a menu then?

"Why should I? I know what I want." Munio shrugged.

"What if they ain't got it?"

"Why wouldn't they have it?"

"Well, for example, this wouldn't be a place to order lobster or, pizza or hell, fried chicken. They ain't even got fried chicken." Eddy waved his arms.

"What kind of crummy restaurant is this, anyway?" Munio broke into a smile. "Why do you not bring me to some nice restaurant?"

"Because you're a stupid motherfucker, that's why. Any more questions?" Eddy laughed and punched Munio across the table.

"You think they will have goat's milk?" Munio asked sincerely.

"Goat fucking milk, are you crazy? People don't drink goat milk! Yuck-kk!" Eddy made a horrible face that wrinkled up his forehead like a Sharpei puppy.

"What's wrong with goat's milk? It's good for you."

"No, it ain't. Goat milk sucks. They ain't got it, I guarantee you. Like I said, Einstein, just look on the menu. If they got it, it'll be there." Eddy flipped a menu in front of Munio.

Munio picked it up and pretended to read it.

"Ah, goat's milk small size one dollar twenty-five cents, large one seventy-five. See." He laughed and pointed triumphantly.

Eddy grabbed the menu and looked to see where Munio was pointing. "Grape juice, grape juice, that's what that says."

"I knew that." Munio smiled coyly, hiding the anxiety he felt from his bad guess.

"No, you didn't neither. You didn't know that. You can't read, can you, Munio?" Eddy looked him directly in the eye. "Tell me the truth. Can you read?"

Munio lit a cigarette. "I can read some, but I read more when I have my reading glasses."

"It ain't a sin, you know. Lots of folks can't read or write. You can learn. There's classes." Eddy spoke gently.

"Oh, it is no problem, really. Thanks, man, but it's no problem. I get along just fine." Munio brushed it off and smiled at Eddy, who continued to stare at him. "Don't worry about it, Eddy, I'm fine." He was relieved when the waitress arrived.

After lunch, Eddy proceeded to get ready for work while Munio lounged on the porch. Munio took off his T-shirt to better accommodate himself to the day's heat. He took his shoes and socks off too and felt his feet sigh. The only part of his body that noticed it was dressed was now the part hidden behind his faded blue jeans. "Ok, ok, I'll change," he said to his legs. He rummaged through one of his big, black plastic bags until he found a pair of cutoffs. He stepped out of the jeans and into the shorts, and as he stood up straight to zip

them, he noticed the dolls all over again.

The battalion of dolls still seemed as strange as they did the first night. His eyes scanned each wall of the room. Munio snapped and entered his fantasy. He pretended to be center stage in a great theater, and all the dolls were patrons who had bought tickets to hear him sing.

With abandon, he broke loudly into song for the crowd with his rendition of "The Impossible Dream". In a solid and beautiful tenor, he sang through every verse with gusto as if it were the performance of his life. The stage lights burned and the orchestra sounded magnificent. On the last verse, he sang in Spanish with such beauty and passion tears escaped down each cheek as he reached the final words. He bowed to the audience and applauded with them for himself and the orchestra.

He laughed and cried. The echo of the applause still rang in his ears as he looked around the room, which, despite its strangeness, appeared flat now after that fantastic experience. Slowly, he backed out of the doll room, went into the kitchen, and splashed some water on his face. His face, buried in the soft dish towel, felt comforted by the darkness. Confused by his emotions, he felt empty and sad, and he did not know why. He never knew why. The crack of the pop-top gave him hope, and the first sip of the cold beer brought him back to center.

"Hey, you want to burn one before I go, pal?" Eddy bopped into the kitchen while buttoning up a shirt over his massive torso. As he worked his way up the buttons, the cloth hid the big red pimples incubating on his chest.

"I would love to be stoned." Munio smiled and ran his hand over his face to further wipe the sadness from it.

It was that time, just past noon on a sunny summer's day in south Georgia, when it gets quiet. Everything and everyone hides and conserves their energy. The bees don't buzz, and the dogs don't bark.

Likewise, Eddy and Munio lay low in the shade of the porch, saying little. Their breathy toking styles dominated the sound waves. Eddy inhaled with ferocious vocalization, but exhaled silently. With Munio, the exact opposite was true.

"Eddy, would you like to hear some music?" Munio said finally.

"Music? You gonna sing for me?" Eddy chuckled through his redeye high.

"As a matter of fact, I will." Munio winked and made way down the steps of the porch to his pickup truck.

Munio opened the passenger door and an incredible blast of heat hit him so hard he stepped back as quickly as if he had stuck his head in an oven. After a deep breath, he dove right back into the truck. He fumbled around through the black plastic bags and unearthed an old guitar case that lay on the floor of the truck.

"Oh lord, me and my big mouth. What am I in for, now?" He moaned.

"My friend, you are one lucky guy to have me to serenade you on this day. I happen to be known as the Eric Clapton of Monkey River Town, mister."

"Monkey River Town? Is that the name of your hometown, man? Well, whoop de do. Monkey River Town's Eric Clapton." Eddy cracked up and threw a meaty thigh over one arm of the rocking chair.

A saturated smell of heat escaped when Munio opened the velvet-lined case. Mother of pearl inlays outlined the body and the center hole of the guitar, which was crafted from a rich rosewood. Munio smiled as he handled it.

After a lengthy tuning session, Munio strummed with a dramatic Spanish-style, and after a minute or so of this, he broke into song. Eddy had thought by the sound of the music that Munio would probably sing something in Spanish, but instead he sang "The Impossible Dream" with the same fervor with which he had sung to the dolls.

Through all three verses, his voice gained momentum like a boulder tumbling down a hillside. He sang with great bravado and passion in a voice strong and clear, except for when it occasionally broke.

Eddy was not so much in awe over the performance as he was hysterical at the fact someone could be so serious about this old and, in his mind, radically hokey song. It was all he could do to keep from falling out of his chair, and he would have, except he did not want to hurt Munio's feelings. When the final note sounded, Eddy applauded and stood, yelling "Bravo, bravo! Let the big dog eat!" Munio stood and bowed with great dignity.

"Go ahead on with yo bad self, Mister Munio. Shit, that was hell, man. You shore got a flair for the dramatic. I tell you what, boy." Eddy sat up straight and felt very relieved to finally release his stored up chuckles.

"Thank you. Thank you. I'm glad you liked it." Munio strummed and picked on the guitar at random now.

Eddy heard the phone ring and sighed as he reluctantly got up to answer it. He reappeared at the screen door shortly to find Munio picking away. When there was a break in the action, Eddy piped up.

"Hey Munio, I got to get going. I got to go over to the midget's house to pick up my growth. I'd take you with me, but they're kind of paranoid. I start work at four so come on over whenever you want to for those free beers, ok?"

Munio turned to face Eddy. "Yes, ok, I'll see you."

# CHAPTER V

Eddy's drive took him way beyond the outskirts of town. He passed the town's water tower that displayed his name, written in black paint along with scores of names of other teenagers drunk enough to climb up and scrawl their legacy. He drove another few miles beyond the catfish pay lake and the grave-

yard where his mama and daddy now resided. At the first dirt road past the cemetery, Eddy turned right, leaving a cloud of red dust in his wake. At the third mobile home, Eddy turned in and stopped.

Immediately, three densely furred and matted red chows came barking out from under the trailer. After Eddy spoke to them, they quieted and glumly returned to the coolness of their doublewide cave. The door opened and a head stuck out just below the doorknob. The little midget child watched Eddy walk across the yard. The boy had long, curly, dark hair that formed a soft halo around his rather large head. He had a poignant look about him that was incongruent with the tiny body that lived below that big head. On this hot day, the child's toplessness revealed his bony little chest with skin so thin that much of his entire network of veins and arteries lay visible just under the surface. Below his cutoff jean shorts, an unusually thick crop of dark brown leg hair grew, which bore testament to the unpredictable side effects growth hormone could produce. Eddy moved up the rickety steps and greeted the boy.

"Hey there, Nate. What you say, boy?" Eddy poked him in the ribs as he passed through the door.

"Nothin'. I ain't doin' nothin'." Nate smiled and followed Eddy into the living room.

"Hey Eddy, come on in."

"Hey Billy. Hey Bibby. How're y'all?" Eddy sat down on a couch that resembled red patent leather. Across from him on a matching loveseat, Billy and Bibby sprawled.

"We're downright tired," Bibby started in. "We went up to Mama's and picked a bushel of okra. Picked two bushels of corn. Went over to my sister Shirley's and picked beans. Picked a bushel of them. Then, on the way home, we stopped on the side of the road and picked about a gallon of blackberries."

"Dadgum, Bibby, y'all ought to be set for a few days, anyhow. That'll be some good eatin', huh?"

"Yeah, I thought I'd make up a cobbler and some corn bread. I'll cut some of that corn up and put it in the bread. It's good that way. Makes it like chunky cornbread, you know? Then I'll snap the beans and put them on. Chop up the okra, some of it anyhow." She laughed at herself. "I'll fry up some of that. I don't know what kind of meat we can have. I reckon I'll end up frying a chicken. Might make some gravy." Bibby rattled on and on. Finally, Billy put on the brakes.

"Hon, I don't believe Eddy rode all the way out here to hear about what we're havin' for supper, ya know?"

"Oh," she laughed, "I'm sorry. I just get to talking, you know. I'll go on and get started because it'll take me til midnight to get done, you know. Let me see. I'll go on and start that cobbler because that'll take the longest. Then I'll go on and put the cornbread in with it in the oven, you know. And-"

"Honey." Billy gave her a look.

"Oh, I'm sorry. There I go again. I'll just go on in the kitchen and get going and leave you boys to talk." She got up and continued her conversation alone.

Little Nate crawled up on his daddy's lap. The boy ran his hands through his thick wild hair, revealing enormous ears. He smiled at Eddy and stretched in his daddy's arms.

"How you doin', big 'un?" Eddy winked at Nate.

"I'm fine. I ain't doin' nothin'." Nate stated.

"How about you, Billy? Anything new going on with you?"

"Ain't a damn thing new but the phone bill." Billy sputtered a laugh at his joke, exposing brown and jagged front teeth. His wit vanished as quickly as it had appeared.

Eddy smiled to be polite although, inside, nausea threatened as well as claustrophobia. Rivers of sweat surfaced when he thought about how it could be him living Billy's life. After all, most of his high school classmates were married and lived in a double wide with two or three kids.

"Well, Billy, I got to go on to work. You think we could settle up?"

"Yeah, uh huh. Come on back in the bedroom. Nate Nate, you stay here, all right?" Billy stood up, leaving Nate nodding and wiggling on the couch. The trailer shook as they walked down the narrow hall to the minuscule bedroom. Billy opened the curtains to let some light into the room, revealing a pasture full of black and white cattle that grazed just outside of the walls. From the top drawer of the dresser he removed a small, clear glass bottle full of yellow liquid.

"Well, there you go, bud." Billy smiled as he handed it to Eddy.

Eddy reached in his wallet and counted out two hundred and fifty dollars that he put in Billy's hand. The two of them shook hands and smiled.

"Sure do appreciate it, Billy. I'm getting big as shit on this stuff." Eddy bowed out his chest as he bragged. "I'm figuring to win the Mr. Dixie contest. If y'all want to go, I'll get you some tickets, ok? It's in Atlanta though."

"All right. Well, I'm glad it's working for somebody. I don't believe it's doing a lot for Nate right now. He still only weighs about thirty-five pounds and half of it's them damn ears." Billy punched Eddy jokingly, and then instantly resumed his deadpan expression. "He'll be nine next month, too. It ain't looking too good. He might just end up being a little ole pip squeak, I reckon."

"Well, hell, Billy, I don't know what to say. It ain't so bad. I mean, at least he can walk and stuff. You know, feed himself. At least, he ain't a spaz or nothing. That'd be worse, don't you think?"

"Yeah, I reckon so. Yeah." Billy looked pained as he stared out the window. The light shone harsh on his weary wrinkled face. Even though they were the same age, Eddy noticed how much older Billy looked.

"Billy, thanks man. I'm going to head on out."

"OK, All right. Let me walk you out."

"Bye, Bibby." Eddy said as they walked towards the door.

Bibby moved like a tennis player, bouncing off the walls of that little kitchen, chopping this, stirring that. Big clouds of steam escaped as she raised a lid off of a pot. She was so preoccupied she didn't even hear Eddy. Eddy looked back at Billy, who waved him on. They both chuckled.

"See you, little brother." Eddy tousled Nate's hair and winked at him. "You eat good so you'll get big, ok?"

Little Nate smiled shyly and hung onto his daddy's leg. "Ok, I ain't doin' nothin'."

Eddy strode gratefully to his car and as he left a cloud of red dust on that little dirt road, he thanked his lucky stars to have his life instead of theirs. The sight of his huge forearm as he gripped the steering wheel caught his eye. He rubbed it up and down with his other hand, nodded approvingly and sped on.

# CHAPTER VI

Destiny poured herself another cup of coffee and curled back up on the couch to view the rest of the talk show that held her absolutely spellbound. The subject was mothers who had run off with their daughters' boyfriends. The topic hit close to home for her because the very thing had happened in her own family. It was not her boyfriend, but her younger sister's who had been nabbed by their sex-crazed mother. Now, Destiny had a stepfather that was too young to buy hard liquor in the state of Georgia.

Destiny offered opinions every few seconds, though not a soul could hear them except the cats.

The phone rang, and Destiny reached across the coffee table to answer. She aimed the remote at the TV and pressed the mute button.

"Hello? Hey. Watching TV. You should see it. It's got people on that's like Mama who have run off with boys half their age and all. Pinched his fingers off? I swear to God. Well, is he all right? Yeah. Uh huh. Is that right? I'll be damn. Y'all need anything?" Destiny rolled her eyes impatiently, as she listened to her caller.

"Lynette, now you know I love you and all, but I broke up with Jimmy Ray a long time ago. Lynette, the man treated me awful now, and you know it. He's finally not followin' me around everwhere, and I swear I hate to get him started back up and all." Destiny's face contorted in a variety of frustrated expressions as her discontentment grew with the news on the other end of the phone call.

"Yes ma'am, uh huh. Well." She paused and sighed. "I reckon I could come over for a few minutes, but you better tell him because I'm sure going to tell him that this don't mean nothin'. I ain't looking to get back up with him,

now, ok? I ain't kidding, Lynette. All right, I'll be over directly, in oh, about thirty minutes, I guess. Ok, all right, uh huh, bye."

"Damn!" she said as she slammed down the receiver.

Destiny started straightening the apartment in high gear. She moved quickly, cursed, and spoke aloud. "Just when I think I'm rid of the bastard, he thinks of some shit to make me feel sorry for him! That son of a bitch and his goddamn mama, too! Shit, I do not want to be doing this! Hell, it serves the motherfucker right! Damn, jive ass preacher!"

Destiny begrudgingly changed from her giant T-shirt, and put on a pair of cutoffs, a tank top, and a pair of navy blue open-backed, low pumps. She brushed her long, shiny, brown hair vigorously for a few minutes, smeared on some tangerine dream lipstick, then stepped back from the mirror for a full-length visual inspection. Her hand caressed the long scar on her face. As if the old wound still hurt, she squinched up her face and her eyes grew anxious in anticipation of pain. It actually did ache at times, but mostly she felt afraid and weak on the rare occasions when she allowed herself to acknowledge it.

"Oh stop, will you?" she scolded, and turned away from her reflection.

A couple of years ago, long before he added the title reverend to his name, Destiny had been engaged to Jimmy Ray. Back then, he was more appropriately called 'Doctor' Jimmy Ray because of his extensive inventory of drugs for sale, both recreational and steroids. That's really how she had come to know him. In the beginning, he sold her a little pot every couple of weeks and maybe a little coke or crank once a month.

One thing led to another, and before she knew what happened, she agreed to marry him. For a brief time, he actually treated her well, but after they became engaged, his occasional slaps escalated to full-scale beatings. The first bone to go was her nose, and a week after that, two ribs. It took ten stitches to close a cut on her leg when Jimmy Ray flung a glass at her, and her wrist broke in two places after she was thrown against a wall in her apartment. The final straw came one night when he staggered around blind drunk, waving a pistol at her, threatening to shoot her if she didn't quit cheating on him, which she was not doing.

For Destiny, the night Jimmy Ray got busted was the luckiest day she had had in a while. A two-bit dealer down in Waycross got popped and narked on him. Jimmy Ray never suspected a thing as he sold the guy a pound of reefer and an eight ball of coke.

For Jimmy Ray, this presented a real good time to tote a bible and pray every hour on the hour. Who knows if it helped or not, but somehow he managed to serve only six months in the county jail, with three years probation. He received so much positive feedback for his born again act that he decided to keep it after he got out of jail.

Destiny called off the engagement while he was in jail. The unspoken reason was her fear of his violence. She said outwardly that she simply could

not bring herself to marry a holy roller. Jimmy Ray had no choice but to accept this decision while he was in prison, but once released, he began to badger her in earnest to get back together with him.

Despite her wishes, Jimmy Ray called on the phone incessantly, came by the insurance agency where she worked, and would appear out of nowhere at times when she was out shopping. He stalked her for months until she threatened him with the law. Such behavior violated parole. So, for four months now, the harassment had ceased.

She pulled into the long driveway that led down to the old farmhouse, and a pack of barking yard dogs greeted her. She sweet-talked them, and they wagged their tails instantly. Jimmy Ray's mama stood on the porch and held the screen door open.

"Come on in, honey. It's so good to see you, darlin." She reached to hug Destiny.

"It's good to see you too, Lynette."

"Well, come on in. He's in here." She followed Lynette down the shotgun hallway.

Jimmy Ray's room looked like a Jesus store. Framed eight-by-ten velvet-backed paintings featured the most famous Jesus poses: Jesus kneeling down by the big rock, looking up to heaven, Jesus by the sea of Galilee, Jesus petting a lamb, and Jesus tacked up on the cross. There were close-ups and crowd scenes of Jesus doing this or that. Alongside, Jimmy Ray displayed a number of photographs for comparison to highlight his perceived resemblance to the alleged son of God. Destiny found it spooky to see that he had actually assembled props for some of them, such as the crown of thorns he donned for one pose. He even had a picture of himself coming out of a squat rack with his arms outstretched on the bar so it looked like he was attached to a cross.

Jimmy Ray looked the perfect Jesus lying in that bed, too, propped up with each arm outstretched and elevated. Both hands were thoroughly bandaged so that he appeared to wear snow-white boxing gloves. This sight eased Destiny's mind; she knew no punches would be thrown today. She forced a sweet smile at Jimmy Ray. He mistook it for gladness to see him, but it was her satisfaction upon seeing the man disarmed and in obvious pain.

"Hey." She sat down on the edge of the bed.

"Hey sugar, thanks for coming. It's so good to see you." He smiled a dreamy barbed-out smile. "Why don't you come over here and give me some sugar, baby."

The bottom dropped out of Destiny's smile. "Because I didn't come here to give you no sugar, Jimmy Ray. I come here just to be nice for a few minutes, and that's that. Don't be startin' nothin."

He unleashed a wicked snarl. "You fucking bitch. You think you got it all figured out, don't you?" He tried to sit up, but instead just leaned his head towards her as far as he could and spoke in a quiet, evil voice, "Nobody leaves

me, woman. You hear that? It won't be today, but it will come to pass that I will teach you a lesson about that."

Destiny laughed out loud. "Well, ain't that a Jesus-like thing to say. Why, you are plum full of the holy fucking spirit today, Jimmy Ray. My, my, my!" She stood up, leaned over the bed and got in his face. "If there is a God, and if there is a heaven, then there probably is a hell, and you know what, Jimmy Ray? That's exactly where you'll go, reverend, because you are one stupid and mean bastard. You will get what's coming to you one day. I hope your fucking hands rot off, you son of a bitch! With all the momentum she could muster, she aimed at Jimmy Ray's crotch level, spit on the bed, spun on her heels, and left the room with a slamming of the door.

"Lynette, I'm going. See ya later, ok?" Destiny called as she moved briskly down the hall past the kitchen.

Lynette appeared in the kitchen doorway. "You sure didn't stay very long. I thought you'd eat with us and all." She looked disappointed.

"I can't. I got to go on to work, hon, but it was real good to see you, Lynette. You take it easy, ok?" Destiny put her hand on Lynette's arm.

"All right then. We'll see you. You come back real soon, ok?" Destiny, already in motion, nodded and waved. Lynette watched Destiny's heels click down the linoleum hall, out the screen door and down the porch steps.

"Mama!" Jimmy Ray hollered. His voice boomed. Lynette's body jerked into motion involuntarily. She hurried down the hall to Jimmy Ray's room. "What on earth is the matter with you, boy? You liked to scared me silly! Hollering like that, land sakes! What on earth do you want?"

Jimmy Ray's thunderous voice deserted him, and he transformed into a gigantic little boy who sobbed uncontrollably. Lynette rushed to his side, sat down on the bed, and patted his head.

"What's the matter, sugar? Tell mama."

He spoke in broken phrases between sobs. "She... talked... awful... to me." He whined and sniffled. He tried to point but couldn't. "She spit! On the bed, Mama!"

"No, she didn't!" Lynette was flabbergasted, not even thinking for a moment Destiny was capable of such a thing, but at the fact her boy could say something so hateful.

Jimmy Ray's sobbing stopped with the return of his anger. "She did done it, mama. I ain't lying."

"Hush up, boy. You better quit talking so ugly. You want another pain pill? I believe you need one. Somebody done got fussy." She walked over to the dresser and shook out a pill from a bottle. She bent over the bed, stuck it in his open mouth, and held a Pepsi can with a straw in it up to his lips.

"She did do it, mama. I ain't making it up. How come you're on her side?"

"I ain't on her side. I just know you have treated that girl awful in the

past, and I just don't know why. She was nice enough to come visit you, and look how you done her. I just know you said something ugly. Jimmy Ray, you beat all. You know that?" With that, she set the Pepsi can down on the night-stand, walked out the door and slammed it.

Jimmy Ray wiggled and kicked his legs under the covers. His arms were still fixed and outstretched, crucifix style.

"Jesus, help me, Lord. Sanctify me today, Jesus. Help me to do thy will. Help me to pass through this bleak and painful time." Jimmy Ray's eyes turned skyward as he prayed aloud. "Lord, I ask you today to please heal me so that I may be witnessing for you real soon. Lord, help me to be thy servant as best I can. In the name of sweet Jesus, yore son and my savior, amen." Jimmy Ray stared straight ahead. He was calm for the moment but did not look tranquil. Then, with humility long gone, he growled viciously, "Thy will be done!"

# CHAPTER VII

Munio scrutinized himself in the full-length mirror. Striking poses from the front, the side, and the back, the more he looked the more he liked what he saw. What he saw was a pair of rust-colored, polyester, double-knit bellbot-toms that swayed free and easy just above the floor where brown patent leath-er, zip-up, ankle-high boots with three-inch heels became visible. A cream-colored silk shirt with an enormous collar was unbuttoned to mid-chest level, to expose his sparse outcropping of chest hairs. He flirted with himself, sang in Spanish and danced around, making quick turns and snapping his fingers.

"Not bad for an old man, eh? Maybe I'll get lucky down at Eddy's bar to-day, hum? Maybe I will." He paused and glanced away, "Maybe I will find true love or true fortune on this day." He laughed, turned his back on the mirror, swished his tight little rust-colored butt down the hall, and set sail for Eddy's bar.

The old country classic "Heartaches by the Numbers" was playing as Munio hit the door. His adrenaline began to surge as the cool, dark, smoky aura of the room encompassed him. He stood just inside, lit a cigarette, and scanned the scene from left to right.

"Munio," Eddy called to him. "What in the hell are you doing, man?"

Munio chuckled and gave Eddy a big smile as he headed for the bar. "A man's got to get his bearings, boy. A man's got to check out a situation, you know. Look around, see what's happening."

"Well, goddamn, Munio, it ain't hard to see that there ain't nothin' hap-pening in this dive." Eddy giggled, ever amused with his new friend. "And where in the hell did you get them damn bellbottoms?"

Munio was as close to an alien being as Eddy had ever met, and he had come to like him very much even in this short time.

"I will tell you two things. Do not joke about my clothes, or I will have to kill you. The second thing is, brother, there is always something going on. Even when you stand alone on a desert, if you look for it, there is action. A man with a true sense of adventure will find it, too. Now, give me a beer please, bartender." Munio slapped his hand flat on the bar and winked at Eddy.

Eddy poured Munio a tall, cold draft. "Well, you either got more imagination than Walt Disney, or else you are one bored son of a bitch if you can find something going on around this joint."

"Thank you and cheers to you, my friend." Munio held the glass of beer in the air, offered a toast in Eddy's direction, and consumed half of it in one long, slow slug. Finally, he set it down hard on the bar, followed by a loud "ahhh".

At this moment, except for the music, the bar was dead because it was, after all, five o'clock in the afternoon on a Tuesday. A total of six people including Munio occupied the place: a solitary man at the bar, three people at a table far away from the bar, and a man throwing darts alone. Like any good hustler, Munio keyed in on him since dart-throwing placed high on the list of his hustling skills. Munio monitored his consistency for a few minutes.

"Hey bartender, a refill if you please."

"All right, coming right up, senõr." Eddy replied.

With a second beer in him, Munio hit his stride and settled into his hustler persona. His even-tempered nature gradually slipped from sight, replaced by a quick-witted, sharp-tongued scoundrel, whose lust required competition. No matter how small the battle, the challenge, Munio had a profound commitment to victory, be it a war of words or darts or whatever else presented itself on his stage.

"You know that man over there playing darts?" Munio asked Eddy.

"Yeah, he's a regular. Pretty nice guy."

Munio snorted, "Good. I hope he will be pretty and nice when I win all his money." Munio laughed loudly.

"Oh, right, you play darts, don't you?" Eddy said thoughtfully. "Well, go on over there and get yourself a game, bud."

"I will, Edward. Oh, I will indeed."

With that, Munio drained his glass and nodded at Eddy. Eddy returned the nod, and filled the glass. Munio toasted his friend again, and backed away from the bar towards the dartboard.

Munio moved close to the man, who looked over at Munio, nodded, and then threw a dart. He looked back over at Munio after he threw, wondering what this Jimi Hendrix/John Travolta clone intended.

The man toked hard off a cigarette and asked wryly. "Could I help you, buddy?"

"No, I was just watching, that's all."

"You play darts?" The man looked Munio up and down.

66

"Yes, I do. I haven't played much in a while, but yes, I play."

"You want a game?"

"Ok, I'll, ah, I'll play a game with you." Munio reacted with hesitance. "How is it you do that? What, ah, do you want to bet? A dollar, maybe?" Munio raised his eyebrows and gave the man his best innocent face.

The man laughed and pulled up his sagging blue jeans. "Hell, a dollar ain't hardly worth the trouble, amigo. What you say we go for, oh, how about twenty dollars? The man gave him a raised eyebrow.

Munio paused a couple of extra beats and scratched his head. "All right, I'll do that."

From the bar, Eddy watched the scene unfold as Munio systematically milked the poor guy for every penny he had on him. After winning, the first game, marginally, Munio granted the man a rematch, and the cycle repeated. With each game, Munio's stealth increased until the man was angry and flabbergasted: he finally realized, too late, that he had been had by the best dart hustler that may have ever worked Rosedale, Georgia. The man slapped his money in Munio's hand and turned in a huff to leave as Eddy watched.

"Have a nice day!" Munio called out tauntingly.

The man stopped dead in his tracks as he neared the door, turned, and shot Munio a bird. Munio laughed heartily, held up his money and shook it at the man.

"You ought to warn people about crooks like him, Eddy. I swear to God! I just lost my goddamn rent money! You ought to have warned me, that's all. It ain't right!"

"Vern, he didn't make you play with him. You done it on your own free will. Now, don't be blaming me for it. You ought to have more sense than to bet your fucking rent money, man." The man shot Eddy a bird and left through the door with a bang.

Munio reseated himself at the bar, looking every bit the part of the cat who swallowed the canary.

"You're pretty proud of yourself, aren't you?" Eddy's face crinkled in a scowl.

Munio lit a cigarette and, without looking at Eddy, said, "As a matter of fact, I am. That man is an adult. He played me out of free choice. I am to feel bad, Eddy?"

Eddy slapped the bar with both hands. "You're right, you're right. Hell, you sure beat the shit out of him. How much did you take him for?"

Munio raised his voice. "I won." He took a long dramatic pause, "Repeat, won, fair and square, two hundred and twenty-five dollar,." He said happily.

"Damn." Eddy's eyebrows shot up in amazement. "I be damned. That ain't bad. That ain't bad."

"You are right, it ain't half bad, and you know what? It is only the beginning, Eddy." Munio jumped off the bar stool and threw his arms open wide,

striking a grand pose. "Before this night is through, I will own this whole town. The whole state of Georgia will walk in fear that I should come to their town and steal away their life savings with my skill at the dart board, eh?" Munio laughed an artificial evil laugh. "Drinks, Eddy, I need drinks."

"You need something. I don't know exactly what, maybe a damn psychiatrist, because you are so goddamned crazy." Eddy set another draft down for Munio.

"I need something more substantial than this, my friend. Let's have some shots of whiskey. No, tequila. Let's have some shots of tequila. You have a shot with me, Eddy."

"I'll have one, but that's about it. I can't get too fucked up while I'm working. I will shore as hell get you one. Here." Eddy set down a shot glass and filled it with Cuervo Gold. "Cheers to ya, bud."

"Cheers to you, my new friend Eddy."

Over the course of the next two hours, Munio entertained himself, Eddy, and a few other people who looked on as the sweet yellow glow of Cuervo Gold washed away all his inhibitions.

His best Don Juan/Tom Jones persona emerged that night. A witty, hip, dancing machine took to the stage. No matter what Allman Brothers or country song came on that jukebox, Munio would do the mamba, tango, and perform any other Latin dance he could think of. Though he danced alone, in his mind, Munio had a different partner for every number, some men, some women. He turned and dipped and swerved his way through the evening, amazing and entertaining the real and imagined crowds.

Eddy, on the other hand, had an exceptional evening as he explained to all the patrons who Munio was, and why he was here, playing out his own Spanish version of Saturday Night Fever.

Finally, Munio sat down at the bar for a break and immediately requested another tequila shooter. He lit a cigarette and spun around on the bar stool to cruise the crowd, which had grown larger. His hands took turns servicing his mouth as one, then the other, brought a cigarette or a drink to his lips. Wound tight as a spring, his eyes darted back and forth like ping-pong balls bouncing on a concrete floor, and his feet nervously tapped out a beat. Suddenly, a Long Island accent blindsided him.

"You certainly have some interesting moves, Mister." The unusually deep, yet feminine, voice came from the tall, dark-featured woman perched on the stool next to him. "My name is Audrey Myers, and yours?"

In case this person proved to be a figment of his imagination, he waited a couple of beats to respond. He had never heard a woman's voice with such depth and resonance.

He took a long puff off his cigarette. At last, he spoke and extended his hand. "Munio, Munio Morelos,"

"Mind if I join you for a drink, Mr. Morelos? I would certainly enjoy the

opportunity to have a conversation with a man whose name is not Bubba. You know what I mean? Oy!"

"Not exactly, no, I do not know what you mean, but," Munio snorted out a halfhearted laugh and looked away from the woman for a second. "I have a feeling I will find out."

"Well, Munio, you say? Is it Munio?" She crossed her long legs.

"That's right."

"Well Munio, I have been in the South for a couple of weeks, and I am… well, I am not exactly what you would call enamored with the Southern thing. You know what I'm talking about?" She nodded her head at him. "So Munio, tell me a little bit about yourself, won't you?" she droned through her large, distinctive nose.

"I am from the country of Belize. I have been in this town only a short time. Eddy, the bartender is my friend. I am staying with him." Munio pointed with his thumb behind him towards Eddy who was busy keeping up with the bar orders.

"I see. How interesting. I suppose that would explain your superior Latin dancing skills. You have very nice timing, Munio, very nice."

"Thank you. I have always been a dancer." Munio smiled at her and turned on his stool to face her, feeling more cordial, especially after the compliment. "Since I was even very small, I remember I learned the steps quickly, and I would dance with the adults often. My uncle, he taught me mostly, and his friends." Munio laughed. "They were, um, dramatic fellows. They would have dance contests at the bars every week. A funny bunch really, homosexual, they were."

"Oh, really now? Would you like to dance with me, Munio?" Audrey batted her eyes seductively.

"I could do that, yes." Munio took her hand and led her out to the dance floor, where they began to tango in earnest to the unlikely beat of the Allman Brothers.

By the end of the song, people had cleared the dance floor to watch. Audrey was a good head taller than Munio, but despite her size, Munio dipped her with ease, and whipped her upright as they tangoed their way through "One Way Out". One misdirected track light allowed their silhouettes to race about one wall with Audrey's nose leading her profile like the bow of a ship. When the song ended, they bowed and curtsied to one another.

"Munio, I cannot tell you how absolutely exciting that was. You are one good dancer, Mister. Yes, you are. Very good, very good. And you're so third world. I love that, so refreshing, fabulous. This music though--oy!" Her accent astounded Munio. He had never heard such an unusual sound or cadence come from a human voice.

"You are, too. I am surprised to find a woman so accomplished in this style of dance here in this little town."

"Well, Munio." She cleared her throat and laid her arm across Munio's shoulde. "You know what? I have a little surprise for you. Number one, I'm not a woman, and number two, I teach this kind of dancing for a living." Munio snorted a laugh and looked away for a second. "Surprising? Yes, I bet it is. It most certainly is, I would imagine. Well, what the hell. Life is surprising, isn't it, Munio? Yes, indeed it is. Bartender, I need a refill over here right away, please!" she called to Eddy.

An ear-to-ear smile was frozen on Munio's face. Finally, he spoke. "Well, I thought you had some highly developed back muscles for a woman, but, well, you never know." He held his arms out and shrugged his shoulders.

"That's not the only muscles I've got highly developed, mister." Audrey winked at Munio, and Munio laughed.

He felt relief that she was a man, because, as a woman, he could not quite relax with her. She was so foreign, so aggressive, his mind could not fit her into any slot of "woman" he had ever known. Besides, drag queens had been his aunts growing up. He knew their energy, their ways. He laughed about how funny it was that he did not detect this fact about Audrey. He was entertained by the fact he was fooled. It was a surprising feeling, as if his foot had gone sound asleep, so numb, like a block of wood, so unlike a foot.

"So Munio, you're not going to call the sheriff on me or anything like that, are you?" Audrey gave him a nod and a smile.

"I think I will not, no. It may surprise you to know, Audrey, that I am most familiar with drag queens. As I said, I was raised around them to some extent."

"Is that a fact? Jungle drag queens in Belize? Stop it!! Who could know?"

Munio laughed out loud. "No, no, not in the jungle, in the cities. There are cities in Belize too, you know."

"Oh well, that's good. Because, drag queens in the jungle???"

"What y'all need?" Eddy appeared and slapped his hands down on the bar. "Munio, you working it on that dance floor, boy. Y'all looked good. I ain't ever seen any dancing like that in person. I saw it on TV a time or two." Eddy smiled big at both of them.

"Eddy, I require a new beer and a new shooter, ok? I am starting to sober up, and I am not ready to do that, ok? For the lady, what ever she wishes to have, I will buy." He held his hand in Audrey's direction, palm up.

"I want a martini, extra dry, no olive, please." She smiled gracefully.

"Ok, y'all, coming right up."

"So where is it you teach this dancing?"

"Well, believe it or not, Rosedale has a country club, and in their minuscule attempt to seek culture, they have offered ballroom dancing classes. Can you believe it?"

Munio listened, fascinated with Audrey's dialect. To Munio, it was an art

70

form.

"So, this friend of mine that used to live in New York, when he was a man, that is, migrated down here after he got it lopped off." Audrey made pointed eye contact, raised her thinly plucked and arched eyebrows high in conjunction as she extended an index finger and used her other hand as an imaginary hatchet. "You know what I'm saying?"

"He had a change in the sex, this man?" Munio asked.

"That's right Munio, a seeeerious change in the sex." Audrey laughed. "It's a long story, but what happened is she moved to Rosedale and joined the country club. Imagine that?" Audrey laughed and slapped Munio on the shoulder gleefully. "If those people only knew, they would die! They would literally just die! So, Paul, now Sandra, and a few other members wanted to take these dance lessons, and I, being the superior instructor and queen of the ballroom," she posed, patted her hair and checked her long, polished nails, "was solicited to make a guest appearance to direct this instruction. We have had the most fun, I swear, Sandra and I, laughing at these rich old rednecks flirting away at us. If they only knew, they would die! They would literally just die!" Audrey sipped at her martini and dabbed at her painted lips with a napkin. "How's my lipstick, Munio, smeared?"

"No, it's ok. It's good, muy bien, muy bien." Munio said with great expression and Latin flair.

"Stop! Would you stop it with the Spanish, already?" She laughed. "You're so third world. I love it. What a kick you are. Who would have ever thought I would find someone like you in this dive? I'm impressed to find a bartender that could make a fucking martini. You know what I'm saying? But you, well, what a surprise, a literal surprise. A gift is what you are, Munio, an absolute gift." Audrey elbowed Munio playfully and giggled, getting an obvious boost from the high-octane martinis. "I have to take a pee. I'll be right back." Munio raised his eyebrows at Audrey.

"Ain't I a lady? Of course, I go to the ladies room. Where else? Don't I look like a lady, and I'll tell you right now, you better just say yes, already." Audrey pointed her finger sternly at Munio as she stood.

"Oh yes, of course, yes you do, a fine lady, yes, yes," Munio blubbered.

"Thank you very much. I'll be back." Audrey, on that note, swished her way to the ladies room.

This particular ladies room was small, a two-staller with only a small mirror for primping. The traffic flow was steady but not overcrowded. Most of the women at the bar dressed jean and T-shirt casual, except for the occasional short-skirted, three-inch-heeled, freshly frosted, high-styled redneck motif that would sashay in. Audrey's New York sophistication, low-cut black, sleek fitting knit dress, and black heels made her the yacht among the rowboats. She finished in the stall and took a place at the mirror, the cosmetic watering hole in a women's restroom. From her clutch, she extracted a silver lipstick holder

and began careful application. A comfortable-looking woman with a ponytail began to wash her hands, and the two made eye contact.

"Hi," the woman smiled.

"Hello," Audrey returned softly.

"I saw y'all dancing out there. Y'all were great."

"Well, thank you. We're having a lot of fun."

The woman fished in her jeans for some change and then approached the condom vending machine that hung on the wall. She fed it some quarters and pulled the lever, which delivered her a neat two-pack of ribbed and lubed protection.

The woman made eye contact with Audrey again. "I think I might get lucky tonight."

Audrey let out a baritone giggle, "You go, girl! At least you've got enough sense to get your equipment together because you know, they never do."

"Ain't that the damn truth. You take it easy now."

"You too."

A woman exited a stall and took her place at the watering hole. She did not offer to exchange greetings with Audrey. She pulled a pick from her purse and while loudly smacking gum, attempted to give her stiff blonde hairdo a good fluffing. Audrey eyed her, greatly amused at the woman's attitude. Audrey pulled out her compact and began to touch up her blush. The woman pulled out a tube of orange lipstick, which Audrey thought atrocious. She decided to have some fun.

"Excuse me," Audrey opened innocently. "Has anyone ever told you that you look a lot like Tammy Faye Baker?"

The lipstick skidded to a dead halt on the woman's lips, and she slowly turned and gave Audrey a blistering glare. "No, has anyone ever told you that you look like dog shit?"

Without further ado, the woman snatched her belongings and strutted for the door. "Damn yankee bitch!" she spat as she swung it open.

Audrey, now alone in the bathroom, laughed hysterically. She stopped and gave herself a serious slut stare in the mirror. "You are bad. You are so bad, you, you yankee bitch you!"

Audrey slid up on the stool next to Munio.

"Miss anything while I was gone?" She punched him playfully on the arm.

"No, nothing, maybe three sips." Munio held his beer glass up. "And how was your trip to the ladies room? Full of ladies?"

"It was full. Let's just say it was full." Audrey sipped at her martini. "How have you been treated since your arrival?"

"Here in Georgia, pretty ok. Well, it's had its moments too, I guess. Texas, not good at all. How about you?"

"You mean for being a drag queen, or for being from New York?" Au-

drey laughed and looked around. "For one thing, I don't think anybody has a hint I'm a man. I dress pretty solid, and I don't have a heavy beard, you know. Um, and I think being from New York and having such a strong voice takes the focus off the details of what I look like. People can't seem to act normal once they hear me speak. I don't think they like northerners at all, at all, I tell you."

"Probably you are correct with this thought. People seem to enjoy my method of speech."

"On the other hand, I have to say," Audrey looked around to make sure no one was in earshot of her. "I do think the reason these people talk so slow has something to do with their intelligence level. I never thought that until I came down here." She used her hands for emphasis and crossed her legs in the opposite direction. "But, here I am, and well, I think it's true. Maybe it's this goddamn humidity. You know what I'm saying? Oy! I have been sweating profusely since I got into this God-forsaken town. Maybe all that sweating drains some vital brain mineral or something. You think? Christ if I know. I don't know what it is, but it's not charming to me, not in the least. I prefer proper grammar. People should have enough self-respect to speak properly. Don't get me wrong, Munio. I know you are not from this country, and you don't know the language very well. You, I excuse." Audrey zigzagged her arm in the air above Munio's head as if she were waving a magic wand of approval.

"I have a proposition for you, Munio." Audrey reached over and ran her finger down his arm and winked.

Munio chuckled. "A proposition from you I am not sure I would live through, lady."

"Stop it! You've such a dirty mind, Munio, really. I want you to come be my partner at this dance class. It's only once a week through the end of October. I'll pay you. Let's say thirty dollars a class, and it lasts two hours. What do you say?"

"I think I could do that. Sure, I would help you."

"One condition." Audrey raised an index finger. "You let me dress you. You look like a Latin John Travolta."

"What is wrong with that? I like how he dresses."

"Oy vey." Audrey looked skyward. She looked at her large silver designer watch. "I've got to get going. I've got some hand wash to do." She smiled and rolled her eyes. "Munio, here is my number." She scribbled on a napkin. "Call me in the morning, and I'll tell you when, how, and all about the class, all right?"

"Ok, I wish you did not have to go. We could dance some more, but ok, I call you."

"Ok, give me a hug." Audrey stood and leaned over to Munio, who reached up and hugged her. With a wave to Eddy, she pranced to the door

with her heels clicking on the hardwood.

* * * * *

Munio tapped out a rhythm on the bar counter as Eddy made a beeline to him.

"You gonna get you some strange, bud?" Eddy popped him on the arm.

"What do you mean?" Munio smiled, knowing exactly what he meant.

"You gonna get it on with that queen, man?"

"How did you know she's a queen?" Munio looked with disbelief at Eddy.

Eddy looked around to see who was in earshot of them. "Hey, I wasn't born yesterday, man. I've been around drag queens before, up in Atlanta. It's cool. I ain't got nothing against them. He looks damn good. I'll tell you that."

"You think anybody else knows she's a he?"

"Naw, I doubt it. People around here would believe he's from fucking Mars before they would believe that a man could dress up that pretty. They just wouldn't believe it. What the hell's he doing here anyhow?"

"She is teaching a dance class at the country club for a few weeks. She lives in New York."

"Oh."

"Guess what? She wants me to be her partner at the classes. She will pay me, too."

"I'll be damned. That's good, man. Who knows, maybe you'll get lucky."

"You will get lucky if I don't get up and kick your ass, Eddy... uh...uh...." Munio snapped his fingers. "You know I don't even know your last name."

"Jackson."

"So like I was saying, Eddy Jackson. I will get up and kick your lucky ass all over this bar if you don't quit teasing me about this queen." He laughed at Eddy who drew back and held his hands up in surrender at Munio's threat.

"All right, all right, all right." Munio threw up his hands. "I think I will have some more drinks now, if you are still working."

"Ok, stud, here you go." Eddy winked at Munio as he set another beer and shooter down for him.

Munio contemplated the fact that he had been fooled by Audrey. His radar was usually so excellent. He slugged down both his drinks, and rapped on the bar with the empty glasses for Eddy to refill then.

"What? Finished already? You gonna slip up and get drunk."

"What is the purpose of drinking alcohol if not to get drunk? I want to get drunk. I love to get drunk."

"All right, but don't be throwing up in my house now, you hear?"

"I don't throw up. I don't waste my booze. Fill them!" Munio rapped again on the bar with the glasses.

Munio sat at the bar and continued to chug five more rounds. His world gradually became a slow motion underwater scene that had no crisp edges or

swift movements. His mind was so saturated that his thoughts were diluted to moments of fear or anger, simple emotions that cropped up and disappeared quickly like bolts of distant lightning. Ultimately, Munio succumbed to a deep inertia that carried relief from all troubling thoughts and resulted in a big crash as he came off that bar stool and onto the floor. Eddy rushed around to the other side of the bar and attempted to slap Munio awake, but all attempts failed. Frustrated, he threw Munio over his shoulder and put him in the back seat of his car to sleep it off.

When he came back in a man seated at the bar said, "Them Mexicans can't drink."

"He ain't a Mexican."

"Where's he from then?"

"Belize."

"It's down there somewheres by Mexico, ain't it?"

"Yeah, I reckon."

"Same difference. They all from the jungles down there, and they all basically Indians, jungle Indians. I'm telling you them Indians can't drink."

"Yeah, yeah, yeah." Eddy threw down a bar towel and moved to the other end of the bar.

This situation did worry Eddy. He had worked at the bar too long not to know what this behavior spelled. Most people get a little drunk and go home. Once in a while, though, he would get one, a dead drunk that invariably had to be thrown out or carried out.

Suddenly, Munio was not the wise cool dude that spelled promise in Eddy's life. He was a middle-aged immigrant with a drinking problem was camped out in his house.

Eddy felt angry and scared about what the future would hold. Had Munio just taken his time to show Eddy his true colors? Should he go ahead and end this relationship quickly? He would have to wait and see what happened. Maybe it was a fluke. Maybe.

Eddy closed up the bar at four a.m. and got in his car five hours after he had put Munio in there.

Still, Munio lay snoring, not twitching a muscle when Eddy slammed the car door and cranked the engine. He rolled down the window and drove into the warm night. Fog had formed in low-lying areas, and the air seemed twenty degrees cooler in those spots. It gave Eddy chills that made the hair stand up on his arms and formed goose bumps on his skin. After he pulled into his driveway, he got out of the car, stood and stared at Munio for a few seconds. Then, without a word, he went into the house and to bed.

# CHAPTER VIII

All through the night, through the early dawn, and even after the sun continued to climb high into the sky, Munio lay crumpled in the back seat of Eddy's car. In his dreams, Munio was far away, far above the car, far above Rosedale. He dreamed he was riding the full and cream-colored moon. He straddled it like a pony as it circled round and round the earth. It was cool up there in the sky, and Munio wore only white shorts and a wide white cloth as a headband. Behind the moon was the sun, a blazing yellow-orange sun with an angry face, that chased them around and around and around as they circled the earth. In his sleep, the tension grew as the sun chased faster and faster. The moon sped on, but slowly the flaming sun gained on them. Munio could feel the heat on his back, hotter and hotter, and occasionally he flinched, as a spark would catch him. Munio's mind stuck on this image like a broken record, and for hours, he just circled and circled, with a growing dread of being burnt alive by the angry sun.

The sound of the front car door opening woke Munio. The opening of the door let an onrush of fresh air into the car. Heat had built up all morning and now at eleven a.m., and it had become dangerously hot in the car. Munio sat up quickly, his heart pounding from the heat, the drama, and the confusion. Eddy looked in and shook his head, not amused.

On the other side of that onrush of air was an out rush of body odor, heat, tequila, beer, and cigarettes. Eddy didn't say anything, but he nearly gagged at Munio's smell.

"Get up. I got to go train."

Munio reacted slowly and just sat there, blinking and running his hands through his wild hair.

"Get up, man! I got to go now!"

"Ok, ok, I'm going. I'm going." Munio opened the back door of the car and pulled himself out. It was an uncomfortable moment for both Munio and Eddy. After a second, Eddy spoke up.

"Listen, Munio, I ain't got time to be nursing no drunk. Now, if you want to stay with me and help me train, that's cool, but this ain't no refugee camp. That was not cool for me to have to carry you out of where I work, man. That ain't going to cut it. You think about it, and figure out what you want to do. I got to go."

"I'm sorry if I caused you trouble, Eddy. I just got a little carried away, you know, and I, ah, was having such a fine celebration." Munio held out his arms and shrugged his shoulders. "I don't do this with habit."

"All right, well, whatever. I'm going to go do biceps and triceps, if you want to come over to the gym after you get your shit together. Do something with that damn hair. You look like you've been shot out of a cannon."

Eddy drove only about a block and then got out and unrolled the backseat windows. "Smells like a stinking drunk in this car! Damn Indian!" He spat out the window as he sped back onto the road.

Munio walked slowly up the porch steps and sat on the metal glider. He gently rocked himself back and forth. He took a cigarette out of his cream colored John Travolta shirt, which was still unbuttoned nearly to his waist. He sat up, unbuttoned it the rest of the way and took it off. His skin sighed with relief to be uncovered and feel fresh air. The longer he sat, the more his mind gained clarity. He remembered the dream, and watched himself in review, riding round and round on that moon with the sun giving chase. He blinked his eyes wide and shook his head. He suddenly noticed his mouth felt parched, bone dry.

His boots resounded across the living room floor. In the kitchen, he opened the refrigerator, reached for a beer. Without stopping, he drank half the can and finished with a big "ahhhhhh." This was followed in a few seconds by a tremendous burp, to which Munio responded with a laugh and a smile. Immediately, he perked up and went back on the porch to finish the drink. The alcohol picked up where it left off, and after the last sip of that beer, Munio was feeling cheerful and human and high.

"I better clean up and get over to that gym and see if I can get Eddy to not have such bad feelings for me. He'll be ok." Munio went into his assigned room to get some clean clothes.

The frozen faces of the dolls left him with a great sense of dread. Just having them, the hundreds of them, perched there, poignant representatives of the dead woman to whom they belonged, bothered him. Like a scene from "The Birds", they waited and watched. Munio hurried about his business and backed out of the room.

After Munio showered and washed his hair, his face took on a totally different look. The fluffy black curls were gone. Now exposed was an older brown face that looked tired and sad. Bags hung under his eyes and many wrinkle lines confirmed that he was no youngster. His head looked small compared to how he looked normally. Without all that hair, he looked very fragile. In the bathroom mirror, he combed it, pulled it back, and secured it with a rubber band in a ponytail.

After stepping into a pair of blue jean cutoffs, he threw on a white tank top, sandals and dark sunglasses, and went to get in his truck. For a minute, he panicked and thought it had been stolen, until he remembered it was at the bar, only a mile away, Munio set out walking. The road was like walking in an oven, and Munio's sunglasses fogged up at first. The blinding light of the noonday sun irritated him and spawned a splitting headache.

It was, thankfully, a short walk, and soon he reached his lonely truck in the bar's parking lot. The heat billowed out when he opened the door. He stepped back quickly as if to not get burned. Reaching into the glove compart-

ment, he took out a bottle of aspirins and tossed four down his dry throat.

Munio walked into the gym, and Eddy smiled when he saw him, which made Munio feel more at ease.

"Hey hoss," Eddy said, "You actually have good timing because I was just starting bis. You got a headache? You sure as hell ought to. Got that damn hair plastered back too, huh? That's mighty attractive. Well, what the hell." Eddy chattered away, and Munio was not sure he could take it.

Eddy led them over to a preacher curl bench where he loaded an ez curl bar with a thirty-five pound plate on each end. He took a seat and put his arms over the padded top of the bench. "On the count of three hand it up, and I'm going to do eight on my own. Then, help me go to failure. Ok, one, two, three!"

Munio hoisted the bar to Eddy. Making loud aggressive sounds normally associated with sex or combat, Eddy worked hard to curl the weight. With each rep, his face grew more red and full of rage. His teeth flashed, and he blew out little spitballs as he exhaled. His biceps grew as they engorged with blood on each successive rep. Munio caught some of Eddy's contagious emotion as he screamed for him to keep going. Finally, the drama and the set ended. Both Eddy and Munio could say nothing until they caught their breath. They walked it off, almost a substitute for "the cigarette after" two lovers might share.

"Good set, Eddy. Good concentration."

"Thanks, man. This ephedrine is kicking in good as shit today."

"What's that?"

"Speed, man, speed. Well, it's cheap speed, over the counter, but what the fuck, it gets the job done. You have to take a ton of em though. You build up tolerance real quick."

"How many you take today?"

"Fifteen."

"Fifteen? Are you crazy? Never mind, I know the answer to that question already." Munio tapped his palm on his forehead in frustration.

"Hell Munio, I'll take shit til my kidneys fall out and my liver weighs fifty fucking pounds if I could turn pro. I could get hit by a truck tomorrow and die. What the hell do I care about what this shit will do to my body when I'm fifty?"

"Well, ok man, it's your life. That's true. Ok, let's get this set in, brother." Eddy nodded, took a couple of big breaths, got his head set, and then counted off.

Eddy's face looked frightening, and with each subsequent rep, his whole head seemed to grow larger. Big thick veins popped out on each side of his temples, and the whites of his eyes turned blood red. He screamed his way through the last rep, threw the weight down with a curse, and then, as quickly as it came, his ferocity dissipated. He struck a front double bicep pose in the

large mirror that was in front of him. His eyes scanned his body like a gun-slinger-art critic. He went into a side tricep pose, and that muscle stood out like a tornado, wide at the top of his arm, tapering to a funnel point at the base near his elbow. He stopped posing and primped, checking his hair and tightening the rubber band that held his blonde ponytail.

"You look pretty enough, Miss Eddy?" Munio leaned against the end of the fixed barbell rack with his arms crossed.

Eddy's face lost its arrogance and intensity and broke into a shit-eating grin. "I reckon. My arms are coming up, I think. I need more delts all the way around, but other than that, I think I'm on track."

"You look fearsome, just fearsome. I have not seen anyone here that is as big as you."

"Thanks man. I don't know. There's a couple of people that look pretty good, but to tell you the truth, they don't look no better than me, not really."

"What is next, my fearsome Edward the great?"

"Standing barbell curls, let's start with a hundred and ten." Eddy picked up the fixed barbell with "one hundred ten" stenciled in white on the end. He got set in front of the mirror and then started the set. He used strict form, and without swinging the weight, kept a good steady rhythm going up and down through every repetition.

"That was easy. Let's go to one fifty."

"Ok, I'll get it." With a good tight arched back, Munio picked up the barbell.

This set was much harder, and Eddy had to work and cheat a little to make the eight reps with it.

"That's not bad. You have to use good form, Eddy. Don't swing the weight. Use your arms, not your back, ok?"

Eddy nodded, looked around, and didn't say anything.

"Ok, now, brother, let's go with eight big ones. You want to grow? Well, grow! Be tough! Come on, Eddy! Squeeze, squeeze!"

Munio and Eddy pooled their passion to a climax with the clang of the released barbell, dismissed to the floor after Eddy's eighth repetition.

"That's it. Nice job, Eddy. That's the way to do it."

"Thanks, man." Eddy smiled, knowing he had done a better job, and the reason was Munio's intensity as a spotter and coach.

"Ok, Munio, now on this next set, I want to go to failure, and from there, help me with three or four, all right?"

"Got it. Whenever you're ready."

"All right, let's go." He snorted like a bull as he took the barbell from Munio.

Munio counted off each repetition aloud. "One, good! Two, concentrate now! Three, stay with it, Eddy! Four, come on, keep going! Five, good work! Six, don't stop now! Focus Eddy! Seven, that's it! Eight, alright now, here we

go! Nine, come on now, a couple more!"

Eddy got the ninth one only halfway up, and Munio touched the barbell just enough to complete the curl. They continued this through three more reps, and then a man walking by bumped Eddy accidentally from behind. Eddy lost all concentration and threw down the barbell. He became instantly enraged, chased the man, and pushed him sharply. The man stumbled on a bench and fell.

Eddy opened fire. "What the fuck is wrong with you, dude? Don't you know to not fuck with somebody when they're in the middle of a heavy set? You stupid bastard! What the fuck are you even in here for? I got more testosterone in my left ear than you do in your whole motherfucking body!"

The man was so startled at first that he couldn't speak, but the longer Eddy insulted him, the more angry he became.

"Ok, man. I'm sorry I bumped you, but let it go, why don't you?"

"You let this go, motherfucker!" Eddy dropped to the floor, straddled him, and started choking him with a vengeance.

Horrified, Munio jumped on Eddy's back, trying to pull his hands away from the man's throat.

"Eddy, stop it! Stop it! Come on, Eddy, calm down! Turn this man loose, right now! You're killing him, Eddy!"

Finally, Eddy came back to reality and released his grip. He sat on top of the man and looked at the red hand marks still embossed on his neck. Slowly, he climbed off and stood. Munio tended to the man, who lay there sucking in air and sobbing. Eddy stared blankly at the floor. Everyone in the gym gathered around to watch him recover.

"I'm, I'm sorry, bud. Hell, I don't even know what to say. I just went into a rage. I couldn't stop it. It was my last set, you know, and I was just focusing on it and all. I really am sorry." Eddy stuck out his hand, and the man took it, neither of them smiling at this point.

"I'm sorry I bumped you. Real sorry!" He chuckled weakly. "My mind was on something else, I guess. That's all right, man. I'm all right."

"Good, you want to go get checked out or anything? I'll pay for it."

"Naw, I'm ok, now that I got some air. I tell you what. You're a bad motherfucker when you get going. Thanks for calling him off." He looked over at Munio.

"No problem, no problem, brother. Eddy has a bad problem with PMS syndrome, you know?" Munio winked at the man, and laughed over at Eddy, who snorted a laugh and shook his head, still reeling from the experience.

"Yeah, right. I know a 'roid rage when I see one."

Eddy and Munio did not have a response to that, because they knew it was true. Munio nodded to the guy and steered Eddy by the sleeve. "You've got one more set to do. Let's do it, brother. Put that behind you. Let's go on." Eddy nodded and powered his way through it. "Let's get out of here, man."

Once outside, Eddy's tension eased, and he took a seat on the stoop. Munio joined him and fired up a cigarette. He pointed the pack at Eddy, who took one out and leaned into Munio's lit match. They both drew a couple of good hits before either spoke.

"You ever had that happen before?" Munio questioned Eddy.

"A couple of times. I mean, no, I never fucking choked nobody, but I've thrown temper fits. I hit one of my old girlfriends once. Broke her damn jaw. She was good about it, knew it wasn't really me. Actually, it was that damn decca. When I do that shit, shoooeee, I near about grow hair on my tongue. I feel like an animal. See, because when I'm doing decca, I'm always doing test and anadrol, and now, hell, on top of all that, I'm doing all that growth. Basically, I'm about as loaded up as a mother fucker could be." He laughed, and so did Munio.

"Maybe you ought to be a fighter, or one of those wrestlers on TV. You put on a really good show." They both laughed again.

"Really, I ought to. I feel bad about that guy. Shit, I liked to have killed that poor old boy. Fucker probably won't be the same for months." They both laughed again.

An old black Cadillac pulled up in the parking lot, and the only thing that Munio could tell about the person inside was that he or she was black.

Eddy spoke quietly. "Speaking of the evils of steroids, here comes the queen bee. You are not going to believe this woman, hoss."

Out of the car came the scariest human being Munio had ever seen. Munio could not fathom that this person was a woman, because her musculature was so immense and she carried more muscle than Eddy. She was black as the blackest sun-drenched African on earth, a rich blue-black that shone in the hot sun. Her weight neared two hundred twenty-five, and she hedged on six feet tall. Her massive amount of hair hung down long, straight, and stiff with thickness below her gigantic silicone trophies, double Ds, at least.

She wore a black and white striped Spandex workout suit. Her back was thick-slabbed with spinal erectors, the crevices between them deep enough to lose your wallet. Her traps nearly covered her ears. Knotted with muscle, her arms were downright freaky, and the quadriceps hung over her knees like bowling balls. The veins at her temples stood out like worms on the edge of carefully manicured eyebrows. Her face was iced with a layer of makeup thick enough to conceal each follicle of her dense closely shaven beard.

Upon her approach, Munio stood instinctively in self-defense because of the frightening power that surrounded her. From this position, he noticed her eyes, colored, by contact lenses an unnatural royal blue. She smiled broadly at them, displaying her large white teeth.

"Hey baby, looking good, looking real good," Eddy jived.

In a pure baritone voice, she responded, "Thank you, thank you. What are you fine boys doing out here? Trying to get picked up?" The woman winked at

Munio, and Munio's asshole twitched.

"Anytime, baby, anytime." Eddy joked back.

"Who have we got here?" She eyed Munio up and down like he was supper. She spoke in a smooth clean manner with a dialect that was unidentifiable to Munio, but was definitely not southern.

"Ida, this is Munio Morelos, my new friend and training partner. This fine lady is Ida Blue."

"Please to meet you Munio, and where might you be from?"

"Belize, originally." He felt incredibly intimidated by this woman, and offered nothing more than a small shy smile.

"Love your country. I spent some time down there. It's beautiful." She smiled and pierced Munio with neon blue eyes.

"And you, where might you be from?" he asked.

She sidled up to Munio seductively. In Mae West fashion, she said, "Darlin', I came here straight from hell." Then she threw her head back and released a deep loud laugh that chilled Munio to the bone and excited him all at once. "No, really darling, I was born in the French West Indies, but moved to the Bronx shortly after. And now? Umm, I am from everywhere, it seems."

"Traveler too, eh?" Munio found his voice once again.

"Yes, I am. So you two are through with your training, I suppose?"

"Yeah, we just got through. You won't believe what I did in there today," said Eddy.

"What?" Ida frowned, drew eyebrows together, and wrinkled her forehead.

"Aw, I was doing a set of curls, and this guy bumped me a little from the back. I went off on the motherfucker, threw him down and started choking his ass." Eddy pointed at Munio. "Munio had to pull me off, or I think I would have killed him."

"Ouuuuweeeee, child." She made a clucking sound with her mouth and shook her head. "What you be doin', boy? No, no, no, let me guess." She shook her head, put an index finger to her temple, and thought a moment. "At the very least decca and anadrol."

"Nope, but I am doing decca, growth, and anything else I can get my hands on." Eddy stated.

"Ok, that would do it. Well, honey, I'm glad you didn't get arrested." She nodded with the sincerity of a scientist. "You're getting to have a curse around here. I heard what happened to that guy, that preacher fellow, big obnoxious cuss. What's his name?" She clicked her fingers hoping to jog her memory.

"Oh, Jimmy Ray. Hell, I done forgot about that myself."

"Well, love, I've got to scoot, guys. Now you, Munio, I would love to talk to you some more and soon. How might I contact you?" She ran her finger down his bare arm, and Munio's every hair stood on end.

"Well, I am staying at Eddy's." he said nervously.

"Ok, I have that number. See you later." She winked again at Munio and turned to enter the gym.

"Well, hey hey hey. You gonna get some of that, are you?" Eddy punched Munio in the ribs. "She's gonna chew you up, and spit you out, Bro'! Ewwwww eeeeee, somebody done up and got lucky!"

"Lucky? I am not sure. If I sleep with her, it may be the last thing I ever do in this life," Munio quipped, and deep inside he felt a sense of dread that was somehow turning him on. It was a passion that he wanted neither to acknowledge nor deny.

# CHAPTER IX

It had now been twenty-four hours since Destiny made her visit to Jimmy Ray's house. Even though she had been proud of her courage in standing up to him, and even though one of the most liberating feelings she had ever known was spitting on that bed, she had spent every minute since then in mortal fear of what the consequences might be. She knew how mean this man could be, and she knew that sometime, somewhere, he was going to hurt her over this. Every woman he had ever had anything to do with for more than a night had been taken to task with Jimmy Ray Jones's fists.

She sat all night and into the next day pondering these things. She chopped line after line of snow-white crank to snort up her nose, and every couple of hours, she would mix up a batch to shoot. Her counter-balance and lone companion, save all the cats, was a half-gallon of Jack Daniels. All this time, the cats were content to observe in silence their mother's agony as she would alternately cry, curse, and occasionally laugh as she channel surfed with the remote control.

On and on her tension built, and her rational mind dissolved. She looked closely at herself in the mirror when she would go into the bathroom to pee. Her cheeks were artificially rosy due to blood vessel dilation, and her mean scar was especially reddened. Her pupils were pinpoints, and her eyes seemed to lose connection with her soul with each trip to that mirror.

Just as Destiny witnessed the sunset giving way to a long, dark, new moon night, she watched the process reverse with the return of morning. The beautiful colors of the sunrise comforted her as she stood and peeked through the curtains. When the dawn gave way to full blown daylight, the reality of her perceived dilemma and the searing brightness were too much to face.

About mid-morning, Destiny had one last staring bout with herself in the bathroom mirror, and then, with great determination, she began to clean herself up. She shook a shower, and even though her body still felt like rubber, a measure of peace came over her as the steamy hot water sprayed her and ran down her body. After applying a full dose of makeup, she put on her favorite pair of jeans, her cowboy boots, and a fresh T-shirt. She ran a brush through

her long brown hair, and aimed a squirt of Lady Stetson cologne on either side of her neck.

A small suitcase was dragged out of the back of her closet, and after filling it with clothes, she reached under her mattress and pulled out an envelope full of cash, which she put in her purse. She sat down and composed a note to her sister, her closest relative. It read, "Louise, I am taking off for a while. Please come over to my house as soon as you get home, and get my cats. Sorry this seems weird, but I'll explain later. Don't tell nobody. Love, Destiny."

She slowly licked the envelope. The glue was thick and had a dull sweet taste that motivated her to find the jug of Jack Daniels and take another swig. She smiled as she swallowed and then went on with her business.

Out of a box of insulin syringes she put two on the table and packed the remainder in a baggie, which she put in the suitcase. Carefully, she stirred up some crank in a spoon for what would be her last dose for a while. She put the top back on the syringe after filling it, preferring to wait until she loaded the car.

Having completed all the loading, she returned to the two syringes. With a sharp rap, she plopped a bottle of nail polish remover down on the table and took a seat. With the skill of a surgeon, she filled the second syringe to the brim with nail polish remover, replaced the top on it, which she patted, gave a smile and put it in her purse. She picked up the syringe with crank, but hesitated a moment and put it down. She got up, hugged, kissed and spoke a few words to each cat. Going back to the table, she quickly tied herself off and fired the crank into her arm with a bang. She sat there and absorbed the wonderful hot rush of the shot and slugged another swallow of Jack Daniels.

With her purse and the Jack Daniels in one hand, she stopped with her other hand on the doorknob. Finally, through tears, she said, "Y'all be good." The cats listened to the deadbolt turn from the outside, the jingle of their mother's keys grow faint, the car engine start, pull away, and leave them all alone.

Another oppressively sunny hot day was under way. In self-defense, Destiny slid on a pair of sunglasses and rolled her window down quickly. The air rushing in as she drove along felt like she had her head in a clothes dryer. Stopped at a light, Destiny took in a big breath of air that almost made her throw up. Rosedale seemed to always have a foul odor to it--a combination of barbecue and the smoky truth that nearly every car in town needed a ring job.

After dropping the note off at her sister's, she wheeled the aging black Oldsmobile into the yard of Jimmy Ray Jones's. Only Jimmy Ray's truck was parked out front, and she hoped Lynette might not be home. She took one last swig of Jack Daniel's, grabbed her purse, and walked across the yard and up the porch steps. The four brown yard dogs gave only about two barks apiece at her.

"Hey boys," she called to them, getting a chorus of tail wags in return.

Giving a good rap on the screen door, she looked inside through the main door. "Lynette? Yoo hoo, anybody home?"

From the back of the house, she heard Jimmy Ray boom, "Yeah, come on in! I'm in the back!" She smiled to herself, and let herself in.

When she appeared in Jimmy Ray's bedroom doorway, he looked away and spat, "What the fuck do you want?" With his arms still outspread and bandaged, he looked like Jesus in a foul mood that the adoring crowds never saw.

"Jimmy Ray, don't be like that. Be nice now. I come to apologize to you for yesterday. I'm sorry I was such a bitch, but hell, I don't know what was the matter with me. It might have been the heat or something. Anyhow, I come over to make it up to you."

He turned and looked at her and grinned. "Baby, I knew you'd come back. You love me after all, don't you? Crazy bitch, I swear you pissed me off though. I tell you what. I was gonna put a hurtin' on you whenever I was to get out of this rig." He laughed.

Destiny slowly strolled over and sat on the edge of the bed. "Well, baby, you don't have to do that." She stroked his head, and he responded by closing his eyes and purring like a kitten.

"Ah, oh, baby, that feels so good. You know I like a good head rubbin'."

"How you feeling?" she asked him softly.

"Hell, all right, I guess. I wish they'd give me something decent for pain. All I got is them damn souped-up Motrins. You ain't got anything, have you?" he asked excitedly.

Destiny smiled seductively and patted her purse. "I figured you might could use some help. The way to some men's hearts might be through their stomachs, but I know the way to yours is through your veins. How would you like a nice hot shot of Demerol?"

"Shit! You're kidding? You got some Demerol?" She smiled and nodded. "Well, load me up sugar, and kiss me good bye because I'm going to sho' 'nuf go night night. I ain't hardly slept a wink. I wish you'd knock me out for a couple of days."

"Oh," she chuckled and nodded. "This'll knock you out all right. Where's Lynette, by the way?"

"She went to the store. She'll be back after while."

"Ok, you ready, baby?" Jimmy Ray nodded eagerly and Destiny pulled the loaded syringe and her rubber tie-off out of her purse.

"Damn, you loaded that thing up, didn't you?" Jimmy Ray frowned a little when he saw the full syringe. "You ain't going to give me too much, are you?"

"Jimmy Ray, I don't think you could do too much. You're such a big old thang. Now, hush and lay back."

Looking like an EMT, she proficiently tied off his left arm just above the elbow. His vein bulged out invitingly, and she removed the cap from the syringe. She hesitated a second and watched Jimmy Ray lying there with his eyes closed. For once, he was so vulnerable. She smiled and went about her business--the business of killing Jimmy Ray Jones.

"Ok, Jimmy Ray, say ahhh." She giggled and winked at him.

"Ahhhh," he chuckled.

The needle silently pierced the vein like a spider in the dark, and blood shot into the syringe. Destiny pushed the plunger slowly and then, with one quick squirt, unloaded it into Jimmy Ray's innocent vein.

He jerked awake and tried to sit up. "Something's wrong! Something's wrong! That don't feel right, baby!"

Destiny stood quickly and watched as Jimmy Ray panicked. His fear was replaced with a convulsion as the nail polish remover made the trip up the river of his blood to his heart and brain. Convinced she had struck a winning blow, she capped the syringe she still held in her hand.

"Good bye, Jimmy Ray. Have a nice day, now you hear?" She coolly and calmly walked out of the room, out of that house, and soon, out of Rosedale.

With no witnesses, Destiny felt pleased this had turned out even better than she had planned. The hot air now felt so good, like a beach breeze, as she found her way onto Interstate eighty-five southbound. Her body's tension had disappeared, and a peace of mind now filled her. No longer would she feel the back-burner dread of Jimmy Ray's meanness, always wondering when and what he would pull next. He was gone, gone, gone.

Back in the bedroom, Jimmy Ray thrashed for a few minutes, and then a massive heart attack set in, ending his short torture. He never said a word, and he lay like another Jesus, a big dead Jesus, for his blessed judgment day had finally come.

# CHAPTER X

Eddy and Munio sat in the kitchen eating very different lunches. Eddy had cooked a pound of spaghetti and mixed three cans of tuna in it. Munio ate from a jar of pickled pigs' feet and washed it down with a can of condensed milk. Eddy slurped his food like a starving dog, while Munio ate slowly, took small bites, and wiped his mouth with a napkin often.

"How in the mother-fucking hell can you eat that, Munio? Jesus fucking Christ, I never saw anything like that in my life. Is that what you was raised on or something?"

"Eddy, you should never criticize anyone about what they eat. People eat what feels sacred to them, to their own body. You have never been to other countries, but believe me, they eat a lot of different things. In Belize, there

were not a lot of cattle or pigs roaming around there. So, much of the meat we get is in the can or the bottle."

"Yeah, well, I reckon you're right, but damn that's weird."

"People in other places in the world eat dogs and cats, even rats. What's the difference, really? An animal is an animal, a drumstick is a drumstick." Munio held up a pig's foot as evidence.

"No, hell, it ain't. It ain't right to eat no dog or cat. That's just plain mean, now." Eddy said.

"In India, people think cows are sacred. They don't have hamburgers in India. They think it's mean the way you eat."

"All right, Mr. history teacher, I got your point. You're putting me to sleep, Munio. Besides, I ain't eating no cow. This is a fucking fish." Eddy got up and washed his bowl out. "I'm gonna take me a shot of test and take a nap."

"Oh no, you don't eat the cow. You run its balls up into your bloodstream." Munio laughed, and Eddy joined him. "Can I watch?"

"Watch me take a nap?"

"No, take the shot."

"Gee, Munio, cheap thrills. You can if you want to see my butt. Come on." Munio followed Eddy down the hall to his bedroom.

Eddy opened a drawer that contained a few small vials and bottles, syringes, and pills. He removed a clear bottle of yellowish liquid and shook it up. It was thick, like machine oil.

"Why is it so thick?"

"Uh, I don't know. Well, see there is oil base and water base. Water base ain't this thick."

"What do you feel like right after you take it?"

"Like I could rip your head off, that's what!" He screamed in fake anger. "Naw, I tell you the truth, Munio. It's the greatest feeling you could ever want to have. I feel like a serious stud. My dick gets hard as a rock, and it'll stay hard too all fucking night. For training, it's great because nothing feels heavy, nothing. You think in your mind there just ain't nothing you can't do. You feel fucking invincible."

Munio smiled at Eddy's testimony. "Well, brother, what good does it do you for your dick to get so hard if you don't ever have a girlfriend?"

"Well, that's a good point, and I ain't, to tell you the truth, had much action in a while. I tell you what. I have had some good times with my thumb and her four ugly sisters about five times a day."

"Masturbate?"

"Hell, yeah. Shit, I have to. I couldn't get out of bed unless I did it a time or two. My dick is so hard when I wake up that it hurts."

"Damn brother, give me a shot of that stuff," he laughed.

"You want one?"

"No, no, not yet anyhow." Munio leaned on the door frame and crossed

his arms and legs.

Eddy took the wrapping off a syringe and stuck the needle through the rubber top on the bottle. He dredged the testosterone until one third of the syringe was filled. He pulled the needle out and pushed on the plunger until a thick drop glistened at the tip and fell to the floor. With his sweatpants around his ankles, he quickly jammed the needle in his hip and emptied the shot. Eddy pulled the syringe out, held it up, and blew on it as if it were a smoking gun.

"Ah, the pause that refreshes." Eddy moved right into his finest nelly queen imitation. "Was it good for you? It was good for me." he joked, touching Munio on the shoulder.

Munio laughed, "You are a real clown is what you are, Eddy."

"Ok, it's nappypoo time."

"Sweet dreams."

* * * * *

Munio went out to his truck and excavated a black plastic bag from the passenger side. He carried it into the doll room and sat down on the floor. The bag contained photographs, many little bundles carefully sorted in envelopes with rubber bands around them. He took the rubber band off one bundle and began to sort through the stack. All of the small black and white prints had white borders cut in a zig zag pattern. He smiled as he flipped through the assortment of groupings of people, some very light brown-skinned, curly-haired dark-featured, on the porch of a little house with chickens pecking in the foreground. In others, the people bore Mayan features with straight black hair, wide faces and distinct cheekbones. Their strong solemn faces gazed out from the photographs. One picture was taken from the top of a hill or a mountain and panned down on a beach scene.

The next photo showed a little church made of snow white stucco with a big white cross iced on the top of it like an ornament on a cake. Munio didn't smile when he saw this one, or the next one, a photo of a priest, a chubby white priest in a black vestment, standing in front of the doors of the little church with his arm around a small curly-haired boy dressed in altar boy attire. He stared intently at this one for nearly a full minute, then put down the whole stack, and went out on the porch to smoke a cigarette.

Seated on the green metal glider, Munio drew hard off his smoke and exhaled with great force. His eyes gazed between the porch's roofline and the distant treetops at the sky, a pure, deep blue void without a cloud to diffuse it.

Thoughts seldom surfaced about those times he spent learning the creed of Catholicism under the tutelage of the missionary men who came to Monkey River Town. There were a few, but only a few, Mayans who surrendered their ancient beliefs of earth and its elements for a rosary and a robe. One of these people had been his Uncle Armando's father.

When the little white stucco church was erected, Alejandro Fernandez was a small boy himself, and he watched the men build it. After it was completed, he observed the goings-on as best as he could from the outside. The bell that would ring throughout the village and the black and white robes the men wore fascinated him. In fact, he made a childhood vow to be a part of that church when he was old enough.

By the time Armando was born, Catholicism had been established as the religion of choice of Belize. Thus he, as well as Munio, experienced similar puberty rituals at the hands of the men in the little white stucco church.

Munio flinched and sweated as he remembered more about those times, the gray clammy hands on his stomach, the priest's poor attempt at Spanish as he spoke lies to Munio. He felt the sharp pains of uncertainty as the priest reminded him that God was a thing to fear and obey, and as God's messenger, the boy must take heed and cooperate.

Munio smelled the hot candle wax in the sanctuary, his eyes glued to those candles as he bent over a prayer bench while the priest practiced his vow of sodomy on the boy, week after week. Somehow, his focus on those candles helped to take away the pain and humiliation Munio felt as that holy man's heavy chest pounded against his back, the priest chanting away in Latin with every stroke.

Munio brought his mind back to the porch, frowned, and wondered why he saved that picture. He had never told anyone about how that priest treated him because, in fact, he had believed it was truly altar boy work. After he reached the age to have a choice, Munio never went back into that church.

Munio thumped his cigarette butt, which flew in a perfect arc and landed midway down the walkway to the house. He retrieved a beer from the kitchen, and then returned to the doll room.

Instead of looking through the rest of the photographs, he put the twist tie back on the black plastic bag they were stored in. He opened another bag that held clothing and a smile crossed his face as he pulled out a pair of black and white patent leather pointed wing tips.

"Ah, it has been a while since I saw you," Munio said to the shoes. "We need to go out dancing. I don't want you to get dry rot." Munio suddenly stopped in his tracks. "Goddamnit! I forgot to call Audrey! Damn, I hope she will be home now. I can't believe I forgot this thing." He slapped himself on the forehead. He pulled out his billfold and found the piece of napkin on which Audrey had written her number.

After three rings, Audrey's unmistakable voice answered, "Hello."

"Audrey?"

"Hello, Munio. You are late, mister."

"I know. I'm sorry, but I just forgot."

"Oh, that's nice. Forgettable am I? Thank you for that, Munio, thank you very much," Audrey kidded.

"No, no, no. You are not forgettable. I am just a forgetful man at times, and I had a rough night."

"Yes, I bet you did. Well, ok, I forgive you then," she honked. "Tonight. Can you come to the class tonight?"

"Yes, I could be there."

"Good. Well, let me give you directions, or would you rather I pick you up?"

"Yes, that would be better."

"All right, where are you?"

"I am at Eddy's house."

"Well, Munio, Jean Dixon I am not. Be a little more specific." Audrey snorted a laugh.

Munio chuckled. "I guess so, ah, let's see. You know, I don't know where it is either. Let's see." Munio looked around the room and spotted some mail on the counter.

"Ok, here it is. Three two five and then," and he spelled out, "b-r-u-n-e-r road."

"Bruner Road, 325 Bruner Road. You can't read, can you, Munio?"

Munio stammered, "Well, I ah, I cannot read English so well."

"English is one of the main languages in Belize. I looked it up."

"Also, there is the factor to consider that I do not have my eye glasses available at this time."

"You can't read, can you?" she repeated. "It's no sin, Munio. You can learn, you know."

"Well, my glasses really are a factor to be considered, but it's true that I do not read extensively."

"You can't read, but you use words like extensively. Interesting."

"Ok then, you will pick me up." Munio moved the conversation along.

"I guess you don't really have the faintest idea where this Bruner Road is, do you?"

"Not really, no."

"That's ok, I'll find it. Munio, I will pick you up at seven o'clock, all right?"

"Ok, seven, that's good."

"Now, about what to wear. Hummmmm, let me see. Do you have a nice pair of black trousers? How about a white dress shirt?"

"Ah, yes, I have that."

"Good. Seven o'clock, Munio, all right?"

"Ok, I'll see you then, and thanks, Audrey."

"You're welcome. Good-bye, Munio.

# CHAPTER XI

The phone rang as soon as Munio hung the receiver in the cradle, and so he answered it.

"Hello?"

Lynette, on the other end of the line, took the receiver away from her ear reflexively, surprised at the unusual voice that answered at Eddy's house. "Is this Eddy Jackson's house?"

"Yes it is, but Eddy Jackson is sleeping at the moment," Munio replied politely.

"Well wake him up! It's an emergency!" Lynette barked angrily.

"All right, hold on a moment."

Munio walked quickly down the hall to Eddy's room and pushed open the door. Eddy was snoring away, covered with a sheet to the waist, his bare chest heaving up and down. Munio paused a moment before waking him.

"Eddy, Eddy, wake up! Some lady wants you on the telephone." Eddy stirred and then woke up rapidly.

"What?" He sat up in bed.

"Some lady on the telephone says there is some emergency."

"Damn, wonder what it is?" Eddy reached over to his phone next to the bed. "Hello?"

"Eddy?"

"Yeah, who is this?"

"It's Lynette."

"Hey, Lynette, how's Jimmy Ray doing?"

"Well, that's a what I'm calling you about. See, I don't know. I went to the store and come back, and when I went to check on him, he just ain't acting right. I was wondering if you would come over, and see what you think. Could you do that, Eddy?"

"Well, yeah, I would, but you know, I ain't exactly no brain surgeon, Lynette." Eddy laughed and looked over at Munio, who smiled.

"I know, but I'd just feel better if you was to come over. Would you?"

"Yeah, I'll come over in a minute. I just got to get dressed. I'll see ya. You need me to bring anything?"

"Naw, I reckon not," she said quietly.

"Ok, I'll see ya."

"Damn, I wonder what's going on over there? That was Jimmy Ray's mama. Says something's wrong with Jimmy Ray. I don't know what she thinks I'm gonna do about it, but I'll go on over there." He got out of bed, threw on a T-shirt and a pair of sawed off sweatpants. "I'll see you afterwhile, I reckon."

"You want me to come with you?" Munio asked.

"Naw, better not."

\* \* \* \* \*

Lynette met Eddy at the screen porch door and led him quickly down the hall to Jimmy Ray's room. Eddy took one look at Jimmy Ray and knew exactly what was wrong with him. His body lay lifeless on the bed. Yellow vomit trailed from his half-opened mouth and disappeared into his dark, brown beard, and onto the bright green sheets below.

"I have tried to wake him up, but he seems to want to sleep. I figured he must need it so I just left him be." She spoke in a voice void of emotion, one robotic syllable after another, softly, with hardly enough air power to make a sound. Her arms held a fixed position, the right covered her heart, the left hand covered her throat.

Eddy began to cry as he absorbed the scene of how pitiful Jimmy Ray and his mama looked. It reminded him of the day he found his own mother face up, dead eyes fixed open, mouth gaping open, lying amongst the dolls. He walked over and put his arm around Lynette.

"Lynette, you really know what's wrong with Jimmy Ray, don't you?"

Lynette's face was filled with confusion. "No, what?"

Eddy cursed to himself and shook his head. "Honey, Jimmy Ray is dead. That's what's wrong with him. He has up and died on us. We gonna need to call somebody to come take him off, ok?"

One look at Eddy's red and streaming blue eyes and Lynette started to whimper, which grew to a sob, which escalated to full scale wailing. They embraced for a few minutes as Jimmy Ray lay unfazed on the bed. Eddy led Lynette down the hall and into the living room, where he sat them down on the couch. Eddy reached over with one hand, picked up the telephone receiver, and dialed 911.

"911 emergency."

"Yeah, uh, I'm over at," he put his hand over the receiver, "Lynette, what's this address? Yeah, sorry, that's 1371 Walkersville Highway. Uh, somebody has died, ma'am. Can y'all send whoever y'all send when somebody dies, please?"

"How did they die, sir?" the operator asked.

"I don't know. He was sick, but I don't know."

"Ok, we'll send someone out."

"Thanks."

He held Lynette, who continued to sob. Shortly, the yard dogs started to howl in harmony, and a sharp rap sounded at the door. Eddy pried himself away from Lynette to answer it. The right shoulder of his shirt was soaking wet with tears. Eddy let the policeman in without a word and led him down the hall to Jimmy Ray's room. The officer walked over to Jimmy Ray and put a finger on the side of his neck to check for a pulse.

"What happened to him?"

"She don't know. She came home from the grocery store, and he was like this."

"I mean what was all those bandages on his hands for?"

"Oh, he hurt 'em in a squatting accident the other day."

"A what?"

"A squatting accident. You know, lifting weights. He was lifting weights, and he got 'em, his fingers, pinched on the bar. He set the bar down on 'em. Broke a bunch of his fingers."

"Did he have heart trouble?"

"Not that I know of."

"Is that his wife or mama in there?" The man pointed back down the hall.

"Yeah, his mama."

"Let me talk to her." Eddy led them back to the living room.

Just about then the yard dogs started up again, and another knock came at the door. Eddy opened it to find a company of EMTs, more policemen, and the fire rescue squad.

"Y'all come on in. He's down the hall here." Eddy led them back to Jimmy Ray's room.

"Hell, I knowed that man." one of the ambulance attendants drawled matter of factly as he checked for vital signs. "I heard him preachin' in a revival last month, uh huh. That there is Reverend Jimmy Ray Jones."

"He's a big ol' boy. We gonna play hell gittin' him out of here," the other EMT said. "Big ol' boy."

Eddy eased on back to the living room where the policeman took Lynette's statement, "Ma'am, did yore son have a history of heart trouble?"

"Well, the doctor did tell him his cholesterol was real high. Tried to get him not to eat no fat foods, but he couldn't never do it. He loved everthing fried."

"Ok, now, was anybody else home when you went to the store?."

"No, nobody. We just live here by ourselves." She dabbed at her eyes with a worn tissue.

"All right, mam. I'm going to call the coroner to come over to the funeral home, and issue the death certificate. Uh, would you like to request an autopsy, ma'am?"

Lynette's grief stricken expression vanished for a moment. "You mean do I want y'all cuttin' my boy up? Don't y'all dare!" She pointed to the clipboard and form he was filling out. "You be sure you don't make no mistakes on that form so that they'll go to cuttin' on Jimmy Ray now. You hear?"

"Yes ma'am, I will."

"I'll tell you something else, too. Ain't nobody gettin' none of his organs neither. Don't even ask. My boy's going home to Jesus in one piece, and that's all there is to it. Now you make sure, mister."

"Yes mam." The policeman nodded sincerely.

"All right then." She glared at him angrily and slapped her thigh. Eddy and the officer exchanged looks, both surprised at Lynette's fierceness.

Eddy sat with Lynette in the living room until the ensemble of people pushed Jimmy Ray down the hall on a gurney with one squeaky wheel. They nodded and bowed their heads as they passed Lynette and Eddy huddled on the couch. Eddy walked back into Jimmy Ray's room and pulled off all the linen, balled it up, and threw it in the trash can out behind the house so Lynette would not have to see those stained sheets.

Eddy returned to the living room and sat with his arm around Lynette once again. "You will help me bury him, won't you?" Lynette asked through her tears.

"You know I will, Lynette."

"He would want you to be a pall bearer. Heck, we're going to need a team of muscle men to lift the old boy, you know?" She let out a little laugh and patted Eddy on the knee.

Eddy laughed too. "Yeah, he was a big old boy. I'll get some of the guys from the gym that liked him if you want."

"Ok, you do that. He loved lifting weights more than anything except Jesus."

"When you want to have it?"

"I reckon, ah, I reckon day after tomorrow. We could have the wake tomorrow night. Have the funeral in the afternoon the day after that."

"Ok, ok. You gonna be ok now by yourself?"

"Yeah, I will, I reckon." She started to cry again.

"I'll stay here with you if you want me too."

"Naw, I'll be all right. I got to make a bunch of phone calls, I reckon."

"Well, you call me if you need anything. Lynette, I sure am sorry. Jimmy Ray was a good old boy. I sure am sorry. I can't believe it. I think I'm still in shock."

She nodded, and he stood up. She walked him to the screen porch door. They both waved as he pulled his car out of the driveway. The yard dogs stood, wagged their dusty tails and stretched.

Lynette looked down the long shotgun hallway of her house. It was dark and empty. The only sound was the old mantle clock and its constant tick. At five o'clock, the old clock began its announcement, "bong, bong, bong, bong, bong." The last sound echoed for a long while in the old, silent house as Lynette sat motionless. The afternoon light drifted slowly away and left her in darkness, with only the company of the ticking clock and her grief.

Eddy stared straight ahead at the road, not even aware that he was driving. The experience of Jimmy Ray's death numbed him, but Lynette's incredible sadness upset him more. Her face was welded in his mind. A gray pallor had overtaken her normally rosy face, and her eyes, that he knew as blue

and bright had faded. He could almost see the life begin to seep out of her. From every pore, her love and will to live seemed to ease away. Jimmy Ray was her everything, and nearly everything she did was motivated by Jimmy Ray. Whether it was cooking, cleaning, running errands for him, answering his evangelistic fan mail, she was always at his beck and call. A fear nagged at Eddy too when he thought about the fact that probably the reason Jimmy Ray died was because of his long standing affair with drugs, especially steroids, and the burden that it put on the dead man's heart.

He pulled into his driveway. Munio strummed his guitar on the porch. Eddy smiled when he saw him, and felt glad somebody was home.

He walked slowly up the porch steps and plopped down in the glider beside Munio. "Man, I can't believe it. Jimmy Ray's dead. He's really dead."

"What happened to this man?" Munio asked.

"He probably had a fucking heart attack. The coroner ain't exactly issued the statement, the uh, death certificate, but that's what probably happened. Hell, he was only twenty-eight years old. Had a fucking heart attack at twenty-eight. I cannot believe this man."

"That is pretty young for that thing to be happening to him."

"Yeah, but you know, the motherfucker lived a hard twenty-eight. I mean, he probably had the guts of a sixty-year-old man with all the drugs and steroids and shit he did in his life. He wasn't no angel even though he walked around saying he was. He wasn't no angel."

"Well, brother, I'm sorry for you to lose your friend."

Eddy's eyes welled up with tears, and he looked up at Munio. Munio slid over on the glider and put his arm around Eddy. Eddy leaned over with his arms on his thighs, covered his face with his hands, and sobbed like a child. Munio just sat there quietly patting him on the back, and soon tears began to silently roll down Munio's brown cheeks, too. After a few minutes, Eddy's tears subsided, and he sat up wiping his eyes. He looked at Munio and winked.

"I appreciate it, man. You being here and all. I ain't had that many people die on me. I think I ain't ever had none of my friends die, you know?"

"It presents a shock, I know. I have lost a few people. You just have to feel sad and go on with your life."

"Yeah, I reckon so. I better call Destiny. She nearly married the guy, although they were not on good terms." Eddy went in the kitchen dialed the number, listened to the phone ring in Destiny's empty house, and hung up. He sat down in a chair at the kitchen table.

"I wonder if his mama done called her?" he said to Munio, who had followed him inside, and who also took a seat also at the table.

"You want to smoke something, Eddy?"

"Yeah, let's burn one for old Jimmy Ray up in heaven." Eddy laughed. "At least I hope he made it up to heaven."

"I'll roll one out of my special stuff. You stay here."

The marijuana smoke drowned out every other smell in the universe, the honeysuckle, and that old foul Rosedale smell, too. Each of them sat with their own flood of thoughts about Jimmy Ray Jones and death. Eddy, in his mind, rolled a tape of the many years he had known Jimmy Ray, and Munio rolled a tape of the one and only day he had ever known of the man.

"Gee, I wonder if his mama would give me his bodybuilding 'medicine.'" Eddy laughed a fast mean laugh that instantly infected Munio with the giggles.

"Well, it is for sure he will not be needing it wherever he has gone."

"No, he ain't. I tell you what, too. If it turns out there is a heaven and a hell, Jimmy Ray is roasting. Basically, he was a son of a bitch. I mean, I loved him and all, but he was a real son of a bitch. He knew it, too. We had a lot of fun. Raised a hell of a lot of hell. Hell, he taught me how to fuck."

"Taught you?" Munio was incredulous.

"Well, not taught me. I mean he didn't fuck me or nothing. See, when we was little, I guess I was about ten and Jimmy Ray was about thirteen, we was hanging out one day around Jimmy Ray's house. They live a little ways out from town on a small farm. They used to raise pygmy goats, little bitty ol' things. Well, I mean you can't put 'em in your pocket or nothing, but they're littler than regular goats. So anyhow, one day Jimmy Ray and me were sitting around on the porch, and Jimmy Ray gets this mean old look on his face.

"'Hey Eddy, he said to me. 'You want to go get fresh with my girl-friend?'

"'You ain't got no girlfriend,' I said to him.

"'Uh huh, I do, too. Come on, I'll show you.'

"So, he took me out back to the barn where the goats were. He scooped up a handful of sweet feed out of the barrel and went up to the biggest nanny goat of all of them.

"'Come on nanny. He called that goat in this sweet voice until she followed him into the barn hoping to get that handful of sweet feed. Jimmy Ray backed his way into a stall, followed by that nanny goat and me.

"He yelled at me to lock the gate, which I did. Then, instead of letting that poor old goat have that sweet feed, he slung it on the ground. That old goat just looked at him. Then, before I knew it, he took his pecker out and grabbed that goat from the back. I had hardly never seen nobody else's pecker before, but buddy, that boy was hung even back then. Anyhow, it was sure bigger than mine. I know that. So, he pulled that old goat to him, stuck it in her, and started fucking away. She cried awful at first, but then shut up. He fucked her until he came. You know he pulled out of her and then gave her a swift kick? I never will forget that. I don't know why he done that. Jimmy Ray had a mean streak to him. He really did. Anyhow, he told me to go on and get me some. You know, Munio, I did indeed fuck that goat that day, but it is one thing I ain't really proud of. To think that the first time I ever really fucked

something was some damn pygmy goat that I basically had to rape. Naw, I ain't too damn proud of that."

Munio smiled and shook his head. "I don't know what to say to that, brother. I know you are strange, but I never expected this from you." He chuckled and winked. Eddy hung his head, took one last toke on that roach, and stared with sad eyes up into the blue sky. "Hey Eddy, I was just kidding. You were only a boy. Boys do things like that. It's not so bad."

"I just wish I had given her that sweet feed, that's all. It was just a mean thing to do, you know?"

Eddy and Munio rocked and glided in their respective seats, out of sync with each other. They gazed out at the cloudless sky above the trees and contemplated nothing.

After thirty minutes, Munio startled himself and Eddy. "Oh! What time is it? Let's see." He looked down at his watch. "Six o'clock, ok, I'm ok."

"You got a hot date or something?" Eddy inquired.

"Yes, I do. I am going to assist her with a dance class."

"Who is her?"

"Oh, Audrey, that queen from last night?"

"Oh right, I forgot. Munio at the country club. That should be a fun scene. You'll fit right in. All them nice honkies will take one look at you and run screaming for the sheriff." Eddy laughed loudly.

"That may be the case, brother. We will just have to see about that. Anyway, it is time for me to prepare. I must get properly dressed for this event. I must shower now. What will you do tonight, Eddy?" Munio stood as he spoke.

"Hell, I reckon I'll, uh, I'm going to try to get Destiny and go over to the funeral home. I hate going to them places, but I reckon I ought to. She's going to freak out. She don't take too well to tragedy, people dying and all. She did love the man at one time, but he done her wrong. He really was a fucking hypocritical son of a bitch, but what the hell."

"Eddy, if you loved that man, you should go to the funeral home. My grandmother, a Mayan, taught me that through death, the living have the opportunity to grow. It is said the magnitude of a person's efforts to honor the dead shows the gods not only how much the person was loved, but also how much more committed you are to living."

"Hey, grow or die!" Eddy pointed at Munio.

"Well, yes, I guess this is true."

Eddy scratched his head and took the rubber band off his long blonde ponytail. He ran his fingers through his hair with an irritated look on his face. "You know what?"

"What?" Munio said standing and rocking from one foot to the other. Although he hated to leave his friend in a time of grief, it was past time for him to get ready to go to the dance class.

"I think I'm going to get this shit cut off. I've had long hair for just about long enough. What do you think?"

"Sure, cut it off, if you want. Get a flat top. That would look good."

"Yeah, I think I'll get me a fucking flat top. I am sick of washing this shit."

"Listen brother, I hate to leave you, but I have made this commitment to meet Audrey in a short while. I must go and prepare now."

"I'm ok, man. Go, go, don't worry about it, man. I think I'm going to the barber shop right now, and get this shit cut the fuck off before I chicken out."

Munio laughed. "You will look like that guy, ah, that bad boy singer, uh, oh, Bill Idol. That's who you will look like." He pointed his finger at Eddy and laughed.

"Yeah, maybe I will. That'd be cool." Eddy spontaneously jumped up and went into a Billy Idol routine. "With a rebel yell, he cried more, more, more!" They both laughed.

"That's good, Eddy. That's good. Maybe you get a job as a Billy Idol impersonator, eh?" Munio disappeared into the house.

# CHAPTER XII

Audrey pulled up in Eddy's driveway precisely at seven o'clock and beeped the horn. Munio burst through the screen door. His rich, brown face was in stunning contrast to his wild and shiny black hair and the glimmering white silk cloth of his shirt. The blousy shirt, with its oversized collar and billowing sleeves, and was unbuttoned to the nipples, exposed Munio's smooth chest. He wore black bellbottom polyester trousers that hung exactly to the floor. The tips of his black and white wingtips stuck out from under the canopy of the pants to complete a stellar image of a ballroom dancing machine. Looking like a Mayan god, Munio struck a pose on the porch.

"Holy mother of God," Audrey quipped.

Munio strode down the steps to the car. "Hello, Audrey."

"And hello to you, Don Juan of Rosedale. You look fabulous."

"Thank you very much, and you too are lovely this evening." He straightened out the legs of the bellbottoms that hung like half-closed umbrellas.

"Muchas gracias to you, senōr. Ok now, let's run over some details. First of all, you remember I told you that my friend Sandra who is a member of this country club got me this job? Well, I forgot I was not supposed to tell you she was a trans so don't mention it, not that it would come up in the course of normal conversation, of course."

Munio laughed out loud.

"Oy, gevalt." Audrey waved her right hand.

"What's that you say?"

"Oy, gevalt?"

"Yes, what is that?"

"Yiddish. It means ah, it means, what the hell or heaven help me. Take your pick!"

Munio chuckled, "Oh, ok."

"What made this man want to be a woman?

"Why is the sky blue? Who the hell knows?" Audrey snapped her long, red fingernails.

"Wow, that is an unbelievable story." Munio joked.

"Believe it, honey. Everybody's story is unbelievable when you think about it."

"Maybe so, maybe so."

" Oh, by the way, button up that shirt a bit. I don't want them to throw you out for indecent exposure."

Munio smiled slightly and shook his head as he buttoned the shirt.

"First, you and I will demonstrate several different styles of dances. For example, samba, tango, mambo maybe. You don't have to say a word. Just look pretty and dance hot. You'll be a big hit. Trust me."

"Ok, boss." Munio smiled and looked out the window.

* * * * *

The country club grounds were impressive with rows of well-manicured boxwoods and dozens of sizable crepe myrtle trees filled with magenta blossoms. With its rambling three-story yellow-orange brick building, shining white trim, and red-tiled roof, the place had the look of royalty. The membership criteria were steep as well were the dues.

A young white tuxedoed man waited in the motor lobby to valet park Audrey's black Chrysler New Yorker. Audrey and Munio entered the lobby and were greeted by several uniformed male attendants waiting to assist members. Audrey's black heels clicked on the marble floor, intermittently silenced as she moved onto the oriental rugs scattered throughout. Munio followed behind her watching her long black dress and slim shapely body sway through the room. Her hair was twisted and restrained in a tight bun.

They entered a large room where a group of twelve people were standing about talking. One woman instantly noticed their arrival and made a quick approach to greet them.

"Audrey, so good to see you!" The large woman said with enthusiasm. "This must be Munio. How are you, Munio?" Each word, enunciated with great profundity, shot at him like verbal bullets.

"Yes, hello," He said politely and nodded.

"Munio, this is Sandra Fugleberg. Sandra, Munio Morelos."

Sandra's large right hand engulfed Munio's as she shook it furiously. Her congeniality overwhelmed Munio, but he subdued his instinct to pull away

and sprint from the building. Instead, he smiled and nodded his head.

"Ok, we must get started, Sandra. Is the music ready?"

"Yes. Oh Munio, we are so excited to have you enhance our class tonight. Everyone," she boomed, like a jet breaking the sound barrier, "this is Munio Morelos from the country of Belize who will assist Miss Meyers tonight. Let's give him a warm round of applause, shall we?" The group responded politely, and Munio smiled and bowed in their direction.

"Ok, everyone, pair off and form a circle, please," Audrey instructed and motioned for Munio to join her. He walked to her side and took her hand.

"First of all, we are going to work on the tango since we have Mr. Morelos's expertise with us this evening. Watch us, if you will, run through the steps slowly without the music. I'll count off. Ready, Munio?" Munio sprang to life, drawing Audrey close to him in the starting position. His body posture held steady with a robotic elegance. "And a one and two and three and four, reverse," Audrey counted off. Audrey and Munio slunk across the floor in slow motion with their bodies close together. Munio's left and Audrey's right arm extended straight as an arrows. On the "reverse" command, they changed direction like the snap of a whip, swift but smooth, their faces nearly touching.

"There now." Audrey stopped for a moment and pulled away from Munio. "That's how it goes. People, this is a sensual dance, a smooth dance, a dramatic dance. I don't want to see any bouncing. Slink, slink is the watchword for this dance, all right? Any questions?" Audrey looked over the group. All of them shook their puzzled faces no. "Very well, Charles, start the music." A young blonde man in a white tuxedo jacket and black trousers stood in the corner next to a sound system. Upon the push of a button, a loud vibrant Latin song changed the shape of the room and the people in it.

The students were middle-aged and older. The men were all bald, and the plump women's stockings created a "whoosh" sound with every step. They took Audrey's direction to heart, and for that instant, in their hearts, became the young, impassioned, lithe dancers who conceived this dance of romance. Their faces filled with staunch resolve, they moved stealthily across the parquet floor. Even Sandra moved with a measure of grace and purpose, as her much shorter, red-faced partner's ear pressed against her large silicone bosom. Meanwhile, Charles, the music attendant, stood in the corner like a member of the Royal Guard, expressionless. Munio, although very much attentive to Audrey and the task at hand, watched the others and in his peripheral vision had to suppress his mirth. He caught Audrey's eye, and she raised one eyebrow sternly as if she had read his mind. This made him snicker, and he had to look away quickly to not lose his composure.

Audrey and Munio dipped, tangoed, and mamboed their way through the two-hour class, and at the end, the students all applauded as they capped the evening off with a solo performance. As children invariably crowd around

a pony, all the students wanted to shake the exotic hand of Munio, hoping some of his natural talent would rub off on them.

"You want to go for a drink?" Audrey asked, knowing the answer as they exited the front gate of the country club.

"Yes, sure, I could use one."

"What would you like to drink?"

"Drink?" Munio snickered, "Lady, I will drink anything. Anything, you want, I will drink it too."

"I don't really feel like going to a bar, do you?"

"It does not matter to me. We could sit on Eddy's porch if you want. That is a such a nice porch. I like that porch. We could stop at the liquor store, and I'll buy us something to drink, eh?"

"All right, that's fine."

* * * * * *

Munio stirred two screwdrivers in the kitchen and took them out to the porch.

"This is a nice porch. Southerners definitely use their porches," Audrey commented. "But, what's not to use? It's five hundred degrees in the house, and no air conditioning? I cannot believe these people don't have air conditioning! I would wilt, literally wilt, if I lived here. Look." Audrey dabbed at her forehead with a paper napkin. "I'm wilting now, as we speak."

"I like the heat myself. I am used to it. I have not known any other climate."

"You have also known pantyhose, mister, and I'm here to tell you a girl could melt here, literally melt."

Munio laughed and downed his drink in one smooth swallow.

"Want another?" Munio asked as he stood.

"No, not yet," Audrey responded, quietly taking note of Munio's thirst.

"Ahhh." He pushed the screen door open. "This sure tastes good. Audrey, your friend Sandra must have been one hell of a man."

"Why do you say that?"

"Because he still has a handshake strong as can be, stronger than any woman I ever met, and nearly all the men, too!" Munio laughed loudly and slapped his black polyester leg.

"Yes, he has. He wasn't tiny by any means." Audrey was a little uncomfortable with the rapid escalation of Munio's extrovertedness. "Have you eaten today, Munio?"

"Eaten? What kind of a question is that?"

"A simple question, Munio, that's what. Have you eaten today?"

"Well, of course, let's see." Munio replayed his day on the fingers of his right hand, mumbling in a low voice that only he could understand. Finally he concluded, "Damn, if I have, I sure can't remember." he laughed heartily, a big smile stuck to his face.

Audrey tipped her drink to finish it. "I need to run along, Munio." She shot him a superficial smile and put her glass down on the small table next to the rocking chair.

Munio was caught off guard and was not happy that she was going to leave him. "You have to leave?" He said sadly.

She nodded. "Here, let me give you this before I forget." Audrey counted out thirty dollars and handed it to Munio.

"Ok, well, thank you, and you call me, ok?" Munio stood and stuffed the bills in his pocket.

"Yes, I will." Audrey coolly moved down the steps and walked to her car.

"You call me, ok?" Munio called to her as she got into her car. Audrey just nodded and drove away in the big black car.

Munio turned to sit down, but then spun around on his heels fast as lightning. He ran down the steps and screamed to the empty street, "You don't have my number!"

Munio's gaiety subsided after he was alone on the porch for a few minutes. In fact, he quickly became depressed. He mixed another screwdriver and rolled a joint.

He felt better once he had fired up a joint. The burning heat of the day had given way to the coolness of the dark, which tonight brought with it a steady breeze. Munio preferred the night. The lightning bugs began to appear. They entertained Munio and kept him company. He picked up his guitar, began strumming softly, and sang the song, his favorite song, "The Impossible Dream", in Spanish. Though he dreamed to one day live a life true to the words of the song, he feared that time would never come. Tears rolled down his face, staining the white silk blouse with little dark spots.

The song grounded him, and when he finished playing, he realized he was starving. After putting his guitar back in its case, he drove to a grocery store. Returning home, put his bag of groceries down on the little table on the porch in front of the glider. One by one he pulled items from the bag: a clear jar of pickled pigs' feet, a can of condensed milk, and a package of saltine crackers. This was one of Munio's favorite meals, and with each bite he became aware of how hungry he was. The food both sobered and cheered him up as he chomped, happy as a child, listening to the crickets chirp and watching the lightning bugs flash.

Eddy's car screeched into the driveway. Like a pair of crazed moons on the run, the headlights blinded Munio temporarily. The now flat-topped Eddy leaped from the car and sprinted up on the porch with a pillowcase full of something. He beamed from ear to ear as he hit the top step of the porch.

"What do you think, man?" He ran his hand back and forth over the top of his inch- long bristled hair.

"Very cool, very cool." Munio wasn't quite ready for Eddy's high energy.

"Come in here! Come in here! I got something to show you. You won't believe what I got! I can't believe what I got." He motioned for Munio to get up and follow him in the house.

Munio sighed and reluctantly did so. Eddy marched down the hall to his bedroom. Turning the pillowcase upside-down on the bed, he poured out dozens of little glass bottles full of liquid. They made rapid and high-pitched clinks as they hit together.

"Steroids," he proudly announced, and held out his arm in introduction.

"That's all steroids?" Munio pointed to the pile.

"Yep, as a matter of fact, that's about fifteen thousand bucks worth of steroids. That's the finest collection of steroids in the southeast, I guarantee. Decca, anavar, anadrol, French primobolin, water base testosterone, oil base testosterone, d-ball, you name it, buddy, and it's here. This is so beautiful, man. To a bodybuilder, this is fucking heaven right here on earth."

"So did you win a steroid lottery?" Munio chuckled.

"Nope, Jimmy Ray's mama gave them to me," he said proudly. "I went over to visit her, and she said she had found some stuff that she didn't know or want to know what it was. She asked me if I would get rid of it. So, we go back in poor old Jimmy Ray's room, and all this shit was loaded up in a drawer. I tried to keep a straight, serious face while I said that I would throw the stuff out. If this pile of shit don't turn me into America's next Arnold Schwarzenegger, I don't know what will. This is the greatest thing that has ever, I mean ever, happened to me!" Eddy's level of excitement coupled with the maniacal look on his face frightened Munio.

"I think I'm going to have a toast to Jimmy Ray right now." He went over to his dresser and pulled out a syringe. He removed the cap, perused the stock, and picked a bottle of anadrol. Pulling a couple of cc's into the chamber, he pointed the loaded gun in the air and pushed the plunger until a little ran down the needle. He lowered his pants down just to the high hip area and shot the yellow liquid into his skin. "Ah, what a jolly good vintage!" he quipped with a mock British accent. "A very good year, indeed! Cheerio to you, Jimmy Ray. Wherever you are, may you remain large!" Eddy let out a loud laugh. "Won't you join me?" Eddy pointed the needle at Munio.

"No, Eddy, that's not for me. If I can't drink it or smoke it, it will not be going into me. Thank you just the same."

"Ok, if you want to be scrawny all your life, if you want your head kicked in the sand, go right ahead! As for me, buddy, I'm going to loom large in this world!" Eddy stomped around the room and assumed the persona of a TV evangelist, shaking his fists and looking up to the heavens. "Life's too short to be small, people! You have got to load up and pump up if you ever want to find salvation in this world, or make it on the cover of Ironman! Can I get an amen?"

# CHAPTER XIII

From Rosedale to Mobile, tears streamed down Destiny's red, wind-burned face. Her brown hair flew in the wind like a tarp, improperly secured for highway driving, but big black sunglasses served her well and kept the hair and dust out of her eyes. The tears were not for Jimmy Ray, but for her home, which she felt she must now abandon in order to avoid prison. The tears represented all the sadness suffered at Jimmy Ray's mercy, and all the times she had felt so helpless, a feeling she had never known until she met him. She cried for the self-confidence that had vanished in the midst of that time, and now she cried for times that would never be again because of her courage earlier in the day. It was not the time to honor herself for that because right now, she was a fear-crazed woman who could absorb no message other than to run.

And run she did, as she held relentlessly onto that steering wheel, and without speeding, made Mobile by mid-afternoon. There was no time to stop at the overlook over Mobile Bay or take any side trips to look at the beach. All she could take note of were the beautiful live oak trees filled with green leaves and gray moss that waved at her as she passed. How many times she had just wanted to take off and visit Mobile. Her mama and daddy took her there when she was just a toddler, but she never made it back on her own.

From Mobile, it was on to New Orleans, and Destiny started crying again when she started over the Lake Pontchartrain bridge because whether it was drugs or not, she vowed aloud that this was the most beautiful sunset she had ever seen. It was a good omen, she thought. She must be on the right road at the right time.

When daylight disappeared and darkness set in earnest, a deep fatigue gripped her. The nuances of the trip, the scenery, the trees, vanished, leaving only headlights, tail lights, road signs, and filling stations to keep her company. This stretch of road from New Orleans to Houston seemed endless, and it took eight hours and three generous shots of crank to make it.

The overload of track marks looked like a rash on her arms. Now she had to go to the smaller veins that stood up on top of her hands. She tried in one restroom to hit a vein in her foot but was not steady enough, could not focus, could barely stand.

When she entered the invariably small and dirty restrooms, loaded with dim fluorescent green-tinged lights, it was hard for her to not flip out after spending so much time whizzing down the road in the comfort and privacy of the darkness. The room buzzed and hummed, and her head would spin so much that she could barely wipe herself. It was doubly worse if some other woman entered while she hit up. Her heart stuck in her throat, convinced

the woman would call the police, as if she could really see what was going on behind that stall door.

About three thirty in the morning, a Houston city limit sign flashed by, and Destiny drew in a great breath and let it out. With it, her tension temporarily decreased long enough for a brief celebration. This meant she was only seven more hours away from the Mexican border.

After Houston, she parted company with the interstate system to pick up highway 77 south through Victoria and on down just west of Corpus Christi. About 7 a.m., the deep dark night gradually succumbed to the palest tangerine at the horizon. Just as at sunset the night before, Destiny had to adjust to the coming of the light. Surrendering her friend, the darkness, for the heat and scrutiny of the morning sun made her even more aware of her impending exhaustion.

The last leg into Brownsville was the loneliest time Destiny had ever known. Her body was functioning on borrowed time, and she was well aware of this fact. Her tolerance to the crank had built up, and the shots weren't lasting as long. She prayed she could just make it those final miles.

As she drove through the desolate prairie south of Kingsville with endless stretches of inaccessible land full of rattlesnakes and cactus, she began to face the fact that Mexico might not be the romantic place she had imagined it to be. Tequila with worms, tacos, and cheap sandals were about all the scoop she had on the country. She chuckled as she recalled the scene on Eddy's porch with Munio, and how she joked about her Spanish speaking ability. She wished she had Munio with her now. She wished she had anybody with her.

It was nine-thirty in the morning when Destiny entered the city of Brownsville, Texas, which rested on the banks of the Rio Grande. Just over that river bridge was the Mexican border crossing at Matamoros, ironically the same spot Munio had gained entry into the U.S. This was the furthest she had ever been from her Georgia home, and she was amazed that she had actually made it here. Something about her accomplishment made her feel proud and secure that she had done the right thing even though, twenty-four hours ago, the hysterical desperate woman who turned onto the interstate had not been so sure. Even though there were places she would rather be, there was solace in the fact that safety from any penalties concerning Jimmy Ray's murder awaited her on the other side of that border.

For more than forty-eight hours now, Destiny had been up, angst, running drugs, and drinking, and her nerves were on a hair trigger. She looked it too. Her face had broken out in several places, and her scar still glowed an angry red. Purple and brown bags hung under her eyes, and her eyes themselves were so glazed and empty that they looked like something a taxidermist might install in a stuffed fox or a coyote.

Before making the actual move of crossing into Matamoros, she stopped at a pay phone to call her sister and see what the score was. Destiny had as-

sumed that the law would somehow know she was the murderer, and within hours, a nationwide search would be enforced.

"Louise?" Destiny said.

"Destiny?"

"Yeah, it's me."

"Where on earth are you?"

"Oh, I went to Florida for a couple of days. I just wanted to call about the cats."

"The cats? Girl, it's what, oh, noon. I reckon it ain't that early, but you know I worked late last night. Are you drunk?"

Destiny laughed, "I've had a few, but I ain't exactly drunk. I passed drunk and moved on into sober again."

"Well, I'm glad you called, honey. Uh, the cats are fine. That new little one is cute."

"Yeah, his name is Jose, by the way."

"Listen, I hate to tell you this over the phone, honey, but something has happened that you might ought to know about."

Destiny's heart thumped wildly, and she could hardly speak. "Yeah, like what?"

"Well, Jimmy Ray Jones has up and died. They think he had a stroke or a heart attack, one or the other. You know he had hurt hisself lifting weights the other day, and they think he was fucked up from that. He was so big and all."

"I'll be dog. I knew he had got hurt, but I didn't know he was that bad off."

"Yeah, well, his mama's pretty tore up about it."

"Was they going to do an autopsy or anything on him?"

"Naw, his mama wouldn't let them do nothing like that. Besides, the man's dead. Whether it was a heart attack or a stroke don't matter now. It ain't like he was murdered or nothing."

A big smile came across Destiny's lips, and the tension broke in her sad face. Tears began streaming from her eyes as she both smiled and cried while continuing the conversation.

"When is the funeral?"

"Friday at eleven."

"Friday? That's four days from now."

"I know. I hope he don't rot too awful bad. Lynette said she wanted him buried on Friday, just like Jesus or something."

"Oh lord."

"Are you going to go?"

"I don't know. I did love him at one time, but he was a son of a bitch. I like his mama though. I don't know if I'll make it back for that or not."

"I can understand that. I'm glad you called so I could tell you."

"Yeah, me too. I reckon I'll go on, then, Louise."

"Ok, be careful, honey. I love you."

"I love you, too."

Destiny hung up the phone and let out a big "Yahoo!" into the morning sky. "Praise the lord!" she screamed as she leaped and skipped around the car. "Yes! Yes! Yes! Shit yeah!" Finally, her exhilaration slowed enough to allow her to drive again.

As she turned that car around with a screech and headed northbound for a change, some feeling returned to her body. It suddenly occurred to her that she had not eaten or slept in two days. A hunger came over her that felt life threatening, and she pulled up to the drive-thru window of the very next fast food joint. When she left the place, there were enough hamburgers, French fries, chicken dinners, milk shakes, and fried pies to feed eight people.

Next door was a cheap looking motel with a vacancy sign, and she checked into room two twenty-two. Her body shook badly as she lugged her overnight bag and all the bags of food up the stairs. Once inside the room, she dropped everything and did a belly flop onto the bed with a bounce. After a few minutes, she got back up, piled the food on the bed, and flipped on the TV. Once she had undressed and put on a big long T-shirt, the feeding frenzy began.

To the light of Sally Jesse Raphael, the fast food bags all were slowly relieved of most of their contents. After Sally Jessie Raphiel ended, Maury Povich picked the ball up with a show about how lesbians' lives had been disrupted by oral surgery. Destiny jeered and laughed her way through both shows, seemingly unaware of exactly what she was putting in her body. She rarely looked down at the food and ate rapidly like a starving dog, chewing little. The small woman swallowed more food than was imaginable until she could not eat one more bite. It was then that she scanned all the deserted containers and wrappers and realized what she had done. She laughed out loud, moaned, and grabbed her stomach in pain. Then, with a mischievous look on her face, she got up off the bed, and walked with purpose into the bathroom. Without having to stick her finger very far at all down her throat, Destiny gave a guttural heave, and the pressure was relieved into the toilet with a resounding splash. A big tight-lipped smile came across her face, and she glanced in the mirror over the lavatory. The sight was rough, so she looked away quickly and rinsed out her mouth.

After a long slow slug of Jack Daniels, she shut off the TV and tucked herself in the other bed, leaving all the dinner debris on the first. Even though it was close to high noon outside, the wall of light behind the mauve curtains did not prevent her from falling, like a stone into a canyon, into the deepest sleep she had ever known.

It was six o'clock in the morning, eighteen hours later, before Destiny woke up. She felt like a ton of bricks had hit her. The energy debt she had incurred on the trip was still overdrawn, even with the long rest. She walked

into the bathroom, cursed herself as she looked at her face in the mirror and checked her waist for fat deposits. A hot shower, an Alka Selzer, and four aspirins allowed her to bear the razor-raw edges she felt, emotionally as well as physically. The dawn was edging in on the night as she shut the door of room two twenty-two and hit the long road back to Georgia.

With all the windows rolled down, the cool morning air got the trip off to a good start. She sang and cried and hollered along with the evangelist preacher on the radio. The decision to not do crank for a while made the trip take longer because she had to take several naps on the side of the road.

At noon the next day, Destiny pulled into her driveway, and just sat there crying. She felt like one of those people on talk shows that claims to have been swooped up by aliens for the weekend. She felt like the past four days had been some paperback book she was reading, not something that really happened to her. Her tears subsided, and she took her bags into the house. The silence that greeted her was comforting, as she dropped back into her little life in Rosedale, Georgia, where nothing much ever happens.

Since it was around noontime, the soaps were on. She flipped on the TV and flopped on the couch. One of her fingernails caught on a seam of a cushion, and when she looked down to inspect the damage, she frowned. She noticed that not only had she torn a nail, but also all of her pink painted nails were chipped and worn all to hell. On the coffee table were all the supplies to give herself a complete manicure, which she began to do. Looking across the room to the dining room table, she spotted what she needed first. She smiled and crossed the room where she picked up the bottle of nail polish remover. She nonchalantly walked back to the couch and plopped down again. With a deep smile that ran all through her body, Destiny uncapped the bottle and took a big whiff. "Wooooo, lawd help me! That's some strong stuff!" She laughed and shook her head. She held the bottle skyward, "Here's to ya, Jimmy Ray." She threw back her head and laughed.

# CHAPTER XIV

As usual, Munio's alarm clock cause him to sit bolt upright in bed, his heart pounding nearly out of his chest, until he realized it was just Eddy's morning howl after taking his shot of growth hormone. Munio peeked out through the curtains of the doll room and saw that it was getting light. Eddy heard him stir and stuck his head in.

"Rise and shine, beautiful, it's shoulder and calf day." Eddy let out a maniacal laugh.

"Oh shit, really? You ready to train?"

"Yeah, baby. I need ya, too. Get on up, and I'll cook up a big ol' breakfast, ok?"

"Eddy, I keep telling you that I would puke if I ate food at this time of day. Coffee only and lots of it, please." Munio rubbed his eyes.

"All right, coming up." Eddy gave him a happy smile and vanished.

Munio's world was spinning, but it usually did if he woke up too soon before whatever he drank the night before had not had time to wear off. His head ached, and his stomach burned. He stood up, pulled on his cutoffs, and grabbed his cigarettes. The crickets were still chirping as he pushed open the screen door and stood on the porch. He studied the one star that remained from the night and the impending peach-colored dawn. The match's acrid sulfur smell and the burning tobacco's powerful scent cut into the dignity of the night. To Munio, however, the smoke tasted much sweeter than any air he had ever smelled. He had smoked since he was fourteen years old and could not imagine life without it.

"Shuuuuuwwweee! Damn, that smoke is strong this early in the morning." Eddy moved quickly out on the porch and handed Munio a cup of coffee. Munio, who was in an introverted state of mind, was irritated by Eddy's verbose presence.

"Thanks," Munio said quietly and took the cup. He drank a long, careful sip and licked his lips, which were dry and cracked. His breath felt thick, and the taste in his mouth was not pleasant.

"Gonna be a purdy day, Munio. Gonna be a good day to grow." Eddy laughed loudly, and the sound almost sent Munio to his knees. Munio nodded back at Eddy and politely forced a little smile across his lips.

"Ok, I'm cooking. You sure you don't want anything? We're gonna be shittin' and gittin' here in a minute. You gonna get hungry."

"I'm ok, really. Trust me. If there is one thing I am not, it is hungry. Thank you, Eddy. I just have to wake up. I am still unaccustomed to rising at this hour."

"Ok man, whatever," Eddy slapped Munio on the back as he passed back through the screen door.

Even after a hot shower, Munio still cringed under the influence of the bright morning light as they drove to the gym. Eddy turned the radio to a hard rock station, which sent Munio's brainwaves scrambling.

Things didn't get better for Munio at the Dixie Ironworks because it was jammed with people who were every bit as exuberant as his charge, Eddy Jackson. The stereo, cranked to the same station as Eddy had on in the car, red-lined an Aerosmith song. The poor-quality speakers responded with muddy vibrations that were almost visible.

Eddy put his bag down and stretched. Munio sat down on a bench and looked around at the action.

"Hello, Munio," said a slow and dark seductive voice from behind him. He turned with a jerk and was startled to see Ida Blue. Her sky blue contacts stung his eyes.

"How are you today?" She moved close to Munio and rubbed her hand up and down his arm.

"Oh, OK," Munio nodded, "OK, it's a little early to tell."

"Not an early riser?"

"No, not at all. How are you?" he asked politely, not wanting to know.

"Fine, thank you, fine. Eddy, good morning, sugar."

"Hey Ida, what's happening?" Eddy replied with a smile as he stretched, holding a broomstick overhead.

"Nothing, doing a little aerobics. I'm down to four weeks until nationals."

"All right, well, you're looking good. You'll have to pose for me soon. Let me check yo' bad self out."

"Ok, ok, I will." She looked over at the stationary equipment area. "Listen, I have to go before somebody gets my bike. I'll check you boys out a little later. Munio, I want to see you today, ok?" She pointed at him.

"Oh, sure, ok." Munio smiled, afraid to refuse her.

Eddy winked at Munio, who shook his head as they walked over to the seated press station.

"Don't say anything!" Munio advised sternly.

Eddy burst into laughter and yelled a hefty pig call, "Yeeehaaaw. Ride 'em!" as he sat down on the worn black vinyl seat.

Munio, who laughed too but tried to suppress it, said, "Don't make me hurt you in front of all your little friends, Eddy. It would not look good for an old man like me to kick your ass, but I will. You may count on this fact."

Eddy warmed up with a hundred forty-five. "I'm sorry, Munio, but if that girl ever gets a hold of you, buddy, I want to be in the closet watching. I can't imagine fucking that woman. Go down on her? She'd crush your head like a papershell pecan with those thighs of hers. Lawd, lawd, lawd! Woman would put a hurtin' on you!" With a clang, he brought the bar to rest on the iron hooks of the rack.

"You know, I might like it just for the experience."

"Chew you up and spit you out, boy. Give me a hand off with this one." Eddy had put twenty-five pounds on each end.

He paused to get focused and gave a nod to Munio, who helped Eddy lift the bar to arm's length. He did ten repetitions, lowering it to his shoulders and then back again to arm's length.

"That felt like nothing. Damn, that good old anadrol is helping me out this morning. Take that twenty-five off and put on a forty-five." Eddy loaded one end while Munio attended the other.

"How can you tell it's the anadrol, and not that growth hormone?"

"'Cause you see, I feel mean. I feel like the baddest motherfucker in the valley. I feel like I could fuck King Kong up, and buddy, when you feel like that, you're jacked up on anadrol." Eddy laughed and slapped Munio on the

back.

Eddy pushed through two more sets of increasing poundages. After a couple of minutes rest, he slid a ten on each end. "If I get this, it will be my all time best. I would love to get a triple with it."

"What is this?" Munio counted up the weight. "Two forty-five? Ok, brother, I'm with you. You will get it. Now, get your head straight, and you can do it. You're plenty strong, plenty strong."

Eddy took his place and went through his psyching up ritual. Finally, he nodded to Munio, and the drama continued.

"That's it, one! Good! Two, Eddy, two! That's it!" Eddy used every fiber of his being to make that bar go up, spewed spit straight up in the air with every exhale through clenched teeth. "One more Eddy! You can do it! All you now, all you! Yes! Good! Good job, Eddy!" Munio patted Eddy on the back as they holstered the bar in the rack for the final time.

Through four more different exercises--seated dumbell presses, lateral raises, the rear delt machine, and reverse flys, Munio coaxed and cajoled Eddy to do good work.

"You boys finished?" Ida Blue sidled up closer than was comfortable to both of them. She smacked a large piece of green gum with a sound like the crack of a whip.

"Yep, fixing to hit the road, girl. What are you doing?"

"Well, Eddy, now that you asked. I want to get that coach of yours to spend some time with me this afternoon. What do you think, Munio?" Ida raised her eyebrows and winked. She ran an index finger with its long red nail slowly down Munio's arm, chilling him to the bone. It drew a smile to his lips, though he was unsure if it was from amusement or fear.

"What did you have in mind, dear?" Munio returned. Summoning up some machismo, he put his arm around her.

"Three o'clock til dark is good for me, honey." She batted the false lashes that hung from of her eyelids like yard rakes.

"Very well, I will do that. When and where, lady, do you want to have this confrontation?"

"Why don't you come over to my place?"

"No, no, no, just tell me. I'd rather you tell me. Write down the address and your phone number, but just tell me the direction."

"Ok, photographic memory, eh?" She laughed as she told him the specifics and handed the paper to Munio.

"Ok, I'll be there at three o'clock," Munio nodded.

"All right sugar, I'll be waiting with bells on." All smiles left her face, and she stared deep into Munio's eyes with a hungry look that compelled him to shiver.

Munio and Eddy watched her ass as she walked away from them.

"Owweee, Munio's gonna get whupped this evenin'. You gonna get your

dick knocked in the dirt! Yep, you're fixing to get yo' clock cleaned but good, son! I hope you got your will wrote down," Eddy joked.

"Not if I return the favor first, Eddy. Do not underestimate my power, my man. I may be old, but I still got a little fight left in me. You'll see."

"She'll throw you and blow you before you know it."

"And this behavior I should try to discourage? Ha! Throw me and blow me, hummmm. This I like, Eddy."

"Ok, don't say I didn't warn you."

# CHAPTER XV

Back in his room Eddy pulled the drug box out of the closet. He set it on his bed and sat cross-legged in front of it. Still in shock from the acquisition, he smiled with glee as he opened it, like a child on Christmas morning. The little bottles and vials created a melody, clinking together as he inspected them. Eddy picked up one and then another and scrutinized the labels, then, like a fine wine collector, he selected two specials of the day. Hopping off the bed, he procured a syringe and proceeded to load it a third of the way with the gold-colored liquid. From the second bottle, he added enough to half fill the syringe. Holding his prize up to the light of the window, Eddy licked his chops and thumped the syringes while the liquids swirled and mixed.

"Ah, tutti-frutti, my favorite flavor!" He laughed and removed his towel skirt. In front of his dresser mirror, he searched for a good spot, high on his hip, to inject his cocktail. The stuff stung as it punctured his skin, and he winced as he emptied the load.

"Shit, that fucking burns! I hope this is really what it says it is. Jimmy Ray." He looked up at the ceiling to speak. "You better not have got a bunch of bad shit here because if I die and go to where you are, I'll kick your fucking ass!" He laughed, then frowned, and rubbed his butt.

Eddy had had a love affair with steroids for five years or so now. Jimmy Ray had indoctrinated him into the way of the juice, so to speak. Eddy sat down on the bed again and reminisced about his first cycle.

Eddy weighed one hundred and eighty pounds and was a fair-sized young man before he ever loaded up. He lifted weights for a few years in junior high and high school, but was overlooked by college football teams for being not quite big enough for a fullback position. It humiliated him to be dubbed too small, and when his old friend Jimmy Ray suggested he had a solution, Eddy was willing.

Jimmy Ray had fired up a syringe with a load of testosterone and had Eddy drop his drawers. Within the hour, Eddy had felt a heightened sense of aggression and power, a feeling of superiority. All of these early side effects brought nothing short of joy to Eddy. By the next morning, he had felt a loco-

motive was running through his veins as his blood pressure elevated. His dick had been so hard upon waking that it became a downright first aid procedure to jack off before he could even get out of bed. The orgasm was unequaled. Eddy figured he had run into the perfect drug. At the gym, his endurance was better, and nothing felt heavy. In fact, he broke all his personal bests on the exercises he did that day. Eddy became forever changed by these drugs and built his whole life around them.

He suddenly stood up in front of the mirror and began posing. With his body fat at only about six percent, in his opinion, he could be contest ready in two weeks. He hit a front double bicep pose and then a side tricep. Turning back to the front, he hit a chest shot and ab pose. His abs were already ripped the best they had ever been. He smiled when he saw them pop out as he exhaled and contracted.

To Eddy, his body was his best friend, his trophy. More than his temple, it was a calling card that fared better than an MBA or a Ph.D. People had an instant opinion about who Eddy was because of that body. He aspired to no greater feat in his life than to be big and ripped. To be Mr. Dixie was to be the God of the South, and from there, who knows? Maybe he could be the next Mr. Olympia. Eddy put his stash away and lay down to dream about winning the title and more muscle.

"Destiny?" Eddy said into the receiver.

"Eddy?"

"Yeah, where on earth have you been, girl? I been trying to call you for days."

"I went down to Florida for a few days."

"Florida? You didn't tell me you was going to do that, did you?"

"Uh uh, I just did it on the spur of the minute kind of thing. How are you?"

"Spur of the minute? You don't ever do anything on the spur of the minute. Going out of town, anyhow. Who went with you?"

"Nobody, just went by myself."

"What?! Since when do you go out of town by yourself."

"Well, Eddy, I'm not a complete idiot. Anybody can read a map, for Christ's sakes!" She twisted her hair around her index finger.

"All right, all right. Well, did you have fun?"

"Yeah, it was all right."

"I don't know if you've heard, but Jimmy-"

"Yeah, I heard he died. Are you ok?"

"Yeah, we was buds a long time. He just lived a fast life. I reckon it wasn't fast enough. Have you talked to Lynette?"

"No, I've got to call her, but I just haven't got up the nerve. I know she's upset."

"Yeah, but she's ok. You know the funeral's Friday at eleven. You want me

to pick you up?"

"Eddy, I just don't know if I can go."

"Well, Destiny, the man loved you more than anybody in this world."

"Eddy, I can't help that. I just get too upset at these things."

"There ain't a more appropriate place in the whole wide world to get upset than at a fucking funeral, Destiny."

"I'll think about it, Eddy. All right? Get off my back, will you?" Destiny spat.

"Ok, ok, you know, I kind of just need you for me, too. I'm going to be a pall bearer and everything. You know you could sit with me and Lynette. She would love that. She thinks the world of you, Destiny. She liked you more than any girl Jimmy Ray ever went out with."

Destiny's stomach turned, and she hesitated and took a breath before speaking. "I'll call her, Eddy. I'll see."

"Ok, honey, I know you're upset."

"I'm sorry about Jimmy Ray. I know you was close with him and all," she said sweetly.

"Yeah, I'm sorry I got so hot there for a minute. You do what you have to."

"Well, let me go. I'll call Lynette now."

"OK, well call me when you decide."

Destiny stared at the telephone and considered what the conversation with Lynette might hold. Should she say she had dropped by that morning? Did he really die right away, or did Lynette return home to see him struggling for life? She had been terrified to ask Eddy any of those questions for fear, in her paranoia, to seem extra curious about such details. With a deep sigh, she picked up the receiver and dialed Lynette's number.

"Hello?"

"Lynette, hey, it's Destiny. How are ya, honey?"

"Lord, lord, sugar, I'm so glad you called. Well, I'm about as good as I could expect to be. It's a awful big shock. I'm telling you. Worst day of my life."

"You sure was a good mama to him, Lynette. Couldn't done no better by him than you."

"I 'preciate you saying that. I really do. I wish I could just get the picture out of my mind of him a laying' up in that bed, layin' there so still and quiet. He never was still and quiet a day in his life til that moment. I'm telling you."

"Nope, he was always into something, wasn't he? I'm sorry things didn't work out for us," Destiny said.

"Yeah, me too. He loved you. I truly believe he loved you. He was stubborn though, and well, he had that mean streak in him. His daddy had it, too. You gonna come to the funeral, ain't you? I'd love you to sit with me and Eddy."

"Yeah, I'll come. I'll be there. I'll meet you at the funeral home."

114

"Ok, I 'preciate it, hon. It starts at eleven."

"Ok, Ms. Lynette, you take care now, you hear?"

"All right then."

# CHAPTER XVI

Munio stepped from the shower and wiped the condensation from the mirror over the lavatory. He stared at himself with the hard fast look a prize-fighter gives an opponent, or someone who is trying to see how they look when they display their most seductive pose. After he worked the towel furiously over his hair, it stood out from his head in a wild black halo of curls. The condensation on the mirror refortified, and the resulting diffusion gave his face the look of a boy's, sweet and innocent. He brushed his teeth, small and yellow, that could not hide their age or wear in any lighting. Several were missing although it was undetectable except through close inspection.

He dressed in worn and snug-fitting jeans, a black vest with no shirt, and black leather sandals. From a brown bag, he took a slug of Jack Daniels. The mixture of the whiskey and the residue of toothpaste went to war in his mouth, causing him to wince. He tried to stick the pint bottle in his back pocket, but his jeans were too tight. He cursed aloud and located a small back pack into which he put the whiskey, along with his wallet. From his suitcase, Munio pulled an ancient bottle of "High Karate" cologne and splashed on way too much of the liquid legend.

* * * * *

"Munio, how good of you to come." Ida Blue said coyly upon opening her door. "Come in. Come in."

Munio smiled nervously, chilled to the bone, again, when he stared into Ida Blue's eyes. Already he wished he had not done this. "Hello, how are you?" he managed cordially.

"Fine, fine, just cleaning up a little. Have a seat, won't you?" Ida Blue waved him to the couch. She breezed past on her way into the kitchen. He caught her scent familiar, like the deep rich pungent scent of freshly cut mahogany wood that he had smelled in the jungle of Belize.

"Would you like something to drink, a soda, or coffee, perhaps?" she asked in her smooth low voice.

"I brought something, actually. Would you like some Jack Daniels?" Munio asked innocently, forgetting that hard liquor is the last thing a bodybuilder would imbibe four weeks before a show.

She threw back her head and laughed, "Yeah, right! If I could have some carbs right now, believe me, it would not come from a Jack Daniels bottle. Go ahead if it helps you to relax. You are a little nervous, aren't you, Munio?" She sat very close to him on the couch and ran her finger gently down his face

Munio nearly bolted out the door for fear he might explode from spon-

taneous combustion her energy felt so volatile, flammable. But he stayed and let her singe him with a fierce pain in his groin, a blue-veined throbber, came to roost in his pants. His hand reached for the paper-bagged bottle on the end table, and the liquor ran down his throat as sweet as spring water.

Her eyesbrows drew close together, and slowly, like a snake, she placed her face close to Munio's as she spoke. "You aren't afraid of me now, are you, sweetheart?" She smiled a knowing smile as she ran her hand down Munio's smooth chest to the spot where his vest formed a v.

Munio shook his head stiffly back and forth like a child, with eyes as wide as if he were staring eye to eye at a coiled and ready diamond back rattler. He took a guarded breath and reached over to get a cigarette, moving slowly so as to not disturb this viper woman.

"You know those things are bad for you." Ida Blue pulled away to let him have his smoke. "I'm sorry if I rushed you, Munio. I just find you luscious. You are so attractive. Do you hear that a lot?"

Munio chuckled, "This? No, I do not hear that a lot. Thank you for saying so." He reached for another drink and held the bottle for the duration of his smoke. "Ok, lady, you want me? Take me!" Munio challenged her as the whiskey had done its job of taking his apprehension away.

"Let's go where we can stretch out." She stood and held out her large hand for him, and then she led him down the hall to a bedroom.

The room was decorated with acrylic cheetah and leopard patterned cloth covering the walls. A red lava lamp, the main light in the room, dripped what looked like large clumps of blood from atop a black lacquered dresser, tinging the air red. Ida Blue closed the door behind them and turned the lock on the knob.

Munio seemed concerned. "Do you expect someone?"

"No, I don't, but you never know these days."

She pulled him close to her as they stood next to the bed, and he began to return her passion with a full wet tongue kiss. A deep rumbling sound came from out of her thick chest. Her thin elastic halter top allowed Munio to realize just how much muscle this woman had. The girth of her back was enormous, and he felt nothing but rock hard striations from her traps to the insertions of her lats. Her spine was buried in a inch-deep groove between her spinal erectors. He felt like he was holding a man.

From the front, her chest presented a whole new set of variables that Munio had never encountered. Like honey dew melon halves, her pecs stood up so that they nearly touched her chin. Her enormous silicone-filled breasts floated under her skin like time bombs waiting to burst.

Because of all his mind chatter, he had neglected to notice that she was squeezing the life out of him. Ida Blue laughed and without warning, flung him onto the soft, furry bedspread, which had a large, sincere-looking male lion embroidered on the front. She followed up her initial assault before he

could defend himself, and in nothing flat, she straddled Munio, her blue black face looming down at him, smiling with that bountiful set of gleaming white teeth.

She undid the buttons on his vest and put her hands on his skin. Her hands were so large they practically covered his chest. Munio reached up and put his hands on her gigantic thighs. Her short skirt now rode up around her waist, disclosing the fact she wore no underwear. Her pubic hair was cropped close, and her steroid-produced, thumb-sized clit stared at Munio like a fat fetus. He wanted to just sit and stare back at it, but Ida Blue was moving along too quickly. He grabbed her buttocks and squeezed them hard. She moaned, hopped off Munio, and began undoing his jean, growling and ripping the zipper down. The pants were tight, and Munio's sweat caused them to cling to him like skin. Ida Blue grew impatient. Her big hands tore at the buckles on his sandals, threw them to the floor, and grabbed the cuff of each pant leg. With all the force she had in her, she grunted and yanked those jeans so hard that Munio's legs stung from friction burns.

Munio lay there bare to the world, his penis waving high in the air. Without warning, Ida Blue straddled him and shoved his penis into her vagina. Making baritone sounds of passion, Ida Blue rode Munio for all he was worth. This situation had moved now far out of his control. The pressure in his gut was painful every time she hit a downstroke. He had been swept away in a raging current, and though his penis was having a good time, the rest of Munio was in trouble. He closed his eyes and hoped to garner some relief from the mounting panic.

*He smelled the smoke and burning wax of a candle that was on the bedside table. Like a flash, Munio vanished into his past. He could see the dark wood of the altar, covered in a beautiful red cloth embroidered all around with gold. The table was covered with brass candlesticks that held white candle,s all aglow in that little white church. No one was there except Munio and the priest. He instructed Munio, as he always did, to take his place in front of the altar. With hesitation, Munio advanced down the aisle, leaned over the edge of the altar, grasped the railing, and planted his feet in a wide stance. For what seemed like an hour, he held that position. Munio prayed to God to take him to hell or heaven, just take him away from that church and that priest. God did not answer Munio's prayers this night.*

*Eventually, the old pink-skinned priest crept up to Munio. He moved like a snake, steadily and quietly as he raised Munio's robe slowly. The cloth tickled his legs as it trailed up to rest in a pile on his lower back. The priest gave a low moan as he saw, in the lovely candle light, Munio's smooth bare buttocks, innocent and wide-eyed. The priest crossed himself while eyeing the stained glass of Jesus hanging helplessly on the cross, and then he rammed the little boy with no mercy. Munio gasped and lost his breath upon the insertion of the priest's penis, but then the candles and the smell of the wax took him far away to the beach*

*where he splashed in the water and felt the sun on his back. The waves crashed on him, and he laughed with delight. Munio played on the shore of the beautiful blue green sea until his consciousness took him back to the little white chapel where the priest now stood over him, speaking loudly and straightening out the front of his red robe.*

*"Munio, you may go now. Munio, do you hear me?" The priest frowned as he bent over to look at the boy who had collapsed on the floor. The priest stood there a moment, pulled out a pocket watch, waved a hand at Munio in disgust, acknowledged the Jesus artwork again by crossing himself, and reverently backed away from the altar a few feet before turning his back and striding away.*

"Munio, Munio, are you ok? Hey, what's going on? Hey Munio, wake up! Are you ok?" Ida Blue shook him and slapped him across the face.

He opened his eyes and felt like he had melted on the bed. He could not feel his body, and for a second, he had no idea where he was or who Ida Blue was. She stood over him looking pissed off, with big furrows in her exaggerated forehead. Finally, he made a move to sit up.

"What happened?" he asked.

"You went off into lala land. That's what happened. You're weird, you know that?"

Munio did not speak as he stood and began dressing. When he finished, he walked into the living room to the brown paper bag. The warm stinging drink felt like a breath of fresh air to Munio, and he smiled as he tipped the bottle to his lips. He picked up his cigarettes, and started for the door.

"Aren't you going to say anything? Didn't that feel good?" Ida Blue was totally baffled.

Munio kept walking and closed the door behind him. He smiled as his face hit the sunshine and the heat. The old Ford truck backfired as the engine cranked. Through the town past the turn off to Eddy's house, he drove and sipped from the bag.

Finally, the scenery settled down to just a double wide trailer every so often. A red dirt road came up that seemed to call to him, and he turned down it. The truck tires spun in the soft dirt and loose gravel. He drove down the road a short while until it ended at the site of a red clay canyon.

It was beautiful, and Munio couldn't believe the magnificence of its color and depth. On the far side of the canyon, massive trains of dark green kudzu vines trailed all the way to the bottom. He turned the truck off and walked over to the canyon's edge. Only the music of the birds could be heard. The vast area and the open sky above it reminded Munio of how long it had been since he had been at the ocean, his solace. For now, this would have to do. Munio felt a wave of sadness rise in him that would fill this canyon. He hurt inside, deep in his heart, but he knew nothing of how to let the pain go. His eyes filled with tears as he sat in the clay and tipped that paper bag until it and his eyes had drained dry.

Munio stayed at the red canyon long after darkness had robbed him of the view. A clear half-moon night and the shooting and twinkling stars gave Munio a focus for a while, until he sobered up enough to realize the mosquitoes were about to carry him off.

# CHAPTER XVII

Eddy woke up late for a change. He did his morning shot of growth, which produced his ritual howling. Munio groaned at the thought of having to get up and train Eddy, but rolled out of bed, nonetheless, and into the kitchen.

"Hey, man!" Eddy said cheerfully.

"Hello, is it time for you to go train now?" Munio rubbed his eyes and yawned like a groggy child.

"Uh uh, I ain't training til this afternoon. I forgot to tell you. I got to go to Jimmy Ray's funeral this morning."

"Oh yeah, right. Ok, then I'm going back to sleep."

Eddy scrambled twelve egg whites and a bowl of oatmeal for breakfast. As he ate, he flipped through a muscle magazine that had all the latest stars, tanned, flexed, and either smiling or grimacing. Eddy scrutinized each page like a scientist. He took a load of vitamins after he ate and a couple of hits of decca orally.

In jockey shorts, Eddy executed the compulsory poses in the full length mirror of his bedroom. He looked big but smooth, because of the weight produced by of all the drugs. His bloated face and morning stubble cast an evil shadow across his cheeks. Diuretics would help, he thought, and remembered the injectables in his stash. He flexed a little while longer, but he could not get that stash off his mind. The little bottles clinked as he opened the drawer. The sight brought a smile to his face as he ran his hands over them. Half of this stuff he had never tried, and who knows, he thought, any one of those foreign bottles might just be the one to bring his body to greatness. Eddy chose Dianabol as the catch of the day and sought a syringe.

He emptied half into one thigh, half, into the other. Since it was leg day, he figured he might as well take the medicine to the source. Immediately, two little lumps began to rise at the point of injection. He winced and rubbed them, hoping that might reduce the stinging, but sloughed it off and hit the shower.

Between the drugs and the training, he never felt relaxed or calm anymore, but the hot water helped, if just for a few minutes. Not that he minded any of the side effects, because they all added up to a price he was willing to pay for that Mr. Dixie trophy. He washed his hair, face, chest and worked his way downwards. His hand stopped with horror as he soaped his left thigh. That little lump had spawned a knot the size of a baseball. He dropped the

119

soap to inspect it, and although there was no pain, it appeared horrendous. His right thigh revealed the same condition. Either he was allergic to the Dianabol, or the thigh was not an optimal place to have it enter the body. Whatever the reason, the situation terrified Eddy. He hurried through the shower and dried himself. To see how his legs felt, he performed several squats. There was no pain, only tightness. With a towel wrapped around his waist, he went into the hall.

"Munio, hey Munio, wake up. I need you to check something." Eddy stuck his head in the doll room. "You up?"

Munio rolled over slowly. "What? What is it, Eddy?"

"Look at this shit." He stood next to the bed.

Munio squinted and drew a bead on Eddy's legs at eye level. He caught sight of the knots and sat up fast. "Goddamn, how did you do that?"

"I'm having some kind of fucking reaction to some D-bol. You think it's all right?"

"Boy, I don't know. Does it hurt?"

"Naw, not really. It just looks like shit. I got to go to that funeral. I ain't got time to mess with this shit."

"Well, put some ice on it, and maybe it will relieve the swelling."

"That's a good idea, but I got to fucking hurry, though." Eddy shuffled out of the room to the kitchen.

After twenty minutes packed in ice, Eddy managed to reduce the baseballs to golf balls. The lumps still showed through his black suit pants. A bad headache came on, and he threw back a handful of aspirins on the way out the door.

All of the excitement concerning his legs had taken the focus off the real business of the day. Suddenly, he felt sad, which made him nervous.

\* \* \* \* \*

The busy parking lot of the funeral home made him laugh. "Son of a bitch, you was a popular mother fucker, wasn't you. There wasn't this many people here when the mayor died." Nodding to people as he walked into the building, he looked for Lynette. In the main chapel, he could see Jimmy Ray's casket opened up. People filed by slowly. Every female in the building had a Kleenex or handkerchief pressed again her nose.

Lynette stood down by her boy, receiving people as they came off the viewing circuit. He stood and watched the procession for a couple of minutes.

Old men, some of Jimmy Ray's uncles and some of the Beulah Baptist church deacons, stood in clumps in the foyer. All balding, bifocaled, and stoop-backed men, they had smatterings of dandruff drifting about the shoulders of their dark suitcoats. Many of them had fixed expressions of struggle like the look of a person caught on a windy, cold day without a hat. One of the

old men approached.

"Hey there, young feller." He smiled without changing his grimace.

"Hey Uncle Lige, how you doing?" Eddy shook his hand and looked down on his gray scalp.

"Doin' all right, all right. I reckon."

Uncle Lige had had an accident when he was a boy. He wore the aftermath of it on his forehead forever. At six years of age, while he milked the family's dairy cow, a wasp stung the heifer on the butt, and she kicked Lige right square in the forehead. The blow cracked a hole clean through his skull. It was a lucky thing for someone to live through such a thing nowadays, but in 1912, it was seen as a downright miracle.

The bone never grew back over that spot, and it left a dent the size of a golf ball. The skin there was soft, and a browner color than the rest of his face. Every time Uncle Lige breathed the spot would rise and fall as if there were air in it. Just as it had when he was a child, it still gave Eddy the creeps.

"Uncle Lige, I'll speak at you later. I got to go help Lynette." He patted Uncle Lige on the shoulder.

"Oh, well, ok boy. I'll see ya later." Uncle Lige grinned up at Eddy, baring the coral- colored gums of his dentures. "Ok, boy."

Eddy hurried through the chapel door down to where Lynette stood. Their eyes met, and they engaged in a close and lengthy hug. When they parted, Lynette's eyes teared.

"I was going to try to not cry so much, but seeing you is like seeing my boy, Eddy."

"It's ok, honey. You can cry. You've been like a mama to me. You been a fine mama to Jimmy Ray, too."

"Lord, look at the crowd. Have you ever seen anything like it?" Lynette said. Every seat in the chapel had filled with twenty minutes yet until the service began.

"I'm serious. Everbody and his brother's gonna show up, I believe. You know that Jimmy Ray knew 'bout everbody in the county," Eddy said.

"I know. I know. You know, I just noticed you got your hair cut all off." She smiled. "Why, look at you. You look like a soldier or something, Eddy. You look so nice."

Eddy chuckled. "Thank you."

"You want to get up and say something about Jimmy Ray when the service gets going?"

"Uh, I ain't so good at public speaking, Lynette. Gee, I don't know. You really want me to?" He face turned red, and he looked worried.

"Well, it'd be nice, hon, if you did. Jimmy Ray sure thought of you like a brother."

"All right, I'll, ah, do the best I can." The fear of this surprise task made Eddy's head pound harder, and he felt he could see his heart beating right

through his suitcoat.

Lynette continued to greet people, and Eddy stood there beside her watching the gospel band put the finishing touches on their setup.

Eddy felt someone's eyes on him, and looked toward the chapel entrance to see Destiny walking towards him. She smiled and raised her eyebrows. Her black velveteen dress fit her body well, and its long sleeves fit tightly on her arms, hiding her bruised and battered track marks. A heavy makeup job served the bags under her eyes well, as she had still not recovered from her epic Texas getaway. Eddy felt aroused, and smiled as he watched her move down the aisle. She hugged him, and then Lynette.

"Look at your hair." She ran her hand over Eddy's crewcut. "I love it. How y'all holding up?" she asked, smiling. Her big scar made her upper lip move in two different directions.

"All right, I reckon. How're you?" Eddy asked.

"I'm ok. Lynette, you need anything? Need me to do anything?"

"Naw, honey, I'm just glad you're here is all. I sure 'preciate it." Lynette took her hand and patted it.

Destiny gulped, took a big breath, and let it out silently. She smiled over at Eddy nervously.

"Lynette wants me to say something in the service. You think I should? What should I say?" Eddy whispered under his breath.

Destiny stifled a chuckle. "Well, you could say how much you appreciate him teaching you how to make your teeth grow apart."

Eddy frowned and grabbed her arm. "They ain't grown far apart. Now, you better shut up, girl. He done more for me than that."

Destiny's arrogant attitude pissed Eddy off.

"Did you come here to be nice or what?"

"The truth is the truth, Eddy Jackson. Jimmy Ray was a good old boy who, for the most part, was up to no good most of the time." She jerked her arm away and smiled at a little old lady that greeted Lynette.

"Well, I'm sorry you feel that way."

"Eddy, I'm sorry for you, and I'm sorry for Lynette, but I ain't sorry for that son of a bitch over yonder in that fucking casket, ok? Now, get off my back!" she spat in a rising whisper that sprayed Eddy like mace.

The funeral director came to Lynette to say it was time to begin, and asked if she wanted to view the body one last time. Lynette grabbed Eddy with one hand and Destiny with the other and led them in front of Jimmy Ray's body.

The snow white satin that lined the coffin looked soft and plush. Next to his shiny thick brown beard and bushy hair, his skin was cherub pink like a child's. A hint of a smile curled his lips. On top of his chest, his big black holy bible with his name embossed on the front in gold had been placed. Lynette started crying, and then Eddy and Destiny, who developed a sudden guilt at-

tack for murdering the man. The funeral director came over and, with a gentle hand, aimed them for the seats on the first row where the other pall bearers were already seated.

The band and choir then performed a rollicking version of "Shall We Gather at the River", and Rev. Howell got up, inviting those who would to come forward and speak about Jimmy Ray.

Gilbert Matheny lumbered up to the podium.

"Uh, I have knowed Jimmy Ray Jones since I was, ah, eight years old. We growed up together all our lives, and I hoped we was gonna grow old together. I reckon we won't, now. I'll shore miss fishin' with him and all. Huntin' too." Gilbert laughed and rubbed his big stomach. "Couldn't nobody drag a big ol' buck out of the woods as quick as old Jimmy Ray. He was a strong old boy. I loved him, and I'll miss him." He bowed his head as he took his seat in the crowd.

Sam Kaufman, owner of the Dixie Ironworks, got up slowly and took his time speaking. "Jimmy Ray started lifting weights over at my place when he weighed no more than a hundred fifty pounds. I knew he was gonna be big, though, because the boy was only in the sixth grade." A gentle unified laugh surfaced from the crowd. "Yeah, he was destined to be a big man, and as it worked out, he sure was. Everbody respected Jimmy Ray 'cause he was fair. Treated everbody the same. You can't fault a man like that, and I am glad I knew the boy." He nodded and strode off to his seat.

Eddy sweated like he was in a sauna, and he tugged at his tie. He looked over at Destiny, and she nodded toward the podium, giving him a stern look. He knew it wasn't going to get any easier, so he stood and stepped over Lynette. The knots on his thighs had begun to ache. At the podium, he glance down at his pants and realized the lumps, having swollen back up, protruded noticeably. He looked at Lynette and smiled. She smiled back at him.

"Lynette, I sure am sorry we have to be here today, but since we are, I think everybody has been real nice. I appreciate y'all saying all that stuff about my good friend, Jimmy Ray. I know he's probably watching us, and thinking we're doing a good job of burying him." Destiny's heart fluttered at the possibility. "Jimmy Ray had a good life. He enjoyed life, probably too much, and he always told me, he says, 'Eddy, enjoy today 'cause that's all you got. You got to be ready to die. Live ever day like it's yore last 'cause it just might be.' Well, that's about all I got to say, except thank ya'll for coming." He looked like a slab of concrete dressed in a suit as he walked carefully down the steps. Destiny's jaw dropped when she noticed the mid thigh protrusion of his pants. He sat down, and she punched him in the ribs.

"What the hell have you grown on your legs?" she whispered.

"They're mosquito bites," he grinned.

"What?"

"Just shut up. I'll tell you later."

The choir sang "Nearer My God To Thee" before Rev. Howell offered the closing prayer. Eddy and a struggling gang of five others carried the three-hundred-pound mass of Jimmy Ray and his coffin out into a spit-shined black Cadillac hearse for the ride. Lynette, Eddy, and Destiny rode in a black Sedan de Ville right behind him. The caravan was two miles long and caused one of the longest traffic jams Rosedale had ever seen. Eddy thought Jimmy Ray would have loved that.

Not much else was said or left to say at the gravesite. A light rain came down at the end as they lowered him into the ground. Lynette dropped a red rose on top of the shiny gray deluxe plastic casket, and Destiny breathed a great sigh of relief. If she ever believed in a God, she did now as she glanced skyward and said a silent prayer of thanks.

# CHAPTER XVIII

It was mid-afternoon before Eddy got back to his house. Munio napped on the glider, with several empty beer cans lined up beside him on the floor.

"Hey, hoss." Eddy looked down at Munio.

Munio opened his eyes, closed them halfway quickly and put his hands up to use as a visor. "What's happening, Edwardo?" Munio smiled.

"Aw, just got done burying old Jimmy Ray. Thought I'd go do legs here in a few minutes. You with me?"

Munio brought himself to a sitting position. "Yeah, yeah, sure, whenever you're ready."

"I'm going heavy now, seriously heavy. Can you handle it?"

"Yeah, yeah, it's no problem, Eddy. I got you, man."

"All right, let me get my shit together." Eddy turned and went in the house.

Munio lit a cigarette and scratched his head. He felt sluggish and foggy. The last thing he wanted to do right now was play strongarm nursemaid to Eddy and his legs, but he would do it. He thumped his ashes and frowned. He thought about Audrey and wondered why she ran off so fast the other night. Tomorrow he would call her. He had to start getting some money together because his was dwindling fast.

The screen door slammed. "Ready, Freddy?"

"Yeah, brother. Let's go." Munio stood up and stumbled a bit as he lost his balance.

"You all right?" Eddy's growing forehead was full of worry wrinkles.

"Sure I am, Eddy. Don't worry."

By the time they reached the gym, the knots on Eddy's legs had disappeared. He stretched for a few minutes, and so did Munio. Eddy tied a black bandanna pirate-style over the top of his head. Black tights covered his mas-

sive legs.

As he continued to stretch, he pulled on a sweatshirt that bore the inscription, "I'm not smart but I can lift heavy objects." His knees ached and cracked as he moved through a set of free standing squats. Eddy winced and popped opened the Advil, swallowing a half dozen. He pointed the bottle at Munio, but Munio shook his head no. Not that he didn't have a headache, but he did not take medicine of any kind if possible. What he really wanted at the moment was a smoke, but that would have to wait.

Eddy warmed up with the bar, one thirty-five, two twenty-five, three fifteen, and four-o-five. With each set, he did ten reps, and with each set, his aggression and intensity increased. The white around his eyes had disappeared, replaced with a thin tomatoey veil as all the capillaries in his eyeballs dilated from the pressure of the weight. His blue irises shone with a glaze of rage, and yet somehow they were at the same time empty, expressing nothing, absorbing no sights at all. By the time he reached four-o-five, Munio did not know this man he was spotting. Eddy had turned into a crimson-faced maniac who acted as if this squat workout was the only thing that would insure his survival.

The next set with five hundred followed, and Eddy screamed and clawed his way through ten reps as Munio stood behind him, shouting alternate messages of praise and humiliation. The bar made a mighty clang as Eddy threw it in the rack. Too winded and exhausted to stand, he dropped immediately to his knees. Munio stood over him, watched and waited to see what he wanted to do next.

Eddy looked up at Munio. "Put another plate on."

"What size plate?"

"A mother fucking forty-five, that's what! There ain't no other plate, man!" Eddy, still laboring for breath, glared up at him.

"You're pushing it, Eddy. What will that be, ah, five ninety? I don't know about that."

Eddy jumped to his feet. "What don't you fucking know about it, motherfucker! Load it up, and I'm gonna show you what I know about the son of a bitch!"

"Hey, fuck you, man! Get out of my face! You want the weight? I'll load it up, but don't fuck with me, Eddy! I'm on your side remember?"

"Ain't nobody on my side, but me! You got it? You fucking drunk ass Indian!"

Munio put down the plate he had in his hand and calmly walked up to Eddy. "I'm going to let that slide because I know you are not in your right mind, but you need to cool out here. You are embarrassing yourself."

"Just load the fucker up, Munio, and shut up. Just don't talk to me now. Ok?" Munio turned and slid a forty-five on each end, a formidable load with six forty-fives on each end.

Five minutes passed before Eddy addressed the last set. In the meantime, Munio recruited some spotters. Sloughing off the insult, Munio started getting Eddy psyched. "Ok motherfucker, let's see it! You think you can do this? Gut check, Eddy! Right here is a fucking gut check! You want it! You got to go for it!" Munio paced back and forth and scratched his head. "Stay tight! Make this the best set right here, Eddy!"

When he took the load out of the rack, Eddy's face instantly turned beet red. He set his feet, took a breath, and came up out of the first rep looking strong. Five more reps passed, and then with sheer steroid-spawned aggression, he managed to make it to ten reps. Again, after racking the weight, he dropped to the floor, and listened to Munio and his spotters congratulate him. When he finally got up, he looked in the mirror. A broken vessel in his right eye left a bright blood trail across his eyeball. He knew he looked like a crazy man, a fugitive on the run. He was. A muscle junky, bound to grow or die.

As grueling as the squat workout was, it represented only the beginning of Eddy's leg work. Munio hustled him through four sets of heavy leg presses, extensions, and hack squats. Nearly three hours later, they exited the Dixie Ironworks exhausted. Munio immediately lit up a cigarette as they trudged over to Eddy's car.

Eddy smiled at Munio as they got into the car. Munio did not return it. "Hey Munio, I'm sorry I got so obnoxious in there. I didn't mean to say everything I said, ok?"

Munio drew hard on his cigarette and stared straight ahead out the windshield. "You should be more careful before you speak. You embarrassed me, and I am pissed off about it." He gave Eddy a hard cold glare with his brown eyes.

"I don't blame you. I'll try not to do it again, but I'm just trying so hard to get in shape to win this fucking contest and all. Another thing is I'm taking all this shit, and I feel like, hell, I feel like a crazy man. What the hell though, I'm getting big as shit, and I was fucking strong today. Wouldn't you say?"

"Sure, yes, you were quite strong, but I guess it's up to you how important all that is." He looked over at Eddy, his eyes softening a bit.

Eddy looked over at Munio with a dead serious look, "Munio, it is more important to me than anything. I don't care what it takes. I don't care if I grow mother fucking horns. I don't care if I have a goddamn heart attack. I am going to win the Mr. Dixie overall title if it kills me."

They drove back to the house, perched up on the porch, and lit into the joint Munio had rolled out of his special stash.

"Damn, that's some good reefer. Why don't you get some of your friends to mail you some of this shit?"

Munio laughed. "I wish I could. If I knew how, believe me, I would do it."

"Wish ol' Jimmy Ray was around. He'd fucking know how to do it. Hell,

he was always smuggling something, 'roids or reefer. Hell, he smuggled in some blotter acid in Bibles once. He dealt a ton of drugs in his career, and only got caught once. All in all, he was a lucky motherfucker. Well, except for now, I reckon."

"Yes, I guess his luck ran out, eh?"

"Yeah, you know what? I feel a serious fucking spree coming on."

"So do you have a girlfriend or what?"

"I ain't got nobody steady. I got a few gals I can call on. I'm gonna have to get on the phone here in a minute, and see if I can't line me up somebody tonight." Eddy leaned back in the rocking chair, looking quite relaxed and thoughtful. Suddenly, he sat up, "Damn, I forgot to even ask you how it went with Ida Blue!"

Munio didn't blink an eye as he looked Eddy square in the face. "She did nothing for me. Maybe for somebody else, but not for me. She did nothing for me. And that clit?" Munio snorted a laug., "What the hell do I do with that, eh?" He waved his hands in the air.

Eddy was laughing hysterically. Finally, he calmed down enough to speak, "What about her fucking clit, man?"

"What about it? It's damn near big as my dick, that's what. Now, if I want to sleep with a man, I sleep with a man, but I don't want no woman with a clit like that."

"Well, what did y'all do? Did she-"

Munio interrupted, "Let me put it this way. We started getting into it. She about bit my dick off. She wanted me to go down on her, and I couldn't get into it so I left with her begging me to come back. She stands at the door speaking to me as I leave, you know?" Munio shrugged his shoulders. "Case closed."

"I'll be damned. Oh well. A clit how big?" Munio holds up his thumb. "Shit, I'd like to see that son of a bitch."

"Trust me. No, you would not."

"I will have to take your word for it. That woman is sho nuf a brick house. I'd hate to have to get her off of me. Umm, umm, um. I'm going to take a nap, and whack off for a while, since that's all I got going at the moment. That is unless you want to suck my dick, Munio."

Munio smiled and gnashed his teeth. "I'll suck your dick all right!" Eddy covered his crotch in mock fear.

"I reckon we better keep this relationship all business." Eddy got up and backed into the house while Munio laughed on the porch.

Munio felt great. He was primed for some action of some kind. He thought about Audrey and wondered if he should call her. Perhaps he should go suss out a place to do a little dart hustle. Not knowing all the bars, he was hesitant to go just anywhere. People might not take to hustling in this little town. Flicking his cigarette over the porch railing, he went into the house.

"Hello." Audrey's distinctive Long Island accent came over the line.
"Audrey".

"Munio, how are you?" she spoke rather coolly.

"Fine, I am fine. You left the other day before I could give you my number, and so I wondered if you might have tried to get in touch with me."

"I see. No, I hadn't, actually." There was a long pause.

"Well, what are you doing now?" Munio asked.

"Straightening up a little," she replied.

"How would you like to go somewhere and have a drink?"

Audrey frowned and rolled her eyes, "Munio, to be honest with you, I have a problem with your drinking."

"Problem? What problem is it for you?"

"I can't take you over to the country club drunk, and I think you just like to drink too much. I can't take a chance. I don't think I can count on you." Audrey spoke abruptly, and her words cut at Munio like a dull knife.

He became defensive. "You don't even hardly know me. Didn't I do good at your class? I thought I did good. Actually, I thought you liked me. I thought those people in the class liked me, too."

"Munio, I do like you on some level, but frankly, I'm not interested in socializing with you on any regular basis. I'm sorry, but I don't think I will be using you again for the class."

A long pause ensued as Munio wondered what to say. Finally, he bounced back in her face. "You think you're better than me? You fucking high and mighty drag queen? Fuck you, Audrey! You are just another fucking white man is what you are, and you don't know nothing about me!" Munio slammed the phone down.

Audrey set the receiver down gently, and stared at the phone intently for a minute. She pulled her white satin robe tighter around her skinny body and looked out through the blinds. Void of all her womanly props except her long fingernails and her hair, she hid behind the walls. With no makeup or sand bagged bra to make her statement about who she was in this world, she was just another white man. She crossed her legs from one direction to the other as she took another sip of Kahlua and coffee.

Munio marched to the kitchen, threw open the refrigerator door, grabbed two beers, and gave the door a hard slam. He burst through the porch door which slammed loudly behind him. Pacing back and forth along the length of the porch, Munio chain smoked, inhaling violently. His face was angry and tense. The veins at his temples were swollen with emotion. After chugging the first beer, he heaved the bottle as far as he could out in the yard. It landed softly in the mesh of honeysuckle vines growing up the fence.

"That fucking bitch. How could she say these things to me? Who does she think she is? She don't know anything about me! Nothing! That was a good thing, us dancing. We danced so good. How could she not want to dance with

me again?" He ranted as he paced, gulping the second beer. "I don't need that fucking bitch, man! I, I do her a favor! For this, she insults me!" He slammed his fist down on the railing of the porch, and with all the power he could muster, threw the second bottle out into the yard and stormed into the house.

Putting on a loose Day Glo lime green, three-quarter length sleeve T-shirt, a tight pair of black jeans, black cowboy boots, and worn black fedora with a red bandanna tied around it as a hat band, Munio hopped into the old white Ford pickup. The tires churned up the loose gravel as he made a speedy exit from the driveway.

He spotted a cold beer sign with flashing lights around it tacked up on the roof of a small building. An old Cadillac, painted hot pink, sat on the lawn for decorative effect. He pulled into the parking lot and turned off the truck. From under the seat, he pulled a six inch stainless steel dagger, which he slid into the tall top of his left cowboy boot.

* * * * *

As he stepped into the room, reality drew its drapes, and the cool black river of the bar scene flowed over Munio's body. It instantly vaporized his doubts and his cares that lay outside that door.

Aretha Franklin sang "Chain of Fools" on the juke box, and several people danced. For the first time in a long time, there were more black people than whites in his company. A couple of Hispanic men shot pool.

The bar stool squeaked and rotated as he took a seat. It startled and irritated him so much that he moved to the next one. By the time he lit a cigarette, the bartender appeared to take his order.

"Whatcha need?"

"Bud." Without another word, the bartender nodded and returned quickly with a cold can of beer.

"I want a bottle please," Munio said firmly.

"You didn't say nothing about no bottle, brother."

"Well, that is what I want, and that is what I will pay for," Munio replied indignantly.

The bartender smirked and frowned simultaneously. "What's your problem, man? I done opened this can for you, and you need to go ahead on and pay me now." He looked over at the man sitting just a few stools down who was catching the conversation. The two made eye contact, and the bartender shook his head while the man chuckled silently.

"I'll take it, Ben. I'm about ready." The man spoke in a calm, deep voice.

"You sure?" the bartender asked, and the man nodded. He set the can in front of him and reappeared with a bottle for Munio. "Two twenty-five."

"Two twenty-five? Sheesh, that is so much!" Munio dug in his pocket.

"Listen, man, don't be coming in here stirring up no trouble. I never seen you before, and the way it's going I'm kind of wishing I never had."

Munio caught himself before saying some smartass comment. "I'm sorry, man. I don't mean to get off on the wrong foot. I'm having a kind of bad day. You know, brother?" Munio smiled disarmingly at the bartender.

"That's cool, man. I know the feeling. We just like to have a good time in here. No hassles, just a little fun, ok?" The bartender gave him a wary smile.

Munio wheeled his stool around, sat with his back to the bar, tipped up the longneck bottle and took big draws off his cigarette. He blew great clouds of the hot smoke into the cool, air conditioned room. He watched it dissolve and mingle invisibly with the rest of the air. He wandered into the game room to see to see what kind of quarry there was to be had.

What had been hidden from view from his barstool perch was the dart board. Four men were playing what seemed to be a very friendly game among friends. They had had just enough liquor to give them almost nonstop silly giggles. Munio glanced over the pool tables. There were three, all occupied by what seemed to be recreational players. "I am going to have to get real friendly to entice any of these people into a hustle," he thought.

Munio took a seat against the wall in order to keep an eye on the dart players, to see if they were any good. If he watched long enough, maybe he could find an opening to get in the game.

He overheard that it was one of the men's birthdays, and that could be the break he was looking for. For one thing, it meant at least one of them had a few bucks to lose. He finished his beer and strolled to the bar for another. As he passed the dart players, he struck up a conversation.

"Excuse me, did I hear one of you say that it is your birthday today?"

"Yeah, it's his." One tall, medium brown-skinned man with long jerri curls pointed to a muscular, dark-skinned fellow with a shaved head, who smiled at Munio, a lazy half-drunk smile.

"Is that right?" Munio stuck out his hand to the man. "It's my birthday, too."

"Hey, all right! How 'bout that?" The men buzzed between themselves at the coincidence.

"Could I buy you a beer? I have no one to celebrate with tonight." Munio asked with his most innocent, charming accent and attitude.

"Can he buy me a beer?" The man laughed at the others. "I ain't never turned down no free beer. Hell yeah, you can buy me a beer. If you're nice, I'll even let you buy me two!" All the men, including Munio, laughed out loud.

"What kind do you want?"

"Bud's cool."

"Ok, you got it. I'll be right back." Munio chuckled to himself and licked his chops as he walked to the bar. This will be fun, he thought. Quickly, he returned with the beers.

"Here you go, ah, what you say your name is?" Munio handed him the beer.

"Howard."

"Howard, my name is Munio." Munio stuck out his hand, and Howard shook it.

"Well, thanks there, Munio. Pleasure to meet you. This is Timmy, Cleveland, and Royce." He pointed to the others, who nodded and smiled.

"Your turn, Howard. You ain't stalling are you?" Royce kidded him. "Birthday or not, I'm fixing to kick your ass here and now in this dart game, boy."

"The hell you say. Not if I kick yours first. You hide and watch, boy," he sparred back. "Watch this shit." He stepped to the line and tossed a bullseye. All the men cheered except Royce, who groaned. Munio purred like a mountain lion perched on a cliff overlooking a herd of sleeping sheep.

Howard tossed again and nearly hit the bullseye. He took his time for the last toss, and with fine style, nailed the bullseye. This brought cheers and ooohss and ahhhhs from his friends.

"All right brother," Howard said to Royce. "Top that, motherfucker." Howard did a soul strut.

"Here we go." Royce enthusiastically grabbed three darts and stepped to the line. The first throw was close to a bullseye. Royce frowned, and Howard laughed. He nailed the bullseye clean on the second toss. There was dead silence among the men as Royce readied himself for the final toss. The dart sailed up in a high arc but landed a good two inches south of the bullseye. The group burst into cheers and applause. Royce shook his head and bemoaned his fate while the others congratulated Howard on the win.

Royce reached in his pocket and pulled out thirty dollars. "Here you go, mofo, happy goddamn birthday. You know I let you win because it's your birthday. You know that, don't you?" He pointed emphatically at Howard.

"Yeah, I know you did that. I know you did that. I want you to know I appreciate your contribution to the Howard fund." They were all still jiving around when Munio piped up.

"Howard, would you like to play a birthday round?"

Howard looked at the others who nodded and gave their go aheads. "Sure, I'll play one with you."

"How about we play the best of three, eh? Ok with you? It gives us more room to play with, you know?"

"That's ok with me."

"Mind if I take a couple of warm-up tosses? I have not played in some time."

"Go for it, man."

Munio tossed five practice darts. "I am ready when you are, Howard. You go first if you want."

"Ok, that's cool." Howard stood at the throw line and was nearly ready to toss when Munio interrupted.

"Oh, say, Howard, you want to make a bet, a small bet?"

"Ok, like what?"

"Ten dollars?"

"Ten, ok, that's cool." He resumed his concentration and tossed. It was a bullseye, and all his friends cheered. The second toss was just outside the bullseye mark, but he nailed the third.

Munio shook his head. "Oh boy, what have I got myself into now. Ten dollars? Did I say ten dollars? I think I said ten cents, Howard." All the men laughed as Munio took to the line for his turn.

Purposely, he threw the first two way outside the bullseye, and on the third toss, he just barely missed the bullseye. He screwed up his mouth in mock disgust.

"Oh well, I guess I am not too good tonight."

"Well, win some, lose some," Cleveland chirped.

"Yeah, and it's a lookin' like I'm gonna be winnin' tonight, y'all! Have mercy!" Howard clapped and laughed as he stepped up to the line to start the second game.

Howard licked his lips, and the smile faded from his face as he concentrated. The first throw arched high and landed a good three inches from the bullseye. "Damn!" He cursed and picked up another dart. The second one rang the bullseye. "Halleluyah!" He threw his arms up in the air, which made his friends and Munio laugh. "Here we go, three! Come on now!" He talked to the third dart. He even kissed it before taking the line. The third dart sailed like a line drive, but just missed the bullseye. His friends cheered, and Howard stepped back and waved like a politician on the campaign trail.

"Not too shabby, Howard, but I feel lucky. I'm getting warmed up now," Munio winked at him as he walked to the board and retrieved the darts.

"Well, I hope you be wrong, Mister. I sho 'nuf do now." Howard jived.

Munio stared at the board, tipped his beer bottle up, and chugged it until the foam dregs drained into his mouth. "Woooeee! Ahhh! I needed that! In fact, I think I'm going to need about twenty more this evening." He chuckled, and the other guys laughed and gave each other the eye.

Munio lit a cigarette and stepped up to the line as it dangled from his lips. The smoke trailed into his face. The discomfort caused him to shut one eye. He drew back and tossed the first dart. It barely clipped the board and hit one of the painted numbers. "Damn!" Munio pretended to be angry.

"Man, you ought to get that smoke out your face, and maybe you could see the damn board," Howard said.

"Yeah, you're probably right. I didn't think about it." Munio took a drag off the cigarette, held it in his right hand, and picked up another dart from the table. "Ok, this will be better." He took his time and nailed the second ring out from the bullseye. "Well, it's better than before anyhow."

The other men said nothing, waiting in anticipation for the third toss

that could give Howard the win. Munio knew he had Howard on the hook. Munio stalled. "Do you mind if I go get another beer right quick? I think it will help my concentration."

"No, that's cool. We ain't going nowhere," Howard lied as he and his friends sat in nervous anticipation.

Munio took his time, too, strolling leisurely to the bar and back. "Ok, here we go. One toss to go." He cleared his throat and let the dart sail. It landed exactly where the second dart had, only on the opposite side of the bullseye. "Ummm, damn!" Howard and his friends high fived him and laughed.

"Well, I guess things aren't looking good going into the third round, eh?" Munio said.

"They looking good for me, man. Looking real good for me," Howard laughed.

"Listen, how would you like to raise the stakes and go three games out of five?"

Howard looked over at his friends, but shook his head, "No, man, I ain't into that. I got to go soon, anyhow."

Munio screwed up his mouth and talked out loud. "Well, I'm going to have to have a hell of a third game to beat you!"

"You sho are. You gonna have to have a three mother fucking bullseye game to beat my bad ass, buddy." Howard's friends and Munio laughed.

"I may be crazy, but what the fuck. I think I can do it."

"Throw three bullseyes in a row? I don't think so tonight. There ain't no way you're going to do that." Howard gave him a look like Munio was crazy.

"Bet you fifty dollars, I can."

Howard gave him a condescending look, and then turned to his friends who elbowed each other and nodded. "I'll take that bet, bro."

"All right, good. You go first again."

Howard plucked the darts out of the board and walked back to the line. He took aim and tossed the first one a couple of rings out from the bullseye. "Shit!" The second he hurriedly threw and hit just one ring closer in than the last. "Dadgum it!"

"Slow down, Howard. Take your damn time. You ain't goin' to no fire," Royce coached.

Nevertheless, a third hasty shot hit the first dart and fell off the board entirely. "I'll be a mother fucker." Howard slammed his fist on the closest table.

Munio smiled knowingly. "You got excited and rushed things, my friend. What do they call that, premature ejaculation, I think?" Munio laughed.

"Let's just see you, dart man. I'm still ahead, and I think you're fixin' to choke," Howard said belligerently.

Munio smiled at his success in rattling the poor man. He loved the thrill of the kill, the manipulation. No one had taught him this. It was a natural talent, his favorite.

"Ok, my friend, we will see." Munio took a long swallow of beer and picked the darts off the board and the one on the floor. While he faced the board, he had a short silent conversation with the bullseye. "I'm coming at you three times. Like a magnet, my darts will come to you." He smiled and winked at the board and backed away. He gave a smile to Howard and the others before wheeling around behind the throw line.

Munio shut his eyes for a moment and crossed himself reverently, while inside he snickered. His eyes sprang open, and without delay, Munio fired one, two, then the third dart deep into the bullseye like bullets from a gun. He looked at the ceiling, crossed himself again, and bowed his head before looking at his stunned opponent and company.

"Thank you, Lord," Munio said.

"How did you do that?" Howard jumped out of his chair and pointed at the board. "I ain't believing you did that."

"Anything's possible with the Lord, Howard. Anything at all." Munio smiled sweetly and genuinely.

This defused Howard, who badly wanted to unload on Munio verbally and physically, but the rooked man was afraid to argue with the power of the Lord. His friends only chuckled while Howard counted out Munio's money.

"Thank you, bro, and God bless you tonight on your birthday. It's been a pleasure." Munio held out his right hand to Howard as he stuffed the money in his pocket with the left. Howard grudgingly stuck his hand in Munio's.

"Yeah, right." Howard and his friends downed their beers and left without another word.

Munio watched them leave and took a seat back at the bar. Only the feelings of satisfaction and power were the after-effects of his self-produced one act play. He felt no guilt or remorse for Howard. Munio took pleasure in the vision of shock or pain on someone's face when the moment of realization occurred that he or she had been had. The adrenaline rush of the hustle plus all the beer he had drunk that day had worn him down. He looked at his watch. It was ten thirty and time to leave, he decided.

# CHAPTER XIX

The night air was cool and relieved of the high humidity that normally persisted. Munio rolled down the window of his truck, lit a smoke, and headed for Eddy's. After a short drive, a police cruiser pulled in behind Munio and followed him closely for a few blocks. Munio got nervous and broke out in a sweat, despite the air rushing through the window. When the blue light came on, Munio drove another block, then pulled over. His mind raced with paranoia. Did Howard call the law on him for the hustle? He had no idea, and he was choked with fear.

The policeman got out of the car, and stayed about five feet from the door of the truck. "Get out of the truck with your hands on top of your head."

"What is wrong here, officer?" Munio asked, not making a move to get out of the truck. "What did I d-"

"Get out of the truck, now!" The cop drew his gun and dropped into a braced stance, prepared to shoot.

"Ok, I'm getting out." Munio pulled the handle of the truck door and stepped out. He put his hands on top of his head and stared at the barrel of the thirty-eight.

"Do you have a driver's license?"

"Yes, officer, I do." Munio went to reach for his wallet, but the cop spat out a warning.

"You keep that left hand on your head and move very slowly. You hear me?"

"Yes I do, but I don't know what I have done t-"

"Shut up and do it!"

Munio reached in, grabbed the wallet and held it in the cop's direction.

"Turn around, put both hands on the truck and spread your legs." Munio complied without protest.

The cop then said, "All right now, I want you to take your license out of the wallet for me, ok?"

Munio did so and held it out from his body toward the cop.

The cop studied it quietly. "Where you from boy, Mexico?"

Munio's face flushed with anger. "Belize. It says so on the license."

"Ain't Belize a town in Mexico?"

"Not to my knowledge, no." Munio turned his head left and then right in frustration.

"Turn around here!" The cop shined the flashlight into Munio's face at point blank range and scrutinized his face. Munio could see the cop's face faintly behind the flashlight, his eyes drawn in concentration, his mouth hanging open. "What you doing here in Georgia, Mr., ah," He looked down at the license again. "More los?"

"That's Mor a los. I am staying with a friend for a while."

"Who is that?"

"Eddy Jackson."

"Where does he live?"

"Down on, ah," Munio thought for a minute, trying to remember the name. "Bruner Road."

"Have you got a green card to be in this country?" The cop kept the flashlight point dead center in Munio's face.

"I have some paper in my wallet."

"Well, let's see it, son."

Munio shuffled through his wallet til he found a white slip of paper and

135

handed it to the cop.

"This is a visitor's visa. It's due to run out in December. Ok. Now, what was it you was doing out this evening?"

"I was just shooting some darts at that bar with that pink Cadillac in the front, you know?"

"Have you been a drinking tonight?"

"I had one beer only."

Just then both Munio and the cop looked behind Munio's truck as they heard the sound of another car pull up and stop. The lighting was not good so the person remained in silhouette. The gravel crunched under foot as the person walked towards Munio and the cop. It was Sandra Fugleberg.

"Munio, how are you?" she said happily, her eyes gleaming behind her thick spectacles.

"Fine, ma'am."

"Officer, what in the world is going on here?"

"I'm just on a routine stop of this man, ma'am."

"Well, let me tell you he is a very special man." Sandra put her arm through Munio's. "He's teaching this old lady to mambo and rumba and tango and God only knows what else. Anything else you need to know?" She gave the cop a playful stern look.

The cop smiled and looked away. "So you know this feller?"

"Oh my yes, he is a new invaluable asset to the community of Rosedale. This man is bringing culture to this town, Officer." She squinted to read his name tag, "What is your name?"

"Officer McKnight."

"Officer McKnight, well, Munio is a dance instructor at the country club, and I am one of his star students." Sandra winked at Munio who returned it with a smile.

"Ok ma'am, if you say so, I reckon you're ok, Mr. More los." The cop handed back his visa and license, tipped his hat to Sandra Fugleberg, and got back in his cruiser.

"Thank you, ma'am, I am not sure what he was going to do to me," Munio said gratefully.

"Glad I was coming by. It is perfect actually because I have been thinking about you since the class, and I would love to get to know you better."

Munio nodded and smiled at her.

"How would you like to come over to my house for a couple of drinks?"

"Ok, I could do that."

She pointed her big frame towards her car. "Follow me then."

Munio got in his truck and followed her late model Lincoln for ten minutes as it wound through a posh little residential subdivision and into the driveway of a large sprawling ranch-style home.

"Come in! Come in, Munio!" Sandra motioned with her big hand for

Munio to follow her inside.

A host of tiny lap dogs offered them frenzied greetings upon entering the kitchen from the carport door. The Yorkie, Pomeranian, and Shih Tzu whined and danced and celebrated while their little toenails clicked like Morse code on the tile floor.

"Hello, hello, babies! Did you miss mommy? Hummmm? Well, God love 'em, uh huh! I missed you too!" She bent down and petted them all while they licked her vigorously in the face, wiggling so hard and fast they could have been having convulsions. "This is Munio, everyone. He is our visitor tonight, all right? Everybody be nice."

Munio stared at the dogs. They did not seem like dogs at all, not like the big brown yard dogs he was accustomed to. These animals seemed like something far removed from dogs. They were so tiny and manicured. Their coats were combed out in long silky strands and sectioned off with colored barrettes. The neurotic energy around them did not endear them to Munio. Their little eyes bulged out as they panted and leaped up on his legs for attention. It was all he could do to not give one or all of them a swift kick across the room.

"They'll calm down in a few minutes. Here, come on in, and let me get you a drink, Munio." Sandra's hefty footsteps clopped across the spotless kitchen floor.

Munio followed her wide flat butt that stretched the material of her flowered dress. She walked like a bow-legged man in pumps. She reached into the refrigerator, pulled out two beers, and held them up to Munio for approval. Without a word, Munio nodded, and they sat at the round wooden table surrounded by tall cane-backed chairs.

Sandra popped the tops on the beers. The pressure inside the can sent a slight spray of beer all over Sandra's unwomanly hand. Neither the feminine silver blue star sapphire ring nor the thin silver watch she wore on her wrist counter-balanced the ample crop of stiff, grayish-brown hairs which grew on top.

"So Munio, do tell me a little about yourself. How did you end up in Rosedale?" she asked in a low-pitched voice.

Munio noticed her voice seemed to vacillate. Sometimes it seemed unusually high, even for a woman, and sometimes it was nearly baritone. At this moment, it was low, a man's authoritative voice.

That tickled Munio, but he tried not to snicker. "I happened to just be passing through this town when I met my friend Eddy. We struck up a friendship, and now I will stay here for a while." Munio held his hands up to indicate that was all the info there was on that subject.

"Well, we certainly did enjoy you in class the other night. My, my, my, how you can dance! It was a thing of beauty, you and Audrey." Sandra's voice went up considerably, and her ample jowls shook as she spoke.

"Thank you, ma'am. It was a fun time." Munio took in a long swallow. "Do you mind if I smoke?"

"Cigarettes?"

"Yes, what else?" Munio chuckled.

"I didn't know if you were going to pull out a marijuana cigarette or a cigar, perhaps." Sandra's gray eyes lit up and looked huge when Munio caught a direct glimpse of them through the bifocal part of her glasses.

"I won't do that."

Sandra shrugged her shoulders and smiled as she raised her beer to her thick pink-painted lips, never taking an eye off Munio. The silence hung heavy between them.

They sipped until Sandra could bear the silence no longer. "Say, I know what we need to get this party going. How about a shot of tequila?"

Munio brightened up. "Sure, why not. That would be great." He smiled encouragingly.

Sandra clapped. "All right! I've got a bottle I brought back from Mexico. It's even got the worm in it. Do you ever eat those worms, Munio?"

"I suppose I have eaten one or two. I am not crazy about it, to tell you the truth."

"Me either. I think it's a filthy practice. The only kind of worm I need to eat is a tape worm." She laughed and patted her ample belly.

She poured them each a shot into rather large shot glasses. They clinked them together in a toast and tipped them quickly into their mouths. They smiled at each other and instantly felt more at ease.

"Tequila is such a fine diplomat, don't you think? A bottle of tequila just gets a party going, you know?" Sandra said.

"Yes, it does. It makes people loosen up, be a little crazy," Munio added, wiggling his fingers.

"Here. Let's have another." She refilled the little glasses, and again they slugged them right down.

Not a word was said through the next two fillings of the shot glasses. The refrigerator motor gently hummed and the distant chorus of crickets chirped on the other side of the sliding glass door. Munio was glad for the quiet, yet surprised because she had been so talkative at the dance class. Sandra, on the other hand, enjoyed the company of someone she had no reason to impress or participate with in any social jousting.

Sandra had moved to Rosedale five years ago to begin her new life as a woman. The social arena in which she had always been involved was upper class and upper crust. She not only enjoyed that, but did not want that to change just because her sex had. She moved here under the guise of being a recently widowed woman who wanted to start a life somewhere that her dead husband was not. It was so painful, the death, is what she had told them when she applied for membership in the country club. She did mourn the death of

Paul, that man that she had been, and it was true that she needed to reside in a place where no residue of that man existed.

Munio had been at Sandra's house an hour now, and as the power of the tequila began to dominate them, their tongues loosened.

Sandra smiled at Munio and looked out the sliding glass door at the lightning bugs flashing in the back yard. She scratched her head hidden under her wig intermingled with gray and brown hair. It moved like a hat under her fingers as she scratched. Munio noticed and smiled.

"What all did Audrey tell you about me?" Sandra inquired of Munio.

Carefully, Munio answered, not knowing if Audrey should have told him about the sex change. "She just said she knew you from New York."

"She told you, didn't she?" Sandra nodded her head.

"What?" Munio returned innocently.

"She told you I used to be a man named Paul. She told me she told you, Munio. It's ok." Sandra chuckled at poor Munio getting caught up in the awkward lie. Her voice lowered and sounded like a man's. Her posture changed, too. She uncrossed her legs, pushed her chair away from the table a little, and leaned on one knee with one arm in a very masculine way.

Reaching up to her ears, she removed her clip-on earrings with a loud snap, displaying her unusually large lobes. After another shot was poured, she walked out of the room momentarily and returned carrying a small picture frame. She set it down in front of Munio.

"That's me, Munio. Actually, that's a young me, a young old me." She laughed at her confusing annotation.

"Wow." Munio said slowly feeling embarrassed because he did not know what to say. He didn't know what she wanted to hear. He was beginning to feel this lady might be a good ally, and he did not wish to offend her over this sensitive subject.

Sandra let out a deep hearty laugh. "You didn't know what you were getting yourself into, did you, Munio? You thought you were just visiting with a little old lady. Well, not tonight, amigo. Tonight Paul is here to visit." She laughed a big deep laugh again.

Munio looked up from the picture at Sandra. The deep voice startled him. Sandra got up again and returned with a photo album that she set down in front of Munio. She opened it to the first page.

"This is my life, Munio. This is the whole story."

Munio quietly turned the pages, looking at photos of a young GI. Further along, he turned to a page with a picture of a big rocket on a launchpad.

"See that?" Sandra pointed to the rocket. "I helped design that thing, the internal air cooling system, particularly. Yep, that was my baby."

"Is that right?" Munio drew his face close to the photograph. Drawing his eyebrows close together, he forced himself to make eye contact with Sandra in hopes his concentration would prevent him from falling from his chair.

His intoxication made it difficult to follow Sandra's dialogue.

Munio kept turning the pages of the book at a steady pace. He stopped when he came to a family portrait of a woman, Paul, and a young boy. Sandra, looking over Munio's shoulder to narrate, tapped her index finger on the picture.

"That is who I used to be, a husband with a son. Hard to believe, huh?" Again Sandra let out a deep belly laugh. "Never know what's going to happen in your life, Munio. You just never know. My son was killed about two weeks after we made this picture. Hit by a car on his bicycle. Killed him instantly." Sandra refilled the shot glasses. "You just never know."

"No, you don't," Munio echoed blankly, feeling a sting in his gut as he looked at the boy in the picture.

Sandra scratched at the wig again, "Do you mind?" she said pointing to the wig.

"Mind? Mind what?" Munio asked.

"Mind if I take this damned wig off." She laughed.

Munio joined in and felt more at ease with Sandra than he had felt all night. Sandra made eye contact with Munio, winked as she reached up and gently lifted the wig off, revealing a slim supply of gray hair on the sides and a big bold, shiny, bald spot that encompassed three quarters of her head. A sticking sound resonated as the glue strips separated from the wig. Sandra reached up and peeled each one off.

"Whew, does that feel better! I tell you the wig thing is the hardest part. The wig thing I do not enjoy. Even when I was a man I never paid attention to my hair, and now I have to if I'm going to look half-way decent. Women, well, what you would call proper ladies, as I certainly want to be considered, have so much more cosmetic maintenance than men. Older women have it worse. I know I look like an old hag half the time, a schmaltzy old hag, but an old hag nonetheless. As a man, people thought I was somewhat handsome, or at least I didn't have the pressure on me to achieve handsome. If I was well groomed, wore expensive clothes, I received respect. Old women are considered fragile, withering, no matter what the hell they wear or do. Old lesbians get by, butch ones anyway, but there you go--they dress like older men. It was a hell of a time in the course of a life to want to be a woman." Sandra filled the glasses, laughed loudly, and slapped her hand on the table. "It's like choosing to be an amputee. That's a thought, huh, Munio?" Munio nodded obligingly.

"You know," Sandra said, "you just don't see amputees any more. I saw a man today, a black man with no left leg, empty pant leg swinging as he hitched down the sidewalk on crutches. People get all these new prosthetics. Can't tell at all, not even a limp, amazing really. They fascinated me always as a child. People don't want to be different these days, Munio. They want to be the same. If I wore a dress without a wig to my next bridge game, there would be mass hysteria." Sandra laughed her big laugh again and punched Munio in the arm;

Munio's mind was a million miles away, thinking about nothing in particular. He moved in his chair, chuckled, and nodded in agreement to what, he had no idea.

"You don't know what the hell I'm rattling off about, do you? I'm sorry. I just don't have much company I can let my hair down with, so to speak." Sandra spewed a laugh over her accidental joke. She got up and replaced their empty beer cans with full ones.

"Munio, what's your claim to fame? What are you really doing in this small, small town, humm?" Sandra coaxed.

"My claim to fame, hummm. Well, I guess that would be when I was in the Olympics in 1972."

"Oh really, in Munich?"

Munio nodded to Sandra's question. "Yes, that's right. I was the first and only, even til this day, the only weightlifter to ever represent Belize in the Olympics." Munio sprang to life.

"How interesting. How did you do?"

"I was fifteenth, but I was not loaded so..." Munio shrugged his shoulders and smiled.

"You weren't loaded?"

"On steroids, you know."

"Oh, oh," Sandra leaned on the table with her elbows, her face cupped in her hands. "They did steroids back then?"

"Oh, sure, they did."

"Hormone drugs are fascinating. I could not believe the changes in my attitude when I first started estrogen therapy. I baked the best brownies." Sandra and Munio cracked up. "But I still didn't give a shit about fixing my hair!" Again, they laughed, and Sandra poured them each another shot.

"God, I am the worst hostess." She suddenly dropped into her high pitched feminine, Julia Child-like voice. "I absolutely forgot the lemon and salt." Munio laughed.

"Anyway, here is a toast to Munio Morelos, ex-Olympian. I have met quite a few American Olympic stars that visited the space center and such, but I never met one from Belize. I have only met one weightlifter. I met Paul Anderson once. So cheers, Munio." Sandra held up her glass and tipped it Munio's way before drinking it.

"Paul Anderson was very strong." Munio reflected.

"I toured the York barbell plant one time. Bob Hoffman had designed an interesting bearing for his barbells that we wanted to use on our rocket simulators' cargo doors."

"I built my own weight set in Belize, and learned to lift long before I ever saw a real barbell, at least in person."

"Is that so?'

Munio went on to disclose his story to Sandra. Sandra's engineering

mind resurfaced, and she was enraptured by the story. With great clarity and eloquence, Munio wove the details of his invention. He included details of the early prototypes that failed, which caused Sandra to laugh with great gusto. This, in turn, encouraged Munio to engage his charm and wit to thoroughly entertain his hostess.

"What an inventive man you are, Munio. Really, and so multitalented are you with your wonderful dancing skills. I'm very impressed. To triumph over such difficult circumstances, remarkable." She reached over and took Munio's hand and squeezed it. "Thank you for coming tonight. I really mean it." Munio gripped Sandra's hand in lieu of any verbal response. A flush of heat traveled through his body, and he felt tears in his eyes. The feeling confused him, for he was unsure if it was that he felt love or the lack of it. At any rate, he felt great compassion for this woman and the man she used to be, this closeted sexual amputee.

"So Munio, you never told me, what you are doing now, or where you are going from here?" Sandra queried.

Munio cleared his throat and lit a cigarette. "I will be here for a while, a few more weeks anyway. My friend Eddy, with whom I am staying, is preparing for a bodybuilding contest, and I am helping train him."

"A muscle head, eh? I like those kind of boys." Sandra wiggled her eyebrows up and down in a flirtatious gesture.

Munio chuckled. "Yeah, he is a big man, strong."

"Then what will you do, Munio? Do you have a trade or something? Will you return to Belize?"

Munio gulped and felt a nauseous wave come over him. It might have been the buildup of tequila, but more likely, it was the pressure of the question. He had no plan that sounded grand, and now was not the time he wanted to be reminded of it. "I am not really sure what I will do. Originally, I had planned to look up a friend in Atlanta. That is where I was going until I met Eddy." Munio gave a nervous thin-lipped smile.

Sandra sensed Munio's anxiety and left the subject alone. "There is another dance class tomorrow night. Will you be assisting Audrey?"

Munio shook his head and laughed. "Audrey is mad with me. I don't know if that will happen again."

Sandra frowned. "Really now? I'll have to talk to that girl, unless you feel like giving me a lesson right here and now." Sandra's face exploded with delight at the thought, and her voice went up two octaves as she spoke. "Would you, Munio, would you? I love to dance. It is the most favorite thing I do in the world. I think it is the reason I got a sex change." Sandra laughed. "So I could wear dresses and be led around on a dance floor."

Munio laughed, and welcomed the opportunity to do anything to change the subject of his life's plan. "Sure, we can dance. Where?" Munio looked around the kitchen and held out his arms.

142

"I know. Let's go out on the patio. There is a huge deck, and I have a speaker so we can pipe in music. What shall we play? Oh, this is great! Come look at my recordings and tell me, ok?" Sandra grabbed his hand again and led him into the darkened living room. She flipped on a floor lamp and walked over to the home entertainment center. From a drawer full of tapes, she motioned for Munio to pick something.

"I don't know what to pick, Sandra. You pick a good one, and we will just dance to that, ok?"

"Ok, that's fine."

The Latin orchestra came on strong and smooth. Any residual tension either of them felt seemed to vanish as music took over their bodies. Sandra led the way to the sliding glass door and went outside along with Munio and her pack of lap dogs. The dogs jumped up on a chaise lounge, huddled together, and watched their mother and the strange man.

Sandra breathed in the cool sweet air and let out a big sigh of relief. Munio followed suit, looking up at the blue- black sky full of twinkling stars. The pulsing music followed them into the night, pouring from the speaker that hung under the eaves of the brick house. Sandra pushed things out of the way and cleared a big path to give them room to dance.

Munio took Sandra by the hand, wrapping his other arm around her waist. She stood a good head and shoulders above him, her baldhead shining faintly in the light of the half moon. Munio's wild hair engulfed his head with shadows and hid the silhouette of his face.

Sandra was like an ecstatic child, tickled to death to be moving in any way at all. She didn't care how bad she was. Bad dancing was just as much fun as good dancing to her. There was a perpetual smile glued on her face. Patiently, Munio coaxed her to slow down and pay attention to him and his signals to her.

Munio felt happy as well. Dancing was his best skill, and his greatest pleasure. Part of that pleasure came from the chance to be close to someone in a controlled way. It was one time that he felt a benevolent sense of power. He felt like a good man when he danced.

They danced for close to an hour until the tape stopped, and when it did, they laughed at how the sudden silence caught them offguard. They pulled each other close for an affectionate hug. They were sweaty and warm and genuine as the lightning bugs blinked, and the lap dogs looked on at the most unlikely couple at the ball.

# CHAPTER XX

Both Eddy and Munio pulled back up to the house within minutes of each other about four a.m. Eddy had called up one of his part-time girlfriends for a fuck. Munio drove home from Sandra's amazingly sober. The dancing seemed to disarm the tequila and beer, as well as throw a net of gladness around this man who had been so full of anger earlier.

Eddy went into the bathroom to take a leak, and he watched in horror as a stream of pure blood curdled in the toilet bowl. For a minute, he could not move; his eyes were paralyzed on that water. Without flushing, he backed out of the bathroom as if creeping away from a rattlesnake, and went into the kitchen to find Munio.

"Hey man, come here. I want to show you something."

Motioning for Munio to follow him, Eddy led him into the bathroom and pointed into the commode. "Check this shit out."

"Jesus Christ, Eddy! What is wrong with you? I don't know what this means, but I can tell you it is not good, man!" Munio's eyes were as big as saucers.

Eddy laughed at Munio's alarm. "It don't hurt or nothing. I have heard that decca will make you do that, and I took a shot of that new stuff from Jimmy Ray. I reckon I'll live, but that sure scared the shit out of me at first."

"At first? You better let it scare the hell out of you forever, Eddy! This is not a good sign! You need to cut it out."

"Sheeeiiitt. You crazy as you look. I ain't about to quit loading now. A little blood ain't nothing." Eddy reached over and flushed the commode and backed Munio out of the bathroom. Both of them returned to the kitchen.

"You aren't going to see a physician or anything?"

"Hell no. what do you think he would say? What would I say? Oh, yeah, I'm throwing back enough steroids daily to choke a horse. Do you think you could give me something for internal bleeding?" Eddy laughed hysterically. "Yeah, that'd be funny." Munio shrugged his shoulders.

"Anyhow, let's quit talking about that. You want some chicken and rice?" Munio nodded, and Eddy got two bowls out of the refrigerator. Eddy carefully spooned some rice into a frying pan and threw four precooked chicken breasts on top of it. He stirred it constantly for a few minutes and then served it up on two plates.

"Thank you, brother," Munio said, as Eddy put a plate in front of him.

"No problem." They ate without speaking for a few minutes, and then Eddy bragged, "Boy, I got me some tonight, Munio. Whooo, I fucked the hell out of this old gal. You can say what you want, but I'll take a little blood any day to keep my dick as hard as it got tonight. You couldn't turn the skin on that son of a bitch with a pipe wrench." Eddy laughed at his joke, and Munio

smiled.

"Is this some young lady you just met?"

"Naw, I've been fucking her for years every now and then. She's got a couple of kids, and I just ain't into that whole scene. I ain't ready for somebody to be calling me daddy, especially if I didn't make the kids."

"Is she pretty?"

"Hell if I know!" Eddy put his hand on his massive forehead. "Like I always say, Munio. Who ever had a piece of face?" Eddy laughed out loud.

Munio did not find Eddy's attitude about this sexual experience pleasant. He had just come from a strange but tender place, and all he could see were those twinkling blue stars above Sandra's patio as they whirled and twirled.

"You know what, Eddy? I think I will go to sleep now. I am tired."

"Oh yeah, I meant to ask you. Where did you go tonight?"

"Out and about really. Played some darts. Went over to this older lady's house for a while. I had a good time. Not a wild time, but a good time for an old man, you know." Munio smiled softly.

Eddy studied him for a moment, "Well, all right man. You sleep good now. We're going to hit it first thing in the morning, all right?"

"Sure, man." Munio washed out his plate and went into the doll room. He did not even turn on the lights to undress. He didn't feel like seeing all those dolls tonight. The sheets felt cool and soft, and Munio dropped off instantly into a long deep sleep.

It seemed that only minutes had passed when Eddy the rooster gave his morning wakeup call, but now it was ten a.m. Eddy was running late. Munio groaned and stretched, wanted to sleep much longer, but he pulled himself out of bed before Eddy burst in with some corny wake up routine.

Munio practically ran into Eddy as he opened the doll room door and went into the hall. They both were naked, and Munio stepped back to view Eddy's massive physique.

"Goddamn, Eddy, you are huge." Munio inspected his body in general now. Munio backed further, frowning in concentration. "Let me see some poses. I cannot believe how you have grown."

"I know, man. It is like motherfucking magic. I love it. This is the best thing that has ever happened to me in my life."

"If it doesn't kill you first." Munio winked at Eddy and shook his head.

"You want breakfast?"

"Yes." Munio counted on his fingers as he spoke. "I want a cigarette, a pot of coffee, and a little Kahlua in that coffee, ok?"

Eddy laughed, "You old buzzard you. I just might have a little Kahlua stashed around here somewhere. God knows I need your ass lively today."

"Good. You work on that. I will be smoking on the front porch, ok?"

"All right. In the meantime, I am fixing me," he counted back to Munio

on his fingers mockingly, "twelve egg whites, three potatoes, and a pound of ground sirloin."

Munio covered his ears halfway through the menu in disgust. "Stop it! Stop it! I am going to throw up on these dolls if you don't shut up!" Munio smiled as he stepped back into the doll room to dress.

He slipped on some underwear and the black jeans he had worn the night before. Munio's mind drifted to scenes at Sandra's. He remembered how dark it was on the patio, and how he loved moving in that darkness, cutting into it swiftly like a bow of a ship splits the water. He smiled when he pictured Sandra's wig hung on a coat hook on the back of the kitchen door next to an umbrella, a raincoat, and the dogs' leashes. He laughed out loud when he thought about how funny the two of them must have looked dancing together, Sandra towering above Munio with her polyester flowered dress swaying in the breeze they created. Munio remembered how soft and comforting it felt to be pressed against Sandra's large artificial bosom.

Out on the porch, Eddy delivered him a cup of coffee. Munio was relieved that it was an overcast day. It was much kinder on his eyes and the fever in his head that burned from all those shots of tequila last night. He thumped his cigarette butt over the railing and went into the kitchen to talk to Eddy.

Munio, nauseated to see Eddy in a feeding frenzy, could not imagine how someone could gag down a bowl of twelve boiled egg whites.

"What do you want to train today?"

"Uh," Eddy said with his mouth full. "chest and tris."

"Ok. How was your pee this morning, any more red?"

"Naw, it was pretty cleared up. I'm all right. Maybe it really wasn't blood. Maybe it was just that shit I took dyed my pee red or something. I have heard of that. I mean, look at those goose eggs that come up on my thighs the other day. They went away fast. It ain't no problem."

"Ok, brother. How much longer are you going to keep doing all of that stuff daily?"

"Til the show's over, or I run out." Eddy scooped an overflowing forkful of egg whites and sautéed sirloin into his mouth and smacked noisily.

At the gym, Eddy and Munio put in two and a half hours of set after set of bench presses, incline dumbell presses, repetitions on the pec deck, and tricep exercises. Munio was nearly as exhausted as Eddy after each workout because of how heavy Eddy always lifted and his love of forced reps.

Back at the house afterwards, the same ritual was repeated. Eddy ate massive amounts of protein--chicken, egg whites, and rice--while Munio nibbled on toast and had the first beer of the day. After they burned a joint on the porch, Eddy went to bed for an afternoon nap before work. Munio strummed his guitar while moving back and forth in the green metal glider, smoked cigarettes, and drank beers.

After a while, Munio decided to give Sandra a call. She had mentioned

needing a little carpentry work done, and Munio offered to do it.

The phone rang, and the Sandra's Julia Childs voice answered. "Hello?" she said merrily.

"Sandra?"

"Yes, Munio." Sandra's heart beat hard.

"Yes, it's me. How are you today?"

"I'm hung over as hell. How about you?"

Munio chuckled. "I got over it."

"I guess there's hope then."

"Yes, I think so. I thought I would see when you want me to do that carpentry work for you?"

"Anytime you want."

"I could start this afternoon if you like."

"Why, that would be fun."

"Ok, I will come soon then."

# CHAPTER XXI

Munio smiled as he hung up the phone, and so did Sandra across town. Sandra had been a certified woman now for well over five years, and it was her undeniable love for men that ultimately was at the root of her decision to make the change. The man she used to be could not find the courage to live as a homosexual in this culture, and thus sprang for the alternative. Although as it worked out, Sandra, as an unusually large and homely middle-aged woman, found no relief from that same culture.

Sandra chose to limit her world and banked on receiving acceptance from the same upper class that revered her as a man. The money she had earned as a man came with her to Rosedale and bought her membership at the country club, which represented the hub and the whole of her social life in this world.

Love had not found a home in Sandra's life, however, and except for her little lap dogs, she had little to live for. Her regular charades at the country club, the dances and other various functions gave no real depth to her life. In that arena, at least she could flirt with the valet parking attendants, waiters, and various other wellheeled hired help that humored her always, just like good help is supposed to do, especially to a generous tipper like Sandra Fugleberg.

Munio presented a totally different story. Despite his obvious lack of financial status and because of his exotic Latin nature, Sandra Fugleberg declared him exempt from her normal discriminating criteria. She knew Munio could use her financially, and she felt his transient state was another safety net to keep her gender secret sacred. No one would believe an itinerant wild-

looking man like Munio. All of these ulterior motives and rationalizations aside, the most important fact was that Sandra Fugleberg had fallen in love with Munio from the moment she first laid eyes on him at the country club. Whether or not it would work out to be a blessing or a curse, Munio Morelos was the man of her dreams.

Munio's thinking was running along the lines of Sandra's in that he was looking forward to using her financially. Whether she would be his sugar mama or he would be her handyman had yet to be decided, but Munio was certain that one or the other or both would occur.

Then there was that strange and unfamiliar feeling that Munio felt when he held her, that tenderness. Whatever that was, Munio wanted to feel it again, and with good intentions, he splashed on way too much High Karate cologne and pointed his old Ford truck in the direction of Sandra Fugleberg's house.

Sandra busied herself around the house, in full femme mode this fine day, changing into a snappy maroon flowered dress. It was sleeveless and, although the neckline did not exactly plunge, it did expose a little more skin than a respectable middle-aged woman's usually did on a weekday. She patted and combed her wig a little, and drew her face close to the bathroom mirror while she carefully lined her lips with a pink coral lipstick. Scanning through her perfume collection, she decided on White Shoulders, an oldie but goodie that she had actually taken from her own mother after she passed away some years back.

The little lap dogs followed her everywhere, watching, hoping she was dressing to take them out for a ride or a walk. Sandra took off her beloved ratty bedroom slippers and exchanged them for a pair of brown backless, low-heeled sandals. They slid on smoothly over her pantyhosed feet. She held her bifocals up to the light of the window and frowned before wiping them thoroughly with the hem of her dress.

When the doorbell rang, Sandra jumped and made a little squealing sound as she hurried toward the door, breathing loudly. She took a moment to compose herself before opening the door.

"Munio, how are you, dear? Come on in." She reached for her highest octave.

Munio smiled and chuckled at the Sandra that was working today. She was a sight different from the bald, baritone, cynical tequila drinker from the night before. "Sandra, how are you?" He gave her a wicked raised eyebrow look as he lifted her right hand to his lips and kissed the top of it.

Sandra blushed and pushed on Munio's shoulder. "Munio, really. Aren't you a devil! You're giving me a hot flash! Heavens!"

Munio laughed and walked into the kitchen. "Ok, lady, let's talk about your little project, now." Very directed, he clapped his hands together.

"All right, as you wish. Follow me." Sandra alternately stomped and shuffled in her sandals as she led Munio out the sliding glass door onto the patio

and into the large backyard.

The yard was thirty yards wide and forty yards deep with a ten foot tall wooden security fence all around it. The lawn was a fescue that did not seem to have a single weed in it. Sandra walked nearly to the back fence before stopping.

"Munio, I was thinking I would like to build a gazebo back here, and put in rose bushes all around it. What do you think about that? Can you do it?"

Munio thought a while. "How tall do you want this to be?"

"Oh," she held up her hands, "about a couple of feet taller than my hands."

Munio nodded, "This is to be a round thing, hexagon, or octagon, maybe?"

"Octagon. Humm. That sounds lovely." She clasped her hands together. "Yes, that's it."

"Ok, octagon." Munio pulled a notepad from his back pocket and drew a hexagon. " Do you want it up off the ground a great distance?"

"A couple of steps will do."

"Ok, two steps." He wrote the number two and drew a step next to it. He shook his head and chuckled. "You know this is more than just a 'little carpentry work', Sandra, but I can do this. It won't be that cheap, but I can do it. You have to use treated lumber so it will not rot or anything."

"That's ok. Use the best materials."

"Let me just figure a minute. Now, show me how big around you want it."

"Oh." Sandra took about seven steps and stopped. "About this big, Munio. This is so exciting. I have wanted to do this for years."

"Ok, let's see." He pulled a retractable metal tape measure from his belt and unrolled it to cover the area indicated by Sandra. "Ten feet say?" Munio looked over at Sandra.

"Yeah, that looks good."

Munio studied the plot and finally spoke. "I don't know how much it will cost because I never built anything here in this country. I don't know how much lumber and so forth costs here. As for me, if you can pay me ten dollars an hour, I will do it."

"Ok, that sounds fair. Uh, are you sure you can build this by yourself, Munio?"

"Yes, yes, I can do it. Don't worry about it. It will be good and sound. I give you my word. If you want, I will sit down and figure what we need, and we could go get it, unless you want to just have me go do that."

"No, that will be fun. I'll go. You want a beer while you figure?"

"Yes, that would be good. I will stay here though to calculate everything."

"Ok, I will bring you that beer then." Sandra hurried through the fescue,

her weight bearing into the soft lawn so that the sandals nearly disappeared with each step.

Munio drew a picture of the proposed gazebo and showed it to Sandra as they sat on lightweight lawn chairs she had pulled up for them. They drank beers and laughed as Munio made more sketches. He had a wonderful hand for drafting, Sandra thought. He drew the layout neatly and accurately. She was impressed with his skill and loved watching his brown eyes study the ground and concentrate on the pad as his hand moved sensuously across the pad.

"Ok, I got it. I know what we need."

"Did you do this work before?"

"I built houses for a while, yes. I learned from a fine builder. Once you learn to do something the right way, you always remember."

"That is probably true. I feel I could reproduce the prints of any circuitry boards I created for NASA even though I have not so much as looked at that material for many years now." Munio glanced over at Sandra, who reverted to her baritone Paul voice for that statement.

"Oh," Sandra's voice climbed back up the scale. "I'm sorry, Munio. I just forget sometimes."

"How come that changes?"

"Because I just didn't want to get massive hormone treatments, damnit! I started, and I do take a modest dose now. I just didn't want to give up every part of the me I used to be. The dick was no problem. The body, no problem, but a total genetic change I could not handle. I was not willing to totally relinquish my mind. You know what I mean?"

"Well," Munio sighed and chuckled. "No, I don't, but that's ok. Whatever you had to do you did, and that's good."

"I don't flub up much in public. An old lady can get away with anything. It is the one advantage of being an old lady. Who's going to question you? It is funny sometimes at, say, somewhere like the grocery store, to tell the bag boy which car is mine in my high voice, and then as he is walking away say, 'Thanks son' in my low voice. His head will nearly snap off as he whips around so fast to get a look at who said that. There I'll be, the good little granny, just waving at him. I'm sure he wonders about it all day. What the hay, Munio. If there is one thing I have bought entitlement to, it is the old ladies get away with anything club." Sandra laughed. "You know what?" She leaned close to Munio, "And I love it." She punched him in the arm and laughed again.

Munio laughed too because he knew nothing else better to do. He did not understand all that Sandra said, but he liked the way she said it.

They walked in from the back yard, and Munio asked, "Do you want to go with me to the lumber yard or hardware store? I don't know where these things are around here."

Sandra, without thinking, said, "Yes, what fun. I'll go with you. Let me

go get my purse." As she went into her bedroom, she started thinking about the consequences of being seen out with a man like Munio. It was not proper for the lady of the house to be seen in the company of hired help unless they were driving them in a limousine. Munio's old white Ford truck was certainly no limo.

"Munio, I forgot that I am expecting a couple of calls this afternoon. Why don't I just give you some cash and direct you to the lumbeyard. Is that ok?" she lied.

"Sure, yes."

With that, Sandra forked over some cash and wrote down on paper the directions to the lumber yard. Munio played a game of his own as he studied the directions as if he knew what they said.

"Those directions make sense?"

"Yeah, sure. Uh, what is the name of the place again?"

"Patterson Lumber Company. It won't take you fifteen minutes to get there."

Sandra sat at the kitchen table since Munio left, in anticipation of his return. She really wished she had had the nerve to accompany him to the lumberyard. When the sound of his truck engine backfired as he turned in the driveway, Sandra jumped from her chair and stood in the carport doorway to greet him.

"Have a good trip?" she called to him.

"Yes, the trip was ultimately successful. I have hand picked some fine lumber with which to build your gazebo." Munio smiled and squeezed her forearm.

Her gray blue eyes, magnified behind gray plastic and silver framed eye glasses, had never been so close to someone as beautiful as Munio. As if she were looking at a newly discovered planet, he became the missing link in her food chain. Big crinkles of skin swelled and stretched around those blue eyes, as she stared at Munio and her gladness compelled her to smile.

Munio's eyes made their way through those glasses like the beam of a welder's arc. He felt drawn by some strange force more powerful than Mescal. As the warmth of their glance filled him with a feeling of joy, his knee jerk reaction to intimacy abandoned him momentarily, and his lips blossomed into a smile that came straight from his heart.

The moment froze, paralyzed them. Without warning, the two locked in an embrace that brought secret tears to each of them. Munio's left ear pressed against Sandra's soft silicone chest. He heard her heart pound. He blinked softly and smiled. Sandra viewed life through the black lace veil of Munio's hair. The top of his head was a perfect height for Sandra's chin to rest on. She inhaled deeply, took in the rich, musky scent of him.

Then, as if a switch had been flipped, they pushed away from each other. Each went through a barrage of unconscious centering techniques. Sandra

cleaned her glasses, straightened her dress, and cleared her deep throat. Munio ran his hands through his hair, dabbed at his nose, and lit a cigarette. As if being awakened rudely from a dream, each became conscious of the rude consequences of rationality. They smiled politely at each other, and offered little nervous laughs.

"So, you got everything?" Sandra clapped her big hands and smiled.

"Yes, yes, everything. Here is your change and the receipt." He handed her the money and paper. "Now, I will get started right away."

"Not before lunch, you won't. You are hungry, aren't you?"

"Yes, I could eat something."

"How about a sandwich, some chips, and a beer?"

"Thank you. That sounds good, Sandra."

"Ok, I will whip it right up. You want to sit and have a beer while I do that?"

"I think I would like to unload the truck first."

After opening the wooden gates that led to the back yard, Munio drove the old pickup through the fescue to the spot for the gazebo. He unloaded everything and stacked it neatly as Sandra, watching through the kitchen window, made their sandwiches on the kitchen counter. Munio stood and stared at the building spot for a bit before walking slowly across the lawn, onto the deck, and through the sliding glass door.

"It's all ready, hon," Sandra said cheerfully, as Munio slid the door open and entered.

"Let me wash up."

They sat and ate in complete and peaceful silence. The only sounds were the crunching of the chips, the beer cans as they were returned to the table after a swallow, and the whining of the lap dogs as they huddled around Sandra's feet, where they hoped for a lucky morsel. Munio ate the most food he had eaten in months, and Sandra ate the least. Each, without thought of it, felt encased in a delicate bubble of contentment. Subconsciously, as if they observed deer, they made small, quiet movements, so as to not frighten the feeling away.

After the meal, until the golden apricot light of dusk fell so deep that he was unable to see, Munio dug square holes for the footing blocks the gazebo's support beams would rest upon. Grandly immersed in the process, he worked deftly and with pinpoint precision. Although he dearly loved and was good at building things, it had been a long time since the opportunity had presented itself. His thoughts of Eddy and the gym faded for the time being, and turned to the art wielded by the shovel. Working as delicately as a cake decorator, he dug not one sprig of fescue more than necessary as he slowly made his way around the site. When he finished, eight little square blocks were buried sans the tops and formed a neat circle ten feet in diameter.

Sandra sat in a lounge chair Munio had carried out to the gazebo area

for her. She alternately read a book on the art of growing bonsai trees and stole peeks at Munio at work. Sandra had brought several citronella candles contained in small galvanized buckets, which she stationed near them for mosquito control. Their yellow flame dispersed a sweet lemony odor into the warm heavy air.

The lap dogs roamed the back yard peacefully. Covering all the perimeters, they sniffed every bush and shrub, and in turn, the three marked each with a stream of urine. Eventually, they all returned to Sandra's lap in the lounge chair where they slept.

Munio liked that Sandra was nearby, but was glad she did not engage him in dialogue. He did not like to talk while he worked because it spoiled his concentration. A few lightning bugs signaled the end of the workday on this evening. Munio had grown attached to the ritual of their arrival as the light of day disappeared.

"Well, that's it for today, Sandra."

"You work well. I'm so happy you are building this for me."

"I will continue tomorrow if you like."

"Yes, yes, let's keep working. What time will you come?"

"Not too early because I must help Eddy at the gym."

"What do you do exactly?"

"I help him work out."

"How is that?" Sandra pushed her glasses high on the bridge of her nose.

"He needs somebody to spot, you know, ah, help him through the heavy exercises. I might hand the barbell to him, or I am there to grab it if he wears out. Did I explain that ok?"

"Yes, I think so. I just never heard of, or never thought of, somebody lifting a weight that is too heavy for them." Sandra laughed. "It doesn't make any sense to me."

"Well, that is probably because it is not a sensible thing to do. Bodybuilding, the way he is doing it, is a strange thing to do."

"Hmm. I would like to meet Eddy sometime. Do you think he would like to come over for dinner with you?"

"Umm. I don't know. I will ask him and see. He eats only certain things. It is a very specific diet he eats now since it is short to the time he will be in his competition."

"Oh, a competition?"

"Yes, the Mr. Dixie contest."

"Mr. Dixie?" Sandra raised her eyebrows and pushed her glasses higher on her nose. "Is he very good?"

"Yes, he is a very muscular man, and he is working very hard to win this title."

"Where is the contest?"

"I don't know, to tell you the truth. I have never asked. We just work every day to build the muscle, and that's all I know about it."

"I met some bodybuilders in New York. They were all gay. Is Eddy gay?"

Munio laughed, "No, no, he is not gay, although he has been so horny lately, he might try it. Who knows?"

They both laughed, and Sandra blew out the citronella candles before they walked back to the house.

"Will you have a beer with me?"

"Sure, I sure would do that."

Sandra popped the tops on two beers and set them on the table. "Munio, you worked so well out there. Do you enjoy this kind of work?"

"I do. It is fun really to build something, especially something as unusual as this gazebo."

"Do you have enough tools?"

"Yes, I think so. I have collected tools all my life. I have quite a few. I might need some more extension cords to reach all the way back there, but other than that, I think I have everything."

"I have miles of extension cords. I have them for the Christmas decorations I use. Last year I had the most lights of any house in town." Sandra snickered as she remembered. "I had the whole front yard laid out in white blinking lights, and in the middle, I laid out a runway made of blue lights. Then, I had sequenced lights laid out in a pattern of the silhouette of Santa Claus and his sleigh that looked like he was taking off down the runway. I had one more silhouette just off the ground so it showed him actually taking off. It was great. My electric bill was enormous." Sandra and Munio laughed.

"That's great. I wish I had seen that."

"Actually, you can. I have a video tape of it." They laughed again.

"No kidding? Sometime I would like to see it."

"Ok, I'll dig it up soon."

"It has always been one of my favorite holidays because of the lights," Munio said.

"How odd. I would not have thought you would celebrate Christmas in Belize."

"Well, the country follows much British tradition, you know."

"I suppose that is true, but somehow I look at you and don't think of you as being very British."

"I feel pretty British in many ways. I know about Mayan ways, Caribbean ways, too. I am a mixture of many people, and I feel it. It is true when they say you cannot judge a book by its cover. Just look at you. You are not an old woman with no brain, no thought. You are an engineer inside of you, still," Munio said.

Sandra cocked her head in surprise. "Why, thank you for saying that, Munio. I have built a life around outward appearances, and to tell you the

154

truth, I am growing a little weary of the effort that it takes. I never talk about being an engineer with anyone anymore. Who would I tell? The people at the country club? I don't think they would like to know that. The only people who know I used to be an engineer are a few queens in New York. Queens like Audrey, queens that you wouldn't go up to and say, "Oh, did you read in Scientific American about the fascinating circuitry of the micro laser installed in the Hubbell telescope?"

Munio laughed out loud. "I do not know what all that is either, but at least now you can talk about wigs."

"Women, wigs, Dolly Parton cologne, some liberation I stepped into, huh?" They both laughed.

Munio looked grave as he spoke and shook his index finger at Sandra. "Sandra, you have to be who you want to be. Do what you want to do."

Sandra said, slowly and sadly, "Well Munio, that is easier said than done. You see, I am used to a certain opulence and a certain class of people with whom I choose to associate. Under no circumstances would they approve of what I have done with my life, my body, and so-" Munio cut her off.

"That is only slavery you impose on yourself. An expensive prison is still a prison. Don't you see that?"

Sandra sat straight up in her chair and put her hands on her thighs. She set her jaw firmly and anger swept across her eyes. For a moment, she almost asked Munio to leave. She thought about what he had said before she spoke. "Munio, I am afraid, sir, you are correct in your assessment." The anger on her face was flushed by a warm smile. She turned her face away. "I do not want to lose my place in line, so to speak, but I don't know how else to live. I have been abiding by this social code for so long. It's not so hard to hide, really, who I am. Anyway, they may be snobs, but they're the only friends I have."

"You have me. I'm your friend." Munio reached out and took Sandra's hand.

"Munio, you are one kind man, and I don't know how to thank you for, for, for just being here. How would you like to have a bottle of champagne with me? I feel like champagne, and we could toast our new friendship."

"Ok, I would be honored." Munio stood up and bowed to Sandra and kissed her hand. Sandra bounded from her seat, giggling like a tickled school-girl.

The cork exploded with such a pop that the dogs barked, and Munio and Sandra laughed hysterically. The champagne hit Munio and Sandra who began to laugh at anything and everything. When the bottle was empty, Sandra pulled out another one from the refrigerator, and by the end of that, they were half drunk.

"Sandra, I have a great idea."

"Yes, what it is? I mean what is it?" They laughed.

"I would like to invite you to dance with me around the proposed gazebo

site. That way we could welcome it into the world, and bless the ground with celebration. It is an old Mayan custom to dance on the ground of a new house or building."

"Really? How fascinating?"

"No, not really. I made it up, but it sounds good, doesn't it?" Munio cracked up laughing, and Sandra joined in after hitting him on the arm.

"Let's do! Let's go dance in the yard. Let's make it our custom." Sandra grinned and nodded at Munio.

"Ok, yes, to the yard!" Munio stood and grandly offered his arm to Sandra. They attempted to walk through the sliding glass door opening side by side, but the effort failed and provided yet another round of giggles for the two.

The air, thick and warm compared to the icy air conditioning inside Sandra's house, was sensuous and rich with sounds of crickets and tree frogs. The night played host to the few lightning bugs that remained even though it was early fall. They made their way through the grass out to the gazebo spot. Their hearing seemed heightened in the darkness, and they both noticed the sound of their footsteps lightly crunching the stiff blades of fescue as they moved along, hand in hand.

"What about music? I could bring out a tape player."

"Shhhhhhh. Listen to the night. There is so much music here for us already," Munio whispered softly.

A heat surge raced through Sandra's body and sweet beads of sweat began to form upon her face. He pulled her close, and they moved in a slow waltz around the pile of lumber. Sandra's heart pounded so that she felt Munio might hear it. She looked up at the sky, full of white twinkling stars, and down at the soft mass of Munio's midnight hair. She rested her chin on top of his head, and without warning, a tear rolled from her heart and out of her eye and into Munio's hair. Their embrace tightened the longer they danced. Munio's body filled with a strange fire. It was an erotic feeling, super charged with electricity. It created a question as to what he was actually feeling, a question he did not want to answer right now. He wanted to just be there with Sandra with no answers at all. He felt her heat as she continued to sweat, little streams down the front of her body. Under those two massive breasts, Sandra felt her skin might glow red in the night through the light flowered dress.

They twirled and twirled slowly on the lawn, undisturbed, until suddenly one of Sandra's low heels hung up in the grass. The two of them, so relaxed, had no ready defense to prepare them for a fall. Down they went like a twin pair of redwoods, hitting the ground with a thud. Sandra let out a little high pitched scream when she realized she would be landing not on the ground but on her beloved Munio. Munio let out a cry of his own also when faced with this reality.

"Munio, are you all right?" Sandra struggled to roll off him, to check for

a pulse.

Munio did not say anything for a moment, but then started a slow round of laughter that built to full blown hysteria. Sandra chuckled a little, and as she saw he was not mortally wounded, joined him in laughter. They lay there in the dew-soaked fescue, happy and wet, huddled together, and watched the stars and the lightning bugs go about their business while their clothes soaked up the night sweat of the earth. For the moment, the two of them cast aside whatever life had gone before, lay like orphan aliens abandoned on this strange new planet called love.

# CHAPTER XXII

"Hey bud, time to hit it." Eddy peeked in the doll room to rouse Munio. "Hey, you no good son of a gun. We gots to go, boy!"

Munio moved a little. "What time is it?" He grumbled under the big comforter.

"It's time to squat, that's what!" Eddy laughed at his own wittiness.

Munio peeked from under the covers. He noticed Eddy's forehead seemed to protrude just a little further than it had the day before, his face dotted with angry pus-filled eruptions. "You gonna make it?" Eddy asked.

"Yes, Eddy, I'm coming. Coffee is what I require. Is there any made?"

"Yeah, I got your coffee, Munio."

Munio rolled over and looked towards the door to see if Eddy was still standing by. His head ached, but still he smiled when envisioning Sandra and himself crashing to the ground. He stretched and sat up in the bed, yawning. "Good morning, girls," he said to the dolls.

"Here, bucko." Eddy rushed in with the cup of coffee. There was a frenetic energy about him.

"You're keyed up this morning, aren't you? I mean more than is customary, eh?" Munio said, and tipped the coffee cup to his lips.

"It's this shit. I hit up a new kind of decca that made me feel like I put on twenty pounds in an hour, man. I mean, I feel like I'm gonna fucking explode or something." Eddy bounced down on the edge of the bed.

"It's no feeling. You probably are going to if you don't watch out, Eddy." Munio pointed his finger at Eddy as he continued to sip at the coffee.

"I am retaining a lot of water. I need to lay off this shit in about another week."

"Another week, hah! That box in your drawer is going to burn a hole in your gut til you use every bit up. With this you act as if you are a child with a sack of candy." Munio sipped delicately from the coffee cup.

"I know. I just never had access to something like this. You're right. I am like a kid in a candy shop. I can't not do this stuff."

"Eddy, it is not candy, and you are not a child. You know you are looking weird as hell, don't you think?"

"I am?"

"Look in the mirror, man! Have you wondered why you have not needed sunglasses lately? It is because your damn forehead is providing shade. It is getting so big, sticking out so much." Munio illustrated with his hands and laughed, causing Eddy to do so. "Look at your face, all broken out. You are looking very scary, man."

"Yeah, but look at this shit. I'll show you scary." Eddy hit a chest shot, pivoted around, and hit a lat spread. "Is that hell or what, man?"

Munio's eyes widened as he looked at Eddy's body, and a cold chill ran through him. "Eddy, you need to be careful. I am telling you. You are not thinking right."

"Yeah, but look at me. I am bigger than a motherfucker. I can't believe it. I am gonna make everybody else in that show wish they had never showed up. I can't wait."

"You are going to do good. I know."

"Not if I don't get to the gym. Now, get up wild man, and let's get going. You ain't gonna eat, are you?"

"No, no, more coffee, cigarettes, maybe a toke or two. You want to have a toke before we go, man?"

"Yeah, I'll hit it a couple of times. I'm going to finish eating." Eddy disappeared from the doorway.

"Ok, I'm getting up right now." Munio stood, naked and dazed, scratched his chest, and tried to decide what to do next. He looked at his soaked and dirty clothes from the night before and smiled.

Munio walked in the kitchen and poured a cup of coffee. He stared out the kitchen window and assessed the weather of the day. The sun was shining, but the sky was full of clouds of all different colors and shapes. A strong, gusty wind blew and swept the clouds across the sky. Munio sipped the coffee, feeling the hot liquid warm him down to the core.

"What the hell did you do last night? You got in pretty late, didn't you?" Eddy mumbled through his mouth full of food. He ate like a starving dog, his mouth stuffed and barely chewing.

"Oh, I was seeing this older lady."

"Older lady, like what, your grandma?" Eddy laughed.

"No, no, she is fifty-eight."

"Fifty-eight? Shit, that's older than dirt! How old are you again?"

"Fifty."

"Well, did you nail her or what?"

"No, Eddy, I danced with he," Munio answered sharply.

"Damn. Danced? Why didn't you fuck her?"

"Hey, just shut up with being so crude about this lady. It is not becoming

158

to speak of a lady in this way." Munio turned away from the window to face Eddy.

"All right man, all right. Well, hell, is she pretty?"

"Not really."

"Rich?" Eddy laughed.

"She's a nice lady, ok? Nobody you would enjoy, I am sure."

"That's about right, I reckon. If I can't fuck it or eat it these days, the hell with it." Eddy laughed.

"You know you are turning into, your head is turning you into a bull! You know that?"

"To that I shall respond with my favorite verse, taken from the scriptures: 'Yea though I walk through the valley of death, I will fear no evil, for I am the biggest son of a bitch in the motherfucking valley'". Eddy let out a loud whoop and looked at Munio for approval.

"You are very funny, Eddy. You are so funny I forgot to laugh." Munio hid a smile and looked at Eddy.

"Look at this shit." Eddy jumped up from the table and pulled his shirt off and struck a chest pose. "Look at the striations on my delts, man, and I'm fat as a pig yet. When I diet down, I'll be so fucking ripped, won't nobody believe it. Dorian Yates himself will blow his brains out knowing the next man has arrived!" He let out another loud whoop that hurt Munio's ears.

"If you don't blow your own brains out first with those needles you have been sticking in you." Munio drained his coffee cup.

"I won't, bud. I won't. This is the best time of my life. I know now what people mean when they say loom larger than life. Can't nothing hurt me." Eddy looked back down at his plate and scraped the last bite of egg onto his fork. "Ok, five minutes, and I'm out of here, ok?"

"Aren't you going to digest all that?" Munio pointed at the empty plate.

"I will by the time we get over there. I got to stretch out and all."

Munio stepped out on the porch just in time for a big gust of wind to surprise him. It blew his hair in his face so that he couldn't even see. He laughed, pushed his hair away from his face, and breathed in the cool fresh wind. He looked forward to starting the gazebo today. After nearly setting his hair on fire, he finally got a cigarette lit. For a change, he sat on the steps instead of the glider. Goose bumps rose up under his clothes on his arms as another gust blew past. The day was unusually cool for late September.

Munio had never been through a fall season. In Belize, the weather was temperate all year long. He wondered if it snowed here, and then he wondered if he would be here when winter came around.

When he thought of Sandra, he changed the subject because at a distance, he was afraid of his feelings about her. When he saw her in his mind, he shivered. She seemed so big and strange and powerful, but when he removed all the pictures, he felt the soft warmth of her, which made him smile and get

chill bumps for a whole different reason.

The door slammed, and Eddy appeared on the porch, clad in blue tights that came to the knee, and a big black three quarter sleeve shirt with the neck cut out of it so that it hung off one shoulder. His crew cut had grown a little and his hair stuck out, spiked all over his head. He looked frightening to Munio because he had grown so big so fast, and he had such a vicious look on his face now.

He broke into a big boyish grin. "Am I bad or what?" He laughed and whooped. "Hey, you got that joint rolled?"

"Yes, I have it with me now."

"Let's smoke the motherfucker on the way."

"You ready?"

"I shore am, bud. I'm ready to grow, my man. I am ready to grow!" Eddy slapped Munio on the back as they went down the steps, nearly causing him to fall.

"Watch it, man. You don't know your own strength."

"I know it. You know last night I fucked this girl? I ain't sure, but I think I cracked a couple of her ribs hugging her. She was going to get an X-ray today. Can you believe that shit?" Eddy laughed proudly, and Munio shook his head.

Eddy pulled opened the door to the gym with all his might. Simon and the bulldog boy were just inside doing leg presses. They both nodded to Munio.

"How are you?" Simon said with a big grin to Munio.

"Fine, thank you."

Eddy strode right past them to a corner where he put down his workout bag and got out his belt and knee wraps.

"Eddy, just don't speak, man. You too good to speak to us now that you done got so big?" the bulldog boy called to Eddy across the gym while Simon and Munio laughed.

Eddy stood up and slowly walked over to the leg press where they were. His face had a vicious look on it. He got right in Jerry's face. "Hello, Jerry." Eddy punched him in the ribs playfully and broke out in laughter.

"You son of a bitch, what the hell are you on?" Jerry grinned at Eddy.

"You name it, and I'm on it. In fact, I'm on some shit I can't even name! I'm a big mother fucker though, ain't I?"

"Yes, you are, dawg." Eddy took off his sweatshirt and in his ragtop gave a quick posedown. "Jesus, Eddy, you're huge. When is your show? Jerry, are you looking at this?" Simon said to the bulldog boy.

"It's the end of October, man. Mr. Dixie, that's me, boys."

"Shit, if you don't win, I don't know who else would. I'm telling you the truth boy. You look huge," Simon said, and Eddy beamed.

"All right y'all I got to get to working these legs. Y'all give me a spot in

160

a while?" The bulldog boy replied. "Sure man, we'll be here." Eddy winked at Simon before parking in front of the squat rack. Munio followed him.

Working through the usual sets of warmups, Eddy looked strong. With each progressive set, his emotional intensity grew, until he was in a meditative rage by the time he reached the top weight for the day, which was six hundred and fifty pounds. As Eddy wrapped for the final set, Munio summoned Simon and Jerry to stand by as side spotters.

Munio screamed, "You go after this mother fucker! Show me something! Gut check right here! Get mad at it, Eddy! Light weight! Light weight! Stay tight! This is what you came here for!"

Simon and Jerry threw in loud insulting phrases too as they rocked nervously from one foot to another. They knew that if Eddy failed with such a heavy weight, it could be very dangerous for them also.

"Come on dawg! Let's fuck this weight, man! Come on Eddy! Focus, stay focused! You got this!" Jerry yelled.

Eddy's face was red before he even stood up. It was red with a rage that was exciting and disturbing to watch for all of them. He was a dangerous man, so revved up emotionally he could have snapped any of the three of his spotters like a twig.

"Showtime! Here we go, motherfucker!" Eddy put his hands on the bar, grunted and screamed a few times before putting his shoulders under it to prepare for liftoff. Finally, he took a great long breath and lifted the bar from the rack. What was left of the whites of his eyes disappeared, and was replaced with a deep blood red that nearly matched his scarlet face. He centered himself and took another breath. He descended slowly and exploded up out of the bottom position. His body shook under the weight, yet he completed rep after rep. Munio, Simon, and Jerry screamed at him through every phase of every rep, along with Eddy, who screamed non stop. The whole scene was a mass of screaming tension until, after ten unbelievable reps, Eddy racked the weight. As soon as he did, he fell to the floor, where he lay motionless.

"Good job, Eddy! Fucking hell set, man! Way to go dawg!" Simon , Jerry, and Munio continued to lavish praise on Eddy for the performance.

Finally, Eddy rolled over, displaying the blood that seeped out of the corner of his right eye and his left nostril. He looked up at Munio and grinned. He held out his hand, and Munio helped him to his feet.

"Shooooeee! I made it! I can't believe it, but I made it. If there is a fucking God, he was in that squat rack with me, son. I tell you what. I didn't feel nothing. It didn't feel heavy or nothing. God, I love steroids! I swear to Jesus, thank you Jimmy Ray Jones!" Eddy laughed and looked up at the ceiling with his hands held together in prayer.

# CHAPTER XXIII

Destiny was working out while watching talk shows. She did pushups, abdominal exercises, and numerous exercises with dumbells. Her cats were stationed somewhere around her to coach and supervise. The, the phone rang.

"Hello."

"May I please speak to Destiny Morris?"

"This is she."

"Miss Morris, my name is Lester McKnight. I am an attorney representing the Jones family, that is, Jimmy Ray Jones. You are familiar with them, are you not?"

She dropped onto the couch like a dead weight.

"Ye, yes, yes sir, I know them."

"Uh huh, how well did you know Jimmy Ray?"

"Well, uh, I knew him pretty good. We went out for a while."

"I see. Well, on behalf of Jimmy Ray, I would like to request your presence to discuss some matters. Could you be available tomorrow afternoon at three o'clock? Is that all right with you?"

"Uh, yeah, I reckon so. Yeah, I reckon. Where will it be at?"

"In my office, Miss Morris, that is at the corner of Oak and Benning Streets."

"Yeah, uh huh. All right, I'll, I'll be over there. Sir, like exactly what kind of matters are you talking about?"

"Miss Morris, it is really not appropriate to discuss this over the telephone."

"Really? Well, ok then."

"Thank you, ma'am, and I'll see you tomorrow."

"What was your name again?"

"Lester McKnight."

"Oh, ok then, ok."

Destiny put the phone in its cradle, and sat motionless except for vigorously gnawing her right index fingernail. The cats, one by one, slunk onto her lap to comfort her,. She began to cry, quietly at first, but the intensity amplified to full-blown sobs. Her sad vocalizations even caused the cats to scatter. When her tears diminished to sniffles, she got up and went into the bedroom, where she pulled out a brown paper bag from her night stand. In it was a ziploc baggy with some crank, an unopened syringe and a spoon. She shook as she mixed up a hit. She shook even more as she tried to load the syringe. It was all she could do to wrap the rubber hose around her arm. On the verge of popping the needle into her vein, she screamed and squirted the shot at the

bedroom wall. The thin liquid raced down the latex paint.

She ripped the hose off her arm, and stomped into the bathroom with the baggy of crank. She flushed it down the commode, and watched the baggy surf on the whirlpool until it spiraled down the drain. Her eyes again filled with tears. She walked back into the living room and sat quietly on the couch. The cats filed over, one by one.

"Well, y'all, mama might end up in the big house after all. I hope not, but I don't know. I'm just gonna go over there and see what that old man wants."

She worked out for another talk show's worth of time, before calling in sick to work, figuring in case it was her last day of freedom, she sure would not want to remember spending it at work.. In a hot bubble bath, she slugged down a bottle of champagne she had been saving for a special occasion that got her good and giddy and took her mind off tomorrow's mystery meeting. Wrapped up in a turquoise terry cloth robe and with her hair turbanized in a red towel, she dialed the phone.

"Hello?"

"Eddy?"

"Yeah, Destiny?"

"Hey, what's happening?"

"Aw, I just got back from training. What you up to? Ain't you got to work today?"

"Aw, I called in sick." Destiny laughed.

"You sound about sick. What's the matter with you, girl?"

"Nothing, I just felt like fucking off, you know?"

"Yeah, well, I wish I could."

"Well, why don't you start today? Why don't you come on over, and we'll get drunk and fuck off. Who knows, maybe we'll even fuck." She laughed again.

"Well now, are you drunk? Sheesh, you ain't wanted to fuck me in a coon's age." Eddy laughed and scratched his crotch.

"Hey baby, maybe this is your lucky day." She giggled. "Come on, Eddy. I haven't seen you in a way long time."

"Hmmm. I was supposed to work later, but I could probably get somebody to cover for me. What the hell. I'll be there. You just hold that thought, and open another bottle or keg of whatever the fuck you been drinking."

Destiny giggled. "All right Eddy, I'll be here."

# CHAPTER XXIV

Munio had lunch with Eddy after the workout and then hurried over to Sandra's to start work on the gazebo. Sandra heard his old truck pull up and raced to the door to meet him. They embraced briefly.

"I'm so glad to see you, Munio. This is all so exciting, the gazebo and everything," Sandra said. "I can't wait til this is finished. I just know it will look great."

"Yes, it will be a spectacular project, and I, too, am glad to see you, by the way. Let me get one thing straight right now, and hear me well, Sandra." Munio pointed a stern finger at Sandra. "I must concentrate on my work. I must have no distractions, at least not at first until I get this gazebo off the ground and organized. Do you understand me, Miss?"

She nodded and as much of a girlish grin as she could manage settled across her large rough face. "Very well, Munio. I respect that in a man. You go right on about your work as if I am not even here."

"That is good. I am glad you see things my way. With that, I will begin." Munio bowed to her and winked. He cranked the truck up, opened the gates and drove past them out to the gazebo site.

Munio moved with the deftness of a fireman. He set up his equipment and strapped around his waist a double-pouch nail apron that was deep tan and soft as a chamois cloth from age. From his truck, he pulled a fine set of well-worn tools stored in a wooden box with cubbyholes custom tailored to fit each item. Within minutes, he constructed a pair of sturdy sawhorses.

Through the afternoon he worked, without a break, though he always had an open beer from which he sipped periodically.

Sandra sat at the kitchen table and watched him work. For her, it was a soft porn movie in progress as she grew more and more aroused observing topless Munio's beautiful brown torso. His cutoff jeans and nail apron hung below his navel, exposing a thick trail of soft black hairs that led to his groin. His wild hair shone like a raven's wing in the bright sun. Sandra's view moved into soft focus with the inevitable sunset. Finally, all she could clearly see was the trail of smoke wafting from the cigarette hanging from Munio's lips.

Sandra grew impatient to be in Munio's company and started to pace the kitchen floor. Every few seconds she stared out the door, thinking surely he would be trudging up any minute. The lap dogs marched right along with her, wondering if she had noticed that it was way past their supper time.

Munio opened his small cooler, removed an icy new beer, sat on a concrete block and stared at the gazebo site. He felt pleased with the day's progress and had enjoyed himself immensely. The solitude, the sun, the work with his hands all brought on a solid feeling of serenity. Munio thumped the final cigarette butt of the day in a bright orange arc across the darkening lawn, pulled on his white T-shirt, and stepped inside the sliding glass door to the sweating and far from serene Sandra. Sandra dabbed at her forehead with a paper towel and struck a nonchalant pose as Munio stepped inside the room.

"Oh, finished already?"

"Yes, the darkness has won for today."

"The time sure did fly. I've been so busy in here. Ah, how did it go?"

"Very good. The surface of the lawn is quite level, which will make setting the footing not so difficult. Today, I sawed all the lumber for the substructure, so tomorrow, the real building will begin."

"Well, have a seat, won't you? Beer? You need a fresh beer?"

"In a minute, I still have some, thank you."

"Would you like to stay and have dinner with me?"

"Sure, I would, and what will you cook?"

Sandra's heart fluttered with delight that he would be staying. She opened the freezer door and then the refrigerator. "I can throw some burgers on the grill. Does that sound good?"

"That is fine, yes."

"I have got to feed these dogs before they gnaw my ankles off." She laughed. "Aren't you hungry babies? Mama has been neglecting you, hasn't she? Yes, she has."

Munio smiled at her sweetness with the dogs. "How long have you had those dogs?"

"The little Pomeranian is ten years old. The Yorkie is six, and the Shih Tzu is five. I got him the day I got home from the hospital after my surgery." She chuckled in her deep voice. "I told my friend who brought me home that I was going to catch a man right away, and so little Jacky here is the guy, I'm afraid."

Munio laughed out loud. "You could have done worse. Just look how bad your taste is now." He held his arms open wide.

Sandra sashayed over to Munio, leaned over, and buried his face in her large breasts as she hugged him.

"You are going to kill me with those tits, Sandra. Suffocate me." They both laughed, and Sandra blushed.

"I know, they're huge, my torpedo tits, but I didn't know what to get. I started to just use socks, but the doctor advised against it. Something about the authenticity is important, but I don't feel I have breasts really. I feel I have four tubes of caulk pumped into my chest. I almost would have them removed if I have the nerve."

"Do they itch or anything?" Munio asked innocently.

"No honey, they just, you know." Sandra put her hands on them and screwed up her face. "They are just always there, always huge. That should be the name of my autobiography, 'Always there, always huge.'" She laughed at herself. "Somehow, in the back of my mind, I thought if I became a woman I would look like Ellen Burstyn. I would be beautiful. I was a nice looking man, distinguished anyway, and I just thought I would look, I would look pretty as a woman, you see." She chuckled. "But that did not quite happen. I am just your ordinary six foot two grandmotherly type." They both laughed.

"What about if you got a blonde wig?" Munio suggested, causing them to both laugh again.

"I would look like Hulk Hogan or worse."

"Black, maybe, you could get a long slinky black wig."

Sandra waved her hands. "No, no. Elvira on steroids. I don't think so."

"Who's Elvira?"

"This tv slut that introduces horror movies."

"Oh."

"Black, though." She thought aloud. "I might try black. I actually tried it at first, but I didn't want to look like one of those older women who didn't act their age. Maybe I could handle it now. I'm going to turn the grill on and get these things started." She held up the plate of burger patties.

After starting dinner, she got a beer from the fridge and sat down with Munio at the table. "So you say Eddy is a bodybuilder?"

Munio laughed, "Oh yes, he's an animal. He's ripped. He's huge. Boy, you should have seen him today. It was a leg day, very dramatic."

Sandra listened intently and pushed her glasses up on her nose. "Really? Why are leg days different than arm days?"

"Well, squats mainly, I suppose. Do you know what squats are?" Sandra nodded. "Today, for instance, Eddy did squats with six hundred and fifty pounds."

"No! My word!" Sandra's jaw dropped. "How can a person, a normal human do such a thing?"

"Believe me, miss, this man is not normal, not now anyway."

"What do you mean?"

"Lots of steroids make him so strong."

"Is that right? Would he not be strong without them?"

"He would not be that strong, no."

"Isn't that cheating?"

"Not in the bodybuilding arena. It is required."

"Now, this is not the kind of lifting you did in the Olympics, is it?"

"No, no, it is not. What I did was the snatch, the clean and jerk and the press, Olympic lifting."

"I remember what those are. I used to watch that on tv. They never seem to have that on anymore. I wonder why?"

"It is a dying sport. It is too hard, and it is not flashy enough, you know. These days people only know about the bench press. When you say you lift weights, people always ask how much can you bench press? Nobody does the overhead lifts anymore. Also, most Olympic lifters don't look real built up. People like to look big these days, cut up, muscle definition."

"You look defined."

"Well, I am unusual," he said proudly, and jutted out his chest in jest.

"You sure are, honey pie. You sure are that." She leaned over him as she got up to turn the burgers, kissed him quickly on the lips, which sent a surge of heat coursing through them both.

# CHAPTER XXV

"Hey there darlin.'" Destiny, in a thin bright red cotton robe that came just above her knee, greeted Eddy.

Eddy pretended to fall backwards, inspiring Destiny to laugh, a little lazy drunken laugh. "Hey back to you, girl. What are you doing?"

"You, I reckon." She laughed out loud, and Eddy walked on in to her living room.

Loud ZZ Top played. A yellow candle flickered on top of the stereo cabinet, and a thin stick of incense produced an inordinate amount of smoke. Destiny motioned for Eddy to sit beside her on the couch.

"What you want to drink?"

"Shit, I don't know. I ain't really supposed to be drinking right now with training and all, you know. I don't know. If I was going to have one drink that could get me drunk what would it be?" he said, thinking out loud.

"Golden grain. That's definitely the one, and I just happen to have a few hits of it. You want it mixed with something?"

"Uh, damn, I ain't supposed to drink no juice or nothing either. I know, naw. Fuck it, I'll drink the son of a bitch straight." He laughed.

"Straight? Shit boy, that'll burn the hair right off your tonsils. Hell, it'll probably take them tonsils right on down with it to that hell hole stomach of yours." They both laughed in tones that harmonized. "You still got your tonsils?"

"I reckon I do."

"All right studly, let me go get that bottle." Eddy watched her walk out of the room He looked around and squeezed his balls while she was gone.

She returned with a quart bottle of crystal clear liquid. She filled a shot glass that had the head of a longhorn cow and "Texas" printed on it, the one souvenir she had bought on the return phase of her aborted exodus. The alcohol made a little gurgling sound as she tipped the bottle up. He picked the glass up and held it up towards her for a toast.

"Here's to ya, baby."

"Here's to you, Eddy." Eddy turned up the shot glass and only got only half down before he gagged. "God all mighty damn! Fuck a goddamn duck! Jesus Christ, that shit is strong! Like drinking mother fucking paint thinner, right there!" Destiny nearly choked on her beer, laughing hysterically at Eddy, who grabbed his throat like a man betrayed by his drink. "Here I go again! Bombs away!" He tipped the tiny glass, and this time, finished every drop. "There we go. Shooooeee! That's some nasty shit!"

"You want another one?" Destiny held up the bottle in play.

"Are you fucking crazy! No honey, I believe that one'll do me. That right

there'll get my ass drunk, pure as I've been lately."

"Pure, ha! That's a laugh." Destiny chuckled. "You're about as pure as swamp water, boy."

Eddy laughed. "I ain't had a drink in a while. I'll have you know."

"If you're so pure, how come there's horns peeking out the top of your head? Looks like you ain't been running short of the juice."

"That is a fact. I hadn't talked to you, but you know what Lynette did? She gave me all Jimmy Ray's stash. All of it, and honey, it was a gold mine. Squatted six fifty today like it was nothing."

"Damn, Eddy. Well, I must say you are looking freaky. You look like Frankenstein's damn love child!" She moved closer to him on the couch. "Look here at this forehead of yours. If it pokes out much further, you won't need no visor when you're out in the sun. You'll have a built-in ledge." She laughed and rubbed her hand over his stiff blond crew cut. "I like your hair like this. You glad you got it cut?"

"Yes, lord, I never realized how much of a hassle it was til I cut the shit off."

"I know. It takes a lot of work to deal with long old hair." Destiny scooted way close to Eddy and put her arm around his neck. "What else you got that's been growing, honey?"

Eddy smiled. "You're fixing to find out." He laughed and kissed her deeply. They stayed lip locked for nearly a minute before breaking apart with a hearty smack.

"It has sure been a while since we did this, hasn't it?" Destiny smiled nervously at Eddy.

"Yeah, it has. Why did we break up? I can't remember."

"You kept being an asshole probably."

"Me? I ain't ever been nothing but sweet to you, baby."

"Uh huh, and cows fly too." She swatted him on the arm.

"Well, I'm fixing to be sweet to you right now." He slipped his arm around her waist and pulled her onto his lap.

Her robe came undone. Eddy looked her body up and down, smiled, and groaned with anticipation as he lowered his head to her right breast. Destiny did a little groaning of her own as Eddy's warm mouth sucked hard on her nipple. She felt his dick grow hard through his pants as she straddled him. Eddy reached up under the red robe and palmed each of her buttocks in his big hands. She felt his rough calluses on her soft skin, but the strength of his hands turned her on.

He moved his mouth over to her left breast, and gave it the treatment for a bit, then raised his head to kiss her again. Their mouths met roughly, and Eddy jammed his tongue down Destiny's throat.

The passion between them grew like some ancient dragon that had been awakened. Its movements were jerky at first as it looked around to discover

168

where it was, but after only a few steps, its memory returned to remind itself of the great power it possessed. The dragon smiled as it took in a great breath and exhaled a long blast of red and orange flames.

Both sounded off with short, anxious and ferocious vocalizations of feral love. They moved from the couch onto the floor, where Eddy topped and entered Destiny. On the carpet, they did a slow horizontal shuffle across the living room. With each furious and powerful stroke Eddy delivered, the pair scooted an inch or two in the direction of Destiny's head. The cats curiously watched on, exchanging glances. They followed the slow parade until the journey came to an end when Eddy and Destiny climaxed together in a fine explosion, just as they reached the linoleum in the kitchen. When they got their bearings, they laughed at the view of the stove and the entourage of cats that gathered around them.

"Uh, what was it you needed out of the kitchen, darlin'?" Eddy inquired.

"Don't know, but while we're here might as well fix us up another drink, don't ya reckon?" They laughed.

"What the fucking hell. I got pretty good mileage out of that first shot. I reckon if I was to drink another one we could fuck all the way out to the driveway," Eddy declared.

"Hell!" She reached under herself and rubbed her butt and gave a scrunched-up face. "I got rug burns on my damn back now! I'm ready to get my ass up off this Scotchguard. Fun as it was and all." She smacked Eddy on the mouth and hopped to her feet.

Eddy lay there on the floor, dragging his body so he could watch her move around. He felt the urge to pee and got up. Without a word, he walked into the bathroom and raised the toilet lid. It made a "clink" sound as it hit the edge of the porcelain tank.

"You put that lid down when you finish, boy!" Destiny hollered from the kitchen. Eddy smiled and looked down into the bowl as the stream started. His blood raced as the clear water turned pink as ribbons of blood-filled urine hit the bowl. Although he felt afraid, he immediately channeled it into denial and flushed the commode. He splashed his face with water and shuddered from the coldness. Thoughts ran through his mind about what to do. There was no pain, yet he feared something was very wrong.

"What are you doin' in there? Did ya fall in?"

"I'm comin'. I'm comin'."

He sat down on the couch and pulled her close to him. He kissed her stomach and bit her navel.

Destiny giggled and slapped him on the shoulder.

"Hey, wait a minute. I need another drink first."

"Drink? You damn alkie. You're as bad as that old Munio. That man's always drinking."

"I ain't no alkie. Besides, you're a damn drug addict your own self."

"I ain't done it. You don't see me running up speed."

"No, you just run up liquefied bulls' balls or monkey glands and weird ass shit like that."

"Yeah, but I'm doing it for a reason. I mean, I'm an athlete. I work hard. At least I don't do drugs just for the sake of getting fucked up."

"You're crazy as you look if you don't think you're a drug addict just as bad as I am, I mean, used to be. I don't hardly do much no more." She repelled him and stood, hands on her hips. She pushed her long brown hair behind her ears.

"You just come here, and let's enjoy this afternoon some more. What do you say?"

She shook her head, looked away from him, and took a great big breath. She let it out with a sigh. "All right Eddy, but I hope you're keeping up with this, this shit you're on. You know it can kill you dead as heroin, speed, or anything else. You know that, don't you?"

"No, it can't. Steroids ain't like none of them drugs, Destiny. I keep trying to tell you. It's natural, in a way. I mean, it's just adding to what I was born with. I'm a man, right? I was born with all these male hormones and growth hormone too. So, it's like taking vitamins really."

"Vitamins, ha! Since when does a goddamn vitamin make your damn ears grow, or did you notice Eddy that your forehead is starting to stick out like a damn monkey's? You go right on ahead and do that shit, but you're conning yourself if you think it's good, for you because it ain't!"

"Are you through?" Eddy grinned a boyish grin, and she fell for it, smiling back.

"I reckon. You want another shot of golden grain?"

"Yeah, I reckon."

# CHAPTER XXVI

Promptly at three p.m., Destiny opened the door to Lester McKnight's office. The receptionist, a thirtyish blonde in a mint green polyester dress, greeted her.

"Mr. McKnight will be with you in a few minutes. Could I get you some coffee or a glass of iced tea, Miss Morris?"

Destiny smiled and shook her head. "No, thank you. I'm fine."

"Glad to see it cooling off?" the receptionist said like a ventriloquist, as she typed at breakneck speed. Destiny, who had had her eyes on the woman, never saw her lips move.

"Yeah, uh huh." She bit the index fingernail on her right hand. What was this guy going to do, she worried. Should she play dumb or insane? Maybe

170

Lynette saw her leave that day and told this guy about it.

"Miss Morris?" Destiny didn't hear the receptionist because she was so immersed in her fantasies of doom. "Miss Morris?" she said again.

"Oh, I'm sorry. What did you say?" Destiny blushed and smiled at the woman.

"He'll see you now." She smiled politely at Destiny, and held her arm out towards his office.

Lester McKnight was bald, except for a long wisp of brownish-gray he hair combed all the way to the front. He swept the cluster off to the side to give him and no one else the illusion he had a full head of hair. Black, horn-rimmed frames held thick lenses which magnified his blue-gray eyes. His suit exactly matched his hair and a light sprinkling of dandruff powdered the shoulders. The grayish skin of his face tightened into many wrinkles as he offered Destiny a smile and his hand to shake.

"Miss Morris, I am Lester McKnight. So good of you to come. Won't you sit down please?"

"Thank you." Destiny licked her lips and crossed her legs at the knee.

He fumbled through a stack of papers in a manila file folder. "Ah, yes, here we go." He squinted as he read over a page, and then gravely began. "Miss Morris, it seems there is some business I must clear up for Jimmy Ray Jones. You say you were close to the man?"

"Well, we had our moments, yessir."

"Well, Miss Morris, you must have had some very fine moments, because Mr. Jones saw fit to include you in his last will and testament. Does this surprise you at all?" He looked over his glasses for a reply.

Destiny smiled as she thought, "Boy does it!", but answered, "I guess so, because I didn't really think he had much to leave nobody, you know?"

Lester McKnight smiled and said, "Well, he didn't have much living, but after he died, he became worth a whole lot more."

"How's that?" Destiny seemed puzzled.

"Jimmy Ray Jones had a $100,000 life insurance policy that came to term upon his death from natural causes, and Miss Morris, he listed you as the sole benefactor of that policy."

Destiny felt a rush of hot blood and a cold chill all at once and almost peed in her pants. She stood right up involuntarily. "He did what?"

Lester McKnight smiled a quick formal smile. "Miss Morris, you have just inherited $100,000." He smiled again as he watched her jaw drop open.

She fell back into her chair stunned. A great flood of tears sprang from her eyes, and she sobbed for reasons Lester McKnight knew nothing about.

He shifted in his seat uncomfortably. "Miss Morris?" There was no reply. "Miss Morris?" Destiny looked over at him. "Are you all right? Do you need me to call somebody? Could I get you--let me get you--." He pushed his intercom button. "Miss Lee, will you bring Miss Morris a glass of water, please?"

He spoke with the grandest of slow rolling southern drawls.

"Right away, Mr. McKnight." The receptionist replied crisply.

"I'm ok." Destiny spoke in a soft high voice between sniffles.

"Uh, ma'am, I need you to sign a few documents if you would." He slid several pages across the desk to her. "Right here on this line, and on the 'x' on the subsequent pages, please."

"Ok." She picked up the pen that lay on top of the pages and signed them. "Now what happens?"

"Well, it will take approximately a month for processing, but the insurance company will mail you a check. Let me make sure I have your address correct. Let's see. 307 Choctaw St., ah, Rosedale, and the zip would be 30172?" Destiny nodded.

He picked up the papers and examined them to make sure she had signed them properly. "Miss Morris, I know this is a difficult time for you with the loss of your good friend, but I am sure in time you will be at peace with everything and all. I do appreciate your cooperation, and that's everything I need." He smiled at her, stood, and extended his hand across the desk.

Destiny stood and shook his hand, all the while chattering to herself. "Difficult time, my ass! I hated that bastard, and I hope he is watching this from hell. 'Preciate my cooperation? Ha! Yeah, it was a whole lot of hassle to come down here and sign up for this fucking free money. My life is set, Gomer."

"Good day, Miss Morris, and good luck."

"Same to you, ah, I'm sorry, I forgot your name."

"Lester McKnight, ma'am."

"Mr. McKnight, thanks a lot." Destiny nodded to the receptionist.

She could hardly keep from jumping up in the air and letting out a serious whoop as she walked down the sidewalk to her car. She managed to suppress her glee and opted instead to stop by the liquor store for a case of champagne. Her old car released a gray trail of smoke that she noticed in her rear view mirror as she pulled away. An ear to ear grin spread across her face as she thought about owning a new car for the first time in her life.

The cats greeted her and stood on the furniture to be more accessible to petting. With her arms full of the champagne, all they got was verbal love.

"Hey everybody! Guess what? We're rich! We are motherfucking, kiss my ass rich, kids! Tonight, we are going to celebrate." She dropped the case on the kitchen counter and loaded the bottles into the refrigerator.

With the toe of one foot, she kicked off the low black pump on her other foot, sending it sailing ten feet across the room. She laughed and repeated the procedure with the other shoe. If there was one thing Destiny believed in, it was wearing comfortable clothing around the house. She unzipped her dress, donned a size triple X T-shirt from the Dixie Ironworks that Eddy had given her years ago, and felt instantly wonderful.

Curled up on the sofa, she dialed her sister's number, but after it rang only a couple of times, she pushed the cut-off button. Her mouth curled up in confusion; she simultaneously wanted to tell everybody she knew, and nobody at all. She continued her internal dialogue, and after a minute, called Eddy at the bar.

"Pee Wee's," Eddy answered.

Destiny disguised her voice and tried not to laugh. "Are you Pee Wee?"

"No ma'am, I'm not. He'll be in tomorrow about nine."

"Well, do they call him that because, well, you know, because, he's got a pee wee, you know what?"

Eddy laughed, "I'm not sure, mam. I ain't never looked at it to tell you the truth."

Destiny cracked up. "Hey, it's me. Did you know it was me?"

"No, not really. What are you doing?"

"Oh nothing. What you doing?"

"Nothing, ain't a damn thing going on in here."

"You want to come over tonight when you get off?"

"You ain't trying to get us back together again, are you, darlin'?"

"What if I am?"

"I don't know. All I can think about right now is that Mr. Dixie Contest."

"Where is that thing gonna be?"

"It's in Atlanta. You ought to go with us."

"Who's us?"

"Me and Munio."

"So, he's still hanging around and all?"

"Yeah, he's ok. He's helped me a lot in my workouts. He makes me use good technique, no cheating. He's great."

"Well, I just might want to go. So, are you going to come over tonight?"

"I can't do no drinking. Seriously, I can tell you that right now. Munio, now, can do some drinking. Y'all ought to link up on the drinking, for real. Ain't you got to go to work tomorrow?"

"Yeah, but I can handle it. I got stamina," she said, in a feigned baritone voice. She could not decide whether or not to tell Eddy about her fortune. She wanted to tell him in person. "I just want somebody to party with tonight, you know? You think Munio would come over?"

"Hell, yeah! If you've got some liquor you want drunk, he's the man to do it. Call him up. He ain't got too much to do. Although I swear, for a man that's only been in town a few weeks, that son of a bitch knows half the fucking town."

"Well, maybe I will call him, but you can come over too when you get off."

"I'll call you. It's going to be twelve or one, and I do have to train early. I

173

probably won't."

"Ok then, I'll talk at you later."

Destiny walked over to the refrigerator and put several bottles of the chilling champagne in the freezer to hasten the start of the party. All the cats followed her, slithering in and out between her ankles, and meowed for dinner.

"Ok y'all, don't grovel. Mama's gonna feed you. Y'all want some champagne, you rich little kitties? Y'all gonna be fat cats now, uh huh. Yes you is." She dumped two cans of food on their community plate and set it on the floor. The four cats looked like the June Taylor dancers from above, spaced evenly all around the plate. Their little chewing and purring sounds all mixed together made her smile as she picked up the phone and dialed.

"Hello?" Munio said in his rich sweet accent.

"Munio, hey, this is Destiny? Remember me? I took your kitty."

"Oh yes, yes, hello. Eddy is not-"

"I ain't calling Eddy. I'm calling you."

"Really? Oh, well, what can I do for you?"

"I was just talking to Eddy, and he said I might could talk you into drinking some champagne. I kind of got a good deal on a case, and I just feel like celebrating. You interested?"

Munio smiled. "Yes, sure, I could help you with that. Do you live far from Eddy's?"

"Naw, you just go like you're going to the gym. Actually, it is the second street past the gym on the left. It's Choctaw St., and it's the first house on the left at the second corner, 307."

"Ok, I got it. Thank you for the invitation, and I will see you very soon. Should I bring you anything?"

"You could bring a joint of that kick ass weed you had the other night."

"Oh, ok, I will."

An hour later Munio knocked on the door. Destiny removed the champagne from the freezer and trotted to the door.

"Hey," she smiled, and motioned with her head, her brown hair swinging. "Come on in."

Munio had just washed his hair, and tied it back with a rubber band. His thin mustache looked lonely on his face.

"Wow! You look different without that hair flying."

"Yeah," he laughed softly. "I guess so. I just washed it."

"Eddy didn't pull you in on that haircut kick, I reckon?"

"No, not me. I always have long hair."

"It looks great, I think. I have always liked long hair on men. I like mine, too, although it is a bother to keep up with. Let me get us some champagne, boy." She slapped him on the shoulder as she walked by.

Munio sat down in a wooden rocking chair. All the cats watched him. He

spotted his ex little kitty and called to him. "Hey boy, how are you, little kitty?" The kitten came forward right away and rubbed against his jeans.

Destiny came in with a bottle and two glasses, Bama jelly jars that had completed their metamorphoses. "Sorry, I ain't got no good glasses for this, but you know, I reckon we can choke it down in these. You want Bugs or Daffy?"

Munio laughed. "I will be Daffy because I am Daffy tonight, and I expect I will get daffier as this night moves forward."

"If we drink that whole case, we will. I don't think I have ever drunk a case of champagne with just one person. I think I might have drunk three bottles by myself though."

"That's pretty good. I think I have done that, about that anyway."

"Well, cheers." Destiny aimed her glass towards Munio.

Munio smiled, "Yes, thank you. Cheers to you. Mind if I smoke a cigarette?"

"Hell no, this ain't no smoke free zone here. Go right ahead. In fact, I'll have one with you if you don't mind. I never have smoked much, but I like to when I drink sometimes."

Munio extended the pack to her, and she pulled one out. He struck a match and held it for her.

"Why thank you, Munio. How have you been getting along in this old redneck town?"

"All right really. I haven't gotten out too much. I mostly help Eddy. Although now I have a job building a gazebo for a lady."

"A gazebo? Is that like a porch or something?"

"Well, in a way. This one is like a little porch way out in her back yard."

"Is that fun to do?"

"Yes, it is. Since I have not done any carpentry work in some time, I am enjoying this a lot."

"Well, old Eddy's sure shaping up, ain't he?" She snorted a laugh, and rolled her eyes at Munio.

He responded with a smile. "Yes, he is. He is turning into a beast."

"Hey, did you say hello to Jose?"

"Who is that?" Munio asked.

"Jose, your ex kitty. See him? He's over there."

"Yes, I did. Jose, huh?"

"Yeah, his first name is No Way."

Munio laughed out loud. "It's good you took him." He turned his glass up and finished it.

"Thirsty boy, are we? Here you go." She poured him another. Munio nodded.

"How did you come about getting this job? Eddy said you've met half the fucking town." She laughed.

"Through this other lady I knew, I met her. I helped the other lady teach a dance class."

"A dance class? What kind of dance class? You are just multifucking talented, aren't you?"

Munio laughed, "Latin dances. Ballroom type of dances. It was over at the country club that I helped with the class."

"The country club? Damn, that old hooty place? I bet they loved you over there."

"Why do you say that?"

"I was just kidding. They are seriously white over there. I wouldn't have thought they would like no immigrant working with them."

"I think they liked me. They seemed to. It was just the teacher didn't like me."

"How come?"

"Aw, she thinks I drink too much or something ridiculous like that." He waved his hands in disgust and shook his head.

"I'll drink to that!" She laughed. "I hope I drink too much all night long. I'm celebrating."

"What is it you celebrate?"

"I'm scared to tell. I'm scared it will go away."

"Are you in love?"

"I'm in love with the world tonight, Munio. Most days I hate it. I hate my life. I hate this town. Tonight though, I like it! I like it a lot!"

"Ready to smoke a number?" he asked.

"Yeah, fire it up."

"Ok, I have to roll it first." He pulled out a baggie of reefer and a pack of rolling papers from his blue jean jacket.

Destiny returned with a new bottle, sat and quietly watched Munio's handiwork as she twisted and turned the cork on the bottle until it popped harmlessly into the small towel she had placed over it. If Munio had rolled one joint, he had rolled thousands. She watched his pretty brown hands as they worked. His fingers were long, like spider legs, and his dexterity captivated Destiny. Finally, he held the cigarette to his lips, licked the glue on the seam of the paper and sealed it neatly.

"Here you go, Miss celebrating lady." He struck a match as she stuck the joint in her mouth.

"Have you ever been married?" Munio asked Destiny.

"I used to have a fiancée. Son of a bitch used to beat me up and everything." Destiny looked at the carpet as she spoke.

"What did you finally do?" Munio looked over at her.

Destiny smiled a secret smile and then looked up at Munio. "I broke up with him, that's what. I, uh, believe he's left the state." She giggled. "I shouldn't laugh."

"Why?"

"Well, because he died."

"Gee, that's too bad."

"No, it ain't. It's good. It's real good news."

"Why?"

Destiny said nothing for a good half a minute, and then jumped up from the couch, yelling so loud the cats scattered, "Cause the motherfucker left me a hundred thousand dollars in his motherfucking will, that's why! Yeeee Haaa! That is my big celebration reason. I am fucking rich."

"Wow." Munio was flabbergasted. "Wow."

"Yep, yep, I know it. It's something, ain't it?" Destiny grinned, nodded her head, and watched Munio's astonishment.

"One hundred thousand dollars?"

"That's what the man said. I talked to him today, the lawyer and all. Jimmy Ray's lawyer."

"Is this the Jimmy Ray Jones that Eddy knew?"

"Yeah, sure is."

"He died just a little while ago?"

"Uh huh."

"They said he died of a heart attack. Is that right?"

Destiny almost swallowed the joint. "Well, I wouldn't be a bit surprised."

"Here." Destiny handed the joint to him. "I'm getting another bottle. I think I'm starting to get a buzz. How about you?"

"Maybe I am. What will you do with the money? Maybe you should make some investment to make that money grow." Munio winced as the smoke drifted into his eye. He took the last possible puff before the cotton wadding began to burn.

"I'm thinking maybe I ought to turn over a bunch of coke or speed or something. Hey, why don't you get some of your friends down in Belize to ship me some reefer?"

"That is not entirely impossible," Munio said coolly.

"No shit? Is that easy to do? Have you ever brought any up here?" Destiny's eyes grew large, excited by this prospect.

"I brought this, didn't I?" He held up the baggy of rich brown weed.

"Let me look at that shit. Do you mind?" Destiny said. She opened the baggie and stuck her nose inside. She inhaled deep and hard, and because she exerted too much snorting power, induced at least a thimbleful of pot to race into her nostrils. She jerked the bag away from her face, simultaneously choking and laughing at her stunt.

Munio broke into hysterics as well and said. "Oh, you would be a cool drug smuggler with that nose of yours. You have the power like an anteater!" They both laughed as Destiny finally cleared her nose of debris.

"I got to pee again. Actually, I got to finish peeing. I done started in my pants. God, that was funny." Destiny got up still giggling. She returned with an unopened bottle in each hand. "All right Munio, let's get serious. I think we ought to have a chugging contest that will be followed by a burping contest. What do you say?" she slurred.

"All right, you must know in advance that I have never been beaten in this form of competition before."

"All right, now, get ready." Both of them sat poised, ready to spring into action. "Get set." Destiny paused "Wa, wa, wait. You know what? Why don't we go out on the carport to do this? We gonna get this shit everywhere. I just know it. We're probably gonna puke too! Come on." She got up and led him out the side door in the kitchen that opened up onto the carport. "Ok now. You ready?"

"Yes, ready!" Munio stood with knees bent and in a braced stance.

"All right, this is the real thing now. On your mark, get set," she spoke the words slowly, "Go!"

They looked like hungry, orphaned lambs sucking at those big green bottles, with the overflow streaming down both sides of their faces. Amazingly, neither relented as the bottles emptied. As the thirty second mark passed, Destiny's empty bottle sprang from her lips with a big pop. Munio's was not half a second behind, but still, he had lost. They moved into the burping phase of the competition. Munio let out a three second display that sounded like a tugboat horn.

"Damn, Munio! That was a good one! You about blew my head off. Like the, what do they call it after an atomic bomb, after blast or aftermath? Hell, I can't remember, but something. Listen to this, though." She let out a good loud one, but it was more of a short blast, a round sound, as opposed to the lengthy display Munio had demonstrated.

The two of them continued the concert until the gas ran out. It was then they realized how much drunker the contest had left them. Night had fallen by the time they went back in the house.

"Wheeew, boy! Are you as wasted as I am? That was fucking work!" Destiny walked slowly through the kitchen. "You want another drink?" She chuckled as she said it.

"I hate to say it, but I think I'll hold off a couple of minutes." He snorted a laugh and coughed. "I think I inflicted internal damage on that one."

"Yeah, really, our livers are probably in shock. Hell, my liver's probably the size of a basketball as it is."

After a short recess, Destiny dutifully retrieved another bottle from the refrigerator. "Here we go, Munio. We have to be strong, persevere. There's only four more bottles. You think we can make it?"

"Yes, I think we can." He snickered. "Destiny. How did you come to have such a name?"

"My mama said that when they come out of doing the pregnancy test at the doctor's, that was the first thing my daddy said after she said, Oh my god, I'm pregnant! He said I reckon it's destiny. So, she said I reckon you're right, and that's the story."

Finally, as the last bottle spilled down their tired throats, Destiny floated to her bed after she giving Munio a blanket and pillow for the couch.

# CHAPTER XXVII

Maybe he heard Eddy cussing across town when he saw Munio had not come home in time to go to the gym for the morning workout, or maybe Munio had finally programmed seven a.m. into his internal clock for rising, but whatever the case, Munio's drunken eyes sprang open at seven. When he sat up on the edge of the couch, his head spun around him like some other planet. He realized he had to pee in a bad way and padded to the bathroom.

Destiny, not used to having people in the house, sat bolt upright when she heard the long stream of water hit the pool in the toilet bowl. Her head was spinning too, but she did have the sense to remember Munio's presence. In relief, she flopped back down in the covers. She listened to his movements, but did not want to talk to him just yet. Jose jumped up on the bed to greet her, and she happily petted him.

Munio pulled on his clothes and left. The air outside was cool and wet. A thick fog hung low, but was in motion southbound, driven by a steady breeze. His truck windows were coated thoroughly with morning dew. With a dirty T-shirt he took out of the bed of his truck, he wiped down the windows. The cloth and glass and dew all in motion sounded like the loud squeals of large hungry baby birds.

Eddy was ready to walk out the door when Munio pulled in the driveway. Munio strode up the porch steps, thumping his cigarette butt on the lawn.

"Hey, I thought you was going to stand me up." Eddy smiled at Munio. "You know I do wish you would bother to call to let me know what's going on with you so I won't waste time wondering if you're coming or not."

Munio stood close in front of Eddy. "Eddy, have I stood you up yet?"

"You was late once."

"Late? So what? I say I will be here. I will be here. My word." He paused. "I am a man of my word. I will do what I say. All right?"

"Ok, ok." Eddy held up his hands in defense and punched Munio on the arm playfully. "Munio, you're doing great. Don't know what I'd do without you, buddy. Did you make it over to Destiny's?"

"Oh yes, I made it." Munio laughed. "That girl can party. We drank a whole case of champagne. We had a chugging contest, and do you know that girl beat me? Beat me, the master of chugging."

"What the hell was she celebrating?" Eddy asked as he tied a turquoise bandanna around his crew cut.

"You didn't hear? That girl inherited one hundred thousand dollars from that Jimmy Ray man. You got any coffee made?"

"He left her what?"

"One hundred gees, brother, one hundred thousand gees! Yes!" Munio nodded to Eddy, who was frozen with his mouth hanging open.

"I'll be dog. I wonder what she's going to do with it. Yeah, there's coffee." He picked his workout bag up. "We gots go, boy. Fix a cup and drink it in the car."

"Ok, ok, I'm coming." Munio trotted into the kitchen.

At the gym, Eddy put down his bag and stripped off his large sweatpants to reveal a red, white, and blue-vertically striped pair of skintight Spandex shorts. With his gigantic white sweatshirt, he looked like a miniature hot air balloon. In front of the large mirror, Eddy posed and flexed his freshly shaven legs. From the front, back and sides, Eddy worked his way around the mirror. Munio chuckled under his breath as he watched Eddy scrutinizing his physique so seriously. Each leg was as broad as Munio's waist, and his hamstrings stood out as much from the back as his quadriceps did from the front, with uncanny symmetry.

"Brother." Munio put his hand on Eddy's shoulder. "If you don't win that contest, I don't know who else will."

"Look good?" Eddy questioned eagerly.

"Oh yes, I never saw bigger or more cut up legs. Let's see up top." Munio pointed to his chest.

Eddy ripped off the sweatshirt and the tank top under it. Munio was so stunned his eyes could not believe Eddy was real flesh and blood. A physique like this Munio had only seen in muscle magazines, where the people did not look real either.

Eddy alternately smiled and grimaced as he milked and pumped blood into those muscles with all his might. Beads of sweat quickly formed on his face. He hit one pose for a few seconds, and like a clock moving around the dial, segued onto the next and the next until finally he had hit them all. He bent over with his hands on his knees to catch his breathe the second he finished. Everyone in the near vicinity who had stopped their workouts to observe Eddy's show broke into applause. Eddy good-naturedly straightened up and bowed. Munio laughed and clapped too.

Eddy covered back up with his sweats, and Munio set a bar up at a bench press station for the first exercise.

"Ok, this is going to be easy. Just stay tight, Eddy. Good form. Don't go down too fast. Find your groove and stay in it, now. Concentrate. Come on, now!" Munio stood behind Eddy, who lay on the bench looking up at the bar. Eddy's eyes were bright with the fire of adrenaline and determination as he

took his last few seconds of mental preparation.

"Ok, one, two, three!" Eddy said in a deep angry voice, and Munio helped lift the five hundred and five pound bar off the rack where Eddy held it firmly over his chest.

His face grew redder with each repetition, and every vein planted under his face had risen like furious blue worms trapped by his skull and skin. Munio felt Eddy's voluminous exhalation as he pushed the weight off his chest each time. It blew Munio's hair in the same spot. Occasionally, a bead of spit would land on Munio's face, but he stayed right there and leaned over Eddy in case he had to take the weight from him. At the end of ten reps, Munio helped Eddy guide the bar safely back into the rack.

"Shit!" Eddy said as he sat up. His head was spinning, and he felt a little nauseated. "How'd that go?"

"Good. You looked strong. You going up?"

"I don't know. You think I ought to?"

"How do you feel?"

"Like shit."

"Ok, we stay here. One more set of ten. That will do for today."

Munio patted Eddy on the back. "Take a good rest."

"One set?" Shit, if I can do one set, I can do two."

"Why do you ask me?" Munio became angry. "You ask me, and I tell you what is best. Still, you must do more. You don't look like you feel well. I wish you would listen to me." Munio waved at Eddy in disgust.

Eddy grinned. "You always got to do more than you can do. Because you know what?" Eddy got in Munio's face and waved his arms as he spoke. "There's always some motherfucker up in Atlanta or way down in south Georgia that's going to do that extra set you don't do! He's going to do it, and he's going to get up on that stage with my extra muscle on his goddamn body and beat my lazy ass!"

"Ok, ok, do the set. Do the set. Let's go before you get cold, preacher man." Munio grinned at him and winked.

"It ain't motherfucking funny, dude. I am serious about this shit."

"Yeah, yeah, let's go. Let's go."

Eddy lay down on the bench and placed his hands just so again, muttering angry motivational phrases to himself. "Come on, you son of a bitch! Fuck this fucking weight! It's my weight! My weight! One, two, three!" Munio lifted the weight into Eddy's hands. He ripped through the set, then quickly racked the weight with Munio's smooth assistance.

"There! Was that easy enough for you?" Eddy laughed and clapped his hands together once with a loud pop.

Munio shrugged his shoulders. "How do you feel?"

"Like shit." Eddy laughed. "This ain't supposed to feel good, Munio. Anybody that says getting ready for a show feels good is a damn liar or a fool,

one. Don't nobody that competes at bodybuilding, or hell, at anything, do it because it makes them feel good. They do it because something inside is driving them. Maybe they just don't feel worthy unless they can win something, you know. It's war. It is personal war. Hell, you ought to know that, Munio. You competed. You went to the fucking Olympics. You tell me how good you felt?" Eddy bit a fingernail.

"Hummm." Munio didn't answer at first. "You are right. I have almost forgotten. It was all life was about at the time. I hurt all the time, my knee, my shoulder. By the time the competition day came around, I would feel awful, so tired. It seemed like an instant later, the big moment would be ended, the meet would be over and I would be saying where did it go?" He snapped his fingers, "That fast, it would end. Many times I would not make the lifts I wanted, and I agonized over it for many days afterwards. My knees and my shoulder felt better after a week or so, and there I would go, back on that platform to train again. I would forget how I had hurt, or how depressed I got after a meet. I never remembered, and so I would get right back out there for years, many years, until I got smart. I finally could quit, but it was not an easy thing to do."

Eddy had been sitting on the bench listening intently to Munio. "Maybe I will quit too one day, but for now, this is just my beginning, Munio. I ain't burned out or run out of drugs, yet. I got enough drugs to cure any depression I might have. I don't come home feeling empty. I win every day. I love doing this."

After the lift off, Eddy popped out eight reps, and on the ninth one, a vessel burst in his nose, sending a bright red stream trickling down the side of his face. He was not even aware of it as he did the last rep and racked the bar.

He sat up and his hand traveled to his face. "Shit, Munio. I have done sprung a leak. You got a plug?" He smiled nonchalantly as he rifled through his workout bag and found a bandanna with which he wiped his face. He tilted his head back and took a deep breath. "Nothing like a little blood letting to make you stronger. Yeah, buddy. You know they used to do this back in the olden days, blood letting. Probably was something to it. Probably was."

Munio shook his head. "Yeah, buddy, and you going to run out of blood soon if you do not watch yourself, Eddy."

"I got a couple of cups left. Don't worry. Hey, put a quarter on each end. I'm going to see if I can get a rep or two with four fifty-five. Ok? Let me go wash this shit off. I'll be right back." Eddy marched toward the locker room with his snout held high, covered with the bandanna that was helping stem the tide.

Munio put a twenty-five pound plate on each end and sat down on the bench. It was the first moment of solitude he had had that morning. He had almost forgotten about his hellish hangover, and that he felt depressed. Leaning with his arms over his knees, he studied the backs of his brown hands.

Several prominent scars stood out, reminding him of fights, accidents. One was from a cat bite he received as a child when he tried to save it from being torn apart by dogs. It didn't work, and that scar stood in remembrance of the last breath that poor cat took. Munio saw the terrified eyes and the ball of black and white fur dripping with blood.

"Hey!" Eddy looked down Munio who sat steadfast and oblivious. "Hey boy, wake up!" Still Munio did not move. Eddy looked around and chuckled nervously to see if anyone else had noticed this strange behavior. They had, and several people grinned back in acknowledgment of the fact that yes, Munio was plenty strange. Finally, Eddy shook him gently, and he snapped out of it.

"What's happening?" Munio jumped to his feet.

"It's ok, bud. It's all right." Eddy had one hand on Munio's back and one on his chest, patting him gently. "You had one of them weird daydreams of yours, that's all."

"Oh ok, I , I, I'm just a, ah, still, you know, ah, hung up, I mean hungover. Heh, heh. I could use another cup of coffee." Embarrassed, Munio smiled at Eddy.

"Ok, ok. Listen, how about we get this last set here, and I'll run or you can run next door to the Magic Market and get you some coffee, all right bud? Yeah, yeah, that sounds good. Go on and get you a cup of coffee. Here, let me give you some money. Get you a biscuit or something, too. You could use a little carbing up. You looking kind of lean here lately." He laughed as he pulled a five dollar bill from his gym bag. "Here, hoss, hurry now."

Eddy had been doing warmups and was up to the one hundred pounders when Munio returned. "Get you a hit there, bud?"

"Yes." Munio sipped through the tiny hole in the plastic lid on the Styrofoam cup, carefully and loudly sucking in a lot of air with the hot liquid in order to cool it by the time it reached his mouth. "Umm, good. Here, have a hit." He handed Eddy the cup.

Eddy took a little taste and made a bitter face. "Goddamn, Munio, that tastes like pure coffee flavored syrup. Yuck! You gonna give me sugar diabetes drinking that shit." He laughed, and Munio did too as he unwrapped a package of sugar-coated donuts. "And eating that sugar coated shit there. Oh boy, you're gonna lapse into a fucking coma any minute. Lord help you, son. You ought to take better care of yourself. You need to eat better than you do. Maybe take a dadgum vitamin now and then. Hell, you ought to let me give you a shot of test once a week." He punched Munio.

"Take care of myself? Sheesh, are you one guy to be talking of such things. You, who is bleeding internally. Oh brother, and you worry about a little donut. Sugar is good for you. Make you able to work a long time."

"Shit, sugar don't make you fucking grow." He sat down on the padded incline bench. "Not like these damn dumbells is fixing to do." He ferried the

huge dumbbells, each weighing one hundred and ten pounds, to his shoulders.

"Good set, Eddy. You are so strong in this exercise." Munio praised him while sipping from the sugary brown drink which was boosting his blood sugar and energy levels by the second. Chills coursed back and forth across his scalp, invigorating as a splash of cold water in the face.

"I know it. I love these. I'm going up to the one twenty's for five. Can you handle that?

"I'm with you, brother."

Eddy picked up one, and Munio, straining, but managed to pick up the other one hundred ten pounder and replace it on the rack. They each grasped one of the one hundred twenty pounders and hobbled the few steps back to the incline bench.

"Shit, man, these things are getting too heavy, Eddy. This is too early in the morning." Munio laughed.

"Eat another one of them donuts, hoss." Eddy laughed and pointed at the package of donuts. "All right, I'm about as ready as I'll ever get."

The dumbells were enormous. Six black ten pound iron plates were tacked on either end, separated by a chromed knurled handle.

"Here we go, Ed," Munio said as Eddy bent over, gathered up one of the monstrosities, and sat down on the incline bench.

"All right, hand me the other one. Remember, I'm going for five. If I need help, just push my elbows, all right?"

"All right, I got you. You just do it. You don't need no damn spot!" Munio pysched him up as he heaved the other one onto Eddy's lap.

"Ok, here we go." Eddy lay back, boosting the dumbells into position on his chest with the help of a thrust of his thighs. "One! Two! Three!" Munio pushed on Eddy's elbows, and the dumbells rose up easy as balloons.

Munio's heart beat as fast as Eddy's as he bent over behind him. He knew that one wrong move on either of their parts could rip a shoulder joint out by the roots. Yet, sure-footed as a trail donkey in the Grand Canyon, Eddy guided the big dumbells in a safe groove over his head, and after five repetitions, sent them crashing to the floor.

"Yes! Yes! Yes! That was excellent, Eddy. Fine concentration, man. Well done!" Munio and Eddy slapped high fives.

"Woooeee. Boy, that was hell. Them things sure looked big up there. All I could think about was if I didn't keep pushing I was going to be wearing them on my face." They laughed.

"Shit, let's do something easy. What do you say, pal? This is too much fucking drama for one morning, huh?"

"I'm with you, brother. You going to make the old man have a heart attack."

"I'm just going to do the pec deck for a few sets. You can go smoke a

184

cigarette if you want to."

A breeze hit the tiny beads of anxious sweat on Munio's face. The coffee had cooled and tasted the same temperature as the breeze. His cigarette smoke blew in crazy patterns in the gusty wind.

Thoughts of Sandra and the unfinished gazebo crossed his mind. He hoped to have the decking on the floor finished today. Maybe tomorrow he could lay out the upright support beams and the railings. He reviewed his plan in his mind. Perhaps he should build the steps today so Sandra could step up on the decking easily. She would like that. When he thought of her, he felt so warm inside, but still, he could not name his intention with her. He did not want to think of defining it. Munio sucked the last swallow of the now cold, sweet coffee through the tiny hole in the plastic lid, lit another cigarette, and changed the subject of his thoughts.

# CHAPTER XXVIII

It was eleven a.m., and the cats could wait no longer for their allotment of sticky wet tuna and crunchy dry cat gravel. All four of them circled like sweet-voiced furry vultures, stepping all over her as she lay in the dark, warm under the covers.

"Ok, ok, I'm getting up." She paused and shut her eyes again. "In a few minutes, anyway." She giggled, and the cats moaned louder.

Destiny, afraid of her hangover this morning, lay very still. She figured if she lay there long enough, it would just go away. She slept way past her scheduled arrival time for work and felt guilty that she had not even called. She smiled when she thought about the possibility of them firing her. Let 'em, she thought. I'm quittin' anyhow when I get that check.

Jose stuck his head down through the hole in the covers where Destiny's head was partially poking out. He meowed right in her ear.

"All right, you little motherfucker. I said I'm getting up. Don't be yapping right in my fucking ear. Mama don't like loud things this mornin', ok?" Destiny sat up in the bed. The cool air in the room made her bare nipples grow so hard so fast, they hurt.

"Ouch." Destiny cupped her breasts. "I believe the frost is on the fucking pumpkin this mornin', y'all. Damn. I'd light up a fire if we had a dadgum fireplace. Maybe I'll buy us a fireplace." She slid into a ratty pink pair of open-backed terrycloth bedroom slippers and continued thinking aloud to the cats. "Maybe I'll buy us a house, or a little farm outside of town. That costs a lot. Maybe I'll deal for a while, make a bunch of money, and then I could buy a place without using up everything."

The cats swarmed around her ankles like mosquitoes, whining incessantly. Destiny ignored them, and her pace was not disturbed by their insis-

tent cries while she got a pot of coffee brewing. When she popped the lids on the cat food cans, the cats went into near hysterics. Destiny, unfazed, took her time, and wasted no energy trying to get them to hush. With the food set on the floor, peace and quiet was restored. Soft purrs mixed with the gnashing of squishy wet cat food, and the hot bubbly sounds of the coffee maker's cycle drawing to an end filled the room.

She flipped on the tv, channel surfed through the morning talk shows, and drank her first cup. The first three she previewed discussed various forms of infidelity. What she settled in to watch featured people who had accidentally killed their children. By the end of the pot of coffee, Destiny had bawled her way through half a box of Kleenex.

The phone rang. She screened the call and intercepted it upon hearing Eddy's voice.

"Hey," Destiny said, still sniffling a little from the show.

"Hey, what are you doing home?"

"Well, why the hell are you calling if you thought I wasn't home, dummy?"

Eddy laughed, "I don't know. Just thought I'd leave you a message. I hate calling you at work. You're always answering other calls and stuff. So anyhow, what are you doing home? You sick?"

"Yes." She sniffled again, but then giggled.

"What's wrong with you, girl? You got a fucking hangover. I know that."

"You don't know nothing. I was watching this sad show. Eddy, this poor woman left her kid sitting on top of a washing machine. The little fucker fell in and died. Ain't that pitiful?"

"Damn. I bet he was a clean little bastard." He laughed.

"Eddy, you are so insensitive."

"No, I ain't. Hey, back to you, when was you going to tell me?"

"Tell you what?"

"You know."

"What?"

"About your big fortune." Eddy hooted.

"Oh, Munio must've told you. Eddy, I just can't believe it. I didn't know Jimmy Ray had nothing to leave nobody."

"Well, I reckon he did after all, huh? How much did he leave you?"

"One hundred thousand dollars!" Destiny exclaimed, punching the end of each word dramatically.

"Dadgum, honey, you want to get married?" Eddy laughed.

"Uh huh. Shoot, I reckon."

"So what did you do, call in sick or just outright quit?"

"No, I didn't quit! I ain't even called in today, though. I feel bad about it. I'll call them in a little while. I ain't gonna quit just yet, anyhow."

"You gonna wait til tomorrow, I reckon," Eddy teased.

"No, Eddy, I want to be smart about this. I would like to think I can do something with this money that will last me for my whole life, you know? I mean, I ain't ever gonna get no better chance than this to, to, to do something. I mean, you know, to be better off. You know what I mean?"

"Yeah, well, baby, I'm happy for you. See, that old Jimmy Ray wasn't so bad after all, was he? You used to bad mouth him so much, and all he did was love the hell out of you."

Destiny's voice grew angry and vicious. "Right, Eddy! All he did was beat the fucking hell out of me! Don't forget that! Don't ever forget that! He got what he deserved!"

"What do you mean by that?"

Realizing she had spouted off a little too much, she tried to reel Eddy's mind back in. "Oh well, all I mean is, I don't know, Eddy. All this is just blowing me away. He loved me, I know, but he was real bad for me. You know that. Look. Let's forget the past, and just go on. You're gonna make me start crying again." she lied.

"All right, all right. I got to go on to work anyhow. Come on down tonight, and I'll buy you a celebration drink, ok? I tell you what. I'll buy you a bottle of champagne. How's that?"

Destiny retched and laughed at the same time. "Eddy, the last thing I want to see on this day is a bottle of champagne. I drank six last night!"

Eddy shrieked, "Six?"

"Yes, in fact, I don't want to see anything bubble today. I tell you what though. I wouldn't mind a shot of Jack Daniels."

"You and Munio ought to get married. Y'all are two pigs in a poke. So, I'll see you later, baby."

# CHAPTER XXIX

Meanwhile, Munio had eaten a small can of pork brains and gravy, smoked half a joint, and made his way over to Sandra's to work on the gazebo. Sandra's car was not parked in the carport, but he pulled on into the back yard and began his work.

She had taken a drive over to Lane Bryant's to shop for some new clothes. Earlier that morning, while she munched her raisin bran at breakfast, she read Cosmo and dreamed about romantic love-making with Munio. All of those dramatic glamour girls spurred her to attempt to update her matronly image. After doing the best makeup job she could muster, she set her wig on top of her head, and put on a pair of black double knit slacks and a pink sweater before setting out on the clothes quest.

Sandra pulled into Rosedale's mall. In the middle of the parking lot was a fountain with a giant watermelon made of stainless steel that had water shoot-

ing out from the middle of it and cascading down its sides.

She walked through the parking lot, her low-heeled pumps clicking rthymically. Her oversized smoked amber sunglasses looked stylish, she thought, as she watched her reflection in the glass doors of the entrance. Although her largeness was unsettling to see full length, she thought she carried herself with class. With her Gucci handbag and those arrogant shades, she felt a tad Jackie O-ish.

A wig shop just inside the entrance caught her eye. The Styrofoam mannequin skulls in the window wore a wide variety of hairstyles. Sandra let out a small giggle as she pictured herself with the black extended braids model, and considered buying the blonde Tina Turner number just for laughs. She wished she had the nerve to just go in and try on a bunch of them for fun, but she could not bring herself to do so with her shiny bald spot. There was a long auburn number that she loved. She pictured it on her head and replayed the scene of watching her reflection in the mall doors. She watched herself walking along, the long red curls falling over her shoulders. Her sunglasses would look even more provocative with this new hair. She suddenly became self-conscious and realized she had been standing there for some time. She looked both ways to see if anyone had noticed her. Then, without any further hesitation, she went into the shop.

The place felt a little creepy with all the wigged heads. A woman with a heavy Asian accent helped her as she bought and paid for the auburn wig. Sandra's heart raced as she left the shop. She could hardly wait to go home and try it on. In fact, she almost canceled the trip to Lane Bryant's, but her sensible side convinced her to carry on.

This big and tall store for women was truly a safe haven for the gigantic female form. Lane Bryant sold clothes that were so large, here Sandra felt like a middleweight.

When shopping here, Sandra was always careful to keep her voice in the alto or above range so as to not frighten the clerks. She neglected to realize that, to these women, she was not strange, only big and tall. In fact, she probably reminded them of some elderly aunt or grandmother with masculine fringe characteristics such as a heavy mustache, a small goatee that needed plucking regularly, or a large mole with a crop of long wiry hairs rising from it, and they treated Sandra with respect.

These clerks also recognized many of their customers by face and honored their shopping habits. As was customary with Sandra, they smiled, nodded, and greeted her as she entered the store, but left her to browse and fantasize on her own.

Sandra started with the first rack she came to, and methodically examined every garment they had in the store. She made a second round for try-ons.

Sandra liked the dressing room accommodations because they were tai-

lor made for big women. Each cubicle's walls were about five feet on each side and gave a three or four hundred pounder room to dance around a little on one leg and pull a pant cuff over a foot. For Sandra, this was a big plus, after having had several humiliating experiences in department store dressing rooms.

Once while shopping in Neiman-Marcus on a trip to Atlanta, in a changing stall scarcely large enough for her to stand in, she attempted to pull a pair of black stretch pants over her women's size fourteen shoe, her first mistake. The second mistake was trying to do it while standing. By some Houdini-like method of transference, she managed to get one big foot over the stretchy cloth, but only got the second pant leg coerced to her instep. Ultimately, she lost her balance, crashed through the stall door and wound up in a heap on the carpet, pantless, with her long legs bound helplessly together by the rich tensile strength of cotton and lycra. Humiliated and rug burned, she gasped from embarrassment as, employees and haughty shoppers watched without sympathy or an offer of help as she writhed furiously on the floor to free the second foot so she could stand.

Now, moving at a snail's pace, she made her way through the racks and gathered a collection of maybes folded across her arm. For an hour, she tried on the potential choices, and as she left the dressing room, she felt more than pleased with the day's hunting.

"Hello, did you find everything all right?" the cashier asked cheerfully.

"Yes, I did. Thank you very much. I am quite pleased." Sandra spoke with a dignified yet pleasant demeanor. Then she chuckled and threw out her hands for emphasis. "Fast track as they say."

"Yes ma'am, it looks like you did real good. Look at all this. Ma'am, would we be charging this, or will it be cash?"

"Oh, ah, I think I will charge it. Let me dig out this card, now." She thumbed through her wallet and handed the credit card to the lady.

The clerk looked at it. "All right Miss Fugleberg, let's see what pretty things you have here." She picked up a royal blue cotton turtleneck and rang it up. A double-extra-large pair of matching sweatpants followed.

"Looks like we're fixing to do some working out," she commented sweetly.

"I thought I might start walking more since the weather is beginning to cool off." Sandra smiled and enjoyed the small talk. The cashier's gentle manner put her at ease.

"Yeah, boy howdy. I am glad, too. I need to get out myself. You have to be careful though." She squinted, and her eyebrows wrinkled as if strung on a string.

"Why is that?" Sandra asked.

"Well, you know crime is getting just awful around here. Might as well live in Atlanta. My neighbor was out walking the other night, and some boys

chunked a near full beer bottle at her. Just drove off laughing. Busted right in front of her, and got her pants all wet. Liked to hit the dog, too." Her eyebrows now formed a wide arc as she disclosed these details.

"Is that so?" Sandra feigned a fear to bond closer with the woman. "Mmmm, mmm, mmm, that is awful." She laid her hand across her mouth,.

"Yes, Lord." The cashier leaned over the counter and whispered loudly. "You just never know who you're dealing with these days. You know? There's all kinds of freaks everwhere, just everwhere."

Sandra smiled smoothly. "Oh, I'll watch out, indeed."

"What a pretty sweater!" The cashier held up a dark long, dark brown button-up number. "Won't this go good with your eyes?"

"You think so?" Sandra got excited.

"Oh yeah, you got real pretty blue gray eyes. Uh huh, sure will. Yeah, that'll look good."

"Well." Sandra cleared her throat, a little embarrassed but flattered none-theless. "Thank you. That is so kind of you to say."

"Why, you are welcome, Miss Fugleberg. Well, I believe that will about do it. If you will sign right here, you can be on your way." She pushed the charge ticket across the counter.

Sandra signed and passed it back.

"You have a nice afternoon now, you hear? You come back to see us!" She smiled as she pushed the large plastic shopping bag full of clothes to Sandra.

"I surely will. You have a good day as well, Miss," Sandra strained and adjusted her eyeglasses to view through the bifocal element at see the woman's name tag. "Miss Reeves." She grasped the top of the bag, smiled, and made for the door. Suddenly, remembering her new wig, Sandra smiled to herself and quickened her step. The anticipation of this secret and potential radical new look gave her butterflies, and for the first time, Sandra Fugleberg thought she understood what it meant to say that she felt like a girl again. Uncontrol-lably, tears began to flow from her eyes. Large amber sunglass lenses provided shield enough for her to keep walking towards her white Lincoln Continental and her strange life far removed from the likes of Lane Bryant.

******

The floor of the gazebo was complete now, and the supports for the roof joists rose like eight thick flagpoles in the air. Today, Munio planned to begin the framework for the roof by bolting two by tens onto the four by the four flagpoles. It was time for him to fabricate a small scaffolding structure.

His mind and body worked well today. He measured and sawed cuts with the blazing accuracy of a surgeon. The day was breezy, and the smell of the change in seasons carried on the breeze. Munio noticed the many unfa-miliar exotic smells of the drying foliage, the kudzu, the grasses, and leaves on the trees that surrendered their sap for the year. Munio had never smelled those smells before. His world had been filled with chlorophyll year round

190

from the rich jungles, or when he was along the coast, the scent of the turquoise water rose like a cloud full of the sweet spices of the sea, its salt, and all of its life below.

He had been working several hours when Sandra's big white car rolled under the carport. He looked up from his sawhorses to see Sandra striding swiftly across the lawn towards him.

"Hello Munio, how are you today, sweetie?" She walked up to him boldly and gave him a hug.

Munio smiled. "I must be doing all right for the boss lady to give me such affection." He sat upon several pieces of two-by-ten that lay across the sawhorses and lit a cigarette.

"I just returned from a very successful shopping trip. I am so excited," she exclaimed in her top register voice. "Wait til you see."

"Tell me, what did you buy, boss lady?" He winked at her.

"Oh." She put her palms together in a most feminine way. "No, I'm not going to tell you, Munio. I'm going to let it be a surprise." She slapped him on the shoulder lightly.

"Won't you at least tell me if I can eat it or drink it?"

"No, you have to wait. You will just have to wait. I'm going in now to tr… nevermind. I'm just going in, and you stay out here. Yes, you stay out here and work, work, work."

Munio held his hands up in surrender. "Ok, I stay. I work. You are some slave driver." He laughed and flicked his cigarette butt on the lawn. He watched Sandra hustle back to the car and remove her thrilling new secrets, and then turned his attention back to the gazebo.

Munio became even more engrossed than ever in his work. It was as if his whole life was dependent on the musical, yet searing, sounds of his saw as it ripped through the sweet-smelling pine. The fine yellow sawdust it threw back on him served as confetti to celebrate this party of building. He loved the sound of his hammer as its head met with a nail.

It didn't take him long to construct a scaffold. The height and length of it were both eight feet, but the width was only three feet. It was just wide enough to not tip over easily and to provide Munio with enough room to stand. After the last nail was hammered, Munio climbed aboard to check its sturdiness. He swayed back and forth and jumped up and down a few times.

Sandra looked out the sliding glass door to steal a peek at Munio just as he executed this ritual. She gasped and ran into the yard.

"Are you all right, Munio?" she exclaimed.

He laughed louder than she had ever heard him laugh. It was a big Ricky Ricardo laugh, a series of lengthy bellows that lasted quite a few seconds. When his hysteria subsided, he explained. "I was testing out my scaffold. I have to see now if it will endure. You just walked out at an odd time." He shook his head and chuckled some more.

"Good Lord, I thought you were having a seizure or some kind of fit. You scared me to death. That's awfully high, isn't it?" She squinted up at him, using her hand above her eyes as a shade.

"It is about eight feet. It is good, very sturdy." Munio tried to shake it again, and then patted it like a good plow mule before climbing down.

Sandra walked around the scaffold, inspecting the design, and nodded her head. Her voice lowered as she said, "Good job on this, Munio. This thing would hold a cow. You are doing a fine job on all of this." She put her hand on the back of his neck as she moved past him.

"Thank you very much. I am proud of it, too. I am also anxious to move on and set the roof joists."

"Well, don't let me slow you down." Her voice went back up again to a more feminine key. "I have things to do myself." She raised her eyebrows, winked at Munio, and marched back towards the house. "Oh, if you want a beer, help yourself."

Munio nodded at her, but his mind had already shifted back to the business of measuring the boards.

Sandra grabbed her bags and went into her bedroom All the little lap dogs followed faithfully. They sensed their mother's excitement, and hoped there might be hotdogs in one of those bags. When she laid the bags on the bed, all three of them leaped up to inspect them thoroughly. Disappointed by the lack of anything edible, they curled up on the bed to watch their mother's fashion show.

Sandra emptied the clothes on the bed and rifled through them until she found the gold and black dress, a fancy dress, to wear at dance class.

She took off her clothes, and when she was down to her four-hook black underwire bra and matching black nylon panties, she stopped. From her dressing table, she procured a small pair of scissors, clipped all the tags off the dress, and put it on. Her glasses had nearly been knocked off in the process, and she had to straighten them before she looked into the mirror. Her face lit up as she looked, because the dress really fit her well. The color was very nice on her, she thought, and the cut did not accentuate anything Sandra did not want accentuated on her large frame. She slipped her short black pumps back on as she picked up the wig bag from the bed.

Despite having lived a life that included a sex change, to Sandra, the purchase of this racy, red wig symbolized her first real act of taking a walk on the proverbial wild side. The way Sandra saw it, redheads had a stigma about them, and for a person to seek entry into the world of the redheads meant something. She was not sure what, but something.

Trying on a wig for the first time was not an event Sandra Fugleberg tread lightly into. After several deep breaths, she pulled the wig from the bag, giggling at how sloppy and silly it looked. How empty a wig's life was without a head, she thought, and wondered why she had had such an esoteric thought.

She wondered if the redhead phenomenon had moved into her brain already. Next thing you know, I'll become a vegetarian, she thought, and chuckled. When its tags were all removed and the glue strips installed, she swung the thing toward her scalp. The mounting was aborted quickly because she had forgotten to remove her other wig in all the fuss. She smiled at her mistake and pulled off the wig, carefully peeling the glued spots from her bald crown. Her head felt so cool. In fact, it felt freezing and naked.

Ready now for the second try, she swung the wig on like a cowboy swings a saddle onto a horse. "Oh my God!" she cried as she took a look. A crooked half-smile spread across her face. After straightening the wig and poofing it up in places, she just stopped and stared. She even removed her glasses and cleaned them. The woman who stared back at her was not the woman she had woken up with. It was as if the pile of curls had brought with it a magic wand. Sandra had the opportunity to see herself as vibrant, sexy.

She jumped to her feet and sprinted down the hall to the living room to put on her favorite Latin dance tape. Then she trotted back to the bedroom, to take in the view once again. The music blasted in from a speaker in the corner, and it thrilled her to hear it. Instantly, she began to dance, twirl around, and stop frequently to catch a glimpse of what she looked like moving in different positions. Fascinated, the lap dogs continued to lie on the bed, watching their mother dance and sing in Spanish to the tape she had played millions of times before without such spirited consequences. At the dramatic conclusion of the first song, Sandra ended it with a hearty "Ole!"

Reminded of her thirst, she hustled into the kitchen to uncork a waiting bottle of champagne. The lap dogs heard the refrigerator open and raced in from the bedroom, thinking there might be something in it for them.

"My little babies want a little snack? Hmmm? Yes, you do, don't you?" They panted and jumped up on her leg anxiously. "Don't do that! You'll ruin mommy's hose, and I'll have to beat you!" She laughed at herself as she reached into the cooky jar on the counter and passed out little biscuits to each of them. She watched Munio from the window over the sink after pouring herself a glass of champagne. He moved like an ant possessed, climbing up and down the scaffold. Sandra was truly amazed by his single-handed progress, and was impressed equally with his skill.

She slugged her glass empty and refilled. Listening to the tape again, she assumed the posture of a junior flamenco dancing girl. She watched her red curls bounce along with the other components of her body in her contorted reflection from the chrome and glass oven door as she moved back and forth. Through the rest of the second song, she danced around in the kitchen.

"Well, kids," She said to the dogs. "Let's go see how Don Juan likes mommy's new hair." She giggled.

She grabbed another champagne glass from the cupboard, the bottle, and her glass. Like Peg Bundy on steroids, she charged onto the patio. "Oh,

Munio!"

Munio had his back to the house as she called his name. He looked up when he heard her voice and turned around. When he did, he dropped his hammer and nearly hit his toe. He jumped out of its way, and felt compelled to say a few words of amazement under his breath in Spanish as he watched the new redheaded Sandra move across the lawn. He stood poised, hands on hips, in very macho stance when she reached him. He lit a cigarette without blinking an eye and said nothing as he looked her up and down. With the rotation of an index finger, he directed her to make a 360 degree turn.

After obliging him, slowly, she watched a smile come to his face. "I like it, Sandra. I like it a lot, mucho gusto."

Sandra moved to embrace him. After a hug, they backed away from each other, and Munio continued to stare. This wig stood up on top much higher than her other wig, and now she topped out at about six foot six, nearly a foot taller than Munio.

"Do you really? Do you think I look ridiculous? Am I too old to wear this?" she asked fearfully.

"No, no, no! Look at you! You look wonderful! You look happy. You look alive. Not that you looked dead before, you see, but ah, you look, you look, like I say, happy. I know no other thing to say to you. The dress too, and the hair make you, well," he stammered shyly, "look sexy."

"You think I look sexy?" Sandra beamed. "You think I look sexy?" She repeated and laid a hand on her chest.

He waved his arms as he said, "Yes, I say so. I say you look sexy."

She chuckled. "Well Munio, I feel inclined to use a southern phrase that I have never used before." She paused, looked up at the sky, and with great enthusiasm shouted, "Praise the Lord and hallelujah!" She laughed and slapped Munio on the arm. "Mister, let's you and me have a drink. What do you say?"

"You got it, lady."

They sat down on the gazebo steps, clinked a toast and started to drink. Munio stopped her.

"Wait, wait, wait, just a minute. I want to propose a toast to you." He stood and held out his glass. "Here is to you and your new hair. Also, here is to the gazebo. May this be the first of many good times that you will have here."

"Thank you, Munio. Thank you. Here is to your fine work, and just, here's to you." They clinked glasses once again and sat there until they finished the bottle.

"Ok, that is enough break for me. I must set these last two beams before I stop the work today." Munio stood up and drained the last drop from his glass.

"Munio, would you have dinner with me after you finish?" Sandra asked.

"Yes, I would do that."

"Wonderful, I'll go get started. Oh, I hope you like seafood. Do you?"

"Of course, I was raised by the sea. Any food from the sea, I like." He ran his fingers through his hair as much as the tangles would allow.

Sandra watched him and smiled. "Oh yes, I forgot," she said quietly. "How about a beer to sip on?"

" Would you mind?" Munio asked.

"No, no, of course not. I'll go get one for you." sandra hurried back to the house.

Sandra watched her new reflection in the sliding glass door as she walked across the patio. She smiled and thought that if she were thinner, a little thinner, she would look like Lynn Redgrave. Audrey would love to hear that one, she laughed to herself. Audrey hadn't crossed her mind in a few days, but she would have to give her a call today. As soon as she got dinner started, she would call her. Sandra had not discussed her growing feelings for Munio with her. Since she had had the operation, Audrey had remained her closest friend and confidante. She assumed Audrey would most likely be negative about the Munio situation, but it wouldn't be the first time they had disagreed, and it certainly was not going to interfere with her plan. She intended to marry that man.

\* \* \* \* \* \* \* \*

"Hello?"

"Audrey?"

"Yes, Sandra, is that you?"

"Who else?" Sandra giggled.

"God only knows," Audrey replied in a very drawn out sarcastic whine.

"Guess what I did today?" Sandra giggled again.

"You got changed back? How the hell do I know?"

"Very funny, Audrey. Nooo, I bought a new wig!"

"Well whoopdeedo. How many salt and pepper wigs do you need, for Christ's sake?" Audrey retorted playfully.

"It isn't salt and pepper, Audrey. It's red. Well, auburn."

"Red? Oh my God! This I've got to see. Red? How long is it?"

"Long! It's Peg Bundy long!"

"No, don't say Peg Bundy." Audrey laughed.

"What are you doing? Why don't you come over right this minute and tell me what you think? Would you please, Audrey? I am so nervous about this, but I think it looks good. It's just, just not like what I usually look like."

"You mean like Grandma Moses?" Audrey hooted. "Let's see. Ok, I'm coming over right now, but I can't stay long. I have a private lesson to teach."

"Oh, really, now? Does a blow job come with that?"

"Yeah, right. Ok, I'll be there in a jiffy."

"Ok, ok, good. Thanks Audrey."

"You're welcome."

It was only ten minutes later that Audrey knocked on the carport door. Hearing Munio's hammer, she looked out in the back yard. Her jaw dropped when she saw Munio and all the construction. Just then, Sandra opened the door.

"What the hell is he doing here, and what in the hell are you building back there, a hotel?" Her head stayed turned to the back yard when the door opened. When she faced the door and Sandra, her eyes got big, and her face looked as if it would explode. "Oh my God, Sandra!" A crooked smile replaced her original look of astonishment. "Look at you!" She walked slowly and circled her like a shark, picking at the wig here and there. She felt its texture and studied the cut.

Sandra laughed loudly. "I know, it is rather large, isn't it? I don't care. I like it. It's going to be a gazebo. Come on in. You look great."

"Thank you." She walked in, not taking her eyes off the wig for a moment. Without a change in expression, she responded, "A gazebo? You planning to rent it out for Bar Mitzvahs?" She fluffed up the sides of the wig.

"No, silly," Sandra laughed. She slapped Audrey on the arm.

"What the hell do you need a fucking gazebo for?"

"I plan to sit out there in the evenings with my little dogs and watch the fireflies and such, the stars."

"Oh well then. Back to this hair." She looked Sandra dead in the eyes as she spoke. "Sandra, it looks terrific. I think it's the best thing you've done for yourself since you made the change. I really do. The dress ain't bad either. I am shocked you made such good choices without me. You did do it by yourself, didn't you?"

"Yes, I did. Just spontaneously and everything. Oh, I'm so glad you like it. I really like it, and I think Munio likes it. He told me I looked sexy. He really did!"

"Oy vay, how is it you've gotten mixed up with this lowlife?"

"He is not. Look at him!" She pointed to the back yard. "He has worked faithfully on that thing every single day since he started. He's really a nice man, Audrey. So what if he drinks a little. I drink a little. So what!" Sandra punched her on the arm again.

"Whatever, maybe you're right. The son of a bitch can dance. That I will give him." She pointed her finger vigorously at Sandra.

"Come on in, Audrey. You want some coffee or something?"

"Sure, you got some made already?" Audrey sat down at the round table. The lap dogs huddled around her, sniffing her to determine how edible she might be.

"Won't take but a minute. I'll have some, too. Don't mind the dogs. They just want to see if you perhaps brought in any food." Sandra laughed.

"So Sandra, what is it you plan to do with this immigrant in the back

196

yard?"

"Really, Audrey, do be kind." Sandra sat down at the table. "I don't know. It is so strange, this life I've gotten myself into."

"That's the truth, but who in the hell doesn't have a strange life? Nobody we know, huh?" Audrey patted Sandra on the forearm. "Have you had sex with him?"

"No, no, I have danced with him at length, however. Passionate dances, Audrey. Ginger and Fred movie dances."

"I hate to burst your bubble, Sandra, but Ginger Rogers, you ain't. I know! I taught you everything you know about dancing." They both laughed, and Sandra got up to pour the coffee.

Sandra sipped at her hot coffee gently and looked out the sliding glass door at Munio, who was working away. She said in a sad voice, "Oh Audrey, I thought the change would make my life fit into my mind. Always I loved men. When I was a man, I thought it was because I was manly. You know?" Audrey shrugged. "That whole 'he's a man's man' philosophy. "Audrey nodded. "I seem to know how to be a man a lot better than I know about being a woman."

"Well, you've had a hell of a lot more practice, honey," Audrey reminded her.

"But I thought, after the change, I would know how. I can tell you this. The world liked me better as a man."

"The hell with the world, Sandra. You are the center of your own world. Look, you practiced being a man for fifty-two years, right? You've only had five years to experience being a woman. You'll get it. In fact, look at you today. Look at that demon wig you're sporting, right there. You are catching on. You've just got to find your own style, Sandra. Don't give up. Besides, what can you do? You can't give up. You can't call that doctor up, and say hey, remember me? You cut my dick off. I want it back." They laughed.

"I know, I know. I feel like a child. I never felt like a child even when I was a child. It's not only awkward, it's terrifying."

"Changing, you're changing, Sandra. Maybe you ought to get out of this hick town, and move back to the city. You might be too weird to live here if you really start being yourself. That is, if that red wig is any indication of who your true self is!"

"But I'm comfortable here, Audrey. I like my house. I like the space. It's easy to walk the dogs, you know."

"It's easy for you to hide here. You got your money. You go to the country club, and the boys wait on you. Tell me, where is that going to get you? What kind of stretch is that?"

"Well, I don't have to park my own car," Sandra kidded. "And they call me ma'am."

"They'd call Earnest Borgnine ma'am, you idiot. Those boys just want a

fucking tip. There's no life here. You know in your heart, Sandra, that Munio character is not for you. Are you ready to go to the country club in his truck for dinner? In fact, have you ever been anywhere with the man besides your back yard?" Audrey gave Sandra the eagle eye as her thin eyebrows molded into wide question marks.

Sandra said nothing, and a deep silence fell upon the two friends. Finally, Sandra spoke. "No, I have not dined out with him, and," she chuckled, "you know I haven't been for a ride in that truck." They both laughed, washing away the tension that had hung in the air just a minute before.

"I didn't think so. I can't believe you let him drive it up on your lawn or even park that thing in your driveway." Audrey sipped her coffee.

"All right, all right, so I'm a snob. I know I'm a snob, but I was born a snob. People born with money are different, and not necessarily better, I might add. Different, that's all. And no, I am not sure how to integrate Munio into my world, but in time, I'm sure the answer will reveal itself."

"Yeah, right, Sandra. The answer will reveal itself when he rips you off, and heads for the border. You can't trust his type, Sandra. He's an illegal alien, for Christ's sake. God knows what the man is really running from down in Puerta Vallarta, or wherever he's from."

"Belize, Audrey. He is not Mexican. Belize is a much more sophisticated country than Mexico. He is quite well spoken. Don't you think?"

"Belize, Smelize, tell me what the difference is? It's the same shade of brown, and it's the same mangoes and papayas. You put them in a lineup, you can't tell the difference. Tell the truth. And well spoken, ha! You obviously haven't seen the man kneewalking drunk. He's incredibly well spoken then. A drunk's a drunk, and don't you forget it" Audrey pointed her finger at Sandra emphatically. "Right there you have an international language that defies all cultures. Two drunks from anywhere on the globe understand each other just fine as long as the bottle holds out. He's a desperate man."

Sandra looked angry. "All right, all right, Audrey. I'm desperate too. Jesus, you sound like Archie Bunker. You are one to discriminate so freely. Maybe if we all weren't so ready to judge, we-"

"Don't come off like some saint about this, Sandra. You are just as high and mighty as anyone I know. You are just as prejudiced as I." Audrey's hands sliced through the air like a martial artist's.

"Maybe I am making a change in that, too. You are right. It's true. I am prejudiced, but this old broad just might be changing her stripes a little." She smiled.

Audrey smiled back at her as Sandra's relaxed demeanor disarmed her sharp tongue. "Well, old lady, I hope you do feel happier. I hope you find love with someone, but you and I both know it could never be with Jose out there." Audrey screwed up her mouth and pointed her thumb out toward the back yard.

"Now stop it, girl!" Sandra laughed. "Just wait and see. I think he is a nice man. Whether or not he wants an old broad like me, well, I will just have to wait and see."

"Keep me informed. You know I want to know every juicy detail. Have you given him a blow job, yet?" Audrey looked excitedly at Sandra and nodded, hoping yes was the answer.

"Stop! No, I have not. That is surprising for me, isn't it?"

"You do have a taste for it. I must say."

"Remember that guy, what was his name?" Audrey squeezed her lower lip as if it would help her recall. "That guy you were seeing occasionally just when you made the change?"

"Oh, Rob, uh, Pappas, he was Greek. Lovely man, lovely dick, too, I must add." They laughed.

"Remember how you didn't tell him you were getting the operation? Didn't you tell him you were going to Europe for three weeks or something?"

"Yes." Their laughter intensified as the story went on.

"That poor man. I just couldn't tell him. He was such a closet case anyhow. Remember? He was married with three kids out on Long Island somewhere. Poor woman did not have a clue." Sandra giggled between her words.

"Oh, right. But then remember the first time he came to see you after the operation?" Audrey asked.

Sandra burst into laughter. "That was so funny, but unfortunately, not to Rob. He came over, and I was wearing a nightgown. The look on his face when his hand went looking for my dick." Sandra and Audrey howled.

Finally, their mirth subsided long enough for Sandra to speak. "I said," she blubbered, "gone gone, and he screamed 'No!' I thought it was going to be a nice surprise for him, but the poor bastard fell apart. He ran right out the door, and I never heard from him again."

"That man probably ran straight to Bellevue and never looked back." Audrey commented.

"Oh, for the good old days. Goes to show you, Audrey. You just got to have a sense of humor in this business."

# CHAPTER XXX

Munio worked until the darkness ruled his work site. As he looked over the day's progress, the little orange glow of his cigarette followed. The gazebo was now a floor with eight beams that protruded vertically, and joists mounted on top of each beam. Each was cut to precision, each angle joined the next flawlessly. It was fine work to have been done by one man alone.

Munio gathered up all his tools and neatly stored them. He slipped on a sweatshirt to offset the coming chill of night, and walked slowly to Sandra's house.

"Sandra?" he called, and stepped in. He peeked into the living room. "Sandra?"

He helped himself to a beer, took a seat at the table in the kitchen, and watched the frame of the gazebo disappear as night fell. That Sandra had not made her presence known began to make him a little uncomfortable. It was puzzling because he noticed there was food cooking in the oven and in a covered pot on the stove. Taking the last drain off his beer, he decided to search the house. Maybe she fell down in the bathtub or something, he thought.

He wandered slowly down the long dark hallway, calling out her name, but got no response. It was unusual that the little lap dogs had not barked at him as they generally would when he first entered the house. Munio's uneasiness increased.

"Sandra? Sandra? It's Munio. Are you here?" he called, and kept walking til the hall ended at the door of Sandra's bedroom. He gasped slightly when he saw Sandra lying on the bed, perfectly still. All the little lap dogs were huddled around her. They looked up at Munio but did not make a sound. Munio's heart jumped because she was so still. Dressed in her new red wig and new black and gold dress, she lay on her back like someone dead, lying in state. He stood over her, afraid to call her name.

"Sandra?" he said softly. "Wake up, Sandra." He squinted to see in the dim lighting in the room. Reaching over to the night table, he flicked on a lamp.

Munio jumped back from the bed and clutched his heart. All the lap dogs stood up, startled by his sudden movement. Held loosely in Sandra's right hand was a long-barreled, chrome-plated revolver. Munio leaned over carefully to survey what he could see of Sandra's body, but no blood was visible at all. Relieved by this, he assumed that Sandra was not dead at all, but napping. Since he had never bedded down with her, he did not know whether it was her custom to sleep with a pistol. After all, that would not be so unusual. His fear returned when he thought that, if he more aggressively pursued waking her, she might mistake him for an intruder and come up shooting

Tiptoeing back to the doorway, he called to her more loudly this time. "Sandra! Sandra, wake up! Hello! Wake up Sandra!" He gripped the doorframe. "Hey lady, wake up right now! Sandra! Sandra!" As his voice got louder and louder, tears began to pour down his face, but he continued his vocal assault. "Sandra! Sandra, wake up! Sandra, please wake up! It's Munio!" He picked up a bottle of perfume from off a dresser top and flung it at the silent woman, but even though it tagged her squarely in the side, she remained motionless.

Munio dropped to his knees, wept loudly, and clutched his hands together in prayer, while rattling off in Spanish desperate cries for help. After no response was forthcoming, Munio stood up slowly and moved toward Sandra's bed. The little lap dogs wagged their tails.

"Sandra? Sandra, it's me, Munio. Wake up Sandra! Are you sleeping?" he said, inching his way along the bed until he stood directly over her. Again, he looked her over, without touching her, for any sign of injury. He noticed a blemish on her forehead, partially obscured by the bangs of the red wig.

He bent over her and brushed her hair aside to disclose a perfectly round hole penetrating her forehead. His hand grasped the red wig and lifted it towards him. The glue strips were strong, but not strong enough to support the full weight of Sandra's head. The wig slipped right off her head and left Munio holding the new hair. Munio's eyes were as big as saucers now, and he jumped back and screamed.

Standing there motionless, he noticed the wig in his hand dripped, from its bottom, a slow but steady procession of rich red blood drops which splattered onto Sandra's new dress. Munio gulped and felt his stomach turn. From the space around the pillow where Sandra's head lay, the wig no longer hid the spreading halo of blood. Absolute terror had taken hold of Munio now as he shook all over, clutching the red wig, with eyes riveted on Sandra's bald head and the pillow beneath. As if it were on fire, Munio inched his hand toward her head. He lay the wig on her chest and used both hands to slowly lift her head forward. When the head moved from the pillow, in a horrible cascade, the back of Sandra's skull and the contents it held spilled onto the pillow like a pot of chili. Munio turned loose of her head and his bowels as he fell back and onto the floor, losing consciousness in midair.

After a few minutes, Munio came to and sat up, disoriented. He forgot what had happened until he looked up at Sandra's profile on the bed. Stumbling to his feet, he felt a thick wetness trail down the leg of his jeans. When he put a hand on his butt, he cursed to realize he had shit all over himself. The lap dogs had migrated to Sandra's face, which they tenderly sniffed and licked.

"Move away, dogs! Move away!" Munio sat on the edge of the bed, dazed by the situation. Tears formed again in his eyes, and he carefully lifted her right hand away from the chromeplated revolver.

"Sandra, Sandra, why you do this? What is the matter? I will finish your gazebo soon. We could dance and dance. It won't take long. You sleep. You just sleep here, ok?" Munio spoke earnestly to the lifeless body.

On the bedside table, he saw a clean white piece of paper. Picking it up, he could not make out what it said. "Dear Munio," the letter began, but Munio could not make sense of the rest. The date he could tell was today. He knew it was probably a suicide note, but who could he have read it for him? In his state of shock, he did not know what to do, except deny the truth of this horrible happening.

He stood and spoke to her body. "I am going to make sure our dinner does not burn up, ok? You just sleep, and I will not disturb you. You will feel better tomorrow, dear." He reached down and repositioned the new wig on her head. His hands became wet and sticky with the blood and brain matter.

He ignored this, wiped his hands on his jeans, and patted the wig so it looked in place.

"There you go. That new wig is real good on you. It looks real good." With that, he put the folded comforter that was at the foot of the bed across Sandra. "You sleep now." He leaned forward, and kissed her lightly on the cheek, before switching off the bedside lamp. Down the hall he walked into the kitchen where sweet smells rose from the pots that bubbled and boiled happily.

He dropped into a chair at the kitchen table. In the darkness, he could see the outline of the gazebo. Munio went to Sandra's well-stocked liquor cabinet and brought out a bottle of whiskey. Quickly, he opened it and drank several gulps. Choking and gasping for air, Munio coughed and grabbed his throat; the brown liquid burned him as if it were poured on a raw wound. After a time, his breathing normalized. For an hour, pacing back and forth across the kitchen floor, Munio strode with that bottle in one hand and a cigarette in the other. The ringlets of tangled black curls stood out from his head like a flag, reflecting his fright and despair.

The thought of calling the authorities was too frightening. It was just like them to think he killed Sandra. It was just like them to put Munio in jail for the rest of his life.

"How could you do this?" Munio wailed. "Don't you know we were so good? How could you do this? Now, I can never tell you! I can never tell you that I love you! What am I to do?"

Finally, he became aware of a burning smell. When he lifted the lids on the pots, a cloud of smoke escaped

Munio threw the lids in the sink and cursed madly in Spanish. Afraid and alone and halfway home to what would be a serious drunk, Munio burst into tears. Arms wrapped around himself, he paced the kitchen. The little lap dogs suddenly appeared in the doorway either because they smelled the food or instinct had them turn their attention to the last living soul in the house.

"Hello, little doggies. Are you hungry? I will feed you. Let me see what I can find here. Don't worry, I will take good care of you until your momma returns. She has gone, but she will be back. Ok?"

Munio opened several cabinet doors before he found a shelf loaded with cans of dog food. He turned the can opener round and round until the lid clicked. The sight of the dog food nauseated him because it reminded him of the condition of Sandra's head. The little dogs danced gleefully, with their sharp toenails clicking on the stylishly tiled floor.

While the dogs gobbled down their supper, Munio sat down at the table and swigged at the whiskey bottle every few seconds or so. His eyes were puffy and red. His forehead was drawn with lines of worry and sorrow. Picking up Sandra's final note, Munio tried once again to read it, but could only discern single words here and there. If only someone could read it to me, he thought. Eddy would, he guessed, but would he let it go at that? Would he ask too many

questions? Would he call the police?

The little dogs finished eating and stood at the sliding glass door, waiting to be let out. Munio obliged them and walked into the cool fall air. The air cleared his head. It felt good to step out of the warm horrors of Sandra's house. He walked back to the gazebo and sat on the steps, smoking. What would become of his beloved gazebo project? He told himself that he must continue for Sandra's sake. She would have wanted him to. The dogs yipped at some imaginary predator lurking in the shrubbery, or perhaps a possum. Munio called to them. It was then he realized he never even knew their names.

The heat rose from his neck and up his face as the tears rolled off his cheeks and onto the gazebo steps. Loud moans came from deep inside his chest, so loud that the little dogs came to Munio's side and sat. He patted their soft, well-tended fur.

"What will we do, doggies? I don't know what we will do now. Your mother doesn't feel so well, and I don't think she will be getting better, to tell you the truth." He smiled between his sobs. "We will just keep on doing what we usually do, and maybe she will get better. Maybe she will get better." Munio wiped his eyes with his sleeve and walked toward the house.

Once in the house, Munio reluctantly moved down the hall towards Sandra's bedroom. The lights were not on, and with the darkness returned Munio's thick fear. As he stood at the foot of the bed, his eyes adjusted quite well to the dark, and Sandra's silhouette was very plain. Watching closely for a slight rise of her chest or a twitch of a finger, Munio studied the body, but nothing, nothing spelled life about Sandra anymore. Tears rolled as Munio got down on his knees at the foot of the bed, and began what was a combination of Catholic prayer and Mayan chants for the dead. As night wore on, Munio held steadfast in that position, while he chanted, prayed, and cried for something to change, for something to make that strange woman sit up in that bed. It was midnight before Munio suspended the ritual he had begun a good four hours ago.

His joints stiff and his body weak, he slowly rose to his feet. Through the whole ceremony, the little dogs slept peacefully, cuddled up to their dead mother's side. Munio sat on the bed beside Sandra. He touched her forearm below the sleeve of her new black and gold dress. Her skin felt cool and strange. He gently moved his body around, and lay down on top of her. Munio let out lonesome awful howls like a coyote. Though her body had begun to stiffen, her silicone breasts maintained their life, their artificial softness Munio remembered as he rested his head upon them. For a moment, he felt aroused and by his thoughts of their few sensual moments. He thought of their dance that first night, and the tightening sweet bond of love that had been circling the two of them for these past few weeks.

Reality set in, and Munio knew that he must have a drink. As he carefully climbed off Sandra, her body rocked stiffly. He bent over and gently kissed

her half-parted lips. Her fixed, blue-gray eyes stared blankly at Munio from behind her thick bifocals. He smiled at her as he backed away from the bed and turned to move down the hall. The little lap dogs watched, and after he left, snuggled down again next to their beloved Sandra.

Confined to darkness for hours and hours, his eyes were hurt by the light in the refrigerator. When the top popped on his beer, the sound seemed to echo through the house. Little bubbles of froth crept out of the top, and Munio took a hefty swig. The taste and feel of that cold beer comforted Munio like a warm bath. He leaned on the open refrigerator, drank the beer in one long gulp, and reached for another.

The wooden chair screeched across the tile floor as Munio slid into it. The bottle of whiskey tipped skyward and burned a trail down his raw throat. Munio picked up the page filled with Sandra's last words. He cursed it and himself for how it haunted him. He had to read it, he thought, but who would do that?

Munio thumbed through a stack of scraps of paper stuck in his wallet. Finally, he stopped at one. Another swallow of whiskey downed, Munio walked over to the counter and picked up the telephone.

"Pee Wee's," the voice said.

"May I speak with Eddy, please?" Munio asked.

"You got him. Munio? Is that you?"

"Yes, it is."

"What are you doing, boy?"

"Well, I , ah, need a favor of you, Eddy."

"What?"

"I cannot read a letter I have, and I want you to read it for me."

"Yeah, I'll do that. That gal write you a love letter?" Eddy chuckled and kidded Munio.

"I don't think so. I don't know, but can I come there now?"

"Yeah, I'll be here til four. Come on." Eddy said cheerfully.

"Ok, I will arrive soon."

Eddy mocked Munio's style of speech and his heavy accent, "All right mon, go ahead on and arrive soon."

\* \* \* \* \*

Munio walked down the dark hall once again to Sandra's room. He carried a white taper held in a brass holder. Its yellow flame flickered wildly as he walked. He set it on the nightstand. "Sandra, I must leave for a short time. I will be back. Your doggies are here, and I will leave this flame to warm you until I return." He kissed her sweetly on the cheek and felt his stomach seize when he caught a whiff of blood, brains and candle wax. A grimace came across his sad brown face as he backed away from the bed.

A small brass key rack was mounted on the kitchen wall next to the car-

port door. Munio reflected on it. He had never handled her keys and looked upon it as an intimate act. When he lifted them off the hook, the jingle signaled the lap dogs. Often Sandra took them in the car. The three bounced and wagged at Munio's feet.

"You stay here with your mother. I will be back soon. You cannot go for the ride, now." They whined, but Munio ignored them.

Instead, he studied the key ring. In addition to keys, the ring held a small Swiss Army knife and a little Plexiglas square that encased a photo of the dogs posed with Santa Claus. Munio smiled as he looked at the ring, squeezed it as if doing so could bring back the warmth of holding her hand. After three tries, he discovered the key for the carport door. After one last swig of whiskey, he carefully folded Sandra's letter, which he put in the back pocket of his jeans.

The little dogs still whined and followed him to the door. "No, you cannot go, I say. I will return. Back up now."

* * * * *

The gray gravel crunched beneath Munio's work boots in the parking lot of Pee Wee's. His footsteps sounded solid and rhythmic on the wooden floor as he walkied over to where he saw Eddy and Destiny at the bar.

"Hey, boy," Eddy said, and held out his hand.

Munio took it and smiled weakly. "Hey, Destiny." He nodded to her.

"Hey, Munio. What's happening?" She smiled at him.

"Oh, not much. I needed to show Eddy something, that's all." Munio gave Eddy a look that he understood to mean this reading must be private.

"Look a here, Destiny. I'm going to take Munio back to the office for a minute. Call if anybody needs something, all right?"

"No problem."

Eddy motioned to Munio to follow him, and they entered a little room behind the bar. Eddy sat in a swivel office chair at the big wooden desk in the room, and Munio sat in a straight back wooden chair which sat beside the desk.

"Now, what's this you got to have read? What the hell smell is that? "

Munio had completely forgotten that he had shit in his pants. "Oh, ah, I haven't taken a shower today. I was sweating a lot. Sorry."

"Damn man, that's some funky ass shit, right there. Whewww! Ok, so let me see this thing."

"I just can't read it, you know? I just can't!" Munio slammed his fist on the desk. Eddy sat up in his chair, worried.

"Calm down, bud, calm down now. It's all right. Lots of people can't read. It ain't no sin. Just inconvenient sometimes. Just calm down. Let me see it," Eddy said soothingly.

Munio pulled the letter from his pocket. "I don't know what it says, man."

Eddy took it and unfolded it. "Damn nice handwriting!" Eddy chuckled and winked at Munio who sat across from him with a frozen look of terror. "Cool it, son. Just simmer down."

"This is serious, Eddy."

"All right, all right. Here we go. ' Dear Munio', it says, ah. 'I am sorry to leave you in this way. My life throughout has held so many unexpected twists, and I suppose this one is no different.

"'Today, after speaking with Audrey, I did some thinking, and I realized two things. One is that I have not had the courage to be who I really was, because if I had, I would have remained a gay man. One can only do what one feels is right on any given day, and since I made my change, I just never have felt right, really. The second thing is the most insurmountable problem I face today. It is an obstacle that is even harder to deal with than having a,'" Eddy looked up at Munio. "'sex change'?" Eddy dropped the letter from in front of his face. "Who is this guy, man?" Eddy snickered as he asked.

Munio leaped to his feet, balled up his fists, and took a fighting stance. "Don't make fun of her, man! Don't fuck with her, Eddy! I'll kill you! I'll kill you!"

Eddy jumped to his feet as well. "Motherfucker, sit down!" He pointed to the chair. "Now, I mean it, Munio! We ain't getting into it. I'm trying to help you, man. Now, this is all just a little weird, so excuse me, but I ain't really never read no letter no sex change person wrote, all right? Just bear with me, ok?" They both sat back down, and Eddy cleared his throat.

"All right, where was I? Oh yeah. 'I was born with a silver spoon in my mouth, and it has worked out ultimately to be a curse more than it has been a blessing. It is one area of my life I do not feel, or rather, I do not know how to change. You met me at the country club, and that environment is all I know. It is not your world, and I do not think it could be. You, Munio, are a wonderfully simple man, and I do not mean that in any derogatory sense at all. Please forgive me, but our worlds could never join. This afternoon I faced that truth.

"'Please notify Audrey of my decision here, and perhaps, she might be of help with the dogs. God knows I feel guilty about them, but I just feel I must go on.

"'Munio, no matter what you ever do in this world, let me assure you I will always love you. These last few weeks have been such a bright spot in my life. With the exception of my son, I have never loved another as deeply as I loved you even in the short time we spent together.

"'Forgive me for this, but I can't bear the shame of my feelings. I hate myself so much, and I guess I always have. Ultimately, I am afraid I always will no matter what I try. Forgive me, and be kind to yourself, Munio. All my love, Sandra.'"

Eddy looked up at Munio who was bent over with his elbows on his

206

knees and his palms cupping his face, streaming silent tears. "Hey man, don't worry about it. This ain't the first time a guy ever got dumped, you know. There will be other women for you. This, ah, gal, ah, sounded kind of mixed up anyhow, you know? Sounds like she done you a favor really, man. You think?" Eddy spoke softly to Munio.

"Yeah, I guess you're right. I guess so. It was just a surprise." He sniffed loudly and tried to regain his composure. "Well, thanks, man, for reading, it, ok?" He stood quickly.

"Well, don't rush off. Why don't you stay and let me buy you a few drinks? Stay and have some laughs with me and Destiny, ok? It'll do you good. You don't need to be off alone when you're feeling so bad." Eddy patted him on the back. "What do you say, man?"

Munio nodded, "Yeah, I could use a drink. I'll stay for a short while."

"Ok, ok, good." Eddy ushered him back out to the bar where he took a seat by Destiny.

"Hey, bubbles." Destiny poked him in the ribs and winked.

Munio chuckled a little and smiled. "Hello girl. How are you?" He spoke with no emotion.

"Swell. Boy, you sure are fired up tonight. You sure you got a pulse?" Destiny cackled and slammed her beer can down on the bar.

Eddy put a beer and a shot in front of Munio. Munio nodded at him in thanks, slugged the shot instantly and washed it away with a fresh cool mouthful of beer.

"Ah, Munio got dumped by some broad."

"Really? I didn't know you was going with anyone."

"I wasn't really. Don't worry about it. It's over." He spoke blankly in hopes they would change the subject.

Munio gritted his teeth. His brown eyes begged to weep again, but he held firm, biting his tongue so hard it bled and formed a salty red pool in the bottom of his mouth. He swallowed it like a shot. The pain he felt was almost comforting as a distraction from the agony in his heart. He knew what he must do, and he would do it. After all, he was a man of honor, if nothing else.

Eddy and Destiny giggled frivolously, completely unaware of the horrendous drama that gripped Munio's mind beneath his wild black curls. Munio barely heard their laughter on the periphery of his consciousness. Where his thoughts were, where his soul was, where his mind's eye focused was in that bedroom with Sandra and with the flickering flame of the lone candle on the night stand.

"Eddy?" Munio said.

"Yeah?"

"I will be staying at this lady's house that I am building the gazebo for. She has been called away, and she wants me to look after her dogs. Still, I will meet you at the gym on time in the morning, ok?"

"Yeah, that's cool. Just get your ass up. Why don't you give me the phone number?"

"No, I don't know it. I'll just meet you. I'll get up, don't worry."

"You ain't got her number?"

"No, I never called her."

"Hey, ain't that woman that done wrote that letter the one you are building that thing for?"

"No, that was somebody else. No, no."

"Damn, Munio. You do know half the fucking town. Damned friendliest foreigner on the planet, by God!" Eddy laughed.

"So, in the morning I will see you, yes?"

"You bet your ass I will. We gots to grow boy! It's almost showtime!"

"Good night, Destiny."

"Nighty night, Munio. See ya. Don't be a stranger. I had fun the other night."

Munio smiled, "Yeah, me too."

* * * * * * * *

The carport door jingled from a single small bell tied to a string looped around the door knob. Before he could get the key out of the door, the lap dogs appeared to greet him.

"Hello, hello, ok, ok. You want to go outside? I let you out." He walked to the sliding glass door, opened it, and they went scrambling for the back yard.

He followed them out, sat down on a lawn chair, and lit a cigarette. A good breeze had kicked up, rustling the drying leaves. The coolness felt good on his hot face and sweaty scalp.

A strange stillness enveloped the house. No music played, no cabinet doors opened or closed, no pots simmered, no teapots steamed in the warm, sweet smell of Sandra's kitchen. Munio listened to the silence and dreaded the trip down that long hallway. A corner of his mouth twitched, and he moved to the liquor cabinet. The mescal called to him. Three shots later Munio had bolstered his fortitude enough to go see Sandra.

A pool of warm white wax now surrounded the taper that stood tall. It provided very little light to view the grim reality. This suited Munio fine, as he only wanted to keep her company for the night.

Lighting conditions could not, however, mask the distinct smell of death in the room. A warm, growing, bitter sweetness emanated from Sandra's body, slowly but surely thickening the air. It was an olfactory plague that sought to overtake every molecule of fresh air. By morning, it would begin its campaign up the hall, drifting, gentle as a cloud, to the other rooms of the house.

Munio's sense of smell was unfortunately and surprisingly keen. His first line of defense was to light a cigarette, and as it burned away while he gazed at her body, he remembered there was a pack of incense in his truck. Firing up

several sticks at once, he soon won the battle temporarily. The smoke rose in tight gray curls, silhouetted by the waning candle's flame.

Shot after shot Munio poured down his throat until half past three in the morning. With the little lap dogs curled up next to Sandra, Munio carefully lay on the untouched, still crisply made, other side of the king-sized bed. He reached over and stroked Sandra's bare left forearm. After feeling how cold she had become, tears began to softly flow again, and his brown eyes shone bright with the candle's reflection. Munio soothingly began to sing his favorite song, "The Impossible Dream", with the clarity of an operatic tenor. When all the words he knew had come and gone, Munio hummed lightly, the sound ebbing away until he was released into sleep.

The first sound Munio heard the next morning was a mockingbird, and he knew he had overslept. Without any thought of the dead woman he had bunked next to, Munio rolled over on top of her to catch sight of the bedside clock. It said seven-thirty. As he rolled back over Sandra, his stomach turned as he grasped her arm. It was as solid as concrete. He tried to pick it up, but rigor mortis had set in. He sighed but kept moving, bounding off the bed and down the hall.

As he strode he spoke. "If you dogs want something to eat, you better get in here. I must leave immediately."

The dogs took him at his word and were right on his heels. He opened a can of food for them, and they wolfed it down in no time. Munio let them out for a bathroom break, and he did the same only indoors.

"Let's go, doggies!" He called to them and clapped for further emphasis. As he shut the door, he called to Sandra, "I'll be back in a couple of hours!"

* * * * * * * *

Munio trotted across the gravel parking lot in order to not be one more second late than possible, and as he flung open the door, he saw that Eddy was engaged in posing. Clad in only a skin tight pair of gray knit shorts, and with the aid of the mirror, Eddy immersed himself in his muscle. Pose after pose he struck, standing tall and staring dead into that mirror with all the gusto of a gunslinger ready to draw.

Eddy had begun in earnest to tan in the past three weeks. For thirty minutes daily, naked to the world, Eddy would, in essence, microwave his skin inside a human waffle iron. The ten violet blue fluorescent bulbs hummed him to sleep while the pigment bubbled in his skin and rendered it a strange reddish brown. Even Munio, who was raised in a land whose people bore many shades of brown, did not think this shade of Eddy's skin was one found in nature.

As he leaned on a wall by the door, Munio watched his friend and, again, felt his tired grief stricken eyes fill with tears. Munio felt Eddy slipping away, buried by layer upon layer of muscle and strangely tanned skin. When

he reviewed the structural changes that had occurred in Eddy's face alone, he cringed. That forehead had grown far over his eyes, and his cheekbones formed peaks on either side of his enlarged and puffy nose. Munio feared Eddy had lost his soul to his inheritance from Jimmy Ray Jones.

"Hey boy!" Eddy called across the room to Munio. "How long you been standing over there?"

"Long enough to catch most of the show, I believe."

"What do ya think? Ain't no mother fucker gonna touch this shit, man. Ain't nobody. I can't believe it's me in the mirror, man. I look like one of them dudes in the muscle mags, man. I can't believe it, and I ain't even carb depleted, yet. It's gonna be awesome, man. It's gonna be hell."

While he put his sweats on over his shorts, people who had seen the posedown praised him profusely. Eddy was friendly and gracious to a point, but today he agreed with every compliment offered. He even pointed out additional nuances that they had neglected to mention.

"Damn, we got to get rolling. Got to greet your public though, Munio. I guess I better be a getting used to it, huh?"

"Yeah, right superstar. Do not forget you are human Eddy. Don't forget that. You have pushed your body to some unnatural maneuvers. It may not accept such behavior always, you know."

Eddy frowned and looked irritated, "What the hell you talking about, man? I feel great. Gotta live for today, Munio. My body likes being like this."

"Ok, ok." Munio held up his hands in surrender. "What is it we shall do today, Arnold Jr.?"

Eddy grinned, "You're funny, buddy, real fucking funny." Eddy studied Munio's face. "You looking burnt, bud. Have a late night with them dogs?" He laughed.

"No, I just feel tired, that's all."

"Ok, well, you can split after we do bis if you want. I'm not going to knock myself out on legs today, and so I don't need no spot."

"Ok, that's good. Start with dumbell curls then?"

"Yeah, yeah, that sounds good." Munio followed behind Eddy as he strode across the gym to the dumbell platform. He moved with the purpose of a soldier headed for battle.

"Good job, Eddy," Munio said after the last of twelve sets of bicep exercises.

"Thanks, man. Wheww, I sure get wore out lately, though. Starting to cut my food some, some carbs. I don't like fuckin' with my food. I tell you what."

"Yeah," Munio answered absently.

"Hey, you know there's a rumor goin' around that Ida Blue might be a fuckin' narc."

"Oh really?"

Eddy sat down on a bench. "Yeah, somebody saw her hangin' out with

this dude that has been known to narc. Got busted a couple of years ago for 'roids and never served hardly no time." Eddy wiped the sweat off his face with his sweatshirt. "You just never know what somebody's going to do, you know?"

Munio smiled and raised his eyebrows. "No, Eddy, you never do." He forced the feelings away. Later, he would have plenty of time to cry and wonder why Sandra had done this horrible thing.

"You heading out?" Eddy asked Munio.

"Yes, I suppose I will get to work. I would like to take advantage of this good weather."

"Yeah, yeah, hey, you ought to take me over there to see this thing. I want to see what you're building."

"Oh, ok, yeah, sometime I will do that after I finish."

"How much longer you think it'll take you?"

Munio put his hand over his mouth to help him think better. "If everything goes good, I hope two maybe three weeks." Munio nodded and smiled at Eddy.

"Hey, right around my show. We'll have to have a party over there. At least you and me ought to smoke a joint in it. How long is that woman going to be gone that you're house sitting for?"

"Ah, I'm not sure. Her mother was sick so she said it might vary, her times."

"Now, what's this woman's name?"

"Sandra."

"Now, I thought Sandra was the one who dumped you. The one with the letter?" Eddy questioned good naturedly.

Munio's adrenaline soared as he realized he had tripped his story up. "Her name is Sandra, too," he covered.

"That's some coincidence, huh?" Eddy chuckled. "Fucking Sandra city."

"Yeah, right. So, I'll see you tomorrow morning, or you want to take off tomorrow? I can't remember the schedule."

"Uh, let's see. Actually, I do take off tomorrow. Just aerobics for forty-five minutes."

"Ok, good then. I'll see you day after tomorrow."

"Well, don't be a stranger. Come by, and we'll smoke one. I'm off from the bar, too."

"Ok, ok, maybe I will just do that. Take care, Eddy." They looked at each other and hugged. Munio needed it, but Eddy laughed at it. "Damn, look at us. We're gonna be riding piggy back if we don't watch out, honey," Eddy kidded.

"Bye, Edwardo, you freak, you!" Munio waved as he walked away.

"See ya. Have a good day, brother," Eddy called out.

# CHAPTER XXXI

The lap dogs were all that was stirring at Sandra's as the little bell rang on the door when he entered the kitchen. Their six brown eyes stared grimly up at him and seemed to want to know why things were so strange in their home.

"What is the matter, little dogs? You want to go outside? You want a food, I mean a cookie or something?" Munio went over to the counter where the cookie jar was located. As the lid clanked lightly, the dogs got more lively. When they heard his hand rattling around, causing those cookies to hit the sides of the jar, they began to dance. "Oh, you like this, eh? Ok, well, here you go." He bent over and handed each one a little cookie, which each took politely with a wag. Munio stood leaning against the counter watching them leave little crumbs on the floor. When they finished, there were no crumbs, no trace of those cookies. "Ok, why don't you dogs go outside, eh? I don't want any dog droppings to pile up in this house. God knows it is already smelling plenty weird around here as it is." Munio snorted a laugh, surprising himself with his humor around this grim subject. The sliding door slid smoothly on its track as he opened it for the little dogs. They trotted right out into the back yard, and Munio followed. He walked slowly out to the gazebo. Stopping about twenty feet from it, he put his hands in his jeans pockets and stopped to study it, rolling a soggy toothpick back and forth across his teeth. Soon, all three little dogs collected at Munio's cowboy boots to notify him of their readiness to return to the inside of their house. "Let's go with you then." he said as he turned on his heel.

Munio walked straight through the kitchen and down the hall to Sandra's bedroom for the first visit of the day. She did not look well at all. Her face was sunken in, and her body had certainly turned the corner on accepting death. Munio could no longer pretend she might be napping. Decay was not just inevitable, it was happening and happening fast. With Munio's sensitive nose, the growing aroma was causing him to salivate heavily as one does when they are on the verge of puking.

Gingerly, he sat down on the bed. "Hello dear," Munio started out. "I fed the dogs, and he is doing fine." He looked around the room as he spoke, not really wanting to look at Sandra directly. "You look peaceful. I hope you feel better today wherever you might be. Don't worry about anything because I will take care of it. I will. I think I know what I will do." He tenderly patted her arm and pretended that the chill of it did not send a sharp reflex of pain starting in his groin and flashing straight up his body to his heart. He took a breath and swallowed as he continued, "So, I have much work to do today, and it will not get done if I am visiting with you all day. You rest, and I will be back."

The little dogs now followed him everywhere, and when he got up to

leave, so did they. Munio walked out of the house and out to his truck. He opened up his toolbox and took out his old worn leather nail apron. Slipping it around his waist as he walked back into the house, Munio pulled out his metal tape measure and strode back down the hall to Sandra's room. Munio leaned over the bed, stretching out the tape measure along the length of Sandra's body. He squinted at the mark he decided on and wrote it on a notepad that he pulled from another pocket of the apron. Then, he moved on to her width, checking the measurements at her hips and shoulders. Finally, he got a reading on her depth and wrote it down as well. Without missing a beat, he walked straight back out to the truck and unlocked the gate in order to pull it into the back yard as usual.

Unrolling the long orange extension cord, he plugged in his saw and set it on the floor of the gazebo. After setting a new four by eight sheet of plywood on the sawhorses, Munio set about chalking some lines. As precise and constant as a beaver, Munio measured and cut six pieces of plywood. It did not take him long to fasten them all together using his drill and screws. In an hour and a half, Munio had constructed the proverbial pine box.

Throwing it over his head, he rested the sides on his shoulders and carried it upside down like a canoe into the house. In the house, however, this canoe did not want to turn corners. This put a cog in Munio's planning, because he wanted Sandra to lie in state in her room, where he was sure she would have wanted to stay. There would be no way in hell, short of removing walls, to carry Sandra out of that bedroom in that box. He did not let this logistical problem impede his progress, and moved right on ahead. He set the box on the floor in the living room.

Quickly, he moved down the hall to Sandra's room and, without a moment's hesitation started wrapping Sandra in the comforter she was lying on. Then he jogged out to his truck and returned with a new fifty-foot package of white nylon rope. From his jeans pocket, he took a pocket knife, cut open the package, and began uncoiling one end. Munio systematically cut lengths of the rope and tied them efficiently at her shoulders, waist, hips, mid thighs, and ankles. Now she looked enormous with all the added bulk of the king sized comforter. He gave a tug on Sandra's ankles and the bundle moved. He smiled and nodded. The little dogs had stood at the entrance to the bedroom and watched.

He pulled on her ankles and moved her diagonally across the bed. Despite his gentleness, a dull thud sounded as her body slid off the bed and onto the floor. On the carpet, the resistance was much greater, and Munio had to lean back on his heels with all his body weight to keep the momentum going. He persisted and within minutes, Munio, Sandra, and the three dogs arrived in the living room. Munio pulled Sandra along side of the pine box.

Munio pointed his index finger at the bundle and chuckled. "Shewww girl, you were sure easier to dance with than to drag, I want to tell you!" The

little dogs looked at each other and wagged their tails.

After that effort, Munio took a break and fired up a cigarette. He also got himself a beer out of the refrigerator. Taking a seat on a white leather couch, Munio had a new perspective on the living room. What he realized was that he had never been in it. Sandra and he had always stayed in the kitchen or out in the back yard. Munio thought about what a waste it was to have such a large room full of fancy furniture where no one ever sits. He thought the decorating was really fine, with the accent on antique white, gold, and overdone. Liberace would have been proud.

When he finished his break, he was up again, turning the pine box on its side with the opening towards Sandra. As gently as he could manage, he rolled Sandra up on her side with her back to the box. Then, a little scoot at a time, Munio slowly backed her body into the box by moving one end and then the other, and by the time he had been through twelve or so go-rounds of this, Sandra's big frame was tucked neatly in the box. When Munio was sure she was as snug as he could get her, he straddled the box and flipped it upright.

"There now," he said, dusting his hands to rid himself of a little sawdust. "How is that? Are you comfortable? Good fit, eh? Yes, a good fit, indeed. Now, see?" He pointed to the kitchen doorway. "You can get more light in here. That bedroom is so dark. If you look up just a little, you can see outside, in the back, the gazebo. I will wave to you while I work."

He knelt down, eased back the comforter from her face, and gulped. With the added effect of the light of day, her skin was gray as a rainy day. Munio stared, and slowly dissolved from able caretaker to a bewildered little child. As he slumped down, with both arms wrapped around his legs, tears and loud wails erupted from the sad man for the better part of an hour. The little dogs shivered at the foot of the box, confused and afraid.

Munio felt this was the saddest thing that had ever happened to him. Pictures of the dance they had that first night streaked across his mind, and that strange new safe warmness that he had felt.

The loud ring of the telephone cut the silence like a machine gun. Munio sat bolt upright, sniffling, wide-eyed. He thought about how powerful the gunshot must have sounded.

"Hello, thank you for calling. I'm not in right now, but your call is important to me. Please leave your name, number, and a brief message, and I'll return your call as soon as possible." Sandra's voice again rang through her house in her pleasant and dignified best femme voice. The dogs and Munio looked at each other and smiled, so glad to hear that voice again.

"Sandra, are you home? If you are, pick up." Munio recognized Audrey's voice. "Call me, will you? I'll be home for, oh another hour, or call me tonight, ok? See ya. Oh yeah, I hope I wasn't too rough on you about Munio yesterday." She giggled. "Anyhow, I'll speak to you about it."

The machine made a few more sounds, and the great wall of silence re-

sumed. The adrenaline rush made Munio's skin tingle almost loud enough to hear. He had forgotten there was a world outside of that house. He had forgotten about people who might call for her. He had forgotten about how unusual his handling of her death might be to anyone in the civilized world.

The phone call sobered Munio. Wiping his eyes, he turned to the pine box once more and worked his way down her body, untying the strands of rope that bound her in the comforter for transport. With each one, he lifted, straightened, and tucked in the satin maroon cloth of the comforter. He finished each section with a couple of tender pats.

"There now, Miss Sandra. Feel better to be relieved of those ropes, eh? Yes, I think so. You rest because we will begin the ceremony tonight. I have much work to do. The dogs are here, and they will be keeping you company as always. Ok, so goodbye."

Munio went into the kitchen and grabbed a beer. As he shut the door, he looked down, and there were the lap dogs at his feet.

"Oh, you people want a snack, do you? Let me see how your cookie supply is holding out.

\* \* \* \* \* \*

With his drill, he began to extract all of the screws that held the center pieces of the gazebo's plywood decking. This left exposed the new yellow pine joists. Munio climbed down to the ground below through the new hole and bounced around on the area as if testing something. The fescue that had been sentenced to death by the creation of the gazebo had faded only slightly since being shadowed by the construction. Lighting up a cigarette, Munio sat back on the floor and let his legs dangle in the open hole. He took several soothing deep breaths, and the tension in his face dissolved. For the next few minutes, Munio measured and, with short wooden stakes marked off a long rectangle on the ground beneath the gazebo. Carefully and neatly, Munio ran thin white twine around the stakes and then tied it off on the fourth one.

"Well, I guess it is time to get going now," Munio said aloud and climbed back out of the hole.

From his truck, Munio took out a small wooden box. He marched into the house, and in the living room, with Sandra and the three little lap dogs, began to undress. He was quickly reminded of yet another nasty bit of reality when he removed his jeans and found dried shit caked all over himself. Disgusted and nauseated, he located Sandra's bathroom and quickly showered.

Back in the living room, he took from the small box a long, soft, cream-colored cloth. Munio began to wrap it around his waist and groin. After several passes, Munio's privates were covered, and he tucked the end into the top where it held firm. It looked like a huge diaper. In the front of the waistband, he tucked a gold cloth with red and black images of catlike humanlike creatures and assorted geometric patterns. Munio looked up into the huge full-length mirror that blanketed one wall of the living room.

Chill bumps exploded from every pore as he gazed at himself. It was a man he had never seen. An ancient man that he had only dreamed of and imagined from stories told by his great grandmother. She would tell him how he looked so much like his grandfather. On his thirteenth birthday, she awarded this loincloth to him. He wanted to wear it immediately, but she warned him not to ever wear it frivolously. It was to be used in the most sacred ceremonies, and only when he became a man would those occasions arise. She said, in fact, that there might be only one occasion in his lifetime that would be so special, and after it ended, he should burn the cloth as an offering to the eternal spirit of the earth to forever seal the moment as sacred.

Strange as it was, nothing, not even his Olympic moment or the parade in Monkey River Town following it, felt as important as this. He looked again at himself and thought how proud and powerful he looked, how right his intentions felt. For the first time in his life, he felt like he was doing exactly the right thing, and he was in the right place to do it.

Munio took a multicolored headband from the special box. It had a few feathers and several short strands of green, white, and red beads attached to it. He wrapped it around his wooly head and tied it in the back. He checked in the mirror and smiled. With each special item he put on his spirits lifted higher and higher.

On his feet, he tied a pair of sandals that were nothing more than flat pieces of leather in the shape of a foot with a rope attached in three places. His feet felt happy to be free from the confines of his heavy socks and boots. He wiggled all of his toes.

"Hello, toe," Munio called to them and laughed.

For the final touch, Munio picked up a small glass jar and stood close to the mirror. He opened the jar and looked inside. It was full of vibrant, turquoise paint. With one finger, he scraped out a small amount and made several horizontal stripes across his chest. Reaching in the jar again, he reloaded his finger and applied more small stripes on either cheek and two upon his forehead. He backed away from the mirror to get a better overall look. On his upper arms, he painted three streaks, and then he put the lid on the jar.

He was turning to the side and back to enjoy his image when he suddenly remembered something. He walked over to the pine box, kneeled down and planted a kiss on Sandra's cheek. His voice lowered, and he spoke forcefully. "I am Nika, the Mayan warrior chosen to love and care for you. There is nothing I will not do to please you."

The coolness of her skin again brought the rain to his brown eyes. The warrior, eyes shut, howled with sadness for the loss of his queen. When he opened them at last, the three little dogs had eased up to his face. He reached for them, and they eagerly accepted his affection, offering their little pink tongues to remove his tears. One of them had a turquoise tongue, he noticed. He pushed away from them and looked in the mirror.

216

"Oh brother," he said frowning when he saw the smeared blue stripe on his left cheek. He went to the kitchen for a paper towel to remove the damaged stripe.

He repaired the stripe and then realized he had forgotten one other accessory. From the pocket of his jeans, he pulled a large silver medallion strung on a thin piece of black leather. On the front of it was cast an image of Kinich Ahau, the Mayan sun deity. Munio put it over his head and centered it on his breast.

Finally, he snapped onto each wrist small leather bracelets with several small copper jingle bells on them. Munio's movement gave them harmonic life with sensual, low-pitched sounds.

Munio withdrew another bottle of mescal, poured a fresh shot, and knelt beside Sandra. In a Mayan dialect, he spoke a few words, then, spreading Sandra's stiff lips as best he could, he poured the liquor into her mouth. He poured himself a shot, and after repeating the same words, drank it down.

He licked his lips and shook his head. "That was so good. I think I'll have another. In fact," he turned to the dogs, "I will drink to include you in this ceremony in honor of your mother who has passed." Munio smiled.

Munio proceeded to pour three more shots and toast each dog. He gathered his cigarettes and the mescal and marched out to the gazebo, jingling all the way. Mescal was sprinkled inside the twined-off rectangle under the gazebo. With the precision of a chef cutting squares of lasagna, Munio used a machete to methodically cut and remove the layer of fescue that covered his rectangle. He stacked the squares outside the hole near the lumber pile.

Laid bare was a rich brown tract of dirt. Munio worked a pick ax all through it, shoveling the loose dirt away. It was not easy because his movements were confined by the floor joist structure, which came to about the top of his thighs. Luckily, the earth was somewhat soft, bearing no stones or roots.

His wrists jingled constantly and loudly. Munio became entranced by their sound and by the work. Like a long distance runner, he found a groove and stayed there. Cigarettes hung from his lips most of the time, and he drank on the run, slugging several swallows at a time. From time to time, he would chant Mayan phrases.

After two hours of digging, the rectangle was knee deep, and at four hours, he was waist deep. The extra depth gave him more freedom to move. He ran out of room under the gazebo to stash the removed dirt and just pitched shovelfuls into the yard.

Only an inch of mescal remained in the bottle, and a big round yellow harvest moon bloomed overhead when Munio was at eye level with the ground. The liquor, exhaustion, his own fear of dying, and claustrophobia weighed on his mind. He began to hallucinate, shadows took on life. He felt pulled by the gods of the underworld that his grandmother hadtold him of

long ago. She said a person could be subdued for evil purposes. Munio jingled his wrists hard to repel them. The sound echoed loudly in the hole.

He held his course and completed the hole, a beautiful, perfect grave in which to retire his dear Sandra. He shinnied his way out and sat on the floor of the gazebo, and dirty legs swinging. One last swallow for him and the grave, and he set the bottle down. He tucked his cigarettes in the waistband of his loincloth. Freezing and caked all over with the moist, he walked slowly toward the house.

The little dogs assaulted him in a frenzy, leaping and whimpering. He realized he had forgotten to feed them dinner, and they had not been outside since the afternoon. Munio trudged, grumbling to himself, to the kitchen table and slumped into a chair with one jingle-belled arm draped over the back, the other hunging straight down, and his leg crossed at the ankle on his other knee. His warpaint smeared, Munio smoked a roach. The little dogs paced back and forth in front of him, whining and glancing at him anxiously.

"Give me a break, will you? I'll feed you. I'll feed you. Jesus Christ." He spoke to them like inconsiderate children. "I been out there digging a grave for your poor mother all day and all night. My back hurts, and my feet are frozen. You just got to give me a minute to recuperate from this work. Let me get a few tokes in, and I'll be better, ok?" The dogs lay down by his chair. He looked at them and felt guilty for speaking rudely. He thought about how they must be so sad because Sandra used to spoil them so. That is all she did, was pamper those dogs.

Without any further thought, he got up and took two cans of dog food from the cupboard. While the dogs relieved themselves, he walked back out to the gazebo. He shivered as he walked and wrapped his arms around himself as he moved up the steps in the moonlight. The orange glow of his cigarette led the way. Darkness obscured the bottom of the hole, and its depth seemed infinite. He jingled quietly as he shook from the cold, his bare skin canvassed in a layer of chill bumps.

Suddenly, the dogs, who had been softly making their way around the yard, looked to the house. They raced towards it, barking to high heaven. Munio jogged and jingled behind them to see what was going on.

* * * * * * * *

As he passed through the sliding glass door, a wall of human screams rang out in the night as Munio collided with Audrey in the kitchen. Audrey, not prepared to encounter, here at midnight, a very dirty Mayan warrior in full regalia, jumped in the air and screamed repeatedly. Munio did the same. After their hysterical vocalizations ceased, they leaned on various things, doorways, counter tops, while their heart rate sought normality.

"Mother of God, Munio, what in the hell have you got on?"

He overrode her question with one of his own. "What in the hell are you

doing here at this time of night?"

"Answer me!" She pointed to him.

"Oh." Munio looked down at himself, "Well, it is a ceremonial costume of a Mayan warrior," Munio answered casually, with panic still burning in his eyes.

"Where's Sandra? I've been calling her all day. She never returned my calls. She never does that, so I thought I would stop by after the dance class. That was another thing. She didn't show up for class. So where is she?" Audrey walked further into the kitchen towards the living room. She started to peek around the corner, but Munio headed her off.

"Don't go in there!" he shouted.

"Why? What's going on around here, Munio?" She started to go in anyway, but Munio grabbed her shoulders and put his body in the doorway.

"You don't need to go in there."

"Where is Sandra?" she asked again, becoming very agitated. "Right now, Munio, I want you should tell me what is going on, and where she is!"

Munio paced back and forth in the kitchen, jingling and shaking his hands. He didn't know what else to do but tell the truth. It was so hard for him to say out loud what had happened. His sadness came upon him like a seizure, and he broke down.

"What's wrong, Munio? You have to tell me, what's wrong?" She walked over and grabbed his bare shoulders and shook him. Pulling her hands away, she made a disgusted face as she noticed the turquoise paint from his arms smeared over both of her palms. "Yuck, does this stuff stain?" With a look of sheer terror in her eyes, she quickly scanned her beige linen evening dress for stains, carefully holding her hands, with fingers spread, far away from her clothing. She walked over to the sink to wash it off.

"So, where is she Munio? Tell me this instant where she is! I demand it!" She stomped her feet and clenched her fists at him, her brown eyes furious.

Munio nervously tried to rake his hands through his hair, forgetting he was wearing a headband. He quickly lit a cigarette. His mind raced. He was in no position to lie to this woman, who already mistrusted him. Surely, if he refused to tell her, she would have the police over in an instant, and he so desperately did not want to have the ceremony interrupted. She was Sandra's dearest friend, however, and he reasoned that she did deserve to know.

"All right, I tell you. Sit down here, please. Just sit down here."

"I'm not sitting any goddamned place, mister! You better tell me right here and right now, Munio!"

Munio exploded in Audrey's face. "You want to know where she is? You want to know? Ok, she's in there! Go, see for yourself!" He stood in the doorway that separated the kitchen and the living room, and pointed directly at Sandra's box.

Audrey, puzzled, walked into the living room. With no light on, all she

could see was the outline of the large box. She looked at him again and pointed to concur that in the living room is where he meant her to go. He nodded at her, his headband feathers shaking and his beads swinging. Further into the living room, she crept towards the box. When she was midway across the room, Munio walked to a floor lamp in the corner and clicked it on.

As quickly as the lamp's light clicked on, absolute collapse set in for Miss Audrey, and she dropped to her knees in shock. She screamed and cried incoherently while Munio and the lap dogs sat on the couch. Munio cried loudly too, but it was drowned out by Audrey's wails.

A few minutes passed before Audrey's hysteria subsided. Disoriented, she looked around, trying to remember what happened before she glanced into that box and saw Sandra's withered face. Slumped on the floor, she sat up suddenly and spun around to find the rest of the pitiful crew who mourned on the couch.

"What has happened here?" she whispered softly.

"She killed herself with a pistol. It happened yesterday afternoon, late in the afternoon. I was working in the back yard. She came out to see me earlier. She was fine. She had a new wig and a new dress, and she brought champagne that we drank. She was going to fix dinner. But I come in when it gets almost dark. I sit at that table in there, in the kitchen. I call to her, but she doesn't come or say anything. Dinner was cooking already on the stove, so everything is ok, it seems. She never came out, though, and finally, I go back to see, eh? I call as I go down the hall, but she says not a thing. No response did I receive from her, but I keep going til I get to her bedroom. Still, I look in and see her. She looks asleep, you know, lying in the bed, face up. I walk up slow to not scare her, and I call to her. Still, no response, and then I speak loud, I scream finally. Nothing happened. It was dark so I reach over and turn on the lamp. That is when I see the pistol laying on her chest, in her hand." Munio became overcome with tears again. "She was so still." He sniffed and sobbed. "I lift up her head, and," his sobs got louder between words, "oh, her head is all messed up. It's so messed up." He could speak no further, and so he leaned over with his arms on his knees and his face in his hands.

Audrey, dumbfounded and still suspicious of Munio, fired, "How do I know you didn't kill her? How do I know that? Why didn't you call me?"

He jumped to his feet. Audrey ducked and covered her head, thinking Munio was about to assault her. "You don't believe me? How could you say that? I thought very much of Sandra, and you don't know this? We were having good times!" Then he remembered the letter Sandra had left on the nightstand. "I know how I prove this to you." He strode into the kitchen in a flash and returned quickly to find Audrey standing with her arms crossed. He shoved the letter in her hand. "There, you read that, and you will see!" He paced the living room back and forth while she read Sandra's farewell address.

220

Tears resurfaced as she read, and now rivers of thick mascara rivaled Munio's warpaint. When she finished, she gently sat down on the floor and leaned back against the firmness of the pine box. She sighed and said, "I'm sorry, Munio. I'm very sorry that I accused you. I don't know what to say. I'm like you in that she seemed happy when I saw her yesterday. She seemed fine, but I did say some things that disturbed her, I know."

"What things did you say?" Munio questioned her.

"Well, we were talking about you, and I, now, I'm sorry about this, but I didn't think you were right for Sandra, Munio. I was just talking about that, and I am sorry about that now. I was wrong, and I'm sorry." She held her hands out, palms up. She looked up at him and made eye contact. "I'm very sorry, Munio."

Munio looked at her angrily, yet still he nodded a silent acceptance of her apology. Just then a wave of exhaustion flooded over him, and he looked down at his dirtcaked body, realizing how cold he had become. He got up to get a drink. "Do you want a drink?"

"Drink? How can you drink at a time like this?"

Munio laughed out loud for the first time in a while. "Audrey, if there was ever a time to drink, it is now. If I had never had a drink in my life, I would choose this time to drink one. Now, do you or do you not want a drink?"

"What the fuck. Yeah, what are you having? I'm guessing not a gin gimlet, huh?"

"What is that? She had a lot of liquor. You can look. Maybe she has that," he said innocently.

It was now Audrey turn to laugh. "Never mind, honey. I'll try whatever you're having, and God, I hope I don't live to regret that." She sat on the couch, crossed her legs at the knee and straightened her long dark hair.

"What?"

"Never mind."

Munio brought a bottle of fine Russian vodka and two glasses. He poured each one half-full while Audrey sat there with her jaw dropped.

"Don't you think we need a mixer?"

"Mixer? You want some orange juice or a Coke? She had that, I think."

Audrey chuckled, "No, yeah, yeah, some orange juice and a spoon to stir it with, please."

Munio returned with a quart of orange juice and a spoon, which he handed to Audrey. Joining her on the couch, he watched her adjust her drink.

"Here's to you, Sandra," Audrey said, and Munio mumbled in agreement as their glasses met.

The high-powered liquor, which happened to be one-fifty proof, took their breath away. Both of them coughed in protest after the first sip. They looked at each other and laughed.

"So, now, why don't you clue me in as to what the hell you are doing

here?" Audrey waved her arm at the box and at Munio. "I mean, this is highly irregular, you know."

"I am executing the Mayan burial ceremony. All day and night I dug in the back yard under the gazebo. I will bury her there. I think she would like that, don't you?" Munio's face was most sincere.

Audrey's eyes got huge, and her jaw dropped again. "Are you out of your ever-loving mind? You can go to prison for doing something like that! You're crazy! Munio, I must call the authorities! You just can't bury people in your backyard! Is that what you people do in Belize?"

"If you had a backyard like this, yes, yes, I would. Audrey, don't think you will stop me from this! Sandra loved that backyard. She was so excited about the plans for the gazebo. This is what she would want, and I am going to do it with or without your acceptance."

"No, no, no, no, no, honey, you cannot do this, Munio. I'm telling you, you can't. You just can't." Audrey's face was stern. She scrambled to her feet as she spoke. "That's it, Munio. This charade is over. I'm calling somebody. If we tell them what happened, I'm sure they'll understand. They might want you to go back to Belize or something, but I don't believe they would give you jail time over this misunderstanding. Of course not, they'll understand." She was moving towards the kitchen when a powerful force pulled her back and hurled her through the air. She landed all the way across the big living room against the front door. She looked up, aghast, as Munio loomed over her.

"Audrey, I never felt so close to someone as I did to Sandra. Even though it was for a short while, it was a strong thing. These things I wear," he motioned to his bod,. "I wait til now. I mean, all my life I wait for this opportunity to show my feelings, you see. Sandra and I had not enough time, and so now, Audrey, it is my duty to achieve a proper ceremony for this woman. This is the only way I can show my feelings. I am telling you that nothing, no one will stop me. Also, I tell you this. I will defend my beliefs with my life." His face bore a strange stormy look.

Audrey collected herself and moved to the couch. "Ok, I heard you, but it can't happen, Munio? Eventually, someone will want to know where she is, and then what? What about her house here? With nobody taking care of it, the neighbors will surely notice she is gone. What about the dogs? You can't leave them here. This just will not work."

"You could stay here. You could keep the dogs. She had no family, only you, only me and these dogs. She cared about nothing else. If someone comes looking for her, you say she is out of town." Munio looked at Audrey and shrugged his shoulders.

"Well, what if-"

"What if nothing! Audrey, you do what you must do, but I am going to bury this woman out in the hole I dug. I am going to do it first thing in the morning when it gets light. Then, I am going to complete construction on the

gazebo just the way she wanted. Outside of these things, I don't know what I will do."

She felt totally helpless to change Munio's mind about this insane plan. The more she considered it, however, the less insane it actually sounded. Audrey knew for a fact that Sandra had absolutely no other family. She could stay here a while longer, perhaps, teach another class in the spring. She was not altogether unhappy in this little town.

Munio, who had been poised in a fist-clenched fighting stance, relaxed and joined her on the couch.

Her heart broke again as she reread Sandra's letter.

"Audrey, would you like another drink?" Munio put his hand on her arm. "I will fix it for you." His brown eyes seemed so gentle and compassionate.

"Yes, please." She forced a small, quick smile.

She finished the letter, but continued to stare at it. Her mind continued its self-persecution. If not for her biting comments about Munio and about Sandra's social orientation, Sandra would surely be alive today, she thought.

"Here." Munio handed her the drink.

"Thank you."

"Are you ok?" Munio asked.

Audrey's face wrenched with pain when she heard Munio's kind voice. Sandra's voice echoed in her mind as she recounted the pure joy she had with Munio.

Audrey walked into the kitchen and pulled a couple of paper towels off the roll. She blotted her eyes and looked at the black stains on the white paper.

"Auuuch. I must look like a raccoon." She blew her nose and went back to the couch.

"It is understandable that you cry. I never knew I had so many tears." Munio smiled at Audrey.

"You know, Munio." She blew her nose again. "Sandra was really crazy about you. Since I have known her, never have I seen her so excited about a man. This thing," she took a sip of her drink, "this thing between you. I mean, had you been spending a lot of time with her? It seemed to have happened so fast between you two."

Munio stood and paced. He stopped in front of Sandra's box and looked at her. "When I met her at the dance class, I did not feel it. I thought I would never see her again." He began to pace again. Audrey studied his brown body, scantily clad, littered with dirt and paint. "Then, the night I encountered her again, three weeks ago maybe?" He held his arms out for expression. "We sat in there." He pointed to the kitchen. "In there, we drank and drank. Then, we decided to dance. We decided to dance, and went out on that patio. It was when we, when our bodies touched that I felt something. I never have been in what I could say was love. Sex, I have had. I loved my uncle and my mother.

This feeling for Sandra was a warm feeling that felt like, like, strong, like anger only sweet, you know?" Munio looked at Audrey. "It was powerful. Only bad emotions have ever felt that strong to me, but this was," he stopped and his voice broke as her continued. "sweet. It was just so sweet." He moved in front of Sandra's box again and looked into it. "I think that I was in love with her."

Out of guilt and the authenticity of Munio's testimony of love came Audrey's decision to agree to his plan. If the worse case scenario came about, she would just deny any involvement.

"All right, so is this hole you dug very secluded?"

"Yes, yes," Munio said excitedly, sitting down on the couch. "It is under the floor of the gazebo, and once it is filled, you won't see it at all. It will be fine. It will stay forever. You want to see?" Munio's eyes lit up with the prospect of showing off his excellent handiwork.

"No, no," Audrey waved, "no, no, I'll wait til in the morning. I'll help you, Munio, but I want you to know that I am not going to take the rap for this. If the cops find out, I knew nothing, nothing about this. You got it?" She pointed at him sharply with her index finger.

"Yes, I understand. I will take all the responsibility. I am glad you will help. Sandra would like it." Munio smiled at her.

"Oy, gevalt! " Audrey threw up her arms. "Sandra, what I do for you!" She walked over to Sandra's box and stared at her old friend. Her composure melted and her body shook as she crossed her arms and held herself. Tears and sadness disrupted her normally sophisticated and sensuous face.

Munio smoked nervously, waiting out Audrey's wave of anguish.

"I loved Sandra, Munio. We have been through a lot. She was my best friend, and I thank you for showing her such respect." Her eyes were swollen, but she sent a thin smile to Munio. "Now, pour me some more of that drain cleaner." She moved to sit on the couch again. Munio grabbed Audrey's empty glass.

As he returned, Audrey quipped, "I cannot believe you have that outfit on. I must say you do a loincloth justice," she said, rising. "I've got to pee." She checked her hair and her makeup as she walked by the big mirror. After smoothing a spot of smeared lipstick, she beheld the view behind her. There was Sandra in the box, and a Mayan warrior with a large bottle of vodka parading by. She took a deep breath and fogged up the mirror with her exhale. "Oy vay."

Munio lit a freshly rolled joint. He noticed two beautiful antique silver candelabras on the white mantle, each holding three long red candles. Up until this point, their purpose had been completely decorative, but Munio moved them to the large dining table next to Sandra's box and lit them. Munio turned off the floor lamp, and as the sole source of light in the room, the candelabras created quite a dramatic effect while they flickered and glowed above the finality of Sandra's life.

224

Audrey sat beside Munio and patted him on the back. "That looks lovely, Munio."

Munio smiled and nodded. He enjoyed several loud tokes before extending the joint to Audrey, who took it eagerly and left rose red stains from her painted lips on it. Munio liked the smell and taste of the lipstick.

In a peaceful stupor, they sat, contemplating Sandra, and watched the hot red wax travel down the sides of the candles, forming small pools on the table. Soon, they embraced while they rocked and wept on the couch. Audrey didn't even mind that Munio ground dirt and turquoise paint into her beige linen dress.

Through the long night, they kept a vigil for Sandra. When the red candles had eventually cooled to crusty scabs on the table, he replenished them with short white emergency ones. As shipwrecked victims hopeful for a dawn rescue, they drank, smoked, cried, and even laughed occasionally, but, in general, said little.

* * * * * * * *

At seven a.m. Munio began to stir. He went into the kitchen and searched the cabinets for what Audrey had no idea.

After the morning ritual with the dogs had been handled, he returned with a can of corn.

"It is time to begin the ceremony."

"Ok," Audrey replied slowly, her face crinkled. "and what does that mean?" She snorted a laugh and extended her arms, palms up.

"First, we eat." He sat down beside her and offered her the can of corn kernels.

She turned her nose up at the thought of corn as finger food, but did not want to cause a fuss or break Munio's ritual. Into the can she dipped her long red, manicured nails and dredged a handful of corn, which she ate. Munio did the same. Then, to Audrey's horror, he took a handful in one hand, and pried open Sandra's frozen jaws with the other hand. He emptied the corn into her mouth along with a bead of jade and a small polished rock of leopard agate. He eased her jaws closed and gently kissed her pale lips. Audrey, moved by the tenderness, put her hand over her mouth and began to cry.

Munio stood and smiled. "She is safe now. She will have food to eat and valuables to spend if she needs it wherever she may go."

Audrey sniffled, "Well, that's good. If there was anything that girl loved to do in this world, it was eat and shop." Both of them laughed.

"Are you very strong? Do you think that you can carry one end of the box?"

"God, in these shoes?" She looked down at her heels. "How much do you think she weighs? Is she wearing much jewelry?"

"Umm, probably two seventy-five, plus the box. It's pretty heavy, now

that I think about it."

Audrey frowned. "I'm not sure. Can't we drag her?"

"No, I know what we will do. If we can just get the box outside, I will set it on the wheelbarrow, and it will be easy. First, I must screw the lid on."

With a drill and a can of galvanized deck screws, he quickly fastened the wooden top.

Munio slowly wheeled the box to the gazebo. Audrey followed him, noting the morning dew displaced their footsteps and the track of the wheelbarrow. The sky featured a red blistery sunrise with wisps of little cirrus clouds all along the horizon. Large flocks of small birds cried overhead on their journey south for the winter. Audrey's breath steamed from her mouth like a dragon's in the crisp air. Last night under the cover of darkness, she felt confident about her decision to go along with Munio's plan. This morning, she felt as if the whole world could see. She watched Munio's chill bumps spread across his back and legs as she trailed behind him.

Once they set the box on the ground, Munio arranged a pulley system with rope to gently lower Sandra into the ground. Audrey admired Munio's exotic beauty, caked with fresh dirt and smeared warpaint.

"Do you have any last words to say to her before I begin?" He pointed back behind him to the hole.

"See ya, San. In fact, I'll actually probably see you next week after they hang us at dawn for killing you. Take care, hon." Her face contorted with pain. "You know what? You were right about Munio. He is a very nice man." She sobbed, took a seat on the steps, and waved Munio on to fill the grave.

Audrey stared at the sky and listened to the steel shovel cutting time after time into the soft dirt, the muffled dullness as the dirt landed in the grave, and the never-ending jingle of Munio's wrists. By nine a.m., the hole was filled, and Munio replanted the squares of fescue back on top of it perfectly.

Munio stood in front of Audrey and slapped his hands together to knock off the dirt.

"Well, that's that. It is finished."

"Sandra would have been proud. I must say that I'm proud too. Now, let's get the hell out of here."

Munio and Audrey both felt a great relief to not have the tension of Sandra's body in the house. The spot in the living room looked so empty to them.

"Munio, I'm going home now. I'm exhausted. If I don't rest, my eyes will look awful." She wrote her phone number on a piece of paper. "Here, you call me this afternoon or this evening, and we'll talk further about all this." She waved one arm around the room and reached to hug him.

"Ok, ok. Yeah, I'm tired, too." He returned her hug weakly.

With a false cheerfulness, she left through the carport door.

Once separated, Audrey and Munio each felt engulfed by a terrific emp-

tiness. Audrey drove home, scarcely able to hold the wheel. Munio sat at the kitchen table, dazed. A vast sadness beyond the salty comfort of eager tears had arrived. A nauseating guilt seeped in, haunting them for being alive, for being on the high side of that grave.

* * * * * *

Munio's body craved water, inside and out. He drank three large glasses without stopping. While Sandra was alive, Munio had never been in this bathroom until last night. He browsed her personal effects, bottles of health and beauty aids on the dressing table, bottles of perfume which he opened and smelled. One in particular he remembered. With his eyes closed, he could smell her neck and the night air when they had danced.

Frozen in the shower's stream, the water nurtured him like a parched plant. A pale blue stream appeared on the floor of the shower as the water whisked the turquoise paint away.

Eventually, he started to wash, starting with his hair. He squirted a handful of shampoo and began working it in with his fingers to a soapy froth. He frowned as he felt various knots of hair, wound tight as wool, because he knew it was going to be painful to dislodge them after they dried.

Working his way down, Munio scrubbed his face with the washcloth and noted how scruffy his face felt. He had not shaved for three days now. He figured Sandra must have a razor since her legs were always shaved. Then again, he realized he had never touched very much of her, had never even touched her calf, and so he really could not say if her legs were smooth or not. It was funny to feel so close to someone, yet when it came to the detail of this woman's body and her life, he knew practically nothing at all.

Unaware that the skin on his knees had been worn away from the rigors of working on all fours during the burial, he now felt the huge raw abrasions on each of them beginning to sting from the hot water.

Munio scrubbed and smiled as he thought of Sandra's son, whom she had loved so. It was his hope they were now together again. That posed a question as to whether Sandra would be Sandra in the hereafter or Paul, her original character. Also, would her son know and acknowledge her as Sandra? Would he be friendly with her? Would Sandra acknowledge him, or would she just act like a new friend coincidentally met there in the other life?

Munio stayed in the shower until the water grew lukewarm. Wrapped in a soft thick white towel, he wiped a hole in the condensed mirror to take a look at himself. His hair, tangled and pressed to his head, looked so tiny and pitiful, like a soaked kitten., Bluish-purple areas as deep under his eyes, despite his tan skin as bruises disclosed his fatigue. An uneven outcropping of beard dotted his face and chin with black and gray stubble. He ran his hand over it. In the mirror, he saw the face of a lonely man growing old. His eyes stayed glued to his reflection so long that his vision blurred and took him

away. His body eased down the vanity, and he sat hugging his legs on the soft furry bathmat in the warm, steamy mist.

*A vision came to him of a giant black raven that picked him up gently but firmly in its claws, and flew him over the landscape of his past. Slowly but steadily, he could see himself as a baby crawling naked over the smooth, gray stones of his mother's kitchen. Her voice rang out sweet with song while she stirred and chopped the food for the day.*

*The sun burned luxuriously on the back of a small brown boy searching on a sugary beach for crabs to sell to the market. The raven continued to fly low for a close view of the old white chapel. Munio smelled the candle wax, the suffocating intensity of the incense and the evil of the priest inside those walls.*

*On and on the raven flew. Munio's wet hair flew in the wind, and he felt young and strong as they sailed over the parade, that wonderful parade the town arranged when he returned from Munich and the Olympics. He smelled the leather upholstery of the red Impala convertible, and the fragrance of the flowers draped around the car, as he waved to the crowd.*

*From there, the raven zoomed away from all he knew to a desert land so hot that it was uncomfortable to breath the air. For miles and years, they traveled. He saw the brown young boy wave and shade his eyes from the sun as the raven carried Munio out of sight.*

*Endlessly and with no explanation, the raven continued over a landscape that never changed, never led to anything familiar. Munio felt a deep fear for the loss of his life, and he knew he had not seen himself in a very long time. His fear segued to despair and to hopelessness and then to nothingness as he released his spirit from that life. He screamed to the raven, "Let go!", and the raven obliged. Munio coasted on the winds like a feather, circling, circling down and down until his head jerked and hit the vanity cabinet.* His consciousness returned to find him drooling, and otherwise damp and warm on the bathroom floor once again.

In an effort to ground himself from the fear he had gathered in the dream, he slipped on a huge pink terrycloth robe hanging on the back of the bathroom door. It felt perfect to his war torn body that had not known any physical comfort for several days now, and, it smelled of Sandra. So long it dragged the floor, the robe engulfed Munio. Into the living room he waded, careful to not trip over the hem, and folded himself up on the couch. The three little dogs joined him. Munio moved over and used the arm of the couch as a pillow, and there he lay as the yellow flames of the white emergency candles dwindled down to their last flicker. For Munio, this signified the finalization of the burial ritual, and from that moment, he would move forward with his life. Fresh tears traveled down his cheek. A deep and sound sleep brought peace.

# CHAPTER XXXII

"Eddy?"

"Yeah?" Eddy said.

"This is Munio."

"No shit."

"I'm sorry I stood you up today. I was sick, and I just woke up, brother. I'm sorry."

"Aw, that's all right. No big deal. I got along ok. What you got, a hangover?"

"No, no, I, I came down with a stomach sickness or something. It's better now. I just slept all day, and didn't wake up or nothing."

"I'm gonna start carb depleting tomorrow. 'Long about ten days from tomorrow, I should be getting righteously ripped. Everything's coming together so good, man. I ain't lying."

"That's great. I'm glad you are pleased. What time do you want to train tomorrow?"

"Tomorrow afternoon about four. I ain't got to work at the bar so I might as well rest in the morning, you know."

"Sure, that's good. I will stay here then and work on the gazebo. I'll meet you at the gym."

"Yeah, take it easy, Munio."

Munio sighed, leaned on the counter, studied the darkness through the window over the sink. He fed the dogs and stepped out on the patio to smoke in the cool air, leaving sliding glass door open enough for the dogs to come out when they had finished their supper. Thick clouds floated rapidly across the sky. The air smelled like rain, and this pleased Munio. It would be good to soak the top grass over the grave to root. It would be good to cleanse away the residue of the upheaval from the past few days.

Through the yard, he tiptoed back to his truck. He chose clean clothes from one of the black plastic garbage bags. Despite the impenetrable ten-foot wooden fence around the yard, Munio looked all around to see if anybody could see him. This irony gave rise to laughter since, just that morning, in full daylight, he had wheeled a homemade casket through this same yard. Shaking his head, he proceeded to change.

He looked at the gazebo and then at the sky. His face wrinkled in thought, he took a drill from his toolbox. Before the rain came, he wanted to secure the pieces of plywood he had removed to dig the grave. In short order, he screwed the pieces back in place, totally obscuring the grave site. With this task completed, he felt enormously relieved. It had disturbed him to remove part of the structure he had worked so hard to build.

Munio went into the living room and flipped on a light. To his surprise,

the fireplace had skipped his awareness. Obviously unused for a long time, the mantle had been decorated with dried flowers, and a small table butted up to its opening. He moved the table and found an ornate, built-in fire screen made of brass with glass doors. Save for a few spider webs, it appeared to be a clean and functional fireplace.

"Hey," he called to the dogs. "This is great! How would you like a nice fire to watch tonight? Ha ha! Maybe we will roast some corn or something." Munio smiled and nodded. "I am going out to get some supplies now. I will return soon."

* * * * *

Luck befell him because, not two blocks from Sandra's house, someone had stacked a big pile of wood from a dead tree on the side of the road. Munio screeched to a halt and loaded up a few armloads in the truck. Feeling happy to find just what he was looking for, he chuckled to himself. He loved a fire, and it had been some time since he had sat in front of one.

For days he had hardly eaten, and now he felt hungry for everything. Munio got busy and put on a pot of rice to cook. From the truck, he unloaded an armload of that wood and set it next to the fireplace.

Strategically, he stacked some small kindling, newspapers, and a couple of medium sized logs, and struck a match under the pile. It caught right away. The little dogs happily joined him in wide-eyed fascination by this new thing that was happening in the room where, when Sandra was alive, they were never allowed to linger.

In a few minutes, after he was certain the fire was in good shape, Munio rearranged the furniture. He dragged one of the long white leather couches to face the fireplace. He smiled at his handiwork, and relocated a coffee table in front of the couch.

With the kitchen garbage can in hand, he emptied ashtrays and threw away beer cans, liquor bottles, various ends of ropes, stray feathers from his warrior outfit, and a huge pile of wadded-up, tear-stained Kleenex with Audrey's lipstick signature. After the room was arranged to his liking, he retrieved a hefty can of lemon Pledge and a dishtowel from the kitchen and dusted for an hour, as the fire burned brighter and hotter and glowing orange coals began to form under the andirons. In one last act of the Mayan burial ritual, he took his well-worn loincloth and tossed it in the fire with great glee.

He peeled back the husks of three ears of corn, saturated the kernals with water, replaced the husks, and gently slid the ears on top of the coals.

"This is good. This is the best way to cook corn or anything, on an open fire. Your mother never cooked in here, eh? I can tell." He spoke cheerfully to the little dogs. Parked in a wad on the white leather couch, they sleepily lifted their heads to listen to Munio. "I can relax now that my work is done. Let's have a little drink and smoke a little toke or two while we wait for our corn to cook."

230

Using a sterling silver tray Sandra had displayed casually on a mantle, Munio rolled a joint of his finest smoke. Twenty-four hours before, this room had stored only emptiness. Suddenly, it was full of warmth and contentment, and was the center of Munio's and the three lap dogs' existence.

Periodically, Munio rose to poke the logs on the fire or turn the corn, whose tin foil shifted from shiny silver to a matte charcoal. He sat on the big white leather couch, socked feet stretched out on the walnut coffee table, and stared thoughtfully into the fire with one arm around the pile of little dogs. It was as if that fire had come to mother them, all of them. It had come to assure them that there was a place for them in this world, and it was right there in that room, tonight.

By the time Munio was ready for dinner, the corn was well roasted, and he set out the best feast he had eaten since crossing the border. Besides the pigs feet, he had the beans, poured straight from the can, that warmed themselves on the hot rice and roasted corn. He ate for two hours, taking breaks to smoke a little more pot and just to let the food digest.

It was after two a.m. when he finished. Sleep called to him, and after he put away all the food and washed all the dishes, he was ready for bed. Looking through several closets, he found some blankets and a pillow. One of the blankets was made of soft acrylic and colored a deep purple. He lay this one down on the couch and tucked it in well. The other was a very old and heavy quilt, of geometric shapes in bright colors of red, orange, yellow, and green. After placing another log on the fire, he took all of his clothes off and lay down under the soft blankets. The little dogs piled up too and slept on the end, keeping his feet warm.

* * * * * *

Across town, Audrey was a bundle of nerves. Though she had abstained for years, tonight she chain-smoked cigarettes worrying all the while about how many wrinkles that smoke would incur on her face. Thoughts of potential consequences of the illegality of a home burial were coming on like a bad acid trip. The worst thing about it was that Audrey had nobody in the whole wide world with whom she could talk this over, except a for half-breed Mayan dancing fool who, at this moment, was snoring peacefully. She thought about calling a hotline, even a suicide hotline in New York, but declined, for fear the phone could be traced.

As nontraditional as her very existence was, Audrey failed to see it. In her mind, she was her mother, a good Jew from Long Island who had class. That fairy tale flew around to haunt her on this chilly evening because, deep in her heart, deep in a heart whose compassion lay uncharted to Audrey, she understood quite well why what Munio had done was a good thing. She knew also that Sandra somehow would have been glad that things turned out this way.

It had been a great worry to Sandra that when she died her secret would be known to distant family members, for whom she never cared. It worried her that circumstances might evolve that would have her dead body lugged back to the wide plains of Nebraska and buried alongside her mother and father. When her gravestone would be assigned the same of Sandra Fugleberg instead of Paul, she figured it would become a tourist trap for local thrill-seekers. To prevent this, she had assigned the job to Audrey, should she out-live Sandra, to cremate her body and sprinkle her ashes amongst some roses somewhere, that she might spur the growth of something beautiful through her demise. Sandra had given her a key to a safety deposit box, which contained adequate funds to accomplish this.

It was so late, and she just wanted to sleep. At midnight, Audrey threw three Xanax down her throat and began to undress. Off came the beige linen dress, so tasteful, so country club, and, after the rigors of this strange day, hopelessly wrinkled. She hung it up on a wooden hanger, assessing the brown and turquoise stains from the tumultuous evening. With every item she removed, moaned in appreciation of the comfort it brought. Down to her underwear, hose, and shoes, she kicked off her two-tone tan heels and slid them onto a couple of berths on a shoe tree.

Her body, slim and lithe with long muscles, was toned, a classic dancer's body. She rolled the taupe panty hose over her long-boned legs. Laying them on the bed, she ran her fingers through her hair to toss it back away from her face.

Each cup of her satin cream-colored French cup bra bore a small pink gel-filled sac, popular devices used by women who had endured mastectomies and, of course, drag queens. The facade continued to melt away as she placed the sacs on the dresser and unhooked the empty brassiere. Her torso was hairless, each of her brown nipples as flat as if painted on her skin.

She slipped off the satin bikini panties that matched the bra, and stood completely naked, save for a wide strip of white gauze that encompassed her right upper leg. In the center of it was a stripe of silver duct tape that subdued her greatest secret. It was this tape that allowed her genitalia to be strapped tight as a six-gun to her leg, so that not so much as a rise could be seen on her pubic bone. Audrey took a couple of deep breaths and held one as she gave the tape a great yank, exhaling simultaneously to reduce the pain. Her dick and balls came bouncing free, still wearing a thin white orthopedic sock which protected them from direct contact with the tape's adhesive. She grabbed them reflexively and cursed the tenderness she felt. After a few seconds, she ripped the tape one more time to detach it from her right cheek. A deep red mark on her butt remained, and on this spot, there could be seen a buildup of callous scar tissue. Audrey rubbed it and frowned.

She walked over to the bureau with the tip of her penis peeking out from the sock. Finally, she reached down and removed it with a sigh. Her body felt

so glad to be out of those clothes. If she had just a thimbleful more energy she would take a hot bath, but she didn't. She didn't even care that she hadn't removed her makeup. She donned a floral flannel nightgown. As always, she took a good look at herself as she passed the vanity mirror that provided a nearly full-length body shot. Her hair was beautiful, thick and long and deep brown trailing down way below her armpits. She picked up her brush and worked her way through her hair. This was, by far, the most relaxing thing she had done all night. Widespread goose bumps formed all down her body from the stimulation. Her eyes inadvertently caught sight of her dick standing at half-mast, tentlike under the flannel nightgown. She screwed up her mouth, uncomfortable with this contradiction. While her body felt good, her mind did not like the picture of her womanly face and that hard-on. Her thoughts turned to Sandra, and she set her brush down and began to cry.

It suddenly dawned on her how hard it must have been for Sandra to have the operation, to go through the change. She cried for her unacceptance of herself, and her sadness about what a betrayal it was to be dissatisfied with one's sex. So many times Audrey had considered the operation, but she could not let go. As the first born son of a Long Island banker, she knew that the day would come when, long hair and all, that dick of hers would entitle her to a fortune. It was a back pocket, ace in the hole she could not renounce.

Her parents had long ago accepted her as homosexual, but because she could come home in jeans and her hair in a long ponytail, they could slough it off, even boast to the neighbors and their pals down at the temple that their son was a dancer, making good money, too. Audrey did not deceive herself about the bottom line truth of the matter, and that was that her parents' love was not unconditional enough to accept a sex change.

Despite the annoyances, such as a half-hard dick, to remind her that she was not the woman she pretended to be, she wanted to remain a man. She didn't mind that the souvenir of her manhood most of the time lay tucked away.

On this night, the two men who loved Sandra Fugleberg the most slept apart on opposite ends of the small town. Audrey, in her nightgown, her worries were released by the Xanax, and Munio, curled up with three little lap dogs, had succumbed to the peace of the fire's warm liquid flames. The object of all their exhaustion, Sandra slept six feet under in a cold, love grave with a chilly chrome-plated pistol still resting on her chest.

# CHAPTER XXXIII

Eddy had just arrived at the gym when Munio pulled up.

"Hey, hoss!" Eddy picked Munio up and spun him around playfully.

"Watch the merchandise. Watch the merchandise, brother." Munio

laughed as Eddy set him down.

"You been working on your thing, over there?"

"Yes, indeed, I have. It is coming along so well. By myself, I set all the roof joists today. The maneuvers were difficult, but I got through it all right."

"Damn, Munio, that's hell, man. I got to come over there and see this bad boy. Where is it, anyhow?"

"You know, I don't even know the name of the street. I just know how to get there, but yeah, yeah, you will come and see."

"Does the lady like it and all?" They walked into the gym as they talked.

"Oh, ah, what lady?"

"What lady? The bitch you be building the motherfucker for, man!"

"Oh yeah, that lady. Uh huh, yes, she is pleased with it." Munio felt a nauseous heat wave pass through his body.

"What's her name again?"

"Uh, it is Sandra."

"Sandra? I thought Sandra was the one that wrote you that fuck off letter."

Munio felt like a man who had swallowed a live grenade. For a second, his panic was so great that he disappeared in it, and came out of the other side of its tunnel disoriented and shaken.

"Well, wasn't it?" Eddy repeated, his eyes narrowing, searching Munio's face.

"Yes, remember? I told you that. We spoke of this the other day. Remember?" Munio recovered. He made eye contact with Eddy and threw out his hands to emphasize the coincidence.

Eddy satisfied with Munio's answer, turned the focus to himself. His world was no wider than the space his body occupied, with no vision beyond the mirror of muscle and tanned skin.

"Check this shit out, man." Eddy took off his shirt, turned to the side, and struck a side tricep pose. "Look at my delt, man. I ain't ever had striations like that. Look at that." He beamed, proud as any papa of a newborn.

"Excellent," Munio responded to the display. "Let's see it from the front."

Eddy hit a chest shot which also highlighted the shoulders, and there, too, the striations on the delt were extraordinarily defined. "Yeah, look at that. I got to slow down on my diet. I'm gonna peak too soon. I been cutting my carbs way back, but I'm gonna up 'em, you know? What do you think?"

"Let me see an ab shot." Munio studied the body and pinched the skin over Eddy's abs. "It's pretty thin, Eddy. I think you're right. You don't have much more to go. Just hold your own right now, I say. Nothing too radical, you know?"

"Yeah, yeah, I think you're right. I'm gonna keep up my test every day, though. I just don't want to lose my edge, man. I just want to stay hungry, you

234

know?"

"Sheesh, Eddy, you are about cooked with that stuff too, I think. You don't want to louse up what you have built, you see. You don't want to start retaining water real bad or anything, man."

"I ain't. I'm all right, man. Hey, let's get to it. Let's do some legs." Eddy punched Munio playfully.

"Ok, just some reps, nothing real heavy, ok?"

The brutal training work was over until after the Mr. Dixie Contest. The lack of intensity was almost painful for Eddy since it was that pain that his body was most used to. He resisted the temptation and stuck to his game plan, still absolutely convinced with every passing day that nobody could beat him, nobody.

* * * * * *

Darkness had fallen by the time the workout was finished, and Munio and Eddy parted company in the parking lot. As Munio drove back to Sandra's, a heavy rain began to fall. Munio thought of Sandra, felt a knee jerk reaction to cover the grave with a tarp or something to keep her warm and dry. He smiled softly, took the thought further, and decided it was a good thing for the sky to shed tears of its own for Sandra, as well as to nourish the grass blanket covering the sacred ground under which she lay.

As he turned onto her street, he saw, above the trees, the faint rotisserie effect of red lights, and when he reached Sandra's driveway, he nearly puked to find a fire truck at the house. Though the fear inside begged him to run the other way, he pulled in the driveway and hurried up to see what was going on. There seemed to be no smoke in the air, but because of the pouring rain, it was hard to tell. The red light revolving on top of the fire truck flashed eerily across the house. Munio's headlights splashed the carport, disclosing the crew of firemen who were gathered by the side door. The little lap dogs put up a fine verbal defense on the other side of the door.

The head fireman turned a bright flashlight directly on Munio's face as he approached them and called out with a deep slow Georgia drawl, "You live here, buddy?"

"No, I am caretaking this house, however," Munio responded with his crisp motley accent.

"Somebody called and said they saw smoke coming out of the chimney, and they said they wadn't used to seeing it. Thought there might be a fire."

"Yes, I made a fire in the fireplace today."

Munio hoped his explanation would send the men on their way. This was not going to happen, however, because these men were suspicious of this strange dark man. Not only that, they wanted to see what the inside of this fancy house looked like. They hoped they might even get a look at the big, strange woman who lived there. Word gets around about the rich people in a small town like Rosedale. Most of the people living there aren't rich, but they

know who is. At any rate, they were coming inside.

"Well, let's us go take a look just in case something ain't right. Who does live here, buddy?"

"Sandra Fugleberg," Munio stated without emotion. "There are little dogs inside. Don't let them escape when you come through the door," Munio instructed.

"Well, son, I can hear them little ole things." The fireman chuckled and winked at the rest of the firemen. "Sounds like you got a pack of them Mexican chiwarwers, don't it? Do they bite?" The other firemen snickered at their leader.

Munio did not respond and unlocked the door instead. The dogs' barks changed to whimpers upon seeing Munio.

"It's ok. It's ok, doggies," he reassured them and himself. He walked past them and flipped on every light in his path to the living room, and pointed. "See? It's ok. Everything's ok."

In the fireplace, a handful of coals remained.

"Yeah, it's drawin' good and all, but you know what, bud? You ort to not leave no coals aburnin' in that thang when you go off. You ort to put them out ever time."

"Yes, I understand. I will do that from now on," Munio said politely, stealing glances around the room to see if any strange items might be lying about, such as a roach or a remnant of any number of recent horrific scenes that had occurred in this room. He was aware that all the firemen stole glances, absorbing everything they could about the house and its contents.

"All right then, Mr., ah, I don't believe I got your name, sir."

"Munio, Munio Morelos." Munio forced a thin-lipped smile at the man.

"Mr. Morelos, uh huh. Well, Mr. Morelos, ah, when is Miss Fugleberg due back?"

"She is uncertain of this. She is caring for a friend who is ill out of the state, in New York, I believe," Munio said calmly.

"Uh huh, well, all right then. We'll be agoin', but you be careful now, you hear?" He smiled automatically and motioned with his head for the other men to file on out of the house.

A deep silent sigh of relief raced through every molecule of Munio's body. "Thank you for coming. I'm sorry if I upset anyone," he said politely. "Have a good evening now."

"Thank ya. You do the same, sir."

Munio watched from the carport until the big truck pulled away and turned off the piercing red light. Shaken, he walked back into the living room where he collapsed on the couch and was joined by the shivering lap dogs.

"Wheeww, doggies. That scared me to death. I thought I was going to have a heart attack. Jesus Christ!" He babbled a few sentences in Spanish and threw his hands up in the air. "I need a drink!" He laughed out loud and lis-

tened to the crash of thunder outside.

# CHAPTER XXXIV

When a knock came at Destiny's door a short while later, she responded, "It's open."

Eddy came in to find her eating from a bag of Cheese-its and watching Wheel of Fortune on tv. "You ought to knock, I mean, you ought not to leave your door unlocked, girl. Some convict or something'll come in here and rape you."

"Oh, like you're fixing to do?" She giggled.

"No really-"

"Hush, I'm trying to solve this." She stopped crunching, studying the unsolved puzzle intently. "What's a saying? Uh, oh, I ought to know that."

"You're crazy for watching that shit."

"Fuck you. Let's see you solve it, smarty pants."

Eddy sat and with his big jaw hanging open and tried to figure out what the puzzle was about. After a minute he said, "Shit, I don't know what the motherfucker is. Something, something, it. Oh, I know. Go fuck it! That's it!" He laughed and punched Destiny who, without looking at him, slapped him on the arm.

"Funny, real funny, Ed. Now hush. Oh, shit, this ought to be easy." Destiny watched anxiously, racking her brain for the answer.

"I'd like to solve the puzzle, Bill," the contestant requested.

"Go right ahead, Wilma from North Dakota!" the host encouraged.

"Easy does it!" Lights and bells and buzzers went off, as did as the tv audience who gave Wilma a great big round of applause.

"Damn, I should have known that one. Easy does it. I usually get these," Destiny lamented. "I ought to go be on that show."

Eddy crowed, "That'd be a hoot. They don't let rednecks from Georgia on that show."

"Yeah, they do. There was somebody from Memphis on it the other day." Destiny snuggled up to Eddy, and he put his arm around her.

"Well, why don't you send off to see if you can? I'll go with you."

"I might."

"Speaking of going somewhere, are you going to go with us to the show?"

"Yeah, hell yeah, in Atlanta? Yeah, I'm going, honey. I hope my little checky poo comes in. If it does, we going to have a fine time."

"Do you care if you, me, and Munio all share a room?"

She cracked up. "God, we'll be a fucking trio, won't we? Seriously. Shit, we'll look like the damn Mod Squad gone to hell."

Destiny laughed. "Munio and that hair. Does he ever comb it?"

"Comb it? Are you crazy? It'd take two days of bushwhacking to get through that mess! He's a cool old boy, though. He's got me through this, I tell you."

"Has he really?"

"Fuck yeah, he has. I mean, you don't realize how important a spot is to a bodybuilder. You just do better when people are around. I don't know. I might could have done it by myself, but I doubt it. You don't push yourself as hard."

"Well, is he gonna leave after this?"

Eddy shook his head. "I don't know. I hadn't talked to him about it. It'd be ok for him to stay as far as I'm concerned. He ain't hardly been no trouble. I mean he drinks and all, but he ain't even been staying at the house lately. He got some work building a, uh," he snapped his fingers to stir his memory, "a, ah, gazebra out in this rich lady's back yard. He's been house-sitting for her, too. She's been out of town, and she's got some dogs."

"Damn, that's funny. What rich lady would want somebody that looks like Munio to stay at her house? I mean, I ain't trying to be mean. He's a good guy and all, but think about it. He's kind of scary looking, you know?"

Eddy laughed, "Hell, I guess you're right. I'm so used to him, and I'm so used to seeing weird looking people between the gym and the bar. Yeah, I don't know. I guess it is odd. Oh well."

"I tell you what. You are weird. I'll be glad when all this hullabaloo is over, and we can party again. You-"

Eddy interrupted, "Hey, after this one, they'll be another one that will be even more important, and after that one, there will be another one. It's a life, Destiny. I want to go pro, and you got to keep going. I got to keep going, you know."

"Are you serious? Why the hell would you want to live like this all the time? Never getting to drink beer or pig out or nothing. Shit, I'd rather be a ditch diggin' junkie than go through the shit you've been through, tannin' and making your fucking ears grow. Jesus. Why do you want to do that?"

"Well, just look at me!" Eddy jumped up in a rage and stripped his clothes off. Naked, he stood in front of Destiny, his veins pulsing at his temples, "Just look at me! Who wouldn't want to look like this? This is fucking awesome, and it belongs to me!" he shouted, slapping his chest. He hit a barrage of poses and grinned maniacally.

Destiny sat there, stone-faced, sipping from the Road Runner glass.

"Well, what do you say to that? Now, do you understand?" Eddy said triumphantly, nodding his head.

Destiny clapped slowly and sneered, "Whoopdedoo. Eddy, it may come as a surprise that no, I am not impressed by this thing," she waved her arms around, "you call a body. You look fucking freaky. You don't hardly looked like a man anymore. You ain't hairy, and you're always doing these prissy pos-

ing moves and all. I ain't into that. Maybe some women are, but I ain't one of 'em. I liked you before you got all weird. I'm sorry, and I hope you win this thing because I know you want to, but to tell you the truth, I hope you don't."

"What! Don't you say that! Don't you ever say that!" Eddy paced around the room, picked a wall and pounded the butt of his hand against it. "How could you say that?"

"Easy, Eddy, easy. Calm the fuck down. Come over here and sit down. I'm pulling for you. I hope you win because I love you and I know you want to. Sit down, just sit down. Chill, bubba." She patted the couch beside her. "I have never seen you this anxed." He sat down and looked over at her and found a smile to send.

Except for the constant flicker of light from the television, they sat for a while in the dark, not moving--staring blankly at Jeopardy. The tv's light reflecting on Eddy's face cast a bluish hue on the round knots of muscle that protruded from his jaws as he flexed and released. His right leg bounced incessantly from the great internal tension he felt.

The fact that he had not trained very hard lately only enhanced his mental discomfort. At least, pain and soreness were conditions he understood. This lonely inertia gave him the space to see or not to see what all these drugs and lifting had turned him into, and subconsciously, it frightened him. Eddy refused to acknowledge this fear and instead labeled it boredom.

Destiny was soon aware of his rocking, too. She glanced up at Eddy's face and his undulating jaw muscles. "What in the world is the matter with you, boy? Why don't you hold still?" She pulled away from his body to look at him. "I was starting to feel like I was snuggled up to a washing machine or something. Jesus."

He grinned. "Hell, I don't know. I'm just restless, bored, you know. I feel so tight. You couldn't drive a ten penny nail up my ass if you had to."

Destiny laughed. "Try me." She winked and tickled him.

"Stop." He pushed her away. "I'm sorry. I love you, Des. You know I do. I just ain't my most gentlemanly self right now. I feel like, I feel like somebody else. I feel like a picture of somebody else. I don't know. It's strange. I'm glad I did all that shit, but I'm about tired of it, too. Hey, want to fuck?" His eyes sparkled with the thought.

Destiny laughed, "You rascal!" She slapped him on the chest. "Only if you go down on me first, and don't bite my clit off, you fucking savage!" They both laughed as Eddy eased off the couch and pulled up Destiny's T-shirt.

Destiny snuggled up to him once again and kissed him on the cheek. "You better kiss me too, you son of a bitch."

"Here, I'll take care of that right now, ma'am." He pulled her head to him and kissed her in the most romantic way he could muster.

Eddy took cues from Destiny's hands as she guided his head like some giant living vibrator. An intense look of growing pleasure that could have just

as easily been pain settled across her face. She began to move in her own rthym, and soon her passion chants culminated in high-pitched, staccato bursts. The evening prime time's string of sitcoms played unaffected by the intimacy in the room. The actors spouted their lines and the canned laughter chorus belched out every few seconds. Meanwhile, down below, Eddy's knees were killing him, but he didn't dare cease his actions to make adjustment. He knew he had her orgasm on the run if he could just hold on a little bit longer. Destiny viciously pulled Eddy's ears as she humped and bucked, giving herself wholly to the moment. Eddy smiled to himself as he tried to hold his position through the squall and worked to keep his lips covering his teeth so he didn't accidentally bite her or get them knocked out while his face slapped against her pubic bone. Then, as calmly as the whole thing started, Destiny stopped moving, and lay sprawled out, moaning.

Now, Eddy was ready for his turn, and standing at attention, he climbed aboard the couch, aiming himself at Destiny. She was open to a good hard fuck now that she had come and welcomed him. For a short while, they rode together in a lost and lusty place, and after their united crescendo, rested while Murphy Brown bitched in the background.

# CHAPTER XXXV

Munio had collapsed on the couch through one whole joint, six shots of vodka, and one beer. With nothing but toast on his stomach, he was blitzed. But when the telephone rang, he sat perfectly upright, momentarily sobered by the harsh bell. The answering machine was still on, and Munio got up and walked slowly into the kitchen to listen to it. After Sandra completed the out-going message, Audrey's voice rang out.

"Munio? Munio, if you can hear this, pick up the phone. Munio, it's Audrey. Are you there?" Munio waited another second and then hurried to pick up the phone.

"Yes, I'm here, Audrey." Munio spoke slowly and carefully so as to not to sound too drunk.

"Oh good, I'm glad you answered. How are you?"

"Fine, I am fine, and you?"

"Oh, I'm a nervous wreck, but ok, I suppose. I want to talk to you. Would you mind if I came over, or would you like to meet-No, I would really rather come over. Do you mind?"

"Yes, come over."

When Audrey arrived, Munio walked her into the living room. "What on earth have you done?"

"What do you mean?"

"I mean, rearranging everything, and this fire. Sandra never made fires

240

in here. This room was a showplace."

"It was not a room to live in before. It was not set up for living. Now, I set it up for living, and," he chuckled and held his arms out, "I'm living here. It's comfortable now with the fire and everything."

"So, is that what you think you're going to do, live here?" she said curtly.

Munio shrugged, "I don't know. I thought I would until I finished the gazebo, and then, I don't know. Do you want to live here?"

"Me?"

"Yes, you were Sandra's best friend. I'm sure she would like you to live here and take care of her little dogs. Somebody's got to live here and care for things."

Audrey sighed and sat down. "No Munio, nobody does. You don't seem to understand. Somebody's sooner or later going to need to know where Sandra is. She's got a lawyer, an insurance agent. I mean she probably has got a stock broker. These matters will have to be handled."

"Handled? What is there to do?"

"Well, I have no earthly idea, but something. This, I know."

"Hmm." Munio looked at the fire and poured another shot of vodka. "You want one?"

"Oh, what the hell, sure." She pulled a pack of cigarettes out of her purse and lit one.

Munio, coming out of the kitchen to get another shot glass, said, "I didn't know you smoked."

"I started yesterday. I mean, I quit a few years ago. I, this whole thing has me so crazy."

Munio laughed, "Maybe you should not worry about it."

"Somebody has to worry about it, Munio. Somebody has to, and it looks like it's got to be me since it surely doesn't seem to be you. I mean, this woman had a will, and we need to find that. The mortgage has been paid on this house. I think her car is paid for too, but who knows. Her affairs must be handled."

"I don't know what to say. I don't know these things."

"I know. I know you don't. What I want to do is look around here and see if I can find anything. Maybe I can figure some things out if I do that. Maybe I could find a copy of her will. Have you brought in the mail?"

Munio shook his head. "No, I haven't."

"Oi vay. Let me go do that. You need to do that every day. We don't want somebody thinking something's up."

"Well, you go and do whatever you wish."

She swallowed the shot and rose. "I'm going to go to work here."

Audrey went into Sandra's study. There was a gigantic rolltop desk, a couple of wooden filing cabinets, and two Queen Anne chairs separated by a small end table. Along one entire wall, a floor to ceiling cabinet and shelving unit was anchored. It was made of a dark, rich, red-brown wood, and on the

with a shiny brass handle. On another wall was a bank of windows with a glass shelf on which lived five well-tended plants. Since the wall was on the back of the house, the backyard and the gazebo could be viewed from here.

Audrey walked slowly over to the window and looked through the supple green arms of the plants looked out into the dark. The strange silhouetted frame of the gazebo stood out against the sky. A flood of emotion rose in Audrey's gut when she thought of her friend's death and her own guilt about the whole affair. She wondered, as she suspected she would wonder for the rest of her life, whether it was her fault Sandra was dead. She shook her head and fought back her tears, feeling helpless to do anything to change history. Sighing, she turned away from the window and took a seat at the large wooden swivel chair in front of the desk.

On the desk was a little heart-shaped picture frame with a photo of all the little dogs in it. Audrey smiled, picked it up for a closer look, and set it down. She combed through every piece of paper she could find.

Even though she had a curiosity about people, and even though she was a dear friend of Sandra Fugleberg's, she knew there must have been some interesting information about her life that had never been revealed to her. For instance, Sandra never would discuss her ex-wife or their son or his tragic death. Audrey did not know exactly where Sandra had been born or reared or what her childhood had been like. For Audrey's friends, this was not unusual. Most of them were drag queens, with a stray dyke here and there in New York, but all in all, they were queens--queens that shared a similar past, a misunderstood, confusing childhood.

Audrey had lucked out more than most. Raised in a Jewish environment, she was loved unconditionally as her parents' only son. It was not a problem that little David was not interested in roughhousing with the boys. His parents were more pleased that he was academically gifted, and he exhibited great enthusiasm for Hebrew school. When he fell madly in love with dancing and insisted that he take lessons, they were happy he showed a flair for the arts.

As a model student, he was praised. His dance instructors sent notes home to his parents indicating how much promise the boy displayed. Although it pained him to not wear the wonderfully sequined, petticoated costumes the girls donned, still he enjoyed the technique of all the dance routines, and all along harbored secret thoughts about how one day he would wear one of those costumes.

When he turned eleven, he shocked his parents and the neighborhood on Halloween by dressing as Diana Ross. He was not exactly what you would call a dead ringer for the super star, but with a hot-pink full-length nightgown of his mother's and a cheap black wig, he walked the walk, as they say. He never forgot that night and the attention he got. Boys in the neighborhood at first thought he was a girl and wolf whistled at him. It was a strange sexual awakening for the boy. Without understanding why, he could not deny that

attracting boys sent an excitement bordering on pain through his young genitals. It was the experience that led him to the life he now led.

Audrey opened one drawer in the desk and found an old snapshot. It was black and white, and the edges were trimmed in a zigzag pattern. It showed a young boy in a suit with a yarmulke perched on top of his head. Tears rolled quietly down Audrey's pretty face as she looked at the child from so long ago. It was just the broadness of his chubby cheeks and a certain look in his eye that had never left, even as a middle-aged transsexual. Nothing can ever change that certain spark, that certain way the light strikes a person's eye. It's like a fingerprint, she thought, so individual and so undaunted by whatever course a life must take. If nothing more, the fumes of that child's spirit haunted the soul forever.

It was an hour later, in one of the filing cabinets, Audrey came across a copy of Sandra's last will and testament. She was surprised and touched to find that Sandra had indeed left her the house, car, and whatever remained of the money in her checking account. She left instructions to cash in all her stocks and bonds and to donate that money to the Transperson Assistance League of New York City. It was a group that had been very helpful to Sandra before, during, and after her change. Though she appointed Audrey to see after the dogs, knowing that Audrey was not a big dog person, she encouraged her to find them a good home together. Her entire savings account was to go to the care of them. That was all she wrote. There was no mention of blood relatives to notify or include. She had stated her desire to be cremated and have her ashes used to fertilize the planting of an oak tree in her front yard.

Audrey looked no further that night. She felt now that she must think about what to do. She could not access Sandra's money without the probate of the will being legally attended to. She didn't know at all what to do, and there was no one she could think of at the moment who could help in this unusual matter.

Tomorrow she would go to the bank and see what was in the safety deposit box. Sandra had given her a key to it a year or so ago. For now, she could pay bills. She could risk posing as Sandra to cash checks, but if she got caught, it would be too fantastic a story to work her way out of. Maybe her father would cash a check if she sent it up there. She started to rise from the chair when she noticed Sandra's Gucci purse on the floor. Exhausted, she did not know if she had the energy for that. Nothing is more intimate than a person's purse or wallet, and so, begrudgingly, Audrey picked up the bag and sat down.

She dumped the entire contents on the desk and set the bag on the floor. Sandra's wallet was the largest item in the pile, so she started with that. The plastic photo strip section held only pictures of the dogs. After searching every nook and cranny of that wallet, Audrey came up with twenty-three hundred dollars in cash. Sandra had stashed four five hundred dollar bills up in

one little compartment.

The hard part came now as Audrey noted the rest of the bag's contents. There was Sandra's lipstick, a frosted coral, her compact, and a small bottle of Toujours Moi. Audrey held it up to her nose and smiled to find it smelled like Sandra. It was sad to look at these things, knowing they would never be used again. She started to throw them in the trash, but just couldn't. She wished she had done this before they had buried her, when she could have sent this purse off with Sandra to the world beyond. Audrey put the contents back in the bag to decide later what would be done with them.

Back in the living room, Munio was as mellow as a house cat. He softly strummed his guitar and watched the fire. His eyes were lazy and ready for sleep. Audrey studied him from the back as she stood silently, listening to the strumming for a few minutes. When she thought back over the past few days, she still could not believe all that had happened. The anxiety she had walked in here with tonight had diminished, though, and somehow she knew things would probably work out ok.

\* \* \* \* \* \*

"Here, Munio." Audrey shattered the soft sounds of the room, startling Munio. Leaning over, she reached around him, brushed his hair with her face, and rested her arms on his shoulders while she stuffed the five hundred dollar bills into his shirt pocket.

He looked into his pocket and then looked around at her, but Audrey, having straightened back up, was in route around the couch to sit next to him. Both of them had been aroused by the contact. Both noticed each other's body warmth, soft breath, and smell, and both of their minds were chattering wildly about these things.

Audrey sat down and cast a pointed gaze over at Munio. This was not the look of an acquaintance, not that of a friend; it was a look of lust, of deep, brown-eyed, fireside lust. Munio felt blindsided by this unexpected emotion from himself as well. Their eyes became riveted on each other, and then, in an instant and with all the power and glory of a lucky spark inadvertently setting off twenty thousand gallons of gasoline, they locked up like toy magnet dogs in a deep kiss. When the kiss broke up, they both bore expressions of wild surprise. This was not something either of them would have ever predicted.

Munio grew hard, and Audrey strained against the silver duct tape that held her under wraps, but still neither spoke. They kissed again, and Audrey left lipstick stains on Munio's face.

Audrey threw her whole body on top of Munio's. The force caused them both to slide off the couch and onto the floor. Their lips locked again as they began to do a horizontal roll around the living room. With legs intertwined, the two rolled and thrashed about. To an outsider, it would have been hard to know if these two were friends or foe. The dogs watched curiously from the couch with every ear perked.

244

It was soon obvious that the bodies demanded more than kisses and friction. Because Audrey's equipment needed some preparation for sex, her mind sobered up from the rug dance long enough for consideration. Not since the night of the dance class that Munio attended had she felt any attraction to him.

Munio, too, felt a blinking protest from his conscience, born out of his loyalty and respect for the dead and buried Sandra, but his argument was weak, helpless to fight against the rising tide of his passion.

"Munio, what are we doing?" Audrey sat up on the floor and straightened her top.

Munio scratched his head as he spoke. "It seems we have been directed to follow the call of our nature."

Audrey chuckled at his sincerity. "Do you want me?"

"Yes! What is it you think? This is a sign of disinterest?" Munio held out his arms as he spoke.

"All right, I hope you're ready for this." She slipped her tight jeans down over her slim hips, revealing the penis in bondage.

"Holy shit!" Munio's eyes grew large as he took this opportunity to undress himself as well. Audrey looked at him and raised her eyebrows as she grabbed the end of the duct tape.

As she yanked at the tape, his eyes grew even larger. "Doesn't that hurt?" he cried, as he watched the hardened penis bounce free. She slipped the white nylon sock from around it.

"Just taking my bra off, honey. You know us girls pay a huge price for beauty." She laughed at his astonishment and winked. "Now, fuck me, you crazy Mayan!" She flipped over on all fours and faced the fire. "But wear this." She tossed him a packaged condom, and sat up on her knees to install one on her own dick as well.

Munio shook with adrenaline as he fumbled to open the package and spring the condom into place. He hurried to mount Audrey but found that, without more lubrication than the condom provided, this would be impossible. After spouting a few heated words in Spanish, he jumped to his feet and sprinted into the kitchen with the lap dogs in hot pursuit. Opening the cabinet above the stove, he grabbed the first thing he saw a can of Pam. He ran back to Audrey's ass and gave himself a liberal spray. Audrey's head whipped around when she heard the hiss from the can.

"Oh my God! I can't believe this!" She dropped her head and laughed. Her long thick brown hair hung down over her face.

Munio gripped with the frenzy to mate didn't reply. His dick slipped in slowly as the pressurized elasticity of Audrey's rectum sucked at him. Initially, as if he had grabbed a live wire, Munio felt he might black out from the exquisite stimulation that gripped him. Adjusting from the initial surge, he slowly moved in short strokes with fine finesse.

Meanwhile, Audrey, whose eyes were glued to the roaring fireplace, gasped for dear life as Munio's penetration engulfed her. Her painted lips hung open as she worked to accept him. Her right hand traveled to her own dick which she held firm and stroked periodically. Although she could have come in a second, she held back, preferring to delay until Munio came.

Munio worked the tempo as both their supple bodies recalled the spirit of their mambo at Pee Wee's the night they met. Munio alternately focused on the fire and the hollow of Audrey's beautiful back.

Orgasm for both men proved rewarding. Munio moaned and lay across Audrey's back and buttocks while she had succumbed to a position resting on her elbows with her butt up in the air as she stared into the fire. Finally, Munio extracted himself from Audrey's binding grip and stood. He slowly moved to the kitchen, where he rolled off the condom and dropped it in the trash can.

When he went back into the living room, Audrey was on her back with her eyes closed. Munio gently lay beside her, face down, with his arm around her waist. The little lap dogs slept in a pile on the couch, accepting, as always, the comings and going of the humans in their world.

Munio and Audrey lay silent for a long while, each man's mind ticking at such a different pace, using such different language. The physical release of this encounter had been immensely therapeutic, considering the tension each had garnered over the past few days. Their bodies enjoyed resting on each other, and neither wanted to break the spell with speech, speech that would diminish the magic of the unspoken language they shared now, speech that would be used as the tool to say, "Why did this happen?" and "What will happen now?" They did dread the moment when, sure as anything, a voice would ring out and signal the end of this sweet and lucky time.

Both of them eventually grew restless and cool in spite of the fire, whose flames were still burning merrily along. Munio wanted a drink and a smoke, and Audrey wanted some clothes back on.

Audrey made the first move, indicating she wanted to sit up, which required Munio to move. She smiled at him and kissed him as her torso made its way up to an upright position.

"Sorry, I'm getting chilly."

"Oh, no problem, I'll get you a robe if you wish." he responded politely.

Just as politely she said, "Oh, that's ok. I'll put my clothes back on." She flashed another nervous smile.

"I think I'll get a smoke. Would you care for one, or a drink, perhaps?"

"Oh, no, thank you." She crawled across the room gathering articles of clothing until she had the complete set.

Even an experienced transvestite like Audrey found a time like this awkward. After the explosion of her costume, her facade, reconstructing it in the presence of someone who was really little more than a stranger was uncomfortable.

Audrey moved to the far end of the room to dress, and Munio, sensing she might appreciate privacy, went into the kitchen to get a beer and smoke a cigarette. He opened the sliding glass door and let the dogs outside to roam around a bit. It was cool, though, so he shut the door except for a couple of inches. He enjoyed that little channel of coolness that the crack provided as he sat in one of the wooden straightback chairs at the table. Soon the dogs reappeared, stuck their little black noses in the crack, and whined.

By the time Munio was through snuffing out his butt in the ashtray, Audrey passed through the threshold into the kitchen in full regalia. Like the proper lady she was or tried to be, she had not a hair out of place and her outfit looked as if it just left the rack at Neiman Marcus.

"Well." She flashed a smile that disappeared as quickly as it came. "I suppose I'll be going."

Munio sat there, started to smile and then shook his head, "Where are you going? Don't you want to talk to me or something? I mean, you know that old thing about was it good for you, it was good for me?" he joked. "Well, don't you want to talk about it or something? Jesus, are you so uptight? You sure seem uptight right now."

Audrey looked through the kitchen window into the darkness and sighed. She didn't know what to say. She had no idea something like this would occur but, since it had, she was inclined to deny it. Complications, she figured, were always the bottom line of situations like this. Though the experience for her had been frighteningly tender and comfortable, she refused to be swept off her feet by this bohemian and his beauty.

Carefully, she walked to the table and sat down. A long pause ensued because she was at a loss for words. "Munio, you are no doubt a very interesting fellow, and I did have a wonderful time with you tonight. I, I just don't know you very well, and I usually don't have sex with people I don't know well. I might look like a slut, but I don't really act like, well, I might act like a slut too, but I don't have sex on--shit! What I mean is I don't ever fuck on a first date."

"This wasn't our first date. I mean, this was not a date. I mean, we never had a date, you know. This, too, I will tell to you. Never had I thought desirable thoughts about you." Audrey jokingly shot him a funny scowl that made Munio laugh, "No, no, not that I do not find you that way. You are beautiful and full of grace, but you understand, the circumstances have not guided us to this place. Besides, remember you don't like me so much since that first dance class, eh?" He bounced her scowl right back with one of his own. "So, do you want to know what I think has happened here?"

"No, I don't," she wryly joked, "but you're going to tell me anyway, aren't you?"

"Yes, I am. I think the god Kayab, the Mayan god of pleasure, sent the vibration for us to be together tonight. I think this night symbolizes that we have moved on past the sad time of Sandra's passing to renewed pleasure and

life. That makes sense, doesn't it?"

"Oh no, no, no, no, Munio, I have had just about all the Mayan rituals for this lifetime I care to experience, thank you very much!"

Munio laughed out loud and slapped the table, "Ok, ok, Miss Know It All, you do not have to believe, but I believe." He pointed at her with an index finger.

He took a sip of his beer and chuckled again. He leaned back in his chair. Audrey was not pleased with the fact that she was finding this man incredibly attractive at the moment. She slid her chair up close to his and put her arm over his shoulder.

"Look, you are a beautiful man, and I would be lying if I told you differently. I just got caught off guard, and I don't know what I think about this. I have got to think about it." She kissed him lightly on the lips, and their brown eyes locked in tight for a few seconds.

"Ok, you do what you want, but I know in my heart," he pounded his fist on his chest, "it was Kayab who visited with us and had these relations between us to occur."

Audrey stood. "Kayab, smayab, it was cupid," she joked.

"Cupid, stupid, it was Kayab, and that's what I think."

"I'll talk to you tomorrow, Munio. I did have a very good time." She pointed at him and raised one eyebrow seductively.

Munio looked at her and paused before speaking. "Thank you for this evening. It was not in my plans to have relations with you either. I am glad I have danced with you in two ways now, and these times I will long remember." With that, he stood up from his chair and bowed dramatically.

Audrey smiled, amused by his chivalry, and in response, hit a classic dancer's curtsey. "Thank you, Munio. Goodbye now." She picked her purse up from the counter and moved toward the door.

"Goodbye," Munio said already standing. He reached for Audrey's arm, pulled her to him, and gave her a little kiss.

Audrey made her exit and drove home in the cool fall night, singing a different song. She rolled the window down, letting the wind blow through her thick hair, laughing out loud when she thought of how her day had changed. There was no telling what would become of Munio, and he would not be the first man to bestow upon her a full sexual symphony and then vanish from her life. She hoped they would meet again in that way. She hoped that she would have the opportunity to have her life meet with any experience that was as blinding and sweet as the one she had had tonight with Munio, the Mayan warrior.

# CHAPTER XXXVI

It was midnight, and Eddy happily put himself to bed, but not before implementing yet another tip he had picked up today from somebody at the gym. This somebody, Scott Burns, met a pro bodybuilder while on vacation in California. This bodybuilder had sworn that winning the contest that turned him pro was due to the growth hormone drip he utilized while sleeping during the last two weeks prior to the show.

The idea hit Eddy like a ton of bricks. He knew that the body's natural release of growth hormone occurs while sleeping when the body is at rest and in repair, and so this setup made perfect sense.

Eddy had a contact at a drugstore who provided him with the paraphernalia. Part of Eddy's love of loading up was the gadgetry and the external mechanics of hitting up. It was sensuous to him, and although he considered himself straight as they come, he saw the relationship of a needle penetrating him akin to that of being fucked. Many times, it turned Eddy on so much that after hitting up he would jack off.

This gh drip arrangement was so exotic, Eddy worried that it was perhaps out of his league. As he mixed and rigged it, he fantasized about dramatic consequences. What if he didn't set the regulator correctly and woke up in the morning, having taken in enough growth hormone to turn a mouse into a Great Dane? Having made it this far on his instincts, he figured it would work out.

He injected a whole vial of growth hormone into the plastic drip bag full of saline solution he had gotten from the drugstore.

He got ready for bed and sat down to hook up the bag. As deft as a blood bank RN, he slid the short needle into the huge vein standing up like a caterpillar at the crook of his right arm. Eddy's aim was true, and when the needle penetrated the vein, the blood squirted into the tubing, forming a little red cloud. It quickly dissipated into a fleeting pocket of pink liquid as it melded with the saline solution. Eddy cursed after temporarily blinding himself by he looking at the light bulb of the floor lamp next to his bed to which he had attached the swinging plastic bag. He squinted to read the dial of the regulator valve, and put it on the lowest possible setting. From the nightstand, he picked up a roll of adhesive tape and made a couple of loops around his arm, the needle shank, and the tubing, so it would remain in place through the night. He laughed nervously to himself, aware of how ridiculous all this rigamarole was, but determined to follow through with it.

Wearing only a T-shirt and a pair of boxer shorts, he crawled gingerly into bed so as to not rip the needle out of his arm or yank the lamp over. He glanced at the clock which read eleven o'clock, and then picked up the

phone.

"Hey, Scott?" Eddy laughed at the sleepy voice on the other end.

"Who is this?" the man growled.

"It's Eddy. Whatcha doin'?"

"I'm sleepin', motherfucker! What the hell you think I'm doin'?"

Eddy laughed again. "Sorry, man. I thought you'd be up or something."

"I got to get up at five, man. I turn in early. What the hell do you want?"

"Listen, I'm sitting up here in the damn bed like Frankenstein all hooked up to this bullshit that you was telling me about."

"That growth?"

"Yeah, man."

The man started laughing a deep belly laugh. "You crazy motherfucker. I ain't believing you did that. You're gonna kill your dumb ass."

"Well, that's why I thought I'd call you just to double check on what that dude said, you know. Yeah, and just to make fucking sure you wasn't joking or nothing."

"Naw, he said he did it. 'Course now, I did not see the motherfucker do it, but you know, he was a big son of a bitch."

"He said he put the big cc bottle of growth in one bag, right?"

"Yeah."

"Then, ah, he put it on the slowest drip thing?"

"Yeah, that's what he said."

"Well, that's what I've done done, hoss. So, in case y'all don't see me for a while, you can tell 'em what happened. Tell 'em I wasn't trying to commit suicide." They laughed. "Yeah, and in case it turns me into some Bigfoot freak, you can take me to the state fair or a carnival or something and set up a fucking side show.  Charge some big money to see my fucked up ass, all right?" They laughed again.

"Well, I reckon I'll let you go, man."

"All right Eddy, good luck."

"I'll see ya."

"Take it easy, Eddy."

Eddy continued to chuckle as he flipped the light off and squirmed down under the covers. In the dark, his eyes slowly adjusted so that he could see the silhouette of the bag swinging from the lamp and a glint every now and then of the tubing as it caught a bit of stray light from the streetlight that snuck through the slats of the blinds. He listened to himself breathe and studied the sensation in his punctured arm as if he could see each drip as it entered his body.

Yawning, he kicked at the covers restlessly and noted how taut his body felt. Each muscle had been granted no mercy for so long that there no longer seemed to be a difference between flexed or not. Under his skin, his muscles strained uncomfortably against each sheath. Each tendon and ligament was

250

stretched to the limit to accommodate each muscle's exaggerated condition. Eddy could no longer rest deeply while his muscles played this strange game of tug of war with themselves. Nonetheless, with the thoughts of that trophy all his efforts would surely bring, he drifted off to sleep.

# CHAPTER XXXVII

The mockingbirds woke Munio up the next morning as they held conversations from their perches in the pecan trees and the television antennae high above the house. Munio stirred and stretched gently. He pulled the blankets around him tighter as he blinked at the lukewarm fireplace. Wishing he could start a fire with his eyes, he smiled at the thought, but then rose with a sigh, spurring chill bumps to shower his naked body.

He loaded the fire pit with fresh kindling, paper, and several small logs. The colorful fire and the heat made him happy at once as he crawled back under the blankets on his couch bed to watch and wake up more thoroughly.

Thoughts of Eddy passed through his mind, coupled with an odd urge to call him. He didn't because he knew he would see him soon, later in the morning, for a training session. Actually, he remembered he would see him sooner than that because he needed to go to the house to pick up some more clothes and some other things. A picture of Eddy's crazed face when he was posing at the gym the other day lodged in Munio and made shiver. He wondered what Atlanta would be like, and what kind of chance Eddy really had to win the contest. His mind wandered to Audrey. He replayed the scene in front of the fire--Audrey's smooth back, her ribs rippling as she moved, her dark hair, her willing ass, the searing sensation of it all. With that, he officially woke, sat up, and addressed his hard-on. He grabbed himself and drew in a long breath with his teeth clenched, creating a loud hissing sound.

When he tried to put his cigarette pack in his shirt pocket, he encountered the five hundred dollar bills. He realized he had forgotten to ask Audrey why she had given him that money. Smiling, he looked forward to joking with her about the fact that he had never ever been paid that much for sex before.

It was a cloudy day outside as he climbed into the old Ford truck. In protest, it backfired and coughed. Munio was a little surprised to find Eddy's car home. He thought he would already be at the gym, riding the bike. For the past six weeks, he had had to do forty-five minutes a day of aerobics to whittle away the last remaining shreds of fat from obscuring his muscles. Lately, he had been doing that first thing in the morning. Munio entered the house.

"Eddy?" he called, but heard nothing. He cocked his head and screwed his mouth up, puzzled. Walking down the hall, he faintly heard some type of music. Eddy's bedroom door was shut. Munio walked to it, turned the knob,

and pushed, but the door only opened several inches, obstructed by something. "Eddy?" Munio called as he peeked in.

There he saw Eddy peddling away on an old stationary bicycle he used sometimes. He wore headphones and was listening to some heavy metal music so loud that Munio could hear the words to the song from two feet away.

"Hey!" Munio hollered and Eddy looked behind him.

He smiled and waved. "Gimme five more minutes, all right?"

Munio laughed and waved him on as he went into the doll room to collect some of his things. Munio opened the curtains in the room to let in some light. The silent presence of the dolls seemed especially creepy in dim lighting. By the time he had gotten what he came for, Eddy strolled into the room with a white towel draped over his neck and bare torso.

"Hey man, what's happening?"

"Hey, why did you have that thing, that bicycle up against the door?"

"Oh, I just wanted to look out the window is all. I hate that old bike, anyhow. I was just trying to make it a little interesting for a change. What are you doing?"

"I am assembling some of my clothes. I have been wearing the same thing for a few days, it seems. It's colder, too. I think I need to buy another sweatshirt or something."

"I got some stuff you can have." He punched Munio on the shoulder. "From when I was little, baby clothes." He laughed.

"Ok, let me see them. I will not wear any shirts with those, what do you call them?" Munio snapped his fingers. "Those ninja turtle characters. I hate those things. Even children in Belize talk of these things. Myself, I do not like them at all."

Eddy laughed, "I don't like the little purple sons of bitches neither, so don't worry about that. I'll dig up what I got today sometime."

"Thanks."

"I got to eat. Won't take long on account of the fact I ain't eating nothing but a chicken breast. I'm ready to do some serious eatin' after this show. I tell you what now. Shit. I don't like to go without food. In fact, you're looking pretty good to me right now, bud."

"I am glad to see you in such high spirits. That is good. You will be eating soon. How do you feel, eh?"

"All right. You won't believe what I did last night. Come here." Eddy motioned for Munio to follow him.

They walked into Eddy's room and over to the bed. "Look at this shit, man. I hooked myself up to a gh drip. It's awesome, ain't it? Wish I'd heard about this a couple of months ago. I'd been doing some serious growin'."

Munio laughed, "If you had a brain, you would be dangerous. Do you know this fact? You would be dangerous. You're big enough. Don't do this stuff. Where did you get this thought from anyhow?"

"This guy heard about some guy doin' it that got real big, turned pro."

Munio shook his head and chuckled, "Boy, I can't believe you sometimes. You are one crazy white boy."

Munio pulled onto the street and headed for the gym. Eddy chewed frantically on the chicken breast.

"You know, this is a great truck. What year is it?"

"It was new in 1973. Now, it has over two hundred-fifty thousand miles on it."

"Damn. Good old truck."

"How's your weight?"

"It's cool. Weight class wise, that is. I'm weighing about two twenty-eight. I figure I'll be down to two twenty-two maybe on the day of the show. The weight class is two twenty-five. I don't care what I weigh at this point. I just want to be ripped."

"What did you weigh when you decided to train for this show?"

"Uh, let's see." Eddy chomped on his last bite of chicken and scrunched his face up as he reviewed the time frame. "Let's see. I believe I was at about two fifty. I wasn't too fat."

"That's good you seem to stay pretty lean."

"Yeah, I'm glad, too. One less thing to worry about."

"How's your routine?"

"It's coming. I ain't too great on that. It's so wimpy. I hate all that compulsory posing and all, you know."

The comment pissed off Munio. "It is like dance, Eddy. It is not wimpy. I want to watch your routine. I should have been watching it before now. I wish you had told me you were having problems."

"I ain't having problems. I just don't like to do it. I don't mind posing, but the music and all. I ain't ever been much of a dancer."

"What kind of music are you using? No, wait! Let me guess. Heavy metal."

"No asshole! Southern rock and roll. 'Free Bird.'"

"What is this? Who sings this song?"

"Lynard Skynard."

"I might know it if I heard it."

"Yeah, you might. It's real famous."

Munio pulled into the parking lot of the gym. As he got out of the truck, Munio noted that the gray gravel was the same gray as the sky.

"Hey, Eddy." A fat man with short red hair and beard to match moved toward Eddy. "Guess who I heard is getting in the Mr. Dixie?"

"Who?" Eddy's face clouded over.

"You remember that guy who won the Mr. Georgia last year, and then moved to Idaho or Montana or something? You know who I'm talking about. Name's Bobby Barclay."

"What class?"

"Light heavy, same as you."

"Yeah, I know who you're talking about. Boy looked all right. I went up to Atlanta for that show. You know him?" Eddy asked.

"No, uh, but I hear he looks better than he did at the Mr. Georgia. How you coming along?"

"I'm in ass whoopin' condition, buddy. That's how I am. Y'all can bring on that Barclay motherfucker or Arnold mother fucking Schwarzenegger, but I'm winning that damn show. That's all there is to it." Eddy winked and turned away.

Eddy continued over to put down his gear with Munio right behind him. He leaned over to get his belt out, and when he stood up, his face was an extraordinary shade of red. It was beyond anything that could have been produced in a tanning salon. It was rage red that was building like a shook up Coca-Cola. Eddy marched over to the dumbbell rack and grabbed a pair of fifteens to stretch out his shoulders a bit.

"What's the matter with you?" Munio queried.

"Nothin'," was his reply.

"You didn't let that guy fuck you up about that man, did you?"

"No, just fucking leave me alone, Munio. I don't want to talk about it." He slammed the dumbbells down, picked up the thirties, and began to press them overhead.

Munio laughed and shook his head. "Boy, don't you know that nobody's gonna take this dream from you? Don't waste your time, don't waste your energy on the words of this man. You are not quite right, you know. You're crazy. Look at you! You're freaky all on your outside. Just look at your skin. Your body has changed so, and now dieting? Don't you think your mind is freaked out, too? Go home and smoke a joint is my recommendation to you, my friend. After you train now, go home and smoke a joint."

Eddy put down the dumbbells and looked over at Munio. "Yeah," he laughed, "I am pretty freaky, huh?" He studied himself in the mirror.

"Yes, indeed you are. And on top of that, you do not need to be an asshole."

"Yeah, yeah, yeah, don't push it, buddy." Eddy continued his presses, moving up to the forties.

The workout continued on a peaceful note after that. For Munio, viewing Eddy was becoming more and more difficult. As he sucked the last bit of fat from his muscled frame, Eddy seemed to be shrinking. His skin fit tighter and tighter around his bones, giving him the look of a strange starving man. No cheeks stuck out, and there was no padding around the chin to produce that softness a face usually has. When he smiled or laughed, his face appeared tortured as the reddish brown skin pulled even tighter across bone.

When Munio was Eddy's age, the winners of bodybuilding contests

looked healthy, robust with depth and fullness. People had not become so perversely inventive. They had not gone to the lengths to which this man had gone. In the muscle magazines of today, the winners pictured were caricatures of human strength and health. Even Eddy looked normal compared to them.

It was hard for Munio to pinpoint just what made Eddy seem so empty, so dead. There was something more to it than how he looked. It was more in the air around him, how he moved through space. It was almost as if he didn't fit here on earth anymore. He had experienced similar thoughts after Sandra died. There was a point when Munio knew her body was no longer connected to this world. These silent thoughts made Munio feel sad as he watched Eddy study himself in the mirror and curl dumbbells in a slow monotonous rhythm. It was then he became aware that death was stalking Eddy.

"Hey Munio," Eddy called to him as he dropped the dumbbells on the floor between sets. Munio didn't answer in words but raised his eyebrows as if to say "what?" "When's the last time you had a decent meal? You're looking kind of scrawny."

Munio chuckled, "It is your eyes, my friend. They deceive you. You are the one who could use a decent meal. It is you who is shrinking before my very eyes."

"Naw, I ain't," Eddy got very serious. "I'm leaning out, man. There's a difference. I'm serious, though. Are you eating enough? If you need some lunch money, I got it for you. Besides, ain't that lady paying you something to build that thing for her?"

"I don't need to eat that much. I live on the air and the wind," he joked, waving his outstretched arms around. "I will eat after this. I might have a steak at the Waffle House."

"You do just that, why don't you? It makes me feel better to know somebody is eating. Hell, you ought to go eat with Destiny. She loves going to them fucking all-you-can-eat buffets. I hate for her to because all she does is puke it up. That's the weirdest damn chick." He picked up the dumbbells again and began another set.

"She pukes up her food?"

"Yeah, man, she's bulimic half the time. The other half she eats more than I do."

"Damn. Why would she do that?"

"It's her own little weight control method. She don't do it all the time, just when she pigs out. She says there ain't nothing wrong with it. Says people been doing it since the mother fucking cavemen days. Hell, she's probably right." He slammed the weights down again.

# CHAPTER XXXVIII

Driving back to Sandra's, Munio thought about the work he wished to accomplish on the gazebo that day. The lumber pile had dwindled as the gazebo had grown, and he needed to get more plywood for decking the roof. Also, he wanted to install lattice all around the bottom to prevent easy access under the gazebo. It would keep the Sandra's grave free from any intruders, yet provide a good airflow.

"Hello. everyone. Hello," he baby talked the dogs. "I have to ask Audrey what your names are. You have no ability to tell me this, no? I will call her and ask. Now, we must make a list for the lumber. Let's go into the back and see, eh?"

He slid open the door, and the dogs raced out into the yellowing fescue. A spirited wind blew Munio's hair in all directions, but it didn't seem to bother him or interfere with his ability to see. On a small piece of paper, he jotted down a list of items he would need.

The trip to the lumber yard was successful and quick. After he backed the truck into the backyard by the gazebo, he locked the gate and let the dogs out to wander around as he worked. It took only a very short time to encase the crawlspace. The lattice gave the gazebo a gingerbread house sort of delicateness that pleased Munio, and he knew it would look even better after he painted it.

The air and sky were friendly and entertaining this afternoon. The wind blew in cool refreshing gusts, and the pale blue-gray sky hosted a constant parade of free-floating clouds of various shades of gray that seemed to fly across in a great hurry. Munio could not keep his eyes off of the sky for more than a few minutes.

Decking the roof, the main task of the afternoon was made precarious by the fickle wind. Twice the wind ambushed the piece of plywood he held. As he was standing up on the scaffold to lay it over the rafters, the sheet was ripped from his grasp and sent flying to the ground. Munio screamed each time, hoping one of the little dogs was not innocently sniffing below .

Five hours later, Munio had dried in the entire roof. He stood on the patio and studied his creation. It looked stylish and strong. The trim and the painting were all that remained to be done, and those tasks would go quickly, with good weather. He smoked a cigarette and drank a beer until the light left for the day. At one point, he held his beer up in the direction of the gazebo in a toast for it and Sandra, who, by now, was settling in to her new world. He smiled at the thought, and realized he seemed to have released all the tears he had for his dear Sandra, though he still regretted she would not be around to enjoy the gazebo he had built for her.

\* \* \* \* \* \* \* \* \*

The night was cool, and the moon a pale cream unfocused circle of light, filtered through the thin, transparent clouds. Munio made several trips from

the gazebo to the truck to put his tools to rest for the night. Walking around on the passenger side, he looked down and noticed that the front right tire had gone flat.

"What do you want to do that for, eh? Go flat on me." He smiled at the truck and patted the hood affectionately. "You could have told me about this when there was more light, you know. Sheesh."

He fumbled behind the seat and extracted a jack and a tire iron. From the bed of the truck he rolled out his spare tire. Munio bounced it on the ground. "I guess you have enough air to roll, eh?"

After setting the jack on two small squares of wood, he began to crank it up. The old truck creaked as the jack began to take the load. The old truck was heavy, and did not rise without a considerable struggle. Munio huffed and puffed as the truck inched higher and higher. The creaking sounds both mesmerized and disturbed him. As the space increased between the truck and the ground, a strange cloud of fear like a fog settled upon him. Munio was suddenly incapacitated by a scene he that had been stored far, far away from his memory. It was a part of the post Olypmic parade in Belize with the red Impala, but a part he had forgotten.

Munio turned loose of the jack handle and grabbed his head with both hands. He groaned in agony. The lost images fired in his mind like bullets. Panic seized him.

Pain pounded through his head as his blood, that felt as if it were at a frothing, rolling boil, raced through his veins. The sweet memories of his finest glory day had deserted him now, and what he did recall of the parade was unbelievably horrible. He finally stood and rushed to the house.

Munio flung the sliding glass door open so hard it bashed into the edge of its frame. The lap dogs, who were lined up for their customary greeting, watched him blow past them and head for the liquor cabinet. He grabbed the first bottle, uncapped it and tipped it straight up. The whiskey seared his throat, and he nearly choked on the breathtaking fumes.

He staggered blindly out to the gazebo. The full moon, focused now, burned a hole through the clouds and followed Munio like a spotlight. He hopped up the steps and paced from pillar to pillar, drinking almost constantly from the bottle. In half an hour, he had consumed half of the bottle, and after forty-five minutes, he fell flat on his face on the floor. The bottle that had been glued to his hand bounced away upon impact, and the remaining contents trickled onto the plywood.

Munio began to sob harder than he had when Sandra died. His mind rolled the parade tape. He cried through the beginning, when the gardenias were tossed to him in adoration, and the '64 Impala slowly drove him through the streets of Monkey River Town while he waved to everyone. It was such a wonderful day. It was the finest day of his life, the one glory day he would recall when he was old.

The Impala rolled slowly through the gray stone streets. People were everywhere, crowding the passageway for the car. The driver turned a corner and, as he did, three small boys leaped onto the hood of the car to ride. Munio laughed and waved at them. The driver was not happy about it and told them to get off. Munio convinced him to let them stay, and so they continued.

A couple of hundred yards down the street the driver took another turn to the right. The boys were not paying attention, and one of them slipped off onto the street. The car rolled right over him. The driver swerved to the right in hopes of clearing his body, but this caused the right front tire to drop off the shoulder into a small ditch. As a result, the boy was trapped with the entire weight of the front quadrant of the car pinning him. The child screamed, as did Munio and the drive,r who dashed from the car. Somehow, the boy was still conscious, and they tried to comfort him until they could figure out what to do.

"I'll get the jack out of the car! We'll jack it up, and free him!" The driver raced to the trunk.

Munio stopped him. "No, wait! It will be faster for me to pick up the car! I can do it! I know I can!"

The crowd screamed. When Munio said that, cheers from the crowd began. "Munio! Munio! Munio! Munio!" Nonstop they chanted.

"Are you sure?" tThe driver said. "What if you can't hold on? What if you slip? It is so uncertain."

"Come on! We're wasting time! I can do it!" Munio ran around to the front bumper.

He ripped off his shirt and put it over his hands to protect his fingers from the sharp edge of the bumper. He looked crazed in the fisheye reflection of the chrome. His adrenaline pumped so hard, he had no doubt of his ability. He grabbed the bumper and, using his legs, began cranking the car higher, one molecule at a time. The car kept heading skyward, and the crowd went wild with its deafening chant. Munio had plenty of strength left as the slightest crack of daylight grew between the red frame of that Impala and the blue gray stone.

The driver screamed, "It's moving! Keep going, Munio! Keep going!"

And Munio did. Higher and higher the car miraculously rose, until the driver waited for the perfect instant to yank the child to safety. The boy's head and one third of his upper body were free when, without warning, Munio's grip slipped, and the car landed with a hideous crunch on the boy's body. The spine was instantly severed, and the ribs, internal organs, and pelvis were crushed beyond hope. The boy made not a sound, but a gush of blood pumped from his mouth and nose onto the stone.

Munio stood there with his helpless empty hands, unable to move, unable to take his eyes off the child. The crowd, as any crowd that loves a hero, turned like a rabid dog on their superstar. The chant turned to a inaudible furious jabber with each person screaming a different insult to Munio. People began to throw stones and hit him with sticks. They might have killed him if not for his

mother, who waded through the crowd to save him. They obeyed her commands to let them pass, and with difficulty, she managed to lead him home.

The town, except for a few people, turned as cruel as they had been adoring, and this condition persisted for a long time. Munio went into a trance, lying in his bed, wide-eyed and silent, for a week following the incident. Slowly, the town forgot, and Munio tried to. Until tonight, he had hidden the secret deep in his soul. Unconsciously, he had grieved over this tragedy every day since it occurred. For twenty-six years, half of his fifty-year life, he had lived with this brokenhearted cancer.

Munio stayed prone on the gazebo floor, writhed and cried, beating his fists on the wood. Like a summer squall that rages one moment and vanishes the next, Munio's tears stopped, and he sat up. He crawled over to the steps and put his feet on the bottom one, resting his arms upon his knees.

He listened to his breath deep and slow. He sniffled and blew his nose. A freight train whistle sounded in the background far away. Munio felt exhausted. He looked up at the moon staring at it, hypnotized. As he continued to stare, a figure began forming. The image grew richer and richer, and the smiling head of a boy appeared, the boy he had killed, and also the boy Munio had been. They were the same child he saw, and the child spoke clearly to him, "I forgive you, Munio. I forgive you." The figure vaporized as effortlessly as it had appeared, and Munio again stared at that full-blown cream-colored moon. He looked away and gazed into the black night sky until it gave way to the coming blue dawn, and the big moon swam away to sleep. Munio crashed on the couch for several hours, and then, after serving breakfast to the dogs, went out in the yard to complete the changing of his tire. He knelt down by the jack. Without incident, he maneuvered the change, feeling no fear, no panic, only a soothing calm filling his heart.

# CHAPTER XXXIX

Despite the facade of all that muscle, Eddy's body was at an extremely delicate point. He did not feel like a whole body. He felt merely the sum of his parts. These visceral experiences provoked a low-key but deep-seated fear in Eddy. When he drank water, the experience did not end in his throat. He felt the water pass down his esophagus, through his chest, and into his stomach. Such nuances of life never caught Eddy's eye because usually he happily trampled right over them. Last night he even dreamed he was an angel.

"Good morning, I see you made it through another night."

"What makes you say that?" Eddy snapped.

Munio noticed the serious expression on Eddy's face and laughed, "Lighten up, brother. Easy, boy, I am just humoring you." Munio stepped behind and Eddy massaged his traps.

Eddy smiled. "Sorry, man, I'm just so, ah, shit, different. I don't know myself in the mirror anymore. Hell, I felt like crying this morning. That gh shit might be fucking my head up, man."

"Maybe. you probably ought to smoke a joint, relax. The hard work is over. You should rest until next week, man. Have fun."

"Yeah, right. I can't eat. I can't drink. I don't feel much like bowling either, Munio," Eddy joked. "Hey, but look at this shit." He yanked off his sweatshirt, pulled his sweatpants down to his pubic hair, and hit an ab shot.

"Wow," Munio smiled, "That's fantastic, Eddy. You are right there, right there."

Every abdominal muscle stood out He looked like an anatomical model for a biology course. His oddly-tanned red-brown skin was paper thin. His somewhat large navel lay there too, perhaps the only part of Eddy that remained unchanged.

"I never thought I'd ever have abs like this, man. Especially not six months ago, when I was slamming pizza and beer every other night? Boy howdy, I'll be glad to see those days again, brother. I'm telling you the truth now!"

Munio laughed, "I bet you will. We'll have a big pizza party for you, Eddy Jackson. After you win the Mr. Dixie competition next week, we will, me and Destiny will have a party for you."

"Sounds good to me. I'll sure as shit show up."

"Hey, I must see your routine. I want to see it today, in fact."

"All right, uh, why don't you come over tonight. Come over to the house. Oh, yeah, you know what else?"

"What?"

"Destiny got her check for all that money she inherited. She told me to tell you she's ready for another champagne blowout with you."

Munio laughed, "Good, good. You tell her anytime."

For just an hour, Munio hung with Eddy while he did his mild leg workout. Afterwards, he posed in the locker room in his underwear.

"Hit tight in that one," Munio said as Eddy hit a front double bicep shot. "Roll your arms forward, at the elbows, so you can flex your lats better. You want to show off everything you got. Just because they say bicep shot, you want them to see everything you got so you show them lats as big as possible. You see?"

"Yeah, man, I see what you mean."

"Hit a side tricep shot."

Eddy pivoted stiff as a soldier on a drill team and hit the shot.

"No, no, no, you look like a fucking robot!"

"That's what I want to look like, a machine!" Eddy laughed.

"No, no, you want to look like a dancer. You want to be graceful as well as powerful. Smooth transitions between poses, Eddy."

"I ain't no motherfucking dancer, man! I'm a muscle man, bud!"

"The posing is not about strength. It is about style and illusion."

"What the fuck are you talking about, man?" Eddy stood there in his jockey shorts leaning on one leg with his hands on his hips.

"You want the judges to see what you want them to see. For you, you have a boxy upper body, short torso. What you want to do is, as much as possible, move through the front shots quickly. Don't stay there long so they have time to notice, 'that son of a bitch is a boxy looking man.' You want them to say, "huge lats, nice transitions, look at that side tricep shot. Look at those delts. You know?"

"Ok, ok, well, tonight, we can work on it some more."

"Yes, and another thing. It is time to weed your garden, man." Munio motioned to his crotch.

Eddy laughed, "Oh, you mean all this shit."

"Yes, you look like you have a tarantula in your pants."

Eddy cracked up. "I know. I'm gonna shave today. I been putting it off. I hate that shit, man."

Munio laughed. "You are no bodybuilder! You are a monkeyman, a monster, Frankenstein."

"Get out of here man!" Eddy joked.

"Ok, I will see you tonight. Maybe seven o'clock?"

\* \* \* \* \* \*

Munio was hungry, so he opted for some of his favorite canned goods. Corned beef hash and sauerkraut hit the spot with a couple of tall malt liquors.

With this fortification, he was prepared and eager to make his final assault on the gazebo. With only trim left to install, he hoped to start painting tomorrow. The little dogs roamed the backyard and then took naps in the lawn chairs all through the afternoon, while Munio measured, sawed and nailed the trim.

About the time shadows began to fall, Audrey came to visit. Munio had his back to the gate and did not see her. She crept quiet as a cat so as to surprise him. She did not even wake the dogs, who usually could hear a pin drop. She made her way across the lawn exercising great stealth until she was within a couple of feet from him.

"Boo!" she cried.

Munio whirled around with the look of a warrior and his hammer held high, prepared to strike. When he saw it was Audrey, he dropped the hammer and ran his fingers through as much of his tangled hair as possible. "Goddamnit! You could get hurt doing things like that, you know!" He smiled at her.

She stood there and covered her laughing mouth. "Sorry, I couldn't resist. Come here." She stepped towards him, hugged him lightly, and kissed him on the cheek. "Still friends?" She smiled at him sweetly.

Munio looked her up and down. She looked hot dressed all in black, stretch pants, turtle neck, and soft leather jazz shoes. "I guess, but don't do that any more." He shook his index finger at her sternly. Munio walked over and picked a cigarette out of his pack and lit it. The smoke tasted good, and he followed it up with a sip of malt liquor.

"That's awful stuff, that malt liquor. How can you drink that?" Audrey put her hand across her chest.

"Full bodied taste." Munio flexed his eyebrows at her and smiled.

"Yuck." She walked around the gazebo and studied the details. After she made a complete loop, she looked at Munio and smiled. "Munio, this is beautiful. It looks like a gingerbread house. Do you know how proud Sandra would have been of you? She would love this thing. It's fabulous, absolutely fabulous."

"Well, thank you. Coming from someone as aristocratic as you, I will consider that a compliment."

"Well, you should. What color are you going to paint it?"

"Paint it? Are you crazy? I'm not going to paint it! And cover up all this beautiful wood with the grain showing and everything? It is fine just how it is now."

"Oh Munio, you can't leave it like this. It'll rot!"

"We all rot eventually." Munio laughed to himself and puffed a big harsh toke off his smoke. "I don't care if it rots. I won't be here to see it!"

Audrey fell for it hook, line, and sinker. "You must reconsider this, won't you Munio? It just doesn't-"

Munio could no longer hold his laughter. "What do you think? I'm crazy? Of course, I will paint this thing! It was a joke for you this time. I got you back quick, eh? For scaring me, huh?" He stuck his tongue out at Audrey playfully.

"Ha ha, funny boy. I guess I deserved it, huh?"

"That is right. Indeed."

"So really, what color are you thinking?"

He rubbed his chin and said, "I was thinking real colorful, you know? Like bright pink for the big parts and purple for the trim."

"No, no, no, too gaudy. It's not an ice cream stand, for crying out loud. It has to blend in with the house and the yard. White is good."

"Humm, you might be right about that. White would be ok."

"Munio, I want to talk to you about some other stuff. You got a few minutes?"

"Yeah, sure, come up here." He motioned her to walk up under the gazebo. He picked a railing and half sat on it.

Audrey did the same, only she preferred to lean with her legs crossed. "I'm not going to stay in Rosedale much longer. I thought about staying here. I mean you know, living here in Sandra's house, and with some help from my

lawyer in New York, I could swing all the legalities. I don't think I want to. The South is just not for me. Anyhow, this leads me to you. Would you be or are you interested in living here? I know Sandra would have liked that if you want to."

Munio didn't say anything for a minute. "I don't know about that notion. As you say, I don't feel this place is my home for long either. I like this house. I like my friend Eddy, too, but I don't know. I would have to think about this proposal."

"Well, do that. No rush. Take your time. Now, the other matter is that of the dogs. I cannot take them with me to New York. My building does not allow pets, and besides Munio, truthfully, I am just not a dog person, you know? I mean, more than anything in the world Sandra would want these dogs to continue to have a pampered existence, and they will, somehow. Only, I will not be the one to do it. Do you want the dogs?"

Munio chuckled and looked over at the lawn chairs where all three were curled up in the sun in a pile together. "I have gotten close with those little dogs. In fact, I have been meaning to ask you what their names are. I don't even know."

"Oh well, let's see." She pointed as she named them. "The Pomeranian is named Jacky. The Yorkie, the long-haired black and tan one, is Ricky. The other one, the Shih Tzu, is named Moo Shu." She laughed. "God, she loved those dogs. You know," Audrey's voice broke as she spoke. "you know, if she had nothing else to live for, I would have always thought she would have lived for those dogs. I just can't believe it. I still can't." She looked away.

Munio studied her beautiful profile, her graceful jawline. "I know," he said quietly. "Sometimes," he hesitated and his experience of last night came across his mind, "you have bad days. You can have a very bad day, and," he sighed, "you just don't make it through."

Audrey smiled. "Yeah, I guess so. You just can't figure people."

"Yeah."

"So, Mr. Morelos, what is it you would like to do with your life?"

"Do with my life?" Munio laughed and shook his head. "Live it until I wake up dead one day. I don't know. I never know. I have no plans."

"Do you want any plans?"

"I don't know. What does that mean? Are you selling plans or something of that nature?"

"Nooo, I just thought. Well, if you want to come to New York, I would put you to work teaching with me."

Munio chuckled. "Oh, again, I am honored to be worthy of the great instructor, Miss Meyers. How nice. Thank you, I appreciate your invitation. I will think of that too, and those consequences."

"Ok. You could stay with me."

"I am a neat freak, you must know."

"Like I'm not!"

"Oh, you know I am going to Atlanta with my friend Eddy next week. He will be in a bodybuilding contest. For a few days, we will be gone. You will need to tend to the dogs then, ok?"

"Ok, that's no problem. I need to spend some time over here. I have to pack up some of this stuff, all of this stuff."

"Ok, whatever."

"That's exciting. Do you think he will do well?"

"Oh yes, he anticipates winning the overall trophy. You should see him. He is freaky."

"I met him at the bar that night I met you. I had been there one other time, too. That was some time ago. I bet he has changed since then."

"Oh yes, he is ripped to shreds. Freaky, is all I can say. He is not graceful though. Tonight, I will work with him on movement. He moves like a stone, like a stone robot."

"Do you need some help? I would meet with you and him if you like."

"That is a good idea. Could you come around seven? You would enjoy seeing him, I think. Being a lover of the male body, you should see this extreme male physique."

"No problem, I have absolutely nothing planned."

"Good."

"All right then, hon, I'm leaving." She walked across the gazebo and hugged him. They kissed on the lips, with only a brief pause.

"Bye." Munio winked and waved. He took a big sip of his malt liquor as he watched her long legs and tight ass stride across the yard and pass through the gate.

Munio completed the trim that afternoon. His ordering had been perfect. Every piece of lumber he had bought he had used, and now the woodpile was gone. He looked forward to the painting, the icing on the cake.

* * * * * *

Munio arrived at Eddy's at seven.

"What's happening people?" Munio said. "I forgot to tell you my friend Audrey is coming here tonight to help with the movement, also."

Eddy, perched on the commode, cocked his head and looked down at Destiny, who was carving away at his pubic hair. He laughed, and so did Munio.

"You better not fucking laugh, Eddy! You want to get castrated, I mean circumcised twice in your life?" She giggled. "Damn, you're a woolly motherfucker!" They all started laughing.

"Eddy asked Munio.

"Yes, she is excellent with such matters of dance, movement etcetera."

"I reckon I better get all the help I can, huh? Destiny, darlin', you are

getting a little too damn close to my balls! The fucking judges ain't gonna be looking there."

A few minutes later Audrey rang the doorbell. Munio trotted down the hall to answer the door.

"Hello, dear." Munio kissed her as she made her entrance. "This way." Munio motioned for her to follow him down the hall. Audrey looked left and right and up and down, cruising the house. When they passed by the door of the doll room, she gasped.

"Munio!" she whispered loudly. "What in the hell is this all about?" Her mouth hung open as she peeked in and turned on the light. "Oh my God! What is this, Tennessee Williams' bedroom?" She burst into hysterics. "This is the strangest thing I," she laid her hand across her chest for emphasis, "have ever, ever seen in my life!"

"Munio?" Eddy called from the bathroom.

Munio laughed at Audrey's shock. "Come on. It was his mother's pride and joy, apparently," he whispered, leading her down the hall to the bathroom.

"Eddy, remember Audrey?"

Eddy almost fell off the commode. "Well, goddamned Munio, you might warn me. This lady might not to want to meet all of me. Well, not just yet anyhow. Sorry, ma'am." Eddy nodded his head. "How are you tonight?"

"Don't worry about that little old thing, honey. I've seen a lot bigger ones than that!" Audrey quipped. They all laughed.

"Audrey, this is Destiny!" Munio said, and the two of them nodded hellos.

"We'll be through here in a minute, Audrey. So you're a dancer, Munio tells me."

"I am." She looked around the bathroom at the ceramic tile. "Some house you have here, Eddy. It is a real classic Southern home."

"Well, I reckon it ought to be. Ain't nobody but Southerners lived in it since it was built in ah, believe it was 1910."

"Is that so? It's held up remarkably without renovation."

"We're neat freaks. I reckon that's why. Always cleaned up the house a lot, you know."

"All right Eddy, you might want to hop in the shower and hose that stuff off," Destiny suggested as she stood, holding up three disposable razors all caked with thick curly hair and shaving foam. "Look at that. Isn't that disgusting?" She giggled. "That was fun, though."

"Ok, y'all clear out. I'll be out in a minute. God, this feels weird. I feel seriously naked as a jaybird, now. I never realized how warm them little hairs keeps ya."

Audrey rolled her eyes at Munio, and Munio chuckled. "Ok brother, hurry up now."

Five minutes later Eddy called down the hall. "Hey, are ya'll ready for my grand entrance?"

"Yes, pretty boy, come on down!" Destiny yelled.

Eddy entered in a Day Glo lime green posing suit. His ripped body was slick as a whistle after the thorough shaving.

"My God in heaven, Eddy! You look like them guys in the magazines! I can't believe how big you are!" Destiny exclaimed.

Audrey was speechless, busy studying every square inch of this extraordinary body.

"You look great. Do you have your music?" Audrey asked.

"Yeah, let me put it on."

"What is it?" Audrey asked.

"You know Lynard Skynard? Freebird?"

"Nooooo, not that! That's not music to pose to, is it? Oi, vay," Audrey said in a disgusted and dramatic tone.

Eddy didn't know what to say. "Uh, well, you know, I just picked something I thought everbody would know, you know? Hell, I figured the music would kind of just be in the background anyhow. Well, now look, y'all. It's what I picked, so work with me, all right?" He grinned and held out his arms.

Audrey agreed, "All right, you're right."

"All right, so I'm goin' to just do it, and y'all watch me, ok?" Everybody nodded, and the music began.

Eddy proceeded to crank out his poses to the slow music and surprisingly, the music wasn't that bad after all. Audrey thought it would work, but Munio was right, Eddy had no sense of style whatsoever. With a shit-eating grin on his face, he bounced through the entire routine. He looked more like an aerobics instructor than a bodybuilder.

"First of all, attitude adjustment. You are not a brick mason. You are a drag queen carved in stone, all right? Macho is not what you have to sell. Think style and charisma. You're grinning like a fucking hyena standing in shit. Change expressions and save your smiles for the height of the pose. You know what I'm saying, Eddy?" Audrey instructed.

"Uh, yeah, I reckon."

"O.K., look. Put the music back on. I'm going to show you what you did, all right?"

"O.K." Eddy put the song back on and Audrey took the stage.

She remembered most of the poses and mimicked Eddy perfectly. Munio, Eddy, and Destiny watched as Audrey camped it up, and the three of them were practically rolling on the floor laughing by the time the last "And this bird you cannot tame" ended. They all gave her a standing ovation.

"Thank you! Thank you! No autographs! All right, you see what I'm talking about?"

"Was I that bad?" Eddy chuckled as he asked.

"Yes! Am I wrong?" She held out her arms to Munio and Destiny. They both shrugged and nodded yes at Eddy.

"Damn! Y'all done got me worried now. You think you can teach me what to do real quick like?"

"God, I hope so!" Audrey rolled her eyes and looked to the heavens.

It wasn't the easiest task she had ever taken on, but it wasn't as hard as teaching the tango to some of those old snobs with two left feet at the country club. Over the next three hours, Eddy listened and learned. He learned how to swish a little and sell his act to the judges at the Mr. Dixie Contest.

"Well Audrey, I sure do appreciate you helping me. Munio was right about you being a good teacher," Eddy said as he sat down on the couch.

Munio chuckled and gave Audrey a teasing look as she said, "You are quite welcome, Eddy. If you want to have another session or two this week before you go, just tell Munio."

"All right, I might just do that."

"Oh Destiny, I forgot to tell you congratulations on getting your check," Munio said.

"Oh, yeah, right." A chill ran up Destiny's spine. "I think I forgot myself. I...it's hard to believe, you know?"

"Yeah, I bet."

"You ready for another champagne party?"

"Yes, ma'am, I am. You know I was thinking that if you wait a couple of more days we could have the party over at my friend's house where I am staying. We could celebrate the completion of the gazebo I built." Audrey threw a rigid look at Munio.

"That sounds good. Have it outside, less puke to clean up!" Destiny joked as Audrey shivered at the thought.

"Audrey, you could come if you want to. I don't know how much of a drinker you are, but me and old Munio here are the best there are!" They all laughed.

"Thanks, I'll keep it in mind," She said coolly.

"Where is that place you're staying at?" Destiny asked.

"Uh, you know I still don't even know the address. I just know where it is." Munio chuckled at his ignorance. "Audrey, do you know?"

"Yes, it is on Chickasaw Drive near Vance. The number is 525, I believe."

"Hummm, kind of hooty neighborhood, Munio. How did you get up with somebody over there?" Destiny inquired.

"Oh, I met her through Audrey. She used to take dance classes from Audrey at the country club."

"She don't no more?" Destiny pursued.

"Uh, no." Munio suddenly felt a little cornered. "She doesn't."

"Why is it you're staying there?"

"I take care of her dogs. She is with a sick friend out of town."

"Oh? When's she coming back?"

Munio answered gruffly, "I don't know."

"Oh, well, yeah, you let me know when you're going to finish. Besides, it's going to take me a few days to get my actual hands on some of that dough, you know?"

"Did you win the lottery?" Audrey kidded.

Now, Destiny retreated. "No, a friend of mine got killed, I mean died, and I, ah, inherited some stuff, some money."

"I'm sorry to hear that. That's difficult, isn't it?"

"Yeah," Destiny said quietly, hoping her cross-examination was about over.

"I better get going. Nice to meet all of you, and good luck, Eddy, if I don't see you again before the contest." Audrey smiled at him and held out her hand. "Destiny, see you again, perhaps." She offered her hand to her as well. "Munio, mind walking me to the car?"

"No, not at all." Audrey and Munio headed out the door.

"You did good with all those question," she said as they walked across the sandy driveway.

"I don't like to talk about it at all."

"That's understandable. I thought I would die when I heard the song Eddy wanted to use. God, how I hate that redneck rock and roll! He did all right at the end. I think it will work ok." She leaned against the car and crossed her arms to defray the cool wind.

"You did great. I don't think I would have done as good with him. He is clumsy, not clumsy, but, ah, not graceful at movement." Munio laughed. "I guess that all adds up to clumsy."

"I like him. I thought Destiny was a hoot, too."

As they continued to chat for a few more minutes, Destiny manned the living room window and spied on them. Eddy had just sprung the news to Destiny that Audrey was really a man, and Destiny was about to pop from astonishment, having never met a "real" drag queen before. To her knowledge, she had never met a homosexual before.

"So, what do they do? Is Munio queer, too?" Destiny interrogated Eddy while she continued to keep her eyes glued on that driveway scene.

"I don't know. I don't think he's all queer. I think he's, ah, you know, acey deucey."

"Acey fucking deucey! I ain't ever met anybody like that before."

"Jesus Christ, Destiny! You would think you have been living out in the fucking woods or something. It ain't such a big damn deal to be queer. People's been queer since the mother cavemen days. Besides, they ain't neither one of 'em trying to fuck you, so what do you care?" Eddy giggled uncontrollably as he watched her.

268

"I'm just excited, I guess, about it. It's like meeting Martians for the first time. It's like, I know in my heart they have invaded us, maybe not Mars, but some place, somewhere has sent people to check out earth. Anyhow, it's like finding out there is some Martian living in your neighborhood. It's exciting. God, wonder what that other one looks like?"

"Who? What other one?" Eddy frowned as he lay on the couch.

"You know, that one that owns that house where Munio's been at. Wonder what she looks like?"

"Maybe she ain't one, Destiny. You're too nosy. Quit staring out of that window. You dadgum snoop, you!" Eddy hurled a throw pillow at her which caught her in the back of the head, causing her forehead to hit against the glass with a smack.

Munio and Audrey both heard the noise and looked up in unison at the house. Destiny dropped like a rock to her knees to avoid detection. She crawled across the floor over to Eddy, hopped on him, and began tickling him for all she was worth.

* * * * *

"Munio." Audrey ran a long finger down his neck. "I think I would like to see you again, soon. How do you feel about that?"

The words hit him like an exploding grenade and sent rays of sexual excitement to every cell of his body. He locked eyes with her with a power that accompanies only lust or rage. "When?" he asked quietly.

"Now."

"I'll meet you in half an hour at Sandra's. You go there now if you wish. You have a key, no?"

"I'll see you." Their brown eyes slapped each other one more time as she got into her car.

Munio jogged back into the house and up the steps. He opened the door to find Eddy and Destiny skirmishing on the couch. "Hey, what are you two doing?" he kidded, sitting down in a big overstuffed antique rocking chair.

"Trying to get this wild ass bitch off me. Help me, Munio! She's gonna ruin me."

"You are ruined, Eddy Jackson. I got news for you!" Destiny said as she climbed off him and sat on the end of the couch.

"Well, Munio, I had no idea you was so, well," Eddy kicked her, hoping she was not going to say something stupid, "adventurous."

"What do you mean?"

"Eddy was telling me about that Audrey was really a man and all, but he sure is good looking. Don't get me wrong, ok? I just never met anybody close up and personal like that, you know?"

Munio laughed, "Well, welcome to the real world. There are many crazier people than her. Like you!" He laughed and pointed at Destiny. He and

Eddy cracked up.

"Ha ha. Now, what's that other girl like? Is she a lesbian or something?"

"She who?"

"That woman over where you've been staying."

"Oh her. She is just a regular woman. She, she is just straight." Munio smiled innocently.

"Huh, well now, Audrey, does he, I mean, does that Sandra girl know about him?" Destiny used her index fingers to emphasize and clarify what it was she was trying to say.

"First of all," Munio said emphatically, "Audrey is to be referred to as a she, ok? Second of all, yes, Sandra knows Audrey very well. They have been friends for many years. Is that cleared up now, Miss Investigator?" Munio laughed.

"Wai, wai, wait a minute. I don't get why, if Audrey is a guy, why does he want everybody to call him a she?"

"He likes to dress like a woman. He lives his life like a woman. He is feminine."

"Is he gonna get a sex change?"

"No, he does not want to be a woman." Munio sighed at the tediousness of the conversation.

"Well then, I don't get it." Destiny shook her head.

"You know what, Destiny? Maybe there is nothing to 'get' as you say. Maybe you just let people be the way they want to be."

"Ok, ok, I ain't trying to insult y'all. I just don't know about all this shit, you know? Now, if you would just answer one more question, I'll-"

"No more questions!" Munio laughed and stood up. "I got to go. You think about the questions I already answered, and maybe I will answer more another time, ok?"

"All right, all right."

"Eddy, tomorrow, do you want to train?"

"Naw, I'm going to just pose, just work on the that stuff I learned tonight. You know posing's a workout enough. Fuck, I sweat like a dog after doing that routine a couple of times."

"Ok, brother. I'm going to work on the gazebo tomorrow all of the day."

"You wasn't offended, were you, Munio?" Destiny asked.

"No, no, it's ok, really." He smiled at her.

"Ok, bye, Munio. Thanks for bringing her over. I like her, by the way." Eddy saluted Munio from his repose on the couch.

"See you two." Munio waved and left, anxious to get to the task at hand.

# CHAPTER XL

Munio looked straight ahead as he drove, not studying the scenery as he usually would. A singleness of purpose now captured and discarded all other thoughts. His face tightened, and his heart quickened while the fury grew within him. Her car was in the driveway as he whipped the truck in. His dick was smitten with an erection that felt like molten lead. He ached from the condition, but the pain only spurred his psychotic passion.

Half-crippled from the hard-on, Munio limped across the carport and flung open the door. The dogs were waiting, but he did not even see them. In the living room he found her. Standing with her back to him, studying a painting that hung on the wall. Classical Spanish guitar music blasted from the stereo, exciting him and adding fuel to the fire.

He quickly moved to her and grabbed her from behind in a powerful and none too tender manner. She gasped  Munio felt hot, his body covered her like a glove, and he began moving with the music. They stalked each other through a seductive flamenco number. The foot sounds were muffled by of the carpet, but the spirit of the dance emerged to bind them to one another in moving foreplay. Their bodies sparred and snapped in sharp movements as they responded to the staccato licks of the guitar and the clicking castanets.

Not like lovers, with sweet, gentle rain, did their urges grow, but with the brusqueness and power of the mating of lions. In their dance, they screamed and clawed and growled their way to the place where their bodies no longer cared about any other body part, except their genitals begging for attention and relief.

It was a night of rug burn that neither would regret or forget as they finally lay motionless, void of energy to lift a finger, to smile, or even blink. Munio managed to drag his blankets and pillow from the couch to cover them. Audrey didn't regain consciousness until morning as Munio held her tightly from the back. Warmed by the heat of his chest, she slept in perfect bliss.

Munio and Audrey awoke feeling much cooler than they had upon falling asleep. Audrey was, in fact, shivering under the blankets on the carpet.

"Jesus Christ, where am I?" she exclaimed, and then laughed.

Munio rolled over, "You died and went to hell, that's what."

"It's not hot enough to be hell, mister." She pinched one of his nipples as she got to her feet. "Oh my God, I'm freezing, and I've got to pee!" She flew down the hall naked to the bathroom.

Audrey returned and demanded a piece of the covers. Munio jokingly begrudged it to her, and she leaped back under them with an air of great desperation. They playfully sparred as Munio wanted to pull away from Audrey's cold body and she wanted to be warmed by his. Finally, Munio gave in and reached around to pull her close to him.

They lay face to face, each aware of the other's warm moist breath as their exhalations landed softly on each other's necks. When Munio blinked, his long black eyelashes tickled Audrey's cheek.

"What caused that awful scar on Destiny's face?" Audrey asked.

"She was drunk and walked through a plate glass window."

"Hmmm. She could get that fixed if she wanted."

"Maybe she likes it. Maybe it is a battle scar to remember."

"I doubt it, Munio. Have you ever met a woman who wanted a full length scar running down her face? Really."

Munio laughed. "It's unique, like a tattoo."

"Aw, honestly, Munio, that girl doesn't want that thing there. Oi,vay."

"Whatever, she is still a nice looking woman, don't you think?"

"Yes, she is, compared to other women I've seen in this town. I would say she is probably the queen of her Wal-Mart." Audrey laughed heartily at her own joke, while Munio reached up and calmly pinched her flat nipple, which caused her to yelp. "You are too much. You have too much arrogance in your attitudes. Is that just you, or is it a condition that all people of New York have?" Munio asked, wrinkling his face and raising one eyebrow suspiciously.

"Hmm. I can't answer for New Yorkers, but I can tell you this. I am the queen of my Wal-Mart! How's that?"

She and Munio giggled.

"You know what?" Munio asked.

"What?"

"Destiny wanted to know if Sandra was a lesbian."

"Sandra would have loved that. What did you tell her?"

"I told her she was just a regular woman." They both burst into laughter.

"That's so funny. What did they think of me?"

"I think they both thought you were a real snob," Munio replied soberly.

Audrey elbowed him in the ribs. "They did not. They liked me."

"Yes, they did. Destiny didn't know until after you left that you were a man."

"Really?"

"She never met a drag queen."

"How touching, meeting your first drag queen. Well, how did she take it? Wait, wait, let me guess. Uh, 'She's so purdy and all,'" Audrey joked in the best cartoonish Southern accent she could muster.

"No, she did not say that." He hooted.

"Ok, here you go. 'Has she cut her pecker off?'" she said in a an excellent performance worthy of Gomer Pyle.

"She did not say that!" Munio could not stop his hysterics. "She wanted to know," he blubbered, " if, if you were going to get the big change." He nodded and raised his eyebrows.

"Oh, well, what did you tell her?"

He wiped the tears from his eyes. "I can't remember exactly. I said something like I did not think you wanted to, that's all." He shrugged his shoulders.

"How about Eddy?" Is he homophobic?"

"No, I don't think he is. He said he had been around some queens in Atlanta." Munio chuckled.

"Oy! Wonder when that was? I might have already met him, or part of him anyway. I went to Atlanta once years ago." Audrey joked. "Actually, I've never been that promiscuous, believe it or not. Since the whole AIDS thing, well, I have been even less so. I always do safe sex, too."

"Do you know people with that?"

"Honey! Are you serious?" Audrey shook her head as she lay on the pillow. "Most of the people I know, men anyway, are HIV positive or have full blown AIDS. It's awful."

"Do you have the HIV positive status?"

"Amazingly no. Knock on wood." Audrey touched the coffee table for good luck.

"Do you?" Audrey asked Munio.

"Me? I don't think so."

"Ever been tested?"

"No, should I? I'm not sick or anything."

"Wouldn't hurt."

They lay there in silence for a while, and gradually drifted back to sleep until the little dogs woke them up by standing right in Audrey's face.

"Don't lick me! Yuck, dog lips!" Audrey wiped her mouth with the blanket as she sat up. "All right, I'm out of here."

# CHAPTER XLI

The sunlight was just beginning to leak in through the edges of the blinds when Eddy blinked awake. A feeling in his gut told him something was wrong. His right hand felt wetness on the sheets and, looking down, he realized the bed was soaked with blood. The IV had come loose in the night, and Eddy, sound sleep, was bleeding to death. He cursed and jumped from the bed as if the bloody mess were fire. As soon as he hit the floor he staggered and fell, weakened by the blood loss. As he sat on the floor, he checked his arm and saw that the spot of puncture had still not clotted, and a stream of his deep red high octane blood trickled down his brown muscled forearm. He grabbed one of his dirty socks that lay on the floor beside the bed and applied it as a compress to try and stem the tide.

He struggled to stand. His head was spinning, and he saw stars as he plopped onto the end of the bed. His heart beat fast and his breath was la-

bored. "Easy, easy, easy," he repeated aloud to help alleviate his panic. He forced himself to slow down his breathing.

After fifteen minutes or so of pressing hard on his vein, he peeked and saw that the bleeding had subsided. He stood and realized he was still very woozy. "Damn!" he spat, as he steadied himself on furniture, the doorframe, and the walls as he wandered down the hall to the bathroom.

After rinsing off the half-dried sticky blood that was all over his arm and hand, the vein started to ooze again. Eddy sat down on the commode and quietly pressed a washrag on the vein for another few minutes. Suddenly, a thought ran across his mind that made him leap up from the commode. Down the hall he ran, into the bedroom. He went to the lamp that held the plastic drip of gh and saline solution, and traced the hose til he found the needle. "Damn!" He cursed as he saw a tiny drop leak from the angled point of the thick silver needle. Like his life depended upon it, he reached up and turned the regulator valve leading out of the bag. He turned it the wrong way at first and the fluid shot out of the needle like a hose until he quickly shut it down.

"Damn! God knows how much of that shit got wasted!" he muttered. "That pisses me off! It ain't like that shit grows on trees! Fuck it! Fuck it!" Eddy stomped his feet, his massive forehead wrinkled in sheer disgust. He stubbed his big toe on the leg of a chair.

"I'll show you! You mother fucker!" He picked the straightbacked wooden chair up over his head and slammed it to the floor, splintering it into total ruin. His eye next caught a bookshelf mounted on the wall. He let out a scream and attacked it. First, he knocked all the books off, and then, with the five foot board that served as the shelf, he began to flog the room. He jammed it into picture frames on the wall. The glass shattered, and then the damaged pictures slid down the wall. Like a madman, he continued to work the room, destroying anything and everything in his reach. Finally, exhausted, he collapsed on the bed with a sigh. After half an hour, as if nothing at all had happened, Eddy gave himself a big shot of test, and fixed himself some egg whites for breakfast.

# CHAPTER XLII

Audrey fell onto her sofa, exhausted and relieved. She kicked her heels off, and they flew across the room end over end like a well-booted field goal. It was ten thirty at night, and she had just spent her most difficult moment at the country club. Her next to last scheduled class had been rehearsing their dance recital to be held next Wednesday. The pupils in the class were not spry, and their ability to perform choreographed ballroom dance frustrate Audrey. Their ages ranged from sixty-five to eighty, and nearly every one of them was hard of hearing. Sandra, oddly enough, had been the youngest and

most able-bodied student of them all. One on one, Audrey could communicate fairly well with them, but to give instructions to the group as they danced in unison was out of the question. After this rehearsal, visual imagery of the recital made her shake her head and roll her eyes. She felt helpless to control the fate of the event.

As if this problem weren't enough, the director of the country club had approached Audrey about Sandra. It seems that her membership had come due, and Sandra had also offered to make a contribution to the annual scholarship award. The director knew that Audrey and Sandra were close, and his attempts to reach her by telephone were unsuccessful.

Audrey performed well, explaining that Sandra, caring for a gravely ill friend up north, had not been her usual responsible self. The director was placated by Audrey's assurance that she would contact him, hopefully tomorrow, and discuss these matters. For the record, she got him to jot down the amount of the dues, and the amount Sandra had committed to for the scholarship.

She had reached an awkward turning point with the consequences of hiding Sandra's death. Bills were coming due. Not just the ones at the country club, but telephone, utilities, insurance. If she decided to pay them by forging Sandra's checks, she put herself in a dangerous situation should the truth ever be known.

Actually, she knew that if the real truth were ever explained to the authorities, she and Munio would be sharing their lives together in a bunk in some south Georgia asylum. Besides, if she were going to jail for a murder and burying a body, how bad could a little old forgery conviction be? The fantasy only got worse the deeper she took it, as she imagined that, somewhere along the line, she would have to give positive ID that identified her as a male. All in all, there was nothing that felt safe about this situation. Nonetheless, here she was with Munio riding the edge of a crumbly cliff. She laughed at the absurdity of it all, and decided to go directly to bed before she blew her own brains out.

Thoughts of Munio crossed her mind. Where was he going to go? She hoped he didn't want to stay here because she feared, deep down, that eventually somebody was going to want to know why the hell Sandra Fugleberg was not accounted for. In a little town like this, they would fry Munio before he could blink twice. Her mind could not stop processing potential solutions to all these problems, and she wondered if her father could be of help. There were other friends in New York as well, attorneys familiar with helping gay people settle estates with their dead lovers. It would work out, she assured herself. As wellintended as all this had been, surely they would not be punished for their love of this dear friend. Her hopes turned to the dreams that she might experience tonight. Maybe some sign would appear to direct safe action.

Audrey quickly pulled her body to the nightstand and slapped the button on her alarm clock. She had slept so soundly she hadn't even turned over

once, and though it had been nine hours, she felt she had just fallen asleep. Falling back on her pillow, she felt her mind focus slowly. Within a few minutes, the internal chatter began.

In the bathroom, she took a seat and pointed herself between her legs and below into the bowl. Afterwards, she checked her face in the mirror and stood brushing her hair, first gently, then vigorously. That woke her up as much as any cup of coffee could. Just the same, she shuffled into the kitchen to put on a pot.

Her special Kenyan dry roasted blend was running low. Because of this, she knew she must either go to New York right away or have a friend FedEx a couple of pounds. She poured some of the hard brown beans into a small grinder and turned the switch, causing a sound as piercing as a dentist's drill. Audrey frowned over this as she frowned every morning, but there was nothing to change. She simply could not drink grocery store coffee, and her tastes were too refined to accept the compromise one makes when the beans are not freshly ground. The coffee machine completed its cycle quickly, and Audrey poured a cup into an ornate bone china cup with saucer. No cream or sugar was ever added, lest it detract from the pure enjoyment.

After one cup was finished, she knew what her course of action would be. Even though she was planning to leave Rosedale soon, on this morning she was not prepared to cause a stir with anyone. The choice was forgery, and she would write whatever checks must be written to keep the bills paid for at least one more month. One month would surely provide enough time to invite more creativity for a permanent solution.

At nine a.m., Audrey called Sandra's bank and solicited a balance. Since she had Sandra's purse with her social security number, there was no hesitation from the employee, and the amount was cheerfully given. There was over twenty thousand dollars available.

A phone rang in a Long Island home. "Hello?" the woman answered, a slow and thick accent powering her speech.

"Mom?"

"David?"

"Hi, mom, how are you?"

"Fine, and you, honey? You haven't called in such a long while, your father and I were beginning to worry." She chuckled. "We wondered if you had been kidnapped to pick watermelons or something. You know, your father and I just saw on that show on "20/20" a story about fruit pickers in the South."

Audrey began laughing. "Mother, really now."

"No, you listen to me, David. They were regular people, and these hoodlums, rednecks, kidnapped people and made them stay endlessly on these farms. There was no escape for them. Do you understand? It was horrible. One man was from Jersey. Seemed to be a nice kid, young, mid-twenties, not

much younger than you, David."

"Mother, I would love to see somebody make me pick watermelons, honestly. That is so hysterical, really."

"You laugh, but you have to watch out. The South is not your turf, David. They do things differently down there, you know. Well, you know, you're there, of course."

"How'sDdad?"

"Fine, your dad's fine. He's swimming this morning before work. He works too much as always, but he's fine."

"Good. And you?'

"I'm ok. My back has been bothering me, but other than that, I'm ok, honey. When will you be coming back up?"

Audrey sighed, "Soon, I hope. My classes end next week. They want me to do another series, but I don't think so. I've had it. I've had it with the South, actually. Although it's been better now that it has cooled off. This is the hottest place next to hell on the face of the earth. Besides, if I don't have a bagel soon, I might just die. I miss New York terribly, Mom. I miss you and Dad, too."

"We miss you too, honey. How's Sandra?"

"Oh, ok, she's fine, Mom."

"When will you be coming up, son?"

"I'll have to call. Not for a couple of weeks."

"Ok, are you all right, honey? You sound a little funny."

Audrey giggled nervously, "No, I'm just waking up, that's all, and I just hadn't spoken to you so I thought I would say hi."

"All right dear. Don't make it so long next time? Watch out for those fruit pickers, too?"

Audrey laughed. "All right, Mom. Love you. Tell Dad hi."

"Goodbye, David."

"Bye Mom."

Audrey sat sadly on the sofa with her hand on the phone. Her white terrycloth robe cinched tightly around her waist, draped open at the front, exposing her long legs. There were people all over this country who, if she requested, would shower her with praise, affection, and support, but she was in such a solitary position that none of those people could help. She chuckled, thinking how she wished Sandra were here to help her. Sandra always had an answer. Audrey dialed another number.

"Mr. Stevens, please," Audrey requested.

"Just a moment, please." The southern belle's voice echoed with the song of her accent.

"Bill Stevens," the voice answered.

"Good morning Mr. Stevens, Audrey Meyers. How are you?"

"Well fine, Miss Meyers, just fine."

"Good. Listen, I have spoken with Miss Fugleberg, and she would like

to renew her membership, of course, and follow through with her commitment to your scholarship fund. The situation has been so demanding with her friend that she unintentionally has neglected some of her own affairs, you see."

"Why yes, I certainly can understand how that can happen, ma'am."

"However, she will be mailing me some checks for you, and they should be here in a few days."

"Well, that will be fine. We appreciate you helping out in this matter. Tell Miss Fugleberg that we wish her well and hope to see her back on the dance floor real soon, now. Real soon, you tell her, hear?"

"Yes, I will, sir. All righty, perhaps you will attend our recital next week?"

"Wouldn't miss it for the world, Miss Meyers. Everyone has so enjoyed your instruction. It is a shame you must return to New York."

"Thank you, Mr. Stevens. It had been my pleasure to be here," Audrey lied through her teeth.

"Good day to you, ma'am."

"Good bye."

Audrey felt a boost in her mood simply because her adrenaline had been pumping throughout that conversation. She put an Anita Baker tape on her boom box and sang out loudly to it while she dressed. Since it was to be a somewhat casual day, she opted not to tape herself, but to wear tight Spandex underwear instead. On top of that, she slipped a pair of old faded blue jeans over her long, smooth legs and slim hips. Her hips were shapely for a man and expressed a slight curve that filled out the line of her jeans perfectly. She tucked in a black long-sleeved T-shirt, and accessorized with a thick black belt and ornately-styled silver buckle.

Onto her feet, she pulled an ankle-high pair of brown suede boots. The small heels made a seductive click with every step. The sound comforted her, as all rthymns did, and reminded her that all movement was dance. Audrey believed that with all movement, there was an accompanying sound, and that sound was the music of the dance. Whenever Audrey was pinned down as to what religion she prescribed, she always said she belonged to the church of the dance of life. People would kid her, and even she felt the statement sounded too newage for her, but she really did believe it, more than anything else that she did believe about life.

# CHAPTER XLIII

By mid-morning the dew had dried and sunshine bore down on the gazebo. Munio set in to finish the painting. As he painted he thought about some way to memorialize Sandra with a plaque or sign on the gazebo, but he decided that could not happen. He thought about the champagne chugging

party. With one full day of curing, the floor would be ready for traffic day after tomorrow. That would also be the day before they left for Atlanta. They could celebrate Eddy's contest although Eddy could not. He laughed thinking about that, and wondered what they would do in Atlanta.

"Boo!" Audrey had snuck up on him again.

"Damn! You got me again! I cannot believe it!" He shook his head. "You know that your payback will be hell, don't you? You will regret this joke you now enjoy, Audrey. Wait and see. You wait and see." Munio shook his finger at her.

Audrey laughed in delight, entertained by his reaction. "I'm sorry, Munio. I just couldn't help myself. You would think you could hear me. I drove up. I slammed the gate. Were you daydreaming or what?" She chuckled.

"I guess so. So what do you think? Doesn't this look great?"

"It does. It really does, Munio. We have to take a picture of it. I'll bring my camera over."

"Ok, yeah, that's good. I'll take your picture tied up to it just before I blow you up for your payback!" He gave her a mock vicious look.

Audrey laughed again. "Well, I came by to go through the mail, and pay some bills. For now, I'm just going to forge a few checks to keep things going until we decide what to do."

"Ok, yeah, whatever." Munio really had given no thought to these things. "I would like to have the initiation party of the gazebo and Destiny's celebration day after tomorrow. Would you like to come?"

"On Wednesday?"

"Yes."

"I'll have to come late. That's my final night with the dance class. We're putting on a recital. I'll drop by afterwards. Is that ok?"

"Yes, it is fine, but I will warn you of something. There will be much drinking, and if you arrive late, there is a very good chance Destiny and I will be drunk as can be. So, you may come if you wish, but don't say I did not warn you."

"Well thank you. Hell, after I get through with them, I'll probably be ready to tie one on myself."

"That's fine, too. There will be plenty of champagne. Do you like champagne?"

"Yes, I do, but not cheap champagne."

"Well, I do not know what she is buying, but I think it will be good."

"I'm going in to do some work. I'll see you later."

"Ok, see you later." Munio turned back to his painting.

He applied the last stroke to the gazebo floor. Before he even stepped back to study his work, he dutifully cleaned his brushes in the kitchen sink. After retrieving a celebratory beer, he sat on the patio and smoked half a joint. The little dogs browsed all about, but surprisingly steered clear of the gazebo.

Munio didn't know if it was the strong smell of the paint or the frightening smell of their mother, who was no doubt getting ripe about right now. Except for the final color selection, the gazebo lived up to Munio's dream of it. On his own, he had never built such a beautiful structure.

Audrey walked into the kitchen for a glass of water and saw Munio on the patio. She watched him for a moment, and admiring his fine facial features. She wondered what he would look like with that hair combed out. Maybe, she thought, one day when she had four hours to kill she would comb it out if he would let her. She chuckled to herself. She opened the sliding glass door, sat beside him.

"I am finished. The gazebo is complete," he announced, and toasted towards her with his beer can.

She smiled, reached over, and kissed his cheek. He felt warm from his work and from the sun. His smell was like a dry towel that had been on the beach, rich with a salty sweet scent, dried by the sun. He smiled at her and noticed that Audrey's eyes were light brown out in this sun.

"I always thought your eyes were browner than they look today."

"They're hazel. You have mostly seen them indoors, and mostly at night." She winked. "It's no wonder."

"Oh, I guess so." He smiled gently at her and looked at the gazebo again.

"You did such a good job, Munio. I know I keep saying it, but I am surprised myself. No offense, but I am so impressed."

Munio smirked and shook his head. "You did not believe in me. You had the wrong idea, that's all. It's ok."

They sat there in silence without interfering with one another's thoughts. It was such a comfortable feeling that both of them forgot the other was even sitting there. Finally, the pack of dogs wandered up to say hello, and Audrey and Munio drifted back into the verbal world, baby talked them and caused tails to wag.

# CHAPTER XLIV

"Eddy?" Munio called as he pushed open the front door.

"Yeah! Down here, Munio!"

Munio walked down the hall to Eddy's room. The room was in shambles from the earlier tantrum, and Eddy lay on the bed reading a muscle mag. "Hey, sit down." Eddy maintained a look of deep concentration as he read.

"What the hell happened here?" Munio chuckled as he watched. He looked around at the debris from the mêlée.

"Tornado blew threw here a little while ago." Eddy looked up from his magazine and smiled sweetly.

"I see."

Photographs smashed in their frames caught Munio's eye. There were

pictures of Eddy as a child with his mother and father. Various trophies lay scattered about. Several had a gold football on top. One displayed a baseball and bat, and another showed a male figure drawing back an archer's bow. There was a solitary photograph of a little boy sitting on Santa Claus's lap. Munio walked over and picked it up. The child looked vaguely like it could have been Eddy.

"Is this you?"

"Naw, my little cousin. He died though. Died right after that picture was taken."

Munio frowned. "That's too bad. So young."

"Yep, playing with matches. Caught the house on fire."

"Wow, that's awful."

"Yeah, it was. Bad thing was I done it. It was me playing with them matches. I burnt up everybody's Christmas presents and Ray. That was his name." Eddy didn't look up from his magazine as he recounted the facts.

Munio stared at him soberly and was surprised Eddy did not display more emotion. He just continued to read. While he did not pass judgment on Eddy's mistake, he could not help but think about what it might feel like to bear such a burden, since he himself had been through it.

"Bitch, huh?" Eddy spoke without looking up at Munio.

"I don't know what to say. It must have been heartbreaking." Munio's arms and hands reached outwards as he spoke.

"Yeah." Eddy continued to read. "Had a little sister, too."

Munio nearly cried at this news.

"Got her. She was asleep in her babybed." Still Eddy didn't offer eye contact with Munio.

Munio looked at the poor smiling child in the photo again and shook his head.

"There was a litter of puppies in the kitchen. They didn't make it either." Eddy's body started vibrating, but still he did not look up from the magazine.

Munio thought Eddy at last was erupting in grief at the memory of this horrible occurrence. Munio's mouth was pursed tensely when Eddy threw down the magazine, leaped up on the bed. He began laughing like a maniac and jumping on the bed like an eight-year-old.

"Gotcha! Gotcha! Gotcha!" Eddy rolled with laughter so hard he was crying.

Munio grinned and shook his head. "You, my friend, are a sick motherfucker. You, Eddy Jackson, need some psychiatric assistance because you are insane! I cannot believe you joke about such a thing!" Munio laughed as he watched the crazy man leaping around on the bed.

"Oh Jesus Christ! I got to sit down. I'm about to pass the fuck out! Shit, that was funny! I was looking up at you just a little, watching your expressions.

You was about to fucking break down, wasn't you, buddy? Yeeeeehaaa!"

"Shit! So sick, so sick. You have been ruined from all those crazy drugs. They have warped your mind in a most terrible way."

"They ain't warped this!" Eddy grabbed his crotch and laughed hysterically. "Ain't warped this neither!" He shot a double bicep pose showcasing those big guns.

"Still, you are fucked up, and you will never be the same. Tonight, your tongue will rot out for concocting such a tale. You are a very bad man, brother." Munio shook his head and laughed.

"Hey, let's go grow! What do you say?' Eddy slapped Munio on the back hard as he hopped up to get his workout bag. "Let's go grow! I'm ready to be somebody today, brother!"

\* \* \* \* \* \* \* \* \*

Eddy drove them over in his car. Munio lit up a cigarette and rolled down his window slightly.

"You're gonna give me cancer from second hand smoke, man. Put that thing out," Eddy joked.

"You going to give me a nervous breakdown with all your foolishness. I cannot believe you told that story today. Still, I cannot believe."

"I'm good, son. I'm real good. My good friends call me guy, and my enemies call me sly! Have mercy right now today, brother!" He slapped the steering wheel with both hands. "Hey, today you are going to finally meet Sam, the guy that owns the gym. He don't hang around there much anymore, but he's supposed to be there today to give me a sweatshirt to wear at the Mr. Dixie. He's hell. Funny as anything." Munio nodded. "Let's go see if he's here yet." Eddy marched through the gym back to a tiny office and stuck his head in the open door.

"Sam?"

A short older man with a horrendous auburn toupee swiveled around in an old wooden office chair. He had half of a big thick cigar hanging from the corner of his mouth, unlit. "Yeah!" he shouted.

"He's kind of deaf," Eddy whispered to Munio. "Hey Sam, whatcha know?" He moved to shake his hand.

"Eddy, how are you, boy? Hear you been working real hard. Is that right?" He grinned, showing a few amber teeth.

"Yes sir, I shore have, harder than I ever worked. Sam, want you to meet my friend Munio. This here is Sam, Munio." The two men smiled and shook hands enthusiastically. "He has been my right hand man. He's helped train me and everything. He's been a big help. I don't believe I would have done this good without him. I tell you the truth."

"Is that right? Well good, good." Sam looked at Munio and smiled.

"Yes sirreeee, and you know what else? Munio was in the '72 Olympics

282

as a weightlifter."

"Is that a fact? Munich? I'll be damned. What country did you lift for?"

"Belize."

"Yeah, I used to do the lifts myself."

"Oh, is that right?"

"Yeah, I never went to nationals or nothing, but I did all right around here. Don't nobody hardly do that stuff any more around here. Great sport though, great sport. You still lift?"

"I haven't, but I can. I hope to lift again sometime regularly."

"You know I got bumper plates and everything?"

"Yes, I did a squat snatch the first day I came in here just to show Eddy what it was."

"Oh yeah, well, hoss, take off them clothes and let me see how you look, why don't you." Sam pulled up his sagging old jeans and tucked in his Banlon shirt.

"All right," Eddy said and peeled off his sweats. After he broke down to jockey shorts, he stepped back a few feet and started his posing routine. Sam and Munio watched as he smoothly hit all the shots, with good transition throughout. Sam finished and stood there, waiting for a response.

"Eddy, go call the sheriff."

"Why you say that?"

"Somebody's done rustled yore calves!" He cracked up laughing, which stirred up the congestion in his lungs. He coughed and wheezed so much he couldn't speak for a couple of minutes.

Meanwhile, Eddy was devastated, thinking he had surely blown it. Sam's opinion concerning physique matters was highly regarded around the gym. Finally, Sam caught his breath and could speak.

"Naw son, I'm just kidding you. You know what?"

"What?" Eddy said nervously.

"You look goddamn good as I've ever seen you look. Shore as hell do. I believe you gonna do all right up there, boy. Need to lose just a little bit more of that butt. How's your weight?"

"Uh, two twenty-six this morning."

"That's good. You're right on it. Just don't do nothing stupid between now and then, and you'll be all right."

"You going to the show?" Eddy asked.

"I think I will. I'll be up there, yeah."

"Good, that's good. You, uh, Sam, you think I look good enough to win?" Eddy asked hesitantly.

Sam paused a minute and chuckled, "Boy, you can't never tell, but I tell you this. You shore ain't gonna come in last! Naw, you just have to wait and see. Just don't do, like I said, don't do nothing stupid between now and then, and you'll be all right. When you gonna carb deplete?"

"Uh, Wednesday and Thursday."

"All right, that's good."

"I been doing a few shots of primabolin. You think that's all right?"

"You just making expensive piss, boy. You ain't gonna get nothing from it that's gonna help you win this contest, except nerve. If you need it for your head, go on, I reckon." Sam shrugged his shoulders.

"All right. It just jacks me up, you know?"

"Yeah, hell, I know. Let me get you that shirt now. What size you need, small or medium?" Sam winked at Munio.

"Small hell! Triple XXX, or double, anyhow!"

"Triple XXX? Shit, my dadgum grandma's biggern you, boy!" he kidded. "All right, what color you want?"

"What you got?"

"Black."

"That's it?"

"Yep."

"Well, I reckon I'll take black. Why'd you ask me?"

"I wanted to see how smart you was."

"I tell you what. I ain't that smart to be doing all this. I can tell you that right now."

"All right boy, here you go. Good luck to you, Eddy." Sam handed him a black sweatshirt with The Dixie Ironworks written across the front in large letters, and across the back the slogan "go heavy or go home".

"'Preciate it, Sam. That's great."

"Hey Eddy, do me one favor, will ya?"

"Yeah, sure, what?"

"Wear it inside out when you're up there. I'm trying to keep a good reputation down here, you know?" Sam winked at Eddy and Munio. Munio laughed.

"Yeah yeah." Eddy shook his head.

"Munio, pleasure to meet you." Sam stuck out his hand.

"Yes, you too."

Eddy and Munio walked away from the office. "All right, I'm just gonna--well, Munio, what do you think? Should I do an overall workout or break it down today and tomorrow?"

Munio thought a minute. "Hmm, I think overall both days to tell you the truth. Light weights, do reps til you get a real good pump. Total workout time about one hour, ok?"

"Yeah, that sounds good." Eddy put his sweats back on and started to work on his upper body first.

They had made the rounds for upper body and were beginning legs when Destiny appeared.

"Hey y'all." She sashayed up, looking happy and happening in her tight

jeans and sweatshirt.

"Hey, what you doing here?" Eddy grinned and she went over and pecked him on the mouth. She gave Munio a hug also.

"Weaallll, I was in the neighborhood, and I thought I would see if y'all was here, which you are."

"How come you're not at work?"

"Weallll, I quit." She looked sheepishly at Eddy.

"Now you said you wasn't going to do that just because you got that money. It ain't going to last forever if you piss it away, Destiny."

"I know, I know, but I just did and so there." She laughed. "I'll get a job. Maybe I'll start my own business or something, you know?" She twirled a hunk of her long hair compulsively and winked at Eddy.

"All right, whatever, might as well enjoy yourself for a while, I reckon."

"I want Munio to get some of his friends in Belize to mail us some reefer to sell."

"Right! Destiny, they make dogs check the damn mail. Don't you know that? Ever package that comes into this country from South America has been sniffed by a fucking dog. That is the truth, too." Eddy pointed emphatically with a finger.

"Well, I don't know. Maybe we'll get them to fly it in." She laughed. "Maybe I'll just have them mail it to your address, Eddy! That's a better idea, huh?"

"Yeah, uh huh, real good." Eddy said as Munio laughed.

"Hey, y'all want to go to lunch after y'all finish?"

"You know I can't eat real food. Munio might. Yeah, in fact, take this man and feed him. He don't eat enough. I need him to get some reserve strength going for this weekend."

"You want to go?" Destiny looked at Munio.

"Yes, I do."

"Go, y'all go on. I ain't got much more to do. Go!"

"Ok, brother, I will. Talk to you later, ok?"

"You got it. Hey, Destiny, maybe you want to come see "big Buck" later tonight?" He winked and nodded.

"Who is big Buck?" Munio asked.

"Oh, that's what's he's started callin' his fucking dick! Can you believe this guy? I swear, Eddy. You are such a redneck! I'll call you!"

\* \* \* \* \* \* \* \*

"You like Italian?"

"Yes, that would be good. They serve beer?"

"Uh huh, sure do. I could use a cold one myself. Hey, we can figure out when to have the party. I'll drive if you want." Destiny offered as they stepped into the parking lot. "It's just down the road. I'll bring you back."

"That's fine." He followed her and got in her car. The floorboard on the passenger side was full of fast food packaging, and Munio stepped gingerly, as if he were stepping in mud. "Sorry about all that shit. It ain't nothing but wrappers. Don't worry. There ain't nothing gooshy." Destiny giggled.

"I hope not. Don't you ever clean out this car?"

"Naa, not really. Once a year maybe."

The drive to Lamar's Italian Restaurant took just five minutes away. It was a little A-framed building that was more in keeping with a Swiss chalet than an Italian restaurant. Inside, empty Chianti bottles hung from the walls along with strands of plastic garlic cloves and bunches of plastic grapes. Behind the cash register hung a black and white framed poster of the leaning tower of Pisa.

"It's buffet style. See, you can go along, and just get what you want. This whole thing only cost three ninety-five at lunch. You can come back as many times as you want to," Destiny informed Munio.

"Oh, beer too?" Munio asked sincerely.

"No, you goonhead." She blew air out of her mouth, making a farting sound, and punched him on the arm.

"Why not?"

"'Cause they'd go out of business the first time you and me came in, that's why!" she laughed.

They ate in silence. By the time Munio was three quarters finished with his food, Destiny's plate was bare, and she got up to fill it again. The beer was absolutely perfect, cold and well carbonated. For Munio, the food was fair, but the good beer made the meal.

"I finished the gazebo this morning."

"Hey, great! So, you still want to have the party over there?"

"Yes, yes. The floor must dry today and tomorrow, but on Wednesday it will be ready. How about Wednesday?"

"I don't have to check my calendar. I'm free as a bird." Destiny smiled.

"Ok, Wednesday evening."

"Well, you got lights out there?"

"No, but let me think. Maybe I could get some candles or something. Audrey wanted to come, but she can't get there until ten thirty or so."

"Did you tell her we'd still be drinking?"

"I already told her that there will be very drunk people at this party. Those people, I say, will be you and me." Munio laughed and Destiny chimed in.

She took a swig of her beer. "What did she say to that?"

"Agreeable, she was agreeable. She understands. She say that on that night, she too might be ready to have a few drinks. She has been teaching a dance class, and on that night, Wednesday, they will have the final class, a, ah, what is it, uh, recital." He snapped his fingers.

286

Munio took the pitcher and poured them each one remaining beer. "Well, I guess this is it. You had enough?"

"Hell, I don't ever get enough. I'm ready to blow this popsicle stand, though. You got any reefer? Let's smoke one, want to?" She ran her fingers through her hair. "My hair's filthy."

"I got a joint, yeah. It's at my friend's house, but you could come there," Munio suggested.

"Ok, or maybe we ought to go bug Eddy. We could go keep him company. Make him do that little posing dance." She laughed loudly and slapped the table. "I'm going to be yelling at him up on that stage. That'll be fun. Let's go." Destiny stood and asked Munio, "So what do you want to do?"

"Let's go see Eddy. He's got some reefer. He won't mind turning us on. Drive me by the gym and let me get my truck. I'll stop and get some more beer and meet you at Eddy's."

\* \* \* \* \* \* \* \* \*

Eddy answered the knock on the door. "Surprise!" said Destiny as she leaped up in the air and flung her legs around his waist. He nearly fell down, since he was not expecting to bear the sudden load.

"Damn, girl! Are you crazy? Break my motherfucking back, why don't you! What you doing here anyhow?"

"Me and Munio thought we'd keep you company." Eddy looked behind her.

"Where is he?"

"Oh, he's coming in a minute. He went to get some more beer."

"Are y'all drunk?" Eddy smiled at Destiny and her goofy grin.

"Who wants to know?" She walked on into the living room and threw her purse down on the couch. "Na, we ain't yet, but we're fixing to be. Hey, you got any reefer? That was another reason we came over was to use up your drugs. You don't mind, do you sweetie?" Destiny laughed.

"Not if I can get a little return on it, if you know what I mean?" Eddy grabbed Destiny's boobs.

"Now stop, Eddy." Destiny slapped his hand. "I don't want to do no fucking. We're just fucking buddies when we're both in the mood. You got that, bud?"

"Well, buddy, I'm in the mood to show you what a good buddy I can be," Eddy said in a fake baritone voice. "All right, guess I'll have to jack off for the fifteenth time today."

"Really? Fifteen? You gonna wear that thing out."

Munio pushed the door open. "Praise the Lord. Munio, save me. This man had immoral designs on my person." Destiny threw out her finest Scarlett O'Hara imitation.

"Well, congratulations. Nobody has even winked at me today."

"Eddy, what are you doing, brother? We came to keep you company."

"I was just dusting."

"Dusting? Some tough stuff you are, dusting." Destiny snorted.

Eddy chuckled, picked up his soft white dustrag and walked back over to the intricately carved wooden shelf full of knickknacks mounted on the wall. Among them were little pink angels whose wings were tipped in silver paint. The paint had worn away in spots from their little eyes and eyebrows from years of cleaning.

Most of them were animals. A donkey loaded with packs on its back had "the Grand Canyon" inscribed on it. A giraffe about four inches tall with "Busch Gardens" written on it stood out above the rest. A kitten playing with a red ball of twine was another one. Several of them were religious in nature featuring Jesus, either standing, smiling sweetly, or nailed to a porcelain cross with that classic hang dog expression.

Eddy gently worked his way to every single one, carefully cleaning out every crevice and crease. Munio and Destiny sipped a beer and watched him. He was so totally focused on the task that he forgot they were even in the room. When he turned around finally to get a clean rag, he was startled by them sitting there.

"Damn, y'all scared me. I forgot y'all was here."

"Getting into that dustin', ain't ya, Ed?" Destiny winked and joked.

"I do it for my mama. She always kept them dusted off. So I figure I better keep it up. I don't mind really. There's really a bunch of cute ones. Have you ever looked at them?" He looked at Destiny and Munio, wrinkling his forehead with a sincere expression.

Destiny spewed a laugh and said obnoxiously, "No Eddy, I ain't ever looked at them." She poked Munio to find some agreement.

She did not get it from Munio, who took up for Eddy. "I think they are nice statues and things. It is good he does this for his mother." Eddy winked at Munio.

"Aw, you guys always stand up for each other. Hey, where's your reefer?"

"I'll get it." He returned with a rolling tray complete with all the accessories. "I think I'll do my hit of primabolin with y'all. It'll be like happy hour." He disappeared and returned with a syringe. "Ready?" Destiny took the first hit off the joint. "Cheers, y'all!" Eddy laughed as he plunged the needle deep into his glute. "Look at this here, Munio. I can't seem to get rid of this little fat spot." He had his sweatpants pulled down around his knees, and he grabbed a tiny bit of his cheek. "See?"

"Yeah." Munio squinted. "I can't even hardly see it, Eddy."

"Hell, I wish that was all the fat I had on my caboose!" Destiny declared.

"I bet if I put preparation H on it on the day of the show, I'll be all right."

288

"Oh my God, preparation H?" Destiny said.

"Yeah, remember," Eddy held up two fingers on each hand to indicate a quotation was coming. "shrinks swollen tissue, reduces pain and inflammation."

"What?" Destiny shrieked.

"You can put that shit on any, hell, any piece of skin or under your eyes if they're kind of baggy, and for a little while, it'll shrink them right up."

"I think that's the most disgusting beauty tip I ever heard of," Destiny replied.

Munio lazily took a swallow of beer. He was reaching a saturation point, a place where he never fared very well. "Light me that joint!" he ordered in a deep and strangely unfamiliar voice.

Eddy's and Destiny's heads turned in unison at the harsh tone in Munio's voice. "Don't be getting obnoxious, boy. Here." Eddy handed him the joint.

Munio shook his head back and forth, mouthing Eddy's words, and took a big toke on the joint. "This pot tastes like shit!" Munio said loudly. "Hey, why don't we put the preparatory H on it, and make it go away!" He laughed hysterically at himself, the strange voice persisting.

Eddy and Destiny looked at each other and rolled their eyes, wondering who this guy was and where Munio had gone. Munio continued to bogart the joint until Destiny walked over and stood in front of him with her hand out. Munio pretended to use her palm for an ashtray. Then he pretended to hand her the joint, pulling his hand away at the last minute.

"What will you give me for it?" Munio let out an evil laugh.

"A black eye for one thing!" Destiny joked and snapped her fingers for him to hurry up and give her the smoke.

"Here you go, so lucky are you to have my spit on the end of this joint."

Eddy and Destiny grew irritated with his behavior. Munio stretched out on the couch, and suddenly passed out cold.

"Damn, was that weird or what?" Eddy said, getting back to his knick-knack dusting.

"Fucking A." Destiny toked on the joint and watched Munio as he began to snore. "I guess he's one of them that just flips on you, you know? One minute they're cool, next they're some maniac. He didn't get that way when we drank that champagne that night."

"Who knows? He got weird one other night when he first came here. Got pretty bad wasted down at the bar. I had to drive him home. He ain't acted up since then."

"Almost there. Almost there," Munio mumbled as he slept.

Destiny and Eddy laughed. "Damn, maybe he'll tell us some dirt." Eddy looked hopeful.

"It's deep enough. Over my head. It's deep enough."

"There he goes again." Eddy tried to encourage him. "What's deep

enough?"

"It's deep enough," Munio repeated. "Goodbye Sandra, goodbye," he called.

"Where's she going?" Destiny asked in a soft high-pitched voice.

Munio answered with snoring that continued for another hour and a half. Eddy and Destiny, unable to talk above the racket, went into Eddy's bedroom, where they fooled around for a while and fell into a deep sleep.

Munio woke up irritated, with a big headache. He felt like he had been clubbed in the head. Fumbling in the dark, he eventually found his cigarettes and smoked with his eyes shut. In the distance, he heard the whistle of a train that made him feel sad. Not timing his next inhalation just right, he coughed on the cigarette smoke.

Eddy, awakened by the coughing, went into the living room to check on him. "You all right?"

"Yes, I'm," he choked and coughed, "fine."

Eddy sat down in a padded chair and threw a leg over the arm. "You got kind of crazy today. Did you know that?"

Munio felt a flash of heat run down him and was grateful there was no light for Eddy to see. "I drank too much, I guess. Sorry, if I was rude or anything."

"Naw, wasn't too bad. Kept talking in your sleep though." Eddy chuckled. "Talking about something's deep enough, and uh, something about saying goodbye to Sandra." He chuckled again.

Munio said nothing. His feelings were reflected only in the fierce orange glow of his cigarette that burned bright as a forge as he sucked on it with all his might there in the dark.

* * * * * *

Tuesday morning dawned, and Eddy's eyes opened at the first crack of daylight. At the thought that Mr. Dixie was one day closer, a jittery feeling sprinkled him with chill bumps. He peed and then got on the scales. Two twenty-six, the dial read. He took his place in front of the full length mirror for the day's first inspection.

It was good. His body was nearly as ripped as it was ever going to get. Intently as a hawk hungrily scanning the countryside for a mouse, he scrutinized every square inch of his frame, searching out new striations that might have developed overnight as his skin drew tighter and tighter around his muscle and bone.

Today his face looked even more like a caricature, his nose and big full mouth of teeth being the predominant features. Eddy couldn't care less about his face. In fact, he didn't even notice it. That was a side effect Destiny, Munio, and the rest of the world would have to bear.

Munio had stayed the night at Eddy's; he woke up on the couch when he heard Eddy in the kitchen. He ambled in and leaned on the doorframe,

watching Eddy mix a protein shake. Munio looked Eddy's naked body over, thinking how unreal it looked. When Eddy turned around, Munio chuckled. His dick hung like a strange pink wart in contrast to the roast turkey reddish brown of the surrounding areas.

"That's some contrast," Munio pointed out.

"Well, good morning to you too, bud." Eddy shook his head and chuckled. "Yeah, they say it ain't good for you to tan them things. Gives you cancer, they say."

"You look damn good, Eddy. How do you feel?"

"Kind of lightheaded. I'm fucking wired. I woke up just a-shakin'. Take a light one today. Pose a bunch. Rest, and that's about it."

"That's good. You've done about all you can do. Just relax. Mind if I fix some coffee?"

"No, go ahead."

"Is Destiny still here?"

"Naw, she went home last night. You slept like a goddamn log. Except for waking up just that little bit, you slept from, hell, five in the afternoon til now. You ought to feel seriously bright-eyed and bushy-tailed."

"Yeah, right. I don't feel that way. Is there a river around this place?"

"Uh huh, right out of town, there is. Why?"

"I don't know. I feel like being by some water. I miss the water bad. I was always around water my whole life. You want to show me where it is? Hang out a while after you train, maybe?"

"Maybe, yeah. If not, I'll tell you how to get there."

\* \* \* \* \* \* \*

Eddy picked up a pair of fifteen-pound dumbells and started limbering up his shoulders.

"You been sleeping ok?" Munio asked.

"Yeah, yeah, I been sleeping fine. Ain't took a shit in three days, but other than that, hey, I ain't too bad off. We'll see how I do during carb depletion time. I'll start that this afternoon." Eddy put down the dumbells and called to a man across the gym. "Hey, Ray, you got your caliper things here today?"

"Yeah."

"Will you check my body fat?"

"Yeah, right now?"

"I got about fifteen minutes left. Is that ok?"

"Yeah, uh huh, I'll be here. I'm waiting for somebody. Your show this weekend?"

"Yeah, uh huh."

"You look fucking ready, man. I swear."

"Thanks man." Eddy did another set and then racked the dumbells. "Nice guy. Been to college and everthing. Works for Federal Express. Good job. I

need to get me a job that good."

"What's wrong with your present job?" Munio asked.

"Aw, it's all right, and Pee Wee is real good to me and all. It don't pay that great and never will, but it's good for training because he lets me work whatever schedule I need to. He gave me a hundred dollar bonus to help with our hotel and stuff, too. He's a nice guy. I ain't got it so bad, really."

"What dream is it that you have?" Munio propped one leg up on a flat bench and leaned on his thigh.

"Me?" He chuckled nervously and grew solemn as he thought. "To win the Mr. Dixie is the only dream I've ever had in my life that was big. I ain't ever wanted anything else. Not that I can think of leastways." He got up and walked across the gym to the leg equipment as Munio followed.

"How 'bout you? What do you dream about, Munio?" Eddy asked as he settled in on the leg press.

Munio laughed and said, "It was going to the Olympics. That was my dream, and it came true. Then, after it did, and…" Munio stopped speaking and looked away out the window when he felt stinging tears intent on clawing their way from his eyes. "Just, ah, after that, I didn't have another dream. I still do not have one." Munio managed to fight the rising emotional tide by gritting his teeth til his jaws ached.

Eddy finished his set, not saying anything even after he finished. He had sensed Munio's sadness. He had felt the rising tears, and through that moment, the thought occurred to him, that one day he might be like Munio, drifting from one cold beer to the next, like so many old men he served at the bar.

"It must have been a big deal to make it all the way up here. You coming all that way from another country. That was a dream, wasn't it?" Eddy said.

Munio smiled fondly at his friend and looked down as he examined his fingers. "It was a migration, like a bird. I escaped. It wasn't a happy time. I have not been a happy man, not deep inside. My friend, you have helped me find the happiest times I have known since I was in those Olympic Games. The people I meet here have shown me consideration. My friend Sandra, Audrey. With them, I have encountered happy times. Destiny too. My dreams?" He laughed again. "Eddy, you, you can have my dreams, ok?" He slapped Eddy on the back.

Eddy grinned and slapped him back, "You're a crazy Indian, you know that?"

"And you?" Munio said, "Your excuse is what? To what tribe do you belong? The tribe of the crazy man, that is your tribe?"

"Fuck you, man!" Eddy's remark was thrown as lovingly as any kiss he could blow or deliver to his friend's cheek. Munio accepted it as such, smiled, and was glad the awkward dialogue about the future had been put back under wraps.

292

Eddy pulled off the paved road and onto a red dirt road which led to another and then another. The roads were well worn, and the tires threw off a red cloud of dust as they sped along. Althought Munio was tickled by the intense speed, his enjoyment of the scenery was compromised, since he could only focus on hoping Eddy would make it around the next curve. Driving wild down dirt roads was a part of every Southerner's childhood. Rules of the road were different for dirt roads, back roads, just like when driving a boat. There is more option for style in this setting. The car spun out as Eddy orchestrated it to do so on the curves of loose gravel. Eddy yelled with delight as he nearly lost control a couple of times. Munio swallowed fast long slugs of cold beer on the straight-aways to avoid a chipped tooth or a cut lip.

Eventually, Eddy pulled onto a road that was more like a tire track path with a rut running down the middle of it. This was not the place to perform driving stunts as the big dips and height of the rut in places required caution. The change of season had begun to kill off some of the undergrowth, but still privet, briars, and numerous other bushes and trees were as tall as the car on either side of the little trail. Soon, the road ended in a very small turnaround.

"We'll have to hoof it from here. It ain't far." Eddy hopped out of the car.

Munio followed his friend down the little pig path through even deeper woods of tall, thin pine trees, sycamore trees with their appaloosa peeling bark, and other hardwoods. Munio rolled the paper bag top tighter as a handle to transport his cold beer.

He felt excitement in his soul and familiarity too as he passed through this land, thick with foliage. Having not seen a bamboo grove in such a long time, Munio smiled upon sighting the green tops of the cane break up ahead. The further they walked, the more Munio could feel the air grow cooler where the brush provided more insulation from the sun, and he could tell the river was very near. He wished Eddy would move a little faster, but he patiently followed him, saying nothing.

Then, without warning, the river's edge appeared. There was no clue, no opening above the trees that Munio detected. Sliding between some large stalks of bamboo, Eddy jogged down a red, sandy bank that was part of a beach area, littered with large, red-stained river rocks.

Munio stood and stared, fascinated with the muddy, vermilion water. Never had he seen a river that was so red. It looked like cream of tomato soup.

"Here you go, bud. The Choctaw River is what it's named, but we just call it the river." Eddy kicked at the sand and walked along the beach, looking at the area in front of each foot. "Found a bunch of arrowheads here. Sometimes, if you kick up the sand, they're right below the surface. This was big Indian country way back when," Eddy informed Munio.

"Where did they go?" Munio asked.

"We either killed 'em or drove 'em off." Eddy skipped a small stone across the top of the water.

"Why did you do that?"

"Hell if I know. We just didn't like 'em or something."

"How do you do that?" Munio asked Eddy as he skipped another stone. "Skip a stone?"

"Skip a stone, eh?" Munio repeated. "Yeah, skip a stone."

"Well, you take it like this." He picked up a small piece of shale. "First, you try to pick a flat one that'll skip good. Light, too. Then, you hold it like this." Eddy showed the proper position to hold the rock in between his thumb and index finger. "You kind of sling it parallel to the water so when it hits, it'll skip, you know?" Munio nodded.

Munio looked at the water's edge for a good candidate. "Like this?" He showed Eddy.

"Yeah, now flip your wrist, and chunk it sidearm almost. Here, watch me again." Eddy demonstrated with a good toss that landed on the beach on the other side of the narrow river after seven stunning skips across.

"Ok, here I go." Munio reared his arm back and tossed. The stone skipped twice and then sunk. "Hey, I see."

"You'll get it. Just practice."

Munio threw a few more times, and then, bored with the game, preferred to sit on a washed up pine log, study the river, and drink a beer. There were no rapids or protruding rocks by which to gauge this river's speed. It was a silent sheet of red glass revealing little about itself. Munio threw a small stick in and watched it ride down the muddy river. It disappeared in no time around the next bend. Up stream, Munio noticed several old tires were washed up on tree limbs that reached out from under the water. On their beach, a child's canvas shoe had made its way from some little foot to this spot. In the crotches of other trees sticking out of the water, debris had accumulated from rainy days of high water. He could see red-stained sticks, beer cans and bottles, picnic supplies, and an abandoned fishing line's fine transparent thread waving in the light breeze. Munio had never seen such a dirty river. The rivers he frequented in Belize did not contain litter like this. Most of them were too isolated, too deep in the jungle for picnicking.

Munio drank the remainder of the beer in a big gulp as Eddy joined him on the log. Eddy's mind was in Atlanta, picturing what would happen at the Mr. Dixie Contest. Hunger pains he had long ignored were growing stronger than his will. He had been eating a restrictive diet for so long. The first thing he was going to have after that show was a cold beer, he decided, and then maybe a big old pizza or a hamburger. Next week he knew he would gain ten, fifteen, or even twenty pounds pigging out on all the forbidden things from which he had abstained while training.

"Shore will be glad to have a cold beer." Eddy looked winsomely at Munio's can.

"I bet. You're probably going to get puking drunk Saturday night, eh?"

"I hope to God I do. Let's go out to a bar, some place with a live band after the show."

"I'm with you, brother." Munio watched the sand displace as he wiggled his shoe through it.

For a while longer they sat quietly and watched the river flow. Loud brassy ravens sent a scouting party to spy on the men. They cawed to each other, making comments, and when they agreed neither was a threat or edible, they flew away on their powerful black wings. On the other bank, Eddy and Munio heard the crunching of leaves. The sounds were loud, made by some substantial animal. The crunch continued toward the river, and eventually, a beautiful tan buck with a ten point rack delicately stepped to the water's edge to drink.

"Bang!" Eddy shouted out, and the terrified buck sprinted away without even taking a sip, his white flagged tail pointing straight up as he ran.

"What did you do that for?" Munio said angrily.

"Fuck, I don't know. I was playing like I was hunting. I didn't hurt the damn thing."

"He had the right to have a drink without some asshole scaring him half to death!" scolded Munio.

"Aw, you sound like some damn woman. Don't hurt the little deers. Poor little Bambi." Eddy took his voice up to his most superior falsetto.

Munio laughed at Eddy and shoved him off the log. "You're just an asshole, Eddy. I wish that deer would return with some of his wolf friends and scare the shit out of you."

Munio popped the top of the last beer in his tall boy six pack. From out of the top, oozed a thick yellowish foam. He promptly tipped the can for a hearty swallow. "Ahh. This is great. Beer always tastes better when you are by the water."

Eddy nodded and looked up from the picture he was drawing in the sand with a slender stick. "Yeah, it does, especially when you're fishing."

"You fished a lot?"

"Hell, yeah, I been fishing forever. Hell, that's about all there is to do around here. Fishing, drinking, yeah, that's about it. Night fishing is real fun. Get damn drunk doing that."

Munio laughed. "What kind of fish do you catch around here?"

"Bass, crappie, catfish. We catch a lot of catfish at night. I remem-"

Munio interrupted suddenly, "Oh shit! I forgot all about the dogs! I forgot about the damn dogs! I left them since yesterday. Oh shit! We have to go right away, Eddy. I can't believe I forgot them! Damn!"

"All right, all right, simmer down, Munio. Them dogs is going to be fine.

You didn't leave them out in the cold, did you?" Eddy hopped up from his seat on the log and headed up the sandy bank to the thin trail, talking as he strode along.

"No." Munio walked fast right on Eddy's heels.

"Well then, so what if they missed a biscuit or two. They's a rich lady's dogs. They could stand to miss a biscuit. Worst thing that's happened is they shit all over everything. You'll get it picked up before that lady comes back."

Munio shook his head in disgust and in response to Eddy. "I am not so good with pets. I don't need any dogs! I just forget. I just can't deal with them."

"Easy, boy, easy. It ain't like they's your dogs, Munio. You just got to feed and water them for a little while."

"You don't understand. She wants me to take care of them forever."

Eddy stopped in his tracks and turned around to make sure he heard Munio. "Forever? Why would she do that?"

Munio pushed Eddy to continue forward. "Because she might not come back at all."

"Sure she will. She's got that house and all. She ain't gonna not come back, Munio. She still owes you some damn money from building that what-chamacallit, don't she?" Eddy giggled as he walked.

"I don't know. I don't want to talk about this anymore. Just please get me back to my truck."

"Ok, ok, ok, we'll be back in thirty minutes. How's that? It's just a couple of dogs, Munio. Jesus, have a damn hissy fit, why don't you?"

Munio leaped from Eddy's car the second it came to a halt in the drive-way. "Bye, Eddy. I will speak to you later."

Eddy casually got out of his car and watched frantic Munio force his poor old truck into action without its required warm-up period. It belched and backfired down the block. Eddy stood listening to that truck even after it was way out of sight. He smiled and shook his head. "Damn dogs. That's one crazy Indian."

* * * * * * * *

Munio fumbled with the keys and dropped them twice trying to open the door. When finally he did get it open, all three dogs were standing there wagging their tails as if nothing had happened.

"I'm sorry, fellows. I am sorry. I am just a drunk asshole who forgot. Let's go outside, eh? Want some fresh air, everybody? Come on."

He opened the sliding glass door, and smiled at the visual treat waiting for him in the back yard. The gazebo, finished at last, shone like a new penny with its bright paint job. He strolled over to it, looking over every detail carefully. With one finger, he reached down and touched the paint on the floor just to make sure it had dried. All three dogs completed their pit stops and

came over to investigate the new structure. Munio sat down on one of the benches he had built into the railings. He was exhausted from the scare he had had at the river when he realized he had forgotten the dogs. Guilt battered his heart, and his mind chattered about how it would have disturbed Sandra to know her little dogs were neglected. He regretted Sandra could not sit here with them. As he daydreamed and punished himself, the little dogs stood at his feet trying to remind him they were hungry.

"Ok, ok, I know what you guys want, and I will give it to you. You can have all the food you want tonight. Let's go, eh?" Munio got up and raced the dogs back to the house. With the crank of a can opener, they recovered from their night of mistreatment.

Munio dialed Destiny's number.

"Hey boy!" Destiny chirped. "Where you been? I was wondering if we was going to do our party tonight?"

"Yes, yes, indeed. The paint is thoroughly dry on the gazebo."

"Well, that's good. What time you want to do it?'

"Anytime is ok with me. Do you want me to go with you to buy the champagne? I will put some money in or something."

"Yeah. You don't have to chip in, but you can help me carry the shit to my car. How about I come get you?"

"Yes, that's good."

"You ready now?"

"I have to clean up a little. Maybe I take a quick shower, ok? Just give me a few minutes."

"All right, that's cool."

"Ok, goodbye." Munio hung up.

He scouted the rooms, looking for any dog accidents, and was surprised to not find a one. "You dogs did better than I would have."

Munio hummed as he made his way back down the hall to the living room after cleaning himself up. The dogs were assembled on his sleeping blankets on the couch. They looked sad, and it was then that it occurred to Munio they needed some affection. He had seen Sandra pet them, carry them in her arms. She constantly lavished them with love and attention.

A knock was heard at the side door, and the dogs lit after it. Munio opened the door to their shrill wails of warning.

"Damn, them dogs is loud!" Destiny walked in. "Hey puppies, it's ok. Good dogs for guarding the house." She knelt down on their level to greet them.

All it took was a woman babytalking for their defensive posture to disappear. They crawled all over her and licked her in the face as she giggled and cooed. Munio stood back and leaned against the cabinet to watch.

"They're so sweet! What's their names?"

"Uh, let's see. I, ah, that big one is named Moo Shu. Uh, I forget the oth-

ers right now."

"You forgot? You been baby-sitting these dogs for weeks. How could you forget their names?" Munio curled up his mouth and shrugged. "That's awful. What's y'alls names, huh?' she asked the little dogs.

"You ready?" Munio asked hurriedly.

Destiny stood up and looked around the kitchen. "This is a nice place. Wow, it's so big." She walked around the spacious kitchen.

"You want to look at the gazebo before it gets dark?"

"Yeah, yeah, sure. Where is it?"

Munio opened the sliding glass door and motioned her ahead of him. She grinned at his gentlemanly gesture.

"Wow!"

"Yes, that's it." Munio stuck his hands in his pockets and rocked back and forth as Destiny stood on the patio, preferring to study the gazebo from afar.

"That's beautiful. You built that from scratch?"

Munio grinned and nodded.

"Damn." She walked slowly towards it. "This is great. I bet she really likes it, huh?"

"Who?"

"Who? Who do you think? Who the hell did you build it for?'

"Oh, right, her. Yes, well, she does like it. She will like it. She, uh, has been, you know, gone. She had not seen it since it was completed, of course. I just finished it day before yesterday, you see."

"Oh right. Well, I bet she'll love it."

"Let's go get the booze, eh?"

"Ok, ok. I'm ready. That thing is sure cool. A gazebo, huh?"

"Oh my gosh, I forgot to call Eddy!" Munio slapped his forehead as he and Destiny were driving back from the store. "I sure am forgetting a lot these days."

Destiny pulled the car into Sandra's driveway. "Call him now. It ain't like he has other plans."

"Eddy, I forgot to call you earlier, but we are just starting the party." Munio said.

"Just starting it, huh? What y'all having, a ribbon cutting ceremony on that gazebra?" Eddy laughed.

"We will be pouring champagne in the gazebra shortly. Gazebra, I like that Eddy. Did you make that up?"

"Brilliant, ain't I? Be over in a little bit."

Destiny announced to Munio, as he hung up the phone, "I got it all in the refrigerator. You know, you really ought to clear some of that old produce and shit out of there. That lady's going to have a fit. That smell would gag a maggot, boy."

"Yes, tomorrow I will do that."

"Yeah, I just bet you will. Hey babies," she said to the little dogs, sitting down on the floor with them again. "Y'all smell my kitty cats? Hummm? I have kitty cats at my house. Have y'all ever seen a kitty cat? Well, they're bigger than you, and would probably rip y'alls little throats out. Uh huh, what do y'all think about that?" The little dogs were in love. They crawled up on her and licked her incessantly.

"Let's go outside now," Munio encouraged.

"Ok, can they come too?"

"Yes, sure they can." Munio grabbed two bottles of champagne from the fridge.

Munio purposely shook the bottle a bit before opening to ensure the cork would fly way across the yard. They laughed as it landed quietly in the grass. He filled the crystal glasses. "Cheers to you and your good fortune, and here's to the gazebo. May it have happy times only."

"Cheers," Destiny toasted, and they sucked their glasses dry with one swallow.

"Yeeehaaa! That was great!" Destiny laughed and reached for the bottle to refill the glasses. "Let the games begin!"

# CHAPTER XLV

Audrey's customary ritual was to venture out of her quarters on performance day as little as possible. Even though she would not be actually performing, as the director, the recital was her creation, her design, and she would be under close inspection this night. Her outfit and accessories had already been selected. The main thing she had left to do was put her hair up. Usually, she had help when she wanted her hair in a bun, but she was much too sophisticated to go to Lulu's Curl Up and Dye or some other local facsimile for assistance.

Early in the day, she stretched and performed basic movement work. Afterwards, she ate a small bowl of oatmeal and wrote in her journal. She wrote concerned thoughts of what she would like to involve herself in professionally upon returning to New York. Perhaps, she thought, it would be a good time to take a few classes in a new discipline. There were some new alternative dance groups that incorporated gymnastics and street dances which had been receiving favorable reviews. She had attended a couple of their performances and found them refreshing.

The day flew by and before she knew it, it was time to dress. She had scheduled a seven o'clock call for all the dancers, and at four-thirty, she began the arduous project of getting ready.

The shower was the shortest part of it all. After she washed her hair and shaved her legs, fifteen minutes of solid blow drying was required.

In this temporary apartment home of hers, she had done little to decorate or customize it. The dressing table was another matter. It was mobile and accompanied Audrey wherever she went. The nucleus of it all was a makeup mirror that was two feet square, with enough round white bulbs to light up a runway at LaGuardia. The heat was intense, but Audrey loved the feel of those bulbs. She loved the excitement of dressing for a show. With the help of all the tubes, bottles, and jars of color and texture, she moved closer to the world of theater that fed her most.

Her hair was the first project. Once it was put up and out of the way she could do her face more easily. Even though she was worried about her ability to do a good job, she managed to twist and pin it into a becoming bun. With a hand-held mirror, she inspected the back and found that no stray hairs had escaped. Her bare neck helped to highlight her beautiful face, which she realized she had forgotten to shave.

Lathered with shaving creme, Audrey laughed at herself; she looked like a cross between Miss America and Santa Claus.

Back at the makeup mirror, a goodly amount of base makeup, custom matched to Audrey's skin color, smoothed out the variety of textures from forehead to chin into a uniform mask.

Using blue-black eyeliner and the steady hand of a tattoo artist, Audrey tiptoed above the top lashes and below the bottom ones. While she traced her eyes with the eyeliner, her mouth fell open, and her lips seemed to have eyes as they moved to the motion of her hand, helping in some mysterious way to steady it. With a Q-tip, she swabbed a couple of areas that were a little thick, then patiently sat, eyes closed, while the heat from the bulbs in the mirror dried the paint.

Mascara followed. Audrey coated her long lashes thickly, and then fit each of them into the slot of the eyelash curler. Once they were driven in up to the hilt, she squeezed the curler. Audrey found the sensation a pleasurable pain. She held the pressure for a few seconds and, after removing the tool, her eyelashes curled like a wave on the Hawaiian pipeline.

For eye shadow, she chose to use three stripes. The one just above her eyelashes was smeared with a yellow gold. Above that, she applied a bright magenta, followed with another stripe of gold. This intensity and boldness of color was not something to be worn to the grocery store. This was strictly theater. Fireworks were in order.

After she brushed on some blush, her entire face was dusted with sweet smelling powder.

It was time to put her undergarment rig in place. Audrey slipped off her the light floral robe. From a bureau drawer, she produced a wide roll of gauze and the roll of silver duct tape cursing because there was only a marginal amount left. Audrey made several passes around her upper thigh with the white gauze. She slipped a nylon sock, with a hole sliced in the tip, around

her dick and balls, and pulled at the tenacious roll of tape. It unwound with a graphic ripping sound. Audrey pushed her dick way back between her legs and started with the first pass of the tape. This part was never easy or comfortable or fun. Just when she finished making the third and final loop, the gray tape ran out. She breathed a grateful sigh of relief that she was able to squeak out just one more dressing.

She pulled a sheer pair of thighhigh hose up her legs. The bra and its accompanying gel packs were next. Time was running out, but something called her to stop and look at herself in the full length mirror. Maybe it was the bitter look of that gray tape, or the tips of the pink gelatinous breasts peeking out over that French cup lace bra, but the sight troubled Audrey. It startled her to see how piece-meal her body looked, bound up with strange social wounds and compromised by her commitment to drag. She shuddered and moved on. Now was certainly not the time to question her whole lifestyle.

The gown she had chosen incorporated a low wide neckline with a snug, off-the-shoulder feature that punctuated her wide and shapely shoulders. The tight-fitting sleeves hugged her arms down to the wrists, and were highlighted by with a thick gold braid cuffs. The cloth was a no-holds-barred magenta, and with hundreds of hand sewn gold sequins and beads, as brilliant as the Christmas tree at Rockefeller Center.

She stepped into her gold three-inch heels. The sound of her footsteps on the hardwood floor heightened her excitement. Long gold and rhinestone earrings slipped through her pierced lobes. They hung like miniature chandeliers, swinging wildly with her every move. The final touch was the lipstick, which flipped the switch as if it to say, "It's showtime." She slid the orange-pink tube across her upper lip and then smacked her lips together to coat the lower lip with the sweet-tasting paint. With a Kleenex, she patted away the excess.

She moved in front of the full-length mirror for final inspection and smiled, turned around and struck poses to check her look from various angles. Gaudy but country club ready, she looked like a gigantic fishing lure. Playfully, she gave the mirror seductive looks and realized she had become the princess her mother always wanted. She was her mother, tall and tacky.

* * * * *

The dancers were all nervous wrecks. Audrey had never assembled such a cast. Since fifty percent of them had pacemakers installed in their chests, she had requested that a paramedic team stand by on the property. On the other hand, it amused Audrey to observe how childlike they really were, spit shined in an array of bold and ridiculous outfits. Like their mentor, most of the women wore dresses adorned with bright and shiny objects. A good core of basic black tuxedos showed up, but here also was a forest green one and an aqua one that Audrey found to be absolutely hideous, though she praised the

old man's sense of adventure. He was celebrating his eightieth birthday that night.

Altogether there were twelve couples and a ballroom packed with spectators. The format of the performance was simple. For twenty minutes, in unison, all the couples moved about the ballroom in a large circle to display the various dances they had learned. At some point during each dance, two couples would move to the center.

Audrey gave a pep talk just before the house manager opened the ballroom to the spectators. "I want everyone to remember to do two things. If you do them, I guarantee you will dance wonderfully. Mr. Mitchell, do you remember what those things are?"

"Uh, why, uh, why yes, Miss Meyers, I believe I do. Let's see. You keep your, you stand up straight, and you breathe." Mr. Mitchell smiled at his fellow classmates around him.

"That's exactly right. I want all of you to stand up proud and tall. Do not forget to breathe, people! It will help you to relax and focus on your steps. Are there any questions?"

"Miss Meyers, have you decided if you'll teach another class?"

Audrey smiled, "No, I'm afraid not. I will return to New York next week."

"Miss Meyers, it's time to open the house. Are you ready?" asked a woman decked out in an elegant black suit.

"Yes, Mrs. Folsom, please. People, let's have fun out there. I don't want you to look like someone has a gun to your head. Fun!" she whispered loudly. "Ok, back stage, everyone. Hurry." She turned on her heel and led her flock into the wings of the ballroom to wait for their introduction.

Audrey stood on the edge of the crowd and watched her students who were now knee deep in their recital. Nothing they could have done would have changed the way she felt about their performance. Missed steps, confusion, hearing problems all contributed to the lack of synchronization of the dancers, but their liveliness and sense of humor won the hearts of their proud instructor and the audience. Audrey beamed as she watched them twirl and dip and occasionally wave to a friend in the audience. She looked over the crowd as she stood with arms crossed. So many tuxedos and Sandraesque women filled the seats. Older women with starched stiff hairdos and more than ample midriffs smiled as they watched through their bifocals at the couples going round and round in their big endless circle.

She saw people in the crowd that could have passed for her parents, and she smiled faintly, thinking that this was the kind of outing they would enjoy. Even with her best efforts, she was very unlike these people. The picture of herself in the mirror earlier wearing her bra and with her dick taped drifted across her mind like a sad dream. Lately, she resented the amount of energy she spent on the upkeep of her facade. She swept the image away and forced

herself to concentrate on the show.

The crowd gave a standing ovation to the couples as the final note of the last song played out. The dancers bowed and clapped. One of the men in the class went back stage and brought out a gigantic bouquet of red roses which he presented to Audrey. She too was applauded as she bowed and curtsied to the crowd.

Behind that beauty queen debutante smile she flashed, all she could think about was the fact that the tape or something had captured several pubic hairs and the feeling was driving her crazy. After hugging each and every student and after a flurry of group photographs were taken, Audrey bade them all good luck, good night, and goodbye.

The recital ended earlier than she had thought. Taking her outfit off was a lot more pleasurable than putting it on. One thing was sure, whatever she wore, she would be swinging in the breeze this evening. Her hair was absolutely wild after she uncoiled it from its hive on top of her head.

With no underwear on at all, Audrey pulled on a vivid pair of floral canvas baggy pants and an extra-large, soft, thick, black sweater. Over black hiking socks, she put on purple Birkenstocks. She smiled as she looked in the mirror to see that she looked as comfortable as she felt.

# CHAPTER XLVI

Eddy heard laughter as he approached the carport. He gently unlatched the gate to sneak up on Munio and Destiny in the gazebo.

"Boo!" Eddy screamed at the top of his lungs, causing a chain reaction of terrified yelps.

Eddy was in stitches, while Munio and Destiny grabbed their hearts. "Gotcha!"

"Eddy! Make us have heart attacks!"

"Jesus!" Munio exclaimed.

Eddy walked around the gazebo and gave it a through inspection. Finally, he took a seat and adjusted himself on it a couple of times. "Damn, if this ain't nice, Munio. You done good, hoss. Bench is a little hard, but that's because I ain't hardly got no more ass."

"Thanks, thanks. You don't want a drink, do you?"

"Naw, shit. Remember, I'm carb depleting today and tomorrow. If I had a drink right now, I'd be fucked bad, I bet."

"Well, we will do your drinking for you. Right, Destiny?" Munio held up a bottle and refilled their glasses.

"Y'all about drunk now, ain't you?" Eddy took note of the empty champagne bottles.

"Hell, we're just getting warmed up. We only had, what, four so far. We

got eight more to go, at least. Tell you what else I got, too." She reached in the pocket of her jean jacket and pulled out a small baggie full of white powder. She waved it around. "Looky what I got," she sang.

"Oh shit. Munio, do you do coke?" Eddy asked.

"I have sniffed a line or two. In Belize, you know, it is our largest cash crop." Munio winked and rubbed his hands together. "Actually, for a time, I was a cocaine tester. People would bring me samples to test and so on. I have expert experience in this. You, madam, you have some cocaine for testing today?"

"Yessir, I have."

Munio grabbed the baggie from he., "All right, ma'am, I will test it to-night, and you call me tomorrow. I tell you what I think about it, ok?" They all laughed.

"Gimme that." Destiny grabbed it back from Munio. "Let's go in the house, and I'll cut us out some lines, ok?"

"All I can do is watch," Eddy whined. "The one damn time you buy coke."

"Baby, believe me, I'm going to be buying more coke this week. I bought an eightball today, and I'll probably buy another one for this weekend. Any-how, why can't you do coke? It ain't got no carbohydrates, no fat, no nothing. What could it hurt?"

"Well, now that you put it that way, see, I don't know. I don't reckon it would hurt. Except, you know what? It'd sure as hell make me want to drink, and I can't do that. I better not. I'll wait. Y'all go ahead on."

The dogs woke up when they heard voices in the kitchen and wandered in. "Hey babies," Destiny called to them.

"These are the damn dogs, huh?" Eddy bent down to pet them. "Little old fru fru dogs. I can't stand fru fru dogs. I like a big old dog."

"They're sweet," Destiny said as she pulled a small mirror and a single-edged razor blade from her purse. She tapped a little of the powder out onto the mirror.

Eddy walked into the living room and drifted further down the hall to snoop.

"Where are you going?" Munio asked, peering around the corner of the kitchen doorway at him.

"Nowhere, I'm just being nosy. Looking around. Nice damn house." He walked into Sandra's bedroom at the end of the hall and turned on the light.

In her dressing room area sat two Styrofoam wig heads with Sandra's old mousy gray standbys. Eddy grinned and grabbed one of them. He put it on his head and looked in the mirror. He ran back down the hall and made a leaping entrance into the kitchen. "Honey, I'm home!" he bellowed in his best falsetto.

Munio became enraged. "What are you doing? How dare you go through

the closets of a dead woman, and play with her personal items! You should never have done that!" Munio shouted, not realizing what he had said. "This is not respectful!"

Destiny and Eddy looked at each other. "Did you say dead?" Destiny asked.

"Dead? I didn't say dead."

"Yeah, you did. You said dead woman. Didn't he, Destiny?" Eddy pointed to Destiny for backup.

"Yeah, that's exactly what he said."

Munio swallowed, grinned, and stammered, "I, I, don't know why. I, what I meant to just say was that you are not supposed to rummage through someone's private areas." Munio held his hands out for emphasis. "That is what I meant to say."

"Ok, then, whatever. Sorry, bud. So is this broad bald or what?" Eddy grinned and Destiny busted out laughing.

"Eddy! Munio's gonna kill you. Don't pay no mind to him, Munio. We all know he's an asshole." She continued to tap away on the mirror.

Munio regained his composure and started to giggle at Eddy, who still had the wig on his head. "You stupid bastard. Look at you. You look pretty good in drag."

"Oh ches, I got a show to do this weekend up in Atlanta, y'all know?" he lisped, prancing around the kitchen.

"Go put that up, will you?" Munio pointed to Eddy to go back down the hall.

"Ok, ok."

Eddy trotted back down the hall, and as he set the wig on the stand, he noticed a pair of beige pumps that were the largest women's shoes he had ever seen in his life. Knowing he risked the certain wrath of Munio, he slipped off his black converse lowtops and put on the pumps. He guffawed to find they were a little big on him. He dragged his feet down the hall and entered the kitchen.

Eddy began to vogue for them, and Munio hit himself on the head, helpless to do anything but laugh. Destiny almost blew all the coke off the mirror she roared so hard.

"Damn Munio, I don't know if I want to meet this gal or not. Her damn feet's bigger than mine. Look at these whoppers." He pulled them off his feet and walked over to Destiny for her inspection.

"Goddamn, they are big. What size?" She looked inside to check. "Fucking thirteen? How goddamn tall is she?" Eddy held the shoe up to Destiny for inspection. While they were getting a big kick out of this, Munio was on the verge of losing it.

"None of your business. You are just laughing at her. She is big, it's true, but so what? You are not going to meet her anyhow."

"Why's that?" Eddy asked.

"Because I don't want you to. You are too rude. That's why." Munio calmed down a bit and tried to make light of it. "Put those shoes away, and don't look anywhere else for nothing. You understand, little boy? No playing around. Come right back!"

"Yes, daddy!" Eddy headed back down the hall.

"How long are you going to tap on that coke? Are you trying to make tortillas or something?" Munio leaned over Destiny and put his arm around her.

"Ok, I'm finished. Here, you go first." She handed him a rolled-up dollar bill.

Munio worked the dollar bill smoothly up and down two lines. He handed the dollar bill back to Destiny, nodding in approval and thanks as he continued to snort and work all the coke to the back of his throat and beyond.

Eddy returned from replacing the shoes with no new tricks up his sleeves. He looked on as Destiny, loudly but expertly, snorted the crisp white lines up the dollar bill tube. "Bravo, bravo." Eddy applauded the deftness of Destiny's technique.

"Munio, want to go again before we go back out?" Destiny offered.

"Yeah, sure." He quickly moved to the mirror and wolfed up another pair of lines. "Feels good. Been a long time since I did much of this stuff."

"Yeah, me too." Destiny snorted two more lines and then put the paraphernalia back in her purse.

Munio grabbed a couple more bottles of champagne, and they returned to the gazebo. His eyes immediately began playing tricks on him. The low light made his hearing intensify. He almost felt like his ears somehow grew larger, and sounds seemed to echo deep down in the chambers of his inner ear.

"Is your hearing different now?" Munio asked Destiny.

"Naw, not that I know of. Is yours?"

"It's echo-y. I can hear real good. It's strange."

Eddy stood in front of Munio, and his lips feigned shouting. He waved his arms around like he was angry.

"Very funny. You know you are real funny tonight, real funny."

"I have contracted a contact high. I am high on drugs. These people have ruint my life, officer." Eddy stood up straight and spoke with the sincerity of a born-again Christian.

Munio snickered but then sat down on the bench, interested in what new things he could hear. The champagne and the coke combined to give him a perfect high. He was very happy and glad to be here in the gazebo. Up in the night sky, the stars twinkled. In fact, he felt he could hear them twinkling, crackling from their intense white heat way up in the wild blue yonder.

"Munio, are you ready?" Destiny, her eyes open so wide they looked like

small, green-yolked eggs, nodded at him.

"What?"

"Chugging contest. You ready?'

"Oh, oh, oh, my my, yes, I am ready to beat you, uh huh." Munio shadow boxed all around her.

"Ok." She uncorked two bottles and handed one to Munio. "Eddy, you got to say 'go', ok? No fooling around either, you hear?"

"Ok, y'all line up." He assumed the persona of a referee. "Do both of you understand the rules?"

Destiny and Munio rolled their eyes at each other. "Yes, you drink the bottle of stuff." Munio replied sarcastically.

"No jokes, no fun, this is serious, people. All right, drinkers take their mark. I am going to say on your mark, get set, go, all right?"

"That would be an appropriate line, thank you," Destiny replied.

"All right, all right. On your mark, get set, go!"

Destiny and Munio tilted their bottles slowly so they would not foam up. They seemed to be neck and neck. A small stream trickled down the sides of both their mouths as they raced on. The bottles pointed higher and higher until, about forty-five seconds into the contest, Destiny pulled her mouth away from the empty bottle. She held it upside down over her head in triumph and danced around the gazebo shouting. Munio was only a few seconds behind her, but the loser nonetheless.

"I proclaim Destiny Morris champion chugger!" Eddy announced and held up her right arm.

"Good show, Destiny, good show." Munio went over and hugged her. "I would like a rematch later tonight, however. Do you agree?"

"All right, you got it. Sheewwwee." She held her hand up to her mouth for a couple of seconds and then let out an enormous burp.

"Jesus fucking Christ, Destiny! Did you lose your liver on that one?" Eddy and Munio cracked up.

Munio was next with an even louder burp.

"I proclaim Munio best burper so far," Eddy declared.

"It ain't over yet, buddy," said Destiny as she summoned up her best effort with another one that was longer than the first.

"Ah, not bad, not bad. Munio?" Eddy challenged.

Munio bounced around trying to coax a blast which erupted with great success. They went a couple of more rounds and unanimously awarded Munio the burping crown, which was a cork from one of the champagne bottles.

"Want another bump?" Destiny smiled at Munio, who nodded back at her. "Come here, and I'll scoop it up on my fingernail."

Munio leaned over as she fed his nose from a scoop of coke balanced delicately on the fingernail of her pinkie.

"Thanks. You want me to do you?" Munio offered.

"No, just tell me when I'm under my nose good, ok?"

"Ok." Munio positioned her little fingernail. "Go!"

"Thanks." Destiny snorted and sniffed.

Munio nodded and sat back on a bench, eager to smoke a cigarette. Destiny and Eddy sat quietly too with their thoughts. Again, Munio focused on his acute hearing, or imagination of it.

Conversations came through his ears that Munio figured to be from inside a neighbor's home or from down the street. From a nearby tree, he heard some little nocturnal animal, a possum or raccoon, clawing its way through the branches. He was puzzled by a subtle but distinct grinding sound, like far away chewing. He had no idea what that could be, and then his mind ran away with him like a wild mustang with no thought of coming back. A sick, hot fever swept through him, and the cigarette suddenly added to his nausea. The sound filled his head and the gazebo and the yard, but no one else seemed to hear it. His mind painted the picture of what the business of that sound might be. It was worms having their way with Sandra down below. Millions of them on their mission to pick her clean. Munio went into a panic.

He wanted to scream and tell Destiny and Eddy what was inside him, but he refrained. Standing up, he walked around, grateful to have his boots drown out the sound. It worked so well, in fact, that he started a flamenco-style dance. This kind of shoe was not optimal for the purpose, but he managed to slap out a fine rthymn. Destiny and Eddy clapped as Munio danced. He worked his way around the circle of the gazebo, snapping his fingers in the air and twisting and turning.

Munio soon forgot what horror had led him to begin this dance and gave himself totally to the experience. His body knew just what to do as his boots stamped out a melody with heel and toe. The wooden floor provided great resonance. For fifteen minutes, Munio danced until his strength gave out and the cocaine's power waned. As soon as he stopped, the extraordinary hearing ability vanished.

Eddy and Destiny stood and cheered and clapped. Munio collapsed on the bench grinning. Sweat poured off his face, and his lungs heaved as his heart pounded. Eddy and Destiny danced around themselves and tried to recreate the art but could not.

"Damn, boy! Where did you learn to do that shit?" Eddy asked. "That was hell! Danced like a man on marbles!" Eddy and Destiny howled. "Like a man squishing roaches!" Eddy chuckled, and Munio gulped as that statement reminded him of what had motivated him to dance in the first place.

\* \* \* \* \* \* \* \*

Eddy had gone home, and Munio and Destiny sat side by side on a bench talking. Destiny kept the bumps of coke coming, which kept the champagne from knocking them out cold.

"Do you ever wonder why you're here?" Destiny asked Munio as he sniffed his last load.

He pondered before answering. "I wonder, yes. I was supposed to go to Atlanta, but I ended up stopping at Eddy's bar."

"No, no, no. I mean here. You know, like here on earth here?" Destiny slurred.

"Oh, here alive here. Oh, well, ah." Munio scratched his chin and pulled the hairs on his mustache. "No, not really, I don't. Do you?"

"All the goddamn time, all the goddamn time. I don't know what the hell my life's all about. I ought to be glad I got a little break getting this money and all. And I am, believe me I am, but don't nothing really satisfy me. Nothing ever has satisfied me. Well," she snorted a laugh, "only one thing I ever done satisfied me. Gimme one of those nasty cigarettes, will ya?" She elbowed Munio playfully.

"Sure, ok, here." He handed her a smoke and then lit it for her.

"Thanks." She exhaled and smoked quietly for a minute while Munio waited for her punch line, but it never came.

"So what was it?"

"What was what?" she asked.

"The thing that satisfied you, you said." Munio looked at her.

"Oh," she giggled, "Oh, that. I can't tell you." she winked and exhaled.

"The one thing in your life that satisfied you, and you keep it a secret?" Munio kidded her.

"Well, I could tell you, but then I'd have to kill you. Know what I mean?" She laughed.

"What? You can tell me. Who will I tell?"

Destiny laughed and counted on her fingers, "Oh, the FBI, Highway Patrol, Sheriff, you know, a few of them types."

"Oh, something illegal. Ah, I understand. Yes, you should keep it a secret, then."

"Yeah, I better. I tell you though. If I was to tell anybody, you'd be a damn good candidate on account of you probably wouldn't give a rat's ass."

"I will take that as a compliment."

The sound of the gate closing startled them until they saw it was Audrey. In the dark, the bright floral cloth of her pants billowed like a jib as she strode across the yard.

"Is there a party back here?" she called out.

"Hell yeah, there is!" Destiny yelled.

"Hello, hello, how are you two getting along? I see the gazebo is still standing. That is a good sign."

"Would you like a drink?" Munio offered.

"Yes, I would, thank you." She walked around all the sides of the gazebo. "He did a great job on this, didn't he?" Audrey said to Destiny.

"I can't hardly believe he did it all by himself, you know? He is more clever than you think. You should have seen this dance he was doing earlier. It was kind of like tap dancing but more dramatic. He was stomping and snapping his fingers and everything. Me and Eddy loved it."

"He is a great instinctive dancer. A real natural talent. If he studied, he would be phenomenal."

"Oh really?" Destiny said.

Munio returned with a glass for Audrey. They toasted and drank. Munio and Destiny felt a little self-conscious with the level-headed Audrey around. She and Munio had been on a crash course for a drunken bash, but now they subdued their merriment, both of them hoping Audrey would catch up.

"How did your recital go?" Munio asked.

"Wonderful. They think I am God." She laughed. "It was good. All those left-footed old people danced as well as they could. And dress?" Audrey rolled her eyes. "I never saw so much gold lamé in all my life. Well, that's not true." She finished off her glass and offered it to Munio for a refill. "Where I'm from, Long Island, that is where gold lamé is mined, if you will." She laughed at herself. "In fact, gold lamé is the official cloth of the Jews. Yes, honey, it's true." Munio and Destiny elbowed each other and laughed at her schtick.

"Is your family real religious?" Destiny asked.

"Not really. We're unorthodox, which means we avoid the temple like the plague. On high holy days, sometimes we would go to temple, but not every week or anything like that."

"What's the difference between orthodox and unorthodox?" Destiny questioned.

"Orthodox means, let's see, one thing is, after Friday night at sunset until Saturday night after sunset, you don't drive or use electrical appliances."

"Electrical appliances? Like a toaster oven?"

"That's right, honey. No microwave. Right there is why I could never be orthodox. Without microwave popcorn, I am a total bitch."

"You know that you're the first Jewish person I ever met?" Destiny giggled.

"Is that right? Aren't there any Jews in this town?"

"There ain't many, and the ones that's here, I ain't ever met. I grew up Baptist. They told us that Jews and Catholics was all going to hell."

"That's probably true," Audrey said dryly, causing Munio and Destiny to crack up.

"All going to hell, eh? You look like you might be headed there yourself!" Munio said to Destiny, creating another round of hilarity.

"I know you're right about that. Speaking of going to hell, Audrey, would you care to do a little coke?"

Audrey curled up her lips and moved her head from side to side in consideration. Then, she threw her hands up. "Why not?"

They all laughed, and Destiny led the way back into the kitchen to cut out some lines. The lap dogs greeted them at the door.

"Hey, sweet babies. What y'all been doing? Huh? We going to party in here for a while. Is that ok with y'all?" Destiny babytalked the dogs while she sat down at the table and got to work. The little dogs danced around Destiny's feet, wagging their tails and whining. "I know it. Mommy's been gone, hadn't she? Bless y'alls hearts. Y'all miss your mommy, uh huh. Yes, you do, precious."

"You sure like dogs, don't you?" Audrey asked.

"Yeah, I do. I love animals period. Rather be with animals than people. I got a bunch of cats, no dogs, just cats." she said, as she chopped on the mirror. "By the way, what are these dogs' names? Munio forgot, the bum." Destiny gave him a dirty look and winked.

"Oh, well, the Pomeranian is Jacky. The Yorkie is Ricky, and the Shih Tzu is Moo Shoo."

"Those are cute names."

"I have never had a pet in my life," Audrey proclaimed.

"Even as a kid?" Destiny asked.

"No, never did."

"Maybe that's because it's harder up in Yankee land, or so I'm told. Not enough grass to walk dogs, and with y'all living on top of one another and all."

Audrey clapped her hands and let out such a roar Destiny looked up from her mirror. "There's grass in New York, honey, and we don't all live twenty people to a room, you know."

"Well, that's what I heard."

"You'll have to come up there and see for yourself."

"Ummm, I don't know about that. I have about as much interest in visiting New York City as I do the moon." Destiny shook her head and smiled as she chopped.

"You might be surprised. It's good to visit other places."

"It's true I ain't got around much, and I am not opposed to getting the hell out of here. It's just that I'm a Southern girl, and I don't like the idea of living out of walking distance from a boiled peanut stand, you know what I mean?"

"Munio, you're awful quiet. What are you thinking about?" Destiny inquired.

"I am enjoying listening to you two talk. I was thinking how similar you two seem to look tonight. Your features are somewhat the same. You from the north," he pointed to Audrey, "and you from the south are much the same. Each of you is so loyal to your native area. You could be related."

Destiny and Audrey looked at each other and cracked up. "Munio, what a thing to say!" Audrey grabbed Destiny's arm.

"See, like now, as you collaborate about what I've said, you are much

alike." Munio laughed and pointed.

"You need some drugs, mister. Walk your little old nose up here to this mirror." Destiny handed him the rolled-up dollar bill.

"Audrey, you go first if you please." He passed the bill to her graciously.

"Well, thank you, Gentleman Jim." Audrey and Destiny giggled. Audrey leaned over and pulled away quickly. "Oh God, I've got the giggles. I'm going to blow this stuff everywhere. Don't get me tickled now." With a smile still on her face, she leaned over like a great heron, slowly yet gracefully, timing her contact with her line perfectly.

"Well done, well done." Destiny clapped for Audrey who, giggling, took a curtsey. "Looks like you've had a little practice at this game, lady. Snorted that up like a real pro."

Audrey tried to give the bill back to Munio, but again, he deferred to Destiny. "Ladies first when I am present," he said proudly, smiling a big high-as-a-kite grin.

"I feel like I'm on a date with Ricardo Montelbaum, or whatever the fuck that Love Boat guy's name is. I ain't used to polite men."

"You should be," Audrey said.

"Hon, if wishes were horses, we'd all ride to town." Her nose lapped up her lines.

They all took up a seat at the table to finish off another bottle of champagne and snorted another round.

"Hey, why don't y'all do some dancing or something? Show me some fancy dance stuff, ok? What do you say?"

Audrey and Munio looked at each other and nodded. "Ok with me. I will find some appropriate music." Munio dashed into the living room to cue up the stereo.

"Did you always want to be a dancer?" Destiny asked Audrey.

"Yes, I really did."

"Did your mama try to make you play football and do boy stuff?"

"No, not really. I think she was glad I didn't want to play rough sports."

"How about your daddy? Did he worry about you turning out sis--I don't mean to insult you or nothing." Destiny chuckled. "But was he worried about you turning out to be a sissy?"

Audrey smiled and replied in a heavy lisp, "Yes, daddy did worry, and look what happened. Boys that don't play football do turn out to be big old drag queens after all."

Destiny punched her on the arm playfully. "No, they don't."

"Honey, let me put it to you this way. Wild horses could not have made me straight. I have been queer since the day I was born. I really believe that."

"Is that right? That's interesting, you know it? That is real interesting."

From the living room, loud, hot Spanish music blared. The powerful speakers produced a wall of sound built of many horns and intricate percus-

312

sion.

"Oh Christ, let's go see what Juan Valdez is cooking up for us." Destiny punched Audrey again.

"I'm rrrready to rrrrrhumba!" Audrey announced and jumped all over the kitchen doing a combo imitation of Tina Turner and Charro.

"Oh God. What have I done?" Destiny looked skyward as she walked toward the living room and gave Audrey a playful panicked look.

Munio, slinking like a big cat, took long, low cross-over steps dramatically in sync with the music. Noticing that Audrey and Destiny were observing him, he put on even a greater show, snapping his head left and right. His face danced with a humorous array of dramatic expressions. Until the selection ended, Munio stayed in character for his audience, who roared over his antics. The little dogs quietly watched him from the couch.

"Muy bien! Muy bien!" Audrey praised him as she and Destiny applauded.

"Come, Audrey, dance with me!" Munio held out his hand.

Audrey took several flying leaps towards her partner, mistimed her last, and almost took Munio out. They started the dance with serious giggles. Destiny chortled from the sidelines with the dogs, who had positioned themselves in or near her lap. Munio and Audrey whipped themselves about the floor. Destiny could not believe they had not rehearsed, since they moved as one with great speed and power. They turned like flexible, super charged mechanical dolls, and at one point, Audrey jumped into Munio's arms for a turn, then a stop, which seemed to instantly transform them into granite. Finally, a slinky march back across the room and a dip ended the scene. Munio held the pose, his arms gripping her body while she coiled tightly in a horseshoe back bend across his bended knee.

"Wow! I'll be goddamned! That looked like something you'd see on Star Search or something! Y'all ought to be on tv! I mean it, y'all!"

Audrey chuckled at her compliment. To a professional dancer such as Audrey, Star Search was not her idea of the bigtime, yet the image tickled her. She saw Ed McMahon meeting Munio. That conversation alone would most certainly be worth the trip. She continued her fantasy for another moment, hearing Ed announce, "And now, a drag queen from Long Island, Audrey Meyers and her Mayan warrior dance partner, Munio Morelos." She chuckled and clapped her hands.

"Hey, girl!" Destiny snapped her fingers in Audrey's ear.

"Oh, I'm sorry. Did you say something?" She giggled.

"Hell yeah, I said something!" Destiny gave her playful nasty look.

"I was picturing Ed McMahon saying, 'And now from Long Island, a big old drag queen. No, no, I mean, and now a drag queen from Long Island!'" This had them all in stitches once again.

"Hey Destiny, want me to teach you a dance?" Audrey offered excitedly.

"Gee, I don't know whether I'm teachable. I know my back can't bend like y'alls. What do I do first?"

"Stand up for one thing. Get up here. I'll teach you the tango. No deep bends here." Audrey manipulated Destiny's position. "Follow me!"

The music was perfect. An accordion led the song with a plodding yet seductive pace. Audrey tried to hold her close, cheek to cheek, but Destiny got the silly giggles as she continually stepped on Audrey's vulnerable sandaled feet.

"Girl, you are going to have me in a wheel-chair if you don't watch out!" Audrey shook Destiny playfully.

Destiny could not stop laughing, nor could Munio on the sidelines. Audrey tried a couple more passes, trying to make snap turns, failing each and every one. At last, Audrey gave Destiny an affectionate shove which sent her falling onto the carpet in a hysterical heap.

"Stop it! Stop it! I'm going to wet my pants!" Destiny begged.

Destiny recuperated on the carpet, breathing heavily from the vigorous movement. The little dogs all took this opportunity to comfort her. One by one, they hopped down from the couch to wiggle and flirt with their new friend.

Audrey and Munio sat on the couch. Munio immediately stood back up to get another bottle of champagne for them. Like a fine waiter, he uncorked the bottle smoothly and made his rounds. The three sipped in silence.

"Whewww, I thought I was going to die there for a minute," Destiny testified. "Should have been here earlier, Audrey. Eddy was a riot. He went in there somewhere," Destiny pointed down the hall, "and came back out with a damn wig on his head, prancing and everything."

Audrey smiled and nodded, while inside, her heart beat very fast from the coke and from the secret she held about the owner of that wig.

Destiny continued. "Then, after Munio got on to him about it, he went to put it back, and came back wearing these fucking gigantic high heels. I swear to God they were big as canoes. They swallowed Eddy's big old hoof." Destiny cackled. "It was so funny. I thought I'd die." She chuckled again, and while she looked down and carefully wiped her eyes, Munio and Audrey gave each other special amused looks.

The conversation lulled, and Audrey chose the opportunity to bow out. She hugged Destiny and thanked her for the drugs and booze and the fun time.

"You know what?" Destiny said to Audrey as she patted her on the shoulder. "I have decided that you are my official favorite queer."

Audrey grinned and bowed. "Well, God knows I'm honored, your highness."

"Well, you ought to be, except there wasn't much competition. I only knew one other queer. Yeah, this boy, I knew from fucking first grade all the way through high school. We was seniors, and he ended up killing hisself."

"God, that's awful!" Audrey exclaimed, wishing she weren't hearing all this.

"Yeah, day before we graduated, his mama found him in the damn garage, hangin' from a beam, wearin' her finest dress. It was a bummer, but a hush hush kind of bummer. I knew 'cause I was pretty close to him and all."

"On that cheerful note..." Audrey rolled her eyes at Munio and Destiny, gave a little wave, and left.

* * * * * * *

Audrey motored home carefully as Destiny's little anecdote echoed through her head. The South seemed to have such bizarre circumstances, she thought. The gazebo, standing in all its grim glory and innocence, crossed her mind, causing her to shudder. What an unlikely town this was in which to meet a man who moonlighted when necessary as a Mayan warrior. She chuckled as she thought how much Sandra would have appreciated all of this certifiable insanity. She laughed remembering Destiny crashing to the floor. Destiny had turned out to be a pleasure, she thought.

Much wider vistas opened up for Audrey's hopped-up, wandering mind. The unsettling picture of herself returned, taped and loaded with silicone packs. Hobbled, it occurred to her that she looked hobbled by the accoutrements required for her persona. For a long time, the procedure had been so freeing.

Audrey's mind drifted back to when she was a young man of eighteen. She had found her way to the drag bars in Brooklyn, thus locating a safe and supportive place to wear the costumes that she had dreamed about for so many years. Rosanna Perez, her mentor, "queen of Brooklyn" as she had labeled herself, took Audrey under her wing and remained a fast friend until she died, just last year. Audrey remembered how, like a newborn colt, she had stood frozen and fascinated by her own image, dressed in a ballgown loaned by Rosanna. How quickly her female persona had slipped into gear and taken over her life. Audrey chuckled to recall that after only five minutes she had moved smoothly in those heels, and in fifteen minutes, she had had an act. His homosexual Bar Mitzvah, she always called that day. Up until now, it had remained the favorite day of her life--the day of the changing pronoun. In honor of her grandmother, she claimed the name Audrey as forever hers.

Home now, Audrey turned up the heat and continued to review and contemplate. There is no shame in change, she reminded herself. For years, her feelings vacillated about the trials of wearing a wig. She remembered how, at first, what terrifically convenient options wigs presented. To instantly be host to a platinum, red, or raven beehive or fall was grand. Eventually, its comfort dissolved, and the procedure felt contrived, itchy, and unnecessary, as long as she could grow hair. Now, no man or woman on earth had anything over Audrey in that department. She had hair that was not only beautiful but healthy, and it occurred to her that her relationship with her hair was the most fulfill-

315

ing one she had with any of her body parts.

Audrey stripped naked in the toasty apartment. Her skin tingled and gave way to waves of goose bumps wrought by the freedom of nakedness and the influence of cocaine. In front of a full-length mirror, she surveyed herself. She posed in a variety of positions. She noted how she felt when focused on her face, and then realized that, when gazing at her pubic area, a catch, a hesitation occurred in her mind. She stared at her penis and began to cry. A sadness came over her, and, she had an awareness of how cruel a life her penis had lived for the last twelve years, like a long neglected child. She was smacked with the truth that passion, spontaneous passion, had been given no room. It was clear to her that the time had come to surrender the tape, and she smiled to remember how she used the last piece just tonight. It was a sign, she felt, a good sign.

Her body hummed from the residual effect of the cocaine. Having no desire to sleep, she decided to begin to pack.

# CHAPTER XLVII

Munio and Destiny revved up another notch after Audrey left. Their philosophy was that a party began and ended when the booze and drugs showed up and ran out, so, they continued to snort, chug and amuse.

"We're going to be in bad shape to drive up to Atlanta tomorrow, you know?" Destiny reminded Munio.

"You are perhaps correct. Maybe you should get some more coke so we will be alert for Eddy. He will probably be a crazy man."

"Ain't that the damn truth. That boy's starting to look seriously wrung out, don't you think? I mean, I didn't want to say nothing, but he's getting pretty hard on the eyes. With that damn face all sunk in, and that weird-ass tan. I'm telling you the truth."

"In my experience, bodybuilding brings out the worst in people. I have been acquainted with muscleheads before, but Eddy is the craziest man I ever met involved with steroid drugs. He had too many choices with all that stuff that man's mother gave him." He lit a cigarette.

"Yeah, I reckon that's true. He's been like a kid in a candy store, and he has sure enough eat too damn much." She laughed. "I reckon he'll be all right. He'll make it another couple of days."

"Oh sure, he'll be fine. I hope he wins, that's all."

"Me too. That'll be a bummer if he does bad."

"Bodybuilding is a funny sport. The kind of competitive lifting I used to do, you lift the most weight, you win the trophy. In bodybuilding, it is not that predictable. The judges judge with their eye, and everyone sees things differently, you know? You can never tell what will happen."

"I hope he handles it better than last time."

"What do you mean?"

"Oh hell, he got second in his weight class, and had a major hissy fit in front of the whole crowd. Just went berserk, mooned the judges and took a couple of swings at the poor guy who won." Destiny laughed. "It was funny, but at the same time, it wasn't either.

They called the cops and everything. It was a little old show in an even littler town than this, if you can believe that." Destiny nodded her head.

"Oh, well, this is encouraging news. If he jumps on anybody now, he will kill them. He does not realize how strong he has become. His emotional nature is, ah, powerful, you know, vicious at times."

"Believe me, buddy. I fucked the guy the other day, and I felt like I was being took by a dadgum wild boar or something."

Munio broke up and blew his swallow of champagne out onto the gazebo floor.

Munio and Destiny continued a never-ending conversation until finally, with classical selections of Latin dance music whispering in the background, the two party animals dozed off.

Munio awoke first at ten. He put on a pot of coffee and got right to work. Moving fast, he rounded up all the bottles and butts scattered throughout the kitchen and the living room. As the dogs took their morning constitutionals, he collected the debris from the gazebo. Still wet from the dew, the empty bottles made him feel sad. Their emptiness reminded him of cold dead Sandra down below. There was no time to contemplate that now, and he brushed the thought from his mind.

For the next hour, he gathered together the things he needed for the trip to Atlanta, and then woke Destiny.

"Destiny? It is time to wake yourself up."

"What time is it?"

"Eleven o'clock," He called from the kitchen.

"Shit!" She sat up quickly, with a look of urgency on her face. "I got to get going. What time did he want to leave?" She ran her hand through her hair and frowned when she hit a snag.

"Noon is what he said originally." He walked in with a bright white delicate cup and saucer.

Destiny smiled when she saw him. "What service. Thank you, Munio. You know, you're a pretty sweet old boy. I think I'll keep you around." She took the cup and drank a sip. "Ahhh, perfect, perfect."

"All right, I reckon I better get my ass in gear." She set the Yorkie aside and stood, then walked over to the full-length mirror. "I look like something the dogs drug up." She laughed. "Audrey was fun last night. I like her. I really do."

"Yeah, she's nice."

"Wish she was going with us."

"She's going to stay here and take care of the animals."

"Damn Munio. You are as much of a neat freak as Eddy Jackson is. He drives me crazy, always putzing around behind you, picking up and stuff."

"I like a place to be orderly. That is just my way," he stated firmly.

"I don't. I like a place to be comfortable, lived in."

"And I don't? Of course, I like to be comfortable. Comfortable to me is neat and clean."

"I mean I ain't a serious scumbag, but, oh God, I just realized I'm going to be stuck in a hotel room with you two. Oh, please, sweet Jesus! As messy as I am at home, I'm twice as bad in a motel. Y'all are just going to have to give me my corner, ok?"

"Ok," Munio laughed. "I doubt Eddy or I will be noticing much about that room until after the show."

"Good." She tipped up her cup, her pinkie extended, and finished off the coffee. "Damn, that was good. Ok, I'm out of here. I'll meet you boys at Eddy's about one, all right?"

Munio took a lengthy shower and called Audrey.

"Hello?" Audrey answered. "How are you? Headache?"

"No, I feel not bad, believe it or not. How is it you feel this morning?"

"This morning? To tell you the truth, my body's still partying. I swear, I'm still speedy from that coke. I am such a cheap date these days, honestly!"

Munio chuckled. "You will remember to care for these dogs, ok?"

"Don't worry, I'll show them a good time. I am going to finish packing up Sandra's things while I'm there."

"Ok. We will be leaving shortly."

"Where are you staying?"

"Let me see." Munio tried to remember what Eddy had said. "Oh yeah, it is the ah, Peachtree Plaza Hotel, under Eddy Jackson. "

"Ok, dear, good luck to Eddy. You have a fun time, and be safe. It is a big city, and you're going with a couple of hicks, so be careful, won't you?"

"They will be ok. I will see you soon, Sunday or Monday."

* * * * * * * *

Eddy's butt was sticking out of the trunk of his car. Munio laid on his horn, and Eddy straightened up.

"Hey."

"Good afternoon. I don't know about anything else, but your butt looks pretty good today."

"Just wait til you see. I'm going to show you in a minute after I clear out this trunk. It's all coming together, Munio. I swear, I look better than I ever dreamed. Come on in." Eddy led the way, hopping up the front porch steps two at a time.

Eddy had stripped by the time Munio walked into the house. Munio

318

had not seen his body in at least forty-eight hours, and was astounded at the change that had taken place. It was as if his paper thin skin had been vacuum-packed on his frame, like a pound of coffee sucked dry of every atom of air inside its foil container. He hit all of the compulsory poses, and on every muscle, the striations had increased dramatically.

A spidery network of vascularity now lay like raised lace under his skin. Small and large, with twists and turns, the vessels that ferried his blood rested so vulnerably. Munio feared for Eddy's safety. All it would take would be a light accidental slice to send an artery or a vein spewing like an oil rig. The thought of it took his breath away.

"What do you think?"

"Eddy." Munio shook his head and chuckled. "You are a monster. You don't look real, like a monster freak, like all those guys in the magazines, brother." Munio clapped his hands and then held his arms wide open. "What can I say? You look like a champion."

Eddy grinned and giggled. "And I ain't even there yet. Wait til I start carb loading. I'm going to fucking bust, man! There can't be nobody better than me. There just ain't gonna be. Fucking right!" Eddy let out a loud war whoop. "Where's that damn Destiny? I'm ready to fucking go!" Eddy clapped his hands so hard he could have broken a hickory nut.

"She will be along. You got yourself packed?"

"Yes, hell, I'm ready."

"Where do you want me to put my stuff?"

"In the fucking trunk, hoss, where do you think I want it?" Eddy fired back.

Munio turned his head at Eddy's tone. "You don't need to talk to me in that tone."

"Who are you, my daddy? I ain't got no TONE!" he returned nastily.

Munio gave him a stern look and said nothing. He walked outside and put an old leather suitcase and a red nylon sports bag in Eddy's trunk.

"Where's that fucking bitch at?" Eddy stood on the top step, posed like a warrior with his hands on hips.

Munio chuckled, "You tell me, superman." He walked by him and slapped him on the butt.

"Hey, don't handle the merchandise!" Eddy turned quickly, grinned, and tried to tag Munio on the butt but missed.

"I tell you what, little brother. You start getting that bad attitude, and I will have to turn you over my knee, you understand?" Munio pointed to Eddy, who followed him in the house.

"Where are you going?" Eddy asked as Munio headed down the hall.

"I've got to pee. Do you mind?" Munio said in a high pitched voice.

"Where is she?" Eddy started paced.

"Eddy, it is five minutes til one o'clock right now. Sit down, relax. Come

out on the porch with me to smoke a cigarette, ok?"

Munio led the way toward the door but stopped. "Say, have you got any beer in there?" He pointed toward the kitchen.

"Yeah, I think you left a few."

"Good, I'm gonna need one right now. My fussy boy is already driving his coach crazy." Munio slapped Eddy on the traps affectionately as he moved toward the kitchen.

Eddy, like a child, sat down in the middle of the top step of the porch to keep a vigil for the first sign of Destiny. Munio, as usual, sat on the green metal glider and popped the top of the beer can. The cold, foamy drink tasted mighty good and left a salt-tinged flavor in Munio's empty mouth. Eddy started singing the old Stevie Ray Vaughan song "Pride and Joy." . Munio watched Eddy and smiled, amused by his bad rendition of the blues.

"You're late!" Eddy yelled. "Late for my trip, girl. You better get on up here. I'm bound to give you a whupping! Munio done told me he'd hold you down, too!" He grinned good-naturedly.

"Well, I ain't that damn late, am I? You wanted me to look good for ya, honey, now didn't ya?" Destiny walked up the steps and gave him a big hug and kiss. "God save Jesus, what did you eat? Your breath smells like a four-day dead hog! Eddy, I'm serious. What in the world made your breath smell that way?" She chuckled, her face contorted.

"Shit, I ain't ate nothing in a while. In fact, I'm due. Oh, you know what? It's that DMSO. It makes your breath kind of garlicky. Is that what it smells like, garlicky?" He ran his tongue all around his teeth in an attempt to swab down some of the film that might have built up.

"Garlicky? Hell, garlic smells like a fucking spring bouquet compared to that shit! I'm telling you, it smells like shit! What the hell grows when you take that?' Destiny gave Munio a look of feigned disgust.

"They give it to race horses for-"

"Oh no you don't, big time. If your dick gets any bigger, you can fuck your own self! Race horse, my ass!" Eddy and Munio guffawed loudly.

"Wait a minute. They give it to race horses to make their joints feel good or something. Jerry gave me some the other day. I ain't tried it before."

"Well, give it back. Eddy, they ain't gonna let us in the hotel with you smelling like that! I ain't lying. Don't he stink, Munio? You tell him!"

Munio had noticed an odd aroma, but he was used to smelling Eddy when he was ripe. He leaned over close to Eddy and sniffed him.

"Damn, Munio, you don't have to deep throat the guy. You can smell that shit clear across the yard! Let us in the hotel? They ain't gonna let us in the city limits. Probably get some toxic waste ticket or something!" As she kept it up, Munio and Eddy were bent over with laughter.

"Yes, Eddy, you do have a peculiar smell about you." Munio said when his breath returned.

"Perfuckingculiar? Skanky bastard is what that man is, skanky! I hope you know we're keeping the windows down the whole way!"

"All right, all right, I'm going to go try to rinse it off or something."

"Boy, you sure are pepped up today. Not hungover, eh?' Munio put his hands in his pockets as he spoke.

"I did me a little bumpypoo. I feel great. You want one?" She grinned and gave Munio a mischievous look.

Munio ran his tongue over his top teeth to help him choose an answer. "Sure, I'll take one." Destiny headed toward the front door and motioned for Munio to follow.

In the kitchen, she pulled a little brown glass vial. She unscrewed the top, which had a small plastic snorting spoon built into I, then scooped out as much powder as would fit on the little spoon. "Ready?"

Munio nodded and, with explosive power, he loudly inhaled.

"Damn, Munio. I believe you could pick up a brick with that nose." She laughed. "Near 'bout lost the spoon. I could see taking you to the emergency room. Uh, yes, ma'am, could you tell me how much y'all would charge to remove the top to my coke thing from his nose, please?"

Munio laughed out loud and pushed Destiny playfully. "I am in pain. You must stop, I beg you! Nothing more funny, please!"

"You better enjoy it, bud. I do my bitch act a lot more than I do funny. Now, hold the other side of that car wash vacuum you call a nose!" Eddy popped in just as they finished.

"All right, now check me." Eddy walked over to Destiny.

She leaned towards him and had the answer right away. "Yes, that is much better. You're not packing any of that shit, are you? I don't know what we'd do if a bottle of it were to break."

"All right, let me get it out of my bag, but y'all, we got to git gone. It's almost two. I ain't hitting rush hour traffic up there."

"Ok, ok, I'm ready. Munio, y'all got any more beers?"

Within minutes, the party was assembled and loaded in Eddy's old cream-colored Monte Carlo.

"Hey, do you know where we go?" Eddy looked over at Destiny, his eyebrows arched in question.

She snorted and blew a big blast of air out of her mouth. "You don't know where to go? Ain't you got a map?"

"Naw, I mean I think you just get on the interstate going north. I'm going to pull up to the Amoco station and get gas anyhow. One of them ought to know."

Destiny looked in the back seat at Munio, who shook his woolly head. "Yeah hon, why don't you just do that." She patted him on the arm. "Ooowweee, aren't you a big old strong boy?" She squeezed his bicep. Eddy grinned proudly as he whipped into the Amoco.

Cruising now at seventy, the Monte Carlo was breezing northbound. Almost instantly, they were out of town. Nobody said anything for a while, each of them enjoying the rush of space and freshness in the anonymous landscape. Munio thought about his last ride on the interstate and how lucky he had been to pick that particular exit to search for beer that summer afternoon. He thought about all the unfriendly stops like that big fat lady's at Crazy Ray's. Squeezing the metal of the half empty can, he raised it to his lips for a sip.

Destiny rested her beer in a corner of Eddy's open glove compartment. Its latch had been broken for years, but it had become far more functional as a snack tray. With an emery board, she shaped her long fingernails. She planned to polish them once they got to Atlanta. She looked forward to it as a fun chore to kill a little time. Destiny was prone to carsickness, and so she was careful not to look down for too long.

Eddy's mind could not relax, he was headed toward the front line to do battle. His mind created better fiction than he had ever read as he fashioned the story of the way he wanted this weekend to work out. It would be a tough competition, but in the final posedown, he had no doubt who the judges would choose. The crowd would oooh and ahh every time he walked out, and after his posing routine, they would honor him with a standing ovation. The other competitors would flash him hateful looks and attempt to bump him unnecessarily during their group posedowns, but he would let the resentments roll off him like water off a duck's back. It was understandable, their disappointment. They had worked hard too, and to have someone as awesome as himself appear was crushing. He smiled as he drove along, picturing himself posing next to the Best Overall trophy. It was six feet tall, composed of solid brass and mahogany, and would have to be tied on the roof to be brought home.

"Eddy! Eddy! Hey!" Destiny looked back at Munio. "Are my words not coming out, or has he gone deaf?"

"I think he is deep in thought." Munio smiled, knowing how it was the week of a competition. There is nothing else in your world until it is over, he remembered.

Destiny punched Eddy, who returned from his daydream. "What?" he said, annoyed. "Quit punching me!"

"Well, I was calling you for the past ten minutes, but you was off in lala land somewhere. I got to pee."

"All right, I'll stop at the next exit. I wouldn't mind stretching my legs. You all right back there, Munio?" Eddy smiled in the rear view mirror.

"Very fine, very fine." Munio smiled back at his friend.

It was a busy truckstop. The parking lot was full of big rigs and their drivers. The cashier, a small, gray-haired man with very large ears, did a double take as he watched them parade by. He adjusted the Atlanta Braves baseball cap on his head and scratched his right ear, looking around to make eye contact with someone else who might have seen this odd crew enter, but no one

was around at the moment.

Destiny bought a large bag of barbecue pork rinds, a bag of Oreos, and a twelve pack of beer. Munio bought a six-pack, two pop-top cans of Vienna sausages, a small box of Premium saltines, and two packs of cigarettes. Eddy checked out last with one pack of sugar free grape bubble gum. The cashier's dilemma was trying to keep himself from getting caught staring at all three of them. His small head bobbed up and down and up and down like a cork in a stream as his eyes bounced from the cash register keys to the trio.

Eddy graced the man with a full-toothed smile and it made the little man take a startled quick breath to see such a large set of white teeth and the large vein that popped out on Eddy's forehead.

"How you?" Eddy said.

"Fine, thank ya. You a muscle man?" The man's face squinched up as he looked Eddy in the eye.

"Yessir, I reckon I am. Goin' up to Atlanta to be in a big contest." Eddy handed the man a dollar for his gum.

"Is that right? You, uh, shore look big."

"I am, mister. I sure am. You take care now." Eddy winked at him and walked out proudly. Eddy smiled to himself, thinking he was going to have to get used to greeting his public.

"How much farther?" Destiny asked Eddy.

The car passed a mileage sign. "Sixty miles, yep, about an hour. You've got just enough time to give me a couple of blow jobs." Eddy laughed a loud dirty laugh.

"You keep on dreaming, buddy." Destiny looked out the window.

In the first hour's drive, the landscape was all rural. Wide, large acre tracts of land were planted with cotton, and in this first week of November, the bushes were brown stick sculptures, stuck in red clay furrows, decorated with soft, white pods of cotton.

Parked on the sidelines of the fields, the massive irrigation machines stretched two or three hundred yards, like gigantic metal praying mantises.

White-faced red cattle grazed peaceably. Cowbirds trailed behind them in flocks. Crisp, straight lines of barbed wire contained them.

The closer they got to Atlanta, the more the land was besieged by urban sprawl. The concrete thickened. The cattle disappeared, replaced by steak houses. The city had a quickened vibration. None of them acknowledged it verbally, but each felt anxious by all the busyness.

"This is some big place, ain't it?" Eddy commented. "I'm a good mind to turn around before it's too late." He smiled and sweated.

"Honey, it's already too late. You can't get off this damn road." Destiny waved her arm at the highway.

"Ever seen any place like this?" Eddy looked in his rear view mirror at Munio.

"Not exactly, no. Mexico City is big, but it does not have this much concrete."

"They have poured a few yards." Eddy chuckled at his understatement. "Wish I had a dollar for every yard of concrete poured in this town. Hell, we ain't even in town just yet."

"Where's the hotel?" Destiny asked.

"Slap in the middle of downtown, supposedly. It's about the tallest building around, too."

They rode in silence, watching the traffic build around them. For most of their ride, the freeway offered only two lanes, but now there were five busy lanes leading them to the heart of the city. Eddy had seen that movie about the L.A. freeway sniper, and paranoia forced him to clench his jaws and grip the steering wheel tighter.

"Eddy, relax. You look like you're scared to death. Look at him, Munio." Destiny laughed, reached over, and rubbed the back of Eddy's neck. "Good God, you feel like a damn piece of granite."

"Baby, I don't think you really want me to relax right here on this goddamn racetrack. One slip, and we'll be on the six o'clock news." Eddy giggled.

"You're doing fine. I should have offered to drive some," Destiny said.

"Oh yeah, you are just the person I would want to be driving right now. I'd rather just go on and take a bullet as to drive with you on this road." Eddy looked into the rear view mirror again at Munio. "Hey, Munio, you ever rode with this bitch?"

"Yeah, but I think I was drunk," he snorted.

"It's a good thing you were because she is the single most terrifying driver I have ever rode with!"

"Oh, I ain't that bad." Destiny defended herself.

"Remember that time you ran some poor eighteen wheeler driver off the road because you was looking down, filing your nails? Huh?"

"Well, he had just pulled onto the road, Eddy. It wasn't like I made the bastard jackknife or nothing." She smiled.

"You tell him that."

"Oh, shut up and drive." She looked over her shoulder at Munio and winked.

"Hey, look at that! Man, that's hell, right there!" Eddy leaned forward as they topped a rise and saw the first view of the downtown skyline.

"Wow! That looks so big. Looks like New York City to me." Destiny leaned forward in her seat for a better view, and Munio rested his arms on the front seat for a closer look.

"Big as you think that is," Eddy pointed at the buildings, "New York City is ten times that big. I ain't lying."

"Well, I don't want to go then. This is big enough for me." Destiny started singing. "If heaven ain't a lot like Dixie, I don't want to go. If heaven ain't a lot

like Dixie, I just soon stay home. Just send me to hell or New York City, be about the same to me!"

"All right, it's coming up fast, y'all. I'm looking for the International Boulevard exit. It's right downtown. Y'all help me look for it. I don't want to miss it. I'd hate to have to turn around. We'd probably end back up in Rosedale." Eddy laughed nervously.

"Ok, I'll keep an eye out," Destiny assured him.

Within ten minutes, their status quickly changed from observer to participant in the web of activity. They were now a part of the city. All three of them became very quiet as the car moved up the boulevard which was lined with the tallest buildings in the city.

# CHAPTER XLVIII

Eddy eased the car into the motor lobby of the hotel. A young man in a black uniform with gold braid and trim on the short waistcoat promptly approached them.

"Good day sir, will you be checking in?" he asked politely.

"Uh, uh huh," Eddy replied.

"All right, fine, sir. If you want to get out, we'll be glad to valet park for you." The young man smiled and opened Eddy's door.

"Can't I park it myself?" Eddy asked.

"Yes, sir, if you wish. Would you like to have the rest of your party wait for you here? We can go ahead and handle your luggage."

"Oh well, I reckon that's ok. It ain't like I'm worried about it getting scratched up or nothing." Eddy handed over the keys.

After checking in, they boarded an elevator that took off like a rocket. They all looked at each other, a little afraid something was wrong. No on expressed this fear aloud, superstitious that doing so might make something happen. They were quickly deposited on the sixty-first floor, and when the doors opened, they hustled out.

"Goddamn! I thought we were goners!" Destiny exclaimed.

Eddy said. "All I know, fans, is I got to shit, and I got to do it right now! Let's go! Come on!" They hurried after him.

He opened the door and found the bellman had just arrived with the luggage. "Jesus Christ, you scared me!" Eddy shrieked as he bolted into the bathroom and slammed the door.

Destiny walked in calmly and smiled at the bellman. "He had to go real bad."

"I understand, ma'am. Do you need anything else?"

"No, I reckon we'll be fine." She pulled two dollars from her purse and handed it to him. "Thank you very much."

Eddy burst out of the bathroom as quickly as he had gone. "Goddamn, I had to shit! Wheeew!" He walked over to the window where Destiny and Munio were standing. "Wow! That's great! Good view, huh?"

"It is. I have never been up this high," Destiny murmured.

"Neither have I, except in an airplane." Munio concurred.

"This must be what it's like up in an airplane." Destiny spoke softly and stared out the window. She felt totally humbled by the experience and a little afraid.

"Well, I'm ready to kick some ass. I don't know about y'all. Want to go down and look at the pool and stuff?"

Destiny moved away from the window and lay back on one of the beds. "I'm kind of tired. I wouldn't mind taking a nap, to tell you the truth."

"A nap? Jesus, some fun you are. I thought you was going to hang with me?" Eddy pulled on her legs, then started jumping on the bed.

"Eddy, stop! I'm going to throw up!" Destiny snapped.

"Munio, what do you want to do?" Eddy asked.

Munio shrugged as he opened beer number three. "Destiny, you want a beer? Maybe it will pick you up."

"Naa, if I take a nap for thirty minutes, I'll be a hell of a lot easier to live with."

"Fuck a nap! Ain't you got no more cocaine? Do you a little bump of that. In fact, do you a couple of big ol' lines. You can sleep tonight."

Eddy started taking his clothes off. Destiny gave him a confused and sarcastic look. "What the hell are you doing?"

Eddy grinned. "I want to see what I look like since we left." He took off everything except his white jockey shorts. "Man, I'm changing like the mother fucking incredible hulk! Look at this, Munio!" Eddy pointed to his shoulder. "Look at that! It's leaned out since three hours ago! Hey!" He looked at his watch. "Another hour and it'll be time to start carbo loading! Y'all will not, I say, will not believe how I'm gonna change then. This is wild, y'all. Right here," He pointed to his body, "Y'all are looking at science at its finest!" He grinned proudly.

Destiny sat up in shock. It had been only a week, but the latest transition Eddy's body had taken since then was nothing short of unbelievable. She felt her whole body tense just looking at him. It was as painful as looking at an injury on the body of a friend. One look at Eddy woke her right up, and now she needed some fortification to forget what she had seen. She started chopping lines.

"I don't know where you are going to end up, brother, but as Destiny said, it is scary. Monster man is what you are. Where do we have to go to get that tanning dye?" Munio asked.

"Uh, there's a gym that ain't supposed to be far. They sell the stuff." Eddy drew close to the mirror and squinted, flexed, and studied his body. "I have

to say I am pleased, y'all. I am so fucking happy I could shit, except I just did. I wouldn't mind pumping up just a little bit, neither. Y'all will go over there with me, won't you?" Eddy asked.

"Sure, we'll go. We're with you, eh, Destiny?" Munio urged.

"Hell, yeah! Y'all ain't leaving me here up in the damn ozone. Oh Munio, don't let me forget to buy a bottle of Jack Daniels while we're out."

Eddy sat on the bed and fumbled through some papers he pulled out of one of his bags. "Oh, right, this place is called, get this, Pumped and Ready." He snorted. "Sounds good, huh?"

Destiny looked at Munio, who gave her a scolding look in an attempt to encourage her to be nice. "Oh yeah, sounds like my kind of joint. Long as I'm pumped, I'm ready. That's what I always say. Yep, pumped and ready." She chopped away.

The sky changed as the autumn sun made its way home for the night. It was no longer bright blue, but pink and golden, as the final sunset fireworks set in. Munio lit a cigarette and watched the sky. The cloud traffic, the big puffy cotton balls moved in synchronized teams for points east. Sandra crossed his mind, and he wondered where she was, and whether she could see him. He smiled as he took a drag and wondered how Audrey was making out with the dogs. Being out of that house made him realize he had not been out on his own in some time. The drama and time consuming work involved with the circumstances of Sandra and her death had totally rerouted Munio's life. Being there on that sixty-first floor, and embracing that big expanse of sky, reminded him that his life was bigger than that experience.

"Hey, space case!" Destiny called to Munio after three attempts to get his attention. He looked toward the table where she sat. "You want a line or what?" She and Eddy snickered.

"Sorry, I was just thinking. Those clouds are so beautiful, aren't they?"

"Uh huh, shore are. Well, y'all ready?" Eddy was growing impatient.

It was luck as opposed to any skill on Eddy's part that they wound up in the parking lot of Pumped and Ready.

"All right y'all, we got to act cool. This is a real classy place, supposed to be anyhow."

"Well, it won't be after we're through with it," Destiny stated.

"Ha ha roar, Destiny. Now, you just act like you worship me, all right?" He pushed her along playfully.

"Whatever you say, darlin'. You know I just worship your big ol' pumped-up ass." She and Munio cracked up.

Eddy was right. The place was classy, or at least classier than the Dixie Ironworks. There was even an attendant on duty. Fast-paced popular music blared. The place was color-coordinated, with teal carpeting, and matching teal upholstery on every piece of equipment.

"Hello, could I help you?" A young woman asked. Her long, blonde,

bouncy hair was pulled back in a pony tail and held firm by a large teal-colored terrycloth hair tie. She had a full face of makeup, and a teal-colored polo shirt with Pumped and Ready tastefully printed over her left breast.

"Hey, ah, yeah, I'm here in town for the Mr. Dixie Contest, you know, and uh, I heard I could buy some of that tanning dye stuff here."

She responded politely, but not in the overly friendly way Eddy would have liked. "Yes, we have some. Let me show you." She moved down the counter to a showcase that contained bottles of tanning dye. "What shade do you prefer?" she asked.

"What you got?" Eddy looked on either side to Destiny and Munio, snickering at them.

"Well, bronze, sepia, burnt sienna, golden brown." She listed the choices.

"What do you think? Have you ever used this stuff?"

"No, I'm an aerobics instructor, but this burnt sienna is our best seller for Caucasians."

Eddy snickered again, but did not manage to get the woman to crack even a faint smile as he said, "Is that what I am, a Caucasian? Ain't nobody called me that all week." Destiny and Munio rolled their eyes. "All right then, ah, how many bottles you reckon I'll need?"

"Generally two. You might not use the entire second one, but it is better to have more than to have less." She issued a perfunctory stretching of her lips.

Eddy, trying to impart some sexual overtone, said, "Yeah honey, I know what you mean." He leaned closer to her and put his elbows on the glass counter top and winked. "I'll take two, please, ma'am."

She pulled two of the bottles from the case and moved back to her original post. "Will that be all?"

"Yeah."

"That'll be twenty twenty-two," she informed him.

"Ouchy uuchy. You hurtin' me, lady." He smiled as he handed her a fifty-dollar bill.

"Thanks a lot." She handed him the change, completely ignoring his poor attempts to humor her.

Eddy located a Sizzler steak house. As Destiny and Munio each had a well-rounded meal, he began the final bizarre food phase of carb-loading by ordering ten baked potatoes. He ate them like apples until he could not swallow one more bite. Having deprived himself of carbohydrates for the previous forty-eight hours, his body sucked up the fuel from the potatoes like a sponge. The results were dramatic. Even Eddy's carb-deprived brain felt affected.

"Y'all, we got to hurry up and get back and watch me grow. I swear, Munio, I can feel it happening. I feel like somebody's got an air needle stuck in me, and they're filling me up real slow." He was as excited as a kid on Christmas morning. "It's like getting a pump when you're not even working out."

"We got to stop at the liquor store first," Destiny reminded him.

Eddy ordered another ten potatoes for the morning, and they made their way back to the hotel after the pit stop for liquor.

"You know that they have a bar on top of that silo we're staying in that revolves around. We ought to go up there," Destiny said, as they cruised through the downtown streets. "Y'all want to?"

* * * * * * * *

They stepped into the glass capsule that served as the elevator car that accessed the lounge. The ride was nonstop, one of the fastest elevators in the world. From the ninth floor atrium level to the seventy-third floor it flew, giving its passengers the thrill and vulnerability of a city view as only birds might see it.

"Oh my God, that was unreal! I was scared to death!" Destiny exclaimed as they stepped out onto the plush carpet.

"I don't feel that great after that. I almost lost twenty dollars worth of baked potatoes. Jesus Christ, I could have done without that." Eddy shook his head and walked with a bit of a limp as he attempted to recover from the ride.

Munio remained quiet, but the ride had exhilarated him. He loved the intense internal stimulation of the fear, and the g-force that stirred his guts as only a bolt of lightning might.

"What did you think, Munio?" Eddy asked him. "Did you swallow your tongue? Been awful quiet since we got here. You feeling all right?"

"Yes, yes, unlike you youngsters with no fortitude, I very much enjoyed that rocket ride. I would like to do it again, in fact." He patted Eddy and Destiny on the back as they walked on to find a seat.

"Yes, may I help you?" A young woman greeted them outfitted in a long tight dress with a slit up the side that stopped just shy of indecent exposure. "Table for three?"

"Yes ma'am," Munio nodded and smiled.

It was as if they were airborne looking down on the earth below with myriad twinkling lights. The buildings to which the lights were attached were indiscernible, making them all anonymous pink or white points. Here the street lights were orangish-pink, unlike the old fashioned cool blue color in Rosedale. Airplanes with their red and green lights seemed to fly close to the hotel.

"I bet this is what it's like to be an air traffic controller. I bet that's a fun as hell job," Eddy commented.

"I don't like being up high myself," Destiny stated.

Eddy looked at Munio and they laughed. "It was you who wanted up to come up here!" Eddy said.

She shot Eddy a bird and shook her brown hair. "I mean I wouldn't want

to do it every fucking day, Eddy. Gaaa."

"How are y'all tonight?" the peppy waiter asked as he slapped down cocktail napkins as fast as a Vegas black jack dealer.

"Good, good. I just want a little water, please," Eddy requested. The man wrote on his order pad without comment.

"I'll have a, uh, 'day at the beach,'" Destiny spouted off like it was the game winning answer on Jeopardy. The waiter chuckled and jotted down the order.

"You, sir?" The waiter looked at Munio.

"I would like a pina colada, please."

"All right fine." He stepped away and hustled to the bartender.

"Do you miss Belize, Munio?" Destiny asked Munio gently.

He reacted with a smile, caught off guard by the question. "I miss the land, the ocean. It is a place I know. My mother, she is there." He flicked his ashes, curled up his lip, and shrugged.

"Do you think you'll go back there?"

He chuckled nervously. "Before my life is over, I will return. Right now?" He paused. "Eh, I don't know."

Eddy watched Munio and listened to him. He had never thought Munio might leave. He figured they would stay a team. Looking at Munio's proud face, Eddy suddenly felt sad for him, but he was not sure why.

The drinks came. Munio's and Destiny's had little umbrellas stuck in the top. Munio was particularly amused with that. In fact, he took his and parked it in his wild hair, and Destiny proceeded to do the same. They toasted to Eddy's championship.

The potatoes were beginning to take Eddy through a physical and mind-altering experience that a person would expect to get on LSD, not carbohydrates. Eddy felt like something had suddenly grounded him in that chair. He could not take his eyes off Destiny and Munio. He watched them and thought about how much he loved both of them. He studied Destiny's scar, which he seemed to never notice anymore. He burped and, behind that burp, a strange bubble of pain pushed its way into his heart. Eddy encountered a flood of emotion. Heat flushed his face along with the urge to cry. He tried to turn it away, but it didn't work. Destiny and Munio stopped talking and stared at Eddy, whose strange brown dehydrated face wadded up like a piece of paper with the arrival of tears.

"What's wrong, Eddy?" Destiny sat up on the edge of her chair, frightened.

He chuckled as tears streamed down his face. "I just love y'all. That's all. I, I, I'm just glad y'all are here. Thanks for coming with me." Munio and Destiny looked at each other with puzzled expressions.

"Geez, you reckon it's all those potatoes?" Destiny asked.

Munio smiled and winked at Eddy. "I bloody well would be crying if I ate

ten potatoes." They laughed.

"I'd be puking!" Destiny roared, and she and Munio toasted.

"Y'all, I don't know what's got into me. I feel like I'm fucked up or something." Eddy's tears now turned into giggles.

"The man shoots himself up with bucketfuls of steroids, growth hormones, and everything else, and it's potatoes that he has a religious experience over! I can't believe you, man!" Munio exclaimed. "Hey, I got an idea! Why don't we take those potatoes that you have there in that bag down to the strip, or wherever they sell their drugs in this town. We sell these potatoes as psychedelic potatoes, man. Sell each one for one hundred dollars. Destiny, we just show Eddy to them if they want to know how fucked up you can get on them." They all laughed, and Destiny beat her hands on the table.

"Yeah, yeah, he can be our demonstrator." She took on the voice of a used car salesman. "Hey folks, are y'all tired of the same old meat and potatoes? Well, how would y'all like to trip your brains out and look good too? Forget Idaho, honey, try our new trippin' taters. Look at this man." She pointed to Eddy. "Why, just a mere twenty-four hours ago he weighed one hundred pounds. But now, he looks like Hercules, and he's trippin' like a mother fucker! Ask for it by name! Do not delay!"

Eddy stuck his napkin in his water glass and wiped down his face. "Jesus, the thing is, I'm 'sposed to eat ten more of the sons of bitches in the morning."

# CHAPTER XLIX

Whether it was getting up to pee, coughing or just loud breathing, the three of them took turns throughout the night waking each other. They were all too wired to sleep soundly in this strange place in one room. When the first hint of light leaked in through the draperies, each was eager to respond.

Eddy made the first move, crawling out of the covers carefully to avoid waking Destiny. He stepped to the window and peeked out.

"What's out there?" Destiny said in a raspy, lazy voice.

Eddy smiled back at her. "It's just another day in Disneyland."

"Is the sun coming up yet?" Munio asked in his sweet accent.

Eddy trying to imitate him said, "Yez, eet iz, mon."

Munio threw a pillow and hit Eddy's naked back. "Did you grow in the night, Mr. Dixie?"

"I ain't looked yet, but I feel pretty filled out."

"I feel pretty filled out myself," Destiny laughed, grabbing her boobs as she thrashed about playfully in the bed. "Hope you ain't shy, Munio, because I sure as hell ain't." She dragged herself to a sitting position and propped up the pillows. Airing her breasts out from under the covers, she relaxed and took a deep breath.

"Not me, I am comfortable with nudity. I have been naked all my life, at some point, every day," he joked. "Give us a demonstration, Eddy," Munio encouraged.

"Y'all really ready to get up?" Eddy asked.

"Yeah, sure, why not, more time in the day to party when you get up early is what I always say," Destiny quipped.

"Ok, I'm gonna open up the curtains then." Eddy sent the wide bank of cloth scurrying for the walls of the room.

"Wow." Destiny sat up, "That's beautiful," she said, moved by the beautiful colors of the morning sky. "I feel like this must be what it's like to be in heaven, you know?"

"I feel like I am on a high mountain," Munio commented.

Eddy, in jockey shorts, took center stage, the gray and pink and red morning sky as his backdrop. Destiny and Munio watched as Eddy ran through his routine, the dance of a madman to the tune of the coming dawn. Since the window was brighter than the light in the room, Eddy remained greatly silhouetted, though this did not mask his size and the acute nature of his vascularity. The network of vessels fastened like spaghetti barnacles on the peaks of his muscles. When he hit a pose, Eddy's silent motion was punctuated by his powerful breathing. He was a Frankenstein ballerina, minus the jumps, turns and twists, as he held the poses and hoped his audience spoke the language of size.

"Well, what do you think?" Eddy asked when he completed the routine.

"I can't believe it, but you look like you have gained muscle size since last night. You are still ripped, too. I have never seen such a thing happen," Munio said.

"Don't even ask me, Eddy, because I don't get this whole bodybuilder deal. If you want to know if I think you're ripped up, then yeah, you're ripped to shreds. That probably means you look great since I just think you look freaky. I'm sorry." She gave him a sympathetic look.

"I know. I know. This is the sort of thing you got to develop a taste for. Hell, I'm glad you think I look freaky. That is a good sign. Now, I got to go look." He trotted to the mirror. His blue eyes grew large. "God o' mighty damn, Munio, I've got fucking veins in my abs." He turned around to the back, and hit a pose while looking over his shoulder. "I got a damn Christmas tree, man!" His lats fanned out and revealed a series of symmetrical striations that resembled the shape of a Christmas tree. This, in the bodybuilding scene, represents the pinnacle of a well-built back. Eddy jumped around the room. "I got a damn Christmas tree! Yee haw! Jingle bells, jingle bells, jingle all the way!" He sang out in one of the most unmelodic voices either Destiny or Munio had ever known.

"Goddamn, don't sing, Eddy!" Destiny grimaced. "Whatever the fuck you do, boy, do not raise up your voice in song because you can't. You got the

most God awful voice I ever heard!" She laughed as she spoke.

The Friday morning sun began to jostle itself from behind giant, clean, billowy, banks of clouds. Looking like a brilliant tangerine lifesaver, it offered stunning red light and heat they could feel through the thick glass of the window.

Destiny got up and walked to the window. "Feel this heat! I can shut my eyes and feel like I'm at the beach! I wish I was at the beach." She looked comfortable in her body as it stared naked out the window with her. "Eddy, we got to go to the beach soon. Next weekend, what do you say?"

"Yeah, maybe we will, if Hollywood don't call." Eddy gave her a wiggle of his eyebrows from his spot in front of the mirror where he still held court with his image.

"Munio, you want to go to the beach, don't you?" Destiny asked.

"Yes, I do. Where do you go?"

"Gulf of Mexico is closest. It's real pretty. It ain't super duper warm this time of year, but it ain't real crowded, either."

"Oh, is that right? I have never been to a cold beach." He laughed.

"It ain't cold as Alaska or nothing."

"Ah."

Destiny put on a red terrycloth robe and sat in one of the stuffed chairs by the window. "Y'all want coffee? I do."

"I do, too," Munio said.

"I'm calling room service. You want anything else, Munio?"

"Toast. Order me some toast with jelly, please."

"Ok, Eddy?"

"I'm fixing to eat me another batch of them trippin' taters. Y'all go right ahead." This brought a round of laughs.

"Oh God, he'll bust through the walls. You're going to grow so much we'll have to take out the window and lower you to the ground with a crane," Destiny fantasized.

She placed the room service order as Munio slipped on jeans.

Eddy dug his boom box out of one of his bags. He set it up on the round utility table and plugged it in. The room filled with the sound of Lynard Skynard's "Free Bird". Over the course of the next two days, Munio and Destiny would grow to hate this song Eddy played it and posed relentlessly. He turned on the tape, trotted in front of the window once again and went into a full dress rehearsal.

Destiny and Munio sat, helplessly trapped, to endure and support Eddy's preparation, but both of them suddenly realized that this part was going to be an absolute drag. Destiny prayed for the room service order to arrive, hoping that coffee would at least help stabilize her temperament before she said something nasty that she would regret. Munio lay across the bed and watched.

Room service broke up the third run-through. Destiny and Munio

rushed for the coffee and gave each other the eye of commiseration.

"Ok, y'all ready for another run through?" Eddy asked eagerly.

"Eddy, Eddy, eat, you need to eat your potatoes, please," Munio directed. "You can rehearse after that. You will lose muscle at this time if you do not eat. It is an important time, eh?" He patted Eddy on his bare, pimpled back.

"Yeah, ok. Yeah, I need to eat. I'm just getting psyched, you know?"

"Yeah, but listen to Munio," Destiny urged. "You're going to get sick of that dadgum song if you listen to it too much."

"Maybe, maybe." He put on sweatpants and a big ragged T-shirt that bore the inscription "I'm not real smart but I can lift heavy objects".

He flopped on the bed and pulled the first big potato from the bag. It was cold and not particularly tasty, but Eddy had eaten meals for so many months without regard for taste or refinement that he did not even think that it was strange or unsightly.

To Destiny, it was not only strange and unsightly, but downright nause-ating. She would not think of eating a baked potato unless it was piping hot from the oven and loaded with butter, salt, and sour cream. The clincher was that he was doing this first thing in the morning.

"Eddy, how can you eat that?"

"Damn, Destiny." Eddy snorted a laugh and looked over at Munio. "This is the tastiest mother fucker I've had in a while. Man, you go without carbs for a couple of days, and you'd damn eat a picture of a fucking potato." He bit off big bites and chewed very quickly.

"Eddy, chew the food. It will assimilate and digest faster. Also, it might upset your stomach for you to eat so fast, ok?" Munio directed. Eddy nodded as he lit into the third one.

Destiny sipped her coffee in a chair over by the window. She looked down on the city, sixty-one floors below, with its morning rush hour. Never had she observed such a web of human activity. It was a sight that was com-pletely foreign to her, like a view through a microscope.

"I can't believe all that traffic. Why do those people do that everyday?"

"I know that's right." Eddy walked over and looked down. "Damn, like a bunch of toy cars, huh?"

Munio did not care to engage in discussion. He was involved with careful application of the rich creamy squares of butter that were wrapped in golden foil. On top of one diagonal of toast, he lavished one square of butter and the entire contents of one little glass jar of strawberry jelly.

Destiny watching Munio out of the corner of her eye, waved at Eddy behind Munio's back to draw his attention to this procedure. Laying his knife carefully on the edge of the small plate, Munio picked up his decorated piece of toast and began to eat in small bites which he chewed an extraordinary length of time. Finally, after one diagonal had been eaten and another pre-pared, Eddy lit into him.

"Munio, you laying tile over there, or are you going to eat that damn toast?"

Munio jumped to his feet and pointed his finger like a weapon in Eddy's face. "Don't fuck with me when I am eating! I do not humiliate or disturb you when you eat your food, and do not ever do that to me! Do you hear what I am saying, man?" he screamed at Eddy.

Eddy backed up and held his hands up in surrender, while trying to stop his giggling. Destiny did not help as she pointed at Eddy and covered her mouth to subdue her mirth. "All right man. I'm sorry, Munio. We was just funning. Chill, brother. Eat your damn toast. Take all goddamn day. That's cool."

Munio sat back down at the table. "I don't like to be disturbed when I eat. I really do not like that. Don't make fun of me when I'm eating."

"All right. We ain't never seen nobody take so long to fix up a piece of toast, that's all. It's like you was some, it's like you was the Queen of England or something." Eddy chuckled.

"Well, maybe that is who taught me. Belize citizens assume many English customs. We learned proper ways of behaving, and so on, you see," Munio explained gravely.

"Oh, uh huh, I gotcha, bud." Eddy appeased Munio somewhat by appearing interested in this information. "Well, now I know." Eddy gave Destiny a funny look that had her in stitches again. He stared down at his own hand that held potato number seven. "I reckon it's obvious I was raised by wolves. I didn't know what a fork was until a couple of years ago!"

Munio smiled at Eddy, and shook his head. "You are some animal that should be kept out of doors!"

Munio chuckled while Eddy and Destiny breathed a collective sigh of relief. The display of such anger had frightened them.

Eddy made his way through all ten potatoes and was so exhausted that he decided to go back to sleep for a while. Destiny and Munio agreed to take a walk on Peachtree Street.

After an hour's walk, they returned to find Eddy working his way through yet another rerun of "Free Bird".

"Check this out!" Eddy halted the music for a moment. I got veins on my butt. "Look!" He pulled down his underwear to display where little vessels had popped up on top of his buns.

"That's great, Eddy! You are there, brother. You aren't even pumped up now." Munio cheered him on.

"Shooowweee! Look at that butt! It looks so cute!" Destiny kicked off her shoes and flopped down on the bed. "So when does the action begin?"

"Tomorrow morning at nine I weigh in and then the prejudging starts. Tomorrow night is the show."

"All you do is weigh in?"

"No, actually. They do all the judging for the individual weight classes in the morning. The overall they judge tomorrow night with the music and everything."

"What in the hell made you choose that song?" Destiny frowned and shook her head.

"What? Free Bird?"

"Of course, Free Bird, what else?"

"'Cause it's my favorite song, that's why. You don't like it?"

"I never have liked that fucking song."

"Well, I have. I had sex for the first time listening to that song." He smiled and they all cracked up.

"You are kidding?" Destiny droned.

Eddy shook his head no.

"Oh my God! I ain't believing this shit! That's why you chose this song? You got laid for the first time listening to it?"

Eddy nodded. "It's my lucky song, I figure. I play it whenever I need something lucky to happen to me."

"Lucky song, humm. Well, by God, you can't go wrong with a lucky song!" She slapped Eddy on the back. "Bless his little old lucky heart!"

Eddy's precompetition tension began in earnest right then and there and like a drowning man, he pulled Munio and Destiny right down into the boiling sea with him. He didn't mean to, but it was inevitable since the mere pretense of competition breeds anxiety in a soul that is more contagious than hepatitis. Eddy had been severely affected by Destiny's comments about the song. Self doubt began to eat him alive. He sat and bit his fingernails for a while and said nothing, then took a shot of primabolin in hopes that would help reverse his mood. He wanted to pose to his song but felt too self-conscious.

Finally, Destiny tried to right the ship. "Y'all, what is going on here? Eddy, what's the matter with you, boy? You look like somebody told you your dog died! Hell, we're all sittin' around acting like he's goin' in for brain surgery." That got a smile out of Munio.

"I'm just nervous, all right? You'd be nervous too if you ever did anything!" Eddy snapped.

"What the fucking hell is that supposed to mean?" Destiny shot back.

"You don't ever do nothing to challenge yourself, Destiny. You don't know what pressure is, girl!"

Munio tried to subdue a smile because he knew a good rumble was about to let loose. Not that he was glad this storm had developed, but he had a nasty streak that now and then could perversely appreciate a scrape between two friends.

"Eddy Jackson, you better just step back and take a couple of deep breaths because you are fixing to--No! You have done said some things that are way, way out of fucking line!" Destiny was on her feet with her hands on her hips.

336

Her cheeks were flushed, her dark blazed.

Eddy did exactly that. He stepped back and took a couple of deep breaths. If he pissed Destiny off, he figured he'd be down to one fan, and everybody needs a couple of groupies. "I'm sorry. I didn't mean to say that shit. I don't know what's got into me. Suddenly, I feel like I ain't got a muscle in my body. My mind keeps telling me I'm a loser."

Munio spoke up. "Ah, that I understand. You must remember that you decided to do this thing long ago, many months. Don't forget where you have come from. Remember all those heavy workouts? Remember how tired you were? Eh, do you Eddy?"

"Yeah." He smiled like a little boy.

"Tomorrow is the day you will get your reward for all that hard work! Tell me something. What if you planted an apple seed, ok. Then you watch and water and care for it. For years, you do this care for that little tree until one day it finally produces a crop of apples. Would you let some lazy asshole pick your apples and sell them at the market? You would not let that man steal your crop, would you?"

"No, I wouldn't."

"Then, you quit this chicken shit bullshit you got going on here! You got work to do, boy! You told me you wanted to win that goddamn trophy, man! Did you lie to me? Well, did you?"

"No!" Eddy screamed. "No, I didn't lie to you! I want that goddamn trophy, man! That's what I fucking came here for, and that's what I'm motherfucking leaving this suck-ass city with sticking out of my raggedy-ass trunk!"

"That's more like it! You got to fight for it, now more than ever! You got to walk out on that stage like you own it, brother!" He slapped Eddy on the back. "Now, take your fucking clothes off and practice that routine while Destiny and I get drunk and watch you!" He smiled and winked at Eddy.

"Go team go, Munio!" Destiny clapped and in a chant yelled, "Free Bird! Free Bird! Free Bird! Free Bird!"

Eddy stripped off his clothes and cued up the boom box.

Ten times Eddy ran through the routine while Destiny and Munio cheered him on through tortured ears.

"Y'all got to put this dye shit on me. You want to do it now?"

"Better I do it before I get too wasted. I'll be spilling it everywhere, and we'll have to buy a rug!" She laughed.

"I will do it if you want. I think it would be fun." Munio giggled. "I feel like an artistic project this evening."

"Ok, I don't care which one of y'all does it. I just know I sure as hell can't do it." Eddy went to the dresser and handed Munio the bottles. "You better read the directions." Munio gave him a stabbing look, and Eddy caught his mistake right away. "Here," he said, grabbing the boxes back from Munio, "let me read it out loud."

Destiny and Munio had a couple of quick shots of Jack Daniels while Eddy narrated. Eddy then took off his underwear and laid down a couple of towels on the carpet. After enduring a round of humiliation from Destiny and Munio about his ultra-pink dick, he put himself at the mercy of a laughing man to paint his skin.

"Now, you got to get it even, Munio. Destiny, you be sure and watch him, will you? Y'all work together on this, all right? I don't want to look striped or something." Eddy smiled nervously.

"Ok, Eddy, here goes." Munio took the glass bottle, held it upside-down and pressed the sponge applicator against Eddy's skin to release the tanning dye. He started on his back, at the base of his neck, tracing a line straight down his back to the crack of his ass. "It's coming out," Munio reported in a sing-song voice.

"Ewwww, that's cold as hell! Jesus fucking Christ! What in the world have I done! Why can't you just lay out in the sun like they did in the olden days?" Eddy's body had chill bumps as big as some of his smaller pimples. "Hey, did you put that plastic glove on?"

"No, he didn't," Destiny informed him.

"Munio, that shit is really dye. You get it on your hands, and it's going to be with you for a few days."

"I'm already brown. What's a little extra brown, eh?"

Eddy and Destiny laughed.

"Don't move!" Munio ordered.

"All right! All right! What does it look like? I want to see it."

"Damn, it's different all right," Destiny commented, making an "oops" kind of face at Munio behind Eddy's back.

"Hold up, hold up. I got to see." Munio held up the action, and Eddy went to check it in the big mirror in the bathroom. "Damn," he said. "You're right. It's weird, but I ain't ever seen nobody look natural or nothing using this shit."

"It's ok?" Munio asked.

"Hell, yeah, carry on." Eddy took his position on the towels.

Munio painstakingly applied stripe after stripe on Eddy's body until he had covered it all, except his genitals, palms, and the soles of his feet. Munio and Destiny had thought that Eddy already looked unnaturally shaded from trips to the tanning bed, but after the tanning dye, he looked pathological. Like a man with a completely new genetic gift, Eddy's skin was a color not found in nature or on any paint chart in the world. The whites of his eyes stood out like two eggs sunny side up, and their brightness seemed out of place. Also, his teeth, which never were particularly white, gleamed like brand new dentures in contrast to the garish yellow-greenish brown shade of his skin.

This only added one more hardship on Destiny's eyes. She wished in her heart she could say, "Wow, Eddy, you look great!", but the application of the

tanning dye served as the last straw, creating the final visual that made it hard for her to even look at Eddy. She had seen a half-man half-alligator at a side show, Siamese twins still hooked together, a man with bad face cancer, and even a pig born with its stomach on the outside of its body, but Eddy struck her as more hideous than any of these things. This would be something she was going to have to fake her way through.

"Damn," was all Eddy could say as he turned around and around slowly in the full-length mirror. "I look weird as shit, don't I? I reckon that's what they're looking for. You know, they judge you on your tan, too." He looked over at Munio and Destiny. "Ain't that something?" He giggled. Destiny and Munio looked at each other and slugged another shot of Jack. "I guess, I guess, ah, I ah, reckon that it's out of our hands now, y'all. We done did about all that's left to do. I'm going to bed," Eddy said quietly.

It was not late, only about nine o'clock. Eddy slid under the sheets, while Munio and Destiny went down to sit around and have a couple of drinks in the lobby. In one of the wide-open atrium lounges, they took a seat. The tall textured concrete walls leading up to a Plexiglas roof were awash from flood lights loaded with multicolored bulbs. From this five- story view, they could see the front desk clearly with the well dressed clerks smiling courteously at the patrons.

Destiny punched Munio in the arm suddenly. "Look at that!" She pointed to a man lumbering across the lobby. He was an Eddy clone, with stylish baggy workout pants, a satin warm-up jacket that bore the name of a gym, and that hulky shape. "Looks like Eddy, don't he?"

"Well, not just like Eddy, but yes, that shape."

"I can't stand it, Munio. It grosses me out. I'm more turned on by, hell, I don't know, dirt than that shit! I tell you the truth. It is hard on the eyes for me!" Destiny looked at Munio and chuckled.

"I know what you're saying." He smiled. "It will be over soon." He patted her leg.

"Not if he fucking wins, it won't. He'll look like this all the time, but hell, I reckon he likes it. Do you think he's going to win?"

Munio shrugged. "I have no idea. We will see who shows up. That's all I can say." He held up his hands, palms up.

# CHAPTER L

Eddy woke up at the same time as the day before. Today, he was unconcerned about waking his friends. In fact, he meant to wake them. As he cranked the cords of the drapes open, he screamed, "It's showtime! It's show-

time, folks!" In James Brown style, he sang, "Get up off of that thang!"

Munio and Destiny struggled to find clarity in their sleeping brains. They pulled themselves to a sitting position, having bedded down in the same bed so Eddy could have plenty of room to toss and turn.

"What the hell time is it?" Destiny rubbed her eyes and yawned.

"I done told you, girl. It's showtime!" he roared in a deep, announcer-style voice. "Ok, let's see. Munio, how do I look today? I got a feeling, I couldn't look no better."

Munio crawled out from under the covers and walked around Eddy, who was hitting a variety of poses. Munio nodded as he studied Eddy's physique. "Eddy, you're there, man. Congratulations, you're ripped." He held out his hand to shake Eddy's.

"Really?" Eddy said, excitedly as he shook Munio's hand. "Let me go look in the bathroom where the light's better. Shoot, I reckon!" he confirmed from the bathroom. "That dye shit is awful, ain't it? I'm ready to go right now. I don't think I have to worry about my weight at all. I think I'm a couple of pounds under two twenty-five."

"I got to pee." Destiny hung onto the bathroom door frame sleepily, peeking in at Eddy. "Goddamn, I can't hardly look at you under that bright light first thing in the morning! Lord, I'm gonna need a nip to get through this day, baby!"

"You can pee," Eddy told her, and she came in, sat down on the commode, and watched him look himself over. "What do you think?'

"I think you are going to win, that's what!" She reached up and slapped him on the butt. "Buns of steel! You could crack hickory nuts on your ass!" She continued to feel his butt.

"Look out now, honey. Don't handle the merchandise!" Eddy kidded her.

"You going to charge me when you get to be Mr. Dixie?" She wiped herself and stood up.

The contrast between Destiny and Eddy was so great they almost looked like different species. Under her pink skin, Destiny's veins could be seen only vaguely with the aid of the harsh blue fluorescent light. Eddy's strange brown skin crawled with them, along with numerous other unidentified lumps and knots of body parts, like lymph glands at his hips that were never meant to be laid bare enough to be viewed by the naked eye.

"Are you going to eat before you weigh in?" Munio asked.

"Naw, I'm going to wait, just in case I'm close. After prejudging, I'm going to hit up some pancakes and eggs and bacon, and oh yeah," he giggled, "and some water-based test."

"All right brother." Munio walked over to the bedside table. "Let's see what time it is here. Eight o'clock. Ok, I am going to take a shower. Destiny, could you order us some coffee again, please?"

"You want some more toast, too?" She winked at Eddy.

"No, thank you."

After the shower, Munio slipped into a new gear that Destiny had never seen, although Eddy was familiar with it. It was why Munio was here now. His coach persona emerged. There was a special energy about him, and a beauty Destiny and Eddy had not noticed before. Today, he was prepared for battle, and in his mind, that required the appearance of his Mayan warrior alter ego, who had indeed arrived, sans war paint.

* * * * *

It was time for weigh-in, which was in a conference room adjacent to the ballroom where the prejudging and the actual contest would take place. Eddy, Destiny, and Munio stepped into the elevator. The elevators dropped just as fast as they rose, and this morning the sensation was especially brusque on their stomachs already full of butterflies.

Every few floors the car would stop for more passengers, and quite a few of them had the earmarks of Mr. Dixie contestants. The tension was thicker than normal for a crowded elevator ride, as all eyes remained glued on the floor indicator while they descended.

Stylish posters, resting on brass easels, directed traffic to the different functions being held that day. Eddy led the way as he followed the Mr. Dixie signs to the door marked "weigh-in". There were already many contestants sitting in chairs or stretched out on the carpet waiting for the contest director to begin the procedures. Eddy stepped up to the table to check in.

"Hello there." The man stuck out his hand and lisped, "I am Howard Drake, and you are?" He smiled at him seductively.

"Eddy Jackson from Rosedale, Georgia, sir. Pleased to meet you. Heard a lot about you." Eddy smiled and nodded.

"Oh really?" The man chuckled. "Well, don't believe a word of it," he joked as he looked up Eddy's name on the roster. "Ah yes, Mr. Jackson. All right, Eddy, why don't you take a seat, and we'll get started in just a couple of minutes." Eddy nodded and shuffled away from the table.

The last contestant checked in, and Howard Drake stood up to speak to the group. "Good morning, everyone! We have a large group this year, and from what I can see, y'all have brought some muscle. We're going to find out who brought the most real soon. What I want now is for everyone who is not a contestant to wait right outside in the foyer. There are chairs out there, and I believe a coffee station is set up, so help yourselves. Thank you. Don't worry, your fellows will be safe with me, girls!" He rubbed his hands together once and licked his lips.

Munio and Destiny reluctantly left Eddy, but Eddy shrugged it off, waving them on. "I'll be out in fifteen minutes, I bet."

"Ok, now, men. I want everybody to break it down into posing suits, and

when your name is called, head right on up here to the scale. Any questions?" Howard Drake looked around, smiled, and continued. "Ok, then. After you weigh in, you might want to go directly to the warm-up room because we will begin prejudging at ten o'clock. Good luck, gentlemen!"

All seventy-two contestants stripped down to their posing suits, which made the heart rates rise and the palms sweat. The posing suits were minute, composed of one half the cloth of a bandanna, in a brilliant assortment of colors. Fast as the flick of a snake tongue, the men's eyes danced over the room. They made mental notes, compared biceps, quads, and everything in-between. Every man felt like every other man was bigger. Panic and dread caused their faces to flush and burn, hidden behind their tanning dye masks.

Silence hung over the room, except for Howard Drake's cheerful voice and an occasional contestant who returned an answer to him at the scale. The men postured with bravado. When Eddy's name was called, he stuck his chest out as far as it would go, held his arms so far away from his body he could have carried basketballs under them, and walked like his legs were big as fifty-five gallon drums. It would have been comical, except since every one of them did it out of sheer terror, the humor escaped them.

"Eddy, hop right up here." Howard Drake directed him to stand on the scale. "Let's see now." He waited for the digital readout to steady itself. "Two hundred and twenty-three pounds. I believe you're going to be a light heavy-weight today, aren't you?" Drake smiled at him. Eddy smiled back. "You can get off now."

"Oh, ok. How many are supposed to be in my class?"

"Looks like fifteen. Ok, you're ready to roll. We will begin the judging on time. Oh, and do you have your music tape?"

"Oh, yeah, let me get it." Eddy trotted back to his bag, dug the tape out, and trotted back. "Here you go."

Howard Drake smiled until he looked down at the selection written on the tape. "'Free Bird'?" he said, with his head still lowered. He peered over his glasses to deliver a distinct look of disgust. Eddy shot him a horrified smile and left the table on the verge of tears.

Destiny and Munio saw Eddy exit the room and walked hurriedly over to greet him. "How did it go? Did you make weight ok?" Destiny questioned anxiously, in the light of his hang dog face.

"Yeah, yeah, I made weight. Two twenty-three." He looked at Munio. "That queen don't like my song either," he said in a small boy's voice.

Munio and Destiny laughed. "What did he say?" Munio asked.

"Nothing. He just gave me a dirty look." He rolled his eyes and allowed a sheepish grin to crawl across his face.

"Did you tell that man that, hey mister," Munio pounded his own chest with an angered passion. "that is my lucky song, not yours. Did you tell that man that?" Munio asked emphatically.

342

Eddy and Destiny giggled at Munio's protectiveness of Eddy. "Naw, I should have. I got paranoid instead."

Munio continued, "You should have said, I did not know this was a dance contest. I thought you want to see how much muscle I have, eh?"

Eddy and Destiny roared out loud.

"Really, goddamnit!" Destiny agreed.

"Fuck it! I'm just ready to do it. You know what? I'm just going to eat a couple of protein bars before prejudging. We ain't got time to go do a whole breakfast deal. Sorry Munio. You want one? Destiny? I got a whole bunch of them."

"No, no, I wait to eat. I'm not worried about that now. We got a show to win, boy! Don't you forget that! I don't want to hear this paranoid shit you are saying! You-"

Eddy broke in. "Sorry to interrupt, but let's go in the warm-up room and let me sit down. Then you can finish yelling at me, ok?" He grinned and slapped Munio on the back.

* * * * *

The warm-up room was already bustling with people, and tension hung thick in the air. In one corner sets of dumbbells, a flat bench, and assorted free weights with barbells were scattered. Eddy scanned the room and chose an abandoned corner in which to set up camp. He plopped down on the carpet and dug in his bag for the protein bars. After he had ripped one open and gnawed off a chunk, he nodded at Munio to continue.

"Yes, well, as I was saying, Eddy. You came out of that room like you were yesterday. Don't worry about everybody else. You worry about what you think. I want you to relax and have fun. You have worked hard for this. You used to move like a bull, a clumsy bull, but you worked hard and now you move like a, ah." Munio started chuckling as he looked over at Destiny, who sat on the floor listening to the pep talk. "Like a, not so clumsy bull, like a girl bull." They all cracked up. "I want you to think about what you're doing. Think feminine, move gracefully. The best bodybuilders don't pose in their routines like the sumo wrestlers or something. They are graceful like dancers. Remember this, eh?" Munio kicked Eddy's foot playfully. Eddy nodded as he chewed quickly. "Hurry up, I want us to rehearse."

"You ready for that surprise, Munio?" Destiny grinned and winked at Eddy.

"Surprise? What surprise?" Eddy looked back and forth from Destiny to Munio trying to figure out what they were talking about.

"Yes, I believe so. Let's do it." Munio clapped his hands and paced a few feet away and then back to them.

Destiny had been carrying the small backpack she used for a purse. From it, she pulled a bottle of champagne and three plastic champagne glasses.

"What is this?" Eddy said. "I can't drink now. I'll get fucked up as shit!"

He howled. "Y'all are crazy!"

"No, we're not. You never heard of this? It is a very common practice for top bodybuilders right before they go on stage, prejudging too, to have a glass of wine. Since your diet has been absent of sugar, this wine, which is mostly sugar, will enhance your hardness. Not that you need it, but you can never be too hard, eh? Anyway, I want it to take the edge off a little. Don't worry, it's ok. Trust me." Munio winked at Eddy.

"All right, hoss, if you say so, by God, I'm gonna do it today. Let's chuga-lug." Eddy, having not had a drink in a very long time, was excited about this and, as Munio had hoped, it distracted him from his concern about the contest.

Destiny filled the little glasses. "Cheers to Mr. Dixie!" Destiny toasted, and they cheered. Their plastic cups made a dull click.

Eddy drank his down in one swallow and emitted a long "ahhh."

"Ok now, boy, get up here. Stretch out real good, eh?" Munio instructed.

"Ok, now what?" He asked Munio.

"Let's go pump up a little. Come over here." Munio led him over to the weights. "Take those thirties, and do some overhead presses. Do them til you feel pumped."

Eddy did twenty reps and set them down.

"Ok, let's do some pushups. Same thing. Do them til you feel pumped." Eddy obeyed. "Good, good. You look great, you know." Munio patted him on the shoulder. "Ok, get those thirties again, and do some bent-over rows." Eddy put the weights down when he finished. "How do you feel? You pumping up good?"

"Yeah, I feel good."

"Ok, let's pump up those legs a little." Munio loaded a bar with one forty-five pound plate on each end. "I'm going to power clean this, and I want you to back up to me and take it on your back for a few squats, ok?"

"Ok."

Munio powered the bar quickly to his chest. Eddy took the bar, got his stance set and did twenty squats with the weight.

"Ok, back up. I got it," Munio said, as he lowered the bar down the car-pet. "You get a pump?"

"Fucking right, man."

"Again, take the thirties and let's work on the bicep, eh? Hurry now, Eddy. What time is it, Destiny?"

"Ten til."

"Ok then." Munio put his hands in his pockets, paced back and forth slowly, and watched Eddy. When he put the dumbbells down, Munio was ready to move on. "Take your warmups off now." Eddy's lime green Span-dex posing suit glowed like a piece of radioactive Key Lime pie. Destiny and Munio blinked twice upon first glance at it. "Ok, now begin the routine. Just

do the first three poses and stop." Without a word, Eddy followed Munio's instruction. "Flow, Eddy, think about dancing, power dancing, strong, passionate! Try it again, and go through the first six poses, ok?"

"Ok." Eddy tried to relax as he ran through the poses. "How about getting me another hit of that champagne, Destiny?"

"Sure, just a second," Destiny said, eager to have something to do.

Eddy slugged down the glass. "All right, that's better."

"Now, go through the entire routine, Eddy. Take your time. You are using a slow song. Take your time hitting your poses, and then hold them, ok?"

"All right. Hey y'all got to grease me up here in a minute." Eddy bent over and toweled off the full brow of sweat he had collected. "Damn, I'm hot. Fucking November, I'm sweatin' like a whore in church, and all I'm wearing is a fucking thong. Shows you how nervous I am." He snickered uneasily.

"You're doing great. You're posing fine." Munio put his arm around Eddy. "I don't see anybody that looks any better than you. Really, I mean it. So, all you have to do is pose as good as you can. You can do it. It will make or break your success today, Eddy." Eddy nodded as Munio pulled away from him.

Just then, Howard Drake moved to the center of the warm-up room. "Listen, everybody! In five minutes, we will begin introductions. When you hear your name called, come line up. We will begin with the lighter classes. As you know, it is in the prejudging that the winners of each weight division are selected, and so go out there and show us something, guys! Best of luck to all of you!"

"Destiny, go reach in my bag and bring out that can of PAM, please." Eddy pointed to his bag.

"PAM?"

"Yeah, uh huh, that's what you're gonna grease me up with. Works great."

Destiny shook her head at yet another hard to believe facet of bodybuilding. She found the PAM and walked back over to Eddy. "Now what?"

"Spray me down real good."

Destiny worked her way around Eddy's body. That PAM made him shine like high gloss lacquer. With this final coat of sheen, she was amazed at how good his skin suddenly looked.

"Man, that stuff looks great, don't it?" Eddy remarked, smiling as he looked down at his shiny muscled-up leg. "Fat free too, you know?" He winked at Destiny.

"Is that it?" she asked.

"Looks good to me. Thanks, honey. Oh yeah, you know, just one more thing. Will you get my number and pin it on?"

"Pin it onto what, your wanger?"

"Whatever," he chuckled.

She retrieved the small white paper circle with a big black number forty-

five on it. Somehow, she managed to safety pin it to the little suit without drawing blood. "All right, Mr. Forty-five, you're ready to go."

Munio kept Eddy posing and stretching. His strategy was to keep him moving so he didn't have time to psych himself out again.

"You know what? I got to pee." Eddy looked around to see if there might be a bathroom adjacent to the room.

"Bathroom's out there in the lobby." Munio pointed.

"Damn, I don't want to go out there like this. I'll mess my grease up if I put on clothes."

"You sure don't want to wet your pants wearing that rag either," Destiny pointed out.

"Is that champagne bottle empty?"

"Yeah," Destiny replied.

"Give it here. I'm hittin' the stairwell." She handed him the bottle and in two minutes, he returned, grinning.

"Where's the bottle?"

"I left the motherfucker out there. Hope nobody thinks it's champagne!" They all laughed.

"Light heavyweights! Line up here please, as I call your name!" Announced the man who was coordinating introductions.

"Well, I reckon we're about ready." Eddy smiled and rocked back and forth on his feet.

"Eddy Jackson!"

"See ya in a minute!" Eddy trotted over to the line that was forming.

All shaved, greased, and dyed like Easter chicks with bright-colored swatches covering their groins, these Georgia boys had come from all over the state to enter this show. Most were loaded up, and they would be the winners when everything was said and done. The ones who weren't looked pathetically smaller. In fact, they looked soft and puny compared to the mass of Eddy's breed.

The small crowd in the ballroom gave the men only a smattering of applause, but there would be a packed house tonight for the real show. Destiny had gone out front to sit and let Munio work with Eddy for the duration of the prejudging. She was glad to get out of that room full of tension.

* * * * *

The announcer worked his way down the line. Each man stepped out and waved graciously to the hundreds of empty chairs. All of them smiled as if that spotlit stage were their favorite place on earth, and they were having the time of their lives sucking their guts in, trying to finagle a way to win that trophy. A sharp pain from the rush of adrenaline rocketed through Eddy's body, causing him to cough just as he stepped forward to be acknowledged.

Destiny got goose bumps all over, jumped to her feet, and clapped for

346

Eddy. She was so nervous for him that when she sat back down, she kept her fingers crossed on both hands for luck.

As Eddy's class moseyed off stage, a long waiting game set in. Since Eddy was in the next to heaviest class, he would have to wait for approximately fifty men to go through their posing routines. Munio had Eddy lie down for a while and do nothing.

One of the contestants, the man who Munio felt was Eddy's biggest threat, was also lying down a few feet away.

"Hey, I'm Jim Dalton." He reached over and stuck out his hand to Eddy.

"Hey, Eddy Jackson." Eddy smiled and reluctantly shook his hand.

"Gonna be a while, looks like." He lay back on his workout bag that was serving as a pillow.

"Yep, shore looks like it," Eddy said.

"This your first?"

Eddy bristled a bit. "Naw, I was in a couple of little shows down in south Georgia."

"Uh huh. I'm really just slummin' doing this one. I need a qualifier for the nationals."

"Oh, is that right?"

"Yeah, plan to turn pro about this time next year."

Eddy felt a flash of anger rise up in him. "Well, so do I."

The man sat up a little, looked at Eddy, and sneered. "This is your third show, and you think you're turning pro?" He threw his head back and laughed.

"You think that's funny? Hey Munio, this man over here thinks he's turning pro, and he ain't even got no legs! That, my man, is funny." Eddy leaned over in the man's face. Munio chuckled prepared to step in if necessary.

Eddy stood up, adjusted his posing suit, and looked down on the man. He stuck out his left leg and hit a razor sharp quad pose. "That there is a leg, buddy." Eddy turned his back to the man. "I got to piss again. I'm going to see if my champagne bottle's still in the stairwell."

When Eddy came back from the stairwell, his ego was pumped and ready. The conversation with Jim Dalton had spurred him on so that he could hardly wait to get out on the stage to kick that man's ass. Munio was so grateful for the incident he wanted to go shake Jim Dalton's hand, but he thought better of it.

Finally, the light heavyweights were introduced. Ten contestants went before Eddy. Backstage, Eddy paced and did a few pushups, a little posing and fired condescending looks at Jim Dalton. He repeated this cycle five times, all the while thinking about how Lou Ferrigno and Arnold Schwartzenegger went at it backstage in Pumping Iron. It was a perfect fantasy for this moment.

"Eddy, I want to go out front to watch you. You will be next. Now, don't

forget-"

Eddy interrupted rudely. "I got it, Munio. You don't have to tell me nothin' else. I'm fucking going to kick some ass. So just go on." Eddy turned his back on Munio, who just stood there for a moment, waved at Eddy in disgust, and went to take a seat by Destiny.

"And now, contestant number forty-five, from the Dixie Ironworks in Rosedale, Georgia, let's welcome, Eddy Jackson," The announcer said enthusiastically.

Eddy stomped out on stage like a caveman. Munio shook his head and slapped himself on the forehead. Eddy grinned like a mule eating briars and went into the routine with a fury. In the second row, Munio and Destiny could hear him breathing and grunting as he put everything he had into maximum muscle contraction on every pose. The network of veins that clothed his muscles made for an eerie yet spectacular display. Although there was no grace to his presence, there was power and muscle. Munio knew those components would be priorities of the judges and would award him first place. The routine lasted for only one minute, and then Eddy bowed to the house and shook his muscled arms over his head like a Saturday night wrestler.

Munio got up to go backstage, and Destiny followed right along behind him. "How do you think he did?"

"I don't know. No one has more muscle than Eddy. This other guy might pose better, though. He might can show what he's got better than Eddy. We will see."

"How did I look? Great or what? I fucking kicked ass out there, didn't I?" Eddy bragged, laughing and slapping Munio and Destiny on the shoulders.

"You looked great, but you did none of the dancing movements as I said for you to do," Munio reminded him.

"Fuck it. I ain't no goddamn dancer like you and your little faggot friends! I just did it best as I could, all right?"

Destiny got up in Eddy's face. "Don't talk to him like that! You fucking asshole! Who the fuck do you think you are? Somebody goddamn special? You ain't God's gift to nothing, you ungrateful bastard!"

"Hey bitch, you better get the fuck out of my face 'fore I knock the fucking hell out of you!" Eddy glared at her.

"I'll be up in the room, Munio. I ain't playing this shit!" Destiny said to Munio as she stormed away.

Munio, feeling that a testosterone overload was the source of Eddy's obnoxious behavior, ignored the scene completely and knew he would most likely apologize shortly. "Let's go watch the other guys in your class. The ones that are your main competition have not gone yet," Munio said.

"Ok, let me get my stuff. I'll meet you out there."

Munio reclaimed his seat and watched the last men pose. Jim Dalton came across very well. Although his muscle was not as massive as Eddy's, he

was more symmetrical and, as Munio feared, a much more experienced poser. He worked his body beautifully, and Munio was not sure how Eddy would fare. It was impossible for Eddy to not place in the top three, he figured, but beyond that, it would remain a mystery until tonight.

Eddy came and took a seat by Munio. "What do you think?"

"I don't know, Eddy. If the judges want muscle alone, you will win, but if they want a more total package, you will lose. There is no way that you will go home without placing in the top three. Of this, I would bet money."

"That guy ain't better than me, do you think?" Eddy growled.

"He handled himself well on stage, Eddy."

"Fuck it! I don't think he did! Who are you for anyhow, you fucking faggot!" Eddy spat the insults at Munio.

Munio sat up in his chair and looked Eddy square in the eyes. "Boy, I have been trying to be patient with your little temper tantrums, but I am running out of patience. What is your particular problem all of a sudden?"

"I ain't got no--You're my particular problem. I thought you was my coach, my support team, you and Destiny. She's done run off, and you're pulling for the other guy. What am I supposed to act like?"

"Eddy, I think you need to eat or something. Maybe that champagne has now made you so grouchy. Just try to not say anything else, and let's go get you a nice meal, eh? We have done our work here. Let us begin our celebration, eh?" He kindly patted Eddy on the back, and Eddy shut up.

* * * * * *

They got on the elevator to go up to the room. "You have made Destiny very angry. She has been here for you, Eddy. I want you to make up with her, ok? That woman is not fun when she is angry, and if the both of you continue to argue, I am going to leave the state!" He gave Eddy a crazy look that made him giggle.

"All right! I just got so hyped up. I want to win, Munio. Man, I just want to win." The car stopped on their floor with a ding.

Destiny was drinking a shot of Jack Daniels and watching Star Search when they entered the room.

"Destiny," Eddy began as he got down on his knees in front of her chair. "I would like to beg your humble forgiveness for the insults I bestowed upon you. If you would continue to be an active member of the Eddy Jackson for Mr. Dixie election committee, I would be honored. Also, tonight after this is all over, you can beat me with a whip or a belt or a towel or something like one of them leather mistresses." He looked up sheepishly.

"I tell you what, you little redneck son of a bitch. You better get on your knees after what I seen down there this morning. Jesus H. Christ! I could not believe you. Have you apologized to this fine gentleman over here?" Destiny pointed to Munio. "Do you even have enough sense to realize all the fucked

up things you said to him? Insulting his friends? You are a fucked up piece of shit, Eddy Jackson!"

"No, I guess I hadn't." Eddy frowned and looked at Munio. "I'm sorry for talking so ugly. I really am," Eddy said sincerely, and walked over to Munio with open arms.

"Apology accepted." Munio smiled at Eddy, and the two of them hugged.

"Now what?" Destiny asked them. "Although I'm scared to ask."

"Let's go eat a big old breakfast downstairs in the restaurant. I'm paying!" Eddy suggested excitedly.

"Then, I'm going!" Destiny said. "Except I got to wait and see who wins the grand prize. It won't be but a minute."

"I hate that shit!" Eddy said. "It's so hokey. Ain't none of them bastards got a thimbleful of talent." He disappeared into the bathroom while Destiny laughed quietly to herself, "Like you do." She looked over at Munio, who smiled and shrugged his shoulders.

After breakfast, Eddy stood naked and scrutinized himself in the full length mirror. "You don't think I'm smoothing out, do you?" Eddy asked Munio.

"Eddy, you have too much imagination. Uh, I mean," he snapped his fingers to try to think of what he meant to say, "hallucinations, that's it." Munio stated.

"I was fixing to say," Destiny countered wryly, "he's got about as much imagination as that rug." She cackled.

"Fuck imagination, who needs it anyhow?" He shot her a bird as he pulled on a pair of cutoff sweatpants and flopped down on the bed. "What's on the tube?"

"Fifty-fucking-something channels, they say, but you know how that goes, and this being Saturday afternoon, probably forty-fucking-nine of them are fishing." She snorted as she thumbed through a tabloid purchased at the gift shop in the lobby.

"Hey yeah, let's watch some fucking fishing, man. Want to, Munio?"

"Watch fishing?" Munio laughed. "Sounds like something Americans would do."

"Hey, don't be putting Americans down, bud. Love 'em or leave 'em, pancho, Eddy responded as he started working the remote control like he was sending a message in Morse code.

"I hate when you do that. Can't you just watch something for a minute, and see what the hell it is?" Destiny badgered him.

"No, I can't."

"Listen to this." Destiny read aloud from her magazine. "'A couple in a small village in the south of Wales claims to have grown a weeping rose bush. It was documented by the National Scientific Society of the United Kingdom

350

that sounds of a distressing nature were recorded coming from the bush. A yellow Graham Thomas variety of English rose, the plant was also reported to excrete a fluid from the center of several blooms in conjunction with its cries. Parapsychologists attribute this phenomenon to the fact that a great battle was fought on the land in the 1600s, and the rose is channeling, from its earth, the tears of the loved ones of the dead soldiers who lost their lives in the struggle.'"

"You don't believe that shit, do you?" Eddy crowed. "Can't you see you're wearing this corsage, and all of a sudden it starts saying shit like "'I want my mama."'

"That is hell. I love these magazines, but why is all this shit always in the south of fucking Wales?"

Listening quietly, Munio smoked and stared out at the drifting clouds. He believed the story of the rose bush and was reminded of the rose garden in the town square in Monkey River Town. An Englishman, Avery James Gibson, started it one hundred years ago. He was a horticulturist from England who was famous for his hybrid roses. During his passage to this new land of Belize, the ship encountered terrible storms that claimed the lives of many onboard. Every member of his family, including his four children, his wife, and his elderly mother were swept overboard and lost at sea. In the hold of that ship, he had brought a dozen of his precious rose bushes. When the ship finally docked at Monkey River Town and his roses were unloaded, only six of them appeared to have a chance of survival. He planted these six in the town square for all to enjoy, and named each after a member of his family who had perished. He bred hundreds of bushes from these plants, and thus, in some way, his loved ones lived on till this very day. Munio smiled at the thought of how Mr. Gibson would have loved to have heard this tale of the weeping rose bush.

"Look at that! Look at that!" Eddy pointed to the tv where a man struggled desperately to land a sailfish.

Munio watched, mesmerized and was sickened by the desperation of the big helpless fish. He remembered the strange dream he had had of the big fish that bit off his head like the tip of a cigar. He got up and walked to the window to avoid the view of the television screen.

"What's the matter, Munio? I thought you'd like this shit, man? Didn't y'all go sail fishing down yonder where you're from?"

"Some did. I did not. I never killed for such a sport. I killed for my supper, but never to let a fish suffer as that fish is suffering."

"Damn, Munio, you turning pussy on me today or what?" Eddy snickered.

"Hey, I'm a pussy, you know, Eddy. It ain't such a bad thing to be. I don't want to see that shit either. Turn it off!" Destiny ordered him.

"Damn, it's just a damn t-"

"Turn if off right now, Eddy!" she repeated.

"All right, all right!" He flipped the station several times before landing on Soul Train. "Here y'all go. This ought to make y'all happy. Look, Munio." Eddy put on a high lispy voice. "Dancing, it's dancing! Come look!" He rolled on the bed, letting off a round of sinister laughter. "I'm going to take a nap, y'all. Here." He threw the remote control to Destiny, who luckily caught it just before it hit her in the face. She was coiled to curse him, but upon seeing he had turned his back, opted to say nothing.

Destiny flipped the stations. Eddy's brutish behavior had left its effect. His mean spirit reminded Munio of many people who had treated him with disrespect. Ordinarily, it was easy to walk away, but not today. Today he was caught up in the net of Eddy's little life, Eddy's little dream. It angered Munio that ultimately Eddy's stupidity, perhaps, had sabotaged his chances to win, but over that, Munio had no control. He decided to go outside and left the room without explanation.

Destiny's heart ached, like it ached when she had been abused by Jimmy Ray. Locked in some silly circumstance with a man again, she felt she had allowed herself to be abducted from her life to serve as an accessory to his. She was disappointed that the humorous light-hearted fun the three of them shared now had disappeared. She felt bad for Munio as she thought of how Eddy had stepped way out of bounds with his words. When Eddy's snoring dominated the room, she abandoned him and sought higher ground down below on Peachtree Street.

Munio wandered to a park and sat alone on a short pink marble wall. It was very windy, and he felt great relief as the stale energy and harsh words were blown off him and into the cool air. As he smoked, the wind blew his smoke away so fast that he could not quite tell if he really was smoking or not.

Destiny arrived a few minutes later and spotted Munio. They watched the abrupt gusts of wind surprise people who walked by or attempted to read newspapers. Destiny pulled a quart of Jack Daniels, shrouded in a brown bag out of her backpack. The clear glass spout stuck up like a sprouting crystal. She took an easy swallow and passed the bottle to Munio. They played oral ping-pong until there was no more sloshing to be heard.

Destiny slapped Munio on the knee. "We'll get through this now, won't we, bud?" She winked at him.

Munio contemplated her scar, which originally had jumped out and stung him like a screech on a blackboard. Today, he felt it was a sign of how fiercely she guarded her individuality. He appreciated her toughness, her standing up to Eddy, and her standing up for him.

"Yes, it will all be over soon. Let us find another bottle of this stuff to help, eh?" Munio elbowed her lightly in the ribs. "I got a feeling we're going to need it."

"Going to need it? Honey, I ain't drinking this shit because I'm thirsty. We're cooped up with the biggest jerk in Georgia. He might not win that Mr. Dixie trophy, but I'm a mind to go have him one made up that reads 'First Place--Biggest Asshole in the State of Georgia.'" Munio laughed as Destiny continued, "I ain't lying. He better hope he has a major attitude adjustment or something. Jesus fucking Christ." She exhaled a loud whoosh.

"I know what you are saying. You ready to go back?" She nodded.

Munio bought two bottles of Jack Daniels. Destiny and he had decided that if bad came to worse, they would have a Jack Daniels chugging contest. Sweet relief would come quickly in the form of drunken bliss or flat-out unconsciousness.

Eddy was up getting ready for the big showdown when they returned to the room. "Hey, where y'all been?" he said cheerfully.

"Hanging out in this park down the street," Destiny said.

"Brother, you ready for victory?" Munio said.

"I am, Munio. I want to get there plenty early. I might want to pump up a lot more for the show than I did this morning, you know?"

"Ok."

"I got a good feeling, Munio. I just think this is about muscle, and I am the man with the muscle. Ain't nobody can touch me." Eddy held his hands up in defense as he saw Munio's eyebrows narrowing in response. " I know, I know, I'll try to pose good and all, but fuck it, I got the goddamn muscle, ain't I? I ain't even worried about it," he lied.

Munio nodded and decided to forego his posing lecture. "Ok brother, ok."

"Well, cheers to you, honey. I hope you win, but you know what?" Destiny got right up in Eddy's face, flashing a sweet smile.

"What?" He put his hands on her hips, smiling back at her.

"I hope above all you don't start acting like an asshole so I'll have to kill you!" She reached down and pinched his dick.

"Ouch!" He grabbed his crotch, scowling. "That hurt, damnit!"

"Well, don't forget it, sugar, because it'll get a lot worse if you don't act right." She winked at him and pretended to take another pass at his crotch, sending him leaping back from harm's way. Destiny giggled happily at his reaction.

"Style, Eddy. You must have style if you want to win."

"Style this, mofo!" He laughed, shoving his big wormy bicep in Munio's face. "I got style. I got class." He moved and started a spontaneous chant. "I'm gonna kick all them motherfuckers in the ass! I got style! I got class! I'm gonna kick all them mother fuckers in the ass!" He laughed enthusiastically while his fan club shook their heads in humored disgust.

The warm-up room was every bit as tense as it had been that morning. This night's outcome would be burned in each contestant's soul as the irre-

versible symbol of what all the thousands of pounds of weights moved and the hundreds of workouts ultimately meant. Each one would win or lose and would be granted validation or humiliation for their efforts. Either way, that moment on stage, not all those workouts, would be played and replayed in each contestant's mind a million times before it would be put to rest.

Saying little, Eddy pumped up with Munio by his side to encourage him. Eddy was hell bent to go his own way in this phase of the contest and virtually ignored Munio's presence. One by one, the lighter classes were eliminated, and the tension began to diminish backstage. The show was nearly over and the warm-up room nearly empty by the time Eddy's turn had come.

"Eddy Jackson, you'll be next." the stage hand informed Eddy.

"Thanks," Eddy said. "Spray me down with that PAM again, Munio. Ok, I'm ready! I'm ready!" He inhaled and exhaled deeply, and gathered up a head of steam just like he did when he was going to squat heavy. He slapped Munio on the palm.

"Style, Eddy! Come on now! This is you! This is what you want! Go get it! Take your time!" Munio reminded him, and Eddy nodded.

"The next contestant is number forty-five. He weighed in this morning at two hundred twenty-three pounds. He is from Rosedale, Georgia, and trains at the Dixie Ironworks! Let's give Eddy Jackson a hand, folks!"

The auditorium was full now, and Eddy was taken aback. In fact, when "Free Bird" started cranking out, Eddy just stood there frozen. He caught up quickly, but he looked like a man caught in a tarpit as he reverted to his old posing habits of powerful yet jerky movements. He even resorted to his old never-ending bounce. Munio cursed under his breath as he watched from the wings, and Destiny cursed and groaned from her seat in the audience. Later, he would explain this to Munio as his attempt to be stylish.

Quickly, his work was over. He padded off stage on his brown-colored feet, waving at the crowd. Destiny clapped and smiled because the whole ordeal was almost over.

"I looked good, didn't I?" Eddy was ecstatic, breathing heavily from exertion and excitement.

"Yes, you did," Munio lied. "We will just have to wait now. Stay up and moving for the posedown."

After the last contestant in the light heavyweight had performed his posing routine, they all were asked to return to the stage as a group for an elimination posedown. Upon the announcer's signal, they all grinned maniacally and hit every best pose they had. After about fifteen seconds, the announcer asked them to stop. When the head judge signaled, the announcer took from him the final top five list.

The men all stood with their hearts about to jump from their chests as the announcer began. "When I call your number, step forward, please. Thirty-six!" With each announcement, cries of approval arose from the crowd.

"Sixteen, forty-one, forty-five." Destiny gave a whistle as Eddy grinned and stepped forward. "And number sixty-two. All the rest of you gentleman, please file off. Let's give them a hand. Now, let's have a front double bicep pose, please." The men complied and held the pose until further instructions. "Side tricep, please." All in a row they strained so hard, they seemed on the verge of implosion. "Rear lat spread." Eddy held taut as an arrow on a bow. "Now, a little free style posing, please, gentlemen." Some racy dance music blasted from the loudspeakers, and the men moved like frenzied seagulls scrambling for crusts of bread, each jumping in front of the other one to be best viewed by the panel of five judges seated below the stage. This kept up another fifteen seconds, until the head judge signaled the announcer. The music stopped, and Eddy felt his breathing could be heard all over the ballroom. "All right, gentlemen, we have the final three. Of course, the first place winner will go on to compete in the final posedown for the overall trophy and the title of Mr. Dixie. In third place, number sixteen, Robert Biltmore!" A nice round of applause arose. Eddy was very encouraged now. "In second place, number sixty-two, Jim Dalton!" Another round of applause rang out. Destiny crossed fingers on both hands for Eddy, and Munio held his breath, hoping for the best. Eddy was just beaming inside. With that Jim Dalton out of the way, he knew he had won. "And now, ladies and gentlemen, the first place winner of the light heavyweight division, number forty-one, Ricky Blalock! Congratulations, Ricky!" The crowd went wild, while Eddy had almost taken a step forward to receive the prize.

Eddy's knees grew weak underneath him, and his body began to shake from the shock. Numbness set in as he managed to clap for the winners and file off stage with the others. Ricky Blalock danced and jumped up and down. Munio put his arms around Eddy and hugged him.

"You did the best you could, Eddy. I'm proud of you, brother."

Eddy walked over to where his stuff was, unable to make eye contact with anyone, especially Munio. His eyes were full of stinging salty tears, and his gut felt as if it were full of broken glass. He wanted to lie on the floor face down and kick and scream, but he didn't dare do that. He was a grown man, after all, who, for this moment, had to, find some grace, swallow his pride and his tears. If he looked down long enough, he could stem the tide welling in his eyes, and in a few minutes, hold his head up. His head and neck felt as if he had been stung by a hundred bees. He was engulfed in a sea of flames fueled by his self-imposed embarrassment and betrayed confidence of his sure victory.

Destiny and Munio waited in the foyer outside the warm-up room for Eddy. He moved like a wounded man, slow and shaken.

"Sorry, Eddy, honey." Destiny went to put her arms around him and hug him, but he recoiled from her touch as if it were physically painful.

"I can't believe it's over," he said in a soft voice. "I want to take a shower.

Will y'all come up to the room with me, please?"

"You know we will, boy!" Destiny assured him sweetly. "We got some partying to do! You sure enough need to get that fucking PAM scraped off you before you start drawing flies." Destiny and Munio laughed. Eddy looked up briefly and managed a hint of a smile as they stepped into the express elevator.

# CHAPTER LI

Destiny chopped out lines while Munio watched. Both of them swilled down shots of Jack Daniels. They were feeling very festive, with little residual sadness about the outcome of the contest.

Eddy stood motionless as the hot shower rained on him. The heat felt good on his body. He soaped up with a washcloth and scrubbed himself. His muscles now felt like rubbery lumps all over him. He bore down with the cloth in hopes that the dye would wash away, but it didn't. It would be Wednesday afternoon next week before that stuff would begin to budge, and until then, he would be yellow-green bronze.

There was nothing to do now but live a life like other people lived. He had no special plans anymore, and he had no reason to do anything. His brain could not quickly adjust the sign on the front of the bus that had read Mr. Dixie or Bust. Without that promise, and without that trophy, his being was taken out at the knees, devastated. The mirror was all fogged up in the bathroom, but it was such a habit for him to look at himself in the mirror that he toweled off a big spot. The light was harsh, and Eddy's face looked awful. Without his spark, his smile, his hardened, leathery skin looked like forty miles of bad road. A man of twenty-three gazed at the face of a much older man. He was a desperado, finally cornered with nowhere else to turn but to himself. Eddy would have to fight himself now for the right to grow or die. If not for the fact the only tool available in that bathroom was a hairbrush, he might have tried to take his own life right then and there. He put the lid down and sat on the commode. The steam from the heat of the shower formed a small gray cloud floating in the warm air of the bathroom. Confined in this space is where Eddy wanted to spend the night, spend the rest of his life. He wished he would never have to see anyone or speak to anyone again. Munio and Destiny were no longer allies. He thought they surely must be out there right now laughing at him for being such a loser. He could never go back to the gym again and face everyone who had expected him to win. Taking a deep breath, he covered his face with the thick, soft, white towel. The darkness felt good and safe. It was a great relief to not be able to see anything at all. With no eyes, he had no sad and weary face to confront, no pimples on his back, no yellow-green skin, no sight of the enormous muscles that had betrayed him

on that stage.

A knock came on the bathroom door. "Eddy?" Destiny called softly. "You drowned in there, baby?"

Eddy sighed, his head still covered by the towel. "No, I'm all right," He replied slowly.

"You coming out anytime soon?"

"I reckon. I'll be out in a little bit."

"Ok, sooner you start drinking, the better you'll feel."

His body moved through the motions of a silent laugh. It was true that he saw his only way out of this state of mind tonight was to get as fucked up as his body would let him. His cloud of doom lifted ever so slightly just thinking about it. "Fuck it," he thought, "I'll try to drink those two alkies under the goddamn table." He said weakly, "Coke, I'll have to load up on a bunch of that coke. I sure hope she brought a bunch." The steam from the bathroom raced out to expand its territory as Eddy opened the door.

"All right, everybody, start pouring and start chopping because I am in need of a major 911 kind of attitude adjustment." He grinned and clapped his hands as hard as he could.

"That's more like it, brother." Munio poured him half a small glassful of Jack Daniels. "Here, have some medicine, eh?" He chuckled cheerfully and handed him the glass.

Destiny chopped out a new set of lines, delighted that Eddy was leaning their way, instead of stuck in some huge funk. "Clear them nostrils, and get over here!"

"Wheewww! This is gonna be fun. I ain't done none of this shit in way too long." Eddy took the rolled up bill, and guided his nose up and down all ten lines on the mirror. It was like he was going for the gold medal run on the giant slalom. "Ahhhh!" he said as he finished.

Destiny looked at him, a little perturbed at his greediness, but sloughed it off. "Goddamn Hoover!"

"Oh, wasn't I supposed to do all of that?" He laughed at his pretended innocence.

"It don't matter. You probably need it."

"I do need it, except for the fact I'm fixing to have a goddamn heart attack. Damn! My heart's beating ninety to nothing. Shit! Give me some more liquor to calm that son of a bitch down." Eddy frowned and held his right hand over his heart.

"Here you go, brother." Munio passed him another glass of whiskey. "You ok?" Munio asked with a look of concern.

"Yeah, oh yeah." He smiled at Munio, but it was obvious that Eddy was worried as well as in some pain. He slugged the whiskey down like apple juice.

"Easy, buddy, sip it slow, why don't you? You're kind of out of practice,

you know," Destiny cautioned Eddy. She looked at Munio, and they shared a frown.

"How do you feel now after that drink?" Munio questioned Eddy.

"Uh, I feel like ah, kind of hot or something. I don't know." Eddy got a strange detached look on his face. He started to stand up, but halfway up a force hit him like a shotgun blast to the chest.

Munio saw something coming as Eddy tried to stand, and moved quickly toward him. Eddy tumbled headlong into the throes of a grand mal seizure. His body transformed into a wild and savage beast. Munio danced around his flailing friend because he could not find the nerve or the right moment to try and hold Eddy down to prevent further injury.

"Destiny, we've got to hold him down, or he'll kill himself! You must help me!" Munio screamed, but Destiny was frozen, her hands covering her mouth. Her eyes looked like they were going to leap out of her body, and it seemed she had not even heard Munio's words. Munio grabbed her and shook her. "Come on! You can't freak out on me now!" She blinked and made eye contact with Munio. "Good! Now, you try and grab his left arm, and I will grab his right. Move now!" Munio jumped on top of Eddy and pinned his right arm to the carpet, subduing his movement. Destiny moved right in also and was able to hold down his left arm.

Eddy's eyes had rolled back up into his head, showing only the whites, marked with many small red capillaries. Blood spewed from his mouth between clenched teeth. Munio knew it was important to try to prevent him from swallowing his tongue, but he also knew he wouldn't have a snowball's chance in hell to open those jaws without loss of a finger to Eddy's mindless teeth.

Eddy's head banged against the carpeted floor repeatedly. Munio did feel like he had to do something about that. He slid his left knee in place to hold down Eddy's arm and transferred his left arm to immobilize Eddy's head. It was a relief to stop that skull flopping so violently.

"Just hold on, girl. He will stop soon." Munio breathed deep. "At least, he better stop soon, or he will kill himself."

Destiny cried quietly as she held down that arm with all her body weight. "He ain't ever had nothing like this happen to him."

"It was all that coke at one time! He should know better than that! But no, no, that's Eddy! He wants to do it all! That is just how he did those steroids!" Munio, infuriated and frightened, spouted off the words, breathing hard from the strain of this spring-loaded man.

To Munio and Destiny, time seemed to pass so slowly. Both of them began to tire, and they prayed relief would come soon. The seizure lasted about two minutes. When Eddy's body quit convulsing, Destiny and Munio were tossed against each other from the force they had exerted. Eddy lay motionless like a mechanical bull whose dollar had just run out.

Destiny and Munio scrambled to sit up. Munio felt for a carotid pulse and found one. They could see his chest rise and fall, and with those two variables in play they rested easier for the moment.

"Eddy? Eddy? Wake up, brother!" Munio cupped Eddy's face in his hands as he called to him. Eddy did not wake up, despite Munio's continued verbal urgings.

Destiny sat with her back against one of the beds. She was still trying to catch her breath and tend to her nose, which was bleeding profusely. In the struggle, Eddy's dangerous arm had smacked her across the face. A peculiar chill racked her body, and she shook uncontrollably from fear and exhaustion.

"Munio, what should we do? He ain't waking up!" she asked in a trembling voice.

"Eddy! Wake up, man! Come on, wake up, Eddy, please!" Munio continued to plead with the inert Eddy. "I don't know. Maybe he just needs to sleep this thing off or something." Munio shook too, overcome by the terror of it all, and at the same time, flashing back to scenes of Sandra. The thought of Eddy dying had his gut bound up in knots.

"Munio, we might ought to call somebody. I mean, I don't know what to do!" Destiny had caught her breath, and now her mind was working its way through the available options of this situation. She too replayed moments of her own recent encounter with death, and even though she loved Eddy a lot, she was not anxious to call the authorities, given that cocaine figured into the equation.

Eddy remained as peaceful as a baby on the floor while time ticked away. It was true that he might just need to sleep it off. Then again, his brain could be hemorrhaging, and very soon Eddy's nap would turn into a permanent condition, minus the heartbeat.

Destiny got right up in Eddy's ear. "Eddy! Eddy! Wake the fuck up, boy! You got to wake up now! Wake up!" she screamed and burst into an avalanche of tears.

Munio moved to her and held her tight. Tears streaked down his face, too. "He just looks so damn peaceful, don't he?" She wept loudly. "What should we do, Munio?"

He sighed and ran his hand through his hair. "We better call for medical assistance. You put all the drugs away in your purse, ok?"

"What do we tell them? Do we tell them he did a damn wheelbarrow full of coke in one snorting? I mean that coke ain't hardly left his nose. We need to tell them, but we don't need to tell them that we did some too." Destiny stood up and bit the thumbnail of her right hand while she paced and thought. Finally, she stopped and just held her arms out. "Hell, we'll just tell them that Eddy did some, but we didn't. We ain't done nothing illegal for them to ring us up on any charges. We'll just say he was in the bathroom a real long time,

and then he, uh, drank a glass of Jack Daniels. Then he sat down, started to stand back up, and started into that conniption fit. Ok? You got that, Munio? We don't know nothing about no drugs. We're just drinking, ok?"

"Yes, all right. I see what you're saying, but we need to call right now, Destiny. It's been a few minutes now."

She began to cry, "I can't believe this is happening! Why is this happening? Goddamnit Eddy! Damn coke hog!" she screamed. "All right, here goes." She walked over, sat on the edge of the bed, and picked up the phone. "Yes ma'am, we need an ambulance up in room 6125, please."

"Ma'am," The operator said, "Let me connect you with security."

"Security, how may I help you?" a man's voice answered.

"Yes sir, my friend, I'm, we're up in 6125, has had a bad convulsion, and he won't wake up. I need y'all to get an ambulance up here right away. Yes sir, ok, thanks." She hung up the phone and sighed. "Eddy! Wake-up, Eddy! They're going to have to take you to the hospital if you don't wake up now!"

"Eddy! Wake up!" Munio screamed in Eddy's face. He grabbed him by the shoulders and shook him, but still no response. Munio stood and looked at Destiny. "How long will it take?"

"Not long probably." She looked at Eddy's naked body on the floor. "Maybe we ought to cover the poor thing up. Shit, I've been so crazy, I forgot that's what they always say to do. Cover them up."

She pulled the comforter off the bed and began to tuck Eddy in when, all of a sudden, his possessed body sprang into action again gripped tight in the jaws of another seizure. "Munio! He's doing it again! Oh shit!"

"Hold him down! Like we did before! Hurry!"

Destiny and Munio jumped on top of Eddy again and watched in horror as the veins in Eddy's face bulged, his eyes rolled, and he seemed to have the strength of ten men. They hung on as long as they could, but this time his powerful motions were no match for them as he slung his only source of help sprawling across the room. Eddy flopped around like an angry wounded crocodile. Blood oozed from his left ear and from the sides of his clenched jaws and mouth.

A loud knock was heard at the door, and a call from the security officer, "Security!"

Destiny ran to the door and opened it. The officer could see she was panicked and desperate. "He's doing it again!"

The officer, a fairly large man, instructed, "Help me hold him down!" The man jumped on top of Eddy with his full weight. Destiny and Munio followed right along and each grabbed an arm. There the three of them rode poor Eddy until the paramedics arrived, along with a couple of security officers.

"Y'all stay right there on him until I can get this sedative started. You're doing fine. Just a little longer, ok? Y'all hang in there, now. He's going to calm right down once he gets a little of this." The paramedic held up a syringe full

of a clear liquid. She squirted a little of the fluid out of the end of the needle. "Let me get right here on his arm." Munio held Eddy's arm straighter to help the paramedic. "Jesus Christ, sure won't have no problem finding a vein on this fellow. What the heck is he, a bodybuilder or something?"

"Yes ma'am, that's right," Munio answered.

The woman plunged the needle into the inviting vein. "That ought to do it." In less than a minute, the seizure subsided, and the demon in Eddy was released.

"Y'all get back now. Let's see what we got here." The woman pulled out a stethoscope, while another paramedic strapped a Velcro cuff on Eddy to check his blood pressure. He pumped the black rubber bulb, and the device pressed tight against Eddy's yellow-green arm.

"Ninety over fifty," he reported.

"Need a pulse," the original paramedic requested.

"Forty," he snapped.

"Let's get this guy moving, y'all." The woman stood up.

They moved together in rhythm, clearing the furniture away to make room for the gurney. Then, with effortless coordination, they picked Eddy up and strapped him tightly in place. They wrapped blankets around him, and he looked very serene for a man knocking on death's door. Destiny and Munio huddled by the window, hugging each other.

The woman turned to them. "What's his name?"

Destiny spoke up. "Eddy Jackson."

"What's his address?"

"Oh, ah," she frowned. "I can't quite remember it. Bruner Road, you can put that down. I'm so upset. I'm sorry. We're all from Rosedale, Georgia."

"Oh, visiting?"

"Yes ma'am, Eddy was competing in the Mr. Dixie contest," Destiny announced.

"Oh, really. Well, from the looks of him, he must have done good." The woman smiled.

Destiny and Munio looked at each other and shook their heads. "Not really, he was real disappointed. He didn't place or nothing."

"Has he ever had a seizure before?"

"No ma'am, I don't believe so."

"Had he taken any drugs or anything that might have set him off?"

"Yes ma'am, he did some cocaine."

"Ok."

"He chugged a big old glass of whiskey. See, he hadn't partied in quite a while on account of training for this contest. He was upset and wanted to blow it out, you know?"

"Yeah. How much coke did he do? Do you know? Did he snort it or do it intravenously?"

"Oh, I believe he snorted it. We didn't actually see him do it. When we come back from the show, he took a shower and stayed in the bathroom for the longest time. Then, he come out, and me and Munio was drinking and looking out the window. He asked us to get him a glass of whiskey. He said he just snorted half a gram of cocaine without stopping. Then, he chugged down that whiskey and sat down. He got this weird look on his face and started to stand up. When he was about halfway up, that's when that convulsion set in."

"Does he have any insurance?"

"No, I don't think so."

"Ok, ma'am, we're going to take him over to Grady Hospital."

"Is that far from here?" Destiny asked in a troubled voice.

"No, ma'am, it's real close. Ah, it's probably only a two dollar cab ride from here."

"Ok, Grady Hospital?"

"Yes, ma'am, uh huh. If you could try to remember his address. They'll want some more information. We need to get going. They've probably got him loaded up by now."

"Ok, thank you, ma'am." The woman smiled a terse smile, nodded at Destiny and Munio, backed away from them, and left the room.

"All right Munio, how did that sound?" She raked her hands through her hair. "God, I need another fucking drink! Want one?" Munio nodded.

"Yes, it was good. It was believable," he said in his soft assuring voice as he took the whiskey bottle.

"Good, all right. Goddamn, I can't believe this is happening. Is he going to die, Munio? Is he?" She looked up at him with her tormented face.

Munio blew air out through his lips as an indication of how far fetched her question was. "No way. He will be fine now. He probably was dehydrated, you know, and once that coke settles down in him, he will wake up. He'll be fine. He'll probably be awake when we get to that hospital."

"Oh God, we better get down there. What if he tells them I gave him the coke? Oh my God, let's split, Munio! Right this second! Oh goddamn, I should have done called a cab. I'll get the operator. Yes ma'am, can you call me a cab, please? Oh, really. Thank you." She hung up the phone. "She said there's a whole pile of cabs waiting in the motor lobby. Hell, I've never rode in a taxi." She snorted a laugh as they quickly left the room.

* * * * * * *

Destiny and Munio hopped from the yellow taxi and sprinted toward the entrance marked emergency room. Destiny stopped at the first desk she came to. "Ma'am, our friend was just brought here. Do you know where he might be?"

"What was wrong with him?"

"He had convulsions."

"Walk down to the next nurse's station and check there."

"Thank you." They strode down the old but highly polished tan linoleum floor. "Ma'am, we're looking for our friend, Eddy Jackson, that was brought here with convulsions."

The nurse studied a list on a clipboard. "Umm, hmm, yes, let's see." She picked up a phone and said to someone, "Yes, the friends of Eddy Jackson are here now." She smiled a comforting smile. "The doctor will be right out to talk to you. Why don't you have a seat over there." She pointed to some aqua and coral molded plastic chairs that looked like of ones Destiny had seen in the bowling alley in Rosedale.

They sat down and didn't speak. Destiny gnawed on her thumb-nail, and Munio bounced his right leg nonstop. Five minutes passed before a small, short-haired woman dressed in a pale green set of surgical scrubs approached them. She adjusted her round wire-rimmed glasses. Her cloth surgical mask hung like a bandana around her neck.

"Hello, I'm Dr. Callahan. You're Eddy Jackson's friends?"

"Yes, ma'am, I'm Destiny Morris, and this is Munio, uh. Munio, I forgot your last name."

"Morelos."

"Why don't you sit down over here." the doctor suggested. Destiny gave Munio a frightened look.

"Well, how is he? Did he wake up? Munio bet that he would by the time we got here." Destiny chuckled nervously.

Dr. Callahan cleared her throat and looked away for a second. "Eddy didn't make it," she said softly, putting her hand on Destiny's knee. Munio and Destiny became paralyzed, and at the same time, they felt like candles melting slowly out of their chairs. They listened to the doctor, but they did not hear her. "He suffered a massive aneurysm that created a tremendous hemorrhage in his brain. There was simply nothing we could do to stabilize him in order to perform the surgery necessary to repair the damaged vessel. This could have been a genetic predisposition, and the extreme neural activity caused by the excitement of the contest and the alcohol and drugs could have just hit him just right. I am very sorry. If you could follow me, we have some papers for you to fill out, so we can release the body to you to make arrangements to take him home. You people are visiting from, ah," she squinted at the chart in her hand, "Rosedale? Do you have any questions?"

Destiny's face flooded with tears. Munio's head rested on his hands, which were propped up on his knees as he leaned over. A steady salty stream of tears dripped from his eyes onto the floor. forming a small wet spot that was rapidly turning into a small puddle.

The doctor stood. "Would y'all like to come with me, now?" Destiny and Munio did not respond or even hear her. "I tell you what. Why don't I have someone check with you in a few minutes. Again, I am very sorry. There was

nothing more we could have done." She put a hand on each of their shaking shoulders as she stood. Both of them briefly looked up to acknowledge her, and she moved quickly down the corridor to the next patient.

As the busy machine of Grady Hospital turned around them, Munio and Destiny held each other's hands and disappeared from sight. Neither was ready or willing to be in the here and now with this unbelievable tragedy. For another hour, as people came and went around them, sitting in the other aqua and coral bowling chairs, Destiny and Munio stayed, barely able to inhale shallow breaths of the disinfectant scented hospital air.

A portly woman, a bereavement counselor, approached. "Miss Morris?"

Destiny looked up. "Uh huh?"

"How are y'all doing here?" She pulled up a chair and faced them.

"Not too good," Destiny sniffled, squeezing Munio's hand.

"I am sure. Death is so hard, but when something happens to take a loved one so suddenly, well, it's especially hard."

"Yes, ma'am, it sure is."

"I'm sorry. I didn't get your name." She smiled at Munio.

"Munio Morelos." He forced a hint of smile to his lips.

"You were good friends with Eddy?"

"Yes." Munio nodded his head.

"As sad as this is, we need to process Eddy's papers, and I need y'alls help, since we don't know anything about Eddy. You understand." She smiled.

Destiny nodded. "Yeah, I reckon."

"Could y'all just follow me, and we'll go get this over with. Then, y'all can rest, or do whatever you need to do." She waddled down the hall with Destiny and Munio following close behind.

"Let's come in here where it's quiet." She motioned them into a small office and shut the door behind them. "All right, now, I need his address."

"Why? He don't need it no more." Destiny started crying again. Munio put his arm around her.

"I'm sorry, Miss Morris. I know this is difficult."

"It's not your fault." Destiny dabbed at her eyes and noticed how sore her nose was from the bop Eddy had accidentally delivered. "Uh, it was 325 Bruner Street in Rosedale, Georgia 84569."

"Ok, now, are you his fiancee or what?"

Destiny chuckled. "No ma'am, we were good friends, occasional fuck buddies." The woman's eyebrows raised, and her pen moved furiously on the form. Munio chuckled slightly.

"Who would be his next of kin?"

"He's got an uncle and really that's it. He's old, too. It was a small family. His folks are both dead. He was an only child."

"I see. What is that uncle's name?"

"Uh, Jeb Boslaugh."

"Could you spell that, please? Also, will you contact him?"

"Yes ma'am, I will." Destiny was being swept by an exhaustion beyond any week-long speed bender she'd ever had. Her mind was not working right. In some way, she felt like she was dying too. She felt her life could never be happy again, having experienced this horrible night. Coupled with the murder of Jimmy Ray, Eddy's death made her feel like she was slipping away from reality. If she could not anchor on some island of denial soon, Destiny felt certain this pain in her heart would kill her as dead as Eddy.

Somehow, she managed to sign the papers necessary to release Eddy's body into her custody. Munio didn't want to, but he could not dissuade Destiny from wanting to see Eddy. A nurse took them into a cold room where there were several stretchers loaded with people covered by the white sheet of death. The nurse pulled back the sheet, and instantly, Destiny wished she had never requested the view.

Eddy was gone from that skeleton bound by all those hard earned muscles. The body that took and took everything dished out to it had finally had its last straw with Eddy's antics. All those big strong bones and big-bellied muscles held up fine. It was that little bitty vein inside his dumb thick skull that, ironically, couldn't take the pressure. Destiny laid one gentle kiss upon Eddy's forehead before pulling the sheet back over his head.

Munio cried again too at the sight of Eddy's repose. Such a waste to see his fine young body lie so still. He wondered why death seemed to be tracking him, and wished he could die to avoid such grief.

"Munio, let's go have a drink." Destiny took his hand, and they walked out of that hospital.

They went back to the hotel room and each collapsed on a bed. Destiny took a long drink and passed it across to Munio. Pulling out his smokes, he extended the pack to Destiny. who gladly took one. It did not take long for them to kill the bottle. Destiny got up and found a new one. By the time that bottle was empty, it was five in the morning. Both of them were lost in a drunken stupor, a speechless stupor that guided them deep into a coma of their own for the next five hours. The telephone woke Destiny on its fifteenth ring.

"Hello?"

"Yes, this is Tom Scott, the hotel manager. I was calling to see how Mr. Jackson was doing." he said in a most formal, but pleasant, manner.

Destiny sighed and didn't say anything for a couple of seconds. "He died."

"Oh, my word! I, I am so sorry. If there is anything I could do, please do not hesitate to ask, won't you?"

"Yes, sir, I appreciate that." Destiny hung up the phone and laid back on the bed, staring at the ceiling. "Munio, you still with me?"

"I am here, dear. I am not going anywhere."

"I got to call Uncle Jeb. Jesus, I don't want to do that. Was this a dream, Munio? How could Eddy be dead? I just can't believe it. We can't go back without Eddy." She began to sob and hug a pillow.

Munio squeezed his eyes tight at Destiny's disturbing sounds. His head ached from whiskey and sadness. His lungs were tired of smoking, yet he could not be without a lit one. He thought of Audrey, and wished he were lying sweetly next to her warm body, watching the flames in the fireplace.

Destiny got up and went in the bathroom. While she sat on the commode, she saw Eddy's clothes lying there on the floor. On top of the pile of sweats was his little lime green posing suit. She leaned over and picked it up. She chuckled to see how tiny it was unstretched. It could have fit a five year old.

She walked out of the bathroom to Munio's bed with the posing suit hanging from her index finger. "Munio, I think we ought to bury him in this, don't you?" She smiled at Munio through her tears.

Tears ran down Munio's face as he nodded. He held his arms out to Destiny, and she crawled onto the bed and into Munio's arms. They hugged each other and wailed.

After a few minutes, Destiny sighed, "This ain't gonna get no easier. I'm gonna call him." She sat up and picked up the phone.

"Uncle Jeb?" Destiny said loudly into the phone receiver.

"Who's this?" an elderly man answered.

"Destiny Morris, you remember me?" She again spoke in an abrasively loud voice. She put her hand over the mouthpiece and whispered to Munio who frowned at her exaggerated volume. "He's nearly deaf, sorry." Munio nodded and chuckled.

"Eddy's girlfriend, ain't you?"

"Yes sir. Uh, Uncle Jeb, I don't know how to tell you this, but I have some bad news." She grimaced.

"What's that, hon?"

"Eddy has, has passed away," she said resolutely.

There was no sound from the other end for a few seconds. "Say he's gone and done what?"

"He passed away last night up here in Atlanta."

"What you saying is he passed away?"

"Yes sir."

"He's dead?"

"Yes sir."

"Ah naw! What in the world become of him?"

"He had a stroke, sir."

"A stroke? How could he had that to happen?"

"Well, he was under a lot of pressure lately because of that contest and all."

"Well, I can't believe it. He's a young man. Young men don't have strokes. Land sakes, that's awful."

"Uncle Jeb, do you know if his mama and daddy made any arrangements for Eddy? You know, for when he passed?"

"Why yes, I believe they did. I cannot believe that boy is dead. Where is he?"

"We're all up here in Atlanta. We got to bring him home."

"Well, I swannee. I just can't hardly believe it. You fixing to bring him home today?"

"Yes sir. Do you think I should get the funeral home there to come get him, or get a funeral home up here to deliver him?"

"Why don't you call over to ours here, and ask them, hon. Either way, you let me know when y'all get back, you hear?"

"Ok, I will."

"I swear I hate to hear that. You ok?"

"I reckon. Believe me, I can't believe this either."

"You call me, hon," he said sweetly.

"Ok, Uncle Jeb," she shouted and hung up.

"Must be real deaf, eh?" Munio smiled and looked over at Destiny on the other bed.

"Fucking right, man. I feel like I've just been in an argument or something, talking so loud." She took a deep breath and sighed. "Jesus, I reckon I'll call the funeral home now."

In the second of many conversations that Destiny would have with friends and acquaintances of Eddy's, she got the funeral director on the phone. She had to listen to his laments about how he had buried Eddy's mother, daddy, and now him. Eventually, the director said he would dispatch a hearse right away to retrieve Eddy.

"Well, we've got a couple of more hours to kill. Feel like taking in a little sightseeing?" she joked.

Munio shook his head. "I don't think so. I've seen everything I care to see here."

"Why don't I order us some coffee, beer, and breakfast, hmm? How does that sound?"

"Yes, that is good. We will need to eat something so we can keep drinking, eh?"

"I'm telling you the truth, boy! Ain't no way I'm getting through this shit sober. Wouldn't want to even try."

So, for the next couple of hours, Destiny and Munio drank coffee and beer and ate eggs, hashbrowns, and toast. The phone rang finally with the voice of Eddy's chauffeur for the return trip to Rosedale, who was waiting at Grady Hospital.

"Well, it's time to hit the road, Munio. That was the guy. Hey Munio,

want to do a couple of lines for the road? I could use it myself. Maybe it'd cheer us up a little bit."

"Yeah, why not, why not?"

They stuck the same dollar bill that Eddy had used up each of their nostrils and launched the fine white coke northbound in search of salvation for their sad souls. They lugged all their stuff and Eddy's down to the motor lobby. Each task of leaving required embracing the surrealness of his death.

As they waited in the motor lobby for the car to be brought up, the new Mr. Dixie was waiting with a group of friends and family. Destiny watched the man, happy, grinning, and oddly tanned. She started to cry, and so did Munio as they looked at him, robust, muscled, and wearing a white satin jacket with "Mr. Dixie 1994" written across the back in big turquoise letters.

The undertaker's assistant was like every undertaker's assistant. A small man dressed in a plain black suit, white shirt, and black tie, with little fanfare or discourse. Destiny arranged to follow him all the way back to Rosedale.

Destiny and Munio waited outside the cold room until the little undertaker's assistant and a hospital orderly wheeled Eddy out in a shiny, gray plastic casket. Both Munio's and Destiny's stomach seized and threatened to empty at first view of that finality. It was very clear that Eddy was never going to wake up on this earth, in this life ever again, and he was never ever going to be Mr. Dixie.

It did not do Destiny and Munio any good to watch the back of that black Cadillac for two hours. Without realizing it, Destiny gripped the steering wheel so hard her fingers fell asleep. She shook them out, and all through the trip, Munio passed her sips of whiskey to fortify her enough to complete the journey. Munio wanted so badly to take Eddy's body and honor it in the same fashion that he had Sandra's. This was not going to happen, and so he distanced himself from the pain. A little time and a lot of drink passed by the time they passed the Rosedale city limit sign. Munio felt numb about the whole affair. He had emptied his heart of love and filled it with stone. It was just that easy.

The first sight of Eddy's old house and that porch spelled the return of a fresh cascade of weeping for the two people that loved him most. Munio carried Eddy's luggage into the house-for what reason, he was unsure.

"Munio, I think he really ought to be buried in his posing suit. I wasn't kidding. What do you think?" Destiny sat down on the couch in the living room.

Munio walked into the living room and set a cold beer on the coffee table in front of Destiny. He offered his can to click in a silent ritual toast. "He would like it. I think it's a good idea. I think we should put his lifting belt and knee wraps in that box, too. All the equipment that he loved."

"Well, we better put that crate of shit he got from Jimmy Ray in there then."

"Yes. He would sure want that." Munio laughed. "That man Eddy was

crazy. He was too crazy."

"I don't know what's going to happen to the house. I reckon Uncle Jeb will sell it. Don't worry, Munio. It will take a while. I'll tell him you're staying and all."

"Actually, I have not slept here for some time. I can take the rest of my things to Sandra's house. Still, I am unsure when she will return."

"Oh, what are you going to do?"

"I have no idea," he said sadly.

# CHAPTER LII

Audrey was not at Sandra's when Munio arrived. The lap dog crew was, and they expressed their delight with his return, wagging their tails and bouncing all around.

"Hello, doggies. Hello," he babytalked them. After taking one out for himself, he put the case of beer he had just bought into the refrigerator.

The day was sunny and cool, in the fifties. Munio opened the sliding glass door. He leaned on the door frame and looked out at the gazebo while the dogs roamed the yard. It seemed like an old friend as he looked at the wood, the detail.

After he sat there for a time, he began to feel his love again for this wonderful thing he had created. It was a octagon of love, he decided, because love is why he started to build it, and it was love that drove him to complete it. He began to cry when he thought of Sandra. At least with her, he had this monument, this personal transaction that would forever stand as a testament of honor to their friendship, to their love. With Eddy, he saw nothing that he could do. He had no ideas of how to hold a similar ritual of expression.

Audrey showed up at Sandra's about an hour after Munio. She knew something was not good by the wet spots she saw on his face, and the hurt look in his brown, bloodshot eyes.

She said softly, "Hello." She wore jeans and a sweatshirt and no makeup. Her hair hung down, luxuriously thick and beautiful in the sun's light. She bent over and kissed his forehead and sat beside him. Munio did not speak, and so she urged him with a question. "How did he do?"

Munio chuckled and looked out at the sky, squinting a little as the light was painful on his sensitive eyes. "Not good, I'm afraid."

"Aw, that's too bad, honey. I'm sorry to hear that." She put her hand on the back of Munio's neck and massaged it. "I'm sorry for you, too. Is he very upset?" she inquired gently.

Munio took a long drag off his cigarette and released it forcefully into the air before he spoke. "Not anymore."

"Well, good. I'm glad to hear he's moved on. It's-"

"He's dead," Munio interrupted.

She stood up in amazement at his words. "He's what?"

He looked into her eyes. "Eddy's dead."

"What do you mean? What happened? Are you kidding me?"

"I wish this was a joke, a big funny joke, but it is not. That man, Eddy Jackson, has died. Last night, after the show, he snorted a whole bunch of cocaine at one time. Destiny had maybe ten lines or so cut out, you see. Eddy came along to do a couple of lines, and he just kept going. He snorted everything on the damn mirror. It was half a gram or something!" Munio stood up and paced, becoming angered as he relived the story. "After that, he chugged down a big glass of whiskey. He sat down on the bed, and then he got this strange look in his eye," Munio stopped, turned, and faced Audrey, "like something out the window was scaring him, like he was seeing death. He started to stand up, and he fell right down and started having the, ah, the seizure. He flopped all around. Me and Destiny tried to hold him down, and finally he stopped. He didn't do nothing, just sleep. He just lay there. We call the ambulance, and then, he started again. They come. They take him to the hospital. We go right behind in a few minutes, eh? The doctor comes to us and says Eddy didn't make it. A brain aneurysm is what she said happened." Munio threw his arms out. His hands slapped his thighs as he relaxed them.

"Tell me, Munio. Have your loved ones always received the kiss of death, or is this a new thing?" Audrey smiled seductively.

Munio smiled and then threw back his head to laugh. "I never thought about that, but you know, you might have a point. Are you concerned, dear?" He flashed her a look of passion that welded a spot in Audrey's gut.

"Stunt love. That's what you are. I should get hazard duty pay for this." She walked over and threw her arms around Munio in a savage embrace.

Munio threw Audrey to the floor of the gazebo where they rolled, kissed and fought each other like wrestlers as they unwound the gifts they had for each other of body and soul.

# CHAPTER LIII

The news of Eddy's death passed like wildfire through the town. Between the crowd that frequented Pee Wee's, the gym crowd, and all the others in-between Eddy had known since his birth in Rosedale, there was only a small percentage of people that had not made contact with him somewhere along the line.

Destiny, Munio, and Uncle Jeb set the funeral for three o'clock Monday afternoon. They all felt like getting the sad task over with and declined to postpone the funeral another day so that they could have a wake. Destiny had gotten Pee Wee to offer the bar as a place they could throw a really good party

in Eddy's honor after the funeral. She thought Eddy would have liked that a lot. Uncle Jeb didn't care if they buried Eddy in his posing trunks, so Destiny took them down to the funeral home.

Monday afternoon at one-thirty, Destiny and Munio went down to the funeral home. Both of them laughed when they took their first look into the coffin. If there was ever a cosmetic aid for the dead, it was tanning dye. In spite of the fact that Eddy's color was drained, it was impossible to tell because his skin remained, albeit putrid, that bright yellow-green bronze. His muscles still looked full and rich. He was as ripped as any dead man ever was. Lying there in that lime green posing suit was such an Eddy way to go. By Eddy's feet, Munio placed the boxes, two shoeboxes full of steroids and growth hormone. Also, he placed inside his lifting belt, knee wraps, wrist wraps, and favorite bandanna he used to wear in training.

The standard custom is to display a corpse from the waist up, but Destiny and Munio agreed to leave Eddy's coffin all the way open so that people could see his legs. His quads still hung like roasted turkey breasts off his thighs.

The chapel in the funeral home was packed. Most who entered the place were crying or had been, but after viewing Eddy's body, they tended to laugh. Eddy would have wanted people to laugh, and how could they not at a tan dead man in a lime green bathing suit?

The preacher from the little country Baptist church where Eddy's mama used to take him as a boy presided over the service. His words were brief, and then he opened the floor for people to say a few words.

Pee Wee was first. "I knowed Eddy since he was twenty-one years old, two years near abouts. He bought his first legal drink in my bar on his twenty-first birthday. He was a good old boy and friendly. We're all gonna miss him down at the bar." He nodded to the crowd and sat down.

"He was a hard worker. I'm sure sorry he didn't win the Mr. Dixie title, but that boy, I say, has the best physique, even lying here dead, than anybody I ever saw in the state of Georgia." Sam from the Dixie Ironworks spoke, and, as he reclaimed his seat, put his new cigar back in the side of his mouth.

Destiny took a breath and got up to speak. "I want y'all to know that I loved this crazy guy a whole lot." She pointed toward the casket. "We had been through a lot, and uh, well, he was my best friend." She paused and looked to the side, out the stained glass window. "He was real sad about losing the show. He really was, and it's a shame he had to die not having another chance to try again. Thank y'all for coming. I know he would have appreciated that. I have a special song to play for Eddy." She started to cry a little. "He called it his lucky song." She smiled and looked at Munio. "Said the first time he ever got laid, he was listening to it." A low cloud of laughter filled the small chapel. "He posed to it at the Mr. Dixie. It wasn't so lucky for him that night, but I think it'll be a good way to send him off. I know he would like to hear this song one more time." She nodded to a member of the staff at the funeral home who had the

tape cued up.

Loud and clear and sweet, Lynyrd Skynyrd filled the room as the song "Free Bird" played. The crowd listened to the sad words of the ballad and either hugged, wept or maintained stoic looks on their faces. "If I leave here tomorrow, would you still remember me? For I must be traveling on now. There's too many places I've got to see." After the final lyric was sung, a rousing five-minute guitar solo ensued. The room became quiet again. The service was dismissed to be continued at the cemetery.

As Eddy's casket was carried out, Destiny remembered how not too long ago Eddy had been a pallbearer at Jimmy Ray's funeral. She recalled the shock of seeing Eddy's legs with knots rising up on his thighs. He said he would explain about them later, but he never did.

Munio and Audrey sat beside Destiny. Munio wore an outfit that was at the very least unique. A purple brocade tuxedo jacket topped his black silk shirt with a big ruffled front. His pants were the fancy black dress linen pair that he had worn the night he went to Audrey's dance class. Eddy would have enjoyed that outfit too, and probably would have said that Munio looked like one of the Temptations.

Audrey was probably the best dressed of any person wearing female clothing. She had her hair up in a severe bun. An expensive contemporary two-piece black suit with an ivory blouse elegantly fit her long frame, complemented by black hose and low-heeled black pumps.

Destiny, Munio, and Audrey shared the Cadillac limo with Uncle Jeb, who drifted in and out of lucidity. He sat across from the three of them and kept adjusting his thick glasses to get a better look at Audrey, who would pet him with a demure smile every so often. He would smile back to her and nod and chuckle.

"Uncle Jeb, how you doing?" Destiny asked.

"Yeah, all right, uh huh."

"That's good."

"Where you from, hon?" he asked Audrey.

"New York, sir."

"Oh, is that right? Knew a feller once from up in there. In the service. We was in the service together, uh huh." He nodded. "Nice feller. Sure was. Reckon whatever happened to him?" He scratched his silver-topped head.

Audrey had elected to go home after the service. Destiny sent Uncle Jeb home with Jimmy Ray's mother, Lynette, who came for the funeral. Destiny was down to her last nerve as she spoke with Lynette, having not seen her since Jimmy Ray's funeral. The majority of the crowd went to Pee Wee's to get drunk after the burial.

Everyone felt like partying except Munio and Destiny. They drank a couple of beers and a couple of shots and then bowed out to the crowd who were doing shots of tequila in Eddy's honor every five minutes. Oddly, the two

of them didn't even feel like drinking tonight. In the past few days, they had drunk continuously because of their state of shock. Destiny dropped Munio off at Sandra's house.

"You want to come in for a beer?" he asked.

"Naa. I reckon not. I'm ready to just be by myself for a while, you know?"

"Yeah, me too. I will speak to you tomorrow. Sleep well." He leaned down and stuck his upper body through the car window to give her a big hug.

"I'll see you, Munio. Thanks for being here."

He smiled and waved as he moved towards the carport door.

# CHAPTER LIV

Munio dutifully tended to the dogs, and then sat on the couch with a beer in hand. He stared at the cold, dark fire pit and promised himself he would make a fire. It was cool enough definitely, in the low forties.

He now realized he had had no time to hear himself think or contemplate his next move. The Mr. Dixie Contest had become his life's goal also. All in all, the time spent in this town had been so mixed, devastating and fantastic, loving and heartbreaking.

The time had come for him to return to a sea, any sea. It was certain that a part of him was constantly unsettled being this far inland. Tomorrow, he would ask some questions about this. Where the closest ocean was he did not know.

He prepared a fire, and in no time, the room was warmed by the yellow-orange flames.

As he picked up his beer, he noticed the cover of the book that was under it. The book had not previously been on this table, and he assumed Audrey must have been looking at it. The title of the book was "Roses", and it was an encyclopedia of them. The cover was designed with color photographs of probably a dozen different types. He thumbed through it and happily found the pages filled with color photographs of roses of every color and size. Many of the names of the roses he could make out, since they were simple words. The photographs were so vivid that he could almost smell them. From his experiences, he remembered how the fragrances varied from color to color. He wondered how a flower, a rose, so beautiful could be so cruel as to tease one by offering no sweet bouquet? It was the palest roses of all, the lavender ones. He found smelled the sweetest.

For four more beers and two large logs, Munio immersed himself in the book. He decided to plant his own rose garden right there in the back yard by the gazebo so Sandra could enjoy it. He remembered that she had even mentioned wanting roses planted around the gazebo.

When the fire had reduced itself to an orange bed of coals, Munio snuggled in his blankets on the couch with the lap dogs in a pile at his feet. He felt happy and home, even though he was neither. At least, he did believe that for this night.

In the morning, bright and early, Munio called up Destiny.

"Hello to you. It is Munio."

"Hey, what's happening?" she said.

"Called to see how you are, and to ask you where I can go buy some rose bushes."

"Rose bushes? What the hell for?" She laughed.

"I want to plant some."

"Where are you going to plant them?"

"Around the gazebo, for decoration," he explained.

"Well, I ain't got much of a green thumb, but you know this town ain't called Rosedale for nothing."

"Oh, really?"

"Yeah, folks are big off into roses around here. There's a festival and everything in June. Yeah, they're pretty and all. I guess I just never lived nowhere to plant none, you know?"

"Uh huh, I see. Well, so where is it I would go to purchase some of these bushes?"

"The best place probably is this little old lady's place out on the edge of town. She is fucking famous for her roses and sells the bushes to people all over the world. She's been wrote up in the paper and all. Little bitty old thing, Jewish. She supposedly lived through being in a concentration camp."

"Really? She must be old. Will you take me there today?"

"Sure, when?"

"Anytime you want, I am ready."

"Ok, I'll see you soon."

Next Munio dialed up Audrey. "Hello."

"Hello, it's Munio."

She chuckled, "Oh really?"

"Yes," he smiled. "It is."

"How are you this morning, Munio?"

"Fine, and you?"

"I'm fine. I'm packing. I am going to leave soon, in a couple of days."

"Hmmm, I will miss you."

"You too. I hope we'll meet again somewhere, Munio."

"Me too."

"What are you doing today?"

"Oh, something exciting. Destiny is to take me to a place where I will purchase rose bushes."

"Rose bushes?"

374

"Yes, I am going to plant them around the gazebo. I want to plant one in honor of you."

"Me?"

"Yes, and Sandra and Eddy and, I will plant eight. So, where was I? Let's see. Oh, for you, Sandra, Destiny, Eddy, me, and one for each of the dogs. Sandra would like that. Don't you think so?" He voice was full of purpose.

Audrey smiled to herself as her eyes welled up with tears. "Yes, honey, I think that is a wonderful, creative thing to do."

"You want to join us in going there? You could pick out your own bush, and help me pick out the others too."

"When are you going?"

"Soon. Destiny is coming here to pick me up."

Audrey looked around her bedroom, which was torn apart because of her packing. She thought of how short her time with Munio was and could not resist. She would enjoy Destiny's company. "Ok, I'll be right there. Wait for me, ok?"

"Ok dear, we will wait." Munio hung up the phone smiling.

He was very excited about this project. Part of his frustration of not getting to bury Eddy himself would be resolved by this ritual. Forever, he would know that Eddy's memory would live on through the life and pleasure that a rose can bring..

"Hi." Destiny came in and gave Munio a hug. The dogs were there to greet her. "Hello! Hello! How is everybody? Hmm? Y'all ok? Y'all ok today? Well, good!"

"Listen, Audrey is to come with us, ok? She will be here soon."

"No problem, no problem." Destiny strolled through the house. "Nice place." She looked at Munio. "Wish I could have a place as nice as this."

"Why don't you buy a little place?"

"Yeah, I might. Right now, I just want to be lazy for a while. If I spend all my money on a house, I'll have to get right to work. I just want some time to figure out what I want to do."

"Sure, sure. That's good."

"You figured out what you want to do?"

Munio smiled at her and sighed. "I don't know exactly, but I know I won't stay here."

She looked out the window, her green eyes trying to steady themselves from an emotional outburst. "Hell." she paused. "I don't blame you. There ain't nothing much going on around here." She crossed her arms tightly across her chest. "It's just that, for me, it's home. It's a habit. Fuck, I don't even know where else to go." She shrugged her shoulders.

He walked up behind her, stroked her hair and put his arms around her. "You will know if it is time for you to go." She stared out the door, while a quiet trail of tears rolled down each of her fair cheeks.

"Hello?" Audrey peeked in the door. "Oh, pardon me!" She camped it up. "I didn't mean to disturb you two lovebirds!" She poured on her finest New York Jew comedic repertoire.

"Roses? We're going to buy roses in the winter? Who would have thought it?" She laughed and gave them a group hug.

"You should like this lady. I was telling Munio. She is real old and lived through being in one of those concentration camps."

"No kidding? She owns a gardening center or something?"

"No, she's only into roses."

"This should be interesting."

"Y'all ready?" Destiny asked.

They drove up the graveled driveway that led up a hill to an old white farm house. Most of the ten acres had been carefully tilled as rose beds. Now, in the off season, a multitude of brown dormant stems slept on their feet, waiting for the signal of spring to return. The three of them imagined how beautiful it must be when the roses all bloomed. They got out of the car and a tiny woman appeared.

"Hello!" she called to them, in an accent that Audrey recognized as Russian.

"Hey," Destiny called to her. "Are you open? We was interested in buying some rose bushes, ma'am."

"Oh, that's good. Wait there. I be there shortly." She held up her hand and went back in the house.

"She's so little." Destiny giggled.

"Isn't she?" Audrey said. "I've seen a lot of little ladies like her in New York. My grandmother is one of them, in fact."

"What, ah, was her accent?" Munio asked curiously.

"Russian, I believe."

The little old lady marched out. "Hello, my name is Fran Micholovich. How are you?" She adjusted her thick round glasses, smiling at them.

"Hi, I'm Destiny. This is Audrey, and that's Munio."

"Well, good. Now, you want you should get some rose bushes? Is that right?" She smiled.

"Yes, I do, ma'am." Munio had brought the rose book to show her what he might want.

"Ah, a good book that is. Their pictures, they are so realistic. You might think what can be hard to take these pictures of flowers? Hard is what it is though."

Munio smiled at her. "This book was so nice to look at. I looked at it for a long time last night."

"Which roses for you should I get?"

"I have still not decided." He opened the book. "Do you have all these roses?"

"Practically, yes, for long time, I collect all of these roses. For the most part, if it is a rose, I will have it for you. So, now for you to select is what is to be done. With your friends, take your time with your selection." She held her outstretched arm toward a nearby wooden bench. "Here, it is nice day. Sit on this bench. Look at your book. I will attend to some things I must do. In that greenhouse over there, I will be when you decide. Ok?"

"Thank you, that's good." Muno said and nodded.

They walked over a to the bench and sat down. Munio sat in the middle and held the book while Audrey and Destiny looked on. They oohed and ahhhed about all the pictures, and they found the names of them intriguing. Audrey got them all giggling over the one named "Golden Showers".

"Here's one for you, Audrey, 'Flaming Queen,'" Destiny kidded. Audrey reached around Munio to slap her on the shoulder, causing a chain reaction of giggles.

"Ok smartass, I've got yours, 'Flaming Peace'. They misspelled it, though. It should be 'piece'." Audrey returned. Destiny reached over to push Audrey, and Munio played like he was having a hard time keeping them separated.

"I got mine. I got mine. Look! Tequila! Isn't it beautiful, just like me." Destiny laughed. "That's it." She pointed to a picture of a bright orange-yellow rose whose name was, sure enough, "Tequila".

"I like this for Sandra." Munio pointed to a deep pink rose with large blooms.

"Ok, that's called 'Constance Spry.' Would you like me to make a list for you, Munio?' Audrey offered.

"Thank you. Yes, that's good. Constance Spry," he repeated thoughtfully.

"I'm going with a classic red, 'Erotica'." Audrey announced.

"This is the one I pick for me. It is like a sunset," Munio said.

"Let's see, oh, 'Apricot Silk'. What a great name," Audrey commented.

"Yeah, that's pretty. Wonder where do they dream some of these names up. Apricot silk, what is that? I don't know what I think when I think of apricot silk." Destiny smiled at the riddle. "I kind of think of a , ah, ah, sweet softness or something. It's nice. Good one, Munio." Destiny patted Munio on the back.

"Now for Eddy. What can we get for Eddy?" Munio pondered.

"Hey, this is perfect, Munio. 'Champion of the World', boy, does that describe Eddy in Eddy's mind! What do you think?"

Munio looked at it. "Yes, that's it. That is what to get for that man. Ok, who is left, eh? The dogs now, that is who. I know I want a white one for Moo Shoo, who is mostly white. How about this one?" He pointed to a big white rose. "The name of this is what?"

"'Ivory tower,'" Destiny informed him. "That's pretty. There's going to be so many colors. They'll look great."

"This yellow one is very nice, Munio. How about that?" Audrey asked.

"Ok, that's good for Jacky. What's its name?"

"'Gold Medal.'"

"Ok, one left to go. How about this two-toned one for the little two toed," He laughed at getting tongue tied. "I mean, two-toned dog, Ricky?"

"'Harry Wheatcroft' is its name. Isn't that pretty? Yellow and red mixed, mmmm, mmm, mmm." Destiny reveled in their beauty.

"Let's go get the lady." Munio got up from the bench and headed into the greenhouse.

"Hello?" Munio called as he entered the glass building.

It was a very old greenhouse with windows that could be cranked open. Pots with little sprouting plants lined the shelves that ran the full length of the building on both sides.

"Yes, you have chosen now, dear?" The little woman appeared before Munio, clasping her hands in front of her.

"We made a list, ma'am." Audrey handed the piece of paper to her.

She looked it over carefully and then said, "How interesting these choices you make. A fine collection they will make, the colors. For these, we must dig. Come and I'll show you." A shovel leaned against the wall, by the door, and as she walked past, she picked it up.

They followed her out into the area where all the bloomless roses waited. She squinted through her glasses at the list and moved midway down one aisle. "One is here, the Champion of the World. The big pink blooms will bring such joy to see for you."

Destiny spoke up. "It's for a friend of ours. He just died. We thought he'd like the name. He thought he was or, as he used to say, he was a legend in his own mind." Destiny remembered aloud, and the others smiled at her.

"Today, will you plant these bushes?" she asked as she dug the shovel into the soft earth.

"Yes, I will plant them today," Munio answered.

"For this one, I shall dig. The next one if you want, you can dig it." She smiled up at Munio with her kindly face. "The difficulty is not great because the earth is soft here, around the roses, you see," she explained.

"I bet it is beautiful here when they're all blooming, huh?" Destiny said.

"Yes, yes, so nice it is. In the spring or the summer, you should come to see, dear. There!" She completed the digging of the root ball of the bush, and with a plastic bag and some twine, she bound the bottom neatly for transport. "One of you please go over by that greenhouse where we were and bring for me the wheelbarrow." She pointed in the direction of the greenhouse.

Destiny jumped at the chance and returned quickly, trotting behind the big, sturdy wheelbarrow. "Here you go," Destiny said cheerfully. "That was fun. I don't think I've ever driven one of them." They all laughed at her.

Down and across several rows, she led them to the next bush. "This Erot-ica has special powers, it has been said." She chuckled. "Be careful to whom

you give the roses. Does someone want to dig this one?"

"I do! I do!" Destiny chirped up, clapping her hands. Audrey and Munio looked surprised at her. She looked at them and explained, "I never dug nothing before."

Audrey looked at Munio, who raised his eyebrows, and they shared a secret laugh. "I have dug plenty, so you go ahead." Munio smiled and winked at Audrey.

"Here, dear, start right here," the woman instructed.

Destiny worked quickly and neatly until she formed a circle around the bush. It was then easily extracted. Destiny looked at them with triumph. Ms. Micholovich bound the bush in the same manner as the other.

"You see, to show you what is wha,t here are these tags." She held up a small plastic tag that bore a color photograph and the name of the type of rose it was.

"That's handy," Destiny commented. "You know, I've lived here all my life, and I've heard about you. I never had any occasion to buy roses so I never got a chance to meet you. I heard you send these things all over the world. Is that right?"

"Yes, I do. All over the world people call me for the roses to buy. Even in the desert of Saudi Arabia, my roses, they grow." She chuckled. "Also, many competitions, rose shows there are. To these, also, I go." she said as she led them over to another rose bed.

"Rose shows?" Destiny questioned.

"Yes, in every place, rose enthusiasts live. Roses, more than any other plant in the world are grown."

"Here is for the Constance Spry, you dig." she instructed Destiny.

"I can't believe I never dug up anything. I kind of like it," she giggled.

"Working with the earth, digging, planting, for you, it is all good. An old woman I am, seventy-five years is my age. Since to this country I came in 1955. For that whole time, with the earth, is where I work. To be outside means, for me, my favorite place."

An hour or so passed before the list of rose bushes had been located, dug up, and bound for transport. Destiny would not relinquish the shovel, insisting on completing all of the digging, and nobody cared to contest her wishes. The wheelbarrow was full of the promise of the beautiful roses featured on the ID labels.

Munio paid for all of the bushes, and they loaded them into Destiny's trunk. Along with the roses, Mrs. Micholovich gave Munio two bags of special enriched soil mix to use when planting. Ms. Micholovich carefully instructed him on the planting and initial care procedures, and gave him a booklet as well. Destiny focused on every word.

"Thank you for you help, ma'am." Munio extended his hand to the sturdy little woman.

"You are welcome. I hope they bloom well for you," she graciously replied.

"You know what? I want to come back out here when all these things are in bloom, ok?" Destiny said, shaking her index finger at Ms. Micholovich.

The lady sweetly smiled and took Destiny's hand. "Young lady, come back to see when they bloom. It will make you so happy. To you I say, you are good at the digging. For more practice, return here and help me."

Destiny reached out and hugged the woman, who was engulfed by her.

"Thank you, dear. All of you are so sweet. How nice today you should come here."

The three of them drove back in silence. All were busy running completely different conversations through their minds. The visit to the Rose Ranch represented a signal somehow for the progression of life to continue, and each of them was engaged in the business of making new plans.

"Destiny," Munio asked as he sat in the back seat of the car, his face propped up on the back of the front seat, "how far is the ocean?"

"Didn't you ask me this before?' she said. "Anyhow, Savannah's the closest. It's about three hours. That's the Atlantic Ocean. Then, the Gulf of Mexico is about six. You in the mood to go to the beach?" she asked innocently.

Munio laughed out loud. "Mood to go to the beach? Yes, girl, it is a suntan that I need." He pointed to his brown skin, jokingly. "No. I want to live there."

"Oh."

They unloaded the bushes and laid them in a pile in front of the gazebo. Munio rustled up his well-used shovel from the back of his pickup truck.

"Gee, I bet the ground's not going to be as soft as hers was," Destiny said in a downcast tone.

Munio smiled. "Oh, it's not so bad really." Audrey had returned with the beers just in time to hear that dialogue and flashed him a fake flabbergasted look, which inspired Munio to chuckle.

"All right, where do you want them?" Destiny said, with the resignation of an old farm hand.

"I'll lay them out like I want them, ok? You can dig the first hole here."

Dusk hedged in as Destiny packed the last shovelful of dirt around the Harry Wheatcroft bush. The dry thorned sticks rose up from the lawn surrounding the gazebo, with no concern for anything except the rain, the air, and the comfort of their dirt blankets.

Destiny went home while Audrey stayed and drank beer with Munio in the gazebo. In spite of the darkness and crisp night air, they stayed for a couple of beers' worth of conversation.

"You know, Munio, there is an ocean in New York," Audrey informed him jokingly. "You're welcome to come there and visit and live or whatever. I'll always be glad to see you. Just so you know." She smiled at him.

"I will come see you someday, but I want a warm climate. Also, I don't want to be around a big city. Someday, I will come. You tell me how to find you, and I promise that I will," Munio said emphatically.

"You are such a beautiful man, Munio."

Munio looked at her with a surprised smile. "You would say that in this darkness."

Audrey laughed, "I guess you have a point, but I can see you out here, honey. This isn't the first time I have looked at you, you know."

"I know." He moved over and put his arm around her. "Thank you. I'm glad you think I am handsome. And you." Munio pushed his body away from Audrey a bit so he could look at her face a little better. "You are a very beautiful man, and I'll always remember this time. The passion we have is so powerful and vicious. It is the most passionate time I ever had with a lover." They then locked in a long, sweet kiss.

"Wow," Audrey said as they came up for air.

They sat quietly for a bit and Munio asked, "Audrey, is it possible that Destiny could live here? She is so good with those dogs. Could that be arranged if she wanted to do it?'

"Destiny?" She stroked her chin. "Have you spoken to her about this?"

"No. I just thought of it, really."

"I have been doing some research on the options of what to do with the property. I have spoken to a friend who is a real estate attorney. He's trustworthy. I've known him a very long time. He would be willing to transfer the property to another person if I am willing to forge Sandra's signature, which I am. Speak with her tonight, ok? That would be the best situation, if you're sure you don't want to live here," Audrey said.

"No. I am ready to go." Munio said.

The phone rang at Destiny's house.

"Destiny, hello, this is Munio."

"Hey, what's up?"

"I need to talk to you about something. Can you do it now?"

"Yeah, sure." She hit the mute button on her remote control and curled her legs up close on the couch. Her cats lined the cushions of the rest of the couch.

"Well, ah, you know, I think I would like to speak about this in person. Can I come over for a few minutes?"

"Oh yeah, that's cool. I ain't doing nothing."

"Ok, I'll be there shortly."

"Ok, bye."

"Hey." Destiny opened the door a little while later.

"Hello," Munio said.

"Long time no see," Destiny joked, as she walked back over to the couch. "I affect people that way. Just can't stay away." She winked. "Now, what is this

big thing?"

Munio laughed. "Ok, now, you know that lady Sandra that owns the house?"

"Yeah."

"Well, she, you know, ah. First of all, if you could somehow, would you like to live in that house? Also, you would have to take the dogs," he said.

"Live there? Well, like for how long or what?"

"Like forever, like if you could own that house, would you like to?"

"Well, hell yeah, I would. That's a nice fucking house."

"How about the dogs? Would you care for the dogs?"

"Yeah, I like those dogs. If I had that much room, hell, I could raise cattle in that much space! Fuck."

"Ok, then, listen to me. A situation is happening with that lady. She is not coming back, and she just wants somebody to take over that house, care for it, and care for those dogs. We can..., I mean, she can fix it, I don't know what you do, but legally, this property will be assigned to you personally, ok? You aren't going to meet her or anything. Audrey is her best friend, and she wants Audrey to coordinate this transfer. I know this is kind of strange, but you just have to say, ah, I don't know exactly what you can say to your friends or relatives. You could say this lady just wanted to up and move somewhere else. She didn't want to take the dogs, but, ah, so, she was rich and ah, just wanted somebody to take care of those dogs, ok?"

Destiny looked at Munio with an incredulous expression on her face as she sat there speechless for a minute. "How much? I ain't got that much money to buy no place like this." She shook her head.

"No money. You don't pay at all."

"You got to be kidding."

"I'm not. It's true. No money, and it will be ok, legal and proper."

Destiny laughed out loud. "Hey," she pretended to zip her mouth closed, "hear no evil. See no evil. Speak no evil, baby. I'll do it, yeah. I'll damn sure do it."

"Ok, I will tell Audrey to proceed."

"When do I move in?"

"As soon as possible. This week? I'll help you."

"You're going to leave, aren't you?" she said sadly.

"Yes," He smiled. "It's time to go."

"Oh, well." Her eyes welled up with tears. "I'm going to miss you."

Munio moved over to the couch and hugged her. They sat rocking in each other's arms, weeping softly.

# CHAPTER LV

A month later Destiny had settled nicely into her reign as the new queen of Sandra's castle. Since her cats had never met a dog, the turf was quite noisy with yelps and hisses, but Destiny passed out enough love for all of them to be happy. She decided to plant more roses around the back yard, and struck up a friendship with Fran Micholovich. In fact, Destiny had started working with her several days a week, to serve as her apprentice, learning the science of roses.

Audrey roamed midtown Manhattan once again and was braving the world without the intricacies of duct tape to tangle her pubic hair or silicone bags under her shirt. For the time being, she divorced herself from the ball-room dancing scene, since her customary role was in direct contrast with her new attempt at life sans drag. Except for her parents, who continued to call her David, Audrey maintained her name because she liked it, and just in case that man Munio should try to find her someday.

Munio left all his tools in the storage room off the carport at Sandra's house. He told Destiny he would get them someday, sometime. He left his truck with Destiny to drive when she needed it, and he got her to drive him to Savannah. With no trouble, he gained passage on a freighter bound for Argentina working as a deck hand. He didn't know if he would really come back to Rosedale, Georgia again. He didn't know if he would even ever go back to Belize again. He did know he never wanted to pass through Texas again in this life as a brown man.

There would be fantastic papayas in Argentina, and he did love papayas. Good smoke would be in Argentina too, and cheap. The way he figured it was that wherever on earth he might roam, if there was cold beer, he would be ok. After all, that was the reason he pulled his truck up to Pee Wee's bar in the first place, and down the road, cold beer would probably have something to do with him meeting the next cast of characters. As the big ship moved down the Savannah River channel and took a southbound turn into the waiting Atlantic, the apricot silk man stood at the bow, at once at home, for the sea to love him again.

The end.

# ABOUT THE AUTHOR...

s. jaen black first published at six years of age when she and her daddy co-authored a jingle for a local milk company in south Alabama. It was a contest and the prize was a Shetland Pony. She lived to tell the tale and learned to always be wary of free horses.

As a trap set drummer, she was a member of Atlanta's theatrical performance band, Moral Hazard, and an actor in the historical Red Dyke Theater.

She performs with world-class musician Bruce Harvie, and along with Harvie and rockin' soul man bass player Jimmy Mudd, plays drums in the band, The Buzzbombs.

A current master's world record holder in the sport of Olympic weightlifting, she became a member of the legendary Coffee's Gym's women's weightlifting team in 1983. As lifter and a USA Weightlifting's Regionally ranked coach, she continues to promote strength pursuits. In honor of her fortieth birthday, she performed a forty kilo squat snatch on roller skates.

She lives on a remote island in the Pacific Northwest with her horse, two cats, and the Colonel.

Printed in the United States
134210LV00003B/4/P